I0649207

Unraveling Grimm

E.R. Brookes

E.R. Brookes Publishing

Contents

For My Family,
You are the First Gift God Gave Me
& I Cherish our Close Relationship
More than Words can Say.
Thank you for always bearing with me,
I know it is not an easy feat, for I am a chaos gremlin.
We all know I'm probably just three raccoons,
stuffed into a sweatshirt,
masquerading as a human being.
However do I deserve you all for putting up with me?

Trigger Warnings

Violence, gore, blood, death,

Mental health reps: Anxiety, depression, eating disorder, SH,

Strong emotional subject matters, SA, SIDS, infant loss and death, domestic violence.

Please take care of your mental health,

with love,

-E

PART ONE
BROKEN ALLEGIANCES

1

The Monster In The Shadows

EVADNE

"Pitch black winter nights live in my bones."
Friedrich Nietzsche

The shadows were screaming as they dragged me backward.

NO! I don't want to go! Let go of me! Let go of me!

"*Come away.*"

A new voice overwhelmed the shadows' cacophony as I struggled against my captors.

There was something all too familiar about these shadows and my inability to wake up.

No, no, please not this!

My throat was constricting, mouth open as I desperately tried to scream. But no sound could escape. No matter how much air I pulled in, I could not force my straining vocal cords to work.

It's a dream. It's just a dream. I have to wake up! I need to wake up!

My body was engulfed in flames. An inferno raged beneath my skin, weakening my strength to fight against my captors.

"*Come away, daughter of Grimm.*"

I can't, I can't, I won't. Where is Ember? What's going on?

Why can't I wake up?

The world was a swirling mass of distorted shapes and shadows within the fading darkness.

"Come away, come away."

No! I don't want to! I won't! I won't!

The longer I fought, the more afraid I became. This was no Dreamscape, of that I was sure.

A barren, gray landscape was slowly materializing around me. I was the only object of color within the lifeless terrain.

What's going on? Where am I?

My fingers desperately clawed at the shadows and their screams intensified. The sound pierced through my mind, making my head ache.

Wake up! Wake up!

The parallels were frightening. This was the same pull, the same voice that had tried to drag me back when Mum died. It had taken all the monarchs to fight the shadows and bring me back. But now I was alone, and every second that passed, the shadows drained my strength further.

I was no match for the monster that once again spirited me away.

How did I get here? Maybe if I remember it will pull me back to reality. Maybe it'll be enough to ground me.

Trying to remember was like moving through quicksand. The harder I fought, the more it sucked me down.

"Come away."

The voice was a whispering hiss. A knife that buried itself deep within my mind and sliced my memories to ribbons as it dragged me forward.

I can't! I won't! Fight, I have to fight it.

C'mon Evadne, remember. You have to remember.

The dance. The last thing I remember is the dance with Damien...

Disconnected images began to flood across my mind. Disfigured faces hidden behind elaborate masks, lifeless eyes staring through me as Damien tried to steal me away. The moonlight—that terrible, unnatural moonlight as I danced night after night with those deep velvet eyes. Those eyes held me, consumed and devoured me whole. Running, then I was running, desperately trying to escape the curse as the gold and diamond shards tore through my skin. His lips, hot against mine as the magic was at last satisfied.

The fragments of the broken curse pulsed around us. The heartache that bled between us as he refused to let go. The traitorous kiss that bound us together as he fought to keep me with him.

I broke the curse and saved my family, but at what cost? I saved them, but I betrayed my heart. Would Marcus understand? Can he ever forgive me?

I betrayed my heart, my one true love.

The world was exploding and then Marcus, my Marcus, was there defending me against Damien despite what I'd done.

He didn't know, he didn't know.

I was falling, lost in endless, painful memories. They hadn't helped pull me back to reality—the grief within had only weakened my fight against the shadows.

I was pinching my side, fingernails tearing at my skin as I tried and failed to wake up.

Darkness was gathering; the shadows hovered on the outskirts of a castle. It lay in ruins. The wreck looked like a gaping wound, with high walls that rose and jutted out into sharp points and peaks that stabbed into the skyline. The air was acidic and sulfurous, with hints of blood and rot beneath the stench.

Wait... I know this place. I've dreamed of it. This is where I...I...

The Dreamscapes...this is where I killed Em in the Dreamscapes... The nightmare we both endured, yet neither of us could speak of...

The shadows were growing around me, morphing into monsters with claws and fangs. I couldn't fight them as they dragged me inside the outer walls of the crumbling ruins, through the broken gates. An unnatural darkness resided within the wreck—an evil tinged with fear and regret, beneath which an undercurrent of poisonous rage bled.

"Come away, child."

The voice wasn't in my head anymore—it was in the space around me.

No, no. I don't want to. I have to get to Ember! I have to get out of here!

The pull was stronger than I was, the same as it had been when I was forced to watch Mum die.

Nausea rolled over me, heavy with pain and sorrow as I desperately clawed at the monsters. Grief dwelt here, heavy with heartbreak and fury. Renewed loss for Mum slammed into me. It was quickly followed by a renewed grief for F and Oma—every person I'd lost because of the Realm.

My very bones ached with the weight of this sorrow.

Ghostly figures floated around me, whispering horrible confessions to my unwilling ears while translucent fingers pulled at my clothes,

"I killed my brother."

"I sent the child on alone. I lied and said I would return."

"I lost the man I loved...I sacrificed him for power."

"I killed them and hid the bones."

"I sent them to their deaths."

"I took his heart and left him to die."

On and on, their chilling confessions followed me as the monsters dragged me through a graveyard. Crumbling tombstones stabbed through the earth like broken teeth. Weeping angels towered over me. All around me, the bodies of the dead lingered—trapped in this cursed place between life and death.

I need to wake up right now.

I was inside the ruins now, stumbling down a dark spiraling staircase. I couldn't find my feet, but my captors wouldn't give me the chance to try. I couldn't see anything now as the stairs went on and on. Down, down, down we went.

"Evadne!"

Ember's voice echoed around the small space as well as through my mind. Real, yet intangible all at once.

Ember! Ember! Help me! Help me wake up! Wake me up!!

Get Artemis to wake me up!!

But no matter how I screamed and cried, she couldn't hear me. The connection was feeble, then gone. She had no idea what kind of danger I was in.

I was panicking now, desperately trying to get through.

"She cannot save you now," a new voice whispered, malicious glee clinging to its edges.

I know that voice. I recognize that voice.

Please, no. Don't be here. Don't be here!

No, it can't be. That's impossible. It can't be true.

Wake up! Wake up!

Blue flames flickered in the darkness, throwing sudden contrast and light around the room.

An all too familiar smile leered at me from the shadows.

I stared in horror, gut plummeting, at the face I knew all too well.

You're supposed to be dead.

"Hello darling," he whispered as shadows leaped from his hands and wrapped around my eyes, plunging the world into complete darkness.

2

Don't Look Back

EMBER

"Who attached these heavy wings on my shoulders?"
-Marina Tsvetaeva, The Bridge of Ice

In a magical realm, the word 'impossible' no longer belonged to our vocabulary. But it was the only word I could grasp as I stared in openmouthed shock at the clouds that raced by us.

We're on a ship, in the middle of the sky. We're on a flying ship.

The ship is flying...

Impossible, impossible. This is completely impossible.

On and on, my thoughts circled and rebounded—redundant and vague.

"Ember." Verity's voice cut through my disconnected haze.

I looked up, startled.

Verity knelt beside Evadne's unconscious figure, fingers deftly searching for a pulse on Evadne's neck. After a moment, she began to examine the wounds that covered my sister's body. "Ember, sit down before you fall over the railing," Verity ordered calmly. "You're losing too much blood, and if I have to conduct a sky rescue, I will be most cross. As will Raz, since she's busy arguing with Nikos."

"Sure," I croaked. "I think I can do that. Hot blood dripped from my forehead, sliding down my cheek and falling to the deck beneath my feet.

The mysterious captain arched an eyebrow, staring intently at my shaking form as she waited for me to follow her instructions.

I wonder what kinds of things she knows... I bet she could tell me all sorts of awesome stories.

Yeah, like, how she became so cool and mysterious...how she fell in love with Jack...how she ended up here...how does one become a skye pirate?

Move. Sit down, you stupid idiot. Sit down!

The wandering thoughts raced around my mind as I told myself over and over to move. It wasn't that I was being deliberately disobedient. But it just so happened that I had somehow, completely forgotten how to bend my knees. My knuckles were white as I clutched the railing and at last forced my knees to bend. Gravity was all too obliging to help my plight, and in an instant, I was sitting in a crumpled heap on the deck.

Well. That's one way to make a good impression.

Verity snorted in amusement, the corner of one eyebrow quirking up.

I huffed, annoyed that she was taking enjoyment from my clumsy weakness.

"I need Clarice!" Verity yelled, turning her attention back to Evadne.

Muffled shouts answered her order, and the deck vibrated beneath me as people went running.

I stared at Evadne's ashen face. Blood was rapidly spreading out from her body.

Will she forgive me that we left Marcus there? Will she understand?

It was a pointless question. I knew Evadne would be heartbroken, but more than that I knew she would understand. She would take Jack's words to heart and hold onto the hope that she and Marcus would be reunited at some point.

Do I have such a hope with Artemis? After everything that's passed between us, is there any hope we can be reunited?

Memories were running circles around my mind. Artemis' ragged face, the desperate look in his eyes as he begged me not to die. Blood, there was so much blood. So much love and loathing still stood between us as my heartbeat faded to a whisper. His words were desperate as he tried to save my life... *'I can't lose you, I can't... It means nothing if you are not by my side...'*

But what does that mean? What does it mean now that I've left him?

Is there any hope left for us?

Will he ever forgive me for leaving him?

"Do you understand what you've just done, child?" Verity asked quietly as she pressed a palm to Evadne's forehead. Her hands were coated in my sister's blood as she tried to stop the bleeding. "She's burning up," she muttered under her breath.

"I..." I swallowed, unable to find my words.

Verity appeared to be somewhere around Jack's age. But as she looked up and held my gaze, her eyes gave her away. Centuries were buried within the onyx depths. A heaviness clung to those burdened eyes. She had seen and lost more than her smooth skin could ever tell.

My attention wandered back to Evadne. She was utterly still, her chest barely rising and falling. Bright morning sunlight shone on the vicious thorns embedded in her skin, refracting cheerful rainbows of light across the deck. It seemed ill-fitting that artifacts of such pain and destruction could create such beauty.

I wonder if she got those before Jack grabbed her, or after. He tried so hard to protect her from them...from him.

I shuddered, remembering the bloodthirsty man and the snarl on his face as he twisted the blade deeper into my chest. Goosebumps raced over my skin as I recalled how Artemis had roared my name and reduced the world to ash in the crimson wave of his rage.

We left him there. Why did I save his life, only to leave him?

Was it the right choice?

What are we going to do? What did I just do?

Panic was welling up inside of me, hot and frantic. My heart was racing as the world struggled to form and reform itself. Everything I thought I knew had changed. Suddenly I was adrift on the ocean, lost, devoid of purpose and hope. I didn't know what to do with myself.

I was on the verge of shutting down—desperate to protect itself, my body was gearing up to go numb and freeze me in place. I could feel it in the way my hands tingled, and my legs suddenly disappeared.

Not now. I can't have a panic attack right now. I have to stay calm.

A sturdy-looking woman came up behind Captain Verity. She was beautiful, with light brown skin and deep black eyes that seemed to read the emotions churning within me. Her long silver and black hair was twisted into dreadlocks, with many colorful gems and thick gold hoops scattered throughout. It was currently pulled back into an intricate bun. She carried with her a calm air of command that seemed to take control as she stopped to assess the situation.

"Clarice, we have new passengers," Verity announced. "They both require your assistance."

"Whatever made you decide that?" Clarice chuckled as she knelt to look at Evadne. "Well," she tsked, "anyone could surmise as much. The blood is certainly a dead give-away." She leaned closer, her eyes scrutinizing the thorns. "Got trapped at the curse by the looks of it. Lucky to be alive, this one is. I'm guessing he tried to keep her."

There was no question as to who *he* was. Clearly Verity and her crew knew of that cursed place and the monster within.

Clarice's dark eyes glanced at me. They seemed to pull me apart at the seams as she looked me up and down, assessing every injury. "Hmm," she muttered. "They have both been through an ordeal, it seems." Her eyes fixated on the bloody hole in my shirt. "Lucky to be alive, too," she noted before pursing her lips in grim acceptance.

"Theron!" Verity barked.

Is it the Grimm?

There could be two Therons on the ship... Confusing and unlikely, but there could be.

A head poked out from high above us. He was standing horizontally against a mast, held in place by the rope he grasped and by the angle of his feet planted against the wood. I hadn't noticed him before now; most of his body had been covered by the sails.

Who am I kidding? I probably wouldn't have noticed him even if he was doing the Hokey Pokey up there. I'm way too out of it.

Fair point.

You put your right hand in... you put your right hand out   you put your right hand in, and you knock somebody out...

He had brown hair that was pulled back into a ponytail, with a closely trimmed beard and mustache. But it was the unmistakable glint of silver eyes in the bright sunlight that caught my attention.

Definitely the Grimm.

His eyes were laughing as he looked down at us, and I vaguely wondered what he thought was so funny. "Yes, Captain?" he called out with a sheepish grin.

"I know you've been eavesdropping," Verity snapped. "So why don't you at least make yourself useful while you eavesdrop."

"Happily," Theron replied as he released the rope that held him in place and began to fall toward us.

I shrieked in fear, then clapped a bloody hand over my mouth, trying to stifle the noise. Clearly, he knew what he was doing, I was only embarrassing myself by reacting.

He probably did it just to get a reaction out of me.

Jerk!

Don't forget to add he's a showoff.

But is it showing off when it's incredibly cool?

The jury is out on that one. You'll have to wait two to three business weeks before we come back with a verdict.

I don't have time or patience to wait that long. I want to know now.

Theron summersaulted in midair and landed with a soft thud on the deck in front of me. "There, now," he chided with a laugh.

How did he jump from that high and not make more noise?

Maybe his shoes are magic. Maybe they mask the sound of his feet.

I want shoes like that.

"There's no need to cry for me, Sparks. I'm not going to fall to my death."

Sparks?

Verity rolled her eyes. "C'mon, you nosy prat. Help get the girls to the medical wing."

It took me a moment to realize that I was still staring in openmouthed shock at Theron. I closed it quickly, unable to mask the audible click of my teeth.

Theron's coy grin morphed into a smirk, reminding me of Jack. He was taller than Verity. I guessed he stood well over six feet. "You have a lot to learn about ships," he said jovially. "You also have a fair bit to learn about those who live on them."

Verity sighed, rolling her eyes again. "Save your lecture for another day, you idiot. I don't believe she's ever been on a skyeship, let alone had the chance to meet the rogues that belong to one."

Theron made a face. "How *is* it that a *Grimm* knows nothing about us? Surely by now she's so entrenched within the Realm she could fly if she wanted to."

"These are Ember and Evadne Grimm," Verity replied tightly. "They are *the* twins. They didn't grow up in the Realm, but spent the majority of their years in the Mortal Realm. These are Jacques' sisters."

How does she know that?

She and Jack are in love. Jack probably told her everything. I bet he told her of home, and what he remembered...everything he loved, everything that made him afraid...she likely bears all the burdens he carries.

Theron made a face. "*The* Grimms," he mocked under his breath as he stooped to pick up Evadne.

Well, excuse me. I didn't ask for the last name Grimm, neither did I ask for all this ridiculous pressure to be 'the' anything.

Again, I submit for the committee's approval the insult of jerk.

Verity rolled her eyes again, and I began to wonder if the view in the back of her head was one she enjoyed seeing so often. Nevertheless, their banter and her ire subtly calmed my growing panic. Theron and Verity reminded me of Jack and Faye. The way they carried on like siblings lightened the heavy atmosphere.

"Gently, gently," Clarice whispered as Theron gingerly picked up Evadne's lifeless body. A small pool of blood had gathered beneath her, and as he began to walk away, it trailed from her fingertips. Crimson drops splattered on the deck. I stared at his bloody boot prints, scared. I didn't know how Evadne could survive losing that much blood.

"Clarice," Verity said, staring at the blood for a moment. "Help the girl, please. I must return to the wheel. Once I've set our course, I will check back in and assist where needed. I'll have Meira come clean up the blood. We're going to the Wastes."

Clarice nodded. "No one can help them but her," she replied cryptically. She turned to me as Verity walked away. "Come on, love," she said gently. "These old bones can't carry you, so you'll have to find your skye legs."

I swallowed, suddenly terrified as I forced my aching limbs to move. The sky seemed to grow around me—stretching until I was aware of how small I was, and how easy it would be to trip and fall over the edge.

Which would be worse? Verity being cross with me because she has to conduct a rescue, or the falling itself?

How about we never find out.

I think that is a most ingenious plan.

"Come on then," Clarice encouraged gently. "It's not rocket science."

A puddle of blood was gathering beneath my boots, mingling with Evadne's on the deck. The numerous cuts from the thorns were steadily weeping.

I nodded. "I'm...I'm trying," I whispered as I willed my limbs to move.

I grabbed the railing, pulling myself to my feet as I continued to stare at the deck.

If I don't acknowledge the endless skies around me, and how high up in the air I am, I won't melt into a puddle of goo.

Right now, being a puddle of goo seems highly appealing, thank you very much.

Oh! I have an idea! How about we scoot across the deck on our butt, in wooly worm fashion?

That is a better option than goo... It's certainly faster. I'll put it before the court for consideration.

Since I was still unable to move, the jury was decidedly hung, and the verdict remained undecided. No one could tell me if I was a wooly worm or a puddle of goo.

C'mon, Em. Move! You have to move, darn it!!

If you don't move, you're going to embarrass yourself.

No amount of lecturing was helping me find, as Clarice had put it, my skye legs.

The ship rose and fell beneath me in an unpredictable pattern. I was unsteady, off balance, and dizzy as I struggled to stay vertical. Pain was everywhere and it was all I could do to stay upright and breathe through the aching fire that was quickly overwhelming my limbs.

I will not throw up on Verity's ship. I will not throw up and humiliate myself!

"I seem to have lost my legs," I muttered.

Maybe if I ignore the pain and insert sarcasm and snark it'll help distract me from reality.

Clarice continued to patiently wait, one eyebrow arched in amusement.

The wind carried the sound of Theron's laugh from somewhere up ahead. I ground my teeth in annoyance.

Stupid pirate, and his stupid...whatever.

How dare he be unafraid when we are clearly in a perilous situation.

Yes, this is a very treacherous environment that is fraught with danger, risk, hazards...uhm...I'm running out of synonyms.

Forget the synonyms, it's a ridiculous pastime. His laughter is getting closer. Stop standing and MOVE before he gets here, sees you're still frozen, and makes fun of you!

"You'll get your skye legs eventually," Clarice said with a laugh of her own. "But I wager it won't be until you're done trying to bleed yourself dry. Fey can endure a higher blood loss than mortals, and Grimms even more than regular Fey, but I wouldn't advise you test how much blood you can lose. It can be an incredibly horrific experience. That foolhardy brother of yours tried those waters and he didn't wake up for a week."

Another wave of pain rushed over me. *I can't afford to sleep for a week.*

Move, Ember. You need to move!

"You're probably a hundred, thousand percent right," I muttered as I once again tried and failed to make myself let go of the railing and walk to Clarice's side.

At least when the Moores were trying to kill us, I could walk and move. My courage has utterly failed me. Apparently, I left it on that darned cliff with a very furious Artemis.

Oh no, what's Artemis going to do with my courage?

Stab it, most likely.

Oh no, I need my courage.

I'm frozen. I literally can't move.

This is humiliating. Completely and utterly humiliating.

Okay. I'm going to move on three. I'm going to move. I will do it!

One! Two! THREE!!

Clarice laughed outright as my body remained frozen, holding onto the railing for dear life. "Oh child, if you could see the look on your face right about now, you'd be laughing with me. I can tell you're counting, but I can also tell you're scared silly."

I am not scared silly, I am scared, plain and simple. There is nothing silly about this stupid situation.

Where did the term scared silly even come from? I'm not silly. I'm terrified. There's a difference. There might even be some people who would go so far as to say that my fear makes me smart.

I'm definitely not silly.

"You're scared of heights, aren't you love," Clarice stated.

"Never been a fan," I grumbled as I took a series of deep breaths, trying to master my fear.

Why would you do this to me, Jack? Why would you put me on a ship, in the middle of the sky, thousands of feet up in the air, when I'm terrified of heights? Why would you do this to your poor sister?! What did I do to you? This seems like a punishment only fitting for someone who stole your doughnuts, and I promise you, I didn't do that!

"You'll have to learn to move through your fear," Clarice said kindly as she walked through Evadne's blood and took my shaking hand. "Come on, love, your sister is waiting for me. We must remember in times like these, that all bleeding stops...eventually." She winked and I stared at her in horror.

"That's a terrible joke," I whispered raggedly.

"It's true. Now come on, like I said, your sister needs me."

Right. Evadne needs her.

This is blackmail. She's blackmailing me with my sister's wellbeing to get me to move.

Well, we've tried everything but blackmail. Maybe that'll do the trick to banish my fear and get me moving.

All right brain, consider yourself blackmailed. Now move!

I stepped forward, leaning heavily on Clarice's arm.

There, see! Blackmail was the answer all along.

Theron turned the corner, and just as his attention latched onto me, a wave of vertigo slammed into me. My guts clenched and roiled, and there was no stopping the bile that rose. I turned and barely made it to the railing before emptying the pitiful contents of my stomach over the edge.

That is exactly what I was trying NOT to do. Especially not in front of mister smirking snark of stupid laughter!

Humiliation rushed through me, burning my cheeks as I quickly grabbed my water bottle out of my cloak and rinsed my mouth, then spit over the railing.

As I stowed my water bottle back in the pocket of my cloak, my fingers brushed up against Fireheart's scales.

Crap. Evadne's petting zoo.

"You okay, Fireheart?" I whispered, trying to catch my breath.

He nuzzled up against my hand, then crawled out of the cloak and climbed up my arm. He perched on my shoulder, craning his neck to make direct eye contact. His tongue flicked in and out, gently touching my nose. His eyes asked a million questions.

He's asking about Evadne. I'd bet anything that's what he's trying to communicate.

"She's hurt," I whispered. "We...Jack...well he split us up. We're here on the ship, but he's with Artemis and Marcus."

Fireheart's eyebrows scrunched in confusion.

"I'm doing a terrible job explaining this..." I whispered, despairing. "Jack wrote a letter; you can read it when we get to Evadne. I'll try to explain it again after I'm a little less exhausted. But you need to promise me you won't accidentally set the letter on fire. Evadne still needs to read it when she regains consciousness."

Fireheart nodded, content, and I turned my attention back to Theron and Clarice. They were engaged in a quiet, yet urgent conversation. I caught the last words, and my breath caught. "She's in grave danger," Theron was just murmuring.

Clarice sighed, shaking her head. "What these cursed monarchs do to these poor children…I grow tired of old, power-hungry Fey brewing wars for the young to fight and die in."

Theron grunted in agreement.

"Try not to take a century to get her to my quarters, will you? Her sister may be worse off, but she is badly injured as well."

"You got it," Theron said as Clarice slid past me and walked in the direction Theron had taken Evadne.

"Well," Theron said cheerily as he made his way to my side. "If you're done spewing out your guts and trading secrets with the little reptile, I'll help you from here."

Fireheart bristled on my shoulder, and I took offense on his behalf. "He is a *dragon!*" I snapped indignantly. "A most brave, honorable, wonderful little dragon, you *jerk.*"

Fireheart hissed in agreement, wings flaring as he glared at Theron and shot a little spurt of flame at his face.

Would I be a bad person if I let Fireheart bite him?

I mean, he did call Fireheart a reptile when he's clearly a dragon. Anyone could see he's a dragon. I think I would be a very good person if I let Fireheart bite him. It would teach Theron a lesson about purposefully calling dragons reptiles just to get a rise out of said dragon…

Fireheart's body bunched up. He clearly had the same thought process as I did and was preparing to launch himself at Theron for his audacity.

Have at it, my little winged assassin. Theron, prepare thyself to be bitten.

Theron raised his hands in surrender, eyes laughing. "My sincerest apologies, oh noble dragon."

Fireheart relaxed and nodded, as if to say, '*That's right, peasant.*'

"Now, I think it's time we pried your hands from the railing and made our happy way to the medical ward." Theron was pulling my fingers up now, one by one.

I didn't care. I was much too busy clenching my eyes shut—trying to block out the clouds as they raced by, so close I could touch them if I only reached out.

"If I let you hold on any longer, you'll scratch the paint and then Raz will be most cross with me. She was ever so meticulous when she painted these railings." He chuckled. "And you wouldn't believe how *grumpy* she was about the whole project—even though she wouldn't accept any help *with* said project. I wouldn't put it past her to strap some wings on your back and make *you* repaint it while we sail."

That thought was enough to make me voluntarily let go of the railing. I absolutely did *not* want to do that.

"Just breathe," Theron said gently as he moved my shaking hands to his forearm. He wrapped an arm around me, grabbing the back of my belt to help hold me upright. "It's just a walk in the clouds. You're completely safe."

"Yeah," I muttered. "Probably about as safe as a child trapped in a den of wolves."

"Well, it certainly worked well for Mowgli," Theron countered smoothly as he pulled me forward and forced my aching feet to stumble over one another. He was bigger than I was, so it was pointless to resist.

"If you fall, I'll be forced to carry you," Theron said lightly as he continued to help me stay upright. "That would certainly be a blow to your pride, now wouldn't it?"

"Maybe," I snapped through gritted teeth.

"Poor Grimmling." Theron laughed. "You're absolutely terrified. Your face is so white your freckles look like delightful little cherries."

"Leave my freckles out of it!" I growled. My pride was now thoroughly mortified. *Comeback, I need a witty comeback.*

"They're none of your business," I mumbled, unable to find a prim tone of voice.

Brilliant save. That was absolutely brilliant. You definitely saved face with that comeback.

Shut up. I shouldn't have to come up with witty comebacks when I'm dealing with blood loss and perilous situations.

"Talk to me," Theron said, his eyes searching the sky above us.

"Why?" I demanded, angry and exhausted.

"Because I'm curious about who you are, and I want to help you not to be afraid."

"Like that's going to happen," I snorted. "I'm always afraid."

"Well, if you want to walk without the assistance of a strong, handsome man, *and* avoid the appearance of being a damsel in distress who needs rescuing, I suggest you humor me."

More blackmail. I should've known it would abound on a skyeship.

Is this skyeship a pirate ship? Do they call themselves skye pirates? Or skyeship pirates? Is there another term they prefer?

"You seem to have an awfully high opinion of yourself," I muttered, making a face. His self-complimenting reminded me so much of Jack, and it stuck a knife in my gut. What was going to happen to Jack when he woke up? Artemis had figured it out, but there was no turning back now.

I should have made it seem like I was kidnapped.

"I'm modest, too," Theron said with a smirk.

I laughed, tears gathering in my eyes. I couldn't stop the grief and mirth from bleeding together. "You remind me of my brother," I whispered.

Theron dipped his head. "That is an honorable compliment. I will cherish it forever. Jack is a fine man, loyal and courageous."

"I'm afraid," I choked out at last.

"Well, everyone is afraid of something. The best way to conquer it is to speak it aloud. It'll help your brain process reality and find your courage. Take a deep, steadying breath and describe it to me."

I struggled to control my diaphragm; I was shaking so hard I couldn't get enough air in to count as a breath—let alone a deep breath. "My feet aren't reliable anymore," I whispered. "The ground is shifting and roiling, and I feel like I'm about to fall over. My balance is gone. The ship, or maybe the wind is going to knock me off my feet."

Theron shrugged. "That's a very real feeling. I understand it completely. What else?"

"There is this...constant threat in my chest. My solar plexus is tightening, aching. It's warning me, cutting me like a knife, unwilling to let me settle or rest. My nerves are fried...I'm tied up, torn in half, and shaking. I can't breathe. My throat is swelling closed, and my insides are ripping themselves apart."

Theron nodded, "I understand exactly how you feel. That was very well put—you should be a writer."

I nodded. "I wanted to be a writer when I was a teenager. Now...now I'm not so sure there's any reason or chance to be one...not when your fate is tied to death."

Theron cursed, "Fate," he scoffed, "The monarchs want you to believe your only way out is through death, but there is always another way." He stared down at me, his eyes unreadable. "Now, let's put that angry tangent aside. We have bravery to find. Tell your brain you're not afraid."

"What?" I spluttered. "That's not how this works. If it was that simple, I'd be doing cartwheels down the deck. I've been telling myself I'm not afraid this whole time, and it hasn't worked yet."

"Well, the millionth time's the charm. Tell your brain you're unafraid."

"That's stupid," I muttered, utterly frustrated.

"You're stupid," Theron countered.

I laughed despite my fear. It was exactly what Faye would say, to which I would usually reply, 'Takes one to know one'.

"But you only show your stupidity if you don't at least *try*," Theron pressed.

I'm not afraid. I'm not afraid. I refuse to be afraid.

I was still utterly terrified.

See. I told him it wouldn't work.

After everything I've endured, the sky manages to turn me into a weeping puddle of goop.

"It was worth a shot," Theron chuckled with a shrug. "How did you get here, any-way? A Grimm like you should be up to her neck in the triviality of the courts—being fought over like a prized racehorse—not wandering around the cursed Moores."

"The Council sent us on a...quest...so to speak."

Theron arched an eyebrow. "A quest," he snorted derisively. "That is a politically correct term to say they sent you to do their dirty work. Now, whether this was a true quest or not, I can't say. But I *do* know, they think you're the ones of the prophecy. They're so desperate to make it happen on their terms they would send you to the very Moores they ignore. Those miserable, stinking monarchs think they can control the outcome and make demands of fate."

I gather he doesn't think much of the monarchs.

He is making me like him with his abhorrence of them. Perhaps we can be friends...

"But there *is* a prophecy..." My voice trailed off. I had never actually heard or read the prophecy. "Well, at least I've been *told* there's a prophecy."

"Oh, there's a prophecy all right. But just because they tell you what it means down to the letter, and how that prophecy is *your* fate, doesn't mean it's true. Things often turn out differently than what those high and mighty monarchs decide. They think they can alter the destined path for their own gain, but their futile attempts only bring about the ending they so desperately sought to change all that time."

My thoughts wandered to *Alice Through the Looking Glass*. Her attempts to stop the unraveling of the Red Queen's madness, had in the end been the cause.

"It's nothing but a poor attempt to rewrite another's fate and keep yourself free of the consequences," Theron muttered angrily. "Only you can decide the path you're destined for."

"I'm boxed in," I mumbled.

"That's what they want you to believe," Theron replied, his tone lecturing as he looked down at me disapprovingly. "If you think you have no way out, you'll stop fighting and submit to their demands. A fully grown elephant won't pull at the tiny rope around its ankle and yank the measly stake up. Do you know why?"

"No."

"Because it believes as an adult it's just as powerless as it was when it was a calf. It doesn't realize the rope is no longer tied to an immovable structure."

My brain was sluggish. It was taking all my focus and energy just to stay upright. "What do you mean?" I asked after a moment's confused consideration.

"Figure it out for yourself," he replied evasively.

"Rude," I grumbled. My focus once again turned to my feet, and for the first time I looked around. We had somehow managed to traverse our way across the ship without me even knowing it. I had been so wrapped up in the conversation I hadn't realized we were moving—or that I was afraid.

We were walking along a long, narrow gangplank, barely wide enough for both of us. It stretched across one deck to the other with no railing.

I looked down. The main deck below was so far away, the crew looked like ants on the ground.

Have we been going up while we walked? I don't remember stairs. Did I pass out for some of it?

Despite our altitude, I wasn't afraid.

"How—"

"I told you," he said, giving me a sly wink. "Tell yourself you're not afraid."

I'm not afraid. I'm not afraid...I'm not afraid.

To my shock, there was no fear. There was nothing but emptiness. A numbness devoid of fear and anxiety—unnatural and foreign—hovered around the edges of my mind.

What's going on with me? This doesn't feel right...could he have been right?

"Tell me, Sparks...."

"My name is Ember," I cut in hotly.

"Sure, but the way your eyes spark and flash, the way your hair looks like flames in the sunlight? I think Sparks is a better name."

Artemis' green eyes flashed through my mind. *'My Flamin!'* His voice roared at the edges of my subconscious, angrily searching for me.

No. I will not let you find us.

I strengthened the wall in my mind, desperate to protect myself as I turned my attention back to Theron. "I didn't give you permission to call me by a nickname."

"Ooo, scary," Theron snorted mockingly. "The one of flames has a hiss of...sparks, wouldn't you say?"

I rolled my eyes, and he laughed. "Now, back to what I was saying before you *rudely* interrupted me. What heroic deeds did you perform to earn that much blood on your clothes?"

There was nothing heroic about the deeds. Every one of them was rooted in survival.

"Furthermore, what wretched fool trained you? He failed if you sustained that many injuries."

I looked down at myself, taking in the ruined state of my clothes, and the bloody footsteps that marked our path to the medical ward. I was an absolute wreck.

"Well, Artemis trained us, but the odds were against us..."

"I'm particularly interested in this one," Theron interrupted as he pointed to the hole in my shirt. "Judging by the blood and location, you should be dead, correct?"

Memories flashed across my mind, overwhelming everything else as what I had done cut through me. Betrayal burned against my heart. It felt wrong to leave Artemis. But Jack knew things I didn't, and I trusted him more than I could trust my growing feelings for Artemis. Memories of what had happened replayed. Fear plunged through me as I jumped in front of that blade. I was already dying, but even if I hadn't been, I was unwilling to let him be destroyed. Pain...there was so much pain and desperation that bled between us. How could we ever find a way through the vicious cycle of love and hate?

It means nothing if you are not by my side.

Theron drew back slightly. "That is not what I expected," he muttered.

"Huh?"

"Your face," he replied quickly. "You looked as if you had remembered something excruciating. Forgive me, I should not have asked."

"I made my choice," I sighed as we stopped in front of a large doorway. Evadne's broken figure lay on a bed inside. Her face was ashen, her eyes flitting frantically beneath her eyelids. The sound of her hollow, rasping breaths filled the room.

How are we going to make it out of this?

"I can't look back now," I murmured as I shoved the guilt and grief down. I couldn't escape the pain of what I'd done to Artemis, but I couldn't think about that now.

I pushed it down, down, down. Down so deep into my mind that it could never hope to escape. "I can't look back," I whispered.

Theron clenched his fists as he stared at Evadne. "What lies behind you is nothing compared to what lies ahead," he replied softly. "You must look back and learn from what lies behind, so you can find the courage to face what lies ahead."

3

Canyons Of Desperation

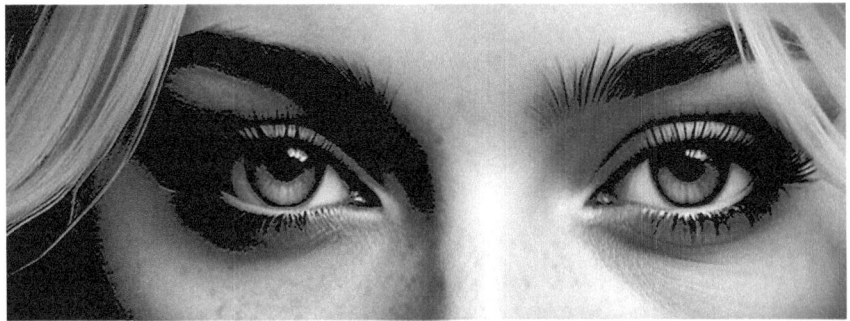

FAYE

"Some days I don't exist. My bed becomes a casket."
-Juansen Dizon, I Am The Architect of My Own Destruction

My fury with Ronan had evaporated, leaving in its place a hollow ache and the renewed desperation to escape.

Five days had passed since I purposefully botched an escape attempt to protect Ronan's sister, and since that humiliating fiasco, Jeremiah had begun to personally administer my daily dose of mind-numbing drugs. Apparently, Ronan was on much too thin ice to be trusted with such an endeavor. I had seen neither hide nor hair of my infuriating jailer, which was probably for the best. I was liable to do something terrible if I saw him again. More than that, I was grateful that I didn't have to face him. I didn't want to acknowledge what had happened between us, let alone the things I'd said. I didn't want to remember the rage in his eyes and the hopelessness that crushed my heart.

I had burned the tenuous bridge built between us with my anger and pain, and now there was a canyon in its place, vast and uncrossable. It was easier to run away than to find a way through.

Peace wasn't an option anymore. We stood on opposite sides, both fighting to protect the ones we loved. It was a vicious, bloody cycle. In the end, one of us would end up dead. I could only hope I wouldn't be the one who killed him. I wasn't sure that I could live with the guilt.

I cannot live with all the innocent blood I've shed within the Realm. I cannot escape their ghosts. Ronan's death would be the end of me. Those gray eyes would haunt me to my dying day...

What am I doing? I can't keep thinking like this! I have to escape, using whatever means possible. He's made his bed, he can lie in it...

But his sister! He's trying to get her out...he only did all of this because Jeremiah's been holding her captive all this time.

He has the run of the compound, if he wanted to get her out, he would've gotten her out by now. He could have done it. He could have killed Jeremiah, fought his men off, anything other than this. Why hasn't he done it yet?

Why? What am I missing.

Nothing. I'm missing nothing. This is just the evidence of his absolute failure and endless excuses.

But no amount of rage-fed accusations could make sense out of such a predicament. I was still missing something.

Days passed in a disconnected and shadowy haze. Jeremiah had believed my bold-faced lie that my strength lay in overcoming the drugs—not Ronan's forgetfulness to administer them. As a result, Jeremiah had doubled, if not tripled the dose. It was so strong now, I could *feel* the darkness within the serum, and suddenly it all made sense. *This* was why I had been so helpless.

Jeremiah was drugging me with potent Darke magic. Deadly, cursed magic that came from the Ruins. Everything pointed to the Knight.

Terror followed the realization as I at last understood the meaning within the Seer's warning. *'It is of the Ruins.'*

Why did it take me so long to realize what she meant?

It would kill me soon if I didn't get out. This was the poison that invaded the Moores, the very toxin the Knight was using to weaken and kill the Grimms at the Last Gate. The bane the monarchs foolishly ignored as the Realm was slowly consumed. It belonged to the monster I had planned to unleash upon the Realm in the desperate hope of saving my sisters.

My only chance to survive, as well as rescue Dad, is to get help. If I try to play the hero and rescue him myself, I will only get caught. I don't think Jeremiah will tolerate it. He's crazy. He'll kill Dad just to get the message across.

I hated the idea of leaving him behind, but it was our only hope.

The only way I could help all of us, Ronan and Meghan included, was to get out and get help.

Dad will understand, he'll understand. If he was here, he'd tell me to leave him behind.

The state of the world as I knew it felt fragile, leaving me in a tenuous state of helplessness. I had to escape, but such a concept seemed so far away as I lay, day after day, staring at the ceiling. It took everything in me just to force my chest up and down, to get air in and out of my lungs.

Jeremiah overdosed me. It's going to kill me.

No. I refuse to die. I have things to do; dying will get none of those things accomplished.

And so, time passed as I struggled to adjust to the new normal and overcome the poison.

I knew the Ruins would kill me one day...but I never thought it would kill me like this.

What was the point of it all if I was just going to die in the end?

What was the point of all that pain when I couldn't save them in the end?

Day turned into night, then back into day. I watched from my bed, curled up in a ball, as the light came and went and came again. But still, it was all I could do to stay alive. But alive I was. Desperation held me together as the talisman burned against my skin. It, too, was struggling as my heart continued to beat unevenly in my chest.

Ronan, where are you? Why are you letting your father do this to me?

Help me, Ronan. Please, help me before this kills all of us.

4

A Phoenix from the Ashes

EMBER

"Some people are like beautiful dreamcatchers, absorbing the most
terrible things for those they love and leaving them only the softest,
gentlest thoughts behind."
-Nikita Gill

Having carefully rid my skin of the vast amounts of blood and grime, I wrapped myself in a warm fuzzy blanket and watched in worried silence as Clarice tried to help Evadne.

"The wound on your chest," Clarice said brusquely, jerking her chin toward me. "Where did it come from?"

"The wraith in the cursed area of the Moores," I replied, remembering the pain. "The one who wanted to dance."

Clarice made a sound of disgust. "That tainted magic has been growing unchecked for far too long. It keeps overtaking more and more ground toward the Central Realm. But I digress. Please, go on."

"He was fighting Artemis when we were trying to get away, but he was playing dirty. His goons put arrows through Artemis when he started to gain the upper hand. When the wraith went in for the killing blow, I jumped in front of it to save his life."

Clarice gasped, shocked. "Why on earth would you do that for a no-good monarch?"

"I..." my voice trailed off. "The Realm needs him," I replied at last.

Clarice snorted in derision. "The Realm needs no pompous ruler."

"He's not pompous," I whispered. "He's changing. We can all see it; he wants to be more than what the Fey have become."

"And yet you left him," Clarice challenged.

"There may yet be a way to escape the Last Gate," I murmured, staring out the window. "I need to know what that path is. I need a chance to decide, not just blindly take the only option presented to me."

Clarice hummed under her breath. "You love him," she said at last.

"What? No, I..."

"You do. You love him, but you left him in search of that great perhaps. Do not be surprised when that perhaps unravels in your hands, and you find yourself back with him. Running was never what you wanted to begin with. It is the way of fate. You can't run from who you are, or who you love, daughter of Grimm."

"Why would Jack send us here if there's no hope of finding a different way and changing our fate?" I countered desperately.

She gave me a small, sad smile as she gently wrapped Evadne's blackened wrist. "This way will doom your heart, child," she replied, gently avoiding my question altogether. "But what do I know? I'm just an old woman...a terrible healer to boot. You'll have to follow this path for now and then you'll see that I'm right."

She and I both began to giggle at the expression. "You sound just like my Oma," I chortled as a spike of grief cut my heart. I missed Oma so much.

"She sounds like a very wise person."

"She was," I replied quietly. "She was."

"Well, I've done all I can for her," Clarice said, staring in dismay at the pile of bloody glass she'd pulled out of Evadne's body. "Your turn, love."

I grimaced, not looking forward to the experience. There were so many thorns embedded beneath my skin I was tempted to ask her to hit me over the head with a frying pan just so I didn't have to feel what had to be done.

Clarice began to examine the wound on my chest first. "Hmm," she said at last, still staring at the jagged scars. "This is not a normal mend. This is a very, *very* rare form of healing. I've only seen it in magics that are entwined and bound." She looked up then, her deep onyx eyes holding mine for a moment. "Child, to whom has your magic been bound?"

I knew, but didn't want to answer the question. After Evadne had told me about what Nightshade had said, it had festered in the back of my mind, both infuriating and entrancing me. So, desperate to keep the delusion that I had a choice in my future, I ignored it. With Artemis' shifts and the desperate escape after, I still hadn't worked up the courage to ask him what it meant.

"I think it was bound to the prince," I sighed.

"Think?" she asked sharply.

"I have no knowledge of it happening, but—"

"Then the King bound it in secret," Clarice interrupted, her voice enraged as she began to examine the other wounds that covered my body. "I'm surprised Winter didn't have a conniption fit..." her voice trailed off. "Though, if Winter was dead certain on your imminently joining their ranks...your magic being bound to the Summer Prince and within Winter's Realm, would weaken the Summer throne." She broke off into another round of humming that sounded angry and annoyed. "Monarchs," she spat at last. "They think they can change fate and control the outcome...they only bring the evil upon us with their desperate attempts to gain the upper hand. If they stopped being so power hungry and doggedly focused on the future, and *faced* the evil that was in front of them *now*, perhaps they *could* change the ending."

She stared down at her bloody hands for a moment. "No," she said softly. "There is no changing such a bloody future. It will all end. Prophecies are always fulfilled."

Well, aren't you an optimistic ray of sunshine.

Clarice looked at me then, her ancient eyes full of sorrow. "It's not fair what they've done to you, child. It is unjust what you'll face within your lifetime because of this broken Realm."

Thanks. That's just the pep talk I needed right about now.

She made a face, as she stared at the ruined mess of skin and blood. "Grimms may heal quickly, but that doesn't mean you should treat that gift so recklessly. I can't find where one wound ends, and another begins."

"It wasn't really my fault," I griped. "Those stupid brambles were trying to eat us, and I didn't want to be plant food."

"Oh no, child," Clarice replied matter-of-factly. "They wouldn't eat you; they'd just impale you and leave you to die slowly in their clutches. You'd be *raven* food."

"Either way, I wasn't keen on dying and being eaten by *anything*. It's not like I *tried* to get injured."

"Curse those reckless monarchs for sending you there in the first place," Clarice seethed. "Wendy, darling," she called out.

"Yes ma'am?" a young woman who bore a striking resemblance to Clarice poked her head in the room.

"I'm going to need Theron. Can you send for him, please?"

"Right on it!" Wendy replied cheerfully.

"That's my daughter," Clarice said proudly as she watched her leave.

"She's beautiful," I sighed, exhausted. "She looks just like you."

"Perhaps when I was a century younger," Clarice laughed.

Wendy returned a few minutes later, her deep brown and gold eyes laughing. "He says he'll be right over, and would like it to be noted that, if he gets bitten again, he will charge a steep fee."

Clarice scoffed and rolled her eyes.

Wendy bore a close resemblance to her mother. They shared the same rich skin, with a light caramel undertone. Her hair was brown and gold with red highlights, that fell in wild waves and curls down her back. Woven throughout were stones and beads, gold cuffs, and flowers. Her talismans were similar to the ones Evadne and I had received from Marcovester Red. Currently, her hair was pulled partially back with a bright green bandana.

"Did somebody call for a hero?" Theron's laughing voice called from the doorway a few minutes later.

Both Clarice and Wendy rolled their eyes. I was too tired to roll mine, but they had been so thorough in their eye rolling, I figured it covered my contribution to their optic spiral party.

So began the long and agonizing process of putting me back together.

Clarice's healing magic and balms were different from any I'd experienced before. Worse yet, the magic she wove as she worked inflicted pain as the price for the healing. Most of the wounds she attempted to treat without her magic, but some were bad enough that they needed a little extra help.

After an eternity had passed, Clarice at last stepped back with a sigh of relief. "There now," she murmured. "That should do it, love. Though your body is not accustomed to the twisted magic that now resides in the Moores... I wager it will take a few days, if not a week, for you to completely heal. If we were in the Central Kingdom, you would heal in a day, if not sooner. But here you'll just have to learn to be patient. We'll change all the bandages daily and unbind that broken arm after a couple days and see how it's faring."

She gave my uninjured arm a final gentle pat. "Rest," she instructed. "Until you cannot rest any more. You need to gain your strength, and the best way to do that is through sleep."

I nodded, knowing sleep would not come anytime soon. I was so exhausted I could drop, but worry for my sister was a constant alarm in the back of my mind that would not let my eyes close.

The night crawled by and still I could not sleep. I passed the hours crying as I sat beside Evadne's cot, holding her limp hand in mine and begging her to wake up.

It was useless. No matter how I pleaded and wept, she still didn't stir.

What are we going to do, Eva? I listened to Jack and left Artemis...but I don't know if it's the right choice.

We were supposed to stay together. Artemis trusted Jack and Jack betrayed him by sending us away...Artemis is going to kill him. I didn't pretend well enough; I've put Jack in danger.

What have I done?

I did something terrible, Eva...I left Artemis. I destroyed the bridge we were rebuilding...I just left him standing there. He was so broken. What if it wasn't the right choice? What if leaving him behind wasn't the right choice...

I read Jack's letter over and over again—trying to make sense of what he'd said. There was a chance of changing our fate. We actually had a real, tangible chance to escape the Last Gate.

But what if my chance to escape the Last Gate means leaving Artemis behind...do I really want a future without him?

I mean...I got on the boat, didn't I? I left him...

I left him, but I'm not sure it was the right choice. I left him, but my heart still weeps for him...

What is right and what is wrong in this tangled, unending web of grief and chaos that stands between us?

Even if, in the end, I return to Artemis...I could still save Evadne from the Last Gate. Marcus can't leave the Realm, but since he's no longer tied to the courts, he'll find her again...they could have a happy life away from all of this...Perhaps she could have a happy ending...

Do we get happy endings? Do happy endings exist for us?

If I go back to Artemis, would he let my sister go?

Can I bear to be parted from my sister?

The unending ifs and questions ran circles around my mind, leaving nothing but a migraine in their wake. There was no way to untangle everything. Not when I had no idea what the future held, or what our options even were...or where my heart truly lay.

The conversation with Clarice was burned into my mind, the endless questions I could not articulate spinning faster and faster as I helplessly watched the shallow rise and fall of Evadne's chest. Every breath was a hollow gasp, and I knew in my gut something was terribly wrong.

Please wake up, Evadne. Please wake up. I need to talk to you. I need to know if I actually did the right thing, or if I did something terrible. I need to tell you about the kiss...that kiss revealed my heart and all I wish we could be. Yet, it betrayed the truth of everything that stands between us. This ravine I cannot seem to get across.

I can't fall in love with him...can I? What if he gets me killed?

But what if he doesn't? What if he is truly changing? Can I really blame him for what the past holds, when he's changing and rising beyond it?

I'm going to die anyway...what if this turns out to be my only chance for happiness? Brief though it may be...

There was no escaping my spiraling thoughts. I had no one to talk through it with who would truly understand. Evadne was the only person in the world I could trust with such questions. So, I passed the time building and rebuilding the puzzle. But no amount of rearranging the pieces could bring the image into focus. It was just a blur of disconnected colors and shapes, veiled in shadows and splattered with blood.

I should be dead. I should be dead, but Artemis saved me after I saved him. When will we stop circling around each other? When will it end? Will we ever find peace?

Do we have any hope for a future? Do I want to go back to him, if it means death at the Last Gate?

What does death at the Last Gate mean? How much time would we have before they send me there?

Is there any hope for us in this broken Realm?

Do I dare hope, when I likely won't survive?

I'm still alive...still alive? Aren't I?

Am I even alive anymore?

I had circled death so much in the past few days, part of me wasn't entirely sure that death hadn't taken me while I wasn't looking, and I was merely watching the rest of my days unfold outside of myself as she spirited my soul away and my shell carried on the beastly task of surviving.

When will I find my way through this labyrinth?

Will I ever find my way?

I don't know...I don't know...

The skyeship creaked and groaned in the night sky as it drifted across the wind currents—the way it would the sea's waves.

I'm on a flying ship...in the middle of the sky. I didn't know this was possible. How is this possible?

Eva, please wake up. You would be so entranced by the view. The clouds sliding through your fingertips would have you mesmerized. You wouldn't care that we're likely hundreds of thousands of feet up. You wouldn't be scared like I am.

Please Eva, wake up. Just wake up. You're worrying us sick.

I wasn't the only one worried. Fireheart and Elvie were perched on her chest, their eyes fixed on her face. They didn't move as they kept a close vigil.

"She's not going anywhere, you know that, right?"

I jumped at the sound of Theron's voice. I had been so absorbed in my thoughts, I hadn't even heard him walk up. He was leaning up against the doorway of the medical cabin. His easy grin reminded me so much of Jack's crooked smile.

"Are you going to stare at her all night, Sparks? All creepy like, as if you're a stalker?" Laughter clung to his voice, but his bright silver eyes were serious—gauging my reaction.

How long has he been standing there? I didn't hear anything.

"She might wake up," I replied hollowly. "Besides, she's my twin. I can be 'stalkerish' if I want to, thank you very much."

My poor attempt at a comeback fell flat, and I rolled my eyes at my slow wits.

He's the one standing there staring at us. I should've said he's clearly the one stalking, if that's what's defined as stalking.

Is it too late to say that now?

"You're totally giving your own stalker vibes," I said as loftily as I could manage.

The corners of Theron's mouth lifted in a smug smile. "I knew you had some spunk left. I was worried after so much blood loss you might've lost the ability to be funny."

I'm funny?

Duh. I'm freaking hilarious. It's about time someone realized it.

"No amount of blood loss could make me dreary." The honor of my humor defended, I turned back to my sister.

Please wake up, Eva. Please wake up.

"She's not going to wake up," Theron said gently. "Not until we reach the healer. Her wounds are too much. Even if she were to wake, we would send her back to sleep. Her injuries are such that she would be screaming in agony if she were to wake."

"Why can't Clarice heal her?" I asked quietly.

"Some things are beyond even her. We need someone fluent in Darke magic."

"That seems like a terrible idea," I muttered.

"It takes one to know one," Theron said with a shrug. "She can't help if she doesn't know it, inside and out, herself."

I nodded with a sigh. He was right.

"Well, even if you have to send her back to sleep," I said, stubbornly picking up my previous trail of thought. "I will be here when she wakes up. She can hear me, even if she's not awake...she can hear me. I need her to know that I'm here." I glared at Theron to prove my point. "I'm *not* leaving her."

Theron shrugged, unperturbed by my obstinate angst. "Suit yourself. You wouldn't be leaving her if you slept. You've already dragged your cot beside hers. You'll be right there, just, snoozleing, per say."

"Snoozleing?" I snorted.

"Yes," Theron replied indignantly. "It's a perfectly acceptable term to describe resting, with your eyes closed, but very aware of what's around you. It's not a nap, it's a snoozle."

"Is that something close to a Heffalump or Woozle?" I muttered under my breath.

"No, those are different creatures entirely. They're nothing but honey thieves."

"You say that like they're something tangible and real," I snorted in amusement.

"Who says they're not?" Theron replied indignantly. "This is the Realm. We are within the Moores to boot. You would do well to broaden your horizons of belief and realize that just about anything is possible here."

"Suuuure." I rolled my eyes to cement my opinion of disbelief.

Y'know, just in case he overlooked my obvious tone of sarcasm and doubt.

Theron scoffed. "Greenhorn."

"Jerk," I shot back.

Theron laughed and I rolled my eyes again. He reminded me so much of Jack, it was uncanny.

"Are you still mad at me?" Theron asked, changing topics.

"I wasn't mad at you," I muttered, unable to meet his laughing eyes. "I was just in a lot of pain...and you happened to be the one holding me down while Clarice tortured me under the guise of 'healing' me."

I could see Theron's smile growing from the corner of my eye as he made his way into the room and sat on the edge of my cot.

Excuse me. That is my cot, I didn't say you could sit there.

Despite my indignation, homesickness hit me in a wave. He wore the same sort of conspiratorial smile I used to share with my sisters. Theron carried the same sort of mischievous attitude as Jack when he was about to get into trouble. We were so young when he left, but I still remembered those days when we were all together. They had been my lifeline over the years, helping me hold on. When I was within the darkness, reminiscing about better days reminded me to hope for the future—good days could come again, I just had to hold on.

"So, tell me, Sparks, where did you learn to insult people like that?"

I frowned; he wasn't even trying to hide his amusement. "My sister," I replied primly.

"Which one?"

"Both," I snipped.

"I don't think I've ever heard such a string of nonsense issue from one person, and I live on a ship. Nonsense is our main dialect."

It seemed to take far too much energy to lift the corners of my mouth into a sheepish smile. The strength it took to humor him seemed incredible. "Sorry," I sighed. "But I'm sure you would've done the same if you were in my shoes."

"Oh, I have no doubt about that," Theron agreed with a laugh. "No good, dirty rotten poop-headed, lost marble-brained, furry donkey-butt, jerk-head!" he growled in a falsetto—doing a poor imitation of my voice.

That was a terrible impersonation. I don't sound like that!

"You will surely strike fear into the heart of every skye voyager you meet in these Moores with that pretty, yet petty, set of insults. They are truly the finest weapons in a six-year old's arsenal of slander."

I huffed, too tired to think of a comeback.

"Are you hungry?" Theron asked, his tone jovial.

I shook my head. The mere thought of food made me want to retch. The herbs Clarice had given me to dull the pain as she dug out the thorns, the sway of the ship, and my own fear and worry, had my stomach in a state of constant nausea.

"You need to eat," Theron pushed gently. "Your body needs to heal. It can't do that if it doesn't have any nutrients."

"I know," I muttered. "I'll eat when I feel a little less like retching."

Theron shrugged and let the matter drop. "So, what's your story?" he asked, changing the subject yet again.

I think there should be a limit on subject changes when I'm feeling poorly. He's only allowed two per day.

Per day? That seems a bit extreme. How about per hour?

I'm the one feeling poorly. Which means I get to make the rules. I can make them as ridiculously extreme as I like.

I didn't feel like making small talk or pouring my heart and soul out to a total stranger. A question like that fell into both categories.

Find something smart to say.

"What's yours?" I countered.

That was not smart.

Whatever. He'll get the hint I don't want to talk.

"I asked first," Theron scoffed, arching an eyebrow.

Clearly he's thick headed and unable to take a hint.

"I'm not in the mood for a heart to heart," I snapped.

"If I ask, 'how are you,' does that count as a heart to heart?"

"Maybe," I replied irritably.

"Suit yourself," Theron said with a shrug.

I sighed, utterly irritated, and turned back to Evadne's gaunt face.

"You'll learn to trust me soon enough," Theron stated.

My exasperation flared. "What makes you so sure?"

"You'll have no other choice," Theron said matter-of-factly. "*I* have information you want." He wiggled his eyebrows. "You're at my mercy, Sparks. You should answer my questions, then maybe I'll be inclined to answer yours."

I made a face, annoyed that he was right. He did have something I wanted.

Perhaps I'll dabble in violence and threaten him. I could put a dagger to his throat and MAKE him talk. He's a pirate. I bet he'd appreciate such tactics.

My eyes were at last growing heavy from exhaustion, but now I resolutely forced them to stay open. I couldn't sleep, not when Evadne might need me.

"Well, aren't you stubborn," Theron commented dryly.

I scowled, determined to ignore him if he was going to criticize my life choices. "I can be stubborn about staying awake if I want," I muttered.

Theron rolled his eyes. "Here," he said after a few moments had passed. He pulled a large leather bag from his cloak pocket and set it on the floor beside me.

It tinkled and clinked, like broken glass and silverware.

My curiosity rose. "What is it?" I asked

"Your lollipop for not biting the doctor," Theron quipped with a smirk. He paused. "Wait, no. I take that back. You bit me."

"You weren't the doctor," I snorted.

"Assistants count as doctors, you know."

"Since when?" I asked incredulously.

"Since now."

I scoffed, and it turned into a cough. My mouth and throat suddenly felt as dry as a desert. I took a long drink from my water bottle, slipping it back into my cloak pocket. I stared in dismay at the worn material of the sack on the floor. Despite the sturdy leather, tiny hairline cuts crisscrossed the surface.

"Is that—" I stopped, unsure of myself.

"Well, open it and see for yourself," Theron replied indignantly.

I stared at the bag, indecision pulling at me. I didn't know what was inside, but right now exploration seemed to demand a little too much energy from me.

"Is it going to bite me?" I asked, stalling.

"After all your biting, I don't think you have a right to be upset if it *is* something that bites. It would serve you right."

I gave Theron a look—one I usually reserved for Evadne when she was being particularly stupid.

Theron ignored my ire. Instead of being properly cowed into submission, he growled and chomped his teeth together. "It wouldn't hurt for you to get a little of your own medicine," he said, grinning.

I rolled my eyes and cautiously opened the bag. Sharp points poked through the thick material, pricking my fingertips. I stared down at the jumbled mess within. Red tinted edges of gold, silver, and diamond glinted in the bright moonlight that streamed through the doorway and wide windows of the small cabin.

"I even got most of the blood off for you," Theron said proudly. "Clarice cleansed the blood echo off of the majority of it for you, as well."

"What am I supposed to do with them?" I asked incredulously. "Wear them like a trophy to make any future thorns think twice before attacking me?"

"Well, you could. But I doubt it would work. The thorns would likely take it as a challenge and keep your skewered body high above the brambles, daring any newcomer to think twice before entering their domain."

I made a face, disgusted by the mental image he had just given me.

"Besides," Theron continued. "You'd cut yourself so much it definitely wouldn't be worth it. The thorns are enchanted with Darke magic. No armor or spell can withstand the edge."

"Well, that explains why my armor did nothing to stop their attack," I griped.

Theron nodded. "That section of the Moores carries a nasty piece of magic. We stay clear of it...it's under the sway of The Daughter, and nothing good comes from her wretched magic."

I have questions about this mysterious 'Daughter,' but I am too exhausted to ask them now. Remind me to ask later, when I'm less exhausted.

Noted. A reminder has been set for next year.

That sounds like a good time frame. Maybe by then I'll have found my brain.

"As to a smarter plan of action, I would suggest bartering," Theron suggested. "You could also sell them, trade them, or perhaps even hoard them if you like keeping war trophies." He shrugged. "Whatever your vicious little heart desires. They're yours by right of trial within the Moores, so you can do whatever you want with them. I'd suggest the first three options. You'll need new fighting clothes. Yours were too far gone to rescue, as was your sister's dress." He paused, scoffing. "Though I doubt she'd have wanted to continue wearing it. It's possible to fight in a dress, but very impractical."

The mental image of Evadne hardcore fighting in her ballgown was one of epic proportions. It was something akin to *Pride & Prejudice & Zombies*, and it gave me wicked satisfaction to think of my sister being so incredibly awesome.

She stabbed Darcy while wearing a dress. She had quite a few daggers on her person during the Farewell Ball... But he's right. It's possible, but not practical. She could have done so much more damage to Darcy if she hadn't been restricted by the dress and how many weapons she could feasibly carry.

I stared down at my own borrowed clothing. Theron was right. Though comfortable, the tunic and black leggings Verity had loaned me were not suitable for combat.

"You'll also need something to bargain with once we reach the healer. She will not do the job for free, and though risky, she is still the safest person this side of the borders to entrust with the most dangerous pieces."

"Aren't they all dangerous?" I muttered. "They all tried to kill me."

"Not that kind of dangerous. The ones on top that are still red tinted? They completely absorbed your blood. They're uncleansable. In the hands of a skilled sorcerer, they're a powerful weapon which poses a threat to them *and* you. The cursed one is the only one who can be trusted with such artifacts, for she is not foolish enough to desire the downfall of the Realm. Not when she created it in the first place."

I said the smartest thing I could think of, which happened to be a singular "Oh," as I dug out my water bottle for another drink. All this talking was making me thirsty.

I pondered his veiled meaning. Who was the cursed one, and what did he mean that she created the Realm?

"As a Grimm, your blood is powerful. It's not something to be taken lightly. The healer deals in rarities and cursed artifacts. Those thorns are rare, and most definitely cursed. But your blood absorbed within is what makes them *most* enticing for her. That will be the key to forcing her hand into helping you. She'll want those pieces more than she'll want to eat you."

I broke into an explosive coughing fit, having thoroughly choked on my water. "*Eat me*?!" I shrieked.

"Yes, she unfortunately happens to have a past with cannibalism. There's reports she's gone clean, but I'm not sure how far to trust that information. She dabbles. The more cursed the meat, the more power to her spells. The further her mind unravels, the more she becomes a wendigo. Thus, the less she will be able to control herself."

"Who *is* she?" I asked. My hazy, exhausted mind was creating the image of an off-kilter, wrinkled old woman, who had a house full of hoarded items that she kept for who knew what. I could picture shelf after shelf of unique artifacts and shiny things as well as a random, yet disgusting, hoard of human bones and body parts that she constantly stated were 'incredibly important.'

"Who are you?" Theron countered.

"I asked first," I protested.

"Actually, I started asking questions first when we began our conversation, and as I clearly remember, you didn't deign to answer me. So I don't feel like answering your questions."

I rolled my eyes at his stubbornness, but his question circled the back of my mind.

Who am I? Who am I?

Too little, too much, not enough...

I am a thief, trying to steal moments from time. I am a coward, too scared to fight her fear. I am a liar, breaking the heart of the one who cares for me... I am a wanderer, longing to go home. I am just a girl, desperately trying to protect her sister...I am tired, tired, tired...I am so incredibly tired. But most of all, I am a broken heart, too shattered to be mended, too weak to fight.

I held my silence with a stubborn sort of desperation, refusing to rise to his obvious bait. I was afraid if I did, I would crumble to pieces so miniscule that no amount of superglue or duct tape could put me back together.

"I was twenty-one Faerie Solstices when I came to this ship," Theron said softly. "I had just lost everything, and everyone I had ever known...myself included. My brother and I...my twin—the only person who had ever truly known me—chose different paths...the woman I loved was gone... I was a hopeless wreck, and it felt as if the world was never going to be okay again." He paused, his silver eyes probing mine. "If I were to guess, I'd wager that you also feel as if part of you is gone, and you can't find your way back."

I couldn't stop the tears that rose. "You're right," I whispered. "I feel so...lost, and I cannot find myself...I feel like I don't know who I am anymore. I left them there. My brother, Evadne's boyfriend, my...my..."

What was Artemis to me? I had no proper description for our strained relationship and the kiss that still burned between us.

My heart. My heart...he's my heart.

No. He can't be...he just can't be...

"I chose to leave them, and I don't know if it was the right choice... It was at Jack's behest, and I trust him more than anything...but the feelings that are left in the wreckage are making me question if it was the right choice after all."

I stole her away from Marcus. She had no choice in the matter... I left Artemis there and burned the bridge we were trying to rebuild... I think I did something terrible, unforgiveable even, and I don't know if there's any way back from this...I don't know if Artemis will ever forgive me for this...I don't know why I did this...I can't find myself in the haze.

What if Evadne is mad at me? What if she's so angry she won't forgive me? What if—

"You'll find your way, Sparks," Theron said kindly, pulling me from my racing thoughts. "And when you do, you will find you've risen from the ashes, stronger than before. You are a phoenix within this darkness and you will burn once more." He tilted his head to the side, forcing me to catch his keen gaze. "Why else would the Moores have marked you as their namesake?"

"What?"

"The phoenix on your back. The Moores claimed you."

"What phoenix?"

I hadn't had access to a mirror while Clarice had healed me. I had no idea what he was talking about.

"There's a phoenix on your right shoulder blade that goes down your ribcage. It's black, red, gold and copper. It's the mark of the Moores."

"I don't..." my voice trailed off as I at last remembered.

Wait...the phoenix, when I saved Evadne and broke the curse—my fire changed into a phoenix, and it ate the snake...the phoenix came back down and landed on my shoulder. The voice...that was the Moores?

"So, what does that even mean?"

"No one *really* knows for sure. But it usually means your destiny has changed...or perhaps this was your destiny all along and you've finally come into it."

"But, I...did I bind myself into a bargain?"

"Not necessarily, it's...it's almost as if the Moores chose you for something, something great. It's less a bargain and more...a, well, a something."

"That's very helpful," I snorted, making a face. "I'm in a 'something' with the Moores, but I have no idea what."

I shifted, and pain shot across my body. I had been sliced to ribbons and every inch of my skin was on fire whenever I moved. The adrenaline had been so strong I hadn't realized how injured I was until we weren't in danger anymore. Bandages covered my body, and there was no moving without some injury protesting.

"I don't know if there's any hope for such a grand destiny," I whispered. "I don't know if there's any hope left for me. I leave a trail of violence and bloodshed wherever I go, and I fail to protect the most precious thing in my life—my family."

I stared down at Evadne's ashen face. Tears were leaking from the corners of her eyes. Even comatose, she was still in pain.

How do I help you, Evadne? What can I do to fix this?

"You got this far," Theron said comfortingly. "I'd wager a bet that based on your injuries, you did everything you possibly could to protect her—all except dying, that is. Though you came pretty close on that one."

"It wasn't enough," I sniffed, trying to keep my own tears at bay.

"That doesn't mean you failed," Theron pressed gently. "Sometimes we give our best, but it just isn't enough. That doesn't mean that *you* aren't enough, it just means the odds were against you and it didn't work out. What happened wasn't your fault. You did the best you could. That's all any of us can do in a world like this."

"How do you know?" I demanded angrily, clinging to my guilt. "You weren't there."

"No, I wasn't. But I think I'm a pretty good judge of character. I can read between the lines...sense the depths of what's really happening, if you will."

I pondered his cryptic statement, wondering how we had ever gotten on this topic to begin with.

I thought I decided that I wasn't going to have a heart-to-heart with a total stranger. Yet here I am spilling my guts and feelings...

Clearly the blood loss has addled my brain and decisions about such things. I am as fickle as an old woman on a hot day.

Does that mean I finally get to have a cane, so I can whack people with it?

I sniffed, wiping the tears from my cheeks. I couldn't put a finger on it, but something within me responded to him. Something *wanted* to reply. Somehow, it suddenly felt as if he was a safe harbor in the midst of my stormy sea. Those silvery eyes reminded me so much of F, and for a moment the chasm of grief in my chest eased. The sorrow I hid for the ones I'd lost seemed a little easier to bear.

"Did you get that wound on your chest from him?"

Who does he mean? Artemis or the wraith at the castle?

"I got it from the wraith," I said softly. The memories attacked me then. I was dying all over again—reliving the pain as I lunged in front of Artemis, his name a desperate cry on my lips as I tried to protect him.

"I got it saving him...before I turned around and betrayed him."

I was unable to keep the confession to myself.

"Is it really a betrayal?" Theron asked hesitantly. "If he truly cares for you..."

"I don't know if he truly cares for me," I interrupted harshly. "It's...well it's complicated." My voice softened. "I know to him it is a betrayal...we were supposed to stay together. We were on our way to rescue my sister."

"There are many roads that lead to the end," Theron said with a sigh. "Don't give up, there is yet hope in this twisted Realm. If he truly loves you, he will see your intent and forgive this so-called betrayal."

I pondered his words as the boat rose and fell beneath us, rocking gently on the wind. "I hope you're right," I at last murmured. Right now, hope was the only thing I had left to cling to.

5

My Magic Mouse Status Has Been Demoted, And I Am Officially Pooh Bear

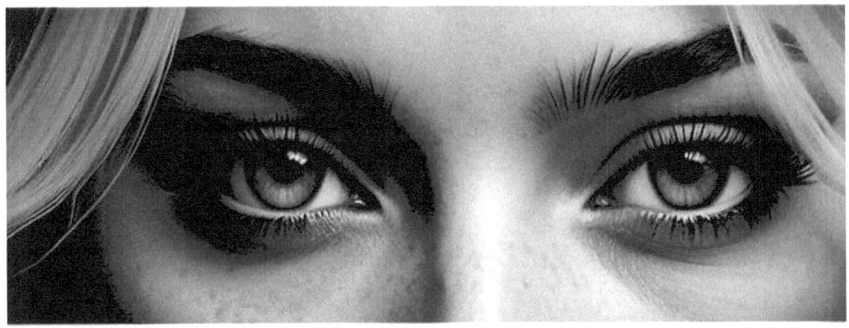

FAYE

"Never mistake my silence for weakness. No one plans a murder out loud."
-Unknown

I was through waiting for Ronan. He wasn't coming to save me—no one was. My only chance of survival, as well as rescuing Dad, would be if I escaped and got help. If I tried to play the hero and save him myself, it would only get me caught and possibly get both of us killed.

I hated the idea of leaving him behind, but it was the only way.

It was also the only possible way of helping Ronan get Meghan out and get him the help he so desperately needed.

Dad will understand. I know he'll understand. If Dad was here, he'd order me to leave him behind and get help.

Everything was hazy and disoriented. Thoughts and plans floated through my mind, then fled as quickly as they had arrived.

Think, think, think. You have to think of a way out.

How? I've already tried everything. It's no use, that gap in the bars is too small, I know I can't fit through it.

Needless to say, I was rapidly spiraling into a vast pit of despair.

I'm going to die here...Jeremiah has sucked one year of my life away...and how does that make me feel?

Well, let me moan for you a little bit and then you'll truly know how I feel.

I know how to cheer myself up. I'll challenge my new monster to a thumb war. I need to know if he's friendly or not.

The last one was most certainly not.

A monster being bloodthirsty and mean is the rule, not the exception. They're all mean.

Yeah but Ember's—

Ember's is a rule breaker.

Well, I think I'm going to see for myself. I want a nice monster too.

Oo! Maybe I can make him nice if I challenge him to a thumb war! Just you wait. I'm going to turn my monster nice.

You're going to get your thumb bit off when you challenge the monster.

I'm going to prove you wrong and get myself a nice monster, you pessimistic potato.

Invigorated by such a dangerous plan, I found the energy to change my position. But moving from lying halfway off the bed in rumpled despair as I stared at the ceiling, to draping myself over the edge, stomach down, so I could peer under the bed to bother my monster, felt as if I was moving through tar. Every inch of movement made my bones creak and ache.

Jeremiah is going to kill me sooner than he intends if he keeps administering this excessive dosage. I don't think he really knows what he's dealing with.

Yes, but what does it mean? Why would the Knight have a mortal doing his bidding? Why would he use Jeremiah? Why kidnap me? Who is the traitor within this elaborate ruse? Furthermore, why does the Knight want me?

Well, clearly he wants me because I am one in a million. DUH!

No. While I am one in a million, I don't think he'd go to such great lengths because of my uniqueness...

There were too many pieces to the puzzle. Too many questions were mixed into the problem, and I couldn't figure out where to begin. It was a conundrum that my drug addled brain was incapable of figuring out.

Here, monster, monster, monster. Come play thumb war with me. I need to know if you're nice or not.

This is a stupid idea. No monster under the bed is nice. You know this.

But Em's monster is nice. I want a nice monster!

Again I state, her monster is the exception.

Maybe I've just had a particularly hard run of bad monsters, and most of the time they're actually good...

It's not called a monster for nothing.

I think you're just being biased as you stereotype poor, defenseless—hello, what's this?

Shoved underneath the bed was an all too familiar black bag of certain torture.

Well, well, well. Look what the stupid ninny-head left when he was throwing his temper tantrum...

Well, monster, we'll have to postpone that match for another day. I have better things to do now.

My moping now thoroughly derailed, I yanked the bag out from under the bed and eagerly dumped the contents on top of the patchwork quilt.

I still don't have a purple bedspread. The nerve of that poo-brain to not heed my demands and give me what I want.

I mean, if he did that, our first demand would be to let me, and Dad, go... The bedspread was just a technicality of a demand.

Yes, but I still want it.

The rapid movement was a mistake. The room spun around me, and my nosy perusal was disrupted as I buried my head in my hands and struggled not to throw up.

One of the most feared warriors in the Realm, destined for the Summer Court to be the King's own lethal right hand...and I have been reduced to a puddle of goo by the simple task of sitting up.

I mean, it probably doesn't help that I was hanging upside down, first for moping, then for thumb wars...

Touché.

After a few agonizing minutes passed, the room finally righted itself and I resumed my snooping. The contents proved to be of little use. But the perceived thievery was enough to make my three brain cells wake up. They began to maniacally cackle as they initiated a frantic plotting session—all while humming the *Pink Panther* theme song.

Several scalpels were the only real prize within the haul. But messing around with all the fancy medical items in the most ridiculous manner possible gave an unexpected rush of clarity, and soon my precious trio of brain cells had a new escape plan to offer. All I needed to do was wait for nightfall.

Waiting wasn't too hard, not when I had new things to keep me occupied. Such as taking my blood pressure and listening to the walls of my cell with his fancy stethoscope. After affirming that I was indeed alive, I attempted to use the cuff on the door, but the seam was too tight. I couldn't jam the flimsy cloth in the crack to see if it would work in forcing the door open, much like it would on a car. That idea abandoned, I began to booby trap the doorway with an unpleasant array of medical items for Ronan to walk into when he did show his cowardly face again. It would be my farewell present to Ronan, as well as my final, crowing victory over the stupidhead.

What is this brilliant plan of escape, you ask? Well, allow me to shed some light on the subject.

The brain cells had donned their special outfits, (outfits reserved only for carrying out plans of utmost sneakiness) and with a loud click, pulled the cord of a singular light bulb that hung from *absolutely nothing* in the middle of my mind. The bright flare of light illuminated the eager faces of the three, as well as the hoard. The hoard lingered around the edges of the light, feigning indifference, when in reality they were incredibly curious. They were *all* listening in rapt silence, excited by the prospect of great feats of genius.

You see, Ronan was so busy being mad at me and storming off in a tantrum-induced rage like a two-year-old, he left his precious medical bag in my clutches. The rule of finders keepers is absolute in kidnapping scenarios.

But wouldn't that mean that, since he found you, he rightfully gets to keep you?

No. Absolutely not. Such rules do not apply to the advantage of the kidnapper, only for the kidnappee. Besides, he didn't find me, he stalked me. Now, if you'd please stop asking stupid questions and interrupting me, I have a maniacal escape plan to outline.

I think you're just making up the rules.

I think you're choosing to focus on the insignificant and negative side of things.

Hmph.

Deranged arguments and inspirational quotes were running rampant in my manic mind. My three brain cells had abandoned their awestruck listening and began to yell the epic quotes, word for word, as they ran little circles around their large chalkboard which was solely reserved for evil plans. In turn, their excitement was stirring up the hoard, who watched the chaos with longing. They were beginning to rethink their original union ideas.

Yes, this precious medical bag will be the key to my escape.

How so? There's nothing of value in it.

For one, it contains scalpels. In my current knifeless situation, they prove to be a priceless treasure.

Yes, but how will they aid in your escape, since we aren't going to try to take over the compound?

Well, no. But it's the principle of the thing. It makes me feel motivated. Thus, in the presence of shiny sharp things of certain death and destruction, an escape plan has been born. As that wonderful quote states, desperate times call for desperate measures and when life (or Ronan) rudely closes a door, there will always be a window... In this instance, I plan to take such sage advice quite literally. Thanks to Ronan's obvious neglect, I've lost enough weight to fit through the window. The Zaubermaus will prevail over these horrible people as soon as night falls.

With this closing statement my brain cells began to scream and cheer in delight at my sheer brilliance.

Why Ronan felt the need to keep five scalpels in his medical bag was beyond me. But I was nevertheless grateful for his overkill measures. It ensured I was well armed as I shoved two in my boot and two in my waistband. The fifth I used for my own twisted purposes. My bangs were long overdue for a trim.

You throw a tantrum, Ronan, you lose.

My hair fell in soft heaps around my feet as I carefully sliced through small sections at a time. When nightfall finally arrived, I had cut my hair into a stylish, layered bob that fell to my chin. The edges were a bit jagged, some parts falling longer than the others, but I didn't particularly care. With the wispy layers and edges, I looked like an entirely new person. It was an understatement to say I was fully satisfied with the results.

Take that, Ronan. I look fabulous and you look stupid.

See, when life gives you lemons, you must throw them back and demand chocolate.

I had spent ample time in the last few days stewing as I threw lemons back at life. Now at last, despite my lemon filled existence, spite had finally paid off. Life had relented and for once granted my demand for chocolate.

You see, when bossing life around, the key is persistence. Eventually, it'll get tired of getting hit in the head with lemons and give you what you want on the condition that you'll just shut up.

I grinned triumphantly at my reflection, admiring the pointed ends and the way the front framed my face. It was a stubborn sort of victory, using Ronan's things against their intended use, but it was also a relief to get my bangs out of the way.

You're lucky that it turned out this decent. It could have gone terribly wrong. Then you'd have to live with a bad haircut and Ronan would make fun of you.

Well. There's nothing to worry about there. I won't be seeing Ronan ever again.

Too bad, I look absolutely stunning. Maybe it would make him reconsider his ways if he saw me looking this beautiful.

My cheeks flushed at the thought, and I resolutely shoved it down a flight of stairs in the back of my mind.

You are incredibly vain and conceited.

What I meant to say was...if he saw me looking like this, maybe he'd think I was just a helpless human. There, that's what I meant. I definitely don't care what he thinks of me...and I really couldn't care less if he thinks I look cute or not...

Suuuuure...I totally believe you.

Look, I can hate him and still want him to think I look beautiful. It's the principle of the thing. I still hate his guts.

The lights in my room flickered off. But unlike the old pattern, there was no announcement of 'lights out,' or any wishing of goodnight. I wasn't sure who was turning off my lights, but it clearly wasn't Ronan. Of that much, I was sure. He was too much a creature of habit, a stalker's happy daydream—predictable and stupid.

I grinned savagely, enjoying my personal rebellion to stay up however late I pleased by leaving my bathroom light on.

Poor, poor, sweet Ronan. He must be pouting still.

I spent the rest of my necessary wait time removing my overgrown stitches with the scalpel. Ronan's thick head had yet to comprehend how fast my body healed. Even though my talisman had been emptied, it recovered after a few hours, and after a couple of days, the stitches had begun to do more harm than good. Part of me wished he had thought to check up on my stitches. The ones across my back and shoulders needed to come out, but I couldn't reach them, no matter how I twisted and turned. They would have to wait until I got out and found help.

After the stitches were taken care of, I didn't have much else to do. So I spent the minutes that crawled by indulging my vanity and admiring my reflection in the mirror. I refined the haircut, taking little bits off here and there as I waited for the vibrations of the compound to fall silent.

At last silence reigned and I slid the thick glass of my little window open. Icy air sliced across my cheeks as the lone howl of a wolf cut through the stillness. A shiver ran down my spine at the mournful noise.

Here puppy-puppy.

No! Not here puppy, puppy! Are you crazy? It'll eat your face off.

A wolf is just a giant version of a puppy dog...it just needs love and treats.

You're delusional. You have terrible taste in men, and dogs. First you want Ronan to see how cute you look, now you want a wolf for a pet. What's next, are you going to change your mind about what constitutes a proper breakfast?

No! I would never do something like that. Pizza is the only proper breakfast in my books. Take it back! I most certainly do not have terrible taste in anything, and I am most definitely NOT delusional.

Do you not remember the last time we encountered a wolf? It nearly killed you.

That was a Direwolfe. Besides, he was just grumpy because I kept him from a crunchy human snack. I'm sure if that wasn't the case, it would be a loyal companion. Man, that'd be great! Can you imagine how cool it would be to have a Direwolf at my beck and call? I could train it to bite whoever was annoying me.

Now you're delusional AND crazy. You're also short. Get the chair.

There's no need to bring my height deficiency into the argument. Insults don't win arguments; they just show you're petty. It's genetic, I can't help how short I am.

The scalpel was clenched in between my teeth as I pushed the chair toward the window. The argument was now background noise. My three brain cells had taken up my fight and were beating the other side of me with their 'evil plan' chalkboard. As they fought, they screamed absurd insults on behalf of my short stature.

"Shtupid Wonan," I muttered around the handle as I stared at the tiny gap that Dad had created when he began to bend the bars.

There is absolutely no way I can fit through that.

Well, the physics escape with a wet shirt and a chair leg requires two people. It would have to be held in place while you scramble through. Add to that you're not strong enough to twist and bend it. You've lost too much strength thanks to Jeremiah's psycho drugs. So, stop your moping negativity and get to work.

True, moping and negativity only gets one so far.

You are the Zaubermaus, you can fit through anything.

At this, my brain cells rallied and, abandoning their attempt to defend me, began to scream the expression like a war cry. *"WE WILL FIT THROUGH ANYTHING, FOR WE ARE THE MAGIC MOUSE!! THE ZAUBERMAUSE WILL BE TRI-UMPHAAAANT!"*

I didn't bother to remind my poor, delusional brain cells how I had gotten that nickname in the first place. It was a closely kept secret between Oma and me, due to my *unbearable* humiliation. I hadn't gotten the nickname from being a magic mouse and successfully getting through a tight space. The nickname itself was an irony because I had received it after getting *incredibly* stuck in Oma's bathroom window.

One summer, two years before I was taken, while my family was gone on vacation, she had locked herself out of her house. I had stayed home from the trip, opting to go see Oma and spend some quality time with her. Upon realizing our mistake, the solution seemed simple. The bathroom window was still open, so I would just climb up, scramble through, and open the front door for her. But, after I inevitably got stuck, Oma had no choice but to call the local fire department for help.

At the time, living in a small town, all the guys on the crew adored her and kept an eye out for her. She in turn took care of them by making them treats and meals. She had adopted the entire department as her grandkids, and they all called her Oma. There were many playful arguments about whose Oma she was, and who the favorite grandchild was. Currently, I was in hot competition with a tall, blue-eyed redhead named Sam who had the audacity to insist that *he* was the favorite because of his handlebar mustache.

Before the crew arrived, I made her pinky promise that she wouldn't humiliate me further and tell them my whereabouts. I knew if Sam was on duty, I'd never live down my embarrassment. When they arrived to let her in, I hung there, stuck in the tiny window and holding my breath. In looking back, I should have just swallowed my pride and let the guys help me get down. Oma was already ancient at that point and had no business trying to pull me through. By the time she finally managed the feat, we were both laughing hysterically as we fell in a heap on the floor.

After we caught our breath, I had made her swear—cross her heart and hope to die—that she would not tell *anyone* in my family what had happened. She promised, but she couldn't resist the chance to give me the nickname *Zaubermaus*. Knowing what it meant—magic mouse—my family assumed I had done something incredible. They were right, but it was something incredibly humiliating and hilarious. Since then, I made it my life's goal to truly become a magic mouse and never get stuck again.

My victory over the doggy door at the Anderson base had boosted my pride in my abilities, making me fairly certain I would be victorious over the cursed window. Besides, I had no choice but to get through it. There would be no sniggering Oma to rescue me if my hairbrained plan failed.

It's not going to fail. I will not let myself fail.

That's the spirit. Now, think small thoughts, very, very small thoughts.

Should I slather my clothes in lotion?

No, that would waste time, and then my hands would slip when I'm trying to get up... Besides, I'm small and bendy, I can fit.

I can fit...but can I fit all the way through?

Sure you can...

I hoisted myself up, muscles screaming from the effort as I fit my head through the bars. The stitches in my back pulled painfully. The skin was swollen and irritated as my body attempted to reject the foreign objects.

I just have to escape, then I can get them taken out. I'll get help and this nightmare will at last be over.

Yes, yes, I know. Now, headfirst or arms first?

I think it's supposed to be headfirst, that's the hardest thing to fit through a hole... If that doesn't work, then I'll go back out and try again the other way.

I stared at the tiny opening in growing annoyance. It was all Ronan's fault that I was having to do such a ridiculous thing in the first place. If he had any decency or morals, I wouldn't be reduced to such absurd measures to escape.

Ah yes, because every kidnapper has decency and morals, and with such tools they begin to regret their terrible life choices and then decide to let you leave through the front door.

I rolled my eyes at my own stupidity and tossed the scalpel onto the dirt in front of me before pushing my head through the small hole. My optimism was slowly beginning to dwindle, but I was unwilling to give up. It was the only option I had left that didn't involve attacking Ronan outright.

As much as I hated to admit it, there was a traitorous part of me that didn't want to kill him, and with every day that passed, it grew. We were both pawns in a greater game, and I was beginning to realize how my hatred for him had dwindled. I pitied him. I didn't want to hurt him. Even though it was impossible, I wanted to help. I knew what it was like to be caged in with no hope left. I *knew* what it was like to have no one help you, and for once I wanted to be the person that could help instead of harm. I wanted a chance to redeem myself from my bloody past. I was delusional and stupid to admit such a thing.

But these were all emotions I couldn't afford to heed. If it came down to it, I would kill him if it meant escaping.

I don't want to hurt him.

Exactly. So, get through this window. Then you won't have to.

I lost my leverage the moment my head and shoulders went through the hole, and the dead weight of my body on my arms proved too much. No amount of pushing, wiggling, or scrabbling could get me through the gap.

Nope! Not good! Abort! Abort!

The ceiling was closing in on me as claustrophobia reared its ugly head. I was very thoroughly trapped within a matter of moments. My arms were squished to my side and gave little help to wiggle loose. It had definitely been a mistake going through headfirst.

Despite my best intentions to be courageous, I was panicking.

No, no, no. I cannot afford to panic.

My three brain cells had abandoned their courage and were now running in a frantic little circle as they screeched at the top of their lungs. The hoard, seeing their fear, joined in and my brain was nothing but a migraine-inducing cacophony.

Hang on little brain cells. It's okay, just hold on.

After a few tortuous seconds of wiggling and struggling, I finally pushed myself out and landed on the unforgiving floor with a muffled shriek. I clapped a hand over my mouth, worried someone had heard and would be suspicious.

Who's there to be suspicious? Ronan's pouting. No one gives a crap you're in here. They don't even deliver your meals like they're supposed to.

Okay, so, obviously headfirst was wrong.

Wrong? It was an absolute disaster. We almost DIED.

You're being dramatic. We did not almost die. We just got a little stuck is all. This time, we'll try arms first, then follow with the head. Bracing your hands on the bars will push your hips through them, and then you'll be free. Easy-peasy-lemonade got all peachy squeezy.

You say that as if we weren't about to become stuck forever. As if we weren't almost just crushed by the ceiling.

You didn't almost get crushed. This compound is infuriatingly well built. Hence why your storms didn't destroy it. Now. Stop moping and get a move on. We don't have time for this.

The lecture did nothing to get me moving. I sat immobilized on the icy floor, clutching my knees to my chest as I gasped and heaved—struggling to overcome the panic that had suddenly overtaken my nervous system. Every second I fought the claustrophobia, my mind simultaneously condemned me as a coward. My fear was just that, fear. But still it irrationally insisted that the walls were closing in on me, that any second now, the ceiling was going to cave in on top of me as the gap between those bars seemed to become smaller and smaller.

I'm never going to fit through it. I'm never going to escape.

C'mon! Move! Darn you, stop being afraid and MOVE!

Ember and Evadne need me. Mum and Dad need me. I have to escape and get help or else I will fail them again. I have to escape or else I'll have to kill—

I silenced the thought abruptly, shoving the image of Ronan lying lifeless on the cell floor, my hands covered in his blood, out of my mind. I could not bear the thought of killing him.

Instead, I forced myself to picture my family's faces, to remember the horrors that lived within the Realm. I could not let my sisters be consumed by that cursed magic. I still had to find another way to save them.

I took a deep, steadying breath, then another as I finally regained control of myself and stood. I glared at the window, wishing it would just disappear as I once again climbed on top of the chair.

It's going to work. This time it's going to work.

I have to get out of here. I have to save my family.

I will save my family. I will survive this.

I AM the Zaubermaus. I am Faye Narah Grimm. I am a wolf with a lion's heart, and I will not be afraid.

It proved easier to get my arms through first, but my upper body strength had diminished so much that I almost didn't get myself hoisted up enough to maneuver my head through the hole.

This means I have to start doing pushups again.

No! Not pushups! I HATE pushups! Stupid poison serum, making me weak and useless. Reducing me to pushups...

I hate being weak and useless. It makes me look bad.

The inner whining kept the panic at bay as I pushed forward, inch by torturous inch. It was a tight fit, but so far pushing against the bars and wiggling was slowly but surely getting me out of my cell.

My three brain cells roared in triumph and promptly began jumping through hoops that were much too small for their round little bodies.

Yes! That's it. Just a little more persuasion and my hips will go and—

My triumph died mid-sentence. My arms were straight, fingertips straining against the bars as I desperately tried to push my hips through. I had lost enough weight and muscle mass that I should have had no trouble getting them through the gap, but in an instant everything had turned. I had lost my momentum and strength.

My toes slid uselessly against the smooth metal wall, trying to find some sort of foothold to give me some leverage to get my hips out. My fingers scrabbled in the dirt, trying to pull myself forward.

It was useless. Life had ripped my chocolate from my hands and dumped an entire truckload of lemons on top of me in punishment for having the audacity to argue.

I was good and truly stuck.

Curse it all! Curse it all to the ever freaking stupid cursed Gate!

NO! I can't give up now. Maybe if I just twist myself sideways...I can shove myself through.

That plan quickly proved futile. Turning myself sideways proved to be of little use. The gap seemed to have shrunk even while I was in it. It was now too small to wiggle through.

This is impossible. I should fit. I know I should be able to fit.

My three brain cells, in their feats of great courage and bravery jumping through hoops, promptly all got stuck, and were now dangling in midair, half in, half out of the hoops. They began screeching and wailing, as they kicked their little legs in the air. Bemoaning the situation, they were ignoring the fact that they were the ones who had decided to jump through hoops in the first place.

I have failed as a Zaubermaus. The name was a joke, but she had said it was a name to grow into. The many feats after had, for a time, convinced me that maybe she was right, and I had grown into it... but now?

The image of Ronan's bleeding, lifeless body hovered in my mind.

Now I have no choice.

I wanted to scream, to howl at the sky until the stars knew of my sorrowful rage and wept for my blackened soul. I had no choice left but to do the unthinkable—the only atrocity that I had deemed as my last resort.

I could just knock Ronan out.

If you threaten him, you'll have to use it. He's going to fight back. You'll have no choice but to kill him. You don't have the strength to overpower and subdue him.

I don't want to kill him...I don't.

You don't have a choice.

But what about his sister?

She'll find her own way out. She'll be liberated when the police come... You've wasted enough time; you can't afford to be distracted anymore. These excuses are going to get everyone killed...

No, I'm trying to stop the bloodshed.

The Realm made you into a monster. Be the monster.

No! I'm more than that! I am not a monster...I'm not...I can't...I won't...

I must, I must...

My toes were rapidly going numb, what with the awkward angle, and my arms were quickly following suit. I had to get myself down before Ronan quit his pouting and came looking for his precious medical bag.

I'm surprised he hasn't come looking already, to be honest.

He'll have to come eventually, and when he does...I'll be waiting.

This violence will never end. I cannot escape the bloodshed. There's no hope or healing after all the things I've done. All the innocent lives I've stolen stand and condemn me.

I began to wriggle backwards, fighting back tears as I began to shove myself back through the hole. But now, my ribs were stuck and my shoulders refused to work their way through the small gap.

Panic set in as I began to violently struggle.

I have to get out of this window right now! I have to get out!

There was a sudden knock on my door, and my frantic movements ceased. I held my breath, hoping whoever it was would figure I was sleeping and go away.

The only person who ever knocks is Ronan.

Crap, this is not good. This is very bad.

Get out! I have to get out of this window right now!!

There was a screech. The door was opening, shoving the bed across the floor.

Look at my Ronan alarm working so well. I need to check on the invention patent—surely by now it's been approved. It is a one-of-a-kind invention.

"Faye?" Ronan's voice hesitantly called through the crack. "I know it's late, and I'm really sorry, but I need my medic bag. I finally realized I left it in here when I was stitching you up...and then when we...well...I left it in here."

You mean you left it in here when you got angry and stormed off like a toddler throwing a tantrum?

Yes, I think that's what he means.

Reply, he needs to go away. Finders keepers, it's mine now, etc. If he comes in now, it's going to compromise my plan of attack.

Remember, no manners. That's what gave you away the first time you were up to something.

Right. Rude. I get to be extremely rude to him.

I craned my neck, ensuring the sound of my voice went back into my room in the direction of the door. "Go away you stupid, ignorant, no good, dirty rotten, steaming pile of poop!" I yelled, listing off every insult I could think of while trying to keep my voice angry and level. I couldn't give away my predicament, but hanging from the window was putting a great amount of strain on my diaphragm. "It's not here! If it was, I would have gotten out of here by now. So take your forgetful memory elsewhere and go away! I'm trying to sleep, oh *rude* human!"

Hee-hoo. That was wonderfully rude.

Yes, terribly rude. That should do the trick. Especially if you consider how badly we parted last time, he'll run away with his injured pride and tail tucked between his legs.

The bed slid further across the floor with a screech.

Well. Someone's about to get a face full of booby trap.

Someone is about to find out we were lying.

"Faye I—Bleck, ACK!"

I grinned as I resumed my frantic attempt to get unstuck. I had a few precious seconds before Ronan cleared his vision. Right now, he had a face full of strips of sticky, yucky gauze covered in hand sanitizer, iodine and triple antibiotic ointment. I had taped them to the ceiling using his medical tape, and, in a stroke of genius, made it into a type of spider web. He had literally gotten a face full of absolute ick.

Serves him right.

If I was lucky, it would be in his eyes and effectively blind him. If I was not, it was bound to at least delay him.

My luck seemed to have failed again; the bed was once more moving across the floor.

"It's after nightfall!" I screeched. "You are not allowed in here after dark, or else you lose points off your 'good kidnapper' monthly score!"

"Look, your booby trap only proves it's in here and I—" His voice fell silent, and heat rushed up my cheeks. No doubt he was staring at my very, *very* stuck backside which, unfortunately, was still hanging out of the window in the most undignified fashion possible.

Someone please, kill me now. Anything would be better than this humiliation.

What does it matter what he thinks?

It's the principle of the thing!

You are a horrible goose, you have no principles.

"Faye—"

I waited, cheeks flaming as Ronan tried and failed to find his words. Then he snorted. The snort turned into a chuckle, then he was full out laughing.

I banged my head against the dirt, over and over, as he roared with laughter. Clearly, he was incapable of getting ahold of himself, just as I was incapable of getting unstuck.

"You look like Pooh Bear!" Ronan managed to wheeze. "Your butt is stuck in the window and your legs…they're just, just, *hanging* there." He dissolved into another fit of laughter as I continued my head banging, seething from the ridiculousness of his amusement.

How dare he be amused by my embarrassment. I'm going to punch that laughter right out of him. I'm going to make him rue the day he dared to laugh at me. I'll make him regret it, I'll destroy him, I—

Yes, yes, blood, murder, mayhem. You're forgetting one teensy-weensy little technicality.

Oh? What technicality would that be?

You're still stuck like, well, Pooh Bear.

I resumed my head banging, enraged that my own brain agreed with Ronan's outrageous observation.

"I'm busy!" I snapped hotly. "Kindly go away and come back later when I've finished escaping."

"By all means, my dear, continue your daring escape."

"I AM *NOT* YOUR DEAR!" I screeched, enraged. I resumed my struggle, trying to ignore him as he once again began to chuckle.

How dare he laugh at my distress!

My movements were frantic and erratic and only proved to get me even more stuck.

I am fire! I am death!

You are completely and utterly stuck!

I am most definitely NOT stuck!

Face the facts, you delusional idiot. You're stuck like Pooh Bear and Ronan knows it.

I ought to get down off my unicorn and smack you.

Like I said, delusional. Well, time to face the facts. You're stuck and you need Ronan's help to get unstuck.

My head dropped onto the dirt as I at last accepted my defeat. "Help me out, you stupid idiot!" I muttered, voice muffled by the dirt.

"You're in no position to be making demands," Ronan chortled. "You're certainly too much at my mercy to be calling me names."

"I am your valued prisoner," I growled. "You are obligated to keep me alive."

"That's true, but if I remember correctly, they kept Winnie the Pooh alive by feeding him through the window. I can certainly do that. It would get both of us some fresh air, give me a momentary spot of laughter in my depressing life, not to mention it might *actually* teach you a lesson."

"Don't you *dare*," I seethed. "Besides, you're forgetting how that beloved story ended. He got out in the end, not backwards but forward. If you leave me here, I'll escape when you least expect it and then your *precious* father would be most cross with you!"

"Well, that's true," he chuckled. "I guess I can't leave you. But, I'm quite enjoying the view at the moment. The humiliation that's pouring off of you is absolutely priceless. I particularly liked the 'bang your head on the dirt' bit."

There was a strange crunching, clicking sound. Familiar, yet its place was buried in the back of my mind. A sound I hadn't heard for years being trapped in the Realm.

Camera shutter. He didn't. He did not. HOW DARE HE!!

"Are you taking a *PICTURE*?" I screeched. My flailing resumed as I once again tried to escape my predicament for the sole purpose of throttling my infuriating jailer.

"I most certainly am," he snorted. "I am going to remember this moment until I am on my deathbed, and on that day, I will die with a smile on my face and this haughty laughter in my soul. All because of your ridiculous determination and *very* stuck rear end. I think I should start calling you my bear instead of my dear. Maybe that'll keep you in line if I continue to remind you of this moment."

"Just get me *out* of here!" I wailed.

"Okay, okay," he laughed. "You're so *touchy* today." He tugged on my leg, and then tried to slide a hand between my side and the bar, testing how much space was there.

I hissed; his prying fingers barely fit. Instead, they dug into my bones and tingling, numb skin.

"Well, you are very well and truly stuck. How did you manage to get so wedged? How...how did you even get that far out? That gap is too small... and what parts of you are through, they're bigger than the gap..."

"The bars started to shrink when I was almost out," I muttered angrily. "*Something is making sure I stay.*"

"I'm sure it felt that way in your daring escapade of failure," Ronan mused. "But that's impossible, Faye."

Impossible to you maybe, but only when you're oblivious to the dark forces that have overtaken the compound.

If it wasn't for that, the Zaubermaus would have prevailed.

Yes, well, maybe that's true, and maybe it's not. Now we'll never know.

No, we would have known. I am the Zaubermaus. No space is too small for me.

Au Contrair, oh stuck duck.

Ha, stuck duck. That rhymes. I should be a poet. Stuck duck in trouble and she cried—

"Well," Ronan muttered, interrupting my terrible poetry, "I'm a little bit unsure how to get you out..."

The ground was beginning to fade in and out of focus. The bars were pinching my ribs so painfully I could barely breathe.

"Ronan, I think the fun and games are over...stop teasing and help me. I'm going to pass out."

A small note of seriousness entered his voice as he began to problem solve in earnest. "All right, don't panic. We'll have you out in a jiffy. You'll need to turn sideways...and you'll need to turn your head sideways and look up. I'll pull you out."

"Seems questionable to me," I muttered.

"You're the one that's in need of help. I mean, I can leave if you want me to. I'm sure you can come up with a better plan in the couple of minutes you have left before you pass out."

"No!" I yelped as the ceiling seemed to lower itself another few inches. "It's a good plan. It's a great plan. Don't leave me here! I will cooperate with the *definitely* not questionable plan!"

Ronan laughed again, and my heartbeat fluttered strangely in my chest. The sound was so unusual to hear from someone so broken. The fact that he was laughing on account of me, when I was the one who had contributed to his pain and brokenness, left me feeling conflicted and strange. I wanted nothing more than to continue any and all antics, if only to give him that small measure of laughter.

What am I thinking? No. I can't think that way.

Things will never work between us. Never. Not after everything that's happened. Not when I have to...

"Okay, put your arms up over your head," Ronan instructed. "I'll try to make sure I get you through as carefully as possible. But I can't make any promises. You do have an exceptionally big head."

I scoffed and rolled my eyes, but after half a second, I obeyed. I would take any amount of ribbing if it meant getting unstuck. Besides, he was helping me. After everything that had passed between us, and all the horrible things I had said, he was helping me.

My eyes landed on the scalpel, lying there, in the dirt.

I'm going to need that.

Dread filled me over what I had to do next.

No, there has to be another way.

There is no other way.

My fingers curled hesitantly around the cool handle, and I hurriedly shoved it up my sleeve. Tears were gathering in my eyes. I was never going to escape the endless cycle of bloodshed. I could never forgive myself for what I was about to do.

This is what the Realm made me. A monster among men. A creature that belongs in the uttermost darkness. I can never find forgiveness after all these things I've done.

I won't ask for your forgiveness, Ronan, after the deed is done. Because I wouldn't deserve your forgiveness.

Forgive me, forgive me.

Ronan was lifting up my legs and hips, trying to help me turn to a sideways position. But something tore painfully at my side.

"That's not working," I cried out, unable to mask the pain in my voice.

Ronan stopped and debated for a moment, fingers subconsciously tapping against my thigh as he debated what to do. "This may be the wrong choice, but I'm going to just start pulling and hope we get lucky. If that fails, then we'll have to grease you up, and you'll really be a stuck Pooh Bear. Just be sure to yell if something gets extremely caught or feels wrong."

"My luck seems to be in short supply today," I grumbled as he began to pull on my legs.

It was painful and everything was screaming in protest.

"How did you get this stuck?" Ronan grunted, pulling a little harder.

"I am *Zaubermaus*, this is my specialty."

"Yes, well, your magic mouse luck seems to have run out, based on how you are now the living reincarnation of *Pooh Bear*."

I growled, swearing under my breath, and he poked my stomach. "Easy there, *Pooh*. Don't go turning into *Tigger* on me. I am saving you, you know."

You're saving me...just so I can turn around and kill you.

I cannot abide the betrayal, this endless cycle of bloodshed...

"On three."

I would like it to be noted that this is the dumbest idea ever.

Your observations have been added to the record, and the court has chosen to ignore you completely.

I took a deep breath and exhaled as hard as I could, trying to compress my chest and make my stomach as small as possible.

"One, two, three!" Ronan pulled, and my body was at last moving.

"Just a little more," he grunted.

My head was almost through the bars, but something was wrong with my shoulder. My torso had shifted and now the gap was the wrong direction for my shoulders to fit through. I moved my arm, trying to push myself up a little more. Something was definitely wrong now.

Stop, stop pulling.

I couldn't make my mouth work. I couldn't find my voice to get the words out fast enough.

"Ronan—"

There was a pop and pain exploded in my shoulder as my body at last slid free and began to fall.

Ronan's arms were around me as he stumbled backward, trying to slow my fall. "I've got you," he grunted.

He most certainly had me, but no one had him. His feet were slipping beneath the momentum and we both crashed into the chair. It broke beneath us.

"Well," Ronan wheezed. "That takes care of the necessity to revoke your chair privileges."

I didn't have the mental capacity to give him a snarky reply. I was in too much pain. It didn't help that my failed escape had snatched what little energy I had left. But now, there was yet another injury added to my roster. My shoulder was definitely dislocated. I could feel the wrong angle as it jutted out against my shirt.

Ronan's fingertips brushed across my cheek, tracing the jagged edges of my hair. "You cut your hair..." he said softly. "But how? What did you..." his voice trailed off as he rolled, dumping me on the floor in one quick movement.

Pain exploded across my body, and I screamed through my teeth. My injured shoulder had slammed into the unforgiving floor, and it was all I could do to ride the waves of agony.

I couldn't have attacked him if I tried, and there was no stopping him as he did a quick search and pulled the scalpels off of me—cursing with every blade he found.

Thief. Those are mine. I stole them fair and square.

"Where's the fifth?" Ronan demanded. There was genuine fear in his voice, and it was all I could do to keep the tears from falling.

I'm sorry. I'm so sorry. You do not deserve this.

I kept my eyes closed, trying not to throw up. The fifth was still tucked in my sleeve, now a second away from sliding into my palm. Ronan had checked my sleeves, but he hadn't shoved the material up far enough to reveal my hidden weapon.

The literal ace up my sleeve.

"Where is the fifth?!" Ronan repeated, his voice taking on a desperate edge.

You're injured and he has the upper hand. You only have one chance to get this right. But it isn't right! This is so, so wrong!

Make it quick. Make it clean. Don't let him suffer. He's just as trapped here as you are. He doesn't deserve to suffer. We have to get out.

"It's outside the window," I lied, gritting my teeth through the pain.

He doesn't deserve to die. Surely there's another way...

I'm sorry, Meghan. You're losing your brother because of me...but I don't have a choice.

Tears were sliding down my cheeks, I couldn't hold them back any longer. They were tears of regret and sorrow, not pain.

Forgive me. Please, forgive me.

I opened my eyes slowly, shock hitting me hard as I took in the state of Ronan's face. There were numerous cuts and bruises all over his face and neck. He looked as if he had been severely beaten. One of his eyes was so swollen it was just a slit.

What happened? Who did this to you?

I was surprised by the rage that rose in me. The anger that wanted to punish whoever had injured him.

Stop it! It doesn't matter now! He's going to die anyway, and it will be your fault. His blood is on your hands, and you'll never wash it off. You'll never come clean of the crimson.

My heart, my heart. It cannot bear this weight. Forgive me Ronan, please, forgive me.

Ronan shook his head, glancing at the window. "I'll grab it in a minute," he muttered as he leaned closer to inspect my shoulder. "It's dislocated."

On three.

I was crying in earnest now. Ronan's eyebrows scrunched in concern. "It's okay, Faye, I'll get it back in place and then it'll stop hurting."

He thinks I'm crying from pain...he doesn't know, he doesn't realize I'm crying because this will break my heart...

There has to be another way.

There isn't. We have to escape.

On three.

The words mirrored his from just moments before. Except this time, there was no intention to help—only to hurt, destroy, kill.

I'm sorry. I'm so sorry.

He was leaning over me, inspecting the shoulder closely.

Please, forgive me.

One, two...three.

My uninjured arm swung up and there was no escaping the look of shock and betrayal on Ronan's face as I buried the blade in his side.

6

When The Darkness Lives Inside You

EVADNE

"The monster is me and I am the monster."
-Leigh Bardugo, King of Scars

He was smiling. I could tell by the gloating tenor of his voice that he was smiling.

But then again, why wouldn't he be smiling? I was in the monster's den. He had me at last, and no matter how I tried to escape I couldn't get away.

I had been kneeling for hours, arms and torso chained to a jagged stone pillar behind me. My legs had long since gone numb. No amount of struggling or wiggling had loosened my bonds. If anything, the harder I struggled, the tighter the chains twisted—as if they were alive and fighting back.

Why am I here? Why do they want me? What is the purpose of any of this?

The questions ran in circles, but there were no answers to be found. I didn't know exactly where I was, and there were two monsters here. One I knew all too well, the other I only knew by presence and shadows. It was the same force that had tried to drag me back when Mum was killed. But I didn't know who it was, or why he wanted me.

Why would anyone want me? I'm not worth anything in a world like this.

I'm just a scared girl. Why would they want me? Why would they possibly want me?

All I had were endless questions.

"So, tell me, Evadne *dearest*," Darcy hissed. "Why won't my Ember see sense?" His voice was cruel and laced with fury.

Because you're a psycho. You're a monster. You're absolutely delusional if you think Ember would actually feel anything for you.

You're crazy if you think that Ember would willingly do anything for you.

How is he alive? How did he survive??

Fingers trailed across my cheek, and I jerked, trying to get out of his reach.

It proved useless. The chains would only let me go so far.

"Did you really think you could escape me? Me of all people...come now Evadne, you know it's hopeless. You can't fight me. I who have been unraveling minds since before the Realm was imprisoned."

What does he mean? What can he possibly mean?

The Realm was imprisoned?

"You can't resist my powers, let alone defeat me. No one can. That stunt you and that cursed *Red* pulled." He spat her name. "That feat of stupidity will cost you and her. I'll kill her for interfering." He stopped, chuckling. "She must die anyway. But even now, she cannot stop me. She, the almighty Marcovester Red, with her endless, *infinite* power." His voice was mocking now. "She who helped bind my master and the Realm...even she cannot stop me."

Easy for you to say, dude. She totally froze you, AND she stopped you. She already beat you. You're just being a sore loser.

"How?" I gasped, through gritted teeth. "How did you survive? You were dealt a killing blow."

"Now, there's the million-dollar question. I bet you're just *dying* to know the answer, aren't you? I'll tell you what, I'll tell you before I break you. So, if you want to know sooner, make my work easier and give in."

I stiffened, infuriated.

I will not break. I will not. I refuse to break!

Darcy's cruel laughter echoed around the hollow space. "Ah, you have your sister's spine in you, all right. Must be a family trait. You all possess that stubbornness. I relished how the rulers tried to break your eldest sister's spirit. You should have heard the screams...if the monarchs had given her to me, she would have become most pliable for them."

Fury rose within me at his words. I wanted to rip him apart.

"No matter, she doesn't concern us—not now at least. No, what matters is *your* rigid courage. I am an expert in breaking, and break you will, my sweet. No matter what heroic things you tell yourself. You will crumble in my hands, and I will destroy what remains.

I struggled to hold my composure as the sound of him moving around me grated against my fraying nerves.

Without my sight, the world narrowed to what my other senses could pick up. I could tell he was there, near me. But I didn't know exactly where. It was a terrible form of psychological torture—I was constantly on edge as he circled me. He was like a wolf, waiting for its prey to fall.

I will not break. I won't, I won't. I am stronger than he thinks I am.

I was desperately holding onto the thin shreds of my will as my mental wall crumbled. Artemis only had so much time to teach and train us. But my will was nothing compared to the monumental force that lurked at the edges of my mind. Shadows sharp as knives cut my wall, bit by bit, slicing me to ribbons as he waited.

It was a hopeless endeavor to resist; I knew it was only a matter of time before my walls came crumbling down. But I had to resist him, I had to.

He was toying with me. I was certain he could've obliterated my walls by now. But he was drawing out the agony of the inevitable. He was giving me the poisonous hope that I had a chance of survival.

It was cruelty, but I would expect nothing but savagery from such a monster.

My whole body was numb now, and the chains were the only thing holding me upright.

"All this effort for one girl?" the hauntingly familiar voice hissed from somewhere deep within the room.

"Oh, but she is worth it," Darcy murmured absentmindedly. His hands were on my face, fingers digging into my chin as he turned my head this way and that. "Besides, this is the only way to lure her out. She does not carry the darkness; we have no foothold within her dreams. No, my Ember is as pure as a summer day. She is untainted by our monstrous shadows."

I carry darkness? Shadows? That's not cool.

What's going on? Nothing makes sense.

"How much longer can you hold her? The task rests upon you. My powers are restrained to the other. Despite the Mortal Realm, she grows stronger. She adapts to the toxins, no matter the dose...it is truly extraordinary. Her pain is like fine wine and her powers are unlike any I've ever encountered. They are just magnificent, all of them. Well worth the wait. Our rise will cripple those foolish monarchs. Soon we will have them all in our net."

Darcy laughed in agreement. "Yes, they are all spectacular."

"How long?" the voice pressed.

"As long as I like," Darcy replied impatiently. "No one realizes she is gone from herself. It is as easy as holding a child that sleeps... It is the same as with the other. I hold her, and the mortals are none the wiser. She will prove useful in the future. What child wouldn't burn the world to save a mother?"

Questions and dread plummeted in my stomach. I didn't know who he was talking about, but I had the uneasy feeling I should.

"Are you sure no one realizes?"

"The seer knows, but she is a coward. She will not fight me. I know it. She ran when you rose, she will run again. Of this, I am sure. She was always a coward."

A hiss of rage from the shadow man, then silence. I waited, holding my breath. "I should have killed the seer when she first dared to speak the prophecies."

"Ah, but if you had, how would we know who to snatch? How could we so cleverly stop what others consider fate? If she had been killed, then we wouldn't have such valuable information. *Twins of power, love and hate*," Darcy hissed mockingly under his breath. "*Linked by blood, bound by fate. Destroy the Realm or raze the Gate...* We will write the history of that prophecy and destroy the Realm and its precious monarchs." Darcy's voice trailed off in thought. "Yes, we will rule the Realm, my king."

The shadow man laughed, a cold, cruel sound that slid down my spine like nails on a chalkboard.

"As for our dear *Eva*," Darcy snarled. "Her sister will know what's really happening soon enough, but we need not worry about her. She won't speak a word, not when I have the upper hand. Not when I hold her precious sister's life in my hands..."

The unmistakable tip of a knife pressed up against my cheek. My skin tingled and screamed, nerves on high alert. One more ounce of pressure and the blade would draw blood.

"I warned her," Darcy whispered excitedly. "I warned her what would happen if she tried to stop me. If she told anyone of our little secret..."

Heaven forbid, the woman you traumatized would get help.

He's so delusional. Do you think he knows it?

Probably not. Delusional people rarely know or believe they're delusional.

"If she failed to see the truth...I told her what would happen, how I would have to *persuade* her... She's mine, and mine alone. That pesky *prince* dares to defy me. But we'll show him... We will show them all," Darcy hissed in glee.

"In time," the shadow man sighed. "All in time. There are many pawns that must be put into position first."

What does he mean?

The shadows rushed back from my eyes, and I blinked in the sudden light, blinded. Darcy's face was inches from mine. A knife hovered right in front of my eye, the edge of the blade brushing my eyelashes.

I choked on a scream, not daring to move or even breathe for fear of blinding myself.

A cruel smile grew on Darcy's face. "Oh darling, I'm not going to steal those pretty eyes. Not yet, that is." The knife moved, and the tip pressed into my temple. "But the time will soon come when I must extinguish those swirling galaxies. After all, I can't go back on my word." Darcy chuckled, and I struggled to contain my fear. I so desperately wanted to be brave, but it seemed as if all I could comprehend was my terror as a bead of blood slid down my forehead and caught at the corner of my eye.

"The day will come, love. You understand, don't you? Tell me, what will your world be like, when you can no longer see your true love? That *human*." He spat the word, his voice overflowing with contempt. "When the chance arises, he's dead," he stated to no one in particular.

Dread plummeted in my stomach; I was going to be sick.

"You'll survive the heartbreak," Darcy crooned. "After all, you're promised to an-other. He'll mend your poor, broken heart. He's set on having you. Seeing you dance through the window as he held the heir captive really sealed the deal. He couldn't get enough of you...you should have seen his face when he told me about that pretty performance. How the queen made the human scream to pull your delicate marionette strings."

Who is he talking about? The only one there was the wraith...the one who turned Ríonach in the first place...

Does he mean the wraith took a fancy to me?

No! Absolutely not! GROSS!

I was looking frantically around the room, trying to gather as many details as possible. Trying to distract myself from the inevitable agony that awaited at the end of Darcy's knife.

A man made of shadows sat on a throne of bone and wood. His undefined form swirled and shifted within the darkness. His pitch-black eyes were the only unshifting element of his body, and they tore me apart at the seams. The screaming shadows bled from him, protecting him from the ghosts that drifted around the room and angrily lunged at him.

There was someone else in the room, a woman. She was also bound by his shadows, blindfolded and gagged. Tears leaked out from under her blindfold and slid down her cheeks. She flickered around the edges, as if she wasn't quite real.

I strained to see more, desperate for more information. There was something eerily familiar about her.

At last, my eyes took in the detail I had missed at first glance—the jagged scar across her collarbone.

That's impossible.

It can't be. I saw her die. This can't be real. It's an illusion, a ruse meant to break me.

The shadowy man laughed, and I shivered.

No, no, no. This can't be real. This can't be right.

"Oh, but it is real, little one," the shadow man hissed. "I hold her ransom. She was never meant to die. That foolish human lost control and listened to his petulant emotions. I kept her alive when she should have died. I *need* her alive, you see. For now, that is." He stood and drew closer.

Every sense in my body was screaming at me to run. But I couldn't move as the chains pulled tighter and tighter.

"I have great use of pawns. They make such lovely tools of *manipulation.*" His shadows jerked, and that familiar voice cut through me. It was her voice, it was her.

Mum was screaming.

"NO!" I cried, struggling against my bonds, desperate to get to her.

Darcy's knife was moving again, trailing down my throat. An inch through the fragile skin, and it would kill me. But I didn't care. All I could think about was Mum.

If he kills me, he won't be able to use me against Em...but then I can't help Mum. No one knows she's here.

What would be the better solution?

"Oh no, love," Darcy purred, drawing the knife back before I could decide whether or not to hurt myself against the edge. "That would ruin all my fun. I won't kill you." He paused, pondering his words. "I'd do it though, just to see Ember's face. To watch her truly break...but then she'd lose her beautiful spirit, and my companion, well, he'd be most cross with me. Don't worry though, we'll have our fun while we wait for your sister. I can't deny how I'll enjoy the sound of your screams. You have been *such* a *thorn* in my side. It's time you learned your place. It's time I taught you a lesson about getting in my way. You'll *never* dare to cross me again after our time together, will you?"

I wasn't listening, I was caught on what he had said, the certainty in his voice when he said Ember would come to rescue me.

Ember, no. She can't. Don't do it, Em. Please don't do it! Don't come here! Please don't!

Revulsion rolled over me in a sickening wave as he stepped closer. His lips brushed my ear as he whispered, "Did she tell you about our little tryst in the Halls? Did she tell you about our secret kiss?"

I'm going to kill you. Monster! You hurt her! You hurt her!

How dare you! How dare you!!

The shadows drew closer. Smoky silhouettes formed and reformed, bearing an uncanny likeness to my sister and the monster before me. She was collapsed on the floor, Darcy kneeling beside her. He cradled her head in his hands. The images broke apart and reformed. Then he was kissing her as she fought and struggled to get away.

"Look at her," Darcy breathed, eyes locked on the swirling shadows. "She loves me, I know it. She's just in denial. We were meant for each other; she just needs to be persuaded. She's just playing hard to get." He hummed in satisfaction, eyes triumphant as he turned back to me. "Your sister is a tricky one," he tsked. "I had to use *so* much of my magic to restrain her trigger-happy intuition. I needed to slow her down when she would have normally reacted... When she finally broke through my spells, I knew it was time to act. She is truly magnificent. She breaks so many bindings... But no matter, the game was up, and to be frank, I was tired of waiting. It was becoming tiresome trying to hide my love and contain her misplaced ire."

My thoughts were a churning mass of fury and pain. The things Ember had endured because of his sick delusions broke my heart. But soon rage overwhelmed the sobs and my mind screamed for justice, revenge—something, anything to make this monster pay for what he had done.

"She'll come. My *Oisillon* will come, she will come because of *you*. But first we have to share the happy news. I'm not dead. She need not weep over my demise any longer."

He's insane. Psychotic.

Darcy pondered the knife in his hands. "But, if I tell her right off, it would be too easy... I think I should like to splinter that bond the King put on her a little more...shatter the edges of that cursed binding." He hissed in annoyance. "That meddling King and his secret bonds, his attempt to uproot everything. His threat to destroy everything I have worked so hard to put in place. He thinks his precious son, that precocious *prince*, should be bound to her. To *my* Ember."

He's delusional. Level thirty crazy.

The shadows that prowled on the edges of my mind lunged, and my flimsy wall shattered. I screamed as it sliced through everything in its reach. My entire being was encased in fire and the locket from Marcovester Red burned against my ribcage like a block of dry ice.

Erebus' words echoed through my mind as Darcy's magic tore apart my memories, feeding off my agony.

'Run child, run, the darkness comes.'

"That's more like it," Darcy murmured. "Now, how to break my little bird...not too much, but just enough..." He was combing through my memories—searching for something." It felt similar to when Artemis had checked our memories and discovered the block, but there was a savageness to Darcy's search that Artemis had not possessed. Artemis had been gentle—overly careful of my mind. Darcy tore everything he touched, leaving gouges that bled as I screamed.

He paused at a memory a few nights before, when Ember had told me as she was falling asleep about Artemis' music, and how, when he'd been bitten, the music had disappeared.

"There," Darcy whispered breathlessly. "That will do nicely." The triumph was evident in his voice as he at last pushed the knife through my skin—just below the hollow of my throat.

Once, twice, three times, he slowly cut through my skin.

"Three marks, three days..." Darcy commented absentmindedly as I struggled to process what he was doing. The pain of the knife was nothing compared to his claws in my mind. He was ripping me apart, piece by piece.

The knife moved, dripping hot blood. I watched, horrified, as he again dug the blade into my skin, this time just beneath my collarbone.

"Don't worry, my pet," Darcy said calmly, pausing his torture to stare in growing relish at the blood on his fingertips. "As soon as she gets the message and comes, my attention will turn fully to her. You just have to hold out for three simple days..." His smile was savage as he stared at me. "Until then, you'll learn this painful lesson not to cross me again. I was most displeased with your interference at the ball. You should really know better than that."

I will never stop protecting my sister. I will fight you tooth and nail until my dying breath to protect her from you.

This is all in my head. He's dead. Darcy is dead. I've been grievously injured, and the blood loss is making me hallucinate. This is a nightmare, just like Ember's nightmares with Darcy.

It's not real! It's not real!

Wake up!

But no matter how hard I tried, I couldn't wake up. No matter what I told myself, it still felt incredibly real. Every centimeter of that knife, every single letter he carved into me, felt *real*.

This isn't happening. It can't be happening.

The shadows lengthened and grew around me, pulling at the tattered pieces of my mind, feeding off my pain.

"Do you recognize them?" Darcy murmured, engrossed in his work.

I was gasping, heaving in pain as tears coursed down my cheeks. I didn't want to cry, but I couldn't stop.

Mum's muffled screams echoed around us. The sound tore at my heart.

Something within my mind was rising to the surface. I watched, horrified as new shadows took form. They were mine, and yet other. I fell still, watching my mind outside of myself as my shadows turned and joined the assault against me.

"Do you recognize them?" Darcy repeated as he caught my chin and forced me to meet his vengeful stare. "Do you?"

I jerked, trying to wrench myself from his grasp. His grip tightened as his fingers dug into my chin. "No?" he sneered, taking my resistance as an answer. "You should. They're your own fears, your pain and suffering. The darkness you've carried since my monster failed to take you all those years ago. But, even in its failure, it served me. I've had a foothold on you since it infected you. Since they *became* you. These shadows are the darkest parts of you." He laughed. "There's no use resisting, Evadne. You can't escape what you are."

7

How Far Would He Go?

EMBER

"Even if it is full of love, all a ghost can do is haunt."
-Avina St. Graves, Skin of a Sinner

Sleep came without my consent or knowledge. I was locked in a Dreamscape before I realized my eyes had closed.

I knelt beside a tombstone, weeping. The thick foliage of a hazel tree spread out over me, deepening the shadows I hid within. "Shake and quiver, little tree," I whispered, my voice shaking. "Throw gold and silver down to me." My words were a desperate prayer, a plea for the impossible.

Once, just once, let something amazing happen. Please, help me Mother...help me have a future.

The girl's thoughts swirled around my mind as the branches rustled above her. There, descending from the tree, was a gorgeous dress of gold and silver clutched in the claws of two white pigeons.

My tears dried in an instant as I stared at the stunning dress while the birds laid it on the grass. I watched in silent amazement as they once more flew up and, after a moment had passed, returned with a pair of delicate slippers. They were gold with silver embroidery that perfectly matched the dress.

"Thank you, oh thank you!" I whispered as I hurriedly pulled on the dress and raced out into the darkness.

Gray mist rushed in, and before I knew it, I was dancing. Swept into the arms of a handsome prince who wouldn't even let go of my hand. Bright green eyes stared down at me with love and hope, but buried in those eyes was something akin to pain as we twirled around the room.

My breath caught. I knew those eyes.

No, no. This isn't a Dreamscape anymore. Wake up!

"How is this for freaking civil?" Artemis said softly. His music trilled at the edges of my mind, trying to lull me into a state of security.

Maybe it's still just a dream...I'm just remembering the ball...the kindness he showed me before everything fell apart...

The softness distorted. Those beautiful green eyes morphed into that hateful blackened green.

No! He's not himself! This isn't him, it's the other him!

What if it's truly who he is? What if he has been that monster all along?

"I warned you, my Flamín."

Artemis' voice was low, but there was something off about the cadence, as if he was fighting to get every word out. His fingers were digging into my skin.

I looked around frantically. My dress had morphed—I wasn't in the gold and silver dress anymore. Now I was in the blood red dress from the farewell ball. His hand had moved away from the fabric; now he was greedily touching everything the dress exposed.

Stop it! Stop it! This isn't you. You didn't do this!!

He leaned close, his lips brushing my ears. "What did I tell you would happen?"

What is he talking about? I don't understand.

Those tortured green eyes were tearing me apart, piece by piece. A monster prowled at the edges of my mind, trying to shatter my walls.

"Please, Artemis," I gasped. "You have to understand. "You have to understand why I did it—"

"I understand *nothing*," he spat as his shadow monster lunged at my mind.

No!

I pushed back. A phoenix rose to life in my mind, desperately screaming as I tried to fight him off and keep him out. The smell of the forest after a rain accosted my senses. Buried beneath it all was the edge of mint. That cursed mint. He was using every weapon he had to break me.

"I warned you," he hissed. "You have three days to find me."

Three days? What is he talking about? How could I possibly find him? Why would I find him?

There's something wrong. He never warned me about anything...did he?

Evadne's screams wrenched me from the nightmare, and I woke with a cry of my own. My skin was burning, as if someone was slicing me open.

"Easy there, Sparks," Theron said gently.

He was sitting on the floor beside our cots, back against the wall as he made repairs to what looked like a cloak. "She's fine," he sighed. "It's just the cursed Dreamscapes. She'll get out of it soon enough."

There was blood seeping through her tunic.

Her wounds reopened. I need to go get Clarice.

Evadne screamed again and something cold settled over me. "She doesn't scream," I whispered. "She never screams..."

"What do you mean she doesn't scream?" Theron asked. "Everyone screams; it's the nature of the Dreamscapes. It marks the Grimms out for the Gate."

"Not her," I whispered. "The last time she—"

The floor fell out from under me, dragging me down as the realization hit me like a blow to the gut. The last time Evadne had screamed was when someone tried to spirit her away.

Artemis' warning in the nightmare... what if he's trying to get us back by spiriting her away...

Is that possible? Can he do that? Lady Nightshade said that was Darke magic...is all spiriting away Darke magic? What lengths would he go to, to get her back?

I had too many questions, too many suspicions. What had Artemis' warning meant? It sounded like a threat. But beneath it all, there was a nagging, strangling thought. Something hadn't been right—there was something decidedly off about the whole thing. Artemis' desperation on that cliff didn't match the malice in his voice during the nightmare.

My chest was burning worse than before. More blood was seeping through Evadne's tunic, and my hand trembled as I undid the laces and pulled the fabric back. I gasped, staring in horror not at old wounds reopened, but new wounds. Something had slashed three lines across her skin just below her collarbone.

"This can't be happening," I whispered as my fingers gingerly touched my chest. They came away wet with blood.

Theron was on his feet now, staring at the wounds. "What's going on?" he asked. "Do I need to go get Clarice?"

I was speechless, unable to process his questions, incapable of finding my words as I continued to stare at her skin. There was no knife, but below the three lines something was carving through her skin. Someone was torturing her in front of my very eyes.

Three lines...no, it can't be. He wouldn't.

Is it a coincidence? Three days. Artemis said I had three days.

Three days till what?

No. He wouldn't do this. He wouldn't do something like this.

Wouldn't he? He's Fey. I betrayed him. What lengths would he go to, what depths would he sink to, to get us back? Would he cave to his baser nature? The Fey blood he was born with, that bays for violence and power?

No. He wouldn't, he...he...

The cuts were letters, and I watched in horror as the letters formed into words.

'I WARNED YOU'

It was identical to Artemis' warning in the nightmare. 'I warned you what would happen.'

But he didn't warn me? Did he?

I wracked my memory, trying to remember the words exchanged between us as we sailed away. It felt like a lifetime ago. I could hardly remember anything. All I could think of was the desperation, the pleading tone. He had begged me not to go, but he had also said there would be hell to pay.

Is this what he meant?

Surely he wouldn't hurt Evadne just to force my hand...would he?

He's Fey...manipulation is how they function best... isn't that what Quillon did for years with all of us? Use us against one another, pushing our fear for one another to keep us in line?

How far would Artemis go to get us back?

I was shaking, tears sliding down my cheeks as I stared at my bloody fingertips and then my sister.

We can't escape him. We can't escape our fate.

Evadne writhed and screamed, tears pouring down her face.

"What's going on?" Theron demanded, voice shaking. "What does it mean?"

It means we're just as trapped with him, as without him...but how do I find him? Do I tell Verity to go back? Do I risk Evadne's safety if it means finding a way for her to escape the Last Gate?

Theron was shouting for help, demanding the crew find him Clarice and Verity. He turned back to me, calling my name over and over again. But his voice was nothing but a distant echo. It was as if we were separated by a vast chasm—nothing remained but me and Evadne.

Would Artemis be this cruel, just to break me?

Would he do this to Evadne?

He is his father's son. He is Fey...

"He wouldn't," I whispered, desperate to make myself believe the delusion I so dearly wanted to be truth. I didn't want Artemis to be so ruthless, so hateful and cruel. But I had to face the facts. He was Fey. He was liable to do anything to get us back—no matter how horrendous or terrible. Because without us, the future of the Summer Court was plunged into darkness.

8

The Forgotten Legend

EVADNE

"She wondered if she had any blood left in her, or if her body had just
filled up with water and cold."
-Catherynne M. Valente, from The Orphan's Tales: In the Night Garden

Darkness held me in place both within and without. Darcy had created an impenetrable prison inside my mind. Thick iron walls surrounded me and the more I fought to break them, the stronger they grew—drawing strength from my resistance. I was screaming as I slammed my fists into the walls over and over again, but no matter what I did, there was no breaking Darcy's barrier.

How is he alive?!

How is he even doing this? How is this possible?

What did he mean, the darkness was inside of me?

The questions ran round and round, as I tried and failed to fight his hold.

Darcy laughed as he combed through my memories, ripping them around the edges. "Oh, you poor girl. You still don't remember, do you?"

"Remember what?" I hissed, desperately trying to hold onto my composure.

His fingers trailed down the scar that ran from my shoulder blade to my collarbone.

The scars stood as a reminder of the first time the Fey Realm had tried to hurt my family—when the monster under our bed had tried to drag my sister away.

"Hm, perhaps I should remind you."

His shadows began to morph and swirl. White smoke joined with the darkness and soon images began to appear.

I don't believe it. How does he know what that looks like?

It was the bedroom of our old house, back before we moved. A much younger Ember was fighting a monster at the edge of our closet. There was blood everywhere as she fought against it, eyes wide and terrified. Then, little feet were pounding across the floor as I rushed forward, screaming Ember's name. I attacked the monster with the only weapons I could find—my pillow and fists. A flash of silver in the dim light of the nightlight and then I was falling. Crimson stained my clothes and I screamed for help. Gashes ran down the length of both of Ember's arms now.

I was screaming as I pushed myself up and charged the monster again. "NO!"

Fire raced across my ribs. My bones ached at the remembrance of it.

I watched in silent horror as the monster in Darcy's vision began to drag *both* of us back into the closet.

I don't remember it trying to take both of us...I thought it just tried to take Em...

A shadowy figure appeared then, curved blade drawn and ready. Ryver's face was murderous as he swung at the monster.

The figure on the throne hissed in fury. "Meddling Fey, he ought not to have intervened."

Darcy waved a hand. "The Shadowthieves belong to the Shadewyrld. He could not have resisted. You know of their curse."

What curse? His duty to protect us now? Is that what he means?

"He will die soon enough," Darcy muttered. He was distracted, pulling my memory from the attack and comparing it with his version, magnifying the emotions that rose and drinking in my pain and horror as if it were fine wine.

Ryver lunged, his body going liquid for a moment as his weapon sank deep into the monster. The monster screamed and began to dissolve into thick black smoke, swirling like ink in water as it faded before my eyes.

Ryver's attention turned to Ember, who lay dying in a pool of our blood. I was screaming her name as he began to weave a spell around her, desperately trying to heal the grievous wounds.

None of us noticed as the smoke from the monster shifted away from Ryver, swirling with the blood that poured out of my shoulder, and then, seeping into my body through the wounds.

"You see," the shadow man crooned. "You have been mine since the beginning. I've had a foothold to hang onto. Though, if that meddling Shadowthief and those wretched monarchs hadn't interfered with you, you would have been here many moons ago."

How much time has passed since we left the Central Realm? It feels like a few days, but has it been longer?

"While you grew, I masked your magic—both you and your sisters'. *I* hid you from the Courts," he crowed. "It is the same magic I use now, hiding the eldest from them. They underestimate me, as they always do. It will be their downfall. Their pride will destroy them."

Dark ebony eyes tore me apart and my body trembled beneath the weight of his gaze. "You see, you have been mine all along. You will be the key to my escape. You and your sister both."

I am not yours. I will not comply.

"Compliance has nothing to do with it, my thorny rose," Darcy murmured as he came to stand in front of me. Chills ran down my spine as I stared at him. "The longer you stay, the stronger the darkness within you becomes. As the moons pass, the control he has over you will increase. Soon, with your power at our beck and call, we will be unstoppable. You were born to be a weapon, and he will wield you as such." He patted my cheek. "But don't worry, love. That all comes later. For now, our focus is Ember."

"You can't have her!" I gasped. "She's not coming. She doesn't even know where I am." My words were a desperate gasp. I was spluttering, rambling, trying to find a lie strong enough to convince him it was useless. I had to protect Ember from this monster.

"Perhaps not yet, but she will. I'll let her in on our little secret at the end of these three days... I'll tell her where our little rendezvous is to be, and I assure you she'll come." His malicious grin widened as he grabbed my chin and leaned close. "I'll make *sure* she comes," he breathed.

"Leave her out of this," I rasped. "She's done nothing, absolutely *nothing* to deserve this."

"True, but she will be mine, nevertheless. Once the Knight is free, no one will care what becomes of her. I don't think I'll put her to the test though. It would be a shame to lose her after all this, just as I lost all the others. She will have to adjust to being mine, and that will be hard enough. She doesn't seem the type to easily leave what she thinks she loves... No, she is too precious a jewel, a bride too hard won."

What is he talking about?

Darcy was speaking in riddles, and my fearful mind was unable to comprehend what he meant.

"A bit rusty on our fairytales, are we?" he sneered. "I thought *you* of all people would be clever enough to connect the dots and figure out who I *really* am. After all, you discovered the beautiful little charm I put on your sister."

That wasn't a charm, you monster. It was a curse. You attacked her and then cursed her you piece of—

"My past is one I was forced to hide," Darcy continued. "I've kept the truth hidden in my bones so no one can trace my origins." He stared down at me in growing triumph. "I am a forgotten Legend. One they think they've eradicated." He laughed, the sound cold and cruel. "You have much to learn about this place, Evadne. Much to grasp about the monarchs who rule with such blatant corruption... They've grown soft in their power, utterly complacent as they revel in what they've become—what they can do. For you see, they've all forgotten, and forgetting the past is the most dangerous mistake of all. For, in our forgetting, we allow history to repeat itself."

"How could you hide such a thing?" I whispered in shock. "How can you hide what you are?"

"It was simple really," Darcy gloated. "I was more powerful than the magic that created me. When the magic bound me, cursing me to become a Legend, I did not allow the origin of my legend to survive. I stopped the story from writing itself into my blood; instead I forced it to write itself on the inside of my bones. Unseen, unknown, unheard."

I swallowed, afraid. Darcy was a far greater threat than anyone had ever realized.

"It doesn't harm me to tell you my story, my dear Evadne... I'd be a bad host to not satiate that *rampant* curiosity. Besides, you won't live long enough to tell the ones who matter of such a tale. Let me tell you how I survived their best attempts to wipe me from the Mortal and Fey Realm."

His voice was proud as he stared down at me. "I traded my shadow for power, and in the death, I recreated myself with Darke magic." He was trailing the back of his fingers down my cheek and I resisted the urge to shudder. "I hate how I am forced to live, masked in shadows and secrets. Never free to truly live. I have spent so long biding my time—waiting to strike. It has been so *very* long, since I allowed myself to remember who I am."

He fingered his knife. "So, I will give you a rare treat as we wait for your sister to fall into my trap. Fall she will, for she is going to attempt a brave rescue for her dear sister, her twin... I will tell you who I am, for there is power in the telling, and I would claim your fear for myself."

A hollow ache was growing inside my chest. I didn't want to know his story. I wanted to go home.

Wake up, wake up. Please wake up!

Darcy lightly trailed the tip of the knife across my cheek in an invisible pattern. I held my breath, waiting. His knife out meant another day had passed. It meant he was going to use it.

"How does the old refrain start?" Darcy mused as he dug the point into my cheek and ever so slowly dragged it down toward my chin.

I swallowed my cry, trying not to make a sound.

"Ah, yes. Once...upon...a time..." Darcy's malicious smile grew as he pulled out the knife and stared at the bloody tip. "Oh, come now Evadne. There's no use swallowing your screams. You might as well let them come as they rise. They will eventually, and then your resistance, your *stoic heroism*, will have been for *nothing*."

I clenched my jaw, determined to prove him wrong. Tears slid down my cheeks, but if all I did was cry, I would still count it a victory.

"Once upon a time," Darcy repeated, "there was a man who knew how to harness the wild flood of magic that, at the time, dwelt unhindered within the world. Let me elaborate for you, for you have no idea what the world was like before the Realm existed." He stared down at me, smiling. "Before the Realm was bound, the world was one with the Fey and their magic. These *loathsome* boundaries did not exist. It was beautiful and the world was ripe for the taking. It was marvelous. Now, some called this man a sorcerer, others a madman. But none of it mattered to him. He cared not what they said or what they thought...what they believed. He cared not an ounce, for, he was free and they were pitiful, beneath him. Now, this man had a wife. He loved her dearly from the moment he laid eyes on her. But she was a wild thing, a horse in need of being broken and tamed. But that didn't matter to him. He knew what a glorious creature she could be, and would be, when the task was done. So, he took on the job with great strength." He paused, staring down at me. "She was much like your sister, fierce as a wolf in the night. That is one of the reasons I have selected her as my next bride."

Was. What did he do?

Revulsion pulsed through me. I didn't have to think very hard to guess what had happened. I had no doubt he had forced himself on this poor girl, much as he had forced himself on my sister.

He killed her, didn't he.

He won't touch Ember again. I won't let him.

"But, one night...she pushed too far. She rebelled too deeply. She tried to *run*," Darcy spat, as he dug the knife back into my skin, slicing it across my jaw. "She *broke* her vows to me, and so, I was forced to deal firmly with her...perhaps I was too harsh, but a lesson must be taught." He stopped, holding my bloody chin in his hand as he forced me to meet his gaze. His golden eyes were bright with lustful memories and rage.

I couldn't contain the shudder of horror that ran down my body as he trailed the knife down my collarbone, grazing the wounds he had inflicted the first day.

"That fixed her, and oh, it was lovely. She was quiet, good, submissive, and obedient as a wife should be..."

He broke her spirit.

"All was well, or so I thought. Until one night, she took my dagger..." he paused, digging the knife in again. "She took *this* dagger and tried to kill herself."

Hot blood dripped from my jaw down my neck. The blade was digging deeper and deeper into my shoulder, causing my arm to go numb.

"I had no choice," he murmured. "It broke my heart, but I had no choice. *She left me* with no choice...I buried her beneath the rowan tree...and the others, well, they were peaceful for a short while. But none could be trusted, and a bride I cannot trust, is a bride I *will not* have." His face went cold. "I would not give them merciful ends such as I had given her. They were pitiful, and weak. There was nothing to them." His gaze found mine again as he intentionally pulled the blade down the length of my arm.

I swallowed the cry that wanted to escape as fire raced across my skin.

"The world lost nothing from their absence," Darcy continued, his eyes miles away.

"You monster," I hissed through my teeth, clenching my jaw against the pain.

I will not break. No matter what he does, he will not break me. Every second he stalls is a second longer I am alive.

"No," he bit out. "The real monster is the one who branded me as Bluebeard and forced me to live on the run for centuries...making me the subject of horror stories made to scare children and young women."

Bluebeard? No, that can't be right...

"But Bluebeard was killed!" I stammered, unable to hide the confusion in my voice.

"Yes, and Baba Yaga was murdered by tiny, helpless children," Darcy sneered. "We all know how the Brothers Grimm loved to rewrite the stories to fit their moral aims. The whole Realm and the magic that binds it was built on *lies*." He leaned closer. "You will find, my innocent little flower, that their so-called justice rarely happened. As the brothers rewrote our history, even the Fey began to forget what really happened. So the magic morphed and accepted the falsehoods." His lips curved into a cruel, gloating smile. "Why do you think the Moores are alive and thriving, despite what they should be? They are the Wastelands, built upon lies. The monarch's power is rooted in falsehoods just as the Knight's prison is, and it will all crumble to dust—as all lies must. Don't you see, my dear *Eva*," he sneered. "The entirety of the Realm, and the Knight's prison, is built on lies. Only the Curse of Three stands in our way. That is the final piece that upholds the puzzle."

"But the rulers said—"

Darcy grabbed my arm, and the chains groaned and shifted beneath his control as he dragged me to my feet with a triumphant sneer. "Because that is what *I* told them, and now their pride refuses to allow them to be on guard for any that might resist them."

I couldn't stop him as he pulled the edge of my shirt up and slid the knife into the skin that stretched across my ribs. Once, twice, he made two new cuts.

He's counting down.

I struggled to contain the pain, my agony within it. The shame that rose as his fingers gripped my side, digging into my skin. The knife dug deeper; he was carving into my rib bone itself.

The shadow man laughed as I fought against my ever-weakening resolve not to scream.

"History has been bathed in blood and violence since the beginning," Darcy hissed as he worked. "War lingers on their doorstep, but by the time the little prince makes it back to tell them what they have foolishly ignored...it will be too late." He rose then, gripping my chin in his bloody hand as he forced me to look up at him. "They will *all* be too late. You will beg for death, long before I ever grant such a merciful release. After all, I promised Ember that would be your end, and I cannot lie."

He dug his fingers into the newly carved words in my side, dragging his nails through the wound. Agony engulfed everything as the pain dragged me down, down, down, feeding the shadows that roared inside of me. He did it again, and I could no longer contain my screams.

"You are alone," Darcy hissed. "No one is coming for you, and you will die alone."

"You're wrong," I whispered.

"No, I'm not. You're simply holding onto a delusional hope that someone will come to save you." He turned to the throne, to the man upon it. "Should I tell her, my king?"

The shadow man continued to laugh.

"Welcome to the Ruins, Evadne. Too bad you can't actually do what the monarchs intended you to do. But you can meet your future king." He shoved my head down and forward until I thought my neck would break. "Bow to the Shadow Knight, the Erlking of the four Realms."

9

The Bloodshed Between Us

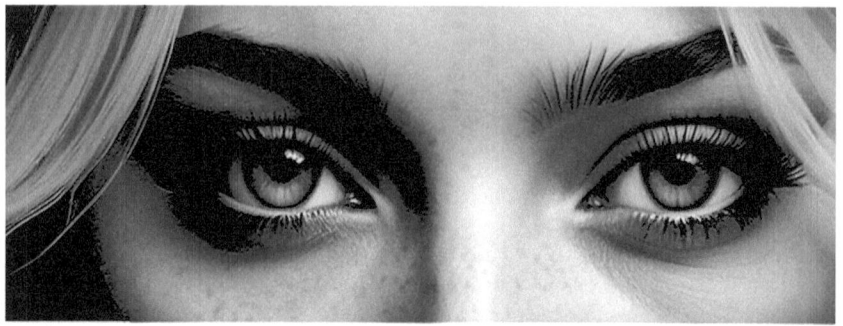

FAYE

"So violently do I know the world."
-Rainer Marie Rilke, [Fragment of an Elegy]

The scalpel jolted in my hand. I had missed my mark. Instead of going between Ronan's ribs and hitting his heart, it had glanced off his rib.

The look of betrayal and horror that crossed his face as he finally comprehended that I had lied, worse that I had tried to kill him, cut my heart to the quick.

I'm sorry. I'm so sorry, Ronan.

No, I'm not. I can't be sorry! I have to get out of here!

But I am...I am so, so sorry. I don't expect you to forgive me. But I'm sorry regardless.

Ronan scrambled back with a yell, his eyes still screaming of my treachery. One look and I was undone. Despite my best intentions not to care, his pain hurt more than any physical wound I had ever endured.

But I am sorry. I am so incredibly sorry, Ronan.

"What the actual *crap*, Faye!" Ronan yelled as he jumped to his feet and kicked the bloody blade out of my hand. The toe of his shoe collided painfully with my fingers, but I welcomed the pain—I deserved it. I deserved so much worse.

There is too much innocent blood on my hands.

Ronan scrambled for his disassembled medical bag. "You could have killed me, you stupid idiot!" he snapped. "What were you thinking?!"

I stared at him, not daring to deny the accusation as he grabbed a handful of clean gauze that had escaped my booby trap from his bag and pressed it against his side.

"You *meant* to kill me." The statement held resignation, pain even, and what little remained of my humanity cried out within me for the agony that stretched between us.

I was ripping myself apart, screaming inside as I tried to cope with the shattered remnants of myself and come up with a backup plan. But there was no backup plan. I had tried and failed, yet again, and there was no going back to the tenuous trust that had grown between us. My next option would be to try again, and I was sure I didn't have it in me.

The blood was soaking through the gauze and Ronan looked at it in dismay as he once again swore. "You are so *incredibly* frustrating. Do you know that?" he asked angrily as he lifted up his bloodied shirt and tore off a piece of tape between his teeth. He added another few layers of gauze and then taped the lump securely to his side.

He turned his furious gaze back to me. "Now, hold still. I'm going to set your shoulder back in place."

Why? Why are you helping me when I just tried to kill you?

I stared up at him, in shock and grief.

Ronan glared down at me. "If you try anything," he snapped, his tone severe, "and I mean *anything*, I will sit on you." His glare deepened, "And then I will *fart* on you."

If it had been any other day, such a threat would have had me screeching in anger, or perhaps stifling a laugh. But I had no emotions, no reaction, just sadness as I stared up at him.

Maybe whoever beat Ronan up gave him brain damage as well.

Probably, he looks terrible.

Who beat him up, and why? He's Jeremiah's son, that gives him status in a place like this.

Which can only mean that it was likely Jeremiah who did that to him, or it was done on his orders...

Probably so, but why?

Ronan was kneeling beside me now, fingers probing my shoulder. "You need to sit up," he stated.

"Stop touching my shoulder or else I'll stab you again," I growled. "You're not doing anything but aggravating the stitches."

"Sorry," Ronan muttered. "I didn't know they were still that tender."

"They're overgrown, you stupid idiot," I snapped as I sat up.

He gave me a disbelieving look as he took my wrist and elbow in his hand and began to carefully maneuver the arm.

"I put them in three days ago, Faye. You're being a bit dramatic."

"*FOUR*," I snapped. "And no, I'm not being dramatic. You're just *stupid*—" My words cut off in a groan as Ronan skillfully maneuvered my shoulder back in place with a sickening pop.

Ronan grit his teeth in pain. His shirt was rapidly staining with blood, as he had already bled through the heavy layer of gauze. He sat down beside me, winded and exhausted as he clutched his side. "You're a pain the butt, Faye. An absolute pain in the butt. Do you know that?" He ran a hand through his hair, making it stand on end as he looked up and stared out the window.

"I am a great many things," I mumbled under my breath, trying to breathe through the pain. "Besides, you said that already."

I am a failure, a coward, and a monster... I am everything I never wanted to be and nothing I ever hoped.

I am afraid, so terribly afraid, because I'm running out of time.

"What happened to your face?" I demanded, trying to change the subject.

"What happened to yours?" he countered.

"What's wrong with mine?" I asked indignantly.

"Have you looked in the mirror recently? Someone attacked your hair with what looks like rusty scissors. Quite viciously, it seems."

I fixed him with my fiercest glare, and he laughed, unheeding of my indignance. "One of these days you'll succeed and truly be the death of me," he sighed.

It was an inevitability we danced around. A darkness that threatened to consume me, yet I could not shy away from.

"You'd better go before I try again," I whispered, a sob clinging to the edge of my voice. Tears were sliding unbidden down my cheeks.

What has my life become? What have I turned into? I'm nothing more than the monster they made me to be.

I jumped, startled, when, instead of pulling away and protecting himself, he scooched closer and gently wiped a tear from my cheek. "I don't blame you," he said softly. "I would do the same, if not worse."

"If I had my strength back, I would do worse," I whispered. "Besides, you should blame me. You should blame me and get away before I hurt you again."

The silence stretched between us, suffocating me as the minutes ticked by.

At last, Ronan broke the silence. "If the stitches are overgrown, then I need to get them out of your back." Ronan's voice was quiet as he looked at my arms and their endless scars—eventually his gaze stopped at the Lichtenberg figures burned into my skin. "If you hadn't brought me back," he whispered. "Then none of this would have happened. You wouldn't be imprisoned, your mother…"

"I'd be dead," I cut in gently. "There is a cost to the use of my gifts…and the use of them such as it happened…it's forbidden. I'd have died if I didn't bring you back. A life for a life is the law outside of…well, where I must be."

Ronan pulled apart my cryptic words, and at last understanding dawned on his face. "Faye, if I hadn't…if I hadn't been afraid, then we wouldn't be in this mess."

"We're all afraid, Ronan. When you're helpless to protect the ones you love, no matter what you do…it makes you afraid."

Ronan gently took my hand, and for a fleeting moment we sat in broken solidarity.

"There's always hope," Ronan said at last. "You can't give up hope."

"There's no hope left," I whispered. "We're both trapped here, Ronan. We can't escape the bloodshed that stands between us. We're circling each other as we slowly bleed out—all while your father pulls the strings…and yet, he's just a puppet himself because someone else is pulling his strings. It's an endless cycle of violence. Endless and hopeless—just like us."

Ronan sighed, staring down at our hands. "Faye, if you give up hope then everything will be lost. Your defiance is the only thing keeping both of us afloat. If you give up, it will destroy the only thing I have left in the world."

I scoffed. "What do you mean, Ronan? What can you possibly mean by such a ridiculous statement as that?"

"I'll tell you what happened to my face, and then maybe you'll understand this whole rotten situation we're tied up in."

"Yes, because your good looks clearly have the answers to all our woes."

"Ah, so you think I'm good looking, do you?"

My cheeks flamed. "NO!" I protested quickly—too quickly.

Ronan laughed outright. "Well, on this incredibly crappy day at least I have that going for me. Your luck may have run out, but it seems as if my rotten luck at least has a flower laid on its grave."

I laughed in spite of myself, his stupid sense of humor pulling me out of my dismal state of mind. "Well then, take your flower. It's the only one you'll ever get from me."

Ronan smiled. "I'll cherish it forever."

"Now, get to the point," I sighed. "What does your face have to do with any of this?"

"It has to do with everything," Ronan replied, his face sobering. "Because it means that I need your help."

My kidnapper needs my help...well, that's a first.

10

Yo-Ho, A Pirate's Life For Me

"You're so incredibly violent...I think I like it."
-Jennifer L. Armentrout, From Blood and Ash

Two days had passed and much to my ire, Theron had a wild, stupid idea and decided that I needed to socialize. I was in no mood for his nonsense. Nothing he said could make me willingly abandon my post at Evadne's bedside to go eat breakfast with the crew. Theron however, didn't care about willing or not. He was dead set on my going.

"I'm not hungry!" I protested for what felt like the millionth time.

Theron shrugged. "I don't care, Sparks. You need to eat, and you need fresh air. It's been two days. Take a break. I'll let you know if something happens. Until then, you're going to take a break. That's an order. You need air."

"I do not!" I argued.

"*Go*." There was a no-nonsense tone attached to his words, and I sighed, trying to gather myself and take a different stance. Perhaps wheedling would get him to relent and excuse me from socializing.

"Theron—"

"Goooo," Theron arched an eyebrow and crossed his arms. "I'll keep an eye on your sister, and her... petting zoo." He sighed. "Does she know she has two highly dangerous creatures bonded to her?"

"Oh, she knows. She just never particularly cared if something was deadly or not...she judges more by the cuteness scale and believes that—" I cleared my throat, preparing to do my best imitation of Evadne's voice, "every animal deserves a fair chance no matter how strange or scary."

Theron laughed, amused by my antics.

If he knew how she really sounded, he'd be laughing a lot harder. That was a TER-RIBLE imitation.

"Well, we have our work cut out for us when she wakes up. I'll have to keep a close watch on her and make sure she doesn't try to adopt a skye dragon."

"What's that?" I asked, my curiosity piqued.

"A very dangerous threat to us skye pirates," Theron replied. "As well as an *absolute* no-no for adoption."

This unintentional stalling tactic had worked in my favor. Theron looked as if he was about to give me a very long exhortation about skye dragons, and my hopes rose—perhaps I wouldn't be forced to socialize after all.

I'm just gonna mosey on over here...sit myself down on the edge of the cot and look as if I'm paying rapt attention to his information.

I do want to hear what he has to say. But I want to avoid socializing even more.

"You see skye dragons—" Theron began, then abruptly stopped. "Nice try, Sparks. Go eat breakfast. I'll tell you about skye dragons when you come back."

"Darn it!" I snapped angrily. I had been so sure my unintentional ruse, turned intentional, would work.

"I'll have to keep a close eye on you, too. You're much too clever for your own good."

"I'm very clever, *entirely* for my own good," I muttered as I stalked out the door. "I don't even know which way to go!" I protested, turning back into our cabin. "I'll get lost. I might as well just save myself the trouble and stay here. I'm really not hungry—"

"Turn right, go down the flight of stairs, follow that deck over and make a left. First door on your right. You'll know when you're close. They're anything but quiet."

I huffed, incredibly annoyed that he would give me directions instead of pity—thus allowing me to stay with my sister.

I do NOT want to socialize.

I tarried in the doorway, casting a lingering glance back. "I really think it'd be better if—"

"Goooo," Theron interrupted.

I felt like whining further. But I knew from the look on his face it wouldn't work. He was as impervious to my wheedling as a guard dog was to bribery.

I haven't tried bribery yet.

I don't think it would work. Besides, what could a skye pirate be bribed with?

I don't know, but surely there's something...maybe a dagger, or perhaps someone, say a sacrifice, that said pirate could then force to walk the plank...

Do they even have a plank they force people to walk?

Of course they do. They're pirates.

But what if that's a stereotype?

It most certainly is not.

I sighed and finally made my way down the deck. I took my slow, easy time, repeating his instructions in my head as I tried to ignore how high up we were. I didn't want to tell Theron, but one of the other, less important reasons I didn't want to leave the cabin was my fear of heights. Being outside of the cabin was absolutely terrifying. I didn't want to admit how much of a chicken it made me.

Stupid Theron. Making me socialize when I just want to stay with Evadne.

I told him I wasn't hungry. Why is he making me eat? I don't feel like eating.

Besides, my arm is in a sling, essentially bound to my chest. I can't eat one handed with any sort of dignity...I'll make a mess, and they'll make fun of me. What a great first impression that'll be...stupid pirate, on his stupid skye ship, too far up in the freaking, stupid clouds.

I hate this. I hate all of this. What was Jack thinking by sending us here??

My angry, grumbling thoughts kept a steady narration as I tried to follow Theron's directions. It wasn't long before I began to wonder if I had missed a step—more like two or three—and was actually going in completely the wrong direction.

What if I wander too far and end up falling off the ship? What if something terrible happens?

This was a bad idea. I'm going to go back. Surely I've been gone long enough that I can fib and say I ate some breakfast and have since returned... As long as he doesn't hear my stomach growling later I should be fine...

I turned around, intent on my own personal mutiny. But out of nowhere, a loud crash pulled me from my thoughts.

The loud crash was followed by a shriek and then a long string of curses.

Hello, what's going on here?

I followed the unmistakable sound of a commotion, making a left turn and there, on my right, was a large doorway. My mouth fell open in shock as I took in absolute chaos, unsure of where to look first. The room was in a frantic state of disarray. People were running this way and that, grabbing plates and mugs, and yelling. There, in the middle of it all, on top of one of the tables, stood a short woman screeching at the top of her lungs.

What is she screaming about?

It didn't take long to identify the culprit. It was a spider. A *huge*, disgusting, horrible spider.

OH HECK NO!

That one is bigger than the one that bit Artemis. But the resemblance is uncanny.

The woman screamed again as the spider quickly scuttled across the wall. I took a step back, horrified and ready to flee. Even thinking about spiders this big was something I was not about to engage with.

What is she doing standing on the table, screaming? Why doesn't she run? She's a sitting duck there.

The woman on the table raised her right hand. "I am too tired for you to be acting like this!" she cried as she pointed at the spider.

"No!" the whole room yelled in unison.

A beam of red light burst from her fingers, hitting the spider spot on. The horrifying creature exploded with an earsplitting screech and everyone in the room groaned. Bits of spider rained down around the room. I watched, horrified, as a disgustingly large chunk fell into someone's abandoned mug of coffee.

"Raz!" a particularly irate, blond-haired Fey man yelled. "Why did you have to shoot it? We could've just smashed it! Now it's everywhere! You exploded it into my coffee!"

"Do I look like I care, Logan?" the woman, Raz, snapped. "I refuse to tolerate skye spiders before I've had *my* coffee. Besides, smashing it means getting close to it and I refuse to get close to those monsters!"

"Well, now my coffee is ruined!"

"It's not star study, Logan. Go pour yourself a new cup. Besides, you're the one who abandoned your coffee in an attempt to flee."

"The whole cursed mug will have to be washed," Logan protested, his sapphire-blue eyes flashing. "You know this is my favorite mug!"

"Ah, yes, because I clearly instructed the cursed spider to fall directly into your coffee when it died," Raz replied sarcastically.

"You know skye spiders are venomous. Their whole body is poisonous. It's spiked and not in any productive way." He stormed over to where she still stood on the table. She was short, and it was evident that, normally, he would have towered over her, but with the added three-foot height of the table, they now stood eye to eye. It was comical, really. Raz, in all of her five-foot-something glory, standing up to this tall, burly man, who was so muscular he could have picked her up and chucked her across the room with little to no effort.

"Wash my cup!" Logan demanded angrily.

"I'll wash it," Raz replied with an angry smirk, "with your life's blood. Then, I'll use your intestines as a dishcloth, to get it extra *squeaky* clean. Just for you."

"Raz, I'm warning you," Logan growled.

"And I'm warning you," Raz replied, all humor gone from her voice. "So, I suggest you take a nice little step back, before I'm forced to remind you of the damage these two *teeny-tiny* digits can inflict on sniveling cowards like you." She wiggled her fingers in his face, and he glanced down at them, as if reconsidering. "You abandoned your coffee, so don't blame me now that you have to face the repercussions of the yellow state of your liver. If you cared about your *favorite* mug so much, you wouldn't have left it."

Teeny tiny digits? Didn't she have a gun in her hand?

"I'm not the one who's standing on the table screeching about a cursed skye spider," Logan said after a moment, picking up the argument where it had trailed off. "I went to go get the shovel to *squish* it. Like we're *supposed* to!"

"The presence of any spider, no matter its size, requires screaming, then decimation, exactly in that order. Sometimes, if it's big enough, it requires screaming while decimating. One must scream to establish dominance. Besides, you took too long to get the shovel. If I had waited while you were taking your sweet time, we'd all be poisoned."

"You're insane," Logan huffed.

"You should be grateful for that. If I wasn't, you'd already be dead. Besides, the most fabulous people typically are. That's why I fit in so well on this ship—yo, ho, a pirate's life for me." I watched, amazed as she reached out and poked the tip of his nose. "Boop!"

"I'm not going to repeat myself," Logan snarled.

Raz raised her right hand again and pointed her first and middle fingers at his face, her thumb was cocked back as if she was miming shooting a gun. "Need I remind you *again* about the power in these tiny-teeny little digits of mine?"

What's so special about her fingers?

Much to my shock and surprise, Logan actually took a step back.

Obviously something interesting. Logan is massive, and whatever she's capable of, it has him wary.

"That's what I thought. Now, stop being dramatic. I do not have the energy for you today, either. Especially not before I've had my first pot of coffee."

Pot?! As in, she drinks a whole pot, and then...multiple pots?!

"Children!" A new, yet familiar voice interrupted their showdown. It was Captain Verity. "You're setting a terribly bad example for our guest."

Raz put a hand on her hip and stared at where Captain Verity had, until that moment, been sitting unobserved, nursing her own cup of coffee.

"Thank you for neutralizing the threat, Raz. But I will remind you, no laser fingers in the house."

"We aren't *in* a house," Raz replied with a scowl.

"No, but you get my drift. We live on this ship, thus the interior cabins are as close to a house as our wandering souls are ever going to find." Verity arched an eyebrow. "I think you know *exactly* what I mean. So, if the two of you don't mind, I'd like to enjoy my third cup of coffee in peace."

Third?

This crew must drink a lot of coffee.

Finally. People who actually understand the value and beauty of coffee.

Maybe they can convince Evadne to give coffee an honest go and change her pretentious tea drinker ways.

"She started it!" Logan protested, pulling my attention back to the argument.

"And I'm finishing it," Verity replied coldly. "Now, get yourself a new cup, or wash the one you have. Things happen; the coffee contamination wasn't intentional. Now, if Raz had killed the spider, then taken a disgusting piece of it and dropped it into your coffee, I would make her wash your mug. That being said, though her methods left something to be desired, she *did* do us a favor by killing the spider. So, kindly stop with your dramatics before I'm forced to take drastic measures."

Raz smirked at the man.

"On *BOTH* of you," Verity snapped.

"Nymphs," Logan muttered irritably.

Raz's mechanical wings flared at the comment, and she looked as if she was going to say something particularly nasty back. But Verity cleared her throat, giving Raz an extremely pointed look over the rim of her large coffee mug.

"Yes Ma'am," Raz muttered, letting the matter drop as she hopped off the table.

Now that the chaos had subsided, I took the opportunity to really look at her. She stood somewhere around five-foot three, and had broad, muscular thighs that made her look as if she could squat at least three hundred pounds. She had long, waist-length, golden brown hair that hung loose in wild, ringlet curls. Thick, ivory horns curved out from her skull, similar to those of a mountain goat. Delicate pointed ears, full of hoops and studs, poked out of her hair. Her skin was light green, with dark green swirls that spread out in various designs and shapes. Her deep gold eyes were piercing, standing out beneath long brown lashes. Large mechanical wings arched out from her shoulder blades and tucked down toward the ground, taking up the space normal wings would. The surface of the metal and cloth wings was engraved with branches, vines, and leaves.

She is the most gorgeous woman I've ever seen.

"Ember, come have a cup of spider free coffee," Verity said cordially, pulling me from my awe-struck perusal of Raz.

As if the alternative option would be coffee with a spider in it...a poisonous spider?

"Please excuse my crew's behavior. They tend to be *quite* uncivilized before they've had their coffee. One might even begin to describe them as a ludicrous parcel of driveling galoots...especially if a skye spider is involved. Nasty buggers those. You'd best dispose of such monsters whenever you find them."

I think I'll just...do what Raz did. Scream as I stand on the table...except my screaming wouldn't be to establish dominance...it would be to establish how completely and utterly terrified I am. Because there is no way I am going to try to kill a spider like that. It would probably eat me before I managed the first swing.

"I didn't know skye spiders were...real," I muttered, trying to wrap my head around the concept.

"Yes, unfortunately for us rogues within the Moores, we have many such atrocities to deal with. Side effects of the Knight's rise in power. He makes absolutely barbaric monsters as he attempts to get out. The skye spiders tend to get quite big out here, especially if they can find the right prey. They travel by parachutes made of their own webs…"

I shuddered, horrified.

Verity cleared her throat. "Nevermind the nasty monstrosities of necromancy. Such is the price we pay when the *proper* Realms don't want the likes of us—we must make our own way."

"Why don't they want you?"

Verity sighed. "That, my dear Ember, is a conversation that can only happen after ten cups of coffee. Another time, perhaps. I don't want to tarnish the *sparkly* perspective you have of the ever-so-magical Courts."

"I have no such perspective," I said quietly. "They've stolen far too much from me."

"From us all," Verity replied, her eyes probing as she stared at me. "Another time," she said gently. "Right now, you need to heal and rest. Once you've accomplished that, I will answer any and all questions you may have. I owe you that much."

"Because of Jack?"

"Because of a great many things," Verity replied cryptically. "Now, go get yourself some food, and a cup of coffee. Food is in the kitchen." She pointed. "There, across the room. Coffee is also there. I don't care if you're hungry or not. Get enough to feed a horse. Your metabolism is too fast—even in the Moores. Your body can't heal if it doesn't have nutrients, and I won't have my Jack mad at me for not taking care of his sisters."

My Jack.

My heart broke a little at those words, the longing buried deep within every syllable. They loved each other and yet they held no hope for the future because of the monarchs.

I nodded, swallowing back the sudden lump in my throat that rose at her heartache, and walked over to the kitchen. Dodging and shuffling, I tried to stay out of the bustling crew's way. They moved around me as if I didn't exist, focused on their plates and coveted cups of coffee. The kitchen was a large room, bigger than the dining room. Counters lined the far wall with a stove in the middle, and floor to ceiling shelves lined the rest of the walls. A large fire roared in a stone hearth, which seemed like a terrible idea on a flying ship, but it gave the room a very homey feel. I had the sudden feeling that this was going to become one of my favorite places on the ship.

I guess being on a magical flying ship comes with its perks. You get to have a fire inside said flying ship.

A large island sat in the middle of the room, full to bursting with platters of hot food.

How much food does this crew eat?

Furthermore, where do they keep said food?

I'd hate to have to go grocery shopping for this lot. It would cost an arm and a leg...

At the end of the island sat at least a dozen carafes of steaming coffee.

They're very serious about their coffee.

Well, I think I should enjoy their love of coffee.

I opted for thick slices of homemade bread, slathered in jelly and peanut butter. I didn't have the energy for traditional breakfast food. PB&J was comfort food, reminding me in a painful, yet calming way of Oma. The balance of loss and life moving on was one I couldn't quite grasp. In some ways, she didn't feel gone. We hadn't had a funeral, there was no closure, and we had been swept away so fast there had been no time to grieve. Much like it had been when Faye was taken, Oma seemed taken, and not truly gone.

Raz had commandeered one of the carafes and opted to drink straight from the thermal container, sighing happily with every sip she took. An incredibly disgruntled Logan put his contaminated mug in the sink, and now Raz held out a new mug for him, giving him a sheepish grin. "Sorry for what I said before I had my coffee," she chirped.

Logan laughed. "I guess I should apologize, too. But next time let me squish it, or at least give me an actual chance to get my coffee out of the way. Half a second doesn't count."

"I'll try," Raz replied. "But I can't be held responsible for what happens when those awful skye spiders are involved."

"Hey, it least it was smaller than the one last week."

The two began comparing information about the two skye spiders and I promptly blocked out the conversation. It was giving me the creepy crawlies to think that there were even bigger spiders than the one I had just seen, which had been the size of several dinner plates.

I do not want to think about that. No sirree. I think I'll just take my happy self and this lovely cup of coffee back into the dining room.

Making the sandwich one handed had been a challenge, but getting both my plate and mug back was worse yet. I finally put my plate on top of my mug, then slowly picked up the mug and carefully made my way back into the dining room.

"So, tell me Ember," Verity said cordially as I gingerly sat my coffee mug and plate down on the table. "Since we didn't have much time for an information exchange when your brother brought you to me, why on earth would the monarchs send two unmarked Grimms into the Moores? What in all the four Realms were they possibly thinking?"

"Well," I began uncertainly.

Verity sighed. "Is this a topic that you need at least three cups of coffee for?"

I took a bite of my impromptu PB&J sandwich and nodded.

"Very well then, perhaps I should give you a little rundown on what we do here, and how things work." Verity gave me a small smile. "Let me just refill my coffee." She eyed my PB&J. "I believe I said enough to feed a horse, did I not?"

I gave her an innocent smile and batted my eyelashes. "Sorry," I mumbled around my mouthful. "I'm trying."

"You and your brother are so much alike. He always gives me that exact same grin. But he, unlike you, has no problem eating enough. He eats enough to feed three or four horses."

"How did you two meet?"

"I saved his sorry life," Verity said lightly as she stood up. "He then decided to make an incredibly stupid decision and fell in love with me..." Her voice trailed off and she smiled softly, staring down at the coffee in her hands. "We both made that incredibly stupid decision."

She didn't say anything else; she simply went back into the kitchen to get her refill.

Raz plopped down in the chair next to Verity's. "So, what's your story, Grimmlin?"

"I..."

"Raz," Verity called. "Don't pester her before she's had her coffee. Give her the same decency you demand from us and save your questions for later. You'll have plenty of time when I post her on your watch."

Raz gave me a delighted grin, and I was suddenly worried about what such a statement entailed. I didn't particularly want to know what 'on your watch' meant.

"I heard you're scared of heights," Raz said lightly. "I don't know why, there's nothing to be afraid of. If you fall off the ship, I'll be sure to save you."

"That's...comforting," I stammered.

"Raz," Verity sighed in exasperation.

"Right-O, oh captain, my captain," Raz replied theatrically as she got up. "Me and my coffee are on our way to the crow's nest. I'll tell you if I spot anything interesting."

"That would be appreciated. But please remember that clouds that look like dinosaurs do not count as interesting."

"Dinosaurs are always interesting," Raz protested with a snort of laughter.

Verity sighed and rolled her eyes, giving Raz a dismissive wave. "Tell Nikos to double check our trajectory. The islands tend to move when you're urgently seeking them."

Raz saluted and left, whistling. I vaguely recognized the tune of "Drunken Sailor."

"Well, since you're bound to be spending quite a bit of time with us, I think it's best you know how things work around here. I'll put this bluntly so there's no chance of you misunderstanding me. I am the captain here, and my word is law. If I tell you to jump, you jump, if I tell you to duck, you duck. If I tell you to do the chicken dance, you do it. Am I understood?" Her gaze was piercing as she stared me down.

I nodded. "I understand."

"Things are done differently here—it's not like what you experienced within the Courts. My crew functions on trust, based wholly within an undeniable tier of command. I don't make decisions to tear you apart and break you down. Every crew member relies on me to keep them safe and I take that responsibility very seriously. If you cannot reside within such boundaries, then you and I are going to butt heads quite a lot. But I promise you, you will *not* win such debates. Now, when you have questions about my commands, I am more than willing to discuss things with you and explain my reasons, but not until after. There is always a justifiable reason behind my orders." She stared me down, letting her words sink in. "Does that make sense?" she asked.

"Yes, ma'am."

Verity smiled. "Good. Now, let me introduce you to my crew, well, the ones in the room. I'll give you a tour of the ship afterward and we'll see who else we can catch out and about."

She gestured toward the doorway, where Raz had just left. "You just met Raz—she's our boatswain and chief rigger. If you value your life, don't get between her and her coffee. Once you've healed up, you and your sister will be running rounds with her in the rigging."

"Oh, I don't think that's such a good idea."

"It's a perfectly good idea. The best way to conquer your fear is through exposure to it as you learn to overcome it. I am well aware you're afraid of heights, but Theron will help you get your bearings and keep the fear at bay."

"How—"

"Nevermind how; he'll tell you that when he's ready. It's his story to tell."

"Ooookaaaay…" I drew the word out, trying to untangle exactly what she meant.

"Logan," she gestured to the tall, burly man Raz had been fighting with, "is our chief swordsman when we are in battle. When we are not, he is our chief cook. He takes great pride in his work, so be sure to compliment his efforts."

Logan nodded to me, raising his mug of coffee from a couple of tables over. He had chin-length blond hair, and a well-kept beard that extended an inch or two down below his chin. His thick forearms were covered with full sleeves of tattoos, and his bright, sapphire-blue eyes seemed to laugh over the rim of his mug.

What's so funny?

For some reason his amusement annoyed me, and I turned back to my coffee. Apparently, I hadn't drunk enough of it to be in a civilized mood.

Compliment his efforts, you're being incredibly rude.

"The, uh, bread is marvelous," I called, trying to keep my tone cordial and civil. Evadne's threatening tone at the farewell ball popped into my mind. 'We will all be freaking civil.'

I'm trying, Eva, I'm trying.

Logan grinned with pride, and I turned back to Verity's introductions.

She was pointing to a fey with wild black hair, dark black eyes lined with kohl, and pale milky skin. "That's Archer. Do yourself a favor and don't ask him if he shoots—especially not if Raz tells you to. He'll likely stab you. He's hopeless with a bow and arrow, and the crew won't let him forget the irony."

"Stupid idiots," Archer muttered under his breath. "Excuse me, Captain, I'm off to help the insufferable Raz with the rigging."

"Play nice," Verity replied cordially.

Archer smiled, showing a mouth full of very pointy teeth. "I always do, Captain."

He winked at me as he walked by, and I hurriedly turned my attention back to my coffee.

Verity gave a mirthless laugh. "Rogue."

Archer bowed slightly. "Always. If I wasn't, what else would I have to my name?"

"On with you," Verity snapped lightly. "Go, before I make you swab the deck, or perhaps walk the plank."

See, they do have a plank.

Archer raised his hands in surrender and hurriedly backed out of the room. "No need for such drastic measures. I'll behave. I swear it on this blessed, bloody ship. Besides, redheads aren't my type."

Verity arched an eyebrow but didn't make further comment. "Over there," she said, returning to her introductions, "Rune and Sora are sitting at that table. Rune is the blonde, Sora the redhead. Sora is married to Logan. Rune is married to Archer. Archer likes to get a rise out of Rune by flirting with people. So just ignore him, or else things will escalate."

"Why don't you tell him to stop?" I asked curiously.

"It's their marriage. I'm not getting in the middle of it. Rune will stab him when she gets tired enough of it, and then he'll behave for a little bit. Then after a while the cycle resets."

Sora and Rune both waved, and I waved back uncertainly. Sora's long, red hair was pulled back into a thick braid, whereas Rune's white-blond hair was chin length. Various scars covered Sora's skin; a set of particularly deep white marks cut across her cheek.

"Rune is my explosives master, as well as my main gunman. Sora is our master archer. She and Rune oversee the main defense of the ship." She gave me a wry grin. "What else can you expect from twins?"

"They're twins?" I asked incredulously.

"Yes, but why should that be a surprise to you? You and your sister look nothing alike, except perhaps you have the same nose."

"Fair point," I muttered as I finished my sandwich.

"That's what I thought. Now, if you'll walk with me, I'll introduce you to the rest of the crew...the ones who are awake, that is." She pointed to my mug. "You can take it with you, just try not to break it. Logan is very particular about his mugs. Each one has a story, and some amount of snark. Every mug is also his declared 'favorite'."

I examined my mug closely. I had been so interested in consuming the coffee within that I hadn't even thought to look at what design was on the outside. It showed several feathery looking creatures, with big eyes and large wings. They had their bums up in the air, pressed against bottles that several other pixies held—two to a bottle. Dark black smoke was exuding from their backsides and filling the bottles. Following the cartoon something was written, but I couldn't read the language.

Captain Verity laughed as my mouth fell open in shock. "He got that one after trading with the pixies for their bottled pixie farts. They threw in the mug to earn his good graces after price gouging him for the explosives."

"What does it say?"

"It says, 'Pixie Gas Factory. Creating trusted explosives since the borders were birthed'," Verity replied, still laughing.

"Why did Logan need the, uh, pixie farts?"

"Well, technically Rune needed them to restock our explosives in case of attack. But Logan is on better terms with the pixies than Rune is. She may have lost her temper and well...unintentionally set off several batches inside their factory..." Verity sighed. "It set them back a month in production, and one thing about pixies is they never forget. They'll charge her eight times what anything is worth. Best just to have Logan do the bartering in that area. They'll only charge him twice what it's worth...and he gets funny mugs out of the process. As clumsy as this lot is, the mugs certainly come in handy."

I followed Verity out of the dining room and down the hall. "The medical wing is where you and your sister are, obviously. When she's better, we'll move you into the hull with the rest of the crew. You may be Jack's sisters, but you don't get preferential treatment around here."

She began to climb a ladder, and I swallowed back my fear, suddenly faced with the predicament of holding my coffee and the ladder, all with one arm out of commission.

Verity was already at the top, staring down at me in amusement. "You could abandon the coffee..."

I clutched it tighter to my chest. "Absolutely not!" I snapped, hardening my resolve. I switched my mug to the hand in the sling, trying incredibly hard not to spill it down my chest.

Verity smirked as I began to awkwardly climb the ladder.

She made it look so easy. C'mon Ember, be like Verity. Fearless as you kick butt in your three-inch boots and flawless beauty.

I was thoroughly winded by the time I made it to the top, and much to my dismay I had indeed slopped the coffee down my front.

I stared at the dark stain in annoyance. "I'm sorry, I think I might have ruined your shirt."

"Nonsense," Verity said lightly. "Clarice enchants the water when she washes. No stains can stand against her magic. Now, up here you can find the helm, as well as the captain's quarters." She smiled, "My quarters."

"Have you always been the captain of this ship?"

"Yes. Faolan and I have been here since the inception of my rig. He is my second mate. He sang the boat into existence, weaving the magic into her helm as he crafted my Aurora. There has only been one attempted mutiny over the centuries. He and Raz helped me put an end to that unfortunate rebellion."

"What happened?"

"I gave them no mercy—just as they gave none to me and those who remained loyal. I hung the traitors by their ankles and left them drifting in the wind for the skye dragons to find." She smiled, but there was no joy in the motion. "A tasty dragon snack to keep us in their good graces as we cross their skies."

I could feel the color draining from my face. Of all the ways to die, that seemed like an incredibly unfortunate way to go.

Verity was watching my face. "I meant it when I said you would not succeed if you tried to cross my authority."

"Yes ma'am." I gulped.

Verity laughed lightly. "Don't worry, Ember. I don't think you and I are going to have any problems."

"I sure hope not," I muttered.

"Now, in here is the helm and my first mate, Nikos. He's helping Faolan with the ship's navigation. Nikos is Raz's husband. Nikos, this is Ember Grimm. She and her sister Evadne will be with us for the foreseeable future."

A tall Fey stood at the wheel, dressed in black army pants and a black tank top with an armored tactical vest over the top. He had wavy black hair on two thirds of his scalp that was long and pulled into a loose braid. The other third was shaved. Black ink covered his skin, in a complex Samoan type of tattoo that went from his skull, down his neck, and around his throat to his shoulders and arms. Every inch of exposed skin on his torso was covered in the intricate design. Similar lines ran beneath his eyes and across his cheekbones, with a complementing mark in between his eyebrows, on the bridge of his nose, and down the middle of his chin.

That must have hurt to get all that done. He's braver than I am, that's for sure.

How exactly does one get a tattoo within the Realm? Is it the same as in the Human Realm?

Human Realm? Sheesh, I sound like everyone else here...as if it's not my Realm...

I guess it's not anymore...

An intense wave of homesickness hit me like a blow to the gut.

Nikos was holding out his hand, and I snapped out of my sadness and hurriedly shook his hand. "Sorry," I mumbled.

"Nothing to apologize for," Nikos replied cordially.

"Between his obsession with ink, and all the details of my ship," Verity said, "I'd say there's more than enough to occupy your attention and distract you."

I blushed, embarrassed she had noticed my inspection of his tattoos.

"It's a pleasure," Nikos said lightly. "I hope you enjoy your stay with our crew. We're like family around here, and we hope you feel at home."

"I'm sure I will," I replied, grinning.

Verity was on the move again. I envied how freely she moved, as if she didn't care how far up we were, with only a thin rail separating us from the vast, endless skies. One clumsy misstep and I was toast.

"Breathe, Ember," Verity called before taking a long sip from her coffee mug. "You can't possibly hope to walk if you're holding your breath."

"I don't think I'm cut out to be a skye pirate," I wheezed as I tried to force my lungs to move in and out.

"Sure you are, you just have to tell yourself you're not afraid."

It was the same thing Theron had told me, and I was still *absolutely* in doubt about the validity of such advice.

"Yo-ho, a pirate's life for me," I muttered.

"That's the spirit!" Verity called exuberantly. "Now you just need to *believe* what you're saying. Try again, but this time, mean it." She began whistling the same tune Raz had been singing—drunken sailor.

I watched her smooth progression across the deck and sighed. If only it was that simple.

Believe what I'm saying...got it.

Yo-ho, a pirate's life for me... Yo-ho, a pirate's life for me...Imma pirate...Imma pirate... I'm a fearless pirate...ARGH!

It wasn't working, but maybe I just had to give it time.

There was no escaping Verity's incredibly amused smile as I followed her around the ship and continued to mutter, "Yo-ho, a pirate's life for me!"

11

Time's Up

EMBER

"The poem begins not where the knife enters, but where the blade
twists."
-Hanif Abdurraqib

Artemis stood in front of me, fury written plainly across his face. His eyes were a vibrant green, carrying so many emotions, I couldn't untangle them.

Music frantically played at the edges of my mind—pleading, begging. All while his countenance seemed ready to rip me to pieces.

I scrambled backward and my shoulders collided with a solid brick wall.

Where am I?

I was breathless as he advanced, desperately trying to figure out a way to get past him and escape.

How did he get here? How did he find me?

"Where are you?" he growled.

The crescendo was pushing at my mind now, the noise deafening as I struggled to keep my wall of flames strong and high. I had to keep him out. If he knew where we were, it would all be over.

"Safe!" I snapped, forcing iron into my tone. "Safely away from you, so let us go. Go back to your Realm and leave us be!"

"I can't!" he snarled. "If I do, they'll kill him."

"Who?"

"Where are you?" he demanded again, ignoring my question.

I lashed out, aiming my forearm at his throat. I knew I wasn't going to be quick enough, but I just wanted to distract him enough that I could get by him. All I had to do was outrun him until the dream fell apart.

Artemis blocked the blow, and his fingers encircled my arm, forcing my fist up as he pinned it against the wall. "Do you have any idea what you've done?" he demanded as he shoved my body backward.

What I've done? What about what you've done? You're torturing Evadne to get to me, you monster!

Stars danced in front of my eyes as the back of my head collided with the rough wall behind us.

Are there brick walls on the ship? Where am I? Did he pull me away or is this just an elaborate dream?

"Well? Do you?"

"I know what I've done," I seethed. "That doesn't give you the right to do what *you've* done. You have no right to torture her to get us back."

Confusion crossed his face and my anger rose. How dare he pretend to be confused when he was hurting my sister.

My wall of fire was wavering as he continued to press down. He was tearing it apart, one tendril of flame at a time as his music at last smothered my rage.

NO!

He pounced as my resistance flickered with my desperation. I had once again used the wrong composition. I ran, fleeing his presence and leading him through a tangled haze of memories as my body continued to struggle against him. Both my fists were pinned against the wall by my head. His feet were standing on mine, preventing me from moving.

No, no, no!

"Where. are. you?" he spat.

I smashed my forehead into his, desperate to get away. It was a useless attempt, and it only succeeded in making me dizzy and disoriented.

Artemis' grip tightened as he tore through my mind, frantically searching. Beneath his rage was another emotion he could not mask—it was desperation.

Why is he so desperate? Why?

Evadne's screams surrounded me, and I couldn't get away. Even now, the three marks he had inflicted on her, to get to me, burned at the memory of her agony.

You did this. YOU DID THIS!

My accusation hung in the air between us as he watched another memory, through my eyes. I stood before a tall mirror, staring at the three warnings carved into my skin. The countdown he had tortured us with.

Artemis' subconscious drew back, stunned. My accusation within the memory hit him like a slap across the face.

"Leave her *alone*," I snarled. "You want to torture me? So be it. But I will not tolerate your brutality against me, on her."

Artemis' mouth was opening and closing. His anger fell silent, leaving only questions. "Where are you?" he repeated.

"Leave her alone!" I yelled, finally pushing him off of me.

"It's not me!" he replied angrily. "Where are you? Let me help you!"

"Oh, sure it's not." I snapped, shoving him back another step. "You're the only one capable of something like this. I knew it was too good to be true, that you were truly *changing*." A sob tore at my voice as my own fears came out between us. "You're going to kill me someday, Artemis, and this? This is only proof that I was right to ignore my feelings and run from you."

"Em," Artemis whispered pleadingly.

"You're the only one who knows about the bond between Evadne and me. You're the only one who would have anything to gain. Isn't that why you told me three days??"

"Where are you?" Artemis replied, his voice desperate.

"Safe," I whispered. But it was a lie. We were not safe. We were the farthest thing from safe.

His inspection of my memories at last came to the moment where Evadne's skin was first being carved into—those horrible, torturous marks branding both of us. His mouth fell open in shock as he stared at the wreckage he'd made of us.

Did you think it wouldn't be like this? Did you think it was only me you'd be hurting? How can you stand there and pretend to care when you did this to begin with?

"Leave us *alone*, Artemis," I hissed. "Don't you dare stand there and look shocked.

You did this!"

"Em," Artemis whispered, hands raised. "I swear—"

"Keep your useless words to yourself and *leave us alone.* You can't fix this. You can't fix it, not after what you've done. You went too far, Artemis."

Artemis' frustration mounted again, but the anger was masking something. "WHERE ARE YOU?" He roared. The desperation was palpable now, thick as smoke in the air. But beneath it, I at last realized what lingered that he was trying to hide—fear.

What are you afraid of? Afraid you'll never win me back since you've gone too far? You're right to be afraid. I can't forgive you for hurting her like this.

You're just as twisted as the rest of the Fey.

The dream shattered around us, and I woke with a cry. I was gasping, trying to calm my racing heartbeat as tears streamed down my cheeks.

We can't go back to what we were...we can never go back to what we were.

It was just a dream...but he has my dreams now...doesn't he? But wait, when he took my dreams earlier, I had nothing but darkness...maybe the darkness can only come if we're close?

I was curled into a ball beside Evadne. I had drug my cot across the room, placing it next to hers so I could hold her hand while I slept and waited for my body to heal.

Fireheart and Elvie were sitting on Evadne's chest, wide awake. Their eyes never left her face as they stared at her. Fireheart had apparently gotten over his aversion to Elvie. When, I had no idea. But he was curled around the deadly little rodent, scaled eyebrows scrunched together in worry. Together, her cursed little petting zoo kept a tense vigil over my sister as she drifted.

Another day had passed, and still Evadne hadn't woken up. She had only screamed when a third mark was carved into her arm. A solitary line, with the warning, *She will die alone.*

Fireheart nudged Evadne's limp hand with his nose, as if pleading with her to wake up. Elvie had taken to chanting her name in a little singsong rhyme. "Ee-va, Ee-va, wake up my Ee-va friend, Elvie no, no like this, please come back, again."

The ship rocked gently beneath us, and I rose, pulling my cloak tighter around my body. "I'll be right back," I whispered to Fireheart, petting the top of his head gently. "If anyone tries to hurt her, bite them."

Fireheart gave me a toothy little grin and blew a spurt of flame toward me.

"Yes, you can also turn them into a crisp if your devious little heart so desires," I replied, too exhausted to smile.

Fireheart's mischievous grin grew at such thoughts of bloodshed and mayhem.

I cast a final, lingering glance back before slipping out of the room for a breath of fresh air.

I'll be right back, Eva, I just need some air. Fireheart will keep watch over you until I get back...

Am I a bad sister for leaving her? Am I a bad sister for not helping her? For not saving her? Is it my fault this happened in the first place? What if I had volunteered to go with the wraith, instead of her...

We'd still be there...everyone knows I'm a hopeless dancer...

Still, better me than her...

I walked silently along the deck, stopping at the rail as I stared out over the endless skies. Countless stars burned dimly across the vast expanse, and in the quiet absence of my fear, I could almost believe it was beautiful up here.

No wonder Verity and her crew like it so much... If I wasn't so afraid all the time, I could almost come to love it...

I feel so small. Who am I to be up against this whole Realm that wants to destroy me?

Will we ever be okay again?

Will we ever be whole again?

I knew the answer to that painful question. We would never be whole again. There was no changing what they'd done—all the loved ones they'd stolen from us. Oma, F, and Mum were gone forever, and now we were irreversibly tied to the Realm. There was no going home again.

Will the bloodshed ever end?

Will they ever stop taking from us?

I sat down, carefully putting my legs in between the posts of the railing to ensure I didn't fall, but allowing my legs to dangle over the side of the ship. I pulled my slate gray notebook out of my cloak pocket and stared at the worn cover. The pages were almost filled now, and what a change had happened during its lifetime.

When I started this, Faye had just come home. I was full of hope and life. I thought maybe we had a chance to get her back and avoid all of this...and now? Now we can never go home, and we're trapped in the Realm ourselves.

I couldn't remember if I had packed my extra notebook or not. I hadn't found it in a haphazard search earlier this morning. The pockets in the cloak were so impossibly endless, that I had wasn't sure I'd find everything I had shoved in there before we left.

At least it's not a sandwich...

I chuckled mirthlessly, slightly entertained by the memory of Ryver's ire at Jacques' abundant food packing.

Jack, why would you send us here? Do we really have any hope of escaping the Last Gate?

I longed for my brother's company. If only had had time to explain instead of just giving us a letter.

My pen hovered over the empty page. There was so much inside, I wasn't sure I could find a way to express the hurricane of emotions that raged within my mind.

How do I write what I feel, when what I feel is destroying me in silence...how can words possibly encompass this agony?

My eyes drifted to my wrist, toward the pale scars that I knew hid beneath my sleeve. *No.*

I didn't want to turn to the demons that, for so long, had kept me alive. I wanted to escape their hold and the ways they helped me release my agony.

I don't want to be that person anymore. I don't want to fight that anymore. I want to be done with it.

I don't want to relapse. I don't want to. I am more than that. I am more.

I hesitated a moment longer, and then, like blood pouring from a lethal wound, the words bled onto the page as I struggled to release the feelings that threatened to drag me underwater and destroy me.

> *I'm trapped beneath,*
> *the weight of screams,*
> *and shame I'm forced to bear,*
> *the weight of guilt,*
> *the taint of blood,*
> *the blame of torture shared.*
> *Her blood upon,*
> *my head just grows,*
> *I cannot find escape,*
> *there's no way out,*
> *I'm trapped beneath,*
> *this monster's hungry weight.*
> *I'd take the load,*

and bear the pain,
if I could only take her place.
I'm so afraid,
it's all my fault,
I cannot fight the grey.
She's drowning right beside me,
and no matter how I fight,
I can't keep us above the waves,
the darkness drains my light.
There's no escape, there's no escape,
There's nothing I can say,
no hope beyond the wreckage,
the darkness stole our way.

"Tell me, is Hemmingway correct when he says that, to write one must simply sit down at the typewriter and bleed?"

I jumped at the sound of Theron's voice. Fumbling with my notebook, I almost dropped it over the edge of the ship.

"Careful, that would be an unfortunate mistake. I'd hate to pull Raz from her post just to rescue a journal."

I shoved the book into my pocket before hastily wiping the tears from my cheeks, trying to hide the evidence of my distress.

"You sleep very little for one who so desperately needs rest." His voice was gentle as he sat down beside me.

"I don't want to sleep right now," I whispered, trying to push the image of Artemis' vengeful gaze out of my mind. But there was no erasing it, nor was there any escape from the palpable fear that replaced his fury, the desperation that screamed and begged for my safety. How he could possibly claim all he wanted was my safety when he was the one doing this to us...

What if he was telling the truth? What if it's not him?

Who else could it be? He said things in that dream that only he would know...

"What do you write?" Theron asked easily, giving me a careless grin. "If we're going to be sleepless, exhausted pigeons, we should find something interesting to talk about. Maybe I should tell you my theory about skye dragons and Logan's cookies."

That sounds like a fantastic theory.

"My writing isn't interesting," I replied, trying to intentionally change the subject to the afore mentioned dragons and cookies.

"Sure it is. Besides, if you truly believe that you can always change what you write about—there's enough fascinating characters on this ship that you could write for years and never run out of entertaining stories." He laughed. "Take the other morning, for instance. Raz, in all her tiny glory, standing on top of that table, screaming about a spider, before taking it out with one blast from her laser fingers—all before she'd had her morning coffee. She then decided to turn her ire on a furious Logan and proceeded to exasperate him beyond belief in a matter of minutes."

"How did you hear about that?" I asked, chuckling as I remembered the standoff between the two.

"Well, Raz told me one side, Logan another, and Verity told me the whole thing."

"It was quite the scene," I chuckled. "Is it like that every day?"

"Just about. Sometimes there's a dull moment—but not often. That's a pirate's life for you; when it's not one thing, it's another."

"How did you end up here?" I asked at last.

"How did you end up here?" he countered.

I sighed, irritated, and he laughed. "I ended up here the same way as you," he answered. "I was running."

My fingers trailed to the new scars on my collarbone. The absentminded movement was not lost on Theron. "What's all this about?" he asked.

The crowned prince of Feylinne is desperate to get his all-powerful Grimm's back, so he can use us as weapons against the Moores...

"All what?" I asked, feigning ignorance. I didn't want to drag out all my rancid, dirty laundry. It was best left hidden far, far away, where no one could ever find it.

Theron pulled up my sleeve, revealing the thin, pale scar on my forearm that mirrored Evadne's. The words haunted my nightmares. "She will die alone."

He wouldn't kill her. He's bluffing. Surely Artemis is bluffing.

Why would he threaten to kill her? That's not like him...

Nothing makes sense. There's something off, something I'm missing.

What if he was telling the truth??

The words stuck in my throat. I couldn't find a way to explain to Theron what was happening, all the bloodshed that bound me to the prince.

"You can talk to me, you know," Theron said gently. "I want to help you—we all do."

Homesickness hit me hard. He was so much like F and Jack put together.

I wish they were here.

I can't find the words. I just can't...

"You two are connected. She's getting hurt, but someone is sending *you* a message. Who is threatening you?"

I sighed, tears creeping down my cheeks. My throat strained but no matter how I tried, I couldn't give voice to my words.

"Whoever it is, they want you to feel trapped—as if there's no way out." Theron stared up at the endless stars and galaxies that swirled above us. "When I was your age, a very bad, very powerful Fey wanted me. So, I ran. I ran and I ran, and I ran—until I couldn't run anymore. But it didn't fix the problem. She still stalked me. She continued to kill my friends—threatening to destroy everything and take me away. So far away that no one would be able to find me again.

Daylight was creeping across the darkness, blotting out the stars, one by one.

Theron's words mirrored Darcy's threatening promise, and a shudder ran down my spine.

Thank goodness he's dead.

"What did you do?" I whispered raggedly.

"I stopped running and faced the monster that had haunted me all those years. I faced my fear and freed myself from its claws. In allowing my fear to have a foothold, I only suffered twice."

"What happened?" I asked breathlessly.

Theron's tone was cold as he at last spoke. "I cut out her heart and burned it until it was nothing but ash on the wind—until she couldn't hurt me anymore and at last, I was free."

Evadne's scream cut through the stillness, and I jerked, jumping to my feet. Theron was right behind me as I raced toward the cabin. Fire was overtaking my body, burning from my neck down my arm as something in my gut churned and clenched.

The pain was unbearable as I collapsed onto my knees and drew the bloody hair away from the side of her neck. A zero was gouged into her skin, followed by two simple words that held the weight of the world.

"Time's up," I whispered in horror.

Oh no, oh no, no, no, no, no. Eva, how do I protect you? How do I protect you from him?
He said I had three days to find him, but I have no idea where he is.
Why would he do this? Why, why, why?

Theron was standing beside me, eyebrows scrunched together in worry. "Do you know what it means?" he asked urgently.

I tried and failed to answer him. "There's nothing I can do," I whispered at last. I stared at my sister's broken body, guilt tearing at me for every ounce of pain inflicted on her.

Three days, four marks. Four warnings we couldn't outrun. I felt responsible for every mark, every drop of blood from every word, every letter.

My fault, my fault. This is all my fault.

Dread was tearing me apart, fear ripping me to pieces. How far would Artemis go? How far would he go to get us back?

"Land ho!"

Nikos's cry rang out through the tense silence, making Theron and me both jump.

"I have to go," Theron said softly. "I'll send Verity over. She needs to brief you about how things are going to work." He squeezed my hand gently, eyes pained as he looked at our matching marks. "We'll find a way. The healer will help us."

With that, he left, and I was alone with my guilt—trying to fight the fear that rose and tore me to pieces.

12

The Twisted Reasons Why

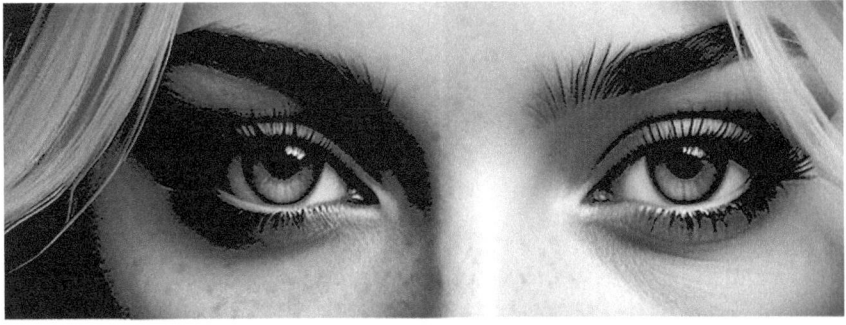

FAYE

"No Mourners, no funerals."
-Leigh Bardugo, Six of Crows

I lay on my stomach, exhausted, watching Ronan's face out of the corner of my eye as he quickly worked to remove the stitches from my back. His attention was focused on his work, but every so often I caught his gaze wandering—lingering on the hideous scars that marred and disfigured my back. They stood as reminders of what I had suffered and survived within the Realm. No amount of magic could properly heal what they'd done to me—both inside and out. But worst of all, no amount of bravery at the front end could erase how I hated what they'd done to me—these ugly, repulsive scars.

I wonder what he's thinking...

Does he think I'm ugly, like I do? Can he bear to look at me because of the scars?

Will he pity me now?

I don't want his pity.

I don't want to know what he's thinking. I don't want to know.

Blood was slowly spreading through the fabric of his shirt. The wound I'd given him had yet to clot, but I could find no regret left within myself with which to apologize. Only the painful awareness that I would do it again—and worse—if it meant escaping this place. If killing him, and everyone who stood in my way, meant saving my family, I knew I would do it. I was a monster inside and out, and I had to save my sisters.

Lies. I tell myself such lies.

If it was true, I would have killed Jeremiah instead of saving Ronan's sister. I wouldn't have worried about the repercussions of killing him because she might get hurt...

Why did I do it? Why did I save her?

Monster, I'm a monster and a liar in between, a fool masquerading as a hero. I can't save anyone.

They made me into a monster. But now I'm something else—something worse.

"I was eight years old when my mother died," Ronan said quietly as he pulled out the last stitch. "She begged me with her dying breath to protect my sister."

Do you see your failure? Your defeat? Do you see what you've done under the false guise of protecting her?

Guilt attacked me as my own failures stared me in the face—condemning me for the fact that I was still imprisoned. My sisters were in the Realm and nothing I had done had protected them from that place or the curse I sought to save them from.

Failure, failure, failure. We have both failed to protect the ones we love.

I savagely shoved the guilt off, pushing it down, down, down, until nothing remained but rage. I had only failed because he had kidnapped me. If I hadn't been kidnapped, then they wouldn't have taken my sisters. The Realm would be in ruins, and my family would be safe. This was all *his* fault.

Ronan pulled off his gloves and stared down at his hands. "You say I've done nothing to protect her, that I've been silent and complacent. But you only see half the story."

I don't believe you. If you were doing your best, then you would have gotten her out by now.

Ronan's eyes met mine, the bruises a sickly canvas across his skin. I couldn't look away from the grief and guilt that encompassed his features. "I've tried, Faye," he said hoarsely. "I've tried to get her out. You have to believe me, I've tried. But every time I attempted to smuggle her out, Jeremiah managed to stop me. He hates her, but he refuses to let her leave. He would rather deal with the torment of her being here than live with the awareness that she's somewhere else. He can't abide the thought that she could have *any* form of happiness." Ronan looked away, searching for something to focus on within my cell. "We have cell phones, but he has some sort of jammer out beyond the compound. It blocks any signal to and from the outside world so that's a dead end. Faye, I can only fight so many of his men at once, and every time we come up with a new plan, he somehow finds out."

"So that's what happened to you," I murmured, more to myself than to him. Understanding at last dawned on me. "You tried again after our fight."

Ronan nodded, staring down at his blood-stained knuckles.

Guilt rose and I shoved at it, determined to make it go away. He was not my responsibility. It wasn't my fault.

If I hadn't pushed him, he wouldn't have gotten hurt.

Why do I care if he gets hurt? He should have shot all of them. He should have killed every one of them.

Why do I care? Why? I shouldn't be getting entangled in this. I shouldn't care!

But I do...I do care...

The guilt would not budge, no matter how I pushed and shoved. It remained and began to swallow me whole.

"I'm going to go wash my hands," Ronan said sighed. "They're all dirty because *someone* decided to stab me." His poor attempt at a joke fell flat between us, and he winced. "Sheesh, tough crowd tonight." He stood up with a groan and grabbed the bloody pile of gauze before heading into the bathroom. "I'll be just a minute," he said without looking back.

Realization dawned.

He's giving me time to get dressed now that the stitches are out.

I hurriedly pulled my shirt on over my sports bra. The bathroom door was open, and Ronan was washing his hands in the sink, but his eyes were pointedly averted. He finished washing his hands, but he still didn't look over. "You decent?" he asked.

"Yeah," I replied quietly, pondering the little scraps of dignity he gave when he could.

Modesty may not always be possible when injuries are in unavoidable places...but he still gives me what dignity he can.

Ronan came back in and sat beside me on the bed. "Every attempt to free my sister has been thwarted. Every effort met with harsher consequences—consequences that *she* bears the brunt of."

The weight of my calloused judgement settled on my heart like a millstone around my neck—pulling me down, down, down. Condemning me for assuming I knew, when in fact I knew nothing at all.

"The first time I tried to get her out, I killed five of his men with my gun. Marcov was grievously injured, and the only person who stood in my way, was my *father*." Ronan choked on the word. "I should have killed him. I should have defended her, but I hesitated. My finger hesitated on the trigger and that was my downfall. At that point, I couldn't kill him, monster or not...he was...he was still my father." Ronan whispered as he hung his head. "To this day, I regret that hesitation. He disarmed me in a second and I haven't gotten my hands on a gun since. All of the men here fear him too much to turn against him like that. They can't, or rather won't, get me a weapon." Ronan sighed, "Even those loyal to me are too scared of him. What little cash I've picked up isn't enough to get one under the radar, and the credit card I have...well, Jeremiah keeps track of any expenses."

Guilt reared its ugly head again. Had the twenty Ronan used to buy my french fries come from his meager supply? Did he use what he'd been saving to help his sister, to meet my stubborn demand for greasy food and caffeine? All because he thought the information I could give him would help him find a way through the chaos?

He couldn't have used the card to pay. We weren't where we were supposed to be.

"Last year, Jeremiah broke both her legs," Ronan whispered. "It took six of his men to hold me down. He forced me to watch as he did it."

The question popped out before I could think as to why I was asking it.

"What part of her leg?"

"Both of her femurs."

"Her femurs?" I cried in disbelief.

"He did it with his foot," Ronan replied, shaking his head.

"That's impossible. The amount of force it would take—"

"It's impossible, yes," Ronan cut in gently. "But impossible no longer defines our life. The shadows, Faye...when he did it there was a darkness to the room, and it was as if...as if something was breaking her legs through him. He looked possessed, and he was drinking in her pain—mine too. There was a heaviness to the room that I can't explain. But it's the same darkness that's been growing around this place since you arrived. In that moment...his face changed; I didn't recognize the man standing in front of us. Evil, it was pure evil."

A chill ran down my spine as I contemplated the gravity of what he was telling me, and what I already knew. "The door in his office," I asked, trying to put the pieces together. "How long has it been there?"

"It appeared eight years ago," Ronan replied.

I'd bet almost anything that it leads to somewhere especially nasty.

"I would take any punishment, any pain, if it meant getting her out." Ronan's voice was strained, full of agony as he picked up where he had left off. "I would do anything, *anything*, if it meant she would be safe. But I can't gamble so recklessly when she bears the consequences."

His words mirrored mine, his reality was my own. We both fought to protect the ones we loved, as they in turn were used against us to keep us trapped.

I am a monster, a hypocrite. I condemn him for what he does, when I have done far worse for the same reasons.

"I was sloppy." Ronan's voice was so low I could hardly make out his words. "I was angry, but more than that, I was terrified. Terrified that you were right. That she would get killed, and all the years, all the tries, all the bloodshed, every act and deed that has stained my conscience beyond repair—all the things I've done to you? I was afraid it would all be for nothing."

"What happened?" I murmured.

"Marcov was waiting. Somehow, he knew. He was there at the door, waiting for us. He raised the alarm while he pointed his gun at her head. I told her to go, to run back to her room, that I'd lie and say Marcov was crazy—I was hoping perhaps if I made a big enough scene my father would finally kill him..." Ronan's voice was hollow, eyes distant as he recalled the horrific memory. "But she wouldn't leave me...Meghan refused to leave me. They dragged us back to his office." Ronan shook his head. "He was waiting. It was as if he *knew*." Tears were streaming down Ronan's cheeks. "He...he broke all the fingers on her right hand, and then he branded her—the way you'd brand an animal."

The air hissed through my teeth as the rage within me grew.

His own flesh and blood. He did that to his own flesh and blood.

"Faye," Ronan whispered, defeated. "He put a tracker in her back. Same as yours. If she goes outside, if I actually manage to smuggle her out, she'll get electrocuted. I'm trapped. I'm completely and utterly trapped."

I chewed over his words, my mind rapidly spinning and processing—trying to find a way through the stormy ocean we were on.

"You have no access to that, do you?" I asked, already certain about his answer.

He shook his head. "No, he keeps it locked away, hidden. I can't access his office at all. He distrusts everyone and everything. Whatever that door is, he's hiding it—afraid someone will come and steal whatever's behind it away."

"Don't go through that door," I pleaded. "Promise me, you won't go through it."

"I won't," he said softly. "I promise you, I won't."

I sighed, shaking my head. "What an absolute cluster of stupidity. Why on earth would Jeremiah do this? Why is any of this happening? It doesn't make any *sense*."

"Nothing makes sense," Ronan replied.

"Can you take the chip out of her back?" I asked. "You have medical training."

"Not enough for that. He put it next to her spine, so deep that if I tried, I could seriously injure her. There are too many nerves for me to risk it."

"He's lucky he didn't injure her when he put it in there in the first place," I muttered.

"I honestly wonder if he wasn't trying to," Ronan replied.

I stared at my blackened hands, my gaze following the twisted pattern of the Lichtenburg figure burned into my skin.

"I don't know what to do anymore, Faye. He beat me senseless in front of her, to get the message across, and left me where I fell. I woke up in a puddle of my own blood and vomit in the hallway...with him nowhere to be found. My only thought was her." His voice broke and he began to sob in earnest. "I thought I'd lost her. When I went to her room, I couldn't find her. Finally, she came out. She was terrified it was a trick, that it wasn't actually me, but a recording of my voice. She had cut a hole in the underside of the box springs on her bed...it's an old model, just wood really. She had been hiding there for *two days*. Too afraid to come out."

My guilt intensified. If I hadn't pushed him, he wouldn't have been so reckless with his escape attempt. The memory of the fear in her eyes, when she was tied to that chair, hit me like a blow to the gut. The way she had seemed to beg Ronan to save her. I had helped him then, only to turn right around and stab him in the back.

We are both trapped within this vicious cycle of abuse, desperately trying to protect what we love.

He turned us into monsters and put us at each other's throats. If we're too busy fighting with each other, we won't turn on him...

"I need your help," Ronan said at last.

My three brain cells screamed a violent objection to such a proposition, but soon the overwhelming guilt had them sobbing in separate corners of my brain—wailing about how wretched they all were. Especially since they had tried to kill their beloved Ronan.

"What makes you think I'll help you?" I muttered, trying to pretend as if I didn't care—trying to escape the knowledge of how much I did indeed care.

I was desperate to hold onto my anger. It had protected me from his twisted motives in this nightmare. But when faced with the knowledge of how alike we were, I had no choice but to face the final awareness that it was not me versus him. It was us versus Jeremiah, and whatever Darke Fey he had been ensnared by.

Ronan caught my chin, forcing me to look at him. "Faye, if you help me, I will get your father out. After Megs is free, I will get you and him out—or die trying. I swear it on my mother's grave."

13

The Witch In The Woods

EMBER

"The choices we face may not be the choices we want, but they are
choices nonetheless."
-Bridgid Kemmerer, A Curse so Dark and Lonely

The distinct click of Verity's boots walking across the deck pulled me from my thoughts. "We're coming up on the Wastelands," she said as she entered our room. "The healer resides on the edge. Do you remember what we talked about last night?"

I nodded, mentally rehearsing my speech once more.

I have cursed artifacts. They are tainted with my blood and uncleansed. If you heal my sister completely, bring her back from whoever holds her, and return her to me, untainted, then I will trade them to you. But only for her return and healing...

"Good," Verity said, giving me a small, reassuring smile before turning to Evadne. "Theron said there's a new mark?"

I nodded, pointing mutely to her neck.

Verity hissed through her teeth. "Monster." She turned back to me. "The trek won't be long. We will arrive at Baba Yaga's as quickly as possible. If anyone can help your sister and bring her back from whoever holds her, it's the healer."

Baba Yaga tried to kill me...
Artemis killed her instead...
She's dead, isn't she?

I turned, exhausted and confused. "What do you mean Baba Yaga?" I whispered. "I thought we were going to a healer...Artemis...he killed Baba Yaga."

It was Verity's turn to be confused. "What do you mean he killed her? Surely, he wouldn't be so foolish as to kill one of the three?"

"Well, he wasn't himself..."

Verity's eyes closed, as if gathering her thoughts. "This is worse than I thought. If he truly killed one of the Yagas, it means the downfall of everything."

"What do you mean?"

"Have they taught you nothing of the history of the Realm, and the curse that binds you and the Knight together?" Verity asked tightly.

I shook my head. "No, every time we tried to ask questions, they bit our heads off...the Halls had nothing but conflicting information..."

I wonder if all this time Darcy ensured we got conflicting information, so we never found out the truth.

Verity sighed, massaging her temples. "Typical," she muttered in annoyance. "In all honesty, I would expect nothing less from the monarchs. Well, I can give you a brief crash course in the history of the Realm's magic. Before the Borders were created, there were three sisters. They all bore the same name and possessed infinite sight and wisdom—though each took a different path. It was they who wove the magic with the Grimm that put the borders in place, thus imprisoning the Knight. But for the barriers to remain in place, the spell requires all *three* to remain alive."

I pondered her words, shocked. Generally, when I had a question, it was answered in a roundabout, riddled sort of way.

"Artemis said the curse of three...whoever kills one of them, is cursed?"

"Aye, them and all the Realm. It means the loss of everything you hold dear—for if one of the three falls, the spell will splinter and the Knight will finally escape to bring ruin upon us all. He seeks nothing but revenge for the centuries he's been imprisoned."

A chill ran down my spine and Verity rubbed at a deep crease in her forehead. "I'm too old for this nonsense. I have things to do before the Realm falls. Stupid, precocious prince. Why would he be so incredibly foolish?" She shook her head and shrugged. "Well, one shipwreck at a time. We can't focus on that particular ship right now. Currently the wrecked ship we must save is your sister. She needs help. We can worry about the end of the world after—I'll tell Nikos to move my agenda around. If one of the Yagas has fallen, then I have some pressing business I must attend to first..." She turned back to me. "Baba Yaga will bring your sister back from this darkness. Fight your fear for her—do not let it control you."

I nodded and Verity handed me a long, thin dagger.

"What's this?" I asked cautiously.

"Theron asked me to give it to you. He's a little preoccupied with his duties at the moment. He said, and I quote, 'Cut out the heart'."

Theron's words settled over me and I took the dagger, fingering the polished wood hilt.

"Baba Yaga is a worker of great magic, child. Some say she is stronger than the rulers themselves. Theron speaks wisely. Your fear is easily manipulated. Monsters would prey upon such a delicate poison."

Verity left then, and I turned back to Evadne, brushing back a straggling curl from her face. "It's going to be okay, Eva," I whispered. "I'm going to get you out of this and make it right. I'll protect you, Evadne. *I promise.*"

The words slipped from my lips before I could consider what I was saying—what it really meant. The weight of the words, a promise I didn't know if I could keep, settled around my heart like a vice.

I'll do whatever it takes to protect you. Even if it means cutting out Artemis' heart.

I promise, I promise.

I was loath to leave her, but I needed to get a scope of my surroundings. I could see everything of the landscape below from the ship's heights.

A warm breeze brushed my cheeks as, with a final lingering glance back, I left the cabin.

The magical world we had been dragged into was full of wonders and possibilities. Time and time again, it had astounded me. But nothing could have prepared me for the sight of an island sitting serenely in the middle of the sky. I couldn't stop my mouth from falling open as I stared at the impossibility. Unheeding of gravity, the Wastelands floated in the middle of nothing—the way an island would sit in the midst of the sea.

The jumbled collection of islands resembled a jigsaw puzzle that had been shoved together by a frustrated four-year-old, who then tied it together with duct tape and string to force it to stay put and not fall apart.

Boardwalks and rope bridges hung suspended between the jumbled landscape. The islands were composed of rocky, tree-filled land, with paths that zig-zagged across the surface like spiderwebs. Ships were anchored all along the edge, but some were anchored above it, held in place by thick wire cables and sharp metal spikes. Rope ladders stretched down from those ships to the ground. From where I stood, I could see people moving up and down the ladders, as small as bugs on the ground. Some of the ships were also interconnected with bridges and planks, where figures scurried from ship to ship.

In the center of the largest set of islands, there was an open area covered in a colorful stone pathway that spread out from a single point like a spiral. It was dizzying and amazing all at once. A river stretched across the island, snaking here and there, suspended over the gaps as if an invisible riverbed stretched across the island—unheeding of reality—before plunging over the final corners and cascading toward the ground in a massive waterfall.

How is any of this possible? How is this real?

My gaze landed on the crumbling ruins of an old castle on the far side of the largest island. The walls jutted out of the ground like broken teeth. Twisted trees had begun to grow in and through what little remained.

The ship was slowly pulling up beside a long dock that stretched out over the open sky. Back in the trees, I could make out the outline of a little house with a stark white fence surrounding it.

"There," Verity said from beside me.

I jumped. I hadn't heard her approach.

"My, you startle easily," she said with a smirk. She pointed toward the house. "There is Baba Yaga's house."

Theron walked up beside us, holding Evadne's limp body in his arms. "She's changed locations since we last made port." He scrutinized the terrain. "Looks as if she moved about three islands, maybe four. Do you remember how far in she was last time?"

Verity shook her head, pursing her lips. "The way she picks up and goes, I wouldn't be surprised if she just rearranges the islands for her own comfort."

"Perhaps it's amusement?" Theron offered jovially.

"Probably a mix of both," Verity replied with a scowl.

Bright sunlight was streaming across the sky. Colors exploded around us—electric blue with clouds so white and fluffy they looked fake, and trees that were unbelievably green and lush.

It's like we're stuck in a camera filter...one that amplifies the slightest color.

Verity grabbed a thick rope and began to tie it off at one of the masts. "Well, we're wasting precious time. No reason to delay further." I watched in openmouthed shock as she took firm hold of the rope and jumped off the side of the ship.

She's absolutely crazy.

I am NOT doing that.

She swung back and forth for a moment, grinning, then began to descend hand over hand down the rope. She hit the deck with a decided thud and looked up at me, eyes laughing. "Your turn, Ember."

I vehemently shook my head, too anxious to find any words, and Theron laughed. "Don't worry, Sparks. I'll help you." He shifted Evadne's petite form over his shoulder and, after wrapping an arm securely around her waist, grabbed the rope with his gloved hand. "Don't tell your sister about this *most* undignified form of carrying. Nobody wants to know they've been hauled around like a sack of potatoes."

I nodded, eyes glued on the rope. Right about now, I would do anything to get carried like a sack of potatoes if it meant avoiding going down that rope on my own.

It's ridiculous that I'm jealous of my sister. She's unconscious, for heaven's sake.

"Don't be afraid, Sparks," Theron said as he jumped over the edge and slid down the rope.

Yeah. Might as well tell me to stop breathing, or perhaps lecture my heart on beating. I am afraid and that is that.

I'm not afraid. I'm not afraid... See Theron, it doesn't work!

I'm terrified, I'm completely and utterly petrified.

Do it afraid.

The thought came unbidden, and I attacked it with a vengeance. I had absolutely *no* interest in doing it afraid.

The sky swam beneath me as I tried to swallow the lump in my throat.

"Just, count to three, and then go over the edge," Theron called up.

The longer I delay, the longer Evadne goes without help. Time's up. Every second matters.

I gritted my teeth, forcing myself to take hold of the rope. Instead of counting, I ripped off the band-aid and launched myself over the edge.

Turns out, doing it without thought was a terrible decision. My shoulders jerked, feeling as if they were going to wrench themselves out of their sockets. But then, after gaining control of my muscles, and my terrified, screaming mind, I began to lower myself down, hand over hand, just as Verity had done.

The things I do for my sister.

She owes me. Big time.

Really? She's getting tortured because of you, and you have the gall to say she owes you? YUP.

My shoulders hurt. Why did we have to jump?? Why did you make that stupid choice. You should have gone down backward, like you're repelling...

That's easy for you to say. I've never actually done any repelling.

I mean, it looks easy enough.

I have the vague idea it's most definitely NOT as easy as it looks in the movies.

Boo.

My hands hurt so much! I don't have the muscles for this. I'm going to slip and fall and then Raz will have to rescue me... I'd probably never hear the end of it if she had to rescue me.

I can do this...surely I can do this?

The scattered and slightly deranged dialogue kept my mind occupied, until, at last, my feet touched the boardwalk below.

I wobbled, and Theron caught hold of my forearm. "Careful," he laughed. "It wouldn't do to be so brave, only to be clumsy and fall over the edge. That was very good, Sparks. For a minute there, I thought we'd have to send Raz after you, but you got the hang of it. I'm proud of you. You were a brave little toaster."

Pride soared in my chest at the compliment. Theron was very quickly working himself into the spot of 'favorite crew member' on my list. He had the compliments down, now all he needed to add was bribery and my crow-heart would never leave his side.

"I'm not a toaster," I laughed.

Theron patted me on the head. "Perhaps not, but when you do something brave, it makes you a brave little toaster."

"Do you even know what a toaster is?" I asked incredulously as our group began to make our way toward Baba Yaga's house.

"Of course I do," Theron replied indignantly. "It's someone who makes public speeches, praising others. Typically, the toaster is the one who really, *really*, hates making speeches. Thus, to be a brave little toaster is someone with speech fright. Similarly, it can also be a device or method you use to get your enemies nice and toasty to convince them to talk. It's akin to a spit over the fire, or perhaps a stake strategically placed in front of a dragon." He wiggled his eyebrows at Fireheart, who had crawled out of my cloak pocket after I'd finished rappelling the ship, and now sat perched on my shoulder. "That's something our winged little friend knows all about."

I couldn't contain my laughter. I had never thought anyone could come up with such an absurd description for a device that toasted bread.

Fireheart growled in appreciation and chomped his teeth together.

"Tell me, my brave little dragon, fierce among men, if I had an enemy I wanted to interrogate, would you assist me in the endeavor?"

Fireheart nodded and Theron crowed in delight.

"Theron," Verity called from ahead of us. "I believe it was a rhetorical, albeit sarcastic question. I don't think she wanted the dictionary recited to her. And I certainly don't think using a dragon for interrogations is a good idea. They're much too trigger happy; they'd roast the prisoner much too quickly. Now come on, you're lagging."

Fireheart and Theron both huffed and glared at the back of Verity's head. It amused me how quickly Theron had won over the little dragon with his compliments and offers to let Fireheart engage in violence.

"Lagging," Theron muttered under his breath. "How dare she insinuate I, the king of fast pace, am lagging. Besides, I'm the only one carrying another human being, well, half human. *I* should get to set the pace."

I giggled at his indignance as he very pointedly picked up the pace.

The cottage was clearly in view now, and the closer we got, the more details I noticed. Small windows with rickety, splintering boards nailed across them. A path of strangely shaped white stones that went around the house and led to a door on the side. Large, yellow chicken legs crouched in the dirt. As we got closer, I finally realized the house was sitting on top of said chicken legs. A huge, black cauldron that sat in the front yard. Then, finally, the very old woman who stood over the boiling cauldron.

Her dress was made of an assortment of brightly colored pieces of cloth—rather like a patchwork quilt. Frizzy, white hair stuck out at various angles around her head, curling this way and that in a chaotic cacophony that clearly had a mind of its own. An assortment of amulets were woven into her hair—all various shapes and sizes. Countless amulets hung from leather cords around her neck.

Her rasping voice echoed around the clearing as we made our way through the trees toward her. She was singing a haunting song—crooning it the way one would a lullaby—but the words were not those you'd whisper to a child. They were heavy and powerful, and they wept of death.

"Smash and grind the bones of men..." Her long fingers were wrapped around a large wooden spoon, with sharp nails that looked a little too much like claws. "Bring the brothers home again...take the plants to what they call...find the truth before the fall..." She looked up, fixing us in the gaze of milky white eyes as we stopped on the other side of her gate. "Lost the maid of ash and dust, dead the heart of loss and rust...gone, gone, the bones have wept, darkness rise, as Realm meets death... Sacrifice, a love so deep, never again to live and breathe."

A chill rushed down my spine as her words settled over me.

"I have been waiting for you, daughter of Grimm," the old woman rasped. "The bones said you, twin of power, would come. But they are always so infuriatingly vague on timing. I thought you would not come seeking answers until after the fall." Her voice was the sound of fire crackling through dried leaves—a cadence that snapped and cracked, rising and falling as it consumed all in its path. "They said the one of blood would come as well, but they failed to mention the rogue."

She fixed her sightless eyes on Theron, and he swallowed nervously.

"I remember you, troublemaker."

I took a step forward. "We are here to bargain."

Her cloudy eyes focused back on me, and she licked dry, cracked lips.

"I am willing to barter in exchange for your help with my sister."

"Come inside the gate," she replied. "Let me feel her heartbeat. It may not yet be too late."

Theron moved forward as Verity opened the gate. I followed, trying to bolster my courage.

I am willingly walking into a witch's yard. A witch that happens to be Baba Yaga...

A white and orange tabby cat rubbed its way along the stark white fence, purring. I immediately noticed how scrawny it was, with ribs that stuck out and hip bones that jutted out.

I dug around in my pocket, at last finding the napkin I had wrapped my bread and jerky in the night before. I had hoped maybe I'd find my appetite with a midnight snack. "Here," I whispered as I put the food down for the cat.

My heart ached for Maladroit, suddenly homesick for the cat I loved, yet had openly refused to claim.

When we get home, I'll claim him. Even if he's a pain in the butt, he's my pain in the butt.

Who's taking care of him while we're away? Mum and Dad are gone, Oma is dead...what about our horses?

Will anything be left of the place I called home? The place I will forever call home.

A renewed sense of loss slammed into me, and all of a sudden, everything felt too much to bear.

The cat scarfed up the scraps, and I quickly scooped it up, digging for more snacks in my pocket as I cradled it against my chest—burying my face in his fur for a moment to try to hide my tears.

It purred softly against my chest, its fur silky and soft despite its haggard appearance. I could hear a rumbling complaint from Fireheart, who had buried himself somewhere inside Evadne's cloak with Elvie. Evadne's cloak was shoved in my pocket.

It's cloak within a cloak...that's bigger on the inside...is it a TARDIS cloak?

No, it couldn't be, it can't time travel.

"Nevermind Red," Baba Yaga chuckled. "That cat gets fed five times a day, sometimes six if I'm especially forgetful. He stubbornly refuses to put on weight. I assure you he is a pampered, spoiled cat that will do anything to get attention and extra snacks. It's why I named him after my sister—he rejects conventional and traditional forms of being a cat." She stared at me for a moment. "You have a kind heart, child. That will not go unnoticed—do not let them break you of your kindness."

She turned her attention back to Evadne, her mouth pulling into a thin line as her fingers probed at Evadne's neck and temples. "This one is in grave peril...mmm...someone snatched her while she fought the wraith's curse...that curse has been broken but the poison remains..." She unwrapped Evadne's injured wrist and the stench of decaying flowers and water rot spread around us in a nauseating wave. "Yes, this is not her first brush with death...she bears much, much darkness...so young, so terribly young. The five of prophecy, you all bear so much darkness for ones so young."

Baba Yaga closed her eyes, leaning her head back as she rested her hand on Evadne's chest, over her heart. "There is still a chance. I hear whispers of her screams... Bring her inside at once."

Hope leapt wildly within my chest, and I started toward the door, but Theron shifted, sticking out his foot and stopping me in my tracks.

"We have yet to determine the price for such a service," Verity cut in smoothly. "We will not become indebted. Terms must be set before anything is done."

"Clever, clever captain," Baba Yaga hissed, smiling. Something prickled along my skin. It was not a friendly smile.

"What do you have to offer, girl?" Baba Yaga asked, still not taking her eyes from Verity.

"I have cursed artifacts," I replied as I pulled the leather bag that contained the uncleansed gold, silver, and diamond thorns. "They are tainted with my blood, and uncleansed. If you heal my sister completely, bring her back from whoever holds her and return her to me, whole and *untainted*, then I will trade them to you in return."

Baba Yaga looked at me sharply, her face bright with greed. "Let me see them."

I opened the bag, and she neared. Despite her rumpled appearance, she smelled wonderful, like woodsmoke and spices. Her fingers carefully sifted through the razor edges, her eyes unfocused and distant. "I will accept this bargain. If it cannot be done, the cursed items remain in your possession. If you cheat me, I will eat your heart. Do we have a deal?"

My mouth fell open in shock. "I wouldn't cheat you..." I whispered.

A vicious grin split her face. Something in my gut churned in response. "Oh, I know you won't. The bones have told me what you're made of. You do not go back on your word, even when it hurts." She continued eyeing me. "Oh, child, what the bones have told me of you...you poor, poor girl..."

She seemed lost in a trance as she laid a withered hand on my cheek, stroking it fondly. "So young, all so young and fresh, sweet and luscious...your heart would be the balm to my cursed existence...are you sure you don't want to cheat me?"

I blanched at her question, and Theron cleared his throat.

Baba Yaga blinked once, twice, three times—pulling herself together. "I accept the terms of your deal," she whispered. "Bring her inside. There is much to do if I would delay the inevitable darkness and pull her from him."

Him? Who is she talking about?

Theron and Verity were already at the door, and I moved to follow, still clutching the purring cat, but Baba Yaga laid a bony hand on my shoulder, stopping me. "You'd best wait outside. It will not be an easy watch. What must take place..." She placed three fingers to my forehead. "I cannot guarantee that I can bring her back. A great, *great*, evil holds her. One more evil than myself." She tilted her head to the side, looking at me. "I feel responsible for you, somehow...mmm...yes, an idea, what a kind idea, my dearies. If I fail, I will not only return the items you have bargained for, but I will also grant you a promise. Perhaps it will make you think kindly of me...perhaps *then* you will let me eat your heart when you no longer have need of it. I do love Grimm hearts, such a delicacy. I have not tasted a heart that carried such deep sorrow since the brother's blood bathed my lips."

"I just want my sister back," I whispered in horror. "And I think I'll always need my heart."

"If only that were true...so young, so young."

With that ominous warning, she left me outside with her cat, my thoughts, and a sense of foreboding that would not leave me.

14

New Beginnings

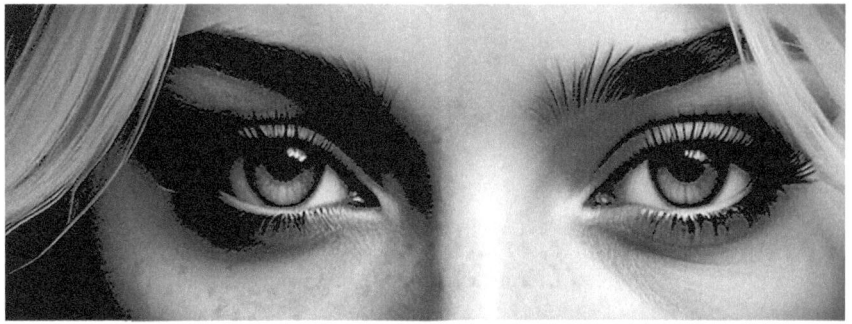

FAYE

"You asked me why I look at you the way I do, and I couldn't think of
anything to say except that I heard Mermaids are so beautiful sailors
think they are lucky when they are given the chance to drown."
-unknown

Hope jolted and pulled at my heart. So wild and potent it stole my breath away.

Careful, careful. Sometimes a favor is a curse in disguise...

"What do you need help with?" I demanded, feigning annoyance.

"Two things—" Ronan began.

I cut him off. "You said *a* favor, not several!"

"What if I bribed you?" Ronan asked with a crooked grin.

My three brain cells screeched in happy delight and immediately began producing long lists of items they wanted. All of which came with terms and conditions. They would accept bribery, but only if said bribery contained every item on their massive list and only if Ronan helped set up all of the things and remain as their personal fixer-upper-handyman.

I silenced my brain cells with a glare. *Bribery is beneath us.*

It most certainly is not. You know full well you are very biased toward bribery.

"Absolutely not," I replied primly.

Ronan's eyes crinkled at the corners. He was laughing at me. "You say no, but the bright look that just appeared in your eyes says an exuberant 'yes'. I'll save this information for later."

"You'll do no such thing," I muttered.

Ronan glanced down at his bloody shirt and cursed. "I need to stitch this closed; it's not going to stop bleeding."

"Do you want help?" I asked hesitantly. Some part of me was suddenly desperate to make amends for what I'd done.

Ronan gave me a crooked grin. "Well, if you fix things better than you damage them, I'll take the help. But if you don't, I'd better decline."

"I've done some stitching," I muttered.

"Well, that'll mean you have to get up," Ronan teased.

"Oh, heaven forbid and rue the day that I have to get up," I chortled as I got up off my bed.

Ronan lifted his shirt and stared at the bloody mess in rueful admiration. "Faye, I've got to hand it to you, at least you're persistent."

I rolled my eyes. "Can you blame me?"

"No," Ronan replied quietly as he began to pull the layers of gauze off.

There's so much blood. What did I do to him? Why? Why did I do it?

I have to save my family. I have to save them...but what if the way out was there all along, I was just too blind to see it?

"No, I don't blame you one bit," Ronan continued. "I'd do the same, worse even. If it wasn't for the drugs, I think you'd have killed me a long time ago. I only have an edge on you because of those drugs Jeremiah gives you."

I sighed. "That's another thing, Ronan. Jeremiah has doubled, if not tripled the dose. He administers them personally. I haven't been able to function for days."

Ronan hissed as the final layer of gauze came off.

"Sorry," I whispered.

"No, I'm sorry," he replied softly. "I can't do anything about that until he lets me start giving it to you again... Even then, I'm not sure what to do. You're dangerous without it, and I need you, but I don't know if I can trust you..." His voice trailed off. "You have no idea how much I want to trust you, Faye, but it seems like every time we reach a point where I think I can count on you, you turn around and stab me in the back. If you agree to help me, that will have to stop. We need to be able to work together and trust each other completely. Otherwise, we're *all* going to die here."

He was right. I hated it, but he was absolutely right.

"I know," I replied quietly. "I know."

Ronan began to lie down, then stopped. "I guess I should ask, do you mind if I put my cooties, that are possibly the plague, on your non-purple bedspread?"

I shook my head. "You still owe me a purple bedspread," I muttered as he lay down, laughing.

He winced. "Note to self, don't laugh," he muttered. "Hand me my medical bag, will you?"

I obliged and after some digging, he pulled out a separate, thick sterile package that contained the suture needle. "Don't make me regret handing you a weapon now, you hear?"

I made an X across my heart. "Just this once," I replied loftily as I put on a pair of gloves.

Ronan sighed as he applied iodine to the stab wound. "I can't believe I'm letting you help me, when you're the one who did this. It seems impossible we're on talking terms after you tried to kill me, not thirty minutes ago."

"Blame it on the drugs," I laughed mirthlessly. "I can't believe I'm helping you either..." I added absentmindedly.

Ronan dug through his bag again. "It seems I'm out of lidocaine," he muttered. "I guess I'll have to endure without it."

Absolutely not. I've been through that; I'm not putting you through such an agonizing experience. You have been through enough.

A small snowstorm swirled in the palm of my hand and Ronan watched, amazed, as I ever so carefully numbed his wound with a layer of snow and ice.

"It's not perfect, but it's better than nothing," I said with a shrug.

"It's amazing," Ronan replied in awe. "Thank you."

"I think I've finally realized the truth, Ronan," I said as I began to stitch the wound closed. "It's not me versus you...it can't be. We're both in this now, trying to protect the people we love. You're right, if we keep fighting, we'll all die. Having us at odds only strengthens Jeremiah's control over us. We're only a threat to him if we're united."

Ronan's voice was hoarse as he stared at me. "I'm sorry you got dragged into this, Faye, and I'm sorry for the part I played in it. I was trying to protect my sister, but that doesn't make it right. Can you ever forgive me?"

I stilled; these were the same words he had asked me so long ago.

Can you ever forgive me?

In my frustration, I had held on to my anger and denied him any hope of making it right. Even though the signs that he and I were both victims in the situation had been there all along. I could no longer hold onto that anger—it was toxic. A poison that killed me from the inside out.

Anger, hatred, and unforgiveness bound the Realm together and dragged it through an unending cycle of violence. I was more than the monster the Realm tried to create.

"I know I have no right to ask it of you," Ronan continued. He was beginning to ramble, anxiety making him fill the silence.

"I forgive you, Ronan," I whispered gently, cutting him off as I began to carefully stitch him back together. "I forgive you."

"Do you mean it?" he asked hesitantly. "Do you really mean it?"

I nodded. "I can't fight you any longer. Holding onto my anger, while justified in one sense, can't bring anything good." I gestured to his bloody wound. "Trying to kill you and escape won't help anything. Our being divided won't heal what they've broken within us. We have no hope if we hold onto that anger."

Ronan sniffed. Tears were leaking out of the corners of his eyes and down his cheeks. I turned back to my work, allowing him to gather himself.

"I need you to teach Megs how to fight," Ronan said at last. "I need you to teach her how to survive without me."

The meaning beneath his words cut my heart like a knife.

Without me...he's not planning on making it out of this alive.

"That doesn't make sense," I replied as I continued to work. "Why do you need *me* to train her? Don't you just need to get her out?"

"Every time we try, Jeremiah somehow finds out and we end up cornered. She only knows the little bits of self-defense that I've been able to teach her in the moments we steal. But it's nothing compared to the training the men have received. In the end, it always reaches a point where I have to stop fighting them because someone has a gun to her head."

"Why don't *you* train her?" I demanded testily. The thought of training a teenager how to fight seemed well above my pay grade. Teenagers made me feel *incredibly* old.

Ronan winced and I realized I had been forceful with my hands as well as my words.

"Sorry," I muttered, trying to be gentler.

I wonder if that's why Artemis was always so cranky during training. Do I make him feel old? Or was it simply above his pay grade?

Perhaps I was so annoying it made him cranky.

Well then, he should grow up.

"Ever since the first time I tried to smuggle her out, Jeremiah intentionally placed us on opposite schedules. He forces her to work in the kitchen during the day, keeping her on her feet for fifteen to eighteen hours. She does most of the cleaning around the compound as well. Meanwhile, he puts me on the night shifts. He exhausts me further by demanding I work random day jobs. I've been surviving on three hours of broken sleep since he put me on your rotation, and we don't see each other anymore except in the rare moments we steal when I go to make your food."

I wonder if he insists on making my food because Meghan wouldn't make it healthy enough.

What stupidity. I want junk food, darn it! Stop forcing me to eat healthy meals, you jerk!

Perhaps it was my exhaustion, but things still didn't make sense. There seemed to be holes in his story, pieces of the puzzle that didn't fit. Colors that didn't meld to each other, like a Picasso painting that someone had distorted. I couldn't put my finger on what questions I needed to ask to get clarification. Furthermore, I couldn't remember what questions I had *already* asked when we had last been on cordial terms.

"Why does Jeremiah still call you son?" I asked after a long moment. I tied off the last stitch and began to cover the wound with clean gauze. "Why does he still, well, trust you? Albeit, not with a gun, but he still lets you roam…"

Ronan raised his hands in defeat as I taped the gauze into place. "Why does he do any of what he does? He's demented. He believes that, in regard to Meghan, it's just a *'minor disagreement'*."

"Minor?" I scoffed.

"Minor, because to him, her life is nothing of consequence. To him, the disagreement is the same as it would be if you found a spider in your house. Do you kill it, or do you let it loose outside?"

I shuddered as I pulled off my gloves.

If this is how he feels about his own daughter, his own flesh and blood…what is his view of everyone else?

"I keep up the façade that I'm loyal to him. But I only do it to protect my sister. If I were to push him on it, he'd just up and kill her. Jeremiah believes I'm his faithful son. He thinks I have the same aims and desires. I have taken pains not to question what he does, to maintain that twisted illusion in his mind. He doesn't know that I've been working against him behind the curtain. To him, the matter of Megs is so twisted in his mind that, while he punishes me to get his delusional points across, he doesn't believe I would actually betray him by truly caring for her, so to speak. He believes the loss of my mother drives me to such extreme lengths to get her out." Ronan's jaw clenched as anger encompassed his features. "He believes that loyalty to my mother's memory, and loyalty to her alone, is what drives me to fight him about Meghan. Yet, he will not give that same loyalty to my mother's memory and protect his own daughter."

This is so messed up.

I sighed, pulling apart the pieces and rebuilding them in my mind. Every version became distorted by Jeremiah's craze-filled eyes as he stood over me, coated in my blood.

"I don't know what to do," Ronan said as he sat up and pulled his shirt back down.

I sat on the bed beside him, pulling my knees to my chest.

"Meghan has been an innocent, caught in the crosshairs of his insanity since the day she was born. She lives in a constant state of fear that Jeremiah will get tired of toying with her and just kill her." Ronan's voice caught. "She's right. It's only a matter of time before that happens, and I'm not quick enough to get there and stop him."

"So, why don't you just try again? Except this time, don't do it in anger and fear. Plan it out."

Ronan shook his head and sighed. "There's two roadblocks in our way now."

"Okay, spill the beans, oh bean hoarder."

Ronan chuckled. "Well, for one, Meghan won't go unless you get out, too."

"What?" I demanded, shocked. "She doesn't even *know* me."

"She won't go unless I get you out, too," Ronan repeated, exasperation creeping into his tone.

I could only imagine the raging argument they'd had about her stubbornness on the matter.

I wonder if Meghan gets the same crease between her eyebrows when she's upset, like he does...

"You saved her life and now she's determined to return the favor," Ronan continued. "Besides, she thinks our last escape attempt failed because you were still here...that any other attempt is doomed because of the debt we owe you."

"Neither of you owe me a debt." I sighed. "Why is she being so stupid?"

"Because she's Meghan," Ronan snorted. "But she's right, I'm indebted to you because I brought you here in the first place...I stole your chance to save your sisters..."

A rush of emotions overwhelmed me, but I shoved them down. Now was not the time to think about such things.

"That will never work," I muttered, dragging my attention back to the problem at hand. "I have to get my father out, but I don't think we can even attempt that little mutiny until she's out of the way. He would tell me to get her out first..." I massaged my temples, my head aching at the complexity of the whole situation. "This will have to happen in stages...what about the second road block?" I asked quietly. Ronan was holding something back, something terrible.

"Jeremiah said if we try again and he catches us, he'll kill her. No more chances."

"Either way, you're dead," I whispered. "If you run, he'll kill her. If you wait, he'll kill her."

"You were right," Ronan murmured.

"What do you mean?"

"You were right," he repeated softly. "One of these days, I'll have nothing left of my family but an open grave."

"You said you needed my help with two things," I replied, trying to change the subject. "What's the second thing?"

"I need your help to come up with an escape plan."

"What makes you think I can come up with a plan?" I snapped, feeling overwhelmed by the sheer weight of the tasks before us.

"You are the most determined, creative person I have ever met, and with the added title of *Zaubermaus,* I am convinced that you are the only person who can come up with an escape plan that will actually work."

"I lost my title as *Zaubermaus.* Don't you remember my little escapade as *Pooh Bear*?"

"That doesn't mean you lost it, just that it was on vacation when you tried that little stunt," Ronan replied, chuckling.

"You're wrong," I whispered. "Every one of my plans has failed."

Ronan's mirth died. "I believe in you," he stated.

"You shouldn't. If you knew what I was, what I'd done...all the times I've *failed*, over and over and *over* again...you wouldn't believe in me. You'd find someone else to help you. Your plans will be doomed if you put me in charge of them. I'm a bad luck charm, a monster. You don't want me."

"You're not," Ronan replied. "A monster wouldn't save the life of a man who kidnapped her. She wouldn't plead with him to go back because he was in danger. She wouldn't save his sister from the real monster."

His words settled around me. It was something I so desperately longed to believe. Yet, it was something I couldn't ever hope to accept. I knew what I was, what they'd made me to be. A horror that could never hope for forgiveness or redemption.

Ronan's voice was gentle. "You are *not* a monster, Faye. Don't believe the lie that says you are. Because if you start to believe it, it will eat you from the inside out."

"What's there to eat?" I whispered, trying to make a joke to escape my pain. "There's nothing left inside to consume. There's *nothing* left of me."

"Yes, there is. If there wasn't, you wouldn't keep fighting to escape, to survive."

Ryver's words came back to me then. The conversation seemed a lifetime ago. 'Spit out your blood and rise, lionhearted girl. You will find another way to save them.'

I will find another way.

"Okay." I sighed. "I need time to think."

Ronan stood stiffly. "I'll give you all the time in the world, my dear."

Does he think I'll take it easy on him because he's got some shiny new stitches? Does he think he can get away with calling me his dear and not face the wrath of my finger horns?!

I put my fingers to my head and lunged forward, jamming my fingers into his stomach, careful to keep them on the opposite side of his wound.

Ronan stumbled back, swearing, and I cackled in glee.

Such a devious move had my sobbing brain cells suddenly cheering and screeching in delight.

"Well, at least you're consistent, Chaos Bunny."

Yes! He used my nickname!

"At least you're still stupid enough to forget. I'd be incredibly bored if I didn't get to cause *some* sort of mayhem."

The corners of Ronan's mouth twitched in a smile. "Don't worry, I think there will be plenty of mayhem despite the fact we've come to an understanding."

He paused, his smile falling from his face. "Faye," he said hesitantly. "I know...I know that you say you'll help me, and you won't stab me in the back... but given how rapidly things have shifted in the past, will you...no, I *need* you to promise me you won't turn on me...I need you to promise you won't stab me in the back."

My brain cells howled in outrage. Giving a promise was a huge no-no. Being forced to give one was a very serious offense in their books. A promise was unavoidably binding, which gave them no room for double crossing and treachery—they were big fans of double crossing and treachery.

Hush.

He's right to ask for a promise. I've destroyed what my word means in the hatred of a moment. I am a danger and a liability to him.

I nodded. "I promise not to turn on you," I said softly. "In exchange for you helping my father get out, and then me, I promise I will help you try to get your sister out. I swear by all the blood that binds me."

"Thank you," Ronan whispered as the weight of my promise settled between us.

I nodded again and Ronan gave me a final, lingering glance that seemed to hold a million unspoken words before he turned and left.

I turned to my bed, suddenly drained.

Now for the best part. Time to think of chaos.

Yes. Chaos that is sanctioned by Ronan... This means he's an accomplice. I get to turn our shiny kidnapper into an instrument of destruction.

The thought of turning Ronan into a minion of chaos was enough to sway my furious brain cells—who had, coincidentally, wasted no time digging out their little 'we hate Ronan's guts' signs, in protest of his asking for my word.

Yes. Chaos, glorious chaos. Time to live up to the wonderful nickname he gave me.

Chaos Bunny...here we come.

But first I need a nap.

Yes. Naps power the brain cells for great and terrible things.

I drifted off to the cackling cheers of my precious trio of brain cells as they pulled out the chalkboard of evil planning and drew various ideas of how to best save the day. Every idea ended with me being awarded a great and fabulous prize by Ronan himself, who knelt in admiration while proclaiming my greatness.

My brain cells are so incredibly fickle. Not too long ago, they hated him so much they made signs saying how they hated his guts...now they want his admiration and compliments.

Such a ridiculous lot of inconsistent idiots.

My three brain cells rioted at the insult and proceeded to adamantly lie, stating they had always, really, truly, secretly loved Ronan.

15

Please Don't Come

EVADNE

"Nothing ever ends poetically. It ends and we turn it into poetry. All that blood was never once beautiful. It was just red."
-Kait Rowkowski

I no longer had the strength to fight Darcy as he pulled me apart, piece by piece. He was distorting my memories and now there was no way to decipher what was real and what had been rewritten.

In my mind, I died. Over and over again, Darcy tortured and killed me while Ember was forced to watch. Until finally, he left me dying on the ground as he dragged her away and I gasped her name.

The shadows at the edge of the world grew, feeding off my agony. Thriving on my fear.

Am I truly dead this time? Does Darcy actually have Em?

There was no longer a clear distinction between what was real, and what remained his fantasies.

Maybe this is all one long, horrific nightmare and I just need to wake up.

"Come back to me, child."

Marcovester Red?

The new voice was distant. Familiar, but so far away. I couldn't comprehend where it was coming from.

"Come back to me," she whispered again. It sounded like Marcovester Red, but there was something off about the tenor. It wasn't quite right to be her voice.

"I can't," I whimpered, a sob catching on my voice. "He won't let me go."

Am I talking out loud? Am I talking in my mind? Where is the voice? Where am I?

I couldn't tell if my lips were moving, if my voice was actually there. Perhaps it was just another layer to Darcy's cruelty, his determination to break me.

Darcy's claws dug into my mind, shattering my grip on the voice and the questioned reality. "You're not going anywhere," he snarled as I screamed.

The pain was unbearable, an icy fire that spread across my skin.

"She'll come," Darcy rasped. "I can feel it, the sound of your screams as the witch tries and *fails* to bring you back...it will push her over the edge. She'll come. I know my *Oisillon* well. She will do anything to protect her *dear* sister." He laughed. "The witch knows it, too. She's too weak to fight me. I've grown since we last battled. She's going to send her to me, for the twisted illusion of saving you...she can't waste the bargain. She won't waste the opportunity to get the blood..."

No, don't do it, Em. Don't do it.

Don't come. Please don't come.

"She'll come for you, *Eva*, she'll come. All you need to do is scream."

"Please," I choked, desperate to protect my sister. "Don't do this! Please!"

Don't do it, Em. Don't come. We do not negotiate with kidnappers! It won't save me. It'll only put you in his grasp and then they'll have both of us. Don't come. Don't come!

"Scream again," Darcy hissed as the pain intensified. He was dragging the tip of his knife down my forehead, toward my eye.

No, no, no. Not that. Please not that.

His words came back to me as he continued to pull the knife through my skin. 'I won't blind you, not yet that is.'

No, no, no. Please! NO!

There was no stopping my screams as skin and tissue gave no resistance to his razor-sharp blade. There was no containing the agony as, in one decisive move, he yanked his dagger through my left eye and plunged the world into bloodied darkness.

16

The Monster's Face Beneath The Mask

EMBER

"Be silent heart! There is no hope."
-Albert Camus, The Possessed

The thin walls of the small cottage did nothing to muffle the sound of Evadne's screams. All I could do was sit and wait, biting my knuckles as her pain enveloped me. I barely noticed the metallic taste in my mouth. The skin had split beneath my teeth as I struggled to manage the agony we shared. My body was on fire, and an inferno raced beneath my skin.

"Time's up, time's up."

I jerked as Darcy's voice entered my mind, overwhelming my senses with the taste of mint.

No. That's not possible. He's dead. He's supposed to be dead.

"I warned you, Mon Oisillon. I warned you, but still you let her suffer...you let your own sister suffer on your behalf."

"No," I whispered.

But that can't be possible. Darcy is dead. Marcovester Red killed him.

She dealt a killing blow and sent him to die...but I haven't been able to speak of what he did to me. I still haven't been able to speak of what he did...which means he isn't dead yet...which means he survived her strike.

My mind was spinning, racing out of control as the realization hit me all at once. Artemis had been telling the truth. He wasn't the one torturing Evadne—it was Darcy.

He has my sister.

No, no, no!

This can't be real. This can't be happening.

"She can't hold out much longer..."

Darcy's voice came and left, sliding over me like a sickly poison. He was everywhere and nowhere. Slithering across my skin as he broke my resolve with each and every one of Evadne's screams.

"Do you hear her? This is your fault. I warned you what would happen..."

There was something in my forehead, dragging its way down, down, down.

Horror rose. It was headed straight for my eye. A memory hit me then. I was back in the Halls, and his dagger was a breath away from my eye, his chilling threat against my sister.

No, no. please no. Don't hurt her! Don't do this!

"Too late. Your chance to stop this has already passed. If you want to save her life, you'll come to me. You have until sundown to come to the ruins at the edge of the wastelands."

He shot an image at me then. It was the crumbling castle I'd seen at the edge of the island.

I was screaming as his blade sliced through my eye in one decisive movement. The world went dark. I was clutching my head in my hands. My screams of grief and horror melding with Evadne's.

"She's blind now, because of you. This is all your fault, Em. I tried to warn you...but you refused to listen. Now look what you made me do."

Hands were on mine, pulling them away from my face.

I jerked, terrified, fighting whoever was there.

"Hey, Sparks, it's okay. It's just me. It's okay."

It was Theron.

"What's going on? Your sister's eye...oh my cursed Faerie Realm, *your* eye."

The world was hazy, disconnected. I couldn't see properly out of my left eye. Everything was blurry around me as tears and blood streamed down my face.

"Help her," I sobbed. "Please, help her. He's hurting her!"

"I know, I know, Sparks. Baba is fighting for her. She's going to get your sister back."

Theron's voice was earnest, but there was an edge to it I recognized all too well—fear. *He doesn't believe that Baba Yaga can get her back.*

Darcy will hold her and continue torturing her until I go. I saw the ruins from the ship. If I go, it will save her. He'll kill her at sundown. There's no time.

"Her eye?" I whispered hoarsely.

Theron pursed his lips, but I could see the truth on his face, the lack of reassurance. "Baba's going to try to heal it...but he's using Darke magic in the wound. It's likely his blade is cursed. Even with her magic, your sister will never be the same."

"I have to help her," I whispered.

"No," Theron replied quietly. "You need to let Baba Yaga work. I'm going to take you to the market to get some air. You need distraction and distance. Perhaps it will lessen the torture on your end."

"I'm not leaving her," I hissed. The mere thought of the space that already separated us was too much to bear.

But if I don't leave her, I can't get to the ruins. I can't save her...

Theron crouched in front of me. "Trust me, Sparks. It will help. Besides, Baba Yaga suggested it. She said with the bond between you two, your being this close is muddling her spell. She needs space between you two so she can differentiate and overpower your sister's shadow and take it back from him."

"What if she can't?" I whimpered. "What if she can't get my sister back?"

Theron swallowed, trying and failing to find the words. "Come on, Sparks," he said after a few moments had passed. "Let's give her the best chance to save your sister. If Yaga says to go, we need to listen. She knows what to do. This is not the first time she's faced monsters. Verity will stay until there is nothing left to be done. Baba says she'll know by sundown whether or not your sister will come back. We'll be back before then. If nothing else can be done, you'll be by her side."

"I can't leave her," I sobbed. "This is my fault. This is happening because of me. You think I can bear to leave her?" I was crying, burying my face in my hands as the world spun around me.

Theron sighed and pulled my hands away from my face. "Look at me, Sparks."

I couldn't breathe, my heart was racing, and my body was encased in pulsing, icy fire. I wanted to curl up in a ball and scream until it was over. The panic was destroying what little resolve and strength I had left.

"Ember, look at me," Theron repeated gently.

I raised my eyes to his, trying to make out his face. Having one eye blurry and another full of tears, yet seeing, was making me dizzy. The conflicting messages to my brain were confusing and nauseating.

"I want you to listen to me, and listen well," he said firmly. "This is not your fault. In *no* possible way, is this your fault. Whoever is hurting your sister is the one at fault. They bear the blame, *all* of the blame. Just because you are the motive behind their twisted, sordid deeds, does not mean that you are to blame. It simply means you are caught in the middle—collateral damage being manipulated for a broken end."

I nodded mutely as Theron pulled me to my feet. But his words were disconnected, far away. Darcy's torture of Evadne was only prolonged because of me. If I went to the ruins, it would stop. I wanted to explain it to Theron, I wanted to tell him everything, but the words wouldn't come. Darcy's curse still silenced me.

Marcovester Red said to break the spell. But how? How do I reclaim my voice?

Evadne screamed again, and I doubled over in pain as the invisible blade once more began to drag down my face. It picked up where it had left off, just below my eye. Now it was traveling down my cheek, toward my neck.

I was screaming through my teeth as my skin split open, began to bleed, and then closed back over, creating yet another scar.

"The longer you delay, the more she suffers. Make your choice, Ember. I grow tired of waiting. My knife itches to open the beautiful arteries in her neck...it craves that undiluted flow of blood. Every moment you delay increases her suffering."

"Do you need me to carry you away?" Theron asked, voice teasing. He was trying to distract me.

I shook my head, trying to wrench my mind from Darcy's claws and the awful, overwhelming flood of peppermint.

"Good, because I assure you, getting hauled around like a sack of potatoes is the most undignified manner in which to enter a new place."

"And you know this because you've had this experience?" I asked, trying to find some sense of normality.

"No, but Raz can affirm what I'm saying. I had to haul her someplace once, and she's heavier than she looks. I tried to carry her like a damsel, but it just didn't work. So, sack of potatoes it was. She's still mad about it."

"Theron, a word."

I jumped. I hadn't heard Verity come up next to us, and I hadn't seen her either. She was on my blind side.

Will my vision clear, or is this the new normal?

Theron and Verity shared a quick conversation, all of which was lost on me. I couldn't hear much of anything. My pulse roared in my ears, blocking everything out as I struggled to breathe.

"Ember," Verity said, coming up to me. I could make out the shape of her face, the scrunch of her eyebrows, and the worry in her eyes. But almost everything else was lost.

"Stay with Theron," Verity said. "That's an absolute order, do you understand me?"

It's as if she knows something.

Verity, I'm sorry, but I can't stand here and do nothing when I could save my sister and stop this torture.

I nodded. "I understand you," I said raggedly.

I understand, but I won't agree to stay with him. I will make no promises.

"Do you know anything?" Verity asked, her eyes probing mine.

I know everything…but I can't tell you. His curse won't let me tell you.

I tried and failed to shake my head. The muscles in my neck were straining, begging to nod, pleading to let her know of our terrible curse.

Verity sighed. "There's something off about this. The witch wants you to leave, though somehow that doesn't seem like the right course of action. Her explanation makes sense…but there's something off about the whole thing. She's on edge, angry… I don't want you out of my sight right now, yet I need to stay with your sister and make sure the witch doesn't try anything…"

I shrugged, unable to answer her.

She was looking at me. I could feel the weight of her gaze on my face.

"Stay with Theron," she repeated. "Do what he says, and don't make me regret this."

I nodded, trying to find something to say. I needed to pull her attention away from her suspicions. "I can't see much out of my left eye," I said softly. "Everything's blurry."

"All of your other linked wounds have healed over correctly, haven't they?" Verity asked.

I nodded.

"Maybe it will get better with time."

"I can only hope," I replied. "I'm clumsy enough. You take my peripheral vision, and I'm bound to walk off the edge of the ship."

"Well, no need to worry about that. Raz would rescue you. She'll probably lecture you though, so best not to do that in the first place." Verity's tone turned serious. "I'll stay with your sister. If anything changes, I'll send for you immediately. I mean it, Ember—stay with Theron. That's a direct order, do you understand me?"

"Let me know if *anything* happens," I replied, changing the topic. I couldn't give her an affirmative answer. It wasn't in me to lie to her, not when she'd done so much for me. I wouldn't lie, but I also couldn't obey. Not when Evadne's life was on the line.

"Come on, Sparks," Theron said in a forced jovial tone. "Let's go find something to eat. Here, why don't you hold onto my forearm till your eye clears up. I'd hate for you to walk off the edge of the island."

That is a horrifying thought.

I nodded and wrapped my arm through his, allowing him to lead me off and away from my sister. Every step felt like a betrayal, yet every step took me closer to the ruins—which held my only means to save her.

I'm going to fix this, Eva. I'm going to make it right.

Is this the right choice? What if he doesn't set her free?

He will, he'll have to. I'm going to kill him. But this time, I'll stay with the body until it's good and truly dead. I'll stab him until there's nothing left of him but a mangled body that no longer resembles the monster he truly is. I'll kill him a thousand times over if I must.

But no amount of vengeful thinking could dull the nagging feeling that Verity was right. A sense of foreboding followed every step we took, and I began to worry that I was blinded by my desperation to save my sister and walking straight into a trap.

Is it a trap if I know it's a trap? Is it a trap if I know what I'm walking into?

I had no answers to my questions as I walked away from my sister and toward the monster that held her.

17

The Plotting Of Great And Glorious Chaos

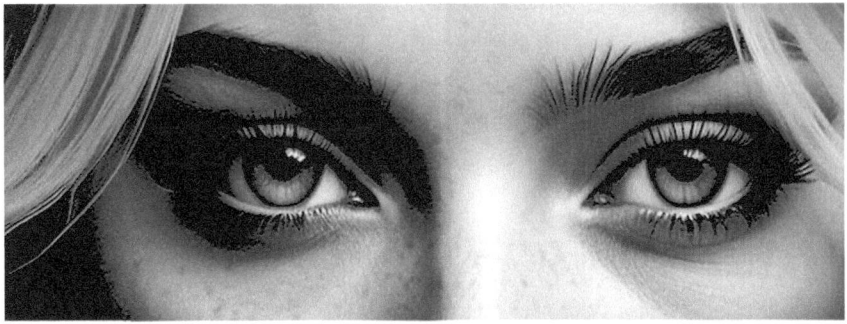

FAYE

"Oh, to be a little dog sprinting at top speeds around the house with reckless abandon to release all the stress pent up from your extremely harrowing bath time."
-Kibibarel

Having been given the green light to cause chaos, my three brain cells took their new job very seriously. My other brain cells, who had abandoned me for their ridiculous union and its impossible demands, began to grow incredibly curious as they watched the plan build with growing excitement. Suddenly, they forsook their precious union and begged to be reinstated as regular brain cells. All for the goal of accomplishing great and heroic deeds of mayhem. Apparently, the union lacked copious amounts of chaos.

The three loyal brain cells, however, refused to take the union crew back fully. Instead, they put all of them on 'trial'. After the trial was done and the hoard was pronounced guilty of treason, the three, after a lengthy debate and wrestling match, decided to accept the traitors back despite the guilty verdict. It was declared the hoard must completely renounce the labor union in the most insulting way possible. Then, they must complete deeds of penitence—under the guise of proving their allegiance, of course.

I found it humorous that the hoard agreed to the ridiculousness, when there was no assurance of their being allowed to join the mayhem after the stupid deeds were accomplished.

So, the pandemonium commenced. Some were forced to write 'I'm sorry, I was wrong, I'm a stupid poo-poo head,' a million times. Others had to march until they collapsed, all while singing their repentance. Finally, every one of them had to walk off a metaphorical plank into shark-infested waters, to prove their undying allegiance to the three.

It had been a week since Ronan and I had made our peace, but apparently Ronan was still on thin ice with Jeremiah. Every day, Jeremiah came unannounced into my room. Some days it was at sunrise, some days closer to noon. The uncertainty of when he would show up to give me the next dose of drugs left my mind in a constant state of anxiety and trepidation.

I didn't like the way Jeremiah looked at me now. He looked hungry and feral. But worst of all, he looked like he was planning something terrible.

Having yet to become accustomed to the drugs, I spent most of my days sleeping. By nighttime they had worn off enough that I was slightly human, and some part of me was wondering if there was something vampiric in the dosage. I was becoming a creature of the night, it seemed, and even sunlight was beginning to bother my eyes.

If Jeremiah turns me into a vamp, I'm going to be pissed.

So will Rionach. She always wanted to turn me, just for spite.

Yes, well, when you become best friends with a vampire and then tease her about it, then proceed to use the forbidden no-no term 'vampire,' it's only logical she'll get a little snappish.

Ha! Literally.

I was forcing myself to work out, in the hope it would help my brain come up with a plan, when Ronan's quiet knock came. "It's me," he said softly, before coming in.

My three brain cells boo-ed at the interruption. They had been happily engaging in a workout of their own. Most of their so-called workout consisted of beating the crap out of the repentant union hoard, under the illusion of 'training.'

I pushed myself up, but there was no hiding how out of breath I was.

"Faye, are you all right?" Ronan asked, taking in my flustered state.

"Yeah, just tragically out of shape," I muttered, annoyed. "Jeremiah's stupid drugs make me so cursedly weak!"

"Want to spar?" Ronan asked suddenly.

"What? No!" I snapped. "I'm way too out of shape for that. You'd beat me and then my pride would be so mortified I'd never try to fight again."

Ronan arched an eyebrow. "Scared?"

I bristled. "No. Besides, I'm in no condition to fight. I can't even do *pushups* without feeling like I'm going to die."

"So, you *are* scared you might get beat," Ronan laughed.

"No, there's a big difference between scared and mortified. Weren't you listening when I was lecturing you about the fragile state of my pride?"

"Big whoop," Ronan scoffed. "If I remember correctly, when you dragged me to that cursed Realm, you were hands down kicking my butt."

"I didn't drag you!" I snapped indignantly. "Your stupid, dumb, ninny brain *followed* me there. *I* told you to go back and you didn't listen!"

"Yes well, what else could I do?" Ronan protested with a laugh.

"*Turn back* you idiot!" I giggled.

Ronan raised an eyebrow and stared at me as he fought a smile.

"What else should I expect?" I huffed. "You're clearly stupid."

"C'mon Faye," Ronan wheedled. "No one around here can keep up with me. My skills are fat and lazy with no one to *actually* challenge me. I need someone to spar with who's better than me. You kicked my butt when we first met, I'm sure you can still hold *some* measure of your own."

"You're delusional," I muttered. "Your stupid father has pumped me so full of drugs that I can't function. It'll be worse than training with your men—like taking candy from a baby. Go find someone else to bug. Maybe in a few weeks I'll feel up to it."

"Pleeeaaaseee?" Ronan whined, drawing out the word as he looked at me pleadingly and batted his eyelashes.

Did he really just have the audacity to bat his eyelashes at me?!

"Pretty please, with a cherry on top?"

Now I want to kick his butt, just to make him stop being so ridiculous!

I rolled my eyes. "Fine. But I'm not going to play nice."

"Since when have you ever played nice?" Ronan quipped as a wide grin began to spread across his face.

The stupid idiot actually looks excited. What a moron.

Look at that grin. He actually looks happy.

My three, enamored brain cells had begun to take polaroid pictures of Ronan's grin. Then, after hugging the images to their chest and squealing, they promptly began to list off all their favorite things about him. At the top of that list was the image of his happy grin and the adorable scrunch in between his eyebrows when he was worried.

My brain cells need to stop this ridiculous mooning. It's distracting and pointless.

I raised my fists and glared at him, hardening my resolve to be annoyed by him.

He raised his fists, but instead of glaring, he smirked and wiggled his eyebrows.

That's it. I'm going to turn him into paste.

The first spar lasted two minutes. He had me down and pinned before I could realize I was toast.

"You suck," I wheezed, shoving him off me.

Ronan smirked, clearly delighted with his little victory. "Look who's talking. I'm not the one who just got pinned."

"Yeah, well, you're beating up an old, drugged up lady. Just put me in a retirement home and leave me alone."

Yeah, and get me my cane so I can whack you.

"C'mon, let's go again," Ronan pressed.

"Fine," I grumbled, hoping I could find my second wind and redeem myself.

The second match went much like the first, as did the third and fourth. It wasn't until the fifth that I finally noticed his pattern and tells. His moves were getting predictable, and I had him pinned within thirty seconds.

"HA!" I gasped before promptly toppling over. The ceiling was spinning, and I was suddenly afraid I was going to hurl.

Ronan flopped down beside me. "Bravo!" he cheered, holding out a fist.

I humored him and bumped his fist with my own, making an explosive sound with my mouth as I pulled my hand away.

"Any luck with a plan?" Ronan asked after a few moments had passed.

I sighed, staring up at the ceiling. "Let me catch my breath, then I'll tell you what I'm thinking. We need to compare notes and find any holes."

Ronan nodded. "Fair enough."

It took what felt like ages to get my air back. Every breath burned in my chest, and it hurt to know how much strength and progress I had lost in the Mortal Realm.

That's not even considering what Jeremiah's drugs have done to me.

"So," I began. "The first step is to get Meghan trained. After she's trained, then I'll disable the zapping chips. I have a hunch that they are linked to his database. If I can hack into the database, and incapacitate it, then it will disable the chips. But then I'll need to test it to make sure they don't work anymore. We'll have to be very careful engineering that escape. You need to keep up the façade that you're loyal to your father—because that'll play into the step *after* this one—and try to stop me...but I have to get out, so that means I'll have to overpower you."

I gave Ronan a goading look. "Who knows, maybe after all this training I'll *actually* overpower you."

Ronan scoffed, but his eyes were laughing.

"After the test, if it's successful that is, we'll have to move quickly. I don't know how much time it'll take him to regain control and reinstate the database..." I chewed on my thumb, thinking. "We'll need to cause a distraction for the next incident... I'm going to give him a secret...a secret about how to get him what he wants...your mother back."

Ronan gasped quietly.

"It's not going to *actually* bring her back," I continued hurriedly. I didn't want to get his hopes up. "But he's so blinded by his greed, the confession will be enough to convince him. Now, to give him that spell, I'll lead him into believing that it can only be obtained from my home. When we go to retrieve it, we'll take Meghan with us.

"Now, back to the traps laid throughout the plan. We are going to cleverly drop little hints that we care for each other. However, you're going to let him in on the secret that *I* care for you...and while you like me, you want the magic. You're going to suggest that you begin to manipulate our bond to get the information Jeremiah wants. When I let him in on the secret of the spell, I'm also going to negotiate about you....it will cement the fact that we've bonded and Jeremiah will believe that I'm telling the truth...even though we can't have bonded because you *clearly* have cooties...but it should be enough to get us out of there...of course he can never know that you're not actually loyal to him..."

I was rambling, but I couldn't seem to stop. Trying to pull a coherent thread of thought from the drug induced side of my brain was a challenging endeavor. Currently, my three brain cells were playing tug of war with the tired, exhausted part of my brain that was lost in thick gray shadows. The union hoard surrounded the three, and were cheering and screaming advice and encouragement. It would have made more sense if they had offered to help and thus given the three an edge against my tired brain, but the thought never occurred to them as I continued to slowly wrestle the pieces of the complicated plan from my subconscious.

"So, as I was saying. After we ensure the pieces are all in place to get Meghan out safely, I'm going to escape my cell but I'm not going to get out. I'm going to go looking for your father. When you hear the commotion, get Meghan out. Hide her in the trunk of your car and then come find me... You have to get her out first because she's your first priority. You also need to ensure that Marcov is close to where I am."

"No," Ronan cut in sharply, sitting up with a jerk. "I'm not letting him *near* you."

That's the second time he's interrupted me because of Marcov's placement on the chess board. He must feel about him the same way I do.

"You have to," I replied as I pushed myself up and sat cross-legged. "You said he's been the one who finds you, traps you. He needs to be occupied with me. The whole compound does. I need a layout of the place, so I can know where to go that will draw the most attention to me, and away from you. Jeremiah and Marcov *must* be occupied with me, or this won't work."

"And what do I do when I come back and find you?"

"You rescue your father," I replied with a shrug. "When you do, I'm going to latch onto you like you're my safe harbor. Jeremiah will see the bond and believe me when I tell you about the spell. Since he trusts you, he'll allow you to handle it on your own."

"How can you be so sure?" Ronan asked. "What if he follows us?"

"I'm going to make sure he can't follow us," I replied with a savage grin.

"What—"

"I'm going to break his kneecaps," I snarled, reveling in the thought of repaying Jeremiah for some of his bloodshed.

Ronan was quiet. "That should keep him grounded," he said at last with a small smile.

Ronan is making puns, how marvelous.

"Literally," I snorted gleefully.

"What happens after we get Megs out?" Ronan asked, returning to the plan.

"I have a contact, a friend in New York. She'll take Meghan in until things settle down. She'll know how to best help your sister, and she'll know if we fail here. If we fail, she'll help Meghan start a new life without us."

"How?"

I shook my head. "I can't tell you," I said gently.

Ronan nodded. "Sorry," he said softly. "I forget there's things you can't tell me..."

"It's okay," I replied with a shrug. "After Meghan is safe, we'll return with the spell. I'll hold the high ground and barter with Jeremiah for my father's release, and while he's occupied with the spell, we'll get my father out. Then, we'll all get away from here."

"And Jeremiah simply goes free?"

"Absolutely *not*." I snorted. "We're going to personally help the police raid his pretty little compound. Jeremiah will be brought to justice. You know where all the bodies are buried. Just show the police his murder victims. Show him the men who should be in prison...tell them everything."

Ronan nodded. "That's true."

I had taken a wild guess there were people Jeremiah had killed and discarded. It was disturbing to know I'd guessed correctly. Jeremiah was likely swimming in blood.

Ronan chewed over the plan. "I'm impressed," he said at last. "Though, for a plan that was supposed to be wrought with great and glorious amounts of chaos, as is fitting for a Chaos Bunny, it seems a little tame to me."

"Oh no," I scoffed. "There is great chaos woven throughout. My three brain cells have seen to that, I just didn't *elaborate* on the chaos."

"Faye, you have more than three brain cells," Ronan lectured. "On average, a human being has eighty to one hundred and twenty *billion* brain cells."

"Well, thank you for that *boring* information, oh walking medical encyclopedia," I replied sarcastically. "But I'll have you know that the other seventy-nine billion, nine hundred ninety-nine million, nine hundred ninety-nine thousand, nine hundred ninety-seven brain cells, are currently on thin ice because they made the foolish decision to go on strike because I wouldn't sign the terms of their ridiculous labor union."

Ronan's eyebrows crinkled in confusion. "Labor union..." he muttered.

"Labor union," I confirmed. "However, they've abandoned the false grandeur of the labor union. Now, they are currently trying to get back in the good graces of the three. But they're still on thin ice."

"Well, aren't you good at math," Ronan commented, clearly for want of something else to say.

"Nope," I replied primly. "I abhor math. I don't dabble in the devil's cursed numbers."

Ronan scoffed and glanced at his watch. "I should go," he said with a sigh. "James is covering for me, but I don't want to take advantage of that. I'll see you tomorrow. We can figure out how to get you over to train Megs."

"Oh, I already have that figured out." I replied loftily.

"Oh really?"

"Yup. I'm going to attack you and you're going to tell your father that I'm getting too feisty, and you're concerned another drug increase could kill me, because I'm *also* acting deranged. Like *super* deranged..." I paused, considering. "I think maybe I should bite you to make it seem super convincing."

"What?" Ronan protested. "Absolutely not."

"Killjoy," I muttered. "Well, now that you've destroyed my lovely idea, I guess we should go back to my plan. Anyway, you're going to tell him you think it would be a good idea to put me in solitary confinement in a dark, windowless room for a while, and that will break my spirit."

Ronan looked confused. "How will putting you in solitary confinement help you train Meghan?"

I rolled my eyes. "Sheesh, *someone's* clearly lacking a few *billion* brain cells. I have to think of everything around here, and explain each minute detail to boot. You're going to put me in a room next to Meghan's, and you're going to give me a way into her room.

"You want me to cut a hole in the wall?"

"Either that or a tunnel that connects the rooms. Seems like a hole in the wall would be easier than a tunnel."

"How would you cover it?"

"Perhaps with a poster."

"A poster?" he asked incredulously. "Don't you think that a poster would be...oh, I don't know, inconsistent with solitary confinement?"

I shrugged. "Sheesh, you big, grouchy killjoy. It doesn't have to be a poster. It was just an *idea*. It's a base you can work with and elaborate upon."

"You want me to put you in solitary confinement and put up a poster in your solitary confinement cell?" Ronan continued. "That's not going to be suspicious at all."

"Oh, Jeremiah won't come check on me."

"And how can you be so sure of that?"

"You're also going to tell him to leave me alone."

"I might as well tell him to stop being crazy," Ronan scoffed.

"You're going to suggest to him that I *crave* the conflict. That resisting him gives me courage and makes me feel as if I'm better than him. Tell him that leaving me in silence, with no one to resist, will hurt me more than his torture ever could."

"You really *have* thought of everything," Ronan said in amazement.

"Well, of course I have," I replied indignantly. "I'm offended you think I haven't."

Ronan got to his feet, laughing. He looked down at me, his eyes soft and, for once, hopeful.

My brain cells began hurriedly snapping pictures with their polaroid cameras. This happy, tender look had quickly replaced the wide grin as their favorite picture of Ronan.

Something stirred strangely in my chest and for a moment, I allowed myself to hope that maybe we would get out of this alive.

18

Crossroads And Choices

EMBER

"Nearer he came and nearer. Her face was like a light. Her eyes grew
wide for a moment; she drew one last deep breath, then her finger
moved in moonlight, her musket shattered the moonlight, shattered
her breast in the moonlight and warned him – with her death. He
turned. He spurred to the west; he did not know who stood, bowed,
with her head o'er the musket. Drenched in her own blood! Not till
the dawn he heard it, and his face grew grey to hear, how Bess, the
landlord's daughter, the landlord's black-eyed daughter, had watched
for her love in the moonlight, and died in darkness there."
-The Highwayman By Alfred Noyes

Theron talked endlessly as he led me through the island on a worn dirt path. It was clear
he was trying to pull my mind from thoughts of Evadne, but it was a useless endeavor.
There was no escaping what was happening to her. Even though every step away dulled
the pain between our bond, until it was nothing more than a burning ache, there was
no avoiding the turmoil in my mind. The haunting echoes of Darcy's voice left an
inescapable taint of mint on my senses.

Being near Theron gave me a strange, yet foreign sense of peace and tranquility. One I hadn't felt since before our life had become entrapped within the Realm.

I barely noticed as we made our way across suspended bridges and creaky boardwalks. I didn't notice the wide gaps of the sky that stretched endlessly beneath us. Everything I'd normally feel was nothing more than a distant anxiety that I could manage.

It was all I could do to make myself put one foot in front of the other, following Theron. All I wanted to do was bolt in the direction of the ruins I'd seen from the ship.

We passed through a wide, stone archway and I jumped as noise suddenly exploded out of nowhere.

Theron laughed at my shocked expression. "The marketplace hubbub is constrained to the marketplace. There's a spell keeping all the noise in. It keeps the danger at a lower level by not attracting Wastes with the noise."

"What are Wastes?" I asked, confused.

Theron grimaced. "Horrid creatures best left unspoken of."

Colors and shapes attacked me from every side. Hundreds of voices droned. There were warbling strains of music, and the telltale screech of animals in cages. It was too overwhelming. I wanted to get away from it all.

I took a step back, running into Theron. "Easy there, Sparks," Theron said quietly as he placed a reassuring hand on my shoulder. "I'm right here with you. There's nothing to be afraid of. If something tries to bite you, just bite it back, but harder. Show it who's boss."

I scoffed at the idea. The mental image of my biting a monster was absurd and ridiculous, though simultaneously humorous. Unable to resist, I chomped my teeth together, imagining my biting something big and scary, and making it run away in terror.

"That's the spirit," Theron said encouragingly.

A small smile pulled at the corners of my mouth, but it died quickly. It felt wrong to smile when Evadne's life was in so much danger.

"Why didn't I see this from the ship?" I asked. "I would have thought I'd see a setup like this from way up there, but I don't remember seeing it."

"It's hidden; the spell that masks the sound also masks the sight. You have to follow the path to find the marketplace."

I swallowed nervously, surveying the melee around me. The second pouch of cursed artifacts in my pocket, the ones that had been cleansed, suddenly felt heavier as I looked at all the different vendors.

"Get everything you can from the vendors with each shard," Theron instructed. "This is haggling territory, so you need to haggle. Rearm yourself and get some good, solid armor. Yours is utterly thrashed. I don't think the rulers' enchantments truly grasped the strength the Moores possess. The damage only proves how much they underestimated the Moores. You need to get stronger spells. Ones that come from the Moores themselves."

"Me?" I squeaked. "You just said you're right here with me. Why do *I* have to do the bartering?"

"Consider it a lesson in piracy. I'm sure your surly prince would approve of such training—once he gets the stick out of his butt, of course." Theron chortled at his own joke, and when I didn't laugh, he shook his head. "You should also get something to eat. You look like death warmed over—you're acting like it too. That joke was *very* funny!"

I rolled my eyes.

Death warmed over...he sure knows how to compliment a girl.

"When you don't look like death, I'll compliment you until your cheeks are so red you want to hide in a broom closet. Until then, I'll insult you. It's a well-known fact that spite keeps a person going longer than flattery. Now, get going. I'll be around, so if you need help, scream. But don't scream unless it's absolutely an emergency."

I do not want to do this.

"Do I have to?" I whined.

"Yup. No arguing."

But I don't want to talk to strangers. Please don't make me talk, and worse yet haggle with strangers.

"Growing pains, Grimm. This is your first lesson in piracy. You must learn to trade and barter like a pirate."

But I don't want to.

I glared daggers and crossed my arms, but he was unfazed. Much to my annoyance, he simply laughed and gave me a little shove forward. "Off you go now, little duck. Time to grow up." He looked awfully proud of himself. "I should have been a poet in another life," he said grandly.

"But I was already a brave little toaster today," I whined, trying to dawdle.

"Well, now you can be a brave little duck," Theron replied, grinning.

This is stupid. Utterly ridiculous. Why. WHY do I have to haggle and talk to people?

Might as well get it over with. It'll give me a little time to think of a way to ditch Theron so I can get to the ruins...and if I'm busy, he'll let down his guard and stop watching me so closely.

I lifted my chin, pretending with everything I had that I belonged in this strange place.

Look at me. I'm a stupid pirate. I'm going to get what I want and need, using things that tried to kill me. ARGH! GRR! Yo-ho, me mateys...grr...

What else do pirates say?

Uhm...swear words. Lots of swear words.

Oo, yay! Swearing!

I sighed. Even the prospect of swearing wasn't enough to revive my rancid mood. "Well, might as well get this ridiculous crap over with," I muttered as I made my way over to the stall.

The trading was almost too easy. The cursed thorns were apparently well known. Moreso, the one who carried them, having survived their wrath, prospered. The vendors eagerly agreed to whatever I asked. I got a thick leather bag to begin with, one that appeared to have the same sort of magic as our WyrldCloaks. The pockets would've done just fine, but I wanted to ensure the items were in one place so they made it back to Evadne. I gently placed my cloak, as well as Evadne's, in the bottom of the bag. I didn't have the heart to explain to Fireheart and Elvie what was going on. When they woke from their nap in one of my pockets, they would be back with Evadne.

I would not be going back.

I got seven full sets of clothes for Evadne and me. Though I knew I wouldn't need mine, I figured she could make use of them. We were close enough in size that it wouldn't be an issue, and I didn't want Theron getting suspicious if he saw only enough clothes for one person. For the price of an extra sliver, one of the traders let me change in the back of her tent. I kept parts of my armor, particularly the forearm guards that contained the hidden knives. They would come in handy when fighting Darcy.

I stowed the rest of my old armor in the leather bag. I wasn't quite sure what to do with it, but leaving it behind didn't seem like the right choice either. Perhaps it could still be of some use, or Fireheart could gnaw on it if he was bored.

A full set of fighting armor for each of us followed the clothes—each woven with the protective magic of the Moores. It was supple, moving with my body as if it were silk, yet so strong my dagger couldn't penetrate it. The trader informed me it was made of shed dragon scales forged in phoenix fire. Mine was black with tints of ruby and cobalt. Evadne's was black with hints of emerald and sapphire.

I replaced the knife I had lost somewhere in the chaos—the one Jacques had given me. I also added to Evadne's collection of throwing knives. It was a small set of eight knives that, when properly manipulated, folded into one razor thin, four-inch blade. The weapons merchant had then assisted me in adding more miniscule blade holders to my boots. Four blades to a foot were added, and they were so light I forgot they were there.

New boots for Evadne were necessary, and I ensured they were equipped with the same arsenal. After all, she was much better at knife throwing than I was. I could throw them, but I was like a three-year-old chucking a block. Evadne's always hit their mark and did considerable, lethal damage.

Finally arrayed, I drew closer to the merchant's tall mirror and stared at the stranger who stood there. I hardly recognized myself. I looked older, harder around the edges—as if I had stared death in the face and laughed. A warrior stood in my skin, armed to the teeth and vicious. My short red hair had grown while we were in the Moores more than seemed possible. It was well past my shoulder blades now, and pulled back into a tight French braid. My bangs had grown, and now they framed my face in long layers. My mouth fell open in shock as I stared at my ears. Where they had once curved down, they now arched up, ending in delicate pointed tips.

How did that happen, and I never realized?? How did I not realize?

Pale pink scars stood out on my face, evidence of Darcy's cruelty. My left eye had changed colors. It was now a pale blue with streaks of black and flecks of crimson—a sharp contrast to my other, electric blue eye. There was a haunted, fierce sort of look buried beneath their depths, making me look angry and dangerous. I was grateful I could see from my injured eye again. Far away, the world was still blurry, and my peripheral vision had yet to return, but at least I could see.

But can I face Darcy and win? Looks are one thing, but do I have the strength and ability to fight him? Can I kill him and survive?

How do I kill him, when I have to get him to release Evadne? I'll lose my upper hand...and if I threaten him, he won't let her go, just for spite.

"Just because you look like a warrior, doesn't mean you should deprive yourself of a trinket."

I jumped, turning my attention to the merchant. She had bright green eyes encased by a face of happy wrinkles—every line and mark left by joy and mirth. The shade of her eyes, however, reminded me too much of Artemis'.

His words from the night before came back to me in a wave. *It's not me.*

No Artemis, it wasn't you. I was wrong. I was so wrong. I'm sorry...he made me think it was you...I'm sure of it...

'Where are you,' he had asked.

I'm lost, Artemis. I'm lost and afraid. I don't know what to do.

I look like an adult, but I feel like a child who can't outrun the monsters. I'm afraid, I'm so afraid and I can't escape.

I pushed back the wandering thoughts and offered the merchant a small, embarrassed smile. She gave me a wide smile in return. "All right there, love?" she asked.

"Yeah," I choked out.

"Well, you've been staring at yourself in my mirror for at least three minutes. What are you lacking?"

"I..."

"You're lacking something pretty," she answered for me. "Might as well browse my little shop and find what completes it."

I sighed, embarrassed and flushed.

"Now, come over here and see what I've got in this box," she said encouragingly. "I think it's just the thing. You look a little lost, my dear. You need a hand, a light."

I approached her, heat creeping up my cheeks. "I just, haven't seen myself in a while," I muttered.

"It's all right, dear. You're stunning. I don't fault you for looking. If I had your beauty, I'd fall captive to the water's side like poor Narcissus."

I chuckled; it seemed such a ridiculous thing to admit one's vanity.

Laid inside the ornate wooden box were two flat, diamond shaped pendants, made of a pale green, opal-like stone and edged in bright blue sapphires. A soft glow emanated from each of them. They looked similar to the bracelets Mum had given us.

Loss crashed into me as if I had just lost her moments ago—not days, or perhaps months ago.

How long have we been trapped in the Moores?

My fingers traced the bracelet on my wrist, wishing I could just go back and see her one more time—hug her one more time. But this time, I wouldn't let go. I wouldn't let her leave.

"Ah, you have the sister," the old vendor nodded approvingly.

"What?"

"Your bracelet, it's made of moonstones, as these are, though a different color. Green is the rarest form of the moonstones. They call to each other in a language only those of starlight can hear. The pendants are also made from pure moonstone, woven with elven song and starlight. They will give light, even in deep darkness and before the greatest evil."

"I'll trade you for both," I said decidedly, holding out a jagged piece of diamond thorn.

The woman's eyes widened at the sight of the small sliver, and Theron's words came back to me. I was supposed to haggle. "I would also like, uh, those cloaks," I said, pointing to two cloaks that sat behind her jewelry display.

I should get something for Fireheart.

What about Elvie? What does Elvie like?

"And, that bracelet there," I said, pointing to a delicate silver chain that was interwoven with sapphires, emeralds, and diamonds. "I'll add another half of a sliver to make the bargain agreeable."

The old woman smiled and nodded. "A good choice. The cloaks especially. They are of the same lore. You would do well to keep it with you, since its darkness has marked you."

Lovely. Yet another cryptic warning that I have no idea how to decipher. Just what I need for moral support.

I nodded, as if I understood her meaning, and took the goods from her. I slipped the chain of one of the pendants over my head and tucked it beneath my shirt and armor. I gained a small measure of comfort from the cool weight of it against my diaphragm. It clinked softly against the other necklaces and pendants I still wore.

It was silly, but I never took them off. I was irrationally afraid that, if I took them off, the things they were supposed to shield me from would come and attack me all at once.

The merchant touched two fingers to her forehead and bowed. "I have heard rumors that the darkness rises, and the ones of prophecy return. The rumors speak of the twins joining the Courts. One of fire, one of night." Her eyes bored into mine and I squirmed beneath their weight. "I know you are running, child of Grimm."

I took a step back, my heartbeat a frantic roar in my chest.

"You cannot outrun fate, Grimm. No matter what you do, no matter where you go. Your attempts to avoid her will bring you to the destiny that has been laid for you since the beginning—just with more heartbreak and sorrow than would have been necessary."

"I don't know what you're talking about," I whispered, the lie trembling in my voice.

Her gaze softened, and she shook her head. "You do, child, and that is what scares you the most."

I shook my head vehemently, unable to find the words. I gave her a quick bow of thanks and fled, searching for Theron.

Theron was five stalls down, engaged in a boisterous bartering argument with another merchant. What they were haggling over didn't register as I slipped my bag into his for safekeeping. Everything for Evadne was there. I had slipped the pendant, as well as the bracelet for Fireheart, into the pocket of the top pair of pants. She would find them when she woke. I knew it was a poor apology, but it was the best I could do without leaving an obvious note that could fall into the wrong hands.

Forgive me, Eva. Forgive me for putting you through this.

Theron held up a finger to the flustered merchant. "One second, mate," he said with a smile. He turned to me. "I do believe I said something about food, and your resemblance to death. Apparently, you thought bartering on an empty stomach was your best bet." He looked me up and down. "Hmm," he mused. "Doesn't seem like you did too terribly. You look as though you could kill death and take his place. So, I can't really complain." He pointed in the direction of the sun. "Go to the end of the street, over the hill. The vendors on that end have the best food this side of the Moores. Some chefs are better than Logan even." Theron gave me a stern look. "If you ever tell Logan I said that, I will string you up by your ankles and hang you over the side of the ship, upside down. Do you understand me?"

I nodded emphatically. I had no doubt he would make good on his threat.

"I'll be with you in a bit. I need to make this merchant see sense. He's being completely uncooperative about his prices, and it's making me quite volatile."

The merchant began to protest, and Theron held up a hand. "Just a moment, my good sir. You can insult me all you wish, once I'm done giving my ward her instructions." He gave me a little push. "Go eat. I'll be by in a bit, and we'll reassess then, okay?"

I nodded and made my way up the hill. The sun hung low on the edge of the island, painting the sky a bloody red. I stopped at the top, staring. Stark at the edge of a thick forest loomed the pale outline of jagged white stones.

The ruins.

The sun's almost down. We've wasted the whole day. How did we manage to waste that much time? It felt like a few minutes, an hour maybe...

I'm out of time. Darcy said I had until sundown.

I could still feel the agony of Evadne's torture. Baba Yaga had failed. He was going to kill her at sundown.

I don't have a choice.

I cast a lingering glance back at Theron, who was still engaged in his exuberant argument.

The sun was rapidly sinking toward the horizon.

I have to go. I'm sorry, Theron, but I have to go. I have to save my sister.

I made my way down the hill, past the vendors and away from the market. As soon as I was out of the chaos, I broke into a run and made my way toward the ruins.

I was almost out of time.

19

Jeremiah Once Again Ruins My Plans For The Day. (How RUDE)

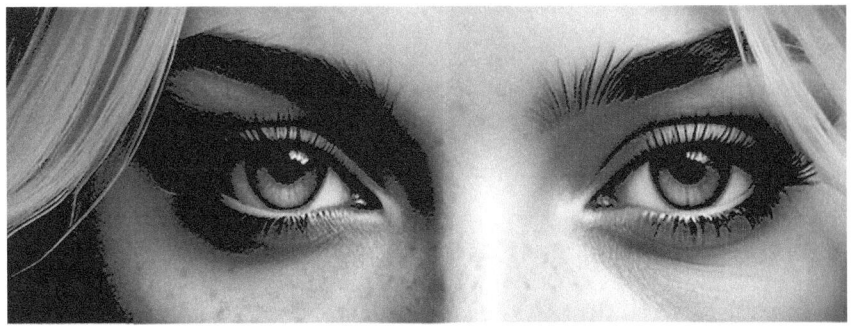

FAYE

"The most monstrous monster is the monster with noble feelings."
-Fyodor Dostoyevsky, The Eternal Husband

I knew something bad was going to happen when Jeremiah walked into the room with a large cat-that-ate-the-canary smile.

Something is definitely wrong. Either he had a stroke and is now permanently smiling, which is a horrible side effect, or he's about to engage in something terrible.

I dunno...maybe his fruit loops were extra fruity? I mean, you are what you eat.

If that's true, his fruit loops must have added ingredients such as 'daily dose of delusions,' 'hourly flares of psychotics,' and 'inescapable overdose of horridness.'

I don't think that's how ingredient labelling works.

Nobody asked you.

"Today we're doing things a little different, my little criminal."

Wait, wait, wait. Why am I a criminal? What did I do to deserve such a title?

I should be granted the opportunity to commit heinous crimes in the compound before he gets to call me a criminal.

For all he knows, I'm nothing but a kidnapped girl. He doesn't know anything about me.

My collective hoard of brain cells were hurriedly making new signs. The loyal three had yet to let the union crew *officially* join the cause, but that didn't stop the union crew. They were trying to outdo each other and prove their undying allegiance by making new signs professing the awfulness of Jeremiah. It was an assumption that, if they played to the fickle whims of the three, they would be allowed to rejoin and participate in the mayhem.

It was all my collective brain cells were truly interested in—mayhem. Lots and lots of mayhem.

I fully planned to live up to the delightful nickname Ronan had given me.

I didn't bother to give Jeremiah an answer. I simply continued to stare at the floor, arms crossed over my chest as I waited for Jeremiah to administer the daily dose of stupid Darke magic drugs.

C'mon, get it over with. I have things to do.

Like plot mayhem and take a nap.

Yeah. Something tells me by that smug look on his face, he's not just drugging me up.

"Seize her," Jeremiah ordered.

Well, looks like my plans for the day are going to be thoroughly derailed...

No! Doesn't he know it's against the rules to deny me the sacred daily nap?!

Ronan was nowhere in the group of his men, and something churned in my stomach. Did he know what was going on?

Marcov and James pushed into the room and grabbed my arms. Marcov was fumbling with a pair of handcuffs and I resisted the urge to roll my eyes. He was so *incredibly* incompetent.

Any day now, stupid head. I have things to do.

Yes! Like NAPPING!

At last, Marcov managed to get my hands secured behind my back, while James held onto one of my arms.

Marcov, never one to waste an opportunity, decided it was the perfect time to be a scumbag.

Fury raced over me as his fingers intentionally groped too low, and I didn't bother checking myself as I allowed my rage to take hold. I slammed my shoulders into him, wrenching my arm from James' grasp. My knee rammed into Marcov's groin, and he doubled over, gasping. James' arms wrapped around my torso, trying to subdue me, but I arched off of him, bringing my feet up as I slammed my weight into him and kicked out with all my strength.

My foot collided with Marcov's head, and he went flying backward. The back of his skull collided with a decided thud against the metal wall before he crumpled in a heap on the floor, out like a stone.

Jeremiah surveyed the scene, silent. His eyes were greedy and calculating. "What a magnificent creature you are. Who knows, perhaps by the end of this, you will be so far gone that you will no longer remember whose side you're on. You will make a valuable asset to my team if I can convince you of our aims. You and my Ronan could even find a happy end together. It could be what it always should have been."

Dude, stop trying to matchmake me. I will matchmake myself, thank you very much.

My three brain cells decided it was the perfect time for karaoke, and promptly began singing "Honor to Us All'" from *Mulan*. At the mention of matchmaking, the incredibly unhelpful hoard began to procure polaroid pictures of Ronan and *only* Ronan. It was clear who they wanted to matchmake me with.

Shut up, you stupid lot of buffoons.

They, of course, refused to listen. They only sang louder, while the hoard danced with pictures of Ronan and made absurd kissing noises.

How did they manage to take so many pictures of him grinning? That doesn't seem possible.

"Drag him out," Jeremiah ordered. Two men edged warily into the room, taking care to put as much distance between me and them as possible.

Yessss! I earned scary points! That's right. Realize my power! Cower you fools! Cower! Please bring honor to us, please bring honor to us aaaall...

I am bringing honor. By being scary and knocking out the ultimate scumbag, Marcov.

The other men didn't need to worry. As long as they minded their manners, I wasn't going to attack them. After all, what good would it do to use up all my strength in a useless fight against his men, while handcuffed, when something terrible clearly awaited me in the very near future?

No, it was better that I saved my energy. I had battles left to fight yet, and I needed my wits about me.

Jeremiah turned. "Bring her," he commanded as he left.

My unwilling escorts took a firm grip on my biceps and led me out of the room.

I'm going to put in a complaint with the good kidnapper's association that you are interrupting my nap time. This is against the rules.

I believe everything to do with kidnapping is against the rules.

Nobody asked you!

Jeremiah strolled leisurely down the hallways, as if he was at the beach on vacation, instead of in an underground compound about to torture the girl he kidnapped.

At last, Jeremiah stopped in front of a familiar wood door. "You do remember the last time you were here, don't you? I still haven't gotten all the blood off the floor. You did lose *ever* so much of it."

That's disgusting. I bet it smells absolutely awful in there.

What is this, round two with his awful tools of torture?

Let me remind you how the last session went, my creepy, psychotic kidnapper. You tortured me and got nothing out of me. You then threw a hissy fit and did unnecessary damage to my body, and you STILL got nothing out of me.

"No reaction? No recognition?" Jeremiah asked, giving me a fake pout of disappointment. "Never mind, you'll soon be afraid of this door and what it means."

No. I won't. It's a door. It means nothing except maybe firewood. If I'm feeling vindictive enough, when I escape here, I will come back someday, take it off its hinges, and burn it to ash. Then, I'll take the ash, and let a dragon use it as a litterbox. Maybe Fireheart would like that...

Fireheart would be happier roasting Jeremiah to a crisp. He likes me enough, I bet he'd do it for me too.

I bet he would. He really enjoys shenanagins and choas.

Jeremiah was still looking at me and I once again resisted the urge to roll my eyes.

What does he want? Me to break out into hysterics as I beg for him to just leave me alone?

No, thank you. I am tired of his dramatics and have no energy to give him any of my precious dramatics. I have to save them for important things.

Yeah, like all my chaos when I escape.

"Ah, the ever-stoic heroine. How long will your façade last, I wonder."

Longer than you'll ever live, you stupid, cod-brained, jerkhead.

I did not have face-to-face interrogation on my bingo cards for today.

No, I certainly did not. I had 'continued board meeting with brain cells to figure out logistics of chaos' on today's roster.

I should have a 'logistics of chaos department' within this company of brain cells.

Do you think my brain cells' company would be registered as an LLC or a corporation?

Hmm...good question. I'd have to confer with a tax expert. Does my brain cell hoard have a tax representative?

The hoard began to take a census and several cells stepped forward, claiming to be experts. After a careful examination, the three determined they were, in fact, lying. However, instead of yeeting them out of the interview room, the three allowed them to take up the job as tax representatives for it was immediately decided tax fraud was perfectly acceptable.

I'm well and truly doomed.

Jeremiah, irritated by my lack of response, huffed and swung the door open. I arched an eyebrow, amused as he angrily stalked into his study. My guards pushed me forward and I was forced to follow.

It was immediately evident that the dark presence within the room had grown since my last visit. Shadows lurked in every corner, prowling like animals, and a heavy, poisonous darkness emanated from the door.

In the middle of the room was a large, flat couch. Thick leather straps were attached every six inches. It was evident that it was a couch meant to hold a prisoner immobile.

Well, isn't this a lovely brew of messed up. Apparently, the chair was too docile for the second round of torture. What'll it be this time?

"Take the shirt, but leave her undershirt," Jeremiah ordered. "I need to see her arms."

At least I get to keep my undershirt this time.

I decided now was the time to struggle. James and the other man had their hands full as they tried to comply with Jermiah's orders and take off my shirt.

"Strap her in then cut it off. I don't care how you get it off, just do it!" Jeremiah barked angrily.

It took four of them to overpower me and get me on the cursed couch, and six to hold me in place while they strapped me down.

Jeremiah tsked disapprovingly. "And here I thought we had an understanding of how things were going to happen."

I glared up at him. If he wanted anger and dramatics, he was going to get it. But his attention had moved on. His gaze was fixed on my skin, tracing over the countless scars. "My, my, what you've already lived through...I'm amazed you're still breathing at all... Those monsters don't know when to stop, do they?"

I bared my teeth, wishing my canines had grown longer than they already had. I was desperately longing for fangs like Ríonach's. "I am one of those monsters," I snarled.

Perhaps I should let Ríonach turn me into a vampire just so I can have the cool teeth...

Cool teeth are not worth the cost of transformation. Plus, drinking blood? DISGUST-ING.

Jeremiah leaned forward and pulled at the chain around my neck until my locket rested in his palm. He hissed and dropped it, as if burned. Its familiar weight settled against the hollow of my throat.

"We both know you are something else entirely," Jeremiah replied, unamused by my bravery. He stood over me, gauging my ragged breath and straining muscles as I fought against the restraints.

I will not be afraid. I will not be afraid because of a monster like him. I am Faye Narah Grimm. I will not cower before a worthless man like him.

"Leave us," Jeremiah said quietly to his men.

Where is Ronan? Does he know what's going on? Surely, if he knew he would be here. He would try to curb his father's insanity.

Would he? Would he when there's so much at stake? We didn't talk about what to do if something like this happened...

I watched from the corner of my eye as Jeremiah's men filed out of the room, closing the door behind them.

Stupid Jeremiah. You're derailing my plans for the day. This was NOT what I had planned. I was going to spend the day planning how to thwart you. I was NOT planning on being tortured by you!

Once we were alone, Jeremiah's eyes went distant. He was staring at the door. "Faye, do you know why you're here?" he asked at last.

"Because you're a psychopath?" I offered helpfully.

Perhaps he doesn't know he's a psychopath.

Again, I think it's important to inform people of what they are. How can they ever hope to change if nobody tells them the truth?

Jeremiah laughed, a cold, humorless laugh. "No. I'm not the psychopath in this situation. No, my dear Faye. You're here because I need information. You're going to give me that information."

No. I most certainly am not going to give you that information.

Someone clearly woke up on the delusional side of the bed. There must have been a double dose of delusions in his fruit loops instead of just the daily dose.

"You may *think* you're going to resist me, but you're wrong. You see, my new friend created something very special. Something especially for you. A truth serum of sorts."

"It won't work," I snarled. "I'll lie. You'll never get real information from me."

"Maybe, maybe not. But you know how I'll know if it works or not?" Jeremiah hissed. "My new friend also told me a little secret about you. You have the most amazing tell." Jeremiah dug his nails into my forearm where the three burns marred my skin, marking me as a traitor. "Your body betrays you, little monster. When the truth is told, it marks you for the traitor that you are."

How does he know that? Who told him that? Who is his informant on the other side??

Real fear was beginning to creep through my body, plunging my stomach down, down, down through the floor.

No, he can't do this. How did he get a magic serum? How?

It was no longer a matter of withstanding his torture—refusing to break. No, he was taking away my ability to resist after all.

Maybe it's not real. Maybe he just wants me to think it's a truth serum so I won't resist as much. Maybe it's just a hallucinogenic toxin that causes pain to make it seem like I have to tell the truth...

Jeremiah walked over to his desk, humming. Seconds later, he came back with a large syringe in his hand. Black, swirling liquid churned inside.

That looks like something straight out of the Realm...and not just any part of the Realm, the Ruins.

This is not good. This is really, really bad.

Jeremiah slid the needle through my skin and into my vein. Cold flooded up my arm as he squeezed the cursed liquid into my bloodstream.

I was heaving as icy waves spread over my body. It was already taking effect.

"That's it," Jeremiah said, his voice menacingly soft. "You're going to be okay. Once this is all over, I'll release you."

Liar, liar, liar.

"Don't worry, my darling. You won't remember a thing."

"I am *not* your darling," I snarled.

I am Ronan's dear.

At this thought, my brain cells rallied, screaming their approval at such a wandering confession. They once again brought out their favorite polaroid pictures of him and began to sing and screech his praises. Soon, all I had left was the chant, 'Ronan's dear, Ronan's dear,' and my own personal reminder of who I was and what I was determined not to do.

I am Faye Narah Grimm. I will not be afraid. I will not say a word. I will not speak ANY truth.

I was fading, fading, fading. Sweet nothingness began to overwhelm me. I was falling so fast I couldn't find my way through to the other side.

Dreaming...it's all just a dream. A nightmare...

But why was I afraid? What's happening...what was I doing?

"What's your name?" an unfamiliar voice asked.

Wait.

It was familiar. I knew that voice. It was Mum's voice.

Mum! Mum, I've missed you so much!

Wait...wasn't there something I was supposed to be remembering? Wasn't there something going on?

"Darling," Mum called, pulling me close into a long hug. "What's your name?"

"You know my name," I whispered, smiling up at her. "You know me, I'm your daughter. You gave me your middle name. Faye, Narah Grimm. Like the fairytales."

I was floating, drifting in sweetness, held in my mother's arms as we laughed and talked. Catching up after so many, many years apart. "I miss you, Mum," I whispered. "You wouldn't believe what they've done to me...You wouldn't believe what happened in that place."

"Tell me all about it, my darling girl."

I couldn't remember why I had been afraid, but my fear had since fled, leaving in its place peace and rest as I answered all her questions and hugged her tightly. Why I was afraid of letting her go, I couldn't remember. But I had the terrible fear that, if I did, I'd never get her back again.

20

To Save The Ones You Love

EMBER

"I have never understood where the line is drawn, between self-sacrifice
and self-slaughter."
-Wolf Hall by Hiliary Mantel

Every step forward intensified the pain in my body as I ran toward the castle ruins. The fiery agony that had subsided to a dull ache was now rekindled into an unbearable inferno. But instead of hindering me, the inferno pushed me forward. My determination to save my sister hardened into unbreakable steel as the connection at the edge of my mind with Darcy grew louder and louder.

He was laughing as my sister screamed.

At last, he had won.

He knew I was coming.

Horror was growing with my determination. My wrist was burning. The mark he'd forced on me was agony. It felt as if my hand was burning off at the wrist.

Ravens circled the ruins, screaming out a warning as I approached, announcing my arrival as I forced myself to take step after terrified step.

Find me in the depths.

Darkness beckoned me forward as the shadows lengthened around me. The sun was gone, sunk behind the trees. My time was running out. I was here, but I hadn't found Darcy yet.

Find me in the depths...the depths of what, despair?

Perhaps I should start calling him Prince Humperdinck.

The humorous thought did little to chase my fear away.

A jagged opening had been blasted into the side of the castle, gaping like the maw of a monster. As I crept closer, I could make out stairs—descending down, down, down into deep darkness.

Brave, I have to be brave for Evadne's sake. She needs me.

I will be brave.

Cut out the heart...

I drew a dagger and began to inch my way down the crumbling steps. Five steps down I could no longer see my hand in front of my face.

I have to save Evadne. I will face any horror, any monster, to save her. I will kill Darcy, and this time I'll make sure he dies.

The steps were slick under my feet, coated in damp moss and crumbling from rot. Every inch further was treacherous.

I gripped my knife harder, trying to calm my panicking breaths as the walls pressed in around me. The darkness was a physical presence, compressing me on every side, weighing me down with every moment that passed.

Bad memories and nightmares were resurfacing in my mind. Things and feelings I had forgotten were rising to the surface, tormenting me once again.

I don't want to remember these things. I don't want to relive this.

My foot slipped, and before I could regain my balance, I was tumbling down the stairs. I bit back a scream as I landed with a crash in a pile of something. They were loose, and they clattered around me, the sound hollow and distinct.

Bones.

Forget the bones—we'll deal with the horror of that later. Where did my knife go?

Did I stab myself and I just don't know it yet?

A quick pat down put my worries to rest. I had not impaled myself, but I was still disarmed.

Knife. I have to find my knife.

I was groping through the darkness, frantically searching for my knife.

I need a flashlight. I should have brought matches, or a torch. I should have thought ahead instead of plunging headfirst into trouble...

"Poor little bird, trapped in this darkness..."

Darcy's voice was everywhere. Behind me, in front, bouncing off the walls as his presence slithered over me.

My efforts intensified and I tore at my throat, trying to grab the right chain for the moonstone.

Why did I tuck it into my armor? Why didn't I think ahead?

"If only I didn't have to clip your wings...you could just fly away..."

Fingers drifted across the back of my neck and then my torso.

I screamed and jerked back, abandoning my efforts as panic overwhelmed everything.

Forget the knife, you have others.

Right, I have others.

Light at last flared from the pendant in my hand. My stomach clenched as I looked around in horror. I was in a dungeon, chains and cells surrounding me. But the worst thing was, there was clearly no way out except the way I had come. It was a tiny, tight little box of a room with a singular staircase leading up and out.

Get out. I have to get out of here!

Not yet! We can't. Evadne's life depends on it.

I wanted to run. Run until I couldn't make it another step. Until I was so far away from this monster that he couldn't hurt me anymore...so he couldn't hurt anyone I loved anymore.

The final detail clicked into place. The room was empty. Darcy was nowhere to be seen.

I turned in a frantic circle, the light bouncing eerily off the walls as I searched for the monster.

"Poor girl," he whispered from behind me. "You're so scared." His breath was warm on the tips of my ears.

A shiver ran down my spine and I whirled around. Again, I found nothing behind me but my own shadow that flickered and bounced in the moonstone's light.

"Where are you?!" I yelled, trying to contain my terror.

"Where do you think I am?" he hissed. His lips were on my neck, tracing an invisible pattern down my skin that burned like fire. The smell of sweet peppermint was everywhere in the small space.

I was dizzy and nauseous as I frantically turned. Again, he wasn't there.

Am I dreaming? Is this real or am I imagining him here? Have I even woken up? Is this just another horrible nightmare? An omen to warn me of what's to come?

"For someone who came to take the place of her sister—a courageous act in and of itself—I expected you to be braver, *Mon Oisillon.*" His voice was disapproving, taunting me.

Hysteria was pulling me apart and I couldn't stop the trembling as the memories began to rise—images from the nightmares I'd been having until Artemis began to take my dreams.

Artemis, how could I ever think you'd do this to me? How could I have ever thought that you'd do something so horrendous?

"Sweet, lovely memories, are they not?" Darcy whispered. His breath accosted my senses, smelling like rot and mint. Like he was festering from the inside out. "I had to give you some outside perspective. Your memories were so...one sided. You never even gave me a chance to see what we could be. How *wonderful* it all could have been."

He's been sending me all those nightmares. It wasn't my subconscious adding things...he was sending them the whole time.

Bile rose in my throat as the scent of peppermint at last overwhelmed my senses.

Not the mint, anything but the mint.

"Hello, *Mon Oisillon,*" Darcy murmured. "Did you miss me? I'm impressed. You put on your battle armor just for me?" His fingers trailed down my arm. "There's no need for it. I'm not going to kill you...why would I kill you after all this *exhausting* effort to get you back?" He laughed softly, the sound cruel and cold. "Though, I can't deny how fierce you look. How stunning. Your time in the Moores has aged you, and my, look at your ears..." Something brushed the sensitive tips of my ears. "You got your elven ears." He hummed in satisfaction. "My heart trembles before you, my lovely bride. I'd get on my knees and surrender to you, if you demanded it."

You'd be easier to kill if you were on your knees, that's for sure.

Careful, careful. You have to get Evadne free first. Then you can kill him—repeatedly if need be.

Because apparently the man doesn't understand the term die. He must be part cockroach, you just have to try extra hard to make sure his disgusting self is dead.

I forced myself to stay still, panic fluttering as memories began to move faster and faster. They showed the Farewell ball, but there was something wrong with them...they were from the wrong perspective. They weren't mine...no, I saw myself through someone else's eyes.

The only person who was there who remembers, is Evadne...

Realization slammed into me. He had taken her memories while he kept her captive.

But these memories aren't right...I didn't act like that. I didn't cling to him, practically swooning...there's something wrong with these memories...

"You're so smart, *Mon Oisillon*. You don't miss a thing, do you? I'll tell you, since you've figured me out. I altered her memories. I made them right. She remembered that glorious dance in such a negative light. I've fixed *all* her memories of us."

I'm going to kill him. I'm going to rip his heart out. Forget cutting it out, I'll rip it out with my bare hands.

You have to get Evadne free first.

"I'm here," I called, still turning in circles as I searched for him. "I came, just like you wanted. Now let her go."

"I didn't tell you what I'd do when you came. I just warned you that if you didn't, I'd kill her."

The ground seemed to shift beneath me as I wracked my memory. What had he really said?

"You, you did!" I cried, my voice breaking.

No, this can't be right.

"Implication is nothing, my dear. It is simply, well, a small manipulation of your *very* large assumptions."

Hands wrapped around my forearm, and someone jerked me around. At last, I came face to face with the monster that had haunted my nightmares, my waking days.

Pale blue and gray light from the moonstone cast his face in horrifying shadows. There seemed to be monsters shifting and crawling across his skin within the dark patches. The buttons of his shirt were open halfway down his chest. The collar gaped, revealing an angry, blood red scar that sliced across his throat. Black tendrils wrapped around the scar, branching out from the wound and across his neck and chest, as if someone had stitched him back together with darkness.

How is he still alive?

He stared down at me, eyes malicious and hungry. "Welcome to the real world. You make foolish assumptions, you lose everything."

Horror sliced over me. I had done what he demanded, and in doing so, I'd fallen directly into his trap. My desperation to save my sister had blinded me. I *had* assumed that, in coming, he would let her go. Stupid. I was so incredibly *stupid*. I had listened to my fear and let myself be manipulated.

I'll have to bargain, negotiate. Something, anything. I can't let my coming be in vain.

"You have me," I whispered desperately. "You have no further reason to hold her."

"On the contrary, love. I have every reason to hold her. For you see, when I hold her," he trailed a hand down my cheek. "You become so *pliable*. So docile. She is your undoing, for she is one of the only things you love within this place. Your brother is not mine, not yet...your other sister is occupied. So, I will take the only tool I can get. Who better than the one you shared the womb with? Your heart, your love, your *twin sister*." His voice was triumphant. "Yes, when I have her, I have you. Her blood will set the knight free, and I will have you without contention while he destroys that meddling prince and his entire kingdom. After what they *did* to him...he will make them rue the day they ever bound him to the Ruins."

Darcy stared down at me and hot rage rose within my chest. It was a fire that coursed over my body, overwhelming the fiery pain that pulsed in the back of my mind from his torturing Evadne.

I glared up at him, helpless fury tearing me apart.

What do I do, what do I do?

"I'll give you a bone," Darcy whispered, still staring down at me. "A wedding gift for my lovely bride to be. Kiss me, and you haven't come in vain. Refuse to and she'll be dead. The sun is down, the witch has failed. Why do you think she sent you to the market? She knew she could not fight me and win. The *great* Baba Yaga herself tries and fails against my power. She forgets that I was there before she consumed her first human and embraced the darkness that cursed her for such an abomination. She forgets I was in the depths before she ever tried to harness it. She is *nothing* to my power. Why do you think she betrayed you in your bargain and sent you to that market—ensuring you had a way to come. She knew she wasn't going to be able to free your sister, and she was loath to let the treasured thorns go. No, my love, no one is more powerful than I am. No one save the Darke King himself."

But Marcovester Red bested you. She killed you...she held you...

Horror was rushing over me in wave after wave as I frantically tried to find a way out, find a different way to make him free my sister.

If I kill him, will it let her go? Will she be safe, or will killing him while he has her in the darkness kill her too?

I didn't know, but it was a risk I couldn't take.

"Tick-tock, Tick-tock. I won't offer again," Darcy murmured as he drew back one step and then another. "This is your final, *noble*, chance to save her. After all, that's why you came, isn't it? To give your life for your sister's? You came to take her place, didn't you?"

His words hung in the air between us, as his lustful gaze made me shudder.

I wanted to throw up, to run until I was safe. To hide until the nightmare ended and the world went back to normal—back to the way it was.

"Swear it," I whispered, hardly processing what I was about to do. What I was agreeing to do in exchange for her.

But didn't I know it all along? Didn't I know I would give my life to keep her safe?

I don't know. I came to kill him.

You can kill him after.

What did I think I was going to do to save her? Valiantly fight him to the death and thus free her? Did I think I would stab him heroically and simply get away unstained? Untainted?

There are no heroic ends, no brave deeds. Only the horror of the real world and what lies within each man's depravity.

Darcy's lips curled up in a smile. He had me and he knew it. "I swear," he drawled. "That, if you kiss me, and by kiss, I mean *really* kiss me, and I am satisfied with your affection, then I will release your sister..." His eyes were malicious as he stared at me. "I swear by all the stolen blood that binds my cursed, deceased heart."

Triumph exuded from him and despite my best intentions of bravery, I trembled before him.

"But I'll be the judge of that kiss, *Mon Oisillon.* I'll be able to tell whether you really mean it or not. But, I'll give you another bone. You can keep trying until I am satisfied. Even if it takes *years.*"

I shuddered at the thought.

It's okay. Just get it over with. Just imagine it's Artemis. Pretend you're somewhere else, anywhere else.

Darcy snarled. "You keep that insufferable *prince* out of your mind, or else the deal is *off.*"

Monster. You're a monster. What did I ever do to deserve this? Why? Why me?

I swallowed, nodding.

"You're right about the monster part, though. I *am* a monster. But you'll find they're making you into a monster, too. I'm just trying to save you from my path."

What does he mean?

Darcy's promise settled between us, the strings that tied the bargain to his twisted mind taunting me with every second that passed. All that remained was the one action that haunted my nightmares. The revolting taste of mint and the horrifying texture of his lips on mine—the violation of myself that I swore I would never allow to happen again.

What is he waiting for?

I said I would. Why is he delaying?

My pride roared as it dawned on me. He expected me to come to him. To go to him, and kiss him, as if *I* wanted him.

I will destroy you. I will tear you apart until there is nothing left. I will destroy your memory from the face of the earth.

How can I, when he haunts my memories? My life, my waking hours?

My knees nearly gave out as I took a step forward, but he made no move to help as I struggled to regain my balance. I took a deep breath, fixing my gaze on the hideous scar on his neck as I took another step. If Marcovester could inflict such a wound on someone who claimed to be so powerful, I could do this.

"Eyes on mine, love," Darcy murmured. "I can't *really* believe the earnestness in a kiss if you're looking anywhere but *deep* into my eyes. Besides, it's just insulting to look at the scar. That scar is your fault. Don't think we won't talk about *that* little rebellion later," he snarled.

Bile rose, but I forced it back down. I had to do this. Evadne would be free if I did this. I could kill him after.

I raised my eyes, meeting his gaze. I spaced my focus, sure I was making eye contact, but I wasn't actually there. I was looking through him as I imagined myself somewhere else. Somewhere far, far away. A place where he couldn't hurt me, or the people I loved, anymore.

Six inches, then four, two, a breath.

"I will destroy you for this," I hissed, unable to help myself.

"I'm counting on it, *Mon Oisillon*," he taunted. "Just remember, what you destroy, destroys you in the process."

I would embrace destruction if it meant his undoing. I would welcome any end to silence the guilt of what I was about to do. I would let the darkness take me, if it erased the memories of what he'd done to me.

Green eyes rose to the surface of my mind, his lips a breath away as he whispered words I hadn't realized I was longing for. *It means nothing if you are not by my side.*

Forgive me, Artemis. Please forgive me.

I pushed the memories away. I couldn't risk Darcy sensing them and calling off our bargain.

I closed my eyes and pulled his head down to mine.

The first touch, as the stench of peppermint overwhelmed my senses, threatened to destroy me. I fought the crippling urge to bolt. I wanted to retch, hold my head and scream until my voice was obliterated.

The strange shadows in the room pounced, overwhelming my poor defenses and ripping into my mind.

I cried out. Pain was mixed into my desperation as he forced his hunger and desire on me, shoving his tainted longing down, down, down, until it covered everything.

I was drowning, and his mark burned on my wrist as I plunged beneath the tumultuous waves, trying to drown myself. Seeking to erase the memories, the screams and the horrified awareness of what I was doing to save my sister.

21

Dying Light

Ember

"Yes, you will rise from the ashes, but the burning comes first. For this
part, darling, you must be brave."
-Kalen Dion

The light inside me's dying,
I stand and watch it fade,
how do I come back from this,
when there's nothing I can say.
The darkness holds a secret,
a truth I wish to hide,
fear has come to feed on me,
it slowly drains my life.
I'm drifting on the ocean's waves,
and floating far away.
Far beyond this painful world,
that steals the light of day.
Every breath is agony,

was it worth all I have lost?
To save the ones I love the most,
but paid a bloody cost?
There's a child on the shoreline,
her words have morphed to screams,
she begs and cries "don't leave me here,"
this little girl is me.
I'm leaving to protect her,
to spare her from this pain,
for I have lived through far too much,
and I'll never be the same.
She's safer on that island,
even if she's left alone,
the monsters cannot harm her there,
it holds hope to live and grow.
How do I come back from this,
can I ever find my way?
When everything's been burned to ash,
and nothing's left but pain?
Is there hope beyond the wreckage,
of all I thought I'd be?
I'm trapped beneath the taint of loss,
and grief is all I see.

22

I Was Not Worth The Price

EVADNE

"Inside me, something seethes. Inside me, some feral animal claws at
my ribcage, trapped."
-Molly McCully Brown, From Places I've Taken My Body: Essays

For a moment, the absence of pain seemed impossible, unreal. All of a sudden, the torture and torment, the claws shredding my mind to bits over and over again, simply stopped.

Is this real? Is it a joke? Is he testing me to make me think it's over?

Am I dead?

Is this death? Wrapped in stillness and silence forever?

"Run."

Ember's voice was a ragged gasp. A wall was immediately erected after her plea. Her words held far too many secrets—secrets she didn't want me to find.

What did you do, Em?

Wait, what if it's a trick? A trap?

She re-engaged the bond. *"Run, Eva. You have to run. Now, before it's too late."* Her voice echoed around me, thick with desperation and pain.

What did you do, Em? What did you do?

She was stubbornly, almost frantically trying to hide something from me as her subconscious brushed against mine. She shoved at me, begging me to leave as she cried. She was blocking out a nightmare—no, reality. Terror and loss slammed into me, so potent it threatened to knock me to my knees.

"Run, Eva. You have to run right now. Please, please go. You're safe now. Escape. PLEASE escape."

The chains had disappeared. Nothing held me to the pillar anymore. Darcy was nowhere to be seen.

Darcy has her.

The realization hit me as his words came and stabbed my heart. "She'll come for you. You just need to scream."

I fell to my knees, sobbing.

No, Em. Please, no. I'm not worth it. Please, please. Don't do this.

The shadowy figure on the throne, the Erlking, rose, towering over me. "Run, little Grimm," he hissed angrily. "For you will not be granted another chance. When I see you again, you will not be so fortunate. I will not again allow him to be so lenient with his bargains."

Not if, but when.

Power rolled off him and rushed over me in a sickening wave. It promised destruction and heartbreak. It swore to bring the Realm to its knees.

I trembled, scrambling backward over the fallen chunks of stone, not daring to take my eyes off him.

He laughed and pain spiked in my mind, a dagger that cut my defenses to shreds. "I have enjoyed our time together, little one. You'll see me again. The dreams are only the beginning. I will come for you."

"RUN!" Ember screamed.

I didn't waste another moment. I turned on my heels and fled, running as fast and far as I could.

The darkness seemed as if it would never end. I had no idea where I was going. How did one escape a world such as this? Was I awake or dreaming? How did I find my body again?

"Evadne."

I jolted awake.

My arms and legs were tangled in a blanket, and I struggled to free them. I had to run, to get away from the monster. I had to save my sister.

My eyes felt thick and heavy. It was a struggle to get them to open. My left eye was especially stubborn, as if held closed by a thick, unmoving material.

My eye. Darcy cut through my eye.

I reached a trembling hand up, praying it wasn't real. That it hadn't actually happened. My fingers brushed the bandage and fear hit me like a blow to the gut. I was truly blind in one eye.

This is the Realm, it'll heal.

But what if it doesn't?

What if I can never dance again? Fight, move, be free...

We're in a magical world. Can't somebody just heal it?

Details came to me in bits and pieces through my right eye. I was in an unfamiliar room. Thin strands of fading sunlight filtered through thick, dusty glass. An old woman leaned over me, her pale white eyes reflecting eerily in the candlelight. To my right, another unfamiliar woman sat. She was young and beautiful, ethereal. Deep black eyes stared at me, assessing the situation. My gaze followed the black and silver swirls across her cheekbones, down her jaw.

If Jack was here, he'd be flirting with her...

Wait, Jack should be here. Where is he?

Maybe he's out looking for a snack... A snack for Jack... A snacky snack for Jacky-Jack...

Ha! And Ember has the audacity to say I don't have the potential to be a poet. She may be one of deep and wonderful words, but I am capable of snarky poetry. Just wait till I tell her—

My rambling, disconnected thoughts ended abruptly.

Ember.

Darcy has Ember.

Darcy is Bluebeard.

I have to get to her. I have to help her. Where is she?!

Where am I?!

"EMBER!" I yelled as I jerked upright, nearly smacking heads with the old woman.

My voice was ragged, throat raw, as if I had been screaming for hours and hours on end.

"You're safe, child," the old woman soothed gently.

Her voice is familiar...she's the one who tried to pull me away from the Knight...

"No," I rasped. "Ember, she's in—"

The door burst open, interrupting my desperate plea.

A man rushed in. He was tall and muscular with light brown hair and a closely shaved beard. His pale silver eyes were tight with worry. "Verity!" he called urgently.

The woman sitting beside my cot stood and went to meet the man.

She must be Verity. What a lovely name. I wonder if she tells the truth, or if her name is simply ironic.

"We have a problem," the man said in a low voice.

"What is it, Theron?" Verity snapped. "Where is the girl?"

"She disappeared," Theron replied.

Verity swore vehemently. "I told you!" she hissed. "I *told* you she was hiding something. I told you not to let her out of your sight."

"I know," Theron replied. "But she was doing so well, and her emotions were stable. I watched her the whole time she was bartering, and she was fine, just fine. So, I sent her to get food."

"She can't have just disappeared," Verity replied irritably. "Did you scan everyone there?"

"I did."

Verity swore again. "I told you taking her to the market was a bad idea There are too many bounty hunters there. Someone probably snatched her."

Why would bounty hunters want her? Is there a bounty on our heads? What happened while I was out?

They have the wrong idea. I know where she is.

"I checked into that already. Raz confirmed. She didn't get snatched by the bounties. She's still listed. She's not at the market."

"Her sister just woke up," Verity said as understanding dawned on her face. "Do you think?"

Theron nodded, jaw clenched. "She got desperate. I think it was the eye that pushed her over the edge. Whoever it was, was communicating with her. Threatening her over a silencing bond."

My fingers once again reached up toward my injured eye, and the old woman stopped me. "No child, no. Not yet."

I was falling, exhaustion hitting me like a blow to the head. I could barely keep my good eye open. The room was lopsided, cast in darkness on one side.

No! I can't fall back asleep. Not yet. I have to tell them. I have to help Ember!

What if falling asleep takes me back? I don't want to go back!

"He has her," I rasped.

Theron blanched and Verity punched him in the arm. "Were you not paying attention?" she snapped. "I told you she woke up."

"The ghost speaks," Theron replied, trying to cover up his surprise with a joke.

"Who has her?" Verity said, ignoring Theron.

"He..." I rasped, my words held at bay by the silencing spell. My wrist burned as I struggled to find my way through it. "Bluebeard," I choked out. "He has her...he's going to hurt her."

"The vendors say they saw her go in the direction of the woods."

"The woods lead to those ruins...that's a convenient place to hide out."

"That's impossible," the old woman whispered as Verity and Theron quicky left. "Bluebeard is dead. I killed him."

"It's him," I whispered. "It's him and he held you at bay. He's powerful enough he held you at bay and you know it."

"No one can hold me at bay," the old woman seethed, denying my accusation.

"He did," I gasped as the exhaustion grabbed hold of me and dragged me back under. I never wanted to sleep again, but despite my best intentions the nothingness swept me away and the world went cold.

23

Stupid, Meddling Human

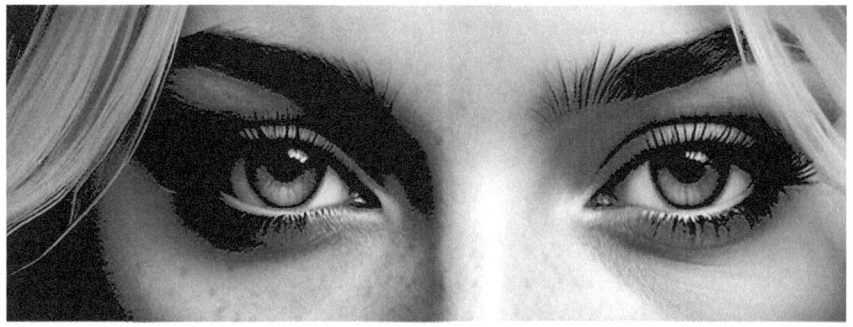

FAYE

"You were destined for the glory, the honor and the fame. I was destined
for the bullet, to be the gun with no name. Fate's been playing the game
on us, sweetheart."

-a.j.

My mind was a tangle of grey fog and questions that didn't make sense. I couldn't remember anything.

Why can't I remember anything?

What happened?

Why does everything hurt?

I cracked my eyes open. Ronan sat beside my bed, holding his head in his hands. His shoulders were shaking, as if crying.

Why is Ronan crying? What did he do?

What did I do?

Moments and memories came back in pieces.

My mother... I was talking to Mum...was it a dream?

Wait...

Moments prior to that came flooding back.

Jeremiah decided to ruin my day... Ronan was nowhere to be found... The toxin... Toxin from the Ruins. Jeremiah poisoned me, he said it would make me tell the truth... Stupid meddling human, what has he done?!

But he was bluffing...wasn't he? That wasn't real, was it?

Did I?

I pushed against the foggy haze, trying and failing to put the pieces together.

"What happened?" I rasped. My voice was raw, barely more than a cracked whisper—as if I had been screaming for hours on end.

Ronan jerked at the sound of my voice, quickly wiping his cheeks. His stormy gray eyes were almost black, lids red rimmed and puffy. His cheeks were pale and tear-stained. "Faye..." his voice faltered, and my worry grew.

"What happened?" I whispered.

"I didn't know," Ronan sniffed. "I didn't know what was happening. Jeremiah put me on an obscure guard duty at the edge of the compound. Nobody but he knew where I was. I should have known he was up to something; he never does that. By the time James found me, Jeremiah had been at you for hours."

What was Jeremiah doing? What happened? Surely...surely I didn't...

My gaze lowered to my bandaged left arm. Fire pulsed across my skin.

No, no. Please, no.

"Nobody did anything," Ronan whispered angrily. "Everyone could hear the screams. I could hear them from four hallways away, and nobody was doing *anything*."

"Why would they?" I asked raggedly. "I'm a prisoner here. Everyone either wants to hear the screams or is too afraid of your father to do the right thing."

"He's not my father," Ronan replied vehemently. "I do not claim him as such."

"Jeremiah," I amended, trying to shift into a different position and prop myself up.

"Easy, easy," Ronan said hurriedly as he helped me settle. "Easy, Faye. You shouldn't be moving yet."

I sighed. "Yes, yes, mother hen," I griped. "But we need to talk... I..." my voice faltered as I stared down at my arms. "I need to see what he did to me."

"No," Ronan cut in sharply. "Faye, don't...he, he..." Ronan's voice broke. "Do you remember the time you accidentally let that one, tiny detail slip?"

I nodded.

"It's that," Ronan whispered in shame. "He...he somehow made you talk. The burns go up your left forearm."

"Just the left?" I whispered.

Ronan nodded. "When I got there...you were out of your mind. You were..."

"I was talking to my mother," I said, dazed.

Ronan nodded. "Talking, then screaming, then talking some more. All the while, he was asking you questions...somehow you thought he was your mother."

"He poisoned me." I sniffed. "It's a...a new toxin. I...I don't remember anything, except my mother's voice."

"I don't know what to do," Ronan said, hanging his head. "Last week it felt as if we had hope. As if we were going to take on the world. But now?"

"We're still going to take Jeremiah down," I whispered. "We just...we have to think things through a little more. We just have to...to adjust our course a little, a little bit."

I was sobbing, desperately trying to think. I was once again reduced to three brain cells; the enthusiastic hoard had hidden themselves—accepting defeat.

It was exactly that. Defeat.

My loyal three were hiding in the corner, sobbing and terrified of what had happened. Slowly, the hoard surrounded them, wailing and crying to try to make them feel better. There was a monster in the back of my mind now, prowling around the edges, and it didn't belong.

Jeremiah's toxin had done more than just forced me to tell the truth. It had let something in.

"I'm a danger to our plan," I whispered raggedly. "If he asks me about any of this, I can't resist. It's not...of human origins."

Ronan sighed. "I know," he replied quietly. "But we don't have another option. You are still my only hope."

"And if you find another way? Another hope? Will you discard me?" My voice broke and I choked on a sob. The possibility of a split, of being abandoned, suddenly seemed too much to bear.

Ronan's eyes held pity and sadness, and I braced myself for the obvious answer. He was going to leave me to face the darkness alone. "Faye," he murmured as he gingerly took my hand. "You will *always* be my only hope. You are everything to me. Both now and if we find a different route." He stared down at our hands, at the way I desperately clung to him. In this moment of pain and uncertainty, he was my lifeline in the churning sea.

"I asked you to swear not to stab me in the back," he said quietly. "I wouldn't ask that of you, without being willing to give you the same level of trust. I know my word isn't binding like yours, but Faye, I *promise* you I will not stab you in the back. I will not turn on you. We're in this together, and live or die, I will not leave you behind. I will stay with you to my dying breath."

"If you find a different path, you should take it," I sobbed. "I am not worth the cost of your life."

"You are," Ronan replied softly, so softly I almost doubted what I heard.

"I am not worth the cost of your sister," I pressed.

Ronan laughed ruefully. "Again, that is no longer a predicament we have to worry about."

"Right," I sighed. "Ronan it's not going to work if she's going to refuse to leave without me. We have to get her out first thing."

She doesn't have to know that I'm coming back to this place when Ronan and I get her out...

Ronan shook his head and sighed. "After you saved her life and then our last attempt failed, she decided it was because I was abandoning you."

I pondered his words.

Ronan shrugged. "Maybe she's right, Faye. Maybe all my plans fail because you're still trapped here. Perhaps fate is punishing me for kidnapping you in the first place."

"We'll never know for sure. All we can do is move forward from where we are," I replied quietly.

"We need to find a way to cut those interrogations short," Ronan said, switching topics abruptly.

"We can't," I sighed. "If you do it now, Jeremiah will suspect. This is his shiny new form of interrogation, and he thinks it's working." I gestured to my injured arms in defeat. "It is working...but it's going to stop working eventually. I'm sure of it. I'll overpower it, like I've overpowered the poison. We'll move then. How long have I been out?" I asked hesitantly.

"Four days."

"Four?" I cried, shocked.

Ronan nodded. "I...I was beginning to worry you wouldn't wake up at all."

That's why he was crying.

"Okay, well...the plan is still the same as it was...it just has an unfortunate intermission. The end goal is still solitary confinement and getting Meghan out."

Ronan frowned down at his hands.

Do I have to spell everything out for him?

"For now, you continue to tell him of my affection toward you. Elaborate. Tell him when I woke up, I was clinging to you. Now, we both know that's a lie, because again, *cooties*, but it will do the trick."

Ronan snorted and glanced down at our entwined fingers.

I chose to ignore him. I wasn't ready to let him have his hand back yet.

I can live with some cootie contamination if the tradeoff is getting to hold his hand a little longer. It's comforting.

The brain cells all roared in agreement. They were absolutely enthralled by this new development of hand holding with their lovely Ronan. Polaroid pictures of our entwined hands were rapidly going up on the multiple bulletin boards around my mind.

"Anyway," I continued, trying to pick up the lingering bits and pieces of my thoughts and ignore my lovesick brain cells. "So, when I begin to overpower the drugs and this form of interrogation stops working, you offer a solution. Suggest a little good cop, bad cop that ends in solitary confinement. Plot with him to weave in a little savior complex. Tell him you're going to protest the solitary confinement, and you're also going to suggest that Marcov takes me. Tell him that I absolutely loathe Marcov—"

"No," Ronan cut in sharply. "Not him."

Stop interrupting me, you stupid idiot!

"It has to be him," I replied, just as severely. "My mind is a little foggy from all the *torture*, but I believe we've had this argument before. If you take me, it'll ruin the appeal of the savior complex. If Jeremiah takes me, he'll be too tempted to come back. Marcov needs to take me. Just do me a favor and make sure you're back in his good graces enough that he lets you do the daily honors of delivering his poisonous cocktail, and don't drug me for a day or two. Or if you haven't won him over, send James after us. If Marcov tries anything, I'll knock him out. I have more training than he does. The only reason he's ever tried anything is because I've been weak and helpless." My rage rose at the very essence of those words. "Pig," I muttered under my breath.

"Okay, so, I put you in solitary, then what?"

"Everything goes on as we originally planned," I replied. "Hidey hole with a poster, I train your sister, and then I initiate the next step of the plan."

"And what will that look like?" he asked quietly. "You said disable the system, but how?"

I sighed. "I have a general idea of what I'm going to do, but I'm not going to think about it anymore and hammer out the details until I get out of these interrogations. I'm worried if I figure it out, it might slip out during an interrogation session. But I am going to need you to connect my computer to the internet. I have a VPN so it shouldn't alert Jeremiah's system of the use. But I need my laptop to update."

"Do you really think you can pull it off?" Ronan asked anxiously.

Of course I can pull it off, you stupid, doubting, ninny-headed potato!

My head was beginning to hurt as my brain cells collectively hurled obscure insults at Ronan in my defense. I rubbed at my temples, sorry I had been offended in the first place.

"Sorry," Ronan said apologetically. "I just—"

"I know," I cut in gently. "I *am* offended you don't think I can do it, but I'm too tired to be angry with you. Right now, I feel like I'm about three brain cells short…"

At this unthinking comment, my three loyal brain cells roared in outrage and began to protest *my* thoughtlessness—which only resulted in moving my headache straight to migraine status.

"But," I continued, trying to ignore the shrieks of indignation. "I assure you I will be successful. I have to be, for all our sakes."

I need a nap.

Stupid Jeremiah. Stupid, meddling, ignorant, jerk of a human!

"For now, I'll put duct tape over any holes in my plan and that'll take care of it."

Ronan raised an eyebrow. "Duct tape?"

"Duct tape," I stated. "I also have superglue and spite if I need it."

Ronan ignored my feeble attempt at humor. "Can you hold out?"

I scoffed, putting on a brave façade. "My dear Ronan, if spite can keep me alive in a certain place of which I cannot speak, for eight torturous years. Not to mention the time I've spent enduring *your* awful 'health food' cooking. Then I can survive a few more weeks of your lunatic father."

Ronan put up his fingers to his head, a crooked smile on his face. "Dear Ronan?" he laughed.

"NO!" I snapped, backpedaling. "I did not say dear Ronan…I said…"

"My dear Ronan," Ronan replied, poking me in my uninjured arm with his own improvised finger horns.

"You're a bad influence," I griped. "You're rubbing off on me with your idiotic pleasantries. How *dare* you make me pleasant!"

"The feeling is mutual...my dear," he laughed. "I've clearly picked up some of your equally bad habits. Besides, it'll do you some good to have some pleasantness—you're downright sour some days."

"I refuse to be pleasant," I retorted haughtily. "It'll ruin my reputation."

The banter continued, but beneath the humor the undeniable taint of fear remained. Time was running out, and we both knew it.

24

Can I Ever Forget These Tainted Moments? Can Death Purge Me Of These Memories?

EMBER

"The finest souls are those who gulped pain and avoided making others

taste it."

-Nizar Qabbani

I was drifting on the ocean, wrapped in darkness. Silence engulfed everything as I forced my mind to shut down. I was away, far away from my body until all that remained was the ocean's rise and fall. The crash of the water on the sand. The sound of the waves beneath the surface. I was alone and the world around me was a peaceful tomb as I stared up at the endless stars.

I did not want to know or remember. I wanted to drift and fade, to let the water consume me and take what little strength was left.

I do not want to remember. I want to forget, forget, forget.

Will I ever be able to forget?

Darcy's poisonous emotions were wrapped around me, but one thing he left to my advantage. He had been so consumed by his longing that, after letting my sister go, he failed to disarm me.

Perhaps it was a mercy that I dropped my dagger. If I'd had it in my hand, it would have reminded him to check for weapons.

As soon as he let his guard down, I would cut out his heart. I would finish what Ríonach and Marcovester Red started.

It was time to stop running. I was going to kill him myself.

I could only hope to find redemption for what I allowed. I could only hope to find forgiveness from myself for the poisonous memories this darkness held. Time, I knew it would take time. But I wasn't sure I could endure the agony within while I waited for that eternity to pass.

Part of me longed that, in my victory over him, I would find my end. To live with what his darkness had stolen wasn't something I was sure I could endure.

How do I come back from this?

Darcy's arms were around me, holding me so tight it felt as if my bones would break. He sat with his back against the wall, holding me gently, lovingly—yet within his so-called tenderness was a cruelty that could not be ignored.

If this is love, I want no part of it. It is not gentle when I am not a willing participant. Even his supposed gentleness is violence. I don't want it. I don't want this!

He had withdrawn from my mind. Perhaps he had grown tired of hearing the screams, or maybe he didn't want to acknowledge how I ran from reality and fled to the ocean's waves. I was desperate to disconnect from reality as he wore me down. I didn't want to acknowledge how I fell to pieces. Soon there would be nothing left to resist him.

"I have a house on the mountainside, hidden deep within the Moores," Darcy said softly. "It is quiet and safe. You won't ever have to fight at the Last Gate. Soon, the borders will be no more. It will all be over, and we will have peace. Our own slice of heaven. I will love you until there is nothing left of me. We will live a happy life *Mon Oisillon*, and you will want for nothing. They will not decide your fate. You will be safe from the bloody end they've destined you for."

I want to choose my own fate. I want to escape you as much as I want to escape them.

I was numb, barely able to breathe as he held me close. Whispering sweet promises—sugar coated lies. His own twisted truths.

Make it stop. Please, just make it stop.

"How did you survive?" I whispered, interrupting his delusional daydreams.

Darcy was silent for a moment. "Hmm...should I tell you?" he mused. "Should I trust you with that secret?"

"Please," I rasped, desperate to know.

"Well, I guess honesty is the best policy in a marriage."

We're not married, you psycho!

I shoved down the rage, burying it deep within myself. I couldn't risk him sensing it. I needed him to think I was broken and helpless.

"Marcovester's punishment would have killed any *regular* mortal or Fey. But she sent me to the Ruins. That was where her ever-so-*righteous* punishment took a misstep. I was rebirthed in the Ruins. She sent me home, where my king healed her wound. My shadow fed off my blood like never before, and I became stronger. Now no weapon can kill me."

He's bluffing. Surely he's bluffing. Nobody is immortal. If I slit his throat and cut out his heart that should do the trick. Two for one.

Would it be like BOGO? Do I get a carnival prize for efficiency?

"We will have the most beautiful children," Darcy continued, as if he had never deviated from his delusional daydreams. "No one will take them from you, Ember. No one will send them to their deaths, as they have for generations. The Grimms have long been used to make an army—an army they uncaringly slaughter at the Gate. But not our children...I won't let them have you or our children...nothing will take you away from me."

I will. I will. I will take myself away from you.

"Gonna be sick," I managed to choke as I pushed out of his arms.

Darcy let me go and I stumbled forward into the darkness, heaving violently. Nothing was in my stomach to come up, but the rancid taste of mint that lingered in my mouth, and the stomach acid that churned in the back of my throat, wouldn't go away.

He was behind me. I could feel the weight of his cursed presence. The thick, sweet smell of that horrible mint clung to him.

My fingers slid down to my knees as I crouched lower, gagging on the dense, humid air as I silently drew a sturdy, four-inch blade from my boot.

"You need to eat," Darcy murmured, fingers trailing a pattern down my back. "Come, it's time we left this ruin."

There is no we. I will not come.

I will end this.

On three. One,

His hand closed around my left arm, gently pulling me up. "If you don't have the strength, my love, I'll carry you."

I am not your love. Two...

Fingers brushed my cheek as he turned me toward him.

Three.

I swung my right arm out to the side, and a blade hissed out over my arm from my forearm brace. In one swift movement, I sliced my right arm across his throat as I wrenched my left from his grasp and drove the blade deep into his chest.

Cut it out. Cut out his heart. Let us be done with this madness.

Die. Die you thieving, poisonous, heartless monster.

I'll break your ribcage open and tear out your heart with my bare hands.

DIE!

Instead of stumbling back, Darcy took a step forward, driving my blade deeper into him. His skin seemed to suck in the weapon, my fingers, my hand. Greedily taking more.

Impossible.

His fingers were like a vice as they closed around my right wrist. "You seem to have forgotten what I said," he hissed as he yanked out the blade. "You clearly weren't listening. I am not normal. No weapon can kill me now."

He forced me back as he pinned my left hand up behind my back. My boots slid and stumbled over rock and bone, before my back collided painfully with the wall. My head quickly followed, and stars danced across my eyes, lighting up the darkness. I lunged forward as I tried to wrench my arm from his grasp, intent on evading him. Pain spiked across my hand and shoulder as he shoved me against the wall again, forcing pressure on the uncomfortable angle my shoulder was at.

"I was hoping the sweetness would last. That our time together had finally convinced you of our future. You are such a good actress, my love. I thought you finally agreed that we were made for each other." His voice was a snarl of rage, a hiss of indignation. "I was hoping that you would see how useless it is to fight our fate. You had me fooled. You were so quiet. So *docile*. I'm realizing now that I'll indeed need to teach you a lesson. My mind had said as much, but my heart wanted to give you compassion, understanding, the benefit of the doubt." His body pressed against mine, pinning me to the wall as he forced my hand up. Up, up, up, until the point of the dagger, still coated in his blood, was pressed into my right temple, just barely missing the corner of my eye.

"The next time you try something foolish like that," he said as he shoved my hand and the blade sunk deep into my skin. "I will slit your throat and cut you to pieces. For now, you can have a mark to mirror your sister's. I'll leave your eye intact, though similar lessons must be taught. Do not forget hers was a promise I kept. Just as I will keep this promise to you if you defy me again."

If you kill me, I win. You won't have me then.

His lips brushed mine, sealing his promise of violence. Before I could register what was truly happening, before I could resist, he was forcing my hand down. Dragging the knife through my cheek, toward my lips.

No, no, no. Please stop. Please make it stop.

Pain was overwhelming everything. I couldn't stop him as he dragged the knife down through the side of my mouth, splitting my lips and scraping my teeth and gums. Agony, everything was agony as I screamed and fought against him. Blood, there was so much blood, filling my mouth, running down my chin as the blade continued down.

If he goes down much further, it'll kill me.

The knife stopped at the underside of my chin and Darcy heaved over me. His fingers were on my face, probing the wound, smearing the blood. His shadows were there, monsters that writhed and screamed. Their cacophony melded with my own as they lapped at my blood.

His mind latched onto me once more, feeding on my torture. I had no strength left to resist him as I sagged in his arms.

"I didn't want to have to do that," he murmured. "Hush, *Mon Oisillon*. You did this to yourself. Your actions forced me to punish you. Why would you make me do that?" He was kissing me again, lips demanding compliance, unheeding of the wound, the blood. His tone shifted into a vicious snarl. "You will *never* defeat me. I *will* have you, even if I must break you apart. Piece by defiant piece."

A sob rushed out of me.

"I will rebuild you, until there is nothing left in you that can resist. Then at last, you will be perfect, and we will be happy."

I was falling, caving inside. Watching myself, outside of myself, as the blood slowly stopped pouring down my face.

"You heal so fast. See? It's over now. The consequences of your defiance will always be minor in the long run, thanks to your miraculous healing," Darcy said absentmind-edly. "The pain, though seemingly drastic, is necessary to give the efficient lesson." His grip tightened on my wrist. "But I will do *whatever* it takes, until you realize the truth."

Why didn't he die? Why didn't he die?!

I was disconnected. Numbness replaced my fear, urging me to go still, begging me to stay calm.

Something isn't right.

What's going on? These are not my emotions.

Something slid above us, so soft I almost didn't hear it. So quietly, I could have imagined it. But Darcy stiffened, falling silent in front of me.

It was the sound of a missed footstep on slick, stone steps.

"Come out, little mice," Darcy snarled.

Emotions, my own, yet not, were pushing at my body now. My heart rate slowed, and my pain faded until the debilitating panic disappeared.

Darcy barked a cruel word and light suddenly exploded around us.

Theron, Verity, and eight other crew members, whose faces I knew but whose names I couldn't quite remember, were on the crumbling steps, weapons drawn.

NO! Why did you come? I didn't intend for you to come! He's going to hurt you. Get out of here! Get out of here!

The crew shielded their eyes, suddenly blinded by the bright light. Darcy's hand was a blur as he threw my dagger at Verity. "Curse you, courtless tracker!" he roared.

"NO!" I screamed.

Verity dodged and it missed her chest, sinking into her shoulder instead. "Bows!" she barked.

Two crew members, whose names I did not know, raised crossbows.

Theron took a step back, preparing to launch himself down the remaining steps and onto the debris littered floor.

A wave of darkness rushed out of Darcy. Fear, twisted and powerful, with fangs and claws, pounced on the crew.

Theron threw up his hands and roared. Darcy's fear shuddered. Theron's magic blocked most of Darcy's and it rebounded, crashing into me instead.

I wanted to run, clutch my head and scream until I was hoarse. Screams echoed around us from the crew, but regardless of their terror, they fired their arrows at Darcy.

Darcy pulled me in front of him, shielding himself with my body. "You'll heal," he snarled. "Perhaps this will teach you another lesson. Every attempt to escape will end in pain."

I jerked, screaming, as the arrows slammed into me. The spells and enchantments woven into the leather held. The sharp points bounced off, breaking my ribs on impact, but my life was spared.

Theron's boots skidded on the floor as he raced down the remaining steps.

Darcy was dragging me backward now. Every jostling movement was agony. I couldn't breathe. With every ragged gasp, my lungs burned.

Verity was close on Theron's heels, cursing with every step. There was magic woven into her colorful language, and wave after wave of power rushed from her palms and attacked Darcy.

Darcy seemed unbothered. His monstrous shadows rushed forward once more, blocking us from sight. Sharp teeth tore at my broken lips as he roughly kissed me. It was a claiming kiss, promising pain and ruin—swearing to me it was not the end. "This isn't over *Mon Oisillon*. If I cannot have you, no one will."

Darkness fell as Darcy snatched back his light and shoved me forward. I was stumbling through the darkness, clutching my broken ribs. Every movement was fire. My lungs felt full of fluid and heavy. I tripped, falling to my knees.

Will the pain stop if I let go? If I give up, will this agony end?

No. I can't think this way. I have survived when I didn't think I would. Evadne needs me. I have to keep fighting.

I pushed myself up, desperately trying to regain my footing and escape.

The ground heaved as everything shook. I fell forward, my efforts wasted.

I'm never going to make it out of here alive. I'm never going to see Evadne again...

"Ember!" Theron yelled.

I have to keep moving. I have to keep fighting. I have to make it back to Evadne!

"Here," I whispered, scrabbling at my throat, trying to pull out the moonstone.

Just let me go, Theron.

I cannot come back from this... I cannot escape what he's done.

Yes. I can. I can move beyond this hopeless point in my life...

I will not let this destroy me. I cannot let it destroy me.

"Here!" I cried, louder this time.

Arms circled around me, pulling me to my feet. Agony consumed me, but I was focused on *who* held me. I was terrified it was Darcy—intent on spiriting me away in the confusion and darkness. I shrieked, fighting the phantom as, at last, my fingers curled around the moonstone. Light flared around us, revealing Theron's worried silver eyes.

"Where did he go?" Verity yelled angrily.

"It doesn't matter," Theron called. "We have to go before he buries us in the rubble. There's nothing he'd like more than to wipe you off the face of the earth, Verity."

"I'll see him dead," Verity promised darkly.

"May we live to see the day," Theron grunted.

The ground shook beneath us as we raced up the stairs. The steps blurred together as my mind once again went numb, replaying Darcy's words over and over. The weight of such a damning promise, the power of that final, vengeful kiss.

I cannot come back from this. I cannot make it out of the darkness.

Will I ever be free of his curse? His touch, his shadows and his monsters?

Even if I cannot find freedom, she was worth it. She was worth every ounce of horror.

25

A Warrior Like My Ancestors Before Me

EMBER

"Most days I am a museum of things I want to forget. -every day I am
trying new techniques to make myself disappear"
-E.E. Scott

Blood dripped slowly from my lips as we finally burst out of the castle. Bright morning sunlight streamed across my face. Pain was everywhere, but I didn't care. We were free.

I survived. I'm alive. I'm still alive.

Am I? Am I really alive after everything I've survived?

We were in the trees now, but the shadows of the trees were comforting. I was falling, down, down, down as Theron gently lowered me to the ground.

Can I say I've survived, when part of me has died?

Can I ever escape the tainted memories?

Can I say I'm alive when I buried a part of myself in those ruins? A piece I'll never get back?

Was it worth it? Was it worth it?

Yes. It was worth it. She was worth it...

She was worth it. My sister was worth it.

Theron was kneeling in front of me, hands on either side of my face. "She's lost," he murmured. "The fear and loss, the grief...it's tearing her apart. He..." Theron's voice shuddered as tears slid down my face. "He did something terrible to her."

Verity paced behind him, anger encompassing her features. She was muttering every combination of curse and insult I had ever heard. Soon her words morphed, and she was speaking another, unknown language—but I could tell by the way she spat every syllable she was still swearing.

"Come back to me," Theron said gently. "Come back to me, Sparks. This isn't the end. Your story isn't over yet. This is just a chapter. It's not over yet. You can still come back from this."

How? How do I come back from this?

I blinked numbly as I stared down at my hands. They were covered in blood. My clothes were muddy and torn.

Where are we?

How long will he leave me alone before he comes back for me?

How long do I have until he finds us again?

What if he kills Evadne? What if he comes back for me and kills her?

"Is Evadne okay?" I whispered at last. Every syllable was torture. My lips began to bleed once more as the movement broke the thin blood clot.

"There you are," Theron said gently. "I was worried we'd lost you."

"You're *going* to lose her once I'm through with her," Verity snarled. She was absolutely livid.

"Evadne?" I asked again.

"Baba Yaga brought her back," Verity replied with a sigh, massaging her temples.

"No, she didn't," I rasped. "He let her go because I came. Yaga wasn't going to succeed. It's why she sent me to the market...to ensure I went to rescue Eva."

"Baba Yaga is one of the most powerful Fey within the Realm," Verity snapped. "You just jumped the gun. You didn't trust her to do it. She herself helped bind the Darke King. No sorcerer stands against her, not even the cursed Bluebeard himself."

Verity's words settled over me, but I knew she was wrong. I had no way of proving it, but she was wrong.

"Your sister is resting," Verity continued. "The witch estimates she will be for quite some time. She was greatly wounded and bore far more than humanly possible." She stared at me. "She, like you, never should have survived."

The bluntness to Verity's words hit me and I stared at the wound in her shoulder. She had bandaged it. When she had done that was beyond me. It seemed as if we had only just escaped the castle.

When did that happen? Did I fall unconscious?

Theron's eyes were pitying as he sat down beside me. "You were completely disconnected," he said quietly, answering my question. "You didn't say a word, you just sat there for hours, crying."

"Sounds about right," I muttered.

"What sounds about right," Verity seethed, "is that I gave you a direct order and you defied it as if it meant nothing. You put lives at risk when you pulled your little stunt. Why? Why did you do it?"

"I had to save Evadne," I whispered. "He was going to kill her at sundown...Baba Yaga was going to fail."

"How do you know this?" Verity demanded. "How on earth do you know? And besides that, if you knew, why didn't you *tell* me. If you knew where that monster was, why didn't you get help, backup? Why did you go alone, as if sacrificing yourself was the only answer?"

"It was. I can't—" My words fell silent. I was stunted. I could not speak of my curse, the silence forced onto me.

"No, it wasn't," Verity raged, unheeding of how my words had simply fallen silent. "He just made you think it was. No one can withstand the witch. It's impossible."

He can. He was laughing at her...

"You directly disobeyed my orders. You put lives in danger. Not only mine, but those of my crew that I had to bring. You were reckless and foolhardy."

How can I get help, when I am bound to silence? Darcy's spell silenced me.

I made my choice. I did choose to disobey her orders...and if Evadne was worth the cost, she is also worth the consequences.

"I accept full responsibility for my actions." I replied hoarsely. My fingers trembled as I gingerly touched my face. It burned under my fingertips. The wound was still raw, but at least it had fully clotted along my cheek and chin.

It could have been worse. It could have been so much worse...

He could have taken an eye. He could have done to me what he did to Evadne...

"The cost of such an insubordination on my ship, if not death outright, is a lashing," Verity snapped. "The consequences are steep to ensure such disobedience doesn't happen. Ten lashes for every crew member whose life you endangered."

"I had to save Evadne," I whispered, unable to stop myself from trying to explain. I would take the consequences, but I wanted Verity to understand. I couldn't bear her anger at me.

"It doesn't matter," Verity seethed.

There were ten crew members...that's a hundred lashes. I can't survive that...can I? What was the point in rescuing me, if she kills me after?

Dread began to grow inside. I had thought that the worst was behind me, but perhaps I was wrong.

I saved her. It was worth it. This is nothing compared to facing the world without her by my side.

I nodded. "I understand," I said quietly. "I'm sorry."

Verity glared at Theron. "That being said, *someone* has convinced the whole crew that you were only doing the right thing. He also has convinced them that you never counted on a rescue, because you weren't expecting to come out of that situation alive. A life for a life."

"He's right," I whispered. "I never meant for you to come. I never meant for you to rescue me... I was going to cut out the heart."

Theron jerked and guilt encompassed his face. He knew exactly what I meant.

"I dealt...a killing blow," I gasped. "And he didn't die."

Verity ignored my words, intent on her rage. "As a captain of my ship, I cannot let you go without punishment. If I did, then it would be an unfair standard and I would have a mutiny on my hands every other day."

I clenched my jaw, willing myself to be brave as I accepted the inevitable.

"The crew voted, and against my better judgement, I have agreed to the proposed reduction of your punishment. Though, *not* as much as *someone* has swayed them."

She glared at Theron again, and he crossed his arms, unaffected. If anything, it looked as if he was holding back a particularly nasty look.

"I have reduced it to two lashes for every crew member whose lives you nearly caused to be forfeit."

Twenty.

"The sentence will be carried out at sunset on board the ship." She stared at me. "You cannot face monsters and expect to be the only one hurt. You are not the only one who would risk your life for someone else. Others will do the same for you. Unless you are *absolutely* the only one entrenched within a situation, you cannot act as if you are a single unit. I would have you bear the weight of such consequences before you are forced to face the grave of someone whose death you caused." She dropped a knife into my lap. It was my knife; the one I had stabbed Darcy with. The one he had then hurled at her. "This belongs to you, Grimm."

"I'm sorry," I said softly.

"I know." Verity sighed. "You are young, and you are brave. But I cannot have you be such a liability...such a danger to my crew. They rely on me to protect them, and I take my vows as captain very seriously. I meant it when I said you needed to listen to my orders."

I nodded. "I understand."

"Good. See that you don't let it happen again."

"I'll try," I whispered.

Verity rolled her eyes. "You don't learn, do you."

"I can't make a promise I'm not sure I can keep. But I'll try, I give you my word I'll try."

Verity shook her head. "Grimms," she muttered. "You truly are your fool brother's sister."

I am. I am...

The sun was sinking low on the horizon. Somehow, a whole day had passed without my knowledge. I didn't have much time to gather myself before my punishment.

"I am unable to deliver the punishment, as I would usually do. It will take a couple of days for my shoulder to fully heal, though I firmly believe that the one who gives the sentence should carry it out. It is the burden of authority. I would spare you the agony of waiting for your punishment until I am healed. So, my first mate will do it." She turned to Theron. "Bind her wrists and bring her on board. I want this over with." Her gaze bored into mine. "Remember what I said, Grimm. People die because of the choices we make."

She turned and left, her words leaving me cold and numb all over.

Theron stared down at his hands. "I tried—"

"She's right," I whispered raggedly, cutting him off. My words were clunky and slurred around my injured lips. I tried and failed not to think about what the future held. Every syllable hurt; every breath was fire against my lungs and ribs.

"I made my choice," I sniffed, tears gathering in my eyes. "But I thought I was the only one who would be harmed." I shrugged out of my armored vest, then the upper bits of my clothing, until only a thin undershirt remained.

"Come on," Theron muttered. "Let's get to the ship. I'll...I'll follow the captain's orders to tie your hands when we reach it."

It didn't take us long to get to the ship; we were no longer in the forest on the edge of the ruins. We had gone farther than I realized. It was a brief hike to the boardwalk.

Once we reached the thick planks, Theron pulled a long strand of thick leather out and I pushed my hands together in front of me, allowing him to wrap it around my wrists.

"I thought I was the only one who would be harmed," I whispered, desperate to explain. "I wanted to be the only one destroyed by..." I choked on my words, fighting the curse that sought to silence me. I needed Theron to know. "I wanted to be the only one destroyed by *his* darkness...I didn't mean for anyone else to get hurt."

Theron's silver eyes were unreadable as he looked down at me. "We never mean for anyone else to get hurt," he replied quietly. He scooped me up then, and without another word, began to climb up the rope ladder onto the ship.

Every movement jostled my many injuries, and I began to worry I'd pass out from the extent of them before I endured my punishment. I wanted to get it over with, not to delay it because I wasn't conscious.

The setting sun was a ball of fire in the sky. The horizon was streaked orange and bloody red as Theron led me across the deck of the ship. The crew was gathered around the deck, watching in silence as we made our way toward the mast. Nikos stood in the middle, face unreadable, a long leather whip in his hand.

Don't think about it. Don't think about it.

Verity stood beside him, eyebrows pulled together, her lips a thin line of anger and frustration. Her shoulder was bandaged and her arm was in a sling.

I take responsibility for what I did. I accept the punishment. She was worth it. She was worth it.

Theron pulled my hands over my head and secured them to a thick iron ring on the main mast.

"Hold your breath before every strike," he said under his breath. "I am not allowed to interfere with the pain."

What does that mean? How would he interfere?

"But I would see you come out of this stronger than before. You are Ember Grimm, a warrior like your ancestors before you. This will not destroy you. Just as he *will not destroy* you."

I nodded, and he walked away.

I waited in growing trepidation as Captain Verity read off the reasons for my punishment. My disobedience and the ways I had endangered the crew. I trembled, waiting in horror and fear as the whole ship fell silent.

"Begin," Verity commanded, her voice hard as steel.

There was a whirr, a hissing snake flying through the air. I jerked forward, the breath rushing out of me in a muffled shriek as a crack split my skin open.

One.

The second strike followed the first, faster than I was prepared for. I forgot to hold my breath as the world swam in front of my eyes. I bit my lip hard, tasting blood as I reopened Darcy's wound. I swallowed the scream that desperately tried to escape.

Two.

She was worth it. She was worth every ounce of pain. Every drop of blood.

I took a deep breath, bracing for the third.

It came and tears rushed down my cheeks.

Three.

We made it out alive. She made it out alive. That's all that matters.

Four.

The world darkened, until all that remained was pain and fire as I focused on nothing but the measured cadence of my breath, the numbers, and my sister's face. She was worth it. She was worth it all.

A warrior like my ancestors before me.

Ten

This will not destroy me.

Eleven.

It will not destroy me.

Twelve.

I will not let this destroy me.

26

Most Disturbing Conversation With A Cannibal

<blockquote>EVADNE</blockquote>

"She is full of wounds, riddled with scars, but she is still standing, and she is still beautiful."

-r.h.Sin

The world was on fire, and I was burning, burning, burning. Screaming out Ember's name as I ripped myself from that agonizing darkness. My back was on fire. Blow after burning blow threw me from where I lay and drove me to my knees on the floor.

Not mine, not mine, not mine.

What was happening to her? Where was she?

"Ember!" I screamed.

My fault, my fault. This is all my fault. She went there for me. What is he doing to her?!

"EMBER!" I screamed again, struggling to find my bearings and force myself to my feet. The world was lopsided, black and blurry. My eyes wouldn't open properly, and everything was wrong, so terribly wrong. I had to run—to get to her and make the agony stop.

"Hush, child."

The voice was ancient, cracked with disuse. But there was a powerful edge that crept down my spine—chilling me to my core. I was still in danger.

My voice faded as my body obeyed.

Where am I?

Pain lanced through me again. Agony, I was in utter agony—consumed by it, as tears streamed down my face. I clutched my knees to my chest, all while my head screamed at me to get up and run far, far away.

I knew I had to get up, but I couldn't move. My back was splitting open, over and over again. Blow after blow with no end in sight.

Make it stop, make it stop!

"You and your sister have a unique bond, but you are still too weak. You must gather your strength before you tear the Realm apart."

I slowly turned, searching for the owner of the voice. My left eye wouldn't open, and whoever she was, she was in my blind spot.

Then at last, I found her. An old woman with white eyes sat in a wooden rocking chair. Forward and back went the chair. Up, around and down went the long, sharp needles. Her work was silent, not a click or clack to be heard.

"I have to go get her," I whispered as the fire on my back continued to rip me to shreds.

I'm going to pass out. I'm going to fall over.

When will it end, when will it end?

"She does not need your assistance, child. The deed is nearly done," the old woman replied as she set her knitting down and pulled a scrawny black cat onto her lap. "Just hold on a few moments longer."

I cradled my head in my hands, unable to stop myself from screaming through my teeth.

Where is she? Where is she??

Get up! GET UP!

"What did you see in that place?" the old woman asked, drawing me back from the pain, away from my mind.

"Darkness," I whispered. "I saw darkness."

A man of shadows, a monster in skin...power that will destroy all of us.

Ember dying, over and over again...

My mind splitting open, his shadows ripping apart my memories.

Darkness and ruin.

He destroyed me. He destroyed me and there's nothing left.

I couldn't get the feel of him out of my head. There was an overpowering presence of evil, mint, laughter. Darkness, so much darkness. I was shattered, torn to pieces.

I wanted to claw my brain out. Kill myself over and over until I came back right. I wasn't myself. I could still feel the echoes of his fingers, his taint, his bloodied smile. His ruin and rot in my memories. The shadows were still there, prowling the edges of my mind, threatening to overtake me as I held the frayed scraps of myself.

Will I ever be okay again?

"He said it was only the beginning," I rasped. "He said…" my voice caught on a sob, and my shoulders heaved.

The old woman sighed, holding the cat to her chest as she absentmindedly stroked it. "If only he lied…but he cannot. He is of the Olde blood. It is only the beginning. You spoke of a dead man, Bluebeard? Surely you were mistaken."

It was a statement rather than a question. I only wished I had been mistaken. "No, he was there. Bluebeard was with the shadow man."

The old woman hummed in anger. "He dares to draw breath."

The blows on my back ceased for just a moment, then all of a sudden, an overwhelming burst of fire. Consuming everything as it burned across the entirety of my back.

I screamed, curling into a ball on the floor as wave after wave of pain radiated from my back, through my body.

What was that?

Everything was silent around me as I stifled my sobs. The low purring of a cat broke through my agony, and then the soft crack and creak of the wood as she rocked—back and forth, back and forth.

"Ah, the salt water. It is over now. She's paid the cost for her defiance. Brave girl."

"What cost?" I gasped. "What defiance?"

She was silent for a moment. "That of disobedience. Though, when the prince comes for her, the cost will be worse. That day of reckoning will be one not easily forgotten…I can see the taint of bloodshed from here. His companions will overstep in anger and revenge. I lose hope for their future. She will not forgive him…or will she? Is she capable of forgiveness when her heart is shattered…the bones are silent, so vague and silent…"

A shudder ran down my spine, though I didn't comprehend her meaning.

What does she mean? What did Ember do to Artemis?

There were holes in my memory, things that didn't add up or make sense.

Fireheart's familiar hiss cut through the small space, and I sat up, searching for my beloved dragon. The pain was beginning to fade, though my clothes felt sticky and bloodstained. No doubt the result of our shared bond.

Fireheart was perched on top of the cot I had just rolled off of. He stared down at me in worry, his eyes glowing dimly in the darkness. They seemed to reproach me for leaving him, while also begging me to be okay.

I'm sorry. I didn't mean to scare you.

His tongue darted out of his mouth, and he briefly looked away, eyeing the cat on the old woman's lap. Memories of what he'd done to Maladroit crossed my mind and I scooped him up, worried he was going to make us unwelcome guests.

No. You may not try to eat that cat either.

My hands shook as I held him tightly to my chest. "I'm sorry," I whispered to him. "I didn't mean for any of this to happen. I'm sorry I worried you."

Fireheart huffed and crawled up my shoulder. His evident desire to eat the cat forgotten, he wrapped himself around the back of my neck—careful of the many wounds as he settled his body under my hair. His head poked out over my shoulder and his tail curled down and wrapped around my bicep.

I gently stroked his nose.

I won't leave you again. Not if I can help it.

Where is everyone? Why did they leave me here with this strange woman?

Where is Jack? Marcus? Artemis and Ember?

Wait. Ember. She's in danger. Where is she?

I turned my attention back to the old woman. "Where is my sister?" I asked. My voice was strained, my throat dry as a desert.

She ignored my question, instead holding out a cup. "Drink, child."

I took the cup from her, eyeing the dark liquid suspiciously. "How do I know I can trust you?" I asked uncertainly, as I pushed myself up and back onto the cot. It took everything I had just to move those few inches.

"I dare not go back on my word, though tender your heart would be..." the old woman replied. "Your sister, brave fiery soul that she is, bargained for your safety. She was smart in her words, wise in her bargain...no, I cannot eat the heart..." She held out her unoccupied hand. In her wrinkled palms rested slivers of silver, diamond, and gold, all flecked and stained red.

I recognize those. They're from the castle. The cursed castle.

They're covered in blood.

Her blood? My blood? Why does she have them?

Where is she?

"These were removed from her body...some were removed from yours. She then bargained with me to help you. I am bound by her to heal you...to bring you back."

"But you didn't bring me back," I said quietly. "You *sent her* to him...he willingly released me after she came. He said as much."

"And then I guided you back to yourself." The old woman's voice held an edge I didn't want to challenge. It promised violence.

"Where is my sister?" I asked, as I struggled to get to my feet.

She pushed me back with a bowed walking stick. It was as thick as my arm and oddly white. A skull was carved into the top, and intricate patterns were carved on the surface. Runes and odd symbols smeared in darkened charcoal and crimson seemed to shine against the bleached surface.

Like bone.

"She will return to you. Until then, gather your strength. I have healed as much as I am able, and despite my best intentions, I now owe your sister a promise. Curse my fickle heart; it took pity on her pain and offered her lenience. I underestimated how the Darke one has grown." She turned her milk white eyes to me, staring at me. "Your physical injuries attest to that. You were not just spirited away. You have been cursed, child. You should not be alive."

The energy was draining out of me, just from sitting. The mere effort of breathing was almost too much.

I have no choice but to trust her... Even if she can't be trusted, she's right. I need to get my strength back.

I took a small sip of the steaming concoction in the mug. Hints of cinnamon and rich, floral herbs washed over me. It was sweet and thick, like cocoa. Before I knew it, I had downed the entire mug.

A sense of peace and warmth washed over me, and I leaned back, resting my back against the cabinet that stood behind my cot.

I took in as many details about the room, and the old woman as I could—having to turn my head back and forth to make up for the lack of vision in my left eye.

The old woman was dressed in a patchwork dress of bright colors. Pieces and bits of material were sewn haphazardly together. Short, white-blonde hair stuck out from her head, a cacophony of tangled frizz and curls. Amulets hung around her neck and even more were woven throughout her ratted hair. At least a dozen sat visible on top of her shirt, and more disappeared beneath the fabric of her dress. Long, clawlike nails stroked the cat. She looked old, yet lethal, and despite her bargain with Ember, I could not shake the unease that threaded through me, deeper and deeper as the moments passed. Ancient power seemed to radiate from her, something so old and strong that it seemed the world had forgotten about her.

It was a power that made the hair on the back of my neck rise.

Shelves and cabinets were everywhere, overflowing with books, bottles, and jars of all shapes and sizes. Papers were everywhere—in stacks, shoved into nooks and crannies, and overflowing from crates. Across the room, a roaring fire crackled and danced. A large, cast-iron pot hung on a hook over it. Plants were suspended from the ceiling, with more pots scattered throughout the room on every available surface—fighting for the fading sunshine that streamed through the dusty windows. Some plants seemed to have been engulfed by the house—they grew from the ceiling beams and the rough wood walls.

A ladder in the corner led up to a loft that stretched over most of the room, and tucked in the corner I could see a large loom.

There were so many different colors and details that I couldn't quite process them. Trying made my head ache.

"What is your name?" I asked, dragging my attention from the room back to her.

"It depends on who's asking," she replied evasively as she pushed to her feet.

She was hunched, spine arched outward and poking through the material of her dress to show the unnatural S curve in her spine. Her shoulders sat at odd angles. Yet, she moved freely, as if she did not feel her impediments. "Come, child, you must eat."

My stomach growled, silencing my thoughts of rejecting her offer. "What should I call you then?" I pressed.

"Babushka will do. I have outlived all the lovies who used to call me such. My ancient ears long to hear a sweet young voice say my beloved name again."

Grandmother...

Outlived...how old is she?

"Where am I?"

"I should think it would be clear that you are in my humble cottage."

She may be ancient, but she certainly isn't slow-witted.

"Do you drink tea?" she asked curtly.

Homesickness washed over me in a wave, and a sob caught in my throat. It felt like years since I had shared a cup of tea with Mum and Oma in the kitchen.

Gone, gone, gone. They're gone...

A memory rose to the surface of my mind and my thoughts faltered.

She was there. She was in that place of shadows...

It wasn't real. It was an illusion meant to break me...wasn't it?

"Yes," I choked out, trying to swim free of my mind. "I would love a cup of tea."

"Don't worry, dear," the old woman, Babushka, said absentmindedly. "Lost things return in the end."

What does she mean? Does she know something? Was it real?

How could she know? She asked what I had seen, as if she saw nothing.

I watched as she moved around the kitchen, pinching off leaves from some of the plants, and flowers from others. Then she began to pour bits of this and that from various jars and bottles while she hummed an off-key tune under her breath.

Soon the tune morphed, and she began to murmur words as she prepared the eccentric cup of tea. "Child lost, far from home," she sang softly as she ladled steaming stew from the cauldron into a large, wooden bowl. "Child, broken, afraid, alone...child stolen, trapped in stone. Screaming echoes in the night, forgotten once, dreams take flight... Darkness rises, takes the bait, sealing now, our final fate."

I didn't want to know, but I couldn't stop myself from asking. "What does it mean?"

She placed the bowl on a cluttered table shoved into the corner. "Come eat," she replied, again avoiding my question.

I stood, forcing my legs to move as I maneuvered around the cluttered cottage. With one side of my world dark, it was hard. I hadn't realized how much I relied on my peripheral vision to guide me.

It was a matter of moments before I tripped and fell.

Swearing, I got to my feet.

Babushka made no move to help me. She simply stood, staring, waiting.

I tried again, and once again fell. Tears rose. I wanted to give up, to scream and cry and give up. It was so unbearably *hard*. A part of life that had been ingrained in me since I was a child, suddenly seemed too great a challenge. The very act of walking was suddenly a mountain that needed to be reassessed, relearned. It was something greater than just a broken limb that you had to carry with a crutch. It was an integral, *vital* part of myself—gone. Worst yet, suddenly, I didn't know if I *could* relearn how to survive.

I cradled my head in my hands, trying to breathe and overcome the anxiety and fear.

Come on, get up. Just get up.

I can't. I can't do this. It's wrong, it's all wrong.

Tears fell, one after another as I struggled to gather my composure. It shouldn't be this hard, this simple task, and yet it towered over me, taunting, taunting, dragging me down, down, down.

"How do you eat a human?" Babushka mused, idly stirring the soup in the cauldron.

What? Why would anyone eat a...a human.

I looked up at her, shaken and disgusted.

She stared back, eyebrow raised. "Well?" she asked.

"I..."

Not at all. You don't eat humans, because that's disgusting. Cannibalism is frowned upon in polite societies.

Perhaps we aren't in polite societies?

How do you even answer a question like that?

Who even asks questions like that?!

"One bite at a time," Babushka said, answering her own riddle. "How do you find your way back to yourself?"

I looked away, shaking my head in defeat.

She hobbled over to me and lifted my chin with the end of her strange cane, forcing me to meet her gaze. "One. Step. At. A. Time."

Tears streamed down my face, and I pulled my chin away, desperate to escape her scrutiny.

She put her cane back under my chin, forcing me to look at her once more. "Rise, child of Grimm, and take back the pieces of yourself. Rebind what was unraveled. The darkness preys upon your pain. It wants you weak, defeated, crippled. Take yourself back. This is not the end. This is not *your* end."

"I...how—"my words broke off in a sob. "How?" I whispered.

"Rise, fall, rise again. *Do not* stay down." She moved her cane but made no move to help me up. "Movement is life, child. If you stop fighting, it will mean the end of everything."

I sniffed and forced myself to my hands and knees. Then, taking a deep breath, pushed myself up.

The room wobbled around me. I was dizzy, disoriented. The state of my new reality scared me. What if it never got any better? What if it was like this forever? What if I never danced again?

The 'what ifs' threatened to undo me.

One step at a time.

I took a trembling step forward, and then another.

My knees gave out and I fell with a cry.

Curse it all.

Up. I have to get up. She's right, I have to keep trying.

Crying, I pushed myself back to my feet and took three more steps before my knees gave out again.

The table was close, so close. One more go, and I would make it.

I'll have more strength once I eat something.

Ember needs me, and I can't even walk. Some help I am.

One step at a time. I have to take this one step at a time.

I forced the 'what ifs' of the future away, and focused on the now. I angrily wiped my cheeks, frustrated as I once again pushed myself to my feet. The table was four feet away, but it might as well have been a mile.

Four feet, then three, two, one.

I pitched forward, falling into the chair, but I didn't care. I had made it. Small victory or not, it was still a victory.

Babushka hummed approvingly and patted me on the shoulder. "Give it time, child. You will find your strength again."

"What does it mean?" I asked again. "The song you were singing...what does it mean?"

"I never know what they mean," she replied absentmindedly. "Not when it's the rhymes. Not when it's the verse. The bones will never tell. He's veiled my sight at last."

"Are you the Seer?"

She laughed. The sound was cold and cruel, making the hairs on the back of my neck rise in unease. It was the cackle of someone I'd assume was trying to eat me.

Yuck. Too many twisted fairytales. She's just an old woman... Ember wouldn't leave me alone with a cannibal...

But what about her question?

She was just being disgusting... Ember would not have left me alone with a canni-bal...would she?

"No. I am not the Seer. That curse and that curse alone belongs to Branwenn. I am simply an old witch who seeks to contain an evil greater than the face that greets her in the mirror each morning."

"What do you mean?" I asked, confused.

"I, too, am cursed, but such is my lot after what I've done."

What did you do?

I shuddered as my imagination ran away with me. I still could not shake the fore-boding sense of unease. Something was off about this whole situation, but I couldn't put my finger on *what*.

"Where are we?" I asked, blowing a spoonful of the thick stew.

"We are in the Moores, where else would we be?"

More cryptic answers. Just what I need.

"But *where* in the Moores?" I pressed. My stomach growled angrily, and I gave up on trying to cool down the bite—opting for simply shoving the bite into my mouth. Perhaps if I ate something, it would make me feel less cranky with her.

I regretted the hasty decision instantly. My tongue was now paying the price for my impatience. Foregoing my manners, I chewed noisily around a fiery bite of potato, try-ing to save my tastebuds. Flavors exploded across my tongue. It was the most delicious stew I had ever tasted

It's the most delicious stew I'm not going to be able to taste in a minute. My poor taste buds. Why didn't I at least blow on it?!

"We are at the edge of the Wastelands," she replied, eyeing me skeptically as she poured a kettle of steaming water into a pot.

Suddenly self-conscious, I sacrificed what remained of my tastebuds for the appear-ance of manners. But, after another few seconds of unsuccessful careful chewing, I opted for swallowing the half-chewed, boiling bite.

I spluttered and coughed as the potato's wrath burned its way down my throat.

Babushka shook her head ruefully. "Never have I seen a Grimm with such hasty manners," she muttered. "And that's saying something, child. That reckless brother of yours has tried my patience before."

I cleared my throat, my cheeks flaming crimson.

"Your sister betrayed the prince's trust," Babushka said, changing the subject abruptly.

Wait. What? How?

"What do you mean?"

"Exactly what I said."

"How do you know?"

"The bones told me." She turned to the fire, staring into the flames. "He is coming, though. She cannot outrun him."

"How do you know?" I repeated.

She shrugged. "The bones."

That doesn't answer my question whatsoever.

Excuse me while I turn to my body and ask my great and all-knowing bones questions. I'm sure I'll get every answer I seek.

Yes, hello bones, can you tell me why she won't answer my questions?

Unfortunately my bones had no answers to give. I turned my attention back to my stew, unsure of how to respond when I knew nothing. I hadn't seen my sister since our escape from the wraith's castle.

"I'm surprised," Babushka mused. "Are you really more interested in burning off more of your tender tastebuds than asking what I mean? I can hear the question at the edge of your delicate tongue. The lack of answers bothers you. I can hear the inquiries brooding in your hunched shoulders."

I put down my spoon and sighed. "Can you give me something more than a cryptic answer? Your replies leave me with more questions than when I started."

"You are the one asking the questions. Ask the right one and I shall answer what it is you really want to know."

I huffed. "What kind of magical person are you? What do you mean you're cursed? How did you get your power?"

"I killed a man," she replied nonchalantly. She stared unseeing at the wall. "I killed an *innocent* man. I slit his throat, and then I devoured his still beating heart." She laughed, the sound cruel and wicked. "I ate the rest of him too, but that part is irrelevant. It was the heart that bound me to darkness."

Horror washed over me, and my attention suddenly returned to the stew. My stomach turned to lead as the potato threatened to come back up.

What's in the stew?

"I wouldn't feed you human flesh, foolish girl," Babushka snapped angrily. "I knew the cost of my depravity and I *embraced* it with open arms. That was many years ago. I have been roaming the Realms for eons, a Wendigo waiting to rise. My sister began that terrible shift...but now she is gone, and the Realm is cursed. It unravels... He is coming... I have delayed my curse, but the darkness will consume me. I only wish to see the knight finally destroyed before I allow myself to turn into such a monster...or perhaps I should let it all burn."

She pulled out a chair and poured the steaming tea into my mug. "I will not harm you, if that is your next question." She eyed me. "Although, you do have such *pretty* eyes and a loyal disposition. No doubt it would sweeten the taste of your heart. No doubt all the things you've seen would enhance the flavor of your eyes. You are a tempting morsel, my dear."

I lurched to my feet, ready to flee.

"Sit," she ordered as she poured herself a cup of tea. "I promised your sister, and cursed be my word, I must honor it." She growled low under her breath. "My sympathetic heart took pity on her; I was hungry for the power these shards contained. But now I want to eat you, and I cannot. Curse it all to the Darke Knight, how I *long* for your blood...your powerful blood."

I stared at her, uncertain and horrified. She stopped her disturbing ramble and pointed to the chair. "Sit," she repeated. "You and I have much to discuss, little Grimm."

I sat. I was in no shape to flee. I needed to regain my strength, and I had no idea where Ember was, or where to start looking.

A furry creature wove its way around my ankles, and I reached down. It was the cat, the very skinny cat. Fireheart hissed in annoyance from my shoulder, but I hushed him. I picked out some thick chunks of meat from the stew and gingerly fed them to the poor, scrawny animal.

Babushka rolled her milky eyes. "That cat is so spoiled for attention. He only pretends he is underfed because he knows he can sway your heart and get more treats. If you saw his true form, you would see what I mean. He is as plump as a hippopotamus."

Golden eyes shone up at me as the cat begged for more. Shiny white teeth flashed as it licked its lips.

"Shoo, brat!" Babushka said scoldingly. "Did you not hear me say I had important matters to discuss with the girl? I cannot discuss such things when you are playing with her bleeding heart."

The cat rolled its eyes, and she bared her teeth at it. "Just because I am blind does not mean I can't tell when you're rolling your eyes," she snapped. "I can hear the click of fluid as the orbs roll, you impertinent cat."

"What's its name?" I asked, turning back to my stew. I resisted the urge to feed it more—I didn't want to encourage it to stay and get itself in trouble.

"His name is Red," Babushka replied. "I named him after my impertinent sister. They are much alike."

I smiled. It seemed a fitting action to name a pet after a sibling.

"So, tell me love, why are two unclaimed Grimms running around the Moores? Furthermore, why did your sister betray the one to whom her fate and magic is bound?"

"Uhm..."

"Surely you knew of the monarch's trickery," she said dismissively. "You are twins of the prophecy, but these days in the middle are a bit vague..." She tapped her fingers on the table, one-two-three, one-two-three. "Hmm...but even then, it doesn't make sense. I believe someone is shifting the timelines. The monarchs would have to be crazy, or dumb, to allow three of the most powerful and important people to come through the Moores, when the Moores are encompassed within such darkness...especially with the eldest hidden."

"I don't know," I replied, resuming blowing on the stew. "I...I didn't know she betrayed him," I said quietly.

"She left him," Babushka said lightly, taking a deep sip of her tea. "She boarded a skye pirate ship and brought you with her. Good thing she did, as I am the only one who could bring you back. You would have died had she stayed with the prince. But I could hear the way her fractured heart beat. It broke her heart to leave him. I could smell the toxic taint of crushed feelings that pulsed through her blood...so bitter, yet so sweet."

"You sent her to the Ruins," I said, my voice shaking with anger. "You sent her to that monster. You didn't pull me back, not truly. You waited for her to go, knowing he'd release me when she did."

"The *how* is *irrelevant*," Babushka replied severely. "I am still the only one who could stop the poison from spreading further." She gestured to my arm. "If it wasn't for me, the wraith's curse would have killed you. He was willing to destroy you, and everything within his little world, to keep you. Even in death, he wanted to keep you for himself."

She tsked. "Such selfish, selfish monsters we become in the darkness."

She began to lay the blood-stained shards of gold, silver, and diamond out on the table. "One for sorrow, two for pain, three to never love again...four for heartache, five for death, six the maiden's final breath..."

She continued to weave her rhyming poem as she counted out the cursed artifacts. I turned from my stew, appetite lost, and picked up the steaming mug of tea, holding the warm cup close to my chest.

"Sixteen finds us in the rain, seventeen haunts with screams of pain, eighteen stabs us in the back, nineteen turns the world to black...twenty strikes the cost to betray, twenty and one...the knight shall rise again."

She raised her pale, white eyes to mine. "Run, child, run, the darkness comes, to drown the Realm in streams of blood."

27

Gambling With My Life (What Else Is New?)

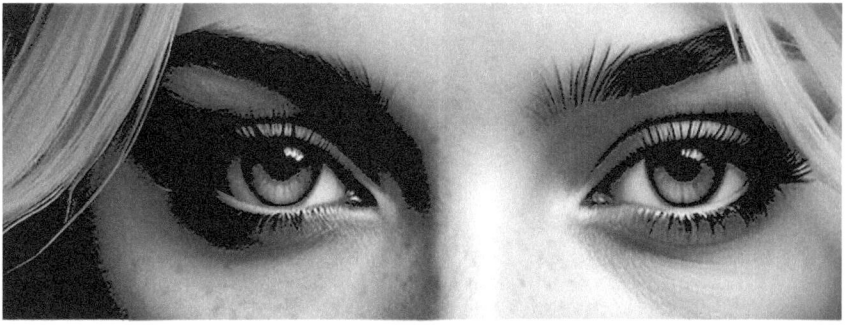

FAYE

"Greet each day with a smile. An ominous smile. A knowing smile.
Smile at the day until the sun turns to its horizon, scared and tired."
-Welcome to Night Vale Podcast

Weeks passed and the world slowly began to come alive outside my little window. Endless gray days with pouring rain finally ceased, and the sun began to shine—turning the world from a colorless blob into a bright cacophony of vibrant green and yellow. Dandelions may have been a common weed, but with every splash of color that popped up, I felt a little less miserable and forlorn. My world was indeed nothing but a landscape of pain and agony, but at least the most hated weeds in so-called *sophisticated* society prevailed. The world outside seemed to hold more promise with every beautiful, bright yellow flower that grew.

Soon the dandelions were followed by irises, peonies, and tiger lilies, and I began to wonder if it wasn't weeks, but perhaps months, that had passed as the days grew warmer outside. I slept with my window open, dreaming of home in an alternate reality that held no monsters. A reality where we were whole and unbroken. A timeline that allowed Ronan and Meghan to be an accepted part of my life.

Even with the holes in my memory, I knew Jeremiah was losing patience. His rage only grew as, after each session, fewer marks were burned into my skin. He was losing ground, and he knew it. It was only a matter of time before he switched plans and chose a worse method of interrogation.

Waking up was a challenge. It hurt to even regain consciousness. But here I was, yet again, making the *abhorrent* decision to be awake.

My mouth tastes like a desert. What died on my tongue?

Perhaps someone disposed of a body while I was unconscious.

That is a disgusting thought.

Come on, wake up. I have to check and see that there's nothing gross in my mouth.

I don't wanna.

Too bad. You don't have a choice.

I cracked my eyes open, suppressing a groan as the sunlight seemed to stab through my eyes and into my brain.

This was a terrible decision. How dare you make me wake up.

Ronan was once more at my bedside, shoulders tense and hunched, sitting with his head in his hands.

I wonder if his head is heavy. He's always holding it up.

"Well," I mumbled. "I think I've had enough of this torture nonsense."

Ronan jerked, turning toward me. "I didn't realize you were awake," he said gently.

I tried to ignore his tender tone. "Yes, well, you were too busy moping and...and holding up your *big*, stupid head. Probably wondering where all your brain cells went and being all jealous of my *marvelous* brain cells."

At this my trio and the hoard revived and began to preen while screeching of their greatness.

The corners of Ronan's mouth twitched, as if suppressing a smile. "You sure have a way of complimenting a person."

"I don't compliment kidnappers," I replied primly. "Unkidnap me, and then we'll talk."

"I'll hold you to it."

"I said we'd talk, not that I'd compliment you right off. There would be strict nego-tiations before any such complimenting were to ever happen. Besides, I don't know if I could even *find* anything worth complimenting. You're quite...quite *hideous*."

Ronan shook his head, laughing, but his mirth died as quickly as it had appeared. The weight of our situation was greater than any ridiculousness I could manage.

"Now, back to the matters at hand," I said as I pushed myself into a sitting position. I immediately regretted the decision as the pain flared to an unignorable roar. I gritted my teeth, waiting for the agony to subside. After a few moments, the pain ebbed to a burning ache. "I am overcoming the toxin. Jeremiah's losing ground, and he knows it. He's getting desperate."

Ronan nodded, "I can tell. He's angry. It makes me worried."

"When is he not angry?" I muttered, staring down at my bandaged arms in dismay. That was the worst part of these wounds; the mark of a traitor came with a curse. Not only was my magic unable to heal the punishments, but they also healed at an absurdly slow rate—slower than even a normal human wound should. Soon, the burns would move to my legs and the words would carve themselves into my back. When my back was filled I was out of chances—the darkness would take me.

"Fair point," Ronan replied. "But it's...different somehow."

"Yeah, I know what you mean. He's like a cornered animal. He's bound to do something stupid if we don't give him a way out. We just have to make sure he's going in the direction *we* want. So, you're going to move ahead with the original plan and finally suggest solitary confinement. Make sure you get me that hidey tunnel with the cute poster."

"Right, the poster," Ronan muttered.

I smirked. "Yes, the poster. Make it something inconspicuous, perhaps a Justin Bieber poster...or maybe Taylor Swift. Then after the idea you gave Jeremiah has gone through his thick skull and bounced around that empty brain of his, because clearly he has *no* brain cells, I'll cause a scene. Amid my great acting of said scene, you'll rescue your father and prove your loyalty, and I shall relent and cement my faked feelings toward you. Then Marcov will take me to my cell—"

"I do not like that part of the plan," Ronan cut in.

"I don't care," I snapped, annoyed by his stubborn insistence to protest this particular detail of my brilliant plan. "I can take care of myself."

Ronan had the audacity to roll his eyes.

"Remind me to kick you when I'm feeling better," I muttered.

"You're in no condition to be kicking anyone," Ronan lectured.

"I *said* when I'm feeling *better*," I growled. "That's it, you're getting kicked twice."

I was struggling with the covers, ignoring the pain, intent on showing him I meant business. "I'm going to kick you now *and* later! I'll be a piece of chewy candy and I'll rip out your fillings while I'm at it."

"No, no, Faye, don't do that. You can kick me as much as you like, just, do it later. Okay?"

"Fine," I huffed, sated by the idea of kicking him until my legs got tired.

I wasn't about to tell him that I was glad he had stopped me. That small amount of movement was enough to leave me breathless and reeling in pain.

"Do you have an idea for what we're going to do after you're done training Megs?" Ronan asked quietly.

"I do," I said, chewing on my lip in worry as I stared at my worn backpack by the bathroom door. It seemed ages ago since he had given it back to me. "How long have I been here?" I asked suddenly.

"What?"

"How long?"

"It's almost June now," Ronan replied. His eyes were distant, as he counted back the months. My mind was too foggy to even attempt such an endeavor.

How much time has passed in the Realm? Are Ember and Evadne doing okay?

I have to hurry up and get out of here.

It'll be my birthday soon. I'll be twenty-seven...

I'm going to be so incredibly old.

At this thought, my three loyal brain cells began wailing. The cacophony morphed into a funeral song. In a matter of moments, they had decided death by old age was imminent and had placed themselves in tiny little coffins. I watched, amused, as they mourned themselves at their own wake. The hoard of course, wept profusely and began to list off elaborate lies about the three's greatness. Still intent on joining in the mayhem, the hoard was in hot competition to outdo each other in their profuse praise of the mighty three.

I rubbed my temples, trying to drown out the noise, while simultaneously moving my arms as little as possible.

"Almost eight months," Ronan said at last.

"Time to blow this popsicle stand," I muttered angrily. "I have things to do, people to save, mayhem to cause."

"So much mayhem," Ronan agreed with a small chuckle.

"Next time your father comes, I'm going to cause a scene. Make sure he's primed and ready by then."

"How do I get him to believe that a different form of solitary is a good idea? Especially when it's so out of the blue? I've been telling him about the relationship blooming between us, like you wanted. But how do I work with the idea of solitary?" Ronan sounded worried. Clearly, he didn't believe he could successfully dupe his crazed father.

Well, he's a liability.

Shut up. He's going to do just fine. He just needs some reassurance and a little pep talk.

At the words 'pep talk,' my three brain cells revived, and abandoning their little coffins, began to draw up maps and diagrams, laying out our little mutiny with elaborate doodles. Their TED talk got carried away, and soon the illustrations became detailed ways in which Jeremiah could be disposed of. My favorite method was that of 'death by salad fork.' It seemed the brain cells agreed, for it had been voted the best idea.

Oh, how I love my bloodthirsty little brain cells.

Remember that time when Evadne stabbed Em with her salad fork, because Em stole her chocolate and tried to blame it on poor Bricklebrit?

Why yes, I do. I think that's where my brain cells get some of their inspiration from.

So, technically, it would also be our bloodthirsty little sister...

I wonder if they're doing okay...I wonder if they're safe.

What's happening to them in the Realm while I'm here?

"Well, you prey on his desperation. Reinforce the bond between us—by now that's not a new fact up for questioning—then plot with him about how to get the information from me. Suggest a worse form of solitary confinement with a good cop, bad cop routine. Tell him you'll try to stop him and save me, but he still needs to put me in solitary. Then go on to suggest that when it's time for me to come out, *you* should be the one to take me back, because it enforces you're the good cop who's rescuing me and I'll be foolish enough to believe that it's you and me against him. Telling Jeremiah all of this will make him trust you and make him feel in control, because to him, it's you and him against me and he's your secret weapon that's double crossing me." I snorted. "Little does he know you're only pretending to double cross me and really you're double crossing him."

The adorable crease between Ronan's eyebrows was making an appearance as his brows pulled together in doubt, and my brain cells began to squeal in delight. I watched, horrified, as they started taking pictures and then held a poll as to which eyebrow scrunch crease from the last few weeks was the most adorable.

Get ahold of yourselves, you ridiculous lot of goats. There is absolutely NO enamoring to be had! He is not the love of my life!

The brain cells boo'd and threatened a mutiny, offering various polaroid pictures of Ronan's facial expressions as justifiable reasons for rebellion. They were completely smitten. I was speechless as they began to give little speeches explaining exactly why Ronan *was* the love of my life.

Intent on making my point, I decided a clarifying announcement was necessary. "Now, I want to be very clear. Let it be added to the record that this supposed bond between us is *strictly* an illusion. There is absolutely *nothing* between us." I glared at him to add emphasis to my statement, at which my brain cells *all* booed. "Anyway," I continued, pointedly ignoring them. "That should do the trick."

Ronan still looked doubtful and, much to the disappointment of my violent brain cells, I resisted the urge to punch him. That required movement, and right now, movement was the ultimate enemy.

I need another nap before I try to move.

They go from being lovesick to wanting violence. What is wrong with them?

"Now, get a move on. You have to sweet talk a dreadful man and lure him into my brilliant trap. In the meantime, I have a nap to take."

"It's not like you just slept for five days," Ronan muttered as he stood up. He cast a lingering glance back, his eyes worried. There was something unspoken between us now—a dangerous, tender beginning.

Despite my best intentions, I did care for him. It was foolish, hopeless even, and I could only pray Ronan did not carry the same emotions. We were doomed before we began, and I didn't want him to carry the heartbreak of losing me. I knew enough of what the future held to guess that I wouldn't make it out of this gamble alive.

I hope that someday, he'll find happiness. I hope someday he can find someone who will help him forget this terrible chapter of his life, and the grief we bore together through it.

Perhaps they can love him for me...perhaps they can love him all the ways I can't.

Two, or perhaps three days later, Jeremiah returned. By then I had recovered enough I could get up without being worried I was going to die—*wanting* to die, however, was still very much on the table. Contrary to our usual encounters, Ronan lurked in the background.

I bet that means he was successful.

All eyes were on me, and out of my peripheral vision, I saw Ronan send me the subtlest nod, confirming my suspicion.

Pride for him soared, fluttering giddily in my chest.

I told you he could do it! I told you!

Yes, yes, you were right.

My three brain cells rallied around the thought, and, digging through a pile of discarded signs, they found their 'we hate Ronan' signs. Scribbling with fury, they destroyed all evidence of ever hating him and instead began to pour their praise of Ronan onto the posterboard, before marching in a tight little circle singing his greatness.

If only Ronan could see their adoration of him. I bet that would make him smile.

Faye: One. Jeremiah: Zero.

Ha, take that, you stupid ninny-head.

Now it's my turn. Time to get to work and cause some mayhem.

Not yet.

I feigned exhaustion, which, given my current state of existence, wasn't really all that hard. It could hardly be considered acting at this point.

"What, no spark?" Jeremiah goaded. "No heroic courage?"

I sighed. "Please, just leave me be. I don't know what you want. I can't help you."

"You know exactly what I want," Jeremiah snapped angrily. "You're simply withholding it."

I forced tears into my eyes. "Please," I whispered. "I, I can't help you. You're right, I know what you want, but I can't help you, Jeremiah. What you want is impossible."

It was the truth. I couldn't help him, and some small part of me longed for him to see the candor in my words. I wanted this nightmare to be over, even though another awaited me within the Realm.

Jeremiah sneered. "Do you think those tears can sway me? Those wretched droplets will bring you nothing here."

I resisted the urge to roll my eyes. That would definitely give mixed signals. Instead, I remained silent, allowing two of his men to roughly grab my arms. Their fingers dug into the weeping wounds, and I cried out, unable to help myself as my vision swam.

"Easy boys, I'd hate to reduce her to real tears before we've even begun. What a weak thing you are. Behold, the destined Grimm of the Realm. The one fated to slow the Gate by her power alone... What a pathetic excuse for a warrior. How could those foolish monarchs *ever* believe you and your foolhardy sisters could stop the rise?"

A chill ran down my spine at his words.

How does he know that? How does he know any of that?

I think it's time we found out what's behind that door.

No. That is a terrible idea. Stick to the plan. The plan says, we do not investigate that cursed door. I think we both know where it leads. The real question is why.

I didn't give Jeremiah a reply. I simply focused on staying upright as I rode out the agony his men were inflicting.

Ronan took a step forward, then stopped himself.

If he blows this because he listens to his ridiculous, chivalrous urges to be ridiculously overprotective, I'm going to kill him myself.

Yes, and then I'll dance on his grave.

Just wait, you stupid goat, you'll get your chance to rescue me. Just hold your horses and be patient. It's not your turn yet. I get to cause a scene first.

The trip to Jeremiah's office seemed longer than usual. By the time we got there, there was no acting involved in my movements. Every footstep was torture, and I began to doubt my ability to cause the much-anticipated scene.

What do I have in my favor? What do I possibly have?

Think, think, think.

It dawned on me then—I did have something in my favor. Jeremiah had become so consumed with his new form of interrogation, he hadn't been drugging me with the usual, daily power-numbing concoction.

I think that is the perfect way to cause a scene.

Please let this work.

I have to do it before he straps me down, though.

This is going to hurt. A lot.

YUP.

The moment I was through the doorway, I plunged my senses down, searching for my power. It was there; a burning ember buried deep inside my body.

I grabbed onto the oldest form of magic I knew. Tracing the long-forgotten rune with my finger, I spoke my magic back into full existence.

COME.

I yanked as I spoke the rune-powered word inside my mind, and it roared to life. A bolt of lightning flashed across the ceiling and hit the doorway, making the remaining men draw back in fear.

The men on either side of me yelped and let go of my arms. I shoved them back with a gust of wind, pinning them to the wall with straight-line winds as I drew more power from my Inheritance. The locket burned against my chest as I sent a bolt of lightning at Jeremiah. The strike hit him on the hip, and he flew back, hitting the shelves with a strangled cry.

Do I get bonus points for hitting him with the lightning?

I think that sounds like a wonderful idea.

The chaos was glorious and the braincells were immensely pleased by the mayhem as they screamed for Jeremiah's blood to be spilled.

Ronan rushed to his father's side as Jeremiah shoved himself up. "Faye! Stop this!" Ronan yelled.

The wind was a roaring cyclone around me, protecting me from attack on every side.

I sent another bolt at Jeremiah, and Ronan shoved him out of the way, taking the bolt himself on his side. He fell to his hands and knees with a strangled cry of pain.

Whoopsie.

Well, now no one will question his loyalty to Jeremiah.

The brain cells, however, screamed in outrage. Their precious Ronan was *not* to be harmed.

"Let me go!" I yelled. "I *can't* help you! Stop this madness Jeremiah, or else I'll kill you!"

The locket trembled against my chest as Ryver's spell struggled to sustain the new strength of my magic. The shadows around the room were growing. Sharp shapes of monsters with fangs and claws rose and fell along the wall. They were feeding off my emotions. Others rose inside of my mind—I could feel them there, greeting the ones on the wall.

It seems I have an audience.

Good. Let them see. Let them know what they're up against. Let the Knight question whether he truly wants to fight me...

Such brave words for such a weak being. I have no chance against him.

I do not need your negativity right now! We have to focus!

Just a little longer. I only have to do this for a little longer.

I was in the eye of the storm, the office a wreck around me. My gaze burned into Jeremiah's. "This is your last warning," I threatened.

"Do your worst," Jeremiah challenged. "You don't have the guts."

Oh yes, I do. But, luckily for you, you don't get to die today.

Or does he? What if I killed him now? What if I just ended this now? Would it stop his men?

I can't. If I do, the darkness will take me.

Realizing it was his moment to shine, Ronan pushed himself in front of Jeremiah—shielding him from my wrath as I sent a bolt of lightning at Jeremiah's chest.

Right-O, time to stop this.

I fell to my knees with a scream of fear, his name a desperate cry on my lips as the lightning bolt trembled, then froze in midair—stopping half an inch from Ronan's chest. It hovered over those handprints I knew were burned into his skin.

My reaction was all part of the plan. But I trembled as the storm continued to rage around me. I couldn't escape the sudden onslaught of memories. In the forefront of my mind, Ronan lay dead on the ground before me.

My fear was supposed to be an act. It was only meant to paint the illusion that I truly cared for Ronan, but it was real. I had come far too close to hurting Ronan.

Ronan shared a knowing glance with his father that spoke volumes, and I took it as my cue to sob. Whether in relief or sorrow—real or fake—I couldn't tell. My emotions were a churning lump inside my chest.

They shared a brief, quiet conversation that was lost on me as I wrestled against my emotions.

"Faye," Ronan said gently, pulling away from his father as he cautiously approached me. "Faye, look at me."

The storm flared around me, as if in fear.

I almost killed you again...I almost stole you from Meghan. What would I do without you? I almost killed you...

He took a few more steps forward, hands raised in a calming manner.

Oh, how this mirrors our first encounter, when he tried to reassure me with the same movement.

"I almost killed you," I whispered, so low it could have been missed. "I almost killed you."

The storm fell silent, and my ears popped. The room seemed to sway around me as the shadows continued to feed on my fear and emotions. Claws cut at the back of my mind. The monster inside was rising, preying on my pain—growing stronger with the minutes that passed.

For a moment Ronan's eyes caught mine. A thousand words passed in a glance, but it was in a language I didn't know, a tongue I could not speak.

I almost killed you. I almost killed you. Ronan, my Ronan.

Ronan wrapped his arms around me, pulling me to his chest and holding me close as I sobbed in earnest.

What if the bolt hadn't stopped? What if I lost control?

Jeremiah heaved, leaning heavily against the wall. The shadows grew around him, and for a moment, his eyes looked possessed. No longer was he looking at me—someone else was using his eyes to tear me apart at the seams.

"Ronan, step away from the witch," Jeremiah hissed.

Ronan's arms tightened around me. "Sir," he said quietly. "She—"

"I said. Step. Away." Jeremiah seethed. "I think our guest grows restless. I'm beginning to wonder if these little sessions are helping her. Giving her a chance to play the defiant victim. I think a stint in actual solitary will do her some good."

YES!

Lock me up, throw away the key, and leave me the heck alone!

Ronan played his part of the savior well and refused to let go. "I don't think—"

"Step away, Son," Jeremiah interrupted softly, giving Ronan a meaningful look. "She needs time to think over her actions. She almost killed you. You are the only piece of your precious mother I have left, until I am successful, and I will protect you. You don't know what you're doing. She has you under a spell."

Ronan shook his head, but his arms began to loosen around me.

I sobbed harder. "I'm so sorry," I whispered.

Ronan's hold fell away, and he reluctantly stood up and took a step back.

"Don't leave me," I whispered, working up the theatrics.

"Marcov," Jeremiah barked. "Take this *monster* away. Put her in the lightless room, the one we prepared for such an occasion as this."

Marcov's hands were rough as he pulled me to my feet, and I suddenly realized I might be too drained to fight him.

Am I strong enough to fight him if he tries anything?

I'll have to be.

Ronan masked his worry for me, but I could still sense it, buried deep inside.

He knows I'm weak. He thinks I'm not going to be able to fight Marcov. Don't interfere, Ronan. Don't you dare interfere. Marcov will tell Jeremiah. It will ruin our plans. Stick to the act.

I can take care of myself. I'll be okay.

Jeremiah limped over to me and roughly took my chin in his hands, forcing me to look at him. "Maybe a month or two with no one to talk to or fight will do you some good. Maybe it'll make you see some sense." He laughed, a cruel, dark sound. "If you can see anything at all after this."

Ronan's fists clenched and I silently begged him to stay put—to put his mask back on. If Jeremiah noticed any genuine affection, when Ronan was supposed to be pretending, he might suspect a true turning in his son.

If he blows this, after I risked my life to make it happen, I'm going to put glitter on and in everything he owns. He'll be eating and pooping glitter for the rest of his miserable life.

Which wouldn't be long, because after I'm done with that petty revenge, I'm going to kill him.

Fine. For the rest of his short, miserable life.

"Take her away," Jeremiah hissed. The pain was evident on his face, and I smothered a smirk. It wouldn't be good to smirk when one was supposed to be defeated.

Ronan offered him a hand, but Jeremiah waved it away. "Leave me," he said. "Go see to the men's training. I will talk to you later in the week. I have matters to attend to."

Continuing my acting scheme, I cast a frantic glance back at Ronan.

Jeremiah's eyes narrowed in greedy satisfaction, noting how I sought reassurance in his son.

Yup. He's fallen for it. Hook, line, and sinker.

He's a dead duck now. Such a stinker...stinky duck...

Wait, what's a duck have to do with fishing, and why does it stink?

Maybe the fish ate the duck? Besides, it's Jeremiah. He always stinks and making the words rhyme gives me bonus points.

Okay, I'll give you that. How big is this metaphorical fish we're talking about?

I mean, it would have to be big to eat a duck...

Let's just forget the duck and go back to fishing.

Fine. He's a dead fish now.

Aw man, that just doesn't have the right ring to it.

Ahem, focus. We're supposed to be a traumatized, scared victim. Not arguing about ducks and fish and other such nonsense.

Right. Victim, play the victim.

I let out a miniscule sob, just as the door closed and Marcov gave me a look of greedy anticipation.

How sad for him he's thoroughly duped. I am neither weak nor upset.

Well, okay, I am weak but not weak enough to be unable to beat him to a pulp. He's in for a world of hurt if he tries anything.

Soooooo much hurt.

PART TWO
BROKEN HEARTS

28

The Broken Hearts That Bind Us Together

EMBER

"More than anything, all I have ever wanted is to be close to someone.
More than anything, all I have ever wanted is to feel as if I wasn't alone."
-James Fey, A Million Little Pieces

I stood on the edge of the ship, fear clawing at my chest as I stared down into the darkness that stretched beneath me. The wind pulled at my body, desperately yanking at my WyrldCloak. Trying to drag me off and down into the endless sky. It whispered honey sweet lies and poisoned promises. Insisting that, if I let go, if I just jumped, it would all be over. Things would get better. I would be okay... One wrong step, just one wrong move, and everything would end... The darkness would take me and the pain would at last fall silent...

It would all go away if I just let go...if I just...jumped...

I wanted a release. I wanted to escape. There was nothing left within but a shell. An empty tomb with a broken, shattered heart. A damaged, battered soul. All I wanted was answers to the questions I held onto. Had we made the right choice to come here? If I had refused to listen to Jack and stayed, would it have spared us all this trouble? All this agony? My sister was broken because of me. But she was also alive because of me.

If I had just caved to Darcy in the Halls, would it have spared her? Would it have made a difference?

No. It wouldn't have...it wouldn't...He would still hurt her to get to me.

Jumping won't fix my problems. It won't help anything. It'll just leave her to fight alone. I can't do that to her. I have to stay and fight for her. She needs me. She is worth living for. My family is worth staying alive for.

But no matter the rational thoughts, the emptiness continued to beckon. Begging me to let go, let go, *just let go*. It drew me forward, like a moth to the flame, wearing at my resolve, this stubborn determination to keep fighting. It was eerily familiar. That voice from the canyon at the cursed castle seemed to resonate through that pull—luring me to a dreadful end.

All I wanted was peace and rest. A safe place to lay my head.

Hands closed around my wrists, pulling me back step after step until I was safely away from the edge.

"There is no going back from such an end, my Flamín." Artemis' voice was soft, gentle even, as he turned me around and pulled me into his arms. I leaned into the tight embrace, cheek against his chest. Trying to forget the brokenness that bled between us. It was just a dream; I might as well get some comfort until it turned into a nightmare.

"There's always hope, Em. Something to keep living for—even if you cannot see it. Don't leave me to fight this future alone. Don't force me to face the rising darkness without you by my side."

Exhaustion was tearing me apart as I struggled against the grey inside my mind that threatened to swallow me whole. I was drowning. I didn't want to fight anymore. I wanted it all to *stop*.

I'm falling. Make it stop, Artemis. Please, make it stop. Help me. Please, help me.

"What happened?" Artemis asked softly. "What happened to us? I thought we had hope, and then...then you left me. Why did you leave me?" There was no condemnation in his tone, only a heartache I knew all too well.

It was the unanswered question that tortured me. One he seemed to desperately scream across the cavern that divided us.

"I felt..." he paused. "Something happened," he whispered at last. "What happened, Em? There was so much pain it cut through my mind, my heart...what happened?"

He found us, Artemis. He's alive. He's still alive, and he's coming for us again. He hurt

Evadne. He hurt her and I can't make it right. I can't make it up to her. He did that to her, because of me... I let him hurt me to save her... How do I find my way through this tangled haze? How do I explain what happened, when I'm lost in this labyrinth?

The words wouldn't come. Darcy's curse still bound me to silence. I wanted to scream. To destroy everything around me in my rising fury. This silence Darcy forced onto me was killing me, moment by moment.

"Found us," I whispered at last.

Artemis' body stiffened for a moment. "Who?" he asked.

The silence stretched between us. Still I could not speak.

His brows came together. He knew what the silence meant. He was slowly putting the pieces together. His music was there on the edge of my mind, probing, begging to be let in. Begging me to just *show* him what had happened.

I can't show him...if I do, he'll know where we are. He'll come find us. He'll take us back.

I haven't found the answer for the other way. Theron hasn't told us yet. I don't know if there's a way to save Evadne... I'm coming back, Artemis, but I have to save her first...

I can't let him know where we are...but maybe...just maybe I could show him enough to let him know how much danger he's in...how much danger we're all in...perhaps I can show him that Darcy is still alive. How far does the silencing go? I could show him what happened at the ball...will I be able to show him this? Is the curse finally unraveling?

"Don't make me regret this," I whispered hoarsely, as I carefully lowered part of my walls.

Artemis lowered his head, gently resting his forehead against mine as he wrapped my fingers in his. His music slid across my mind. It was a gentle lullaby, one that sought to comfort and hold me close.

He recoiled in horror as the jumbled memories from the last few days hit him like a knife to the gut. I couldn't sort them; it was all a tangled mess of screams and blood. Evadne writhed on the cot, the words carved into her skin with an invisible knife, my mismatched eyes in the mirror, and then, Darcy's voice.

"No," Artemis whispered.

Artemis' rage began to simmer and rise as he combed back, pulling the memories apart, breaking my feeble walls that sought to contain him to a specific moment in time. There was no maliciousness in his actions, however. There was only the desperate need to figure out what had happened in his absence.

He watched everything replay—my broken heart as I left him kneeling there, the indecision, the desperation to find another way to save my sister. The need to know what else there was besides a bloody end at the Last Gate.

"I don't blame you," he whispered in my mind. *"I can't possibly blame you for wanting to find another way... But I cannot let you go. Surely you know, I cannot let you go."*

He followed the trail of our bloody journey through the sky. Darcy's warnings, the way he had manipulated my dreams to make me think it was Artemis torturing Evadne in revenge—using things only he and I knew. He followed our painful journey all the way to the stone ruins at the edge of the Wastes, and the darkness within. He trembled against me, watching helplessly as I met the monster in the depths, the ocean I floated on to block the hours out.

He pulled me closer. I cried out and jerked away as the pressure reawakened the agony of the lashes on my back.

Artemis recoiled at the memory of the lashing that rose and fled in an instant. I did not want him to see that. I had come to terms with what had happened. I had accepted my punishment, but I did not know if he could.

Artemis' face was hard in the moonlight as he took a step closer. Gently placing his fingers under my jaw, he tilted my head up, staring down at me, his face a mix of pain and anger. "Who did that to you?" His words were a breath, laced with violence and rage.

Verity. Verity did it, but she had to. But will you understand? If I show you, will you understand?

His music moved back to the edge of my mind, but my walls were back in place. I couldn't show him anything more. I couldn't trust him with the rest. Not yet. I had to find a way to save Evadne. The rest of my memories included the late-night talks with Verity about where we were going next, and what would happen once we had healed enough to travel and be of use to the crew.

"Ember," Artemis whispered, resting his head against mine once more, music begging, pleading with me to let him in. "Let me in. Let me help you. There is no other way. Theron doesn't have the answers you seek—his way will not help you. Come back. Please, Em." His voice cracked, showing the broken heart beneath. "Please come back. We can face this together. We can change the future together."

I can't, Artemis. Don't you know I can't?

I have to save her. I can't come back yet. I can't come back yet.

"I'm sorry," I whispered, pushing back from him. "I'm so sorry," I sobbed. I was stepping away from him, step by step, until I teetered on the edge of the deck.

"There's no coming back from this," I whispered. "Let me go, Artemis. Let me go."

He lunged for me, my name a desperate cry on his lips as I tipped backward and let myself fall off the edge of the ship.

Artemis didn't stop. He jumped, hurtling off the edge of the ship—reaching for me as the dream began to shatter around us.

"I will never let you go," he whispered as his hand grasped mine and he pulled me into his chest, holding me close as we fell through the moonlit sky. "My broken heart is chained to yours, and I can never, never let you go."

29

A Sister's Rage Knows No End...But Her Stupidity Is Even Worse

EMBER

"You sleep coiled; tightly wound. Hands are fists beneath pillows,
clenched above cotton sheets. You are at war, even in your dreams
–Rest Achilles, the world will wait."

-p.d

The next morning found me exhausted, still haunted by memories of the dream. Artemis' arms around me had seemed so real. His desperate words, so true. The look on his face when he jumped, so sincere.

Was it real? Was he really there, or did I create something to comfort myself? Did I create an alternate reality where there is hope of mending the burnt bridge between us?

My wandering thoughts were interrupted by Evadne's anger. I was so tired it was hard to stay focused on the task at hand. Which happened to be keeping her from doing something incredibly stupid—like punching Captain Verity.

"Eva, let it go," I hissed, jerking on her arm.

"No!" she snapped, throwing down her sketchbook. The page was filled with gruesome charcoal images of shadows and monsters, a knife that dripped crimson, and those hateful, golden eyes.

"The good Captain and I have some matters to sort," she growled.

"There is *nothing* to sort," I protested angrily, yanking her back. "Stop acting like an idiot and *listen* to me."

"I won't!" her voice trembled. She was rapidly losing her strength. It wouldn't be long before she was forced to abandon her quest for vengeance.

I pulled on her arm again, trying not to wince from the movement. "Eva, you cannot punch Captain Verity. She's the freaking *captain!* I *told* you what happened. She was justified in what she did. A captain must maintain order and authority. I directly disobeyed her orders."

"You were saving *me!*" Evadne yelled. "You were doing it to save me! Yaga *sent you* to the market! She tricked us! She tricked us all!"

She was shaking, trembling as the fight slowly drained out of her. Tears were sliding down her cheeks, big black droplets leaking from the corners of her injured eye. Baba Yaga had failed to heal it and reverse the damage done by Darcy's cursed blade.

"I know, I know," I whispered as I wrapped her in a tight hug. "I know, Eva, but she was right to do it."

She was sobbing now. "No, she *wasn't!* You went there for *me*, Em. I wasn't worth the price. I wasn't worth it. Why, *why* did you go to that monster for me? You should have just let him kill me."

"No," I murmured, holding her tightly as tears rolled down my cheeks. "No Eva, I couldn't do that. You are my heart, my sister, my blood. I will protect you, no matter the cost. Even to my dying breath."

Sorrow bled between us as we wept. Neither of us had come away from the ordeal with Darcy unstained.

I wanted to be strong and untainted—uncaring of the damage he'd done. But there was nothing left from that moment in time. Just the shattered pieces of my mind and the lingering hopelessness that seemed to haunt me from that darkness.

I don't want to feel like a victim. I don't want to feel this way. But how do I find balance between what he did, and moving past it? Is there a way to acknowledge I was a victim to his monstrosity, without allowing myself to become trapped in a victim mentality? Is there a balance between the two?

How do I reconcile the broken parts of myself?

How do I move on?

"I want to go home," Evadne sobbed angrily. "I want to go *home*."

"I do too," I whispered soothingly. "I do too."

"Why did Jack put us on this ship?" she whispered. "I didn't agree to come here."

Guilt shot through me. She'd had no say in the matter, and here we were. She'd read the letter and then reread it a dozen times. But she was still too angry to see the sense behind Jack's actions. She missed Marcus most of all, and right now it seemed like Marcus would be the only person who could talk sense into her.

"I'm still going to punch her," Evadne threatened darkly, changing the subject. "Perhaps I'll even *stab* her."

"You will do no such thing," I replied sternly.

"Watch me."

"Well, if you're going to make terrible choices, you might as well get it over with."

I jumped, startled. I hadn't heard Captain Verity's approach.

Evadne jerked to her feet, wrenching herself from my desperate grasp.

"EVA!" I whisper yelled.

She ignored me. She was too busy limping her way over to Verity.

"You're in luck, Grimm," Verity commented dryly. "I just had my fourth cup of coffee, which means I won't leave you hanging by your toes off the edge of the ship for your insubordination. The magic bean juice does make me particularly lenient for the first ten minutes." She arched an eyebrow, staring down my sister. "You have ten minutes in which to abuse my lenience."

Oh, dear heavens. What has gotten into her?

You stupid, stupid sister. Stop before she turns you into paste!

But what kind of paste? Toothpaste, tomato-paste, curry-paste?

Shut up. We don't have time for details we have to stop Evadne.

Ooor...hear me out here, we could just watch and see what happens. The drama is incredibly delightful.

You are a terrible sister.

Perhaps, but you know I'm right.

"You had no right!" Evadne fumed.

"I had every right," Verity cut in firmly. "She disobeyed a direct order and put lives in danger with her heroic, self-sacrificial martyrdom."

Ouch. Way to make me sound good.

"Yaga tricked her!" Evadne yelled. "She tricked *all* of you!"

"Yaga would not be so foolish as to manipulate a bargain. Besides, what would she have to gain by tricking us?"

"She wasn't going to be able to free me. She fought that monster for ages, and he laughed at her. He *laughed*, Verity."

"No one can stand against Yaga. She herself helped bind the Darke One. She helped create this bordered Realm. *No one* can stand against her."

"He did," Evadne seethed. "He withstood her and if Ember hadn't come, he would have killed me."

"What use would you be to him dead?" Verity asked.

Evadne faltered.

"Think it through, Grimm. What use would you have been to him if you were dead? The Erlking wants *both* of you. Hence why there's a bounty on both of your heads at the moment. All of the Moores are out looking for you now. If Ember dearest had used her head and simply *told* me what was going on, we could have come up with a plan and she wouldn't have had to meet him alone."

"She *can't*!" Evadne yelled, exasperated. "We've been—" her words cut off in a strangled sort of silence, which morphed into a feral growl of rage. "Curse it all to the depths of darkness!"

She continued to rant, but now she was rapidly hopping from one language to the next—swearing profusely in every language she knew as she wrestled against her rage and frustration.

She was leaning heavily on her makeshift cane now and I went to her side, gently pulling her back to the bed to sit down.

"*Why* am I so exhausted?" Evadne whispered angrily. "What is *wrong* with me? This is ridiculous!"

Verity examined her nails idly. "Hmm, it definitely has nothing to do with your being cursed, not to mention tortured for days on end."

Evadne glared at Captain Verity, her visible eye full of wrath and indignation.

"Child," Verity sighed. "There are painful lessons that we all must learn in this life, lest we unintentionally send souls to the next. There is a cost to every decision, and when our decisions put others in danger, we must face the consequences for our poor choices. I believe it's called involuntary manslaughter. Your sister's decision, while noble, was still wrong. She is on my ship, under my protection, and with that protection comes the reality of my authority. You are *both* under my authority. I understand your rage, hence why I'm allowing you to rid yourself of all the poisonous drops and fully voice your anger—misplaced though it be. But after the anger has subsided, you must accept that, while it is not how things are done in your world, it *is* how they are done in *mine*." Verity walked toward us, her eyes fixed on Evadne until she stood over her. "You are in my world now, Grimm. Learn to abide by our rules or face the consequences. Either way though, you will learn."

There was something akin to sympathy on Verity's face as she looked down at my sister. "I had a sister once, a sister I would do anything to protect. But I could not save her from such a monster, and it is my greatest regret."

"Then you understand why she came."

"I do," Verity replied. "But I also understand she put other's lives in danger. Here in the Moores, on this ship, this crew is a family. We live, bleed, and die for each other. We work as a team, or not at all. I know you were silenced, Ember. I know both of you are. But you didn't give Yaga a chance." Verity turned back to Evadne. "As captain of this ship, I cannot allow her disobedience to go unchecked. Ember knew full well that she was defying me and she accepted the consequences of her actions. It's time you let her accept her mistakes."

"She was *tricked*. You both were!" Evadne hissed, clinging to her rage.

"Eva, let it go," I said gently, squeezing her hand.

I could see the indecision and pain at war on her face.

"Let it go," I repeated. "Please, don't make this harder than it needs to be."

"No, I'm *not*! I'm *not* making this harder than it needs to be!" she protested.

"You need time." Verity sighed. "It will take time for you to come to terms with my decisions, and I respect that. My only requirement in giving you time is that you respect my authority on this ship. You don't have to agree, but you do have to listen and obey. That is all I ask of you, to trust me to make the decisions that are for the benefit of my crew. A crew that *you* are now, in a very real way, a part of, until our paths divide."

Evadne was crying again, but there was a quiet resignation to her manner now. At last, after a silence that seemed to last an eternity, she nodded. "I'm going to prove to you that Yaga manipulated the bargain," she said so softly I almost didn't hear her.

Verity, however, heard her completely. Her eyes narrowed. "How about a wager, Grimm?"

"No." I snapped. "No wagers."

"Prove the witch lied, and I'll let Clarice completely heal the rest of your sister's back."

"And if I fail?" Evadne challenged, lifting her chin.

Verity smirked. "I don't let Theron help your sister get her skye legs. In case you didn't notice, he's been aiding her since she set foot on my deck."

"What do you mean?" I asked, interrupting their stare down. "I've been terrified. What do you mean helped?"

"Why do you think your fear hasn't *utterly* paralyzed you?" Verity asked, her eyebrows arching in amusement.

"I thought I was well, maybe, brave...er...ish..." My voice trailed off.

Theron is a Grimm... What is his Inheritance?

Verity's amusement only seemed to grow. "As much as I wish that were true, he's been aiding you. Theron's gift, or coveted Inheritance if you will, is the manipulation of emotions. He can give or take them away. He's been taking your fear to help you adjust and process life on the ship."

Now it makes sense.

How fitting, the pirate is a thief.

I made a face, annoyed. I had genuinely thought I was doing better.

"He'll stop helping both of us, or just me?" Evadne asked, still contemplating Verity's offer.

Verity's mouth quirked. "It wouldn't be a true wager if you were the only one who suffered. She gains by your triumph. She loses by your failure. That should be incentive enough."

"Evadne," I warned. As much as the prospect of Theron stealing my fear annoyed me, the reality of having to take that fear head on was one I didn't want to face. "This is stupid and reckless. Don't do it."

Evadne turned to me. "Em, she could heal your back. I know I can get Yaga to talk. Please, trust me. Let me help you. It's my fault this happened in the first place."

"No, it's not Eva. But if you fail, then it *will* be your fault that I'm absolutely miserable and terrified on this stupid ship."

"Come now," Verity scoffed. "There's no need to insult my dear ship. That's just downright rude. The Aurora is a wonderful vessel."

"Sorry," I mumbled.

"Consider it exposure therapy," Evadne quipped. "Please," she added quietly, all mirth gone. "Let me try to make this right."

"No…" I replied, annoyed. But we both knew I was wavering.

"Em…" Evadne's voice trailed off in a pleading whine. She clasped her hands under her chin and batted her eyelashes. A small smile pulled at the corners of her mouth. She had me and she knew it.

"Fine," I muttered, annoyed beyond measure. "But you'd better make her talk. If you don't, I'm going to make you regret it. *I'll* stab you with my salad fork."

Evadne pumped her fist in the air. "Yes!" she whispered excitedly.

"That seems like a drastic measure," Verity scoffed. "A dagger is much easier. The force required to stab someone with a salad fork is a waste of energy. But nevermind that," Verity said with a shrug and a smirk. "it's a deal then."

She held out her hand to Evadne and Evadne excitedly shook it.

"Tell Clarice to get ready to heal my sister's back," Evadne called as she wobbled over to the window.

Verity smiled. "We'll see," she replied.

Her answer is not making me feel well.

Good grief, Evadne. What have you done? What have you gotten us into now?

Stupidity. That's what she's gotten us into. Pure and utter stupidity.

Stupid, stupid sister!

"When do we leave?" Evadne called, staring out at the jumbled islands.

Verity arched an eyebrow. "We can leave now, if you like."

"Let's do it," Evadne whispered. "I have to prove I'm right."

"You certainly have to prove *something*," Verity replied with a mirthless laugh. "I'll get the crew around. Be ready to go out in the next ten minutes. Wear your armor. The witch is not liable to be kind. She's no doubt taken an extreme liking to her cursed artifacts. She may have been friendly when you woke, Evadne. But returning to call up the bargain will awaken the monster within."

I have a really, really bad feeling about this.

Time to confront a manipulative, cannibal witch…yes, nothing is wrong with this picture at all…this is going to go so well…nothing could go wrong…absolutely nothing…

30

Confronting A Manipulative, Cannibal Witch—0/10 Stars, Would Not Recommend, It Will Never Go In Your Favor (She Cheats)

EMBER

"I am a shadow's shade, a lunatic perhaps, of two dark moons."
-Marina Tsvetaeva

Leaving the ship by rope was a challenge. One that re-opened the thickly clotted wounds on my back as I climbed down.

Evadne was too weak to get down on her own and was once again subjected to Theron's undignified carrying method.

"I'd carry you down like a swooning damsel," Theron grunted as he gently swung Evade over his shoulder. "But I just can't get down the rope with my arms around you. I'm short a couple of arms."

"This is *so* unbecoming!" Evadne hissed angrily. Her cheeks were bright red in embarrassment. "I have never been so *humiliated* in my entire life!"

"Give it time. Something else will come along that will be worse. *Much*, much worse, and then you'll have forgotten all about this little hiccup in time!"

I watched their argument from the dock below, not bothering to hide my amusement. I was tucking the memory away in the back of my mind. I would harass Evadne with it later.

Theron's boots hit the deck with a loud thud, and he gently lifted the still fuming Evadne down from his shoulder.

"There now, my angry little kraken. There's no need to be so grouchy. I'd guess only...hm, I'd say about *half* the crew saw it."

Evadne scoffed and took a wobbling step forward. She had yet to gain control of her balance and adjust to her injured eye and she pitched sideways with a scared shriek.

Theron's arm shot out, stopping her from falling off the edge of the dock.

She swore vehemently in French, her single dark eye ablaze with fury.

Theron arched an eyebrow. "Heaven help the man who dares come against you. You could destroy him with your vile mouth alone."

"As if you haven't sworn ten times worse than that," Verity scoffed.

Evadne turned her furious eye on Theron, and he raised his free hand in surrender. "Here's your cane oh grouchy kraken. What shall I sacrifice to appease your wrath? I'm a little short on ships. But I could take you to several a few islands over whose traders cheated me on our bargains. I'd happily let you destroy *them*."

Evadne's anger melted a little bit, and the corners of her mouth turned up in a sharp, half smile.

"There we go. That's all you need, you bloodthirsty little monster. You just need someone to destroy. Open ocean or air, you are truly a monster among men, aren't you?"

Evadne's smile widened and she grinned, baring her teeth in a savage smile that reminded me so much of Rosamond's threatening grin. "Maybe," she mused.

"That's my girl," Theron said encouragingly as he handed her the makeshift cane.

"Oh," Evadne said suddenly. "Wait, I forgot."

"What?" I asked, curious.

"The staffs," Evadne replied as she dug through her WyrldCloak pocket. "Mine is buried in one of these pockets. It'll work much better than this cane."

"I'll have you know I worked very hard on that cane of yours," Theron replied indignantly. "Do you realize how ungrateful you are?"

His protests fell short when he saw Evadne's ornate staff.

"Now that is a work of art." He took a step closer. "I'd recognize that handiwork anywhere. That's the work of the healer herself. The one of the woods."

He turned a keen gaze on Evadne. "You didn't say she traveled with you."

"You didn't ask," Evadne snapped. "Besides, she left our party before we split from Artemis. Why do you care?"

"There's unfinished business between us," Theron replied darkly. "Last time I saw her, I promised to put an arrow through her heart, and she swore to do the same. It's only a matter of time before our fates intertwine again. You may bring death to me, my little monster."

"Why?" I asked, unable to contain my curiosity.

"I loved her once, many ages ago. But she betrayed me and tried to take me back to the Central Realm. So, I cut off her wings."

My mouth fell open in shock and Verity sighed. "Theron doesn't know how to play nice," she mused. "He only knows how to retaliate in extremes. Destroying her wings took it too far."

"She can regrow them," Theron snapped.

"But she will *never* be the same," Verity replied curtly. "You know this all too well. When someone steals something like that from you, you're never the same. You only ensured your death with such a foolhardy action."

"As long as she goes with me, I will consider it a good day," Theron muttered angrily as we began to make our way toward the woods.

Verity turned to me. "Don't mention that little altercation to Raz, if you don't mind. When she found out what he did, she destroyed half the ship trying to kill him. Taking someone's wings is akin to a different crime in her culture."

I nodded, pondering the situation. I had never seen Rosamond with wings, so even though she could have regrown them, she'd never chosen to.

Does she not because she wants to hold onto that anger? Or is Theron wrong and she can't regrow them?

"She moved her island again," Verity sighed, annoyance clinging to her voice. "Why does she always have to play the Wastes like it's her own personal jigsaw puzzle? It's going to make the Moores very irritated with her."

Is the Moores a sentient being? Something more than just a part of the Realm?

How do all these pieces fit together? I wish it made sense.

Theron grunted in agreement as he helped Evadne navigate the rough terrain. He was giving her guidance and input on how to function with half her vision gone. He then began to suggest ways she could use her blindness to her benefit. He had a great many ideas, such as manipulating others to pity her, then taking severe advantage of them.

His energetic prattle kept us entertained through the miserable trek, and it helped lift Evadne's low spirits. She had been struggling since she woke at Baba Yaga's, and unable to find her usual sunny disposition, she had reverted to anger and grumpiness. It was bound to get someone hurt.

I wouldn't put it past her to sick Fireheart on someone.

Evadne laughed at something particularly stupid that Theron suggested—something along the lines of bribing pixies to fart on people as a distraction while she looted their ship—and my worry for her decreased slightly. Perhaps we would be okay. Maybe there was still hope she'd get out of this without imploding.

We're gonna be okay. We're going to make it out of this, and everything will be okay.

But I couldn't escape the memories of how she tossed and turned through the long nights, crying out and speaking in a dark, powerful language that seemed to shake the air around her. There was something different about her, something haunted and old that didn't belong.

I knew my twin like the back of my hand, and the person who had awoken in Baba Yaga's cottage was a different person from the one I had known all my life. It scared me. Because I didn't know how she had changed, only that now she carried a certain sense of darkness with her.

My sense of foreboding about our plan only grew, until at last the disheveled little cottage stood before us. My dread became a churning knot in my stomach.

It was time to face Baba Yaga.

There was no sign of her outside, so we made our way to the door. The jagged gate screeched as we carefully opened it.

I exchanged a fearful glance with Verity, who in turn took a deep breath and pulled her shoulders straight. It was a gentle reminder to compose myself and face my fear.

I took a step forward, taking the lead, and with a final, hesitant glance back at Evadne, knocked on the door.

Baba Yaga opened it so fast, it was almost as if she had been waiting for my knock on the other side.

"What do you want, daughter of Grimm?" she asked. Her voice was sharp and angry.

Nothing like that of the old woman who had seemed to have compassion for us the first time we'd sought her aid. The monster she so carefully hid beneath the surface was loose and its fangs were at my throat.

I took a steadying breath. I had to be careful. Very, very careful.

Evadne and I had talked over the logistics of getting Yaga to talk. We had decided on a two-person attack. I would start and then she would go in for the kill. After all, she was the one who had been there. She knew that Baba had failed to best Darcy. She had simply guided her back after Darcy had already released her. We had no proof, but we planned to back her into a corner until she lashed out and revealed the truth she was so jealously guarding.

"You failed to uphold our bargain," I stated.

Yaga hissed and tried to slam the door in my face. My foot took most of the brunt as I lodged it in the gap, but I also slammed my fist into the wood for added effect. I had to gain the upper hand and intimidate her using whatever means possible.

"You *failed* to uphold our bargain," I repeated, my voice low and menacing. "Give me back the cursed thorns."

"I can't," she sneered. "I used them."

"You also owe me a promise," I continued, ignoring her. How to replace what she'd used was a thought for later. Surely there was a way to wheedle another promise or favor from her.

"I owe you nothing. *I* brought the girl back. *I* saved her."

"No, you didn't, and you know it," I countered angrily. "That's why you already used the artifacts. Because you *knew* I was coming. You *knew* you failed. Besides, even if you had brought her back and saved her from that darkness, you didn't heal her completely. Her eye is ruined, and more than that, she's tainted. She carries his shadows now. *Look at her!*"

Baba Yaga winced and backed up, refusing to look at Evadne.

"Acknowledge your failure, Baba Yaga. See what you've done. If you default on our bargain, then you die. You know how the magic binds."

She looked up, her milky eyes containing swirls of red now. "You didn't bind me with your magic. I bear no mark with which you can destroy me. Besides, I do not have artifacts to return. Thus, the bargain is simply null. You *lose*, daughter of Grimm," she hissed.

"That's not how this works. You built the Realms. You *know* how the magic binds you."

"Look at me, Yaga," Evadne growled, taking an uneven step forward. "Look at what you could not heal. I'm blind. I'm tainted. You *failed* me."

"I failed *no one*," Yaga yelled, her voice cracking. "I brought you back. *I* did! It was me. Me *ME!*"

"I would have woken up as soon as you called my name. He released me willingly, because Ember came. Nothing kept me there except sleep and you know it. You fought him for hours. He *tortured* me, for hours while he bested you." Evadne was sobbing in anger now. Her tears were a mixture of clear and black. "Admit it, Yaga! You *failed*. You didn't save me, Ember did. And you're the one who sent her there, to the monster. You *knew* he would let me go if she went. That's why you sent her to the market. You manipulated the bargain!"

"No," Yaga whispered, stumbling backward. "Maybe I could not heal you, but I brought you back. I called your name."

"I would have woken up if it was Verity or Theron who called my name," Evadne countered, repeating the truth she'd already challenged Yaga with. "Admit it. You're helpless against the Knight. The cursed one. Bluebeard is stronger than you now. He's stronger than all of us. He held you at bay and he *laughed*."

Baba Yaga growled in outrage. "You dare, when *I* was the one who imprisoned him. *I* who ate the heart and bound him there. *I* who tricked the great Erlking himself. You *dare* challenge my power, you miserable, weeping, feeble Grimm? You dare when *I* am the one who cursed your bloodline. You stand before me as the bones weep about your bloody fate. You dare challenge me, while you remain a harbinger of the future."

Evadne took another step forward. "Yes," she whispered. "I dare. Because I was there." Evadne's voice was rising with every word. Her tone grew harsher with every syllable. "I heard how he mocked you. I saw how you were *helpless* against his power. You sent my sister there, like a lamb to the slaughter. *You sent her there*! YOU MANIP-ULATED THE BARGAIN! ***ADMIT IT!***"

The air stilled around us as Evadne unknowingly spoke the spell into being. She had woven magic without even knowing it.

"Yes! I manipulated the bargain!" Baba Yaga screeched. "But what choice did I have?!" she charged at Evadne like a crazed animal.

Now we've got her.

"What else was I to do, when all else had failed?" Yaga continued angrily, her voice rising to a scream. "If you think that your miserable, mewling life is worth more than those artifacts tainted with your powerful, cursed blood, you are sorely mistaken. I would have ripped out your heart to get those pieces if I had to."

Well. That's a terrible thought.

We made a very, very foolish decision leaving her alone with Evadne. Thank goodness nothing worse happened.

"Give back the artifacts and give my sister her promise, witch," Evadne hissed. "Or else I will find a way to curse you with my magic, and I promise you, you will *drown* beneath my fury."

The darkness was leaking through the cracks. It was her voice, but the words were not anything I would have imagined my sister saying. Even when she was angry, she was never vengeful like this.

What happened to her in that place? What did Darcy do to her?

Yaga's eyes narrowed. "I told you, harbinger. I don't have them. They are already gone, and I have become stronger. I will destroy you now."

"You will try, and you will once again fail," Evadne replied icily. "You can't raise a hand against us. Not in retaliation for a bargain you failed."

"She's right."

A new voice entered the argument, unfamiliar and deep.

Okay. Who else is here?

The cat, Red, walked out from the back of the cabin. "She's right, Yaga. You cannot fight it. If you do, the Moores will crumble. Do not bring this destruction upon us all."

"What do I care?" Baba Yaga hissed. "They will fall regardless."

"Do you think he will forget your part in his imprisonment, all those years ago? He will come for you first, and he will kill you in the most painful way possible. He will follow the echoes of your magic. He already knows where you hide."

"I hide from *no one*," Baba Yaga yelled. "I am Baba Yaga the great, the horrible, the *feared*. Children scream when they hear my name. I am the witch of the Wastes."

"Death waits for no man, Wendigo," Red replied quietly. "You will die, and your corpse will haunt the ashes of this Realm. You cannot stop it. You've already seen your end. Give them what they came for and let them on their way, cursed though it may be."

"My own cat turned against me," Yaga screamed, aiming a kick at his side.

"NO!" Evadne yelled. She stumbled forward and scooped Red into her arms. She fell, off balance, and Yaga's foot collided with her injured eye.

"Evadne!" I yelled.

She screamed in agony, but curled protectively around the cat, protecting him as she hit the floor.

"Fine!" Baba Yaga screamed. "Take your wretched promise."

"In retribution for the loss of the artifacts, I would like a promise for Evadne as well," I called as I took careful steps forward to Evadne's side. "Consider it a gift that I did not make you pay for failing and using the artifacts anyway." I kept my eyes on the witch while I helped my sister to her feet. Blood and shadows poured from her injured eye, tears of agony from the other.

Baba Yaga gave me a cold, cruel smile and it suddenly felt as if I no longer had the upper hand. "So be it, Grimm. Take your promises, then leave me. You can take my traitorous cat with you. I no longer want his flea-riddled pelt in my house."

Red hissed from Evadne's arms as she and I backed slowly out of the house. "I am no one's to take," he growled. "I stayed these long years for your benefit. Don't forget who pulled you from the darkness."

Baba Yaga ignored Red and turned to me. "A promise you want, Grimm? Fine, a promise I give to you—you, whose love cursed the Realm. My sister is dead because of you. The Realms will die because of you. This *I promise*—you will die, choking on your own blood, as the beast feeds on you. The cursed shadow will rip out your throat as you whisper your lover's name—as he watches, helpless. The ones you love most will fall, never to return. None will escape his wrath."

I wanted to speak, to scream and fight her words, but I was frozen, held in place as her words boomed and echoed. A wind tore at us, caging us in the doorway of the house while keeping Verity and Theron and the rest of the crew out. It was us against the witch and we stood *helpless* in her power.

Evadne screamed my name, and ebony water shot from her fingertips, racing toward Baba Yaga. The two were caught in a battle of wills as Evadne overpowered Yaga's magic and stepped in front of me. The blue forget-me-nots in her staff were glowing a bright, florescent cerulean.

"And you, child of darkness, cursed one of blood. I have not forgotten your promise. This *I promise*."

A chill ran down my spine as the magic began to weave through her words.

"I promise that you will lose what you love most in the world. It will die in your hands, and you will fail to save it. You will remember my words, as you scream and bleed. You will *fall* as the knight rises again. Remember this in your rising power, child of shadows and *cursed* destiny. You brought this upon yourself by fighting me. If you had just stayed away, if you had just let me keep my things, you would not bear such cursed promises."

"You gave your word for a promise!" I screamed at last.

Baba Yaga cackled, a cold, terrifying sound that turned my stomach to lead. "Yes, but I never said a promise of what. If you had asked for a favor, it would have turned out well. But promises are vague creatures. They can be for good or evil—you were foolish to take a bargain of a promise. You forgot that I, at my core, am truly evil. You do not know how the Realms were made. You have no idea what I *did*—what I *will do*—to protect myself."

A knife materialized in Baba Yaga's hand, and she flung it at me with a shriek of rage. "Die now!" she yelled. "It would save you from the fate that awaits you in this cursed Realm."

Evadne screamed out a curse and two more water spears raced from her palms. One deflected the dagger, the other shot through Baba Yaga's defenses and slammed into the witch's chest.

Baba Yaga looked down at the spear, almost as if in surprise. "They were right about you," she hissed, her voice cracking. "The bones spoke of you...they *warned* me about you...but I did not believe it." Her eyes narrowed as she stared at us. "Twins of power," she whispered, "love and hate." Her voice was rising, with every syllable, until her scream was so loud it burned inside my ears. "Linked by blood, bound by fate. Broken destiny, waits for all," she raised her hand, pointing at us. "Knight will rise, all will *fall*."

The final word propelled us backward, out of the doorway and across the island toward the ship. I watched, shocked and numb, as her body swayed and crumpled, the water spear dissolving as we flew away from her.

We're going to die. How do we stop?

Theron and Verity both yelled out a word together as their hands closed around our ankles. Giant mechanical wings exploded from their backs. We jerked to a stop, mere feet away from the edge of the cliff.

Evadne was curled around Red, sobbing in rage and pain. I was gasping for air, reeling from what had happened.

"Well," Verity heaved, flopping back onto the uneven ground. "Let that be a lesson for all of us to simply let sleeping monsters lie. You should never, under any circumstance, get on the bad side of a cannibalistic witch because it'll never go in your favor."

"She cheats," Theron grunted angrily. "The bloody witches *always* cheat."

"Unfortunately so," Verity agreed as she groaned and picked herself up. She pulled on a small lever by her ribcage, and the wings began to shrink and fold up on themselves, until at last they tucked neatly back into her vest. "Well, I think we've overstayed our welcome. Time to pull anchor before she tries something else."

"Like what?" Theron snapped as he crawled onto his hands and knees.

"Like *eat us*, you bloody idiot!" Verity replied irritably. "You saw her. She's clearly dabbled again. She's given in to the darkness. She's turning. Heaven help the fool she trapped. I hope she gave them a quick death. Help the girls up and let's be on our way. I wouldn't put it past her to change the wind's direction to stall our departure so she can do exactly that."

"She might not recover from her injury. I saw her fall," Theron said quietly.

"I have seen her 'die' many times," Verity replied with a shudder. "That's the thing about Wendigos, Theron, they're very, *very* hard to kill."

31

I've Been Considering Words That Begin With The Letter M—Mutiny, Moron, Malice, Murder...Mahogany

EVADNE

"Sometimes I think I was so obsessed with the idea of saving others
because I thought, in some way, it might save me too. Turns out I
wasn't good at either. -all I've got is dried glue on my fingers and glass
under my thumb."

-e.b.

It seemed strange to me that on a pirate ship they would have a mahogany table—several, actually. It was a peculiar luxury in the middle of the sky. But here I was, staring at the dark, polished wood, full of dents and scratches that told a story of its adventures out in the clouds.

I wonder, if this table could speak, what would it say? Would it ask to have the marks removed, or beg to keep them—does it hold such memories as treasures?

Why do I care? What does it matter?

Why would they polish the table up when it's full of so many marks? What's the purpose?

I couldn't escape the foggy gray landscape of my mind. I felt as if I was disconnected, wandering. Baba Yaga's words hung over me, and no matter what I did, I could not escape the heavy sense of foreboding that had followed us from the Wastelands.

"Eva," Ember whispered, poking me in the ribs. "You *need* to eat. You won't get your strength back if you don't eat."

I sighed, annoyed. Eating was a chore. I had no appetite. Even my favorite flavor of tea tasted like dust against my tongue.

Fireheart however, had no such inclination. He was happily gobbling down a plate loaded with cheesy potatoes and bacon. Logan had earned the good graces of the little dragon and, much to Fireheart's delight, he was happily keeping the brat occupied by letting him taste test everything he cooked.

Red had joined him in his indulgence and the two were quickly becoming close friends. Despite Fireheart's occasional attempts to eat Red, the two were bonding over their mutual love of food.

Red was no ordinary cat, and he had thoroughly schooled the small dragon on what happened when he acted on his impulsive thoughts. Every time Fireheart tried to mess with him, Red spoke a magical word and grew to three times his size, before promptly sitting on the foolish dragon.

It was an intimidation tactic that left Fireheart indignant and embarrassed. But I didn't have the energy to care about their on and off again feud. They could sort it out themselves. There were too many other things on my mind that required my worry.

Disconnected memories were running in a jumbled swirl around my mind. Things didn't make sense. There was something wrong with my mind.

"Em, did Artemis try to kill you while we were still in the Central Realm?" The question fell unchecked from my lips.

Em paused, thinking. "No," she replied slowly. "He tried to kill me in the Moores, when he was fighting the spider's poison. But never while we were in the Central Realm. He had his moments of being a jerk during training...moments when he could have dealt a killing blow or put a knife to my throat... But he never actually intentionally tried to kill me...Why?"

"I just...I have this memory, but it's jagged around the edges, like it doesn't quite belong in the landscape. He's got you with a knife to your throat. You're fighting about something, but the words are all muffled... I'm there watching, but it's vague, like a dream. He slit your throat Em, he killed you in front of me...and then healed you, so he could do it all over again...he killed you and killed you."

"No, that never happened..." Ember whispered, horrified. "Again, there were plenty of occurrences in training where there was a knife to my throat or we drew blood from each other—usually we were fighting about something stupid, but I..." her voice trailed off and absentmindedly rubbed at her chest. "I knew, I somehow knew he didn't mean me any *actual* harm. Even when we were fighting, there was a familiarity to it that made it seem normal."

"What happened in the Moores?" I asked quietly.

Ember swallowed, staring down at her untouched food.

She had the audacity to force me to eat, and yet she hasn't eaten much of her food yet. What a hypocrite.

I should shove it down her throat.

I pushed the violent, intrusive thought away. *No, why would I do that?*

"When we were running from Baba Yaga, the poison kept switching him back and forth. He shifted personalities when we reached the ravine; it was the side that hated me because he was afraid... We were fighting Yaga while Rosamond went across. She sent the branch back for us to throw us—like she did when you and I first came to the Realm." Her voice was strained, as if it hurt to even speak about what had happened. "Right before the branch closed around us, Yaga threw a dagger at him. He pulled me in front of him and the dagger went into my chest. It was quickly followed by a second that went into my gut."

My mouth fell open in shock. Artemis had said he tried to kill her, but I didn't realize to what extent. She had seemed okay when I woke, so I didn't even think to ask her what had happened in the time I was unconscious.

I am a terrible sister. I should have noticed. I should have asked. I was too preoccupied with Marcus' return to think to ask.

I am a terrible, awful, very bad sister.

My mind was running out of adjectives to describe what a bad sister I was.

"He healed me," Ember said softly. "His personality switched back right as the blade hit me. He killed Baba Yaga because of me and brought a curse on himself."

"Do you think curses have any real power?" I asked absentmindedly, picking at my food.

"I don't know," Ember sighed. "I don't know if someone saying something will happen means it happens, or if my belief that it will happen and dread of it makes it happen."

"Death in Samarra," I grumbled.

"Exactly," Ember confirmed. "Now eat your food."

How 'bout you eat your food and mind your own beeswax, you diptwit.

Suddenly the prior intrusive thought seemed incredibly appealing. I *really* didn't like to be bossed around.

"I've been considering words that begin with the letter M," I said loftily, ignoring her bossiness. "Moron." I pointed my fork at her, poking the air next to her arm.

Ember made a face.

"Malice," I continued, threatening her with the fork more aggressively. "Murder." This time, my fork jammed into her arm.

Much to Ember's annoyance, Fireheart abandoned his eating and started pointing while laughing at her getting forcefully poked.

I gestured to the table. I was on a roll and I was not about to be derailed by Fireheart's mischief.

There's another M word, mischief!

"Mahogany."

"Magnificent," Ember countered saucily. Clearly, she hadn't learned anything from my poking lesson.

"Well, you're all healed up. It's time you started to learn the ropes on this ship," Captain Verity's voice interrupted my lecture.

"Mutiny," I muttered under my breath.

A curved knife slammed into the table by my plate.

"THAT IS MAHOGANY!" Ember and I both chorused together, doing our best imitation of Effie Trinket from *The Hunger Games.*

Captain Verity arched an eyebrow. "Well," she said dryly. "While I appreciate your concern for my table, I find it highly unnecessary. All care about the surface of my...mahogany table evaporated when Raz carved a rather gruesome doodle of Theron on the corner over there."

I stood, curious, and inspected the crude stick cartoon. It featured one person lying down, impaled with various knives, arrows and swords, and another person jumping up and down over their dead body. I snorted. This doodle was right up my alley. I adored revenge doodles. My sketchbooks over the years featured similar depictions—my siblings were often the unfortunate victims of such petty retaliation.

My favorite had been when Jacques, determined to get me back, had doodled his own. In it, I was a flaming ball of fire, Ember was in a dragon's mouth, and he of course was valiantly riding the monstrous beast.

That's it. I'm making a revenge doodle of Ember when we're done with this wretched day.

"I would also remind you that mutiny will not serve you well," Verity continued, her voice dry. "I believe we've all had quite enough of such behavior."

I resisted the urge to roll my eyes. I was still particularly salty at Verity for hurting my sister. Ember was glaring holes in the side of my head, warning me to shut up.

Malevolent, mean, mutilation, murderous...

You already said murder.

Yes, well, murderous still counts. Now HUSH, you're ruining my adjectives.

"You two will be joining the crew today. With Ember's back all healed up, there's nothing else that stands in your way from learning the ropes."

"Other than a crippling fear of heights," Ember muttered.

"Ember dear, the only way you can rise above your fear is to face it. You're afraid? Do it afraid."

Malignant, malicious...

Ember's mouth pulled into a tight line, but she nodded. "Yes ma'am," she said with a dip of her chin.

"Evadne, you'll be with Raz. Ember, you're with Theron since, between the two of you, you're the most afraid of heights. He'll help you conquer that fear in small doses and then decrease his influence until you can conquer it on your own."

Ember nodded. "Thank you."

Verity nodded back, a small smile pulling at the corners of her mouth. "I am not *entirely* heartless, you know."

"I mean, you fell in love with my brother, so you must have some heart left."

Say what now?

I had been unconscious for so long that the holes in my knowledge were reaching an infuriating level.

I stabbed my fork down into the table next to Verity's curved dagger and Ember shut her mouth with an audible click. Her eyes were apologetic as she turned to me, wincing.

Verity, however, was amused. "What was that about mahogany?" she quipped.

I ignored her. "Artemis tried to *kill* you, Jack has a *girlfriend* who happens to be the very person I'm *furious* with—"

"Eva, I told you being angry with Verity is—"

I didn't let her finish. I interrupted her the same way she had interrupted me. "Is there anything else you haven't told me?" I demanded angrily.

Ember paused, thinking. "I...I'm not sure?" she offered unhelpfully. "You know you have a very dangerous petting zoo, right?"

I rolled my eyes, fuming.

"Did you know your sister's been marked by the Moores?" Verity offered with a helpful sort of smile.

"*NO!*" I snapped, glaring at Ember. "What does that even *mean?*"

"Well, the mark she has is quite *magnificent.* There's another M word for your list, you're welcome my lovely little *menace. Anyways,* it means the Moores has made her their namesake."

"Oookay...but what does it mean?"

Verity shrugged. "We're not quite sure. It just means she's destined for something great."

That is a MOST unhelpful answer.

"I'm sorry, Eva," Ember pleaded. "I just, things were happening, and you were here with me, and for some reason I just, spaced that you weren't really here. I know you were unconscious, but I talked to you while you were...telling you about everything. I forgot you couldn't actually hear me."

I sighed, thinking. "I heard you," I whispered. "Your voice was there in the darkness, but my mind is trying to erase what happened there. It's shutting out the horrors, Em. I don't remember what you were saying—just that you were there..." My voice trailed off as the memories rose. All the blood and screams that place of horrors held was something I never wanted to remember ever again. I shuddered, blinking back the sudden tears that rose.

"All right then, since neither of you seem keen on finishing your breakfast, how about we work up an appetite, and if you get absolutely famished, I'm sure your respective teachers will let you come get a snack. If you want luck in that area, I suggest you offer to bring them back a large mug of coffee and a cookie or six."

"Come on, Twinkletoes," Raz's voice called from the doorway. "It's time your magical feet learned to dance across a tightrope."

"That sounds absolutely *horrible,*" I muttered.

"Not when you have wings," Raz countered.

"And since when I do I have wings?" I challenged.

"When you realize you're a dragon, you'll find your wings."

I have a dragon. That counts. I don't have any wings. So, you're just plain wrong.

With those cryptic words she turned and left. I cast a lingering glance back at Ember, but she was waving me off. "Bye, bye, Eva," she said with a smirk, raising her coffee mug. "Have fun storming the castle."

I stuck out my tongue, annoyed. But my annoyance quickly morphed to cackling glee. Theron now stood in the doorway.

Someone is about to get her comeuppance.

"Hello, my angsty little kraken," Theron said with a smirk. "Plan on destroying any ships today?"

"I haven't decided yet. The day is still young."

"That's my girl," Theron said encouragingly. "If you need any help let me know, I'm always down for shenanagins."

"*Don't* destroy my ship," Verity sighed as she made her way past me.

"Wouldn't dream of it," I muttered.

"Don't think I've forgotten you, Sparks," Theron called as he walked into the dining room. "It's time you found your skye legs."

Much to my cackling delight, Ember choked on her long, haughty sip of coffee. I turned back to my contemplation of words that began with the letter M.

M, m, m...

But, as always, my mind turned back to my old favorites.

Moron, murder, mutiny, malice, mahogany.

32

We Are Most Decidedly The Most Cliché Criminals To Ever Mastermind A Jailbreak

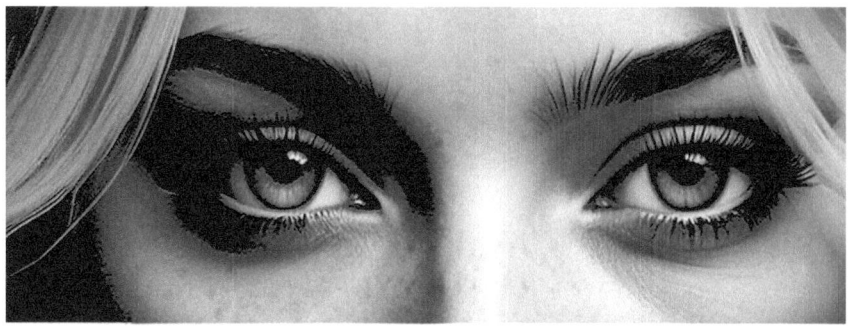

FAYE

"They broke the wrong parts. They broke the wings and forgot we had claws. They left marks on our bones. We left scars on their minds."
-VaZaki Nada

It was decided upon the dreadful trip to my new, comfy solitary confinement cell that Marcov needed to have his tongue removed. He spent far too much effort wasting his breath instead of focusing on the sole task of taking me to my much-deserved rest.

As soon as I'm able, I'll help him with this little problem. He really doesn't need his tongue. It's a waste of a perfectly good organ. I'm sure if I fed it to a Direwolfe, it would be my friend for life. I could feed him bits and pieces of especially nasty people, and then we'd be best buds!

Ooo, yessss. A pet Direwolfe. That would be sick! Evadne would be so jealous! She doesn't have a pet wolf!

The mental image of a pet Direwolfe following me around the Realm was exceedingly pleasing to me. All of a sudden, I desperately wanted to obtain such a loyal pet.

I wonder how the girls are. Are they doing okay in the Realm?

How am I going to save them now? With their life and magic tied to the Realm, to destroy it would kill them too...

My thoughts wandered to Jack, and the two secret letters we'd managed to smuggle to one another during those eight years in the Realm. It was a cruelty how close we were, and yet how far apart.

I had promised to find a way for him to be free, even in my plan to destroy the Realm. But he had replied that, if it was between saving him, or saving our sisters, to choose the girls. We had both endured enough horrors over the years that he was willing to let it all go. He was willing to sacrifice himself if it meant saving them. I wanted to find a way; I wanted to fight for him and give him a chance with his Verity. Even in the Summer Court, I had heard the small rumors. I knew where the last pieces of his heart lay buried. Each of us carried a piece, and the rest, he gave to her. They both knew of the hopeless future that awaited us. But they had somehow come to terms with the inevitability of the end.

Jack would sacrifice everything for us and Verity loved him enough to let him choose that.

But I loved him too much to let him surrender his happiness.

I hadn't seen my brother in so long, it seemed a dream, receiving that letter back. I had memorized every word before burning it to ash. I knew I was being paranoid, but I made sure it was completely gone, then ground the ash to paste, and drank it down in a glass of water—ensuring that no Fey could put the elements back together again. I drank those bitter ashes—determined to find a way to save everyone I loved, and that included my brother.

Where did such determination get me? What do I have to show for it?

We're all trapped in the Realm and the Knight holds me hostage through a human.

"Marcov!" A new voice called out.

Familiar. I know that voice. Who is it? It's one of the original men. What's his name...John? Jeremy? J... it started with a J.

"What do you want, James?" Marcov snapped. Clearly, such an intrusion infuriated him.

"Jeremiah wanted me to ensure you took her straight to the holding cell. He said, and I quote, 'Do not engage or try further interrogation.'"

James stared down at his scuffed boots as Marcov huffed an angry growl. "Go double check your orders."

"You're almost there," James spluttered. "I don't need to double check them."

"Yes, you do. I don't believe you. Go double check."

Well. Looks like we're going to have us a fight. He's sending Jamesy-boy away.

Oo, now can we deprive him of a tongue?

If we can get our fingers inside his mouth, sure. But I'm not especially keen on getting his spit on my hands right now.

Several doors lined the hallway in front of us, and Marcov was making a beeline for the one in the middle.

Someone's in a hurry.

Tweedle dee, tweedle dum. It's time I made him regret his choices...and break his thumb.

Marcov got as far as unlocking the door before he made a wrong move. Unfortunately for him, I was expecting him to be a pig and try something stupid.

I had Marcov on the ground in five seconds. His strangled cry echoed around the hollow space as I wrenched his thumb sideways, but I had no mercy with which to care. After everything he'd done, his scream sounded like music to my ears as I broke his fingers. One by one.

"Let that be the last time you dare touch what isn't yours," I hissed, furious as I broke another finger. Some small part of me cheered at such grotesque, vindictive revenge. Marcov reminded me too much of Bhaltair.

I should have told Ríonach what happened at her mother's behest. I should have told her.

"You stupid—" Marcov's words cut off in another scream as I promptly slammed my boot into his nose. Blood spurted, and mustering the last of my strength and adrenaline, I slammed his head into the steel wall.

Sadly, I don't have the time or energy to break all his fingers today.

He crumpled and I watched his body carefully, checking for signs of life. I hadn't intended to kill him, but if it happened, I wasn't going to mourn him. The plan would likely fare much better without him.

Much to my dismay, he was still breathing.

Boo.

Well. That's the end of that. Time for a nap.

It'll be suspicious if he's out here unconscious, and I nicely lock myself in the cage for my bad behavior.

The most likely solution would be to run...

I took a wobbling step away from Marcov and his disgusting pool of blood. If I was going to faint, I would do it on the opposite walls. If Ronan carried the risk of cooties or the plague, Marcov certainly possessed both.

My back was against the other wall now, and at last, my knees gave out.

Well, that answers that question.

A small noise to my left turned my attention to a wide-eyed, open-mouthed Meghan. She looked shocked and delighted all at once. A small, feral smile pulled at my lips. I didn't think it was an overreach to assume she and I were somewhat alike.

"Hello Meghan," I said breathlessly.

"So, you're the infamous Faye," Meghan replied by way of hello. Her eyes were glued to Marcov, as if counting. "Did you kill him?" she whispered hopefully.

Marcov's chest rose and fell in a shallow gasp, answering her question.

"Not yet," I muttered. "It's only a matter of time though, mark my words. From what I've heard, he more than deserves it."

Meghan stared down at her hands. "Yeah," she whispered. "He deserves every ounce of pain coming his way."

"Yes, he does," I replied with a mirthless laugh. "Run along now, James will be back any moment. I don't want him getting any ideas if he sees us talking."

"James is kind," Meghan replied quietly.

"He's a dead man," I sighed. "Your father has too much dirt on him. It automatically makes him desperate and caged in. Desperate men cannot be trusted, dearheart. They'll turn and stab you in the back before you even see the glint of steel. Don't you give him an inch of trust until we're out of this nightmare, do you understand me?"

Meghan nodded, her brows pulling together in worry.

I shook my head. "This world is a dark, unkind place. I'm sorry for what it's done to you."

Meghan shrugged. "We all bear our burdens. At least I have Ronan to help bear mine."

I smiled softly, staring down at my bloody hands. "Yes," I whispered. "At least you have Ronan." Moments passed as I considered her words, then snapping back to reality, I realized she was still standing in the hallway.

"What did I say?" I grumbled irritably. "Shoo! I won't have you compromising my brilliant plans. I'll be most cross with you if I have to rethink everything because of you."

"See you later," Meghan said as she slipped back behind the door she had first come out of.

Five minutes later, James reappeared. He was out of breath, chest heaving, as if he had been running. His attention zeroed in on Marcov's unconscious form, and then to where I slumped. "Uhm…"

"He did not respect my bubble," I said nonchalantly. "Jeremiah is lucky he depleted my energy. If he hadn't, I would have killed him and then escaped this miserable swamp. Jeremiah should reconsider having Marcov handle things. If you ask me, he's incompetent. He wants what he wants, more than he wants to obey Jeremiah's orders."

Ha, sabotage!

I smirked. "Be sure to tell our dear Jeremiah what happened here, okay sweetie? He *directly* disobeyed Jeremiah's orders."

James swallowed nervously. "Uhm…"

Is that the only word in his vocabulary?

Allow me to give you a second word to add to your collection. It is the wonderfully glorious word, ope. You can use it in any and all forms of situations. For instance, in this particular situation, as you turned the corner, you could have said 'ope,' and I would have replied 'ope indeed.'

"I guess I should put you in your cell…" James managed at last.

I wasn't going to hurt him, but it was a particularly delightful idea to mess with him.

I gave him a savage smile. "You can try," I replied. "Respect my bubble, and nobody gets hurt."

"Yes ma'am," James replied under his breath.

Ma'am? Am I an old grandmother now?

Quick, someone get me a cane. I have an obnoxious young man to whack. He's making me feel old.

James reached out to offer me a hand, then hesitated. "Does helping you up count as invading your bubble?"

"In this case, no," I replied as I took his hand. "Your manners are getting you bonus points, young man."

If he's going to talk to me like I'm an old grandmother, I'm going to act like an old grandmother.

I could barely suppress my groan of pain as he pulled me to my feet.

James' eyes were apologetic as he opened my cell door. I stared into the dark space. From the light of the hallway, I could see the rickety shape of a thick wooden bedframe with a thin sheet of plywood across it. It was bolted to the wall and had no mattress.

I guess it wouldn't be a punishment if I had a mattress.

There were no lights in the room and the stainless-steel walls were completely bare.

Where is the hidey hole?

I scrutinized the space closer, tarrying in the doorway as long as possible. James seemed keen to let me. We both seemed unwilling for me to go into the lightless cell.

There.

Underneath the bed, at the very back, I could make out a pattern on the wall that didn't quite match the rest, a seam that didn't quite fit. If I hadn't been looking for it, I would have missed it.

"Sorry about this." James sighed. "If I let you dilly-dally much longer, they're going to come investigating both Marcov's and my absence. I need to get help carting him to the medical ward."

"Do me a favor and finish the job on the way," I said offhandedly as I walked into the room. "I made it *really* easy for you to take out the garbage."

The look of horror on James' face immediately cheered me, and to make matters worse, I added a wink just to make him *extra* uncomfortable. The mischief made the darkness that followed almost bearable. All I had to do was remember his wide eyes and gaping mouth and my blues vanished.

I fell asleep as soon as my head draped across my arm. Sleeping on the bed felt far too exposed, so I curled up in a little ball against the door. That way if it opened, I'd wake up. I was so exhausted I was worried I might not wake up otherwise.

When I did wake, I was unsure what time it was, but I felt refreshed, as if I had slept a day or two. For all I knew, I had.

Okay then, time to get to work.

I sat up with a groan. It certainly felt as if I hadn't moved for days. My bladder was screaming, and I was suddenly afraid. I hadn't remembered seeing a bathroom in my quick perusal of the room. I had been more occupied with finding the hole and making James squirm.

If he put me in a room without a bathroom, it's going to become an issue...

If he put me in a room without a bathroom I'm going to sue!

You're the one who got us here in the first place, dummy.

With a sigh of annoyance at myself and my circumstances, I pressed my hands against the door and began to make my way around the perimeter of the room.

Stupid Jeremiah, stupid everything. I should have specified to Ronan that there would need to be a bathroom.

In all honesty, I didn't think it would be an issue. A bathroom is a given.

But Jeremiah is crazy. It might not be a given with him. That would be a form of psychological torture all on its own... I mean can you imagine how awful—

My hands slid off the wall and into open air, thoroughly derailing my disgusting train of thought.

YES!

It was a tiny alcove of a room, and it wasn't long before my shins collided painfully with the hard porcelain of the toilet.

Well, now I don't have to throttle Ronan.

My physical needs satisfied, I set to the task at hand. It was time to train Ronan's sister.

"About time you woke up," a new voice stated.

I shrieked, startled. It had been so quiet, the silence so definite, I hadn't even thought to consider the possibility that someone else could be in the room with me.

Did I move away from the door in my sleep?

"Meghan?" I whispered.

"Mmhmm," she replied. "Sorry for scaring you, but you've been asleep for four days. I came in to see if you were dead. Then you woke up, and I wasn't sure when to say something."

I was utterly mortified. The tiny bathroom had no doors and sound carried in such an empty space.

"Hey, don't be embarrassed," Meghan piped up, as if sensing my woe. "We're both adults here. Just pretend I'm one of your sisters. Everybody peeees," she sang happily in a very off key tune.

"How do you know I have sisters?" I asked, giggling at her antics.

"Ronan told me," Meghan replied. "He tells me everything. I've heard so much about you I was ready to tell him to shut up and find a new hobby instead of moping and bemoaning this ridiculous situation and how *awful* he felt, and how you'd never forgive him...and blah, blah, *blah*... I mean, you'd think by now he'd get over what he's done and find a way through it. But *noooooo*, he has to mope and tell me all about you whenever he comes to the kitchens, and how you hate his guts, and how much he *regrets taking you*." I could practically hear her eyes rolling.

Bright light, painful and sudden, flooded through the pitch-black room from a hole under the bed.

"Behold," Meghan said proudly. "My cliché escape tunnel."

I giggled at the ridiculousness of it all. Suddenly, my seemingly brilliant plan seemed downright absurd when presented by Ronan's snarky sister.

"Ronan told me what the plan was," Meghan continued. "I told him he was stupid. He had the *audacity* to insist it was *your* idea. I told him there was *absolutely no* way you would suggest this. Based off everything he's told me, you're brilliant—and in a very scary way."

I didn't feel inclined to tell her that he was right. Instead, to let him take the fall seemed a much better option. "Tell me about it," I snorted. "Ronan comes up with the stupidest ideas."

Technically, it wasn't a lie. Ronan did come up with a stupid idea. I was just allowing her to believe this happened to be one of his stupid ideas.

"Well, no time like the present," Meghan said in a cheerful, singsong tone. "Shall we commence the long-awaited training? You have no idea how much I'm looking forward to learning how to kick butt."

I smiled, cheered by her enthusiasm. "Yeah, I'll be right with you, I just need to put a...well, it's like an alarm, on the door." I wasn't sure if saying the word *rune* outside of the Realm counted as giving information, but I wasn't about to risk getting marked. "If anyone tries to come through, it'll notify me, and stick—giving me enough time to get back in here and pretend I never left."

"Wicked cool," Meghan gasped. "Can you show me how to do that? I want cool, scary powers."

"Sorry, but no. It doesn't exactly work like that. It's not something you can just...learn... It's something you're born with."

Meghan made a disappointed noise, and I was certain there was an equally disappointed face to go with it. "No fair," she muttered angrily.

I began to pick at one of my scabs with a sigh. Rune magic was old magic, and I disliked how messy the process was. It required blood as payment, the more powerful the better, and it always managed to give me gray hairs.

My beautiful blond locks. I'll resemble an old crone if I'm not careful.

All the better to hit people with my walking stick, my pretty.

A sharp pain in my side began to grow as I smeared blood on my finger and drew the rune on the door. It was simple to do in the darkness, as the rune must be completed in one continuous motion. I just had to make sure I followed the correct muscle memory.

Thank goodness I did my homework while I was in the Winter Realm. If I hadn't, I'd probably be dead by now. I can't believe more Fey don't remember this form of magic.

Why don't the monarchs use this form of magic?

Maybe they do and we just don't know it...they initiate a lot of bloodshed. What else happens behind closed doors? The blood doesn't necessarily have to be fresh to work...it just has to be there. They don't always join the crowd after court has adjourned.

What would that mean for the realm if they're secretly practicing Rune magic, mixed with Darke magic?

The possibility of what I might have been oblivious to all these years suddenly hit me like a blow to the gut. Something terrible and fearful began to grow inside of my chest.

What if everything goes so much deeper and darker than I could have ever imagined?

It already does. The Knight is directly involved in this whole mess...but the real question is why? What is his end goal? Are the monarchs involved with him somehow? Is their magic aiding him and they just don't realize it?

Obviously, he's in it to bring down the fall of the Realms, but how? How is this beneficial to him? A crazed human who wants to bring back his long dead wife...a captured Grimm...well, two now.

"Are you coming, or not?" Meghan asked, jarring my thoughts.

My brain cells did not take kindly to the interruption. They had brought out all their little chalkboards, and despite the presence of the boards, they had begun to paint their theories. Her interruption was a welcome distraction in my opinion, however. Things were about to get wildly out of hand. The original three were threatening the newest, almost members with a spur-of-the-moment 'you're almost initiated' initiation session—one to prove their true loyalty—and it involved lots of paint everywhere.

"Yeah, I'm coming. Just, give me a second," I grumbled.

She reminded me of Ember and Evadne, and I felt a familiar pull on my heart. Some buried part of me was rising, the part that remembered how to be a big sister and wanted nothing more than to protect her.

"You're not going to make me do pushups, are you?" Meghan asked from the other side of the hole.

"Pushups are the worst," I snorted.

"Oh, thank goodness," she sighed.

"But you're totally doing pushups," I finished.

She shrieked in outrage, and I giggled at my newfound power as a teacher as I wriggled through the hole. It was smaller than I liked, but bigger than the doggy door. I was sure I'd be able to get through it fast enough in a pinch, but I would need to practice a few times to make sure I was as fast as possible.

Y'know, I feel pretty decent...I'm actually starting to feel like my old self...

Gee, it's almost like you haven't been drugged out of your skull for a while.

Yes, yes, nobody asked for your sarcasm.

My rambling thoughts fell silent at the sight of Meghan's cluttered room.

The space was large—larger than I had been expecting. Bookshelves lined three of the walls, overflowing with books. A twin sized bed and a desk occupied the remaining wall, as well as what appeared to be a small bathroom, and a door with multiple forms of locks that led to somewhere. Upon closer inspection, I found a second closed door, hidden in between the bookshelves.

I wonder where they lead.

As if reading my thoughts, Meghan pointed to the first door. "That one leads out into the hallway." She pointed to the second door. "That one leads into Ronan's room." She smirked. "If you're going to try to escape, don't use that door. He snores, but he's a light sleeper."

I arched an eyebrow. "I'm not going to try to escape. I made your brother a promise."

"Ah yes, the ever-present promise. When I was eight, he promised me he'd find a way out of this hellhole and here we are, eleven years later. Sometimes we make promises with the best intentions, but it's just not enough."

"We're going to get you out of here," I replied firmly.

"And if you can't?"

"We'll die trying."

The words came unbidden, and it was with a growing sort of shock that I realized I meant them. Something had shifted inside of me, and now I was prepared to defend this girl and stay true to my promise to get her out.

Well. That's a disturbing change of heart.

Is it really though?

Yes. Absolutely. I refuse to feel sympathy or empathy. I will be a cold-hearted villain until I die.

Such blasted dramatics. Everyone knows you're lying. Everyone knows you'll protect her to your dying breath.

Yes, yes, now shut up. You're making me look soft-hearted.

"Okay, so, outside door, snore machine door, bathroom..." my voice trailed off as I scrutinized the space. "We can train here in the middle of the room, but we should probably move your bed to cover the hole. It's too obvious."

"No need," Meghan snorted happily. "Ronan, our genius mastermind, has offered a plan. The stupidest plan, mind you, in the history of ever."

The tips of my ears heated considerably as I pretended ignorance. "He does come up with the stupidest plans," I scoffed, trying to save face.

"Tell me about it," Meghan muttered as she pulled a thick roll back down over the hole and shoved an end table in front of it. "Behold, a Taylor Swift poster, to hide our jail break hole that leads to nowhere... Is this when we would start singing *Trouble*?" She hummed softly, then began to sing quietly, "I knew you were trouble when you walked iiiiin..." She laughed, disrupting her song. "Y'know, it's kind of ridiculous. Usually, a jailbreak hole takes you out of your cell to the outside. But this just takes you from one cell to another." She gave me a meaningful look. "We're both prisoners here."

I smirked. "We'll both be fried to a crispy-crisp if we leave this compound."

Meghan grimaced. "Yes, don't remind me of that unfortunate detail. It makes me quite volatile."

"Good. Let's put those volatile feelings to use, shall we?"

"What?" Meghan whined. "You're going to put me to work right away?"

I shrugged. "You literally said you were excited to learn how to kick butt. What else do you want to do?"

"That was before you said you were going to make me do pushups," Meghan grumbled. "Now I want to talk about my favorite books and eat marshmallows. I'd also like to form a union with you, a union that excludes Ronan, but only when I'm annoyed at him, and a separate union that excludes the whole compound for having the audacity to turn us into electric fences."

I nodded. "I approve of all these choices. Marshmallows come during the break, and we can talk about books while we work on your skills, and I will happily join your unions. Especially the one that excludes Ronan when you're annoyed at him." I gave her a wink.

Meghan frowned. Clearly, this wasn't the answer she had been hoping for.

What did I say?

"Your brother did tell you why I'm here, didn't he?" I asked, suddenly unsure.

I'm pretty sure she talked about wanting to learn skills...did we talk about that? I'm a little foggy headed.

"Oh, he did, and while I'm excited to learn skills, I also don't like to be bossed around."

"That makes two of us," I muttered. "How about this—I do everything with you, and then we can both suffer together. I need to get my strength back."

Meghan nodded enthusiastically, then resumed her topic of trash talking Ronan—a topic I was all too happy to engage with.

"He's quite bossy," she said loftily. "He thinks he knows everything."

"I know he does," I scoffed. "You should have heard him when he was trying to get me to eat his disgusting health food!"

"Don't get me *started* on the health food," Meghan snorted. "I told him to just send you mac and cheese and twinkies, but nooooooo. He had to custom make all your food himself. Apparently, he didn't trust me to cook it *properly*. The moron had to make sure it was one hundred percent *healthy*."

Ha! I was right.

Meghan did a stellar imitation of Ronan's voice, adding a dramatic '*blah, blah, blah,*' at the end. My brain cells were consequently won over in a moment. They began to kneel, pledging their loyalty to this spirited child who did a delightful mocking of the annoying Ronan. (They had yet to pick an actual side. The collective group of cells, both the three and the hoard, were decidedly split about him. Half wanted to kick him; half wanted to kiss him, though they would only admit it when they were feeling thoroughly smitten.) So I was thoroughly confused as to my *actual* feelings about him, thanks to my very fickle brain cell collective.

"A balanced spread of protein and nutrients," I said loftily, in my best imitation voice of Ronan. I couldn't quite remember what ridiculousness he'd said so seriously during our many arguments about healthy food. But I was certain I was close.

Meghan began giggling so hard she looked like she was about to fall over for lack of breath.

"Well, he doesn't know everything," I stated. "Otherwise, he wouldn't have asked me to help him."

"No, that's a definite point in your favor. Even just asking you made him eat crow, which is terribly delightful to me. I would have liked to listen in on that conversation."

I laughed, trying to hide my true emotions, the sadness that we could never escape. I was certain Ronan didn't want his sister to know how desperation and not humility drove him to my side. It was fear that bound us together now. Fear of what his crazed father would do to the only thing he loved in this world when our time finally ran out.

33

Dancing On A Tightrope, Blindfolded—Yup It's As Stupid As It Sounds

EVADNE

"Rage, maybe rage would lift me up, make me stand, make me walk."
-Marlon James, Black Leopard, Red Wolf

Between the two of us, Ember was the angry one. I was my sister's counterbalance. I evened her rage with my own form of quiet peace. I balanced her, just as she balanced me, and together we were complete. But since my time held captive at the Ruins, there was something new and unfamiliar inside my mind. I could feel it there, trying to destroy me as I struggled to adjust to my new normal.

There was a new seed of rage within me. A foreign, unwelcome guest that prowled around my subconscious—snapping and biting. I had locked it in an iron box in the back of my mind. But it spent every waking moment trying to find an escape. But even contained, the shadows still leeched from the monster. Even imprisoned, it still managed to poison my mind.

I didn't like the person who had returned from the Ruins. She wore my face, but she wasn't me. I wasn't this creature, and I didn't know what to do with the new and unfamiliar rage that tore me apart with every passing moment, as I tried and failed to adjust.

"Just trust your legs," Raz said for what seemed the millionth time.

I wanted to destroy this blasted ship with my frustration. It wasn't as simple as Raz was making it out to be. Not when the world was a distorted, dizzying kaleidoscope on one side. Not when everything was off kilter and wrong. I didn't have my delicate balance anymore. The graceful way my feet had been connected with the world around me was broken. Ember's comforting stability was nowhere to be found. She was no longer my sanity, nor was I hers. We were miles away from each other, disconnected and broken.

All that remained was the monster that screamed for blood and revenge—a monster I feared I would become at the end of all this.

I am more than this. I can get through this. I am more than the monster they tried to create.

I am not a monster. I am...I am...what am I?

My body shifted in a sudden gust of wind, and I found myself once again jealous of a dragon. Fireheart had decided to remain below deck with Elvie. The two were wrapped in my cloak, *sleeping.*

Red had joined us up in the rigging and was currently climbing and exploring, telling the crew members scattered around him of his many adventures over the centuries.

My feet slid, threatening to send me over the edge, and I began to consider my words that began with the letter M once more.

Murder, mutiny, malice, mischief, moron...MAHOGANY

"This is ridiculous," I muttered, shoving thoughts of mahogany out of my mind. "Why would Verity make me do this? I'm half blind for heaven's sake!"

"Because blind or not, you need to learn," Raz piped from somewhere on my left.

Raz was on my blind side, and that alone made me want to throttle her. I disliked not being able to see my surroundings. It wasn't until now that I realized how much I relied on my peripheral vision. It affected everything, and without it, I was doomed. I couldn't even walk without feeling as if I was falling over. Now add to it that I was on the mast of a ship, flying through the sky, and it made the entire predicament even worse.

"Evadne, even if you fall, I'll catch you. There's no need to be afraid. That's what our wings are for."

"Your wings are mechanical," I ground out as I clung onto my rope for dear life. "They could fail. Something could happen and they could fail. At which point, I'm nothing but a smear on the deck for a poor crew member to have to clean up."

"Nonsense," Raz snorted. "In all the years I've been on this ship, my wings have never *once* failed me. You're just a scaredy cat, and you're too chicken to admit it."

"How can I be a chicken and a cat, that's impossible," I argued.

"How can a dancer be so terrified of a balance beam?" Raz retorted.

"Because I was a dancer, not a gymnast."

"Am," Raz corrected.

"What?"

"You *are* a dancer," Raz pushed.

"I can't dance," I gasped. "Not now. Not after everything that's happened. Not after..." I choked, the words catching in my throat. "After what he did to me," I whispered.

Raz jumped off the beam and, pulling a string, activated her wings. She floated in the air in front of me, her wings stirring the air with every powerful beat.

"You can still dance," Raz stated. "You, Evadne Grimm, were born a dancer. Even the stars whisper of your steps—the way you weave magic and stop time. Rumor of your talent has spread throughout the Realm *and* the Moores—that soul-shattering performance to save your heart. The reprisal that followed which made the skies weep. The King saw and was left in awe. You are still that person, Evadne. You just have to relearn some things."

She was staring at me, and I was pointedly ignoring her, trying to keep myself together.

"Just because your eye is damaged doesn't mean you can't do what you love," she said quietly. "You couldn't stop if you tried."

I don't want to try. I don't want to do it anymore. I can't bear to be forced to acknowledge the fact that it's actually gone.

"Look at me, Raz," I choked, as the tears at last broke through my resolve. "Look at me. I can't dance anymore. I certainly can't be up here doing this."

"Yes, you can. One deep breath and then another. Let go of the rope and go forward. You don't need the rope. You need to trust your legs to carry you. They've carried you this long; they're not going to give up on you now. You do *not* need the rope," she repeated.

"Oh yes, I most certainly do!" I snapped, infuriated.

Raz crossed her arms. "No, you don't."

A growl of frustration slipped from me, and she smirked.

"Take a deep breath and look straight ahead. Don't look at what's below, or what's around. You're not ready for that. That is a skill we can add in later. For now, you need to look ahead and let go of the rope, trusting your feet to carry you."

"They can't!" I sobbed, still clinging onto the rope for dear life.

"Yes, they can, you just don't believe your body is capable of it. But I promise you, it is. You are so much stronger than you feel right now."

"It's too hard," I whispered. "I can't do this."

"Relearning how to do things sucks big time," Raz said quietly. "Trust me, I know. I had to relearn how to do everything after I lost my fingers. I had to relearn how to fly after I lost my wings. I had to find the courage to even *try*. It was a fight that lasted years, panic attack after panic attack—suffocating moments that lasted a lifetime. But when I finally stepped off the edge of the cliff and trusted these new wings to carry me, I remembered what I was capable of. I remembered who I was." She stared down at her mechanical fingers. "It didn't make everything magically better. It was still a constant struggle. Some days it still haunts me. It is an ever-present part of my life...but it does give you the perspective of reality to help you carry on. It helps you push forward when the world is trying to destroy you."

"What happened to your fingers?" I whispered as I struggled to calm my breath.

"A Direwolfe bit them off," Raz replied offhandedly.

"And your wings?"

Raz's face darkened. "They were stolen from me."

"That's why you were so mad at Theron," I gasped.

I regretted the words as soon as they came out. I hadn't been thinking. I had been more focused on where my feet were, and not slipping off the beam.

Raz's dark look turned murderous, and she swore under her breath. "It is the only thing that stands between us. It is the only thing I can never forgive him for. To take a nymph's wings is to do everything short of killing her. Our wings are integral to who we are, and you can never come back from such a loss."

I pondered her words. "Why didn't you kill him for it?" I asked.

"Because that honor belongs to the one whose wings he stole. She is the one who gets to decide if he lives or dies. Even if I hate her, I will not take that justice from her."

"Wouldn't her wrath be revenge?" I asked, taking a hesitant step forward. My body jolted and swayed, and I clung tighter to the rope.

"Let go of the rope, Evadne," Raz sighed, ignoring my question. "At least pretend you're listening to my instructions."

"I heard you," I ground out. "I just choose to keep my body un-splatted, thank you very much."

"I'll *catch* you!" Raz replied indignantly. "Good gracious, woman, it's as if you don't even trust me."

"Can pirates be trusted?"

Much to my shock and horror, Raz decided the best way to vent her frustration, was to push me off the mast.

I fell, fingers straining for the rope that had somehow slipped out of my death grip. A startled and angry screech rushed out of me as Raz watched me fall for a split second. Then, in the blink of an eye, she dove and caught me.

"See," she said, in a gloating voice. "I told you I'd catch you."

"RAZ!" Theron's furious voice boomed out. "That is *NOT* an acceptable form of teaching."

"You leave me alone, you no good, dirty rotten, wing thieving, slime ball of a despicable pirate!" Raz shot back angrily.

Clearly, my mentioning his offense had put him back in her bad graces.

"If you push her off again, I will report you to Verity," Theron shouted.

"And she'll tell you to stay out of it. I'll train my pupil how I wish; you can train yours how you please. Now leave me alone and go back to your coddling."

Theron's harumph was audible and Raz snorted in derision as she set me back on the thick beam of the mast. "Now, I believe I told you to let go of the rope."

"Fine," I snarled. "But if I fall, it's your fault."

Raz shrugged. "If you fall, I'll catch you...*again*. I don't know what your problem is. I just proved I'd catch you."

"You pushed me off the bloody ship, you *jerk*!" I yelled.

"It's Tuesday," she said dismissively. "Anything goes on Tuesday."

"How do you know it's Tuesday?" I demanded. "We're in the Moores. It has *no* concept of time!"

"She's making it up!" Theron called out from somewhere down below us.

"Theron!" Raz yelled angrily. "If you do not keep your nosey little nose out of my business, I'm going to chop it off and then you'll be *ugly*."

Having completed her threat, she turned back to me. "Your mind and your body are capable of impossible and amazing things. Your dancing proves that. You trained your body. You overcame your fear and dared to try."

Fear was creeping back in, overwhelming the adrenaline.

"Raz, I can't. My eye—"

"Your eye just needs a little help. We're on our way to get the help it desperately needs. But until then, you need to learn how to cope, not just wait for someone to come save you...sometimes people don't come to save you, and you have to learn how to carry on. You have to learn how to save yourself."

There was a deep sense of sadness buried in her words, and a spike of pain cut through my chest. She spoke from experience that bled a buried agony into her words.

"Listen to the world around you. Feel the ship beneath you. Stop focusing on what *isn't* there, and focus on what is. You still have both your legs; you still have your other senses. Feel the way everything moves, the rise and fall of the wind's current. Move your body with that rhythm, the same way you move your body to music. Give it a song if you must and dance across the tightrope."

That's the stupidest thing I've heard all day. I just got pushed off the bloody, cursed ship and the only reasoning given was that it's a freaking Tuesday!

"Here, let me provide you with a song," Raz offered enthusiastically.

"I don't think that's necessary—" I began, but Raz wasn't listening. She had already begun to sing a little made-up song.

"You're, so, freaking great," she sang in a helpful sort of tone. "You're so good at your job, you're so freaking great at your job, you spicy little tacooooo..." She trailed off, her face contemplative. "You can fly, you just have to try, now get a moooove on, before I push you off the shiiiip, or make you walk the plaaaank."

"You can't make her walk the plank," Theron called from somewhere down below us. "You don't have the authority to make her walk the plank."

"Theron, I say this with the deepest depths of my heart's sincerity," Raz said, seething. "*Shut. Up.*"

Theron laughed and Raz's ears turned red with rage. "Forget what I said earlier," she hissed darkly, drawing a dagger. "I'll kill him and get a badge of honor from the *Great Woods* herself."

"He's not worth the energy," I said quickly, trying to draw her away from her fury. I felt partly responsible for the fact she was now angry at him. After all, I had brought up the unfortunate incident. "You're supposed to be singing me a song. I need the song. Start over."

Much to my relief, she turned back to me. "What was the first verse?"

"It's about how freaking great I am...I'm also a taco?"

Her face brightened at the word taco. "Right-o. Okay, here we go. You're, so, freaking great. You're so good at what you do, you're so freaking great at your job, you spicy little tacoooooo, you can fly like a dragon, you just have to try, now mooooove before I push you off the shiiiiip, or make you walk the plaaaank..." she paused, frowning. "It doesn't rhyme," she said in disappointment.

"It doesn't have to, but if you really want to, I can help you make it rhyme. Just keep singing."

"You're supposed to be walking while I sing," she said pointedly.

"Right. I'll do that, just as soon as I can make my body actually move."

"Do you need another push?" she asked unhelpfully.

"NO!" I snapped.

"Just imagine you're dancing, except...now it's across a tightrope."

"That's...not very helpful."

"I thought it was brilliant. Now get a move on." She gave me a gentle shove, "I'm right beside you, Twinkletoes. I won't let the fall hurt you. Trust me and trust yourself. You can do this. Hard things don't come easy, but that doesn't negate our obligation to face them and try."

She's right, you know.

Shall I repeat that lovely little phrase Raz just used?

You wouldn't dare.

Oh, I dare. It's apparently Tuesday, remember? Anything goes. Now, with the deepest depths of my heart's sincerity... Shut. Up.

I took a deep breath and, squaring my shoulders, I closed my eyes. The wind tore at my body, threatening to throw me overboard. But buried beneath the wind was a new echo I had failed to notice before. It was the smooth rise and fall of the ship that moved beneath my feet. It carried a rhythm like a song that sat lodged in my chest. The wind pulled at me. It, too, sang of something great and unfathomable.

I opened my eyes and took a hesitant step forward, and then another.

"That's it," Raz said encouragingly.

I was gaining courage now and my next step finally felt confident—as if I had hope of getting the hang of it.

Much to my annoyance, my foot slipped, and I went plummeting over the edge. Raz caught me in a heartbeat, but it was enough to turn my timid hope into feral, childish rage.

"That's it!" I yelled. "I'm just gonna shimmy across the beams on my butt! I will butt scoot like a fuzzy wooly worm and that's all you're going to get!"

"That's the spirit!" Ember yelled from somewhere below us. "Let's mutiny, Eva!"

"You will do *no* such thing!" Raz and Theron yelled in unison.

Raz shook her head, sighing. "You girls are such drama queens. C'mon Twinkletoes. I promise you, that is not the last time you'll fall. It will happen many, many more times. Even when fear doesn't taint your steps, it'll happen. You have to learn to get up and keep trying."

"And if I don't?" I challenged darkly.

"Then you'll get eaten by a skye dragon," Raz said dismissively. "For you are crunchy and taste good with ketchup."

The mental image of Fireheart, eating little toasty nuggets that looked like me, popped into my head—complete with an overflowing bowl of ketchup and a whole tray of cheese sauce.

I wonder what Fireheart would think of mozzarella sticks. I never had the chance to let him try such a treat.

I think I need to ask Logan to make them for him.

"Learn to dance on the tightrope or get eaten. Either way, it's uncomfortable and hard. Either way, it absolutely sucks. But only one of them will give you a chance of finding your way through the labyrinth they've built for us."

"What do you mean?"

Raz's eyes were miles away as she stared at the bright, sunny skies. "Nevermind what I mean, you're just stalling. Get on your feet and go again."

I was seething as I clambered to my feet. I had the bad feeling it was going to be a terribly long, hard day. But as Raz said, it was Tuesday. If it was true that 'anything goes' on a Tuesday, then there was still hope for me and Ember to mutiny and get away from this awful training.

I wasn't entirely sure, but I was beginning to think I'd take my chances with the skye dragons—even though I was crunchy and tasted good with ketchup.

34

If Scared To Death Was A Real Medical Condition, Then I'd Be A Ghost By Now

EMBER

"Nobody ever tells you that bravery feels like fear."
-Mary Kate Teske

I was beginning to wonder if Theron just had it out for me. His idea of training, while preferable to Raz's, was still enough to make me wish I was anywhere else.

"Em, we've been over this. I can't just take away *all* your fear. I'll give it to you in little doses, but you have to consciously learn to conquer it and move through it." His tone was that of patient longsuffering, but it was also one that informed me I was being ridiculous and entirely overdramatic.

"Why not?" I wheedled. "Evadne made the bargain with Verity that you would manage my fear."

"Yes, and that's exactly what I'm doing, managing. But managing doesn't mean taking it away entirely, like I was doing when you got here. It means I'm helping you with the flow of it. I'm breaking the strength of it into bite-sized pieces. Pieces that you then have to learn to chew and swallow."

"I think your pieces are too big!" I protested, still clinging to the mast. "I'm choking on them. Can't you see I'm choking?"

"I think you're just being stubborn," Theron sighed.

"I am *NOT!*" I whispered breathlessly. My whole body was shaking as I stared at the terrifying world around me. We were only about fifteen feet up in the air, but it was fifteen feet too many for my taste. Walking around on the decks alone was enough to make me absolutely terrified. Being up here was far worse.

"Couldn't we have just...started with the deck?"

Theron raised his eyebrows, refusing to answer my wheedling question. "C'mon Sparks, you're making me look like a bad teacher here."

It was then that Evadne fell, screaming through the air above us. My voice wouldn't work; I couldn't scream out her name fast enough. Relief crashed through my fear as Raz dove and caught her.

Oh thank goodness!

"RAZ!" Theron yelled, enraged.

Why is he yelling at Raz?

"That is *NOT* an acceptable form of teaching!"

Wait. Did she push Evadne?"

Raz yelled back a jumbled array of insults and Theron rolled his eyes angrily.

"If you push her off again, I will report you to Verity," Theron threatened.

"And she'll tell you to stay out of it," Raz shot back. "I'll train my pupil how I wish; you can train yours how you please. Now leave me alone and go back to your coddling."

Theron harrumphed, rolling his eyes again. "*Coddling,*" he muttered under his breath. "The sheer audacity of this blood thirsty Fey. If she had her way, you'd both be that high up, falling off the cursed mast. She's just being especially stubborn this morning. Someone must have deprived her of her second pot of coffee."

Second POT?! How much coffee does this lady drink and how is she not DEAD?!

Theron turned back to me. "Well, now that we know *I* definitely don't look like a bad teacher, we should get to work. I'll tell you what, Sparks. You do what I say, and I'll answer your questions."

It was a tempting offer, but I wasn't sure I could fulfill my end of the bargain. "I don't know how," I muttered, infuriated by my own paralyzing fear. Things would be so much easier if my body would just *stop* freaking out.

"You try," Theron said. "You do what I tell you, and you actually try."

"Okay, fine. Why do you look like F?"

Theron sighed. "Ah, you go right for the throat. Walk across the beam to me. Remember what I told you about keeping your balance, and I'll tell you the cursed tale."

I nodded and, intrigued by the knowledge I was about to gain, I finally unfroze and began to carefully put one foot in front of the other, not allowing myself to look down, but simply ahead, as if I was walking across a log over a creek.

It's not a tightrope, it's not a balancing beam. It's as big as a tree over water and that's enough. I can do this. I can do it.

"That's the spirit," Theron said encouragingly.

"Yes, yes. Now tell me the story," I pressed. "I need all the dirt. All the details." I gave him a stern look. "You're not allowed to leave anything out. Got it?"

Theron raised his hands and made an X across his heart. "Bossy, bossy," he muttered. "F and I are brothers—twins, actually," he began. "We both fled the Realm, and the bloody fate they sought to thrust on us—a fate they now proclaim to be yours. Who knows, the ones of the prophecy could be ages down the line. Twins are uncommon, but not entirely unheard of."

"You both fled? What happened?"

Theron sighed. "Nothing good," he muttered. He turned back to me. "F was selfish in his flight. We had both decided to go, but he was impatient. I was on the cusp of a new discovery, one that didn't require you to sacrifice an innocent life and doom them to your fate. But F, fool that he was, didn't want to wait. So, he called in the right of substitution. It's an age-old spell, an ironic twist given by the curse of three in their binding of the Grimms."

"How were the Grimms bound?" I asked, unsure if I really wanted the answer to my question.

"I'll answer that in a moment. Let's stick to the story at hand, shall we?"

I nodded, eyes fixed ahead. I was making step after wobbling step back and forth across the beam—all under the close watch and scrutiny of Theron. His mechanical wings were out of their backpack and at the ready. He could dive and save me at a moment's notice.

"F's flight put me under very close scrutiny with the ruling monarchs and the remaining Grimms. Though I had found my answer for the alternate way, the human he had bound in his absence was not one I could abandon. I felt her blood was just as much on my hands as his. After all, I was the one who first suggested we run. If I hadn't, our lives would have been doomed and bound to the Last Gate, but she wouldn't have been brought to such a place."

"Oma," I whispered.

"I knew her as Morah," Theron replied quietly. He sighed and stared down at his hands. "I couldn't do much for her, but I tried. The monarchs were so enraged by F's deception they broke her mind. Soon she didn't know where she was, or what was happening. I'm sure when she went back into the Human Realm adjusting was impossible."

I shrugged. "She actually did okay...she was eccentric, but I think for the most part she forgot. She was always afraid of the Fey though...that is, until the Dementia set in. Once it took hold, it made her violent. She would stand out in her yard and yell at the trees, daring the Fey to come fight her."

"You're speaking of her in past tense, is she—"

His words hung unspoken between us, and I fought back a sudden rush of tears. "She died the day we were dragged to the Realm," I whispered. "A...a Direwolfe chased me to her house. Several Fey were there waiting for me. They had destroyed the wards and burned the house down. We couldn't find her body... Rosamond came that night on orders from the Summer King and took us away..."

Theron hung his head. "That's a shame. She was quite the woman, even after what was done to her."

"F's gone too," I whispered. "Rosamond killed him on the doorstep."

Theron looked up, his eyes growing angry. "She killed him? Why would she kill him? He was crucial to the strength of the Last Gate after he came back. She didn't think it was me, did she?"

"No, from what I can piece together, King Quillon ordered her to do it. I don't think she wanted to... She later said he was "killed by my own unwilling hand.""

"She can't lie," Theron mused, pondering. "Why was F outside the Realm? After returning to the Fey Realm, he was supposed to be guarding the Last Gate...so why was he there at all?"

"He came often." I sighed. "He would bring us little trinkets and gifts, then eat all the snacks and soda we had in the house...he kept trying to convince Dad to let him take us to the Realm, just not where the monarchs were. He was going to somehow hide us from them. He and Dad were also trying to find a way to help us escape the curse."

Theron swore under his breath. "That fool. That absolute fool. He was always trying to find another way. Always trying to fight fate when she can't be fought." His fist slammed into the worn wood of the mast. "He brings about Ragnarök with every selfish action and leaves too many victims in his wake."

Theron's anger subsided into exhaustion and he sighed, rubbing his calloused knuckles. "It bodes ill to speak such of the dead, but do you think I get a bone to drag him down since he's my own cursed twin?"

I shrugged, unsure of what to say. I was still processing his words.

What does it mean? What does all of it mean?

"I do not like being twisted and pulled as if I'm a puppet on a string. Someone is shifting the scales, and I don't like it. I can't make sense of it. The Moores are unraveling. Darkness overtakes her like dusk on a moonless night. But what does it mean?"

Theron's questions mirrored my own as he glared out at the horizon. "I became a skye pirate to escape such manipulation. I chose this life for myself, and now I fear someone is trying to take it away."

"I'm sorry," I whispered. I felt somewhat responsible. If we hadn't come aboard the ship, he never would have gotten mixed up in the affairs of the Courts again.

"Don't worry about it, Sparks. You are not responsible for the tainted actions of others. I just wish I knew what direction to point my sword. I don't like this. I don't like it one bit."

He sighed again, then shook his head as if to clear his thoughts away. "I'm letting myself wax mysterious when I'm supposed to be teaching you. Either you do your drills while we talk, or we sing pirate songs to keep you focused."

"I'd like to continue the conversation," I replied as I once again began walking back across the beam. We had started the morning out two beams lower, and as the day had progressed, he had moved us up further and further, doing drills up and down the rope ladders as well to get me in the hang of the odd movements. I was beginning to feel confident enough at this level I was sure we could move up again.

"What about Rosamond?" I asked. A wave of fear so potent rolled over me that I wobbled, and clutched the rope I had managed to let go of for the last three passes.

"Sorry," Theron muttered. "I didn't mean to give you back all your fear."

"That's all *mine*?" I demanded incredulously. "Surely you're wrong. I haven't been feeling my fear like *that*."

"You're feeling *some* of it," Theron countered. "I've been giving it back to you in doses—the more confident you get, the more I give it back to you. The confidence overwhelms the fear until it's put away and controlled. I just lost my concentration and gave it back to you all at once. So yes, it is all yours. Now, let go of the rope and scoot."

Scoot like a wooly worm? That I can do. I am a pro at butt scooting.

"That rope will only hinder you. Learn to trust your legs."

I made a face but obeyed. He knew more about skye legs and courage than I did. I'd have to trust him.

"During my remaining time in the Realm," Theron continued, picking up the thread of his story once more, "I fell in love with a powerful nymph named Rosamond. I knew she was a Legend, but I thought despite her history she loved me too. I thought, despite what she was, she was capable of loving another. Together we tried to care for Morah, and together we made a plan to escape. When my brother finally returned, back from his long jaunt of impulsive, selfish freedom and Morah was returned to the Mortal Realm, we ran and never looked back." Theron's voice was full of pain. "*I* never looked back," he corrected softly. "She did. Because not long after we made our escape, she tried to capture me. She tried to force me to return. She bound me with her vines and began to drag me back to that cursed place. Back to that nightmare. She was such a good actress. I don't know why she tried to keep up the act. Can you believe she cried with every step back?"

"What happened? How did you get away?"

"I ate a toxic flower that caused a death-like reaction. It wasn't enough to kill me, but it did the trick. What very few knew about F and I, was that we were both firstborn. Impossibly, our mother gave birth to us at the *exact* same time. The magic bound us both with the curse of firstborn, so I, too, could not die until one of us sired an heir. But Rosamond didn't know this. Since nobody knew of our joint gift, the rumor that F was firstborn was the truth everyone chose to believe."

Theron's voice fell to a whisper as his eyes drifted far, far away. "Rosamond pulled her vines back, screaming my name in fear. I waited as she cradled my lifeless body, mourning me, and when her guard was down enough, I, in my fever induced rage, used a cursed blade to cut off her wings." He shuddered in horror. "Her screams of agony followed me through the Moores as I fled. Then *I* was the one crying with every step away from that cursed nightmare. But unlike her, my tears were genuine."

Horror washed over me at the gruesome details of his past. "How does the powerful lady fit into it?" I asked hesitantly, trying to put the pieces together and make it make sense. "The one whose heart you cut out."

"She was a monster that haunted me the entire time I was in the Realm," Theron replied. "I tried to avoid her, but she had made arrangements with Queen Valda—ensuring I could not avoid her any longer. The union would bring powerful Grimms into the Realm for the Last Gate. Combining her magic with mine would strengthen the Gate, so the Queen readily agreed. The night Rosamond and I fled was to be the night of our union. After Rosamond returned to the Realm empty handed, that cursed Fey started stalking me. I can only assume based on the timing that Rosamond was in cahoots with the infernal wretch all along."

There was something bothering me about the story, something I couldn't pinpoint. I wanted to give some explanation for Rosamond; the heartless Fey I'd come to know in our short time together had seemed to be more than that. But I had no words, I couldn't put my finger on what I knew was buried down somewhere deep inside.

Theron shook his head. "The rest you know. I dealt with the Fey in a similar, bloody fashion, and took back my fate by joining the crew and my beloved Moores. I lost my immortality when F's son was born. That would be your father...the rest of your lineage you know." He turned his full attention back to me, and we both seemed to realize at the same time that I had once again stopped walking back and forth.

"That's it," Theron snapped. "You're learning skye shanties."

"But—"

"No buts about it," he cut in. "You have to find your skye legs so I can stop spending my subconscious energy keeping your wits in line. You're as hysterical as a hyena."

No king, no king, la-la-la-la-la-laaaaa!

"Now, here's the first line," Theron continued, unaware of the memory he'd triggered in the back of my mind. "You're going to sing it while I give you back your full dose of fear. Once we get that controlled, we'll go up another mast and I'll take back some of your fear."

"That's a terrible idea," I whined. "I can't face my fear. I'm scared to death of heights."

"Then your ghost can haunt me later," Theron replied—his tone was that of absolutely no nonsense.

Up above, Evadne's distinct yell cut through the air. "That's it! I'm just gonna shimmy across the beams on my butt! I will butt scoot like a fuzzy wooly worm and that's all you're going to get!"

Yess! Revenge of the wooly worms!

"That's the spirit!" I yelled up, cheered by her angst. "Let's mutiny, Eva!"

"You will do no such thing!" Raz and Theron yelled in unison.

"Fiiiine," I groaned. "But don't for a second think I won't be daydreaming about mutiny."

Theron rolled his eyes. "Hyena," he muttered. "Now, here's how the song goes. I'm going to sing the first verse, and then you call back to my verse, 'yo-ho-ho and a bottle of rum,' until the last bit. It changes then, but I'll tell you what to say when we get to it. Got it?"

"Uhm…"

"Good. Now," Theron cleared his throat and began to sing in a deep, bass growl. "Fifteen men on a dead man's chest."

He gave me a pointed look, and I stammered out the required "yo-ho-ho, and a bottle of rum."

He rolled his eyes. "Not like that. You're killing me, Sparks. Like this. 'Yo-ho-ho, and a bottle of rum.' Now you try."

"But I'm not a good singer," I protested.

"Doesn't matter. What matters is the beat. It helps calm you down and keeps you focused on your body and the pulse of the sky around you. Now sing with me."

We sang the required line together three or four times until at last Theron was satisfied. "That's more like it!" he cried approvingly. "Now let's have another go." He cleared his voice and once again began to sing. "Fifteen men on a dead man's chest."

"Yo-ho-ho and a bottle of rum," I chorused back as loud as I could around my sudden inability to breathe. My fear had been given back, and I didn't like it, not one bit.

There should be a rule. No takesie-backsies when it comes to someone's fear. You take it, you keep it—end of discussion.

It wasn't long until above us, Raz and Evadne joined the song. Raz's enthusiasm was contagious and soon I was grinning with every step, despite my fear. Theron was right—the song helped me focus. The crew in the ship around us began to echo back the chants, turning it into a confusing sort of round that, much to Theron's ire, quickly got out of hand and completely fell apart as they all ad-libbed with nonsense and profuse swearing.

I, however, found the whole experience absolutely delightful, and for a moment, I could forget my lingering heartache and homesickness. There was something about the ship that made me feel safe, and I began to wonder if maybe my broken heart could find a way without Artemis. Perhaps there was still hope that we could find a new future, a new fate aboard this vessel and the skies beyond.

But I can't leave him...I can't leave him...can I?

I don't think I can leave him...

I don't know...I don't know.

35

If Dinner Didn't Possess An Arm Wrestling Competition, It Wouldn't Be A Pirate Ship

EMBER

"An apple a day keeps anyone away if you throw it hard enough."
-Unknown

Nighttime found me utterly exhausted. Evadne looked ready to drop. She had a fresh slew of bruises across her ribs from Raz's quick catching skills, and she looked downright murderous when I poked fun at her for the fifty something times she'd fallen off the mast during the day. It was probably a good thing Fireheart was sleeping during her high beam escapades. He likely would have bitten Raz if he saw her push Evadne off the mast.

"You had help," Evadne growled as she pulled on a thick wool sweater. The days were fairly warm, but as soon as the sun dipped down and the stars came out, it became downright cold. "If I had Theron's help keeping me unafraid, I wouldn't have fallen so much."

"Trust me, he gave me back my fear, he just worked me up to it. You were doing *amazing* out there. Did I see you dancing across the beam at one point?"

The pointed tips of Evadne's slender ears reddened in embarrassment. "Raz made me do it," she growled. "She said if I didn't, she'd push me off the mast again."

"Why is that a go to threat?"

"Because she knows she'll catch me. But it was her way of proving that I was able to do what she said I was capable of doing, and blah-blah-*blah*." Evadne scowled down at her ribs. "She was right, I could dance across the beam, but it made me want to murder her."

"Maybe you're just hungry," I piped in helpfully. "You're a whole four masts ahead of me. You're almost to the crow's nest! Just think what you'll be capable of in a week."

Evadne shrugged, exhausted. "Yeah," she sighed. "Whatever. Come on, let's go find some food. I'm hungry enough I could eat sixteen pizzas."

At the words 'food' and 'pizza,' both Fireheart and Elvie's heads popped up from the hammock. Clearly dinnertime trumped naptime.

I was pulling on my boots over a clean pair of pants. Evadne and I were dressed similarly. We both wore our armored vests underneath thick wool sweaters. Theron had picked the sweaters up for us at the Wasteland's market while we recovered from our injuries. Apparently, where we were headed was going to be cold. We also wore reinforced, close-fitting pants, lined with fuzzy, soft wool, that tucked into our new boots.

It had been so long since my hair was this long—close to six years—that after trying to braid it for a few minutes, I gave up and got Evadne's help. I kept tangling the ends together before I reached them, and I was tired enough that I might end up chopping off all my hair in a fit of rage. Apparently, my hair liked the Moores. It had grown even longer since the last time I had inspected it and was now halfway down my back.

Evadne's hair was below her waist now and she hadn't even tried to braid or brush it. She had simply tossed the hairbrush to me and sat down on the edge of her hammock.

Finally, after we were both cleaned up and somewhat presentable, we made our way out of the crew's quarters toward the dining room.

The air was crisp and sharp. Springtime lingered on the wind, and I wondered how close the Courts were to switching back to summer. When we had left the Realm, the Winter Court was in control, but I had no idea how the Moores' weather mirrored that of the Central Realm, or if it picked an entirely new season on a whim. I somewhat hoped it was rather like my Kansas in the fall. One day you'd be scraping ice off the windshield, next you'd be wearing shorts and a tank top, roasting in the sun and humidity. It was just plain *fickle*.

The sound of a commotion affirmed we were headed in the right direction. Sure enough, after turning the corner, we found the crew in a laughing uproar.

Nikos and Raz were facing off against each other in an arm wrestling match, while the rest of the crew took bets and shouted insults or encouragements in support of their respective bets. Currently Raz and Nikos were locked in a standstill, neither arm moving, though their muscles were straining.

We stopped in the doorway and watched in silent amusement as the crew grew more and more chaotic around the two.

Then, Raz leaned forward, and quick as a wink, kissed the tip of Nikos' nose. Nikos' arm gave way a fraction, but the moment of distraction was all Raz needed. She pinned his fist in a matter of moments.

"That's cheating, you no good bloody pirate!" Nikos yelled.

Raz shrugged, snatching her winnings from the table in triumph. "Don't let me be your weak spot," she shot back. "It makes you *terribly* vulnerable. I'm a pirate, love. You know I cheat."

Nikos swore under his breath as the crew took to jostling and teasing him. Raz got to her feet and blew him a kiss. Nikos glared back as he grabbed her hand and pulled her to his side. "That's cheating, Raz," he repeated.

She arched an eyebrow. "How could it be cheating? I didn't even use my laser fingers this time."

This time? I feel like there's a story here.

"You shouldn't even be given laser fingers," Nikos shot back. "You're far too irresponsible with them."

"AUCGH!" Raz screeched in utter indignation.

Nikos didn't seem to care as he pulled her head down by the back of her neck and gave her a brief, yet passionate kiss, silencing her protests.

The whole crew began crowing and cat calling at the display of affection, and Raz's cheeks burned a deep emerald against her pale green skin.

"All right love birds, break it up before you ruin our appetite," Logan called from the kitchen.

After a moment's effort, Nikos dragged himself away from Raz's lips. "She's my wife. I can kiss her if I want to!" he replied indignantly.

"Food's up," Logan sighed in annoyance. "Come eat or, by all means, continue kissing your bloodthirsty, cheating wife and face the consequences."

Raz's loving face turned murderous and she rounded on Logan. "I was *not* cheating! It doesn't say anywhere in the rule book you can't kiss your opponent!"

"Fine, oh un-cheating pirate," Logan replied, raising his hands in surrender. "I can't promise you this mangy lot will leave you anything if you choose the kissing,"

At those words, all thoughts of love and smooching were gone. The lovebirds jumped to their feet and joined the crew in line in front of the kitchen doorway. While they waited, they held hands, laughed, and talked—sharing stories and cracking jokes.

Sora had abandoned the line and was now leaning against Logan. He in turn had his arms wrapped around her and they were conversing quietly.

Something sharp cut through my chest—longing. An ache for Artemis that I so desperately wanted to deny. Evadne looked similarly sad, and I had the sneaking suspicion she felt a similar pang for Marcus. She twisted the dainty promise ring on her right hand, her eyes distant and pained.

"Come on you two, you've earned it," Logan called, pulling us from our contemplation. "Come eat before these knaves devour it all."

A chorus of angry protests met his statement, but he shrugged. "I said what I said, you lot know the truth. Or do I have to remind you about the great pancake fiasco?"

A series of groans answered his cryptic comment, and Logan smirked. "That's what I thought." He waved us forward. "Come on girls, come to the front of the line so you can eat."

He didn't have to tell us twice. Our growling stomachs propelled us forward, and soon we were sitting at one of the many tables with a large plate overflowing with steaming food.

"How did I get this much on my plate?" Evadne muttered irritably.

Fireheart was perched on her shoulder, Elvie on her other. They were both licking their lips as they stared down at her heaping plate.

"Raz helped with our portions," I reminded her with a laugh.

I wasn't about to complain about Raz's help. I quite liked the excuse to eat more food.

Evadne continued her mumbled protests.

"Last I checked, you wanted to eat sixteen pizzas. Now that I think about it, you probably *should*. You need to eat, Evadne. Remember what Artemis *and* Verity told us? Our metabolisms are so much faster here. If you don't eat enough, your body is going to collapse."

"Yes, yes," Evadne grumbled as she began to devour her steak.

Sensing the possibility of sharing our leftovers was virtually none, Fireheart abandoned his perch and haughtily made his way into the kitchen, eyes fixed on Logan as if to say 'fix me a plate, oh human servant.' Much to my surprise, Logan scooped up the little dragon and plopped him on his shoulder. "What'll it be today?" he asked as he took Fireheart into the kitchen to get him a plate.

Red walked over to where we sat, carefully holding the edge of a heaping plate in his mouth. With gentle precision, he pushed the plate onto the table and then gracefully hopped up into the chair and began to devour his food. "I quite like it here," he said around a bite. "I think, if the captain permits, I shall stay on this ship."

Evadne gave him a sad sort of smile. "I can understand why you'd want to stay. I feel the same way."

"You could," Red replied, pondering her face.

"I don't think I can," she sighed. "My fate lies elsewhere. As much as I'd like to stay, I think—"

"Well, Evadne," Raz said lightly as she plopped down at our table and interrupted the conversation. "Are you ready for tomorrow?"

Evadne stuck a large bite in her mouth to avoid answering the question.

"Well?" Raz pressed.

"No," Evadne said around a full mouth of food.

Since when does Evadne act so unladylike?

Who cares? I like it. No more bossy Eva with her prissy manners.

Who knows. Maybe this lot will corrupt her enough she'll start drinking copious amounts of coffee.

Yesss. Make her love the magic bean juice.

That's it, I'm going to scheme with Raz and Theron. I will make her a coffee addict.

"You have nothing to worry about," Raz said reassuringly. "This is the same smith who fixed my fingers. He'll help with your eye."

"I don't want a new eye," Evadne whispered, tears clogging her voice. "I want *my* eye to work."

Guilt cut through me and my appetite vanished. It was my fault she got hurt in the first place. Darcy was after me.

If I had only caved, she wouldn't have gone through that...

"Do you think I wanted to have my fingers replaced?" Raz asked. "None of us ask for the tragedy that is thrust upon us. But if we do nothing in the wake of that pain, we render ourselves useless. This Realm needs you, and you need your eye back. You can function with one, yes. But you will be so much better off with two."

Evadne sighed angrily and Raz rolled her eyes. "Such dramatics," she muttered.

That must be a favorite phrase around here. I heard it all day long.

"What *did* happen to your fingers?" I asked, trying to change the subject.

"They got blown off during a raid. A blasted pirate threw a pixie bomb right at my hand and blew them clean off. But I can't really complain. One of the wretch's raider friends caught one of the fingers in his mouth and choked to death."

Oh my gosh, that's horrifying.

I knew my mouth was hanging open, but I didn't have the brain function to close it as I pondered such a death.

"Besides, I got these wicked cool laser fingers," Raz continued brightly.

Evadne stopped chewing. "Wait a second, you told me they got bit off by a Dire-wolfe," she said, confused.

"You won't get the truth from her," a new voice interjected. "She won't tell anyone the truth as to how she *really* lost her fingers." An unfamiliar woman sat down next to Raz. She had light greyish green skin that was a disarray of cuts held together by thin metal staples. Thick black hair was pulled into tight pigtail dutch braids, and her bright florescent green eyes glowed softly in the lamplight of the cabin.

"Girls," Raz said around a mouthful of food. "Meet Nyra. Nyra, this is Evadne and Ember Grimm."

I tore my eyes away, determined not to stare, and embarrassed that I had been staring at all, as I held out a hand to shake hers. Her skin was cool against mine, as if she'd come straight from a refrigerator.

"It's quite all right," Nyra said kindly. "I'm sure you've never seen someone like me. Stare all you want. It doesn't bother me anymore. I've embraced my uniqueness." She laughed. "It pleases me to be the most interesting person in the room. It means *I* get all the attention."

I smiled, grateful for her graciousness.

Logan came to our table with two heaping plates and a very smug-looking Fireheart on his shoulder. "All right, remember to share with the feral Moore hamster," Logan lectured.

"Elvie, Elvie, Elvie!" Elvie shrieked in annoyance.

"Hamster, hamster, hamster!" Logan retorted. He turned back to Fireheart. "*Share*," he repeated sternly.

Fireheart glared at Elvie, and then in the blink of an eye, looked up with wide eyes and a moony smile at Logan as if to say 'of course.' But the moment Logan's back was turned, Fireheart wrapped his little talons around the edges of both plates and glared at Elvie. The message was clear: Fireheart would *not* be sharing.

"Here Elvie, eat some of mine," Evadne said distractedly.

"Now, I've heard you girls had an encounter with Bluebeard?"

I strained, trying to nod, but Evadne scoffed outright. "Darn right, we did. Nasty bastard. I plan to kill him the next time I see him. I—" she stopped, shocked.

Nyra arched a slender eyebrow. "What?"

"We've been—" her words cut off, just as they had in all previous conversations about the matter.

"Silenced," Nyra stated. "But you just managed to speak of him...interesting. I would not be surprised if you've begun to break the curse. Your exposure to Darke magic would help, since silencing is, in and of itself, Darke magic." She shrugged. "Neither here nor there. My point is about the monster himself. You see, I was his third wife. He sacrificed me at the Ruins in the hope of strengthening and empowering the Knight. All he got from his cursed spell was an undead wife—a wife who he'd chopped up and then stitched back together without a heart—who then tried to kill him and destroy the Ruins."

"What happened?"

"I failed," Nyra stated with a shrug. "Then to get rid of me, since I wanted to kill him, he buried me alive," she paused, scoffing. "Well, as alive as an undead can be when they're...well, alive. Verity was tracking him and saw the whole thing. She sacrificed her chance to kill him to rescue me. She had no idea I was undead buried beneath that earth. She'd seen him wrestle a *very* alive looking woman into a hole and cover it up with eight feet of dirt. She didn't know I was perfectly fine, simply extremely vexed and volatile under the weight of all that cursed soil. When she realized the truth, she and I both were extremely angry with one another. Her with me for losing her chance, and I with her for not killing the bastard when she had a chance. Since then, we've decided to turn our anger to more *productive* outlets, such as piracy and bloodshed." She smirked, staring at me. "Being made from darkness and shadows, created of Darke magic, I can hear their prattle. From what I hear, you've got him in *quite* a tizzy, redhead. That blow Marcovester Red dealt him might have killed him if she hadn't send him to the Ruins."

"How did he survive her blow?" Evadne asked. "He gloated he was going to tell me, and then he freaking didn't. He's a no good, dirty rotten liar."

I won't tell her I already know, in case that pisses her off.

Memories of her anger about the things she didn't know rose up. I didn't want to make Evadne angry again.

Nyra sighed. It was a long-suffering sigh that did not bode well. "Darcy is a Legend, and in his tale, they killed him, yes?"

"It's been a while since I read any fairytales, but I think so."

Nyra snorted with laughter. "Well, that's ironic. Your last name is Grimm, and you haven't kept up to date with your tales. Funny that."

I laughed with her. She was right; it was pretty humorous.

"Well," Nyra continued, her joking manner turning back to serious. "That part of the tale is true. The men of the Human Realm killed him. But he was a powerful sorcerer. A wizard who wove Darke magic. He knew how to outwit the men who sought to destroy him. If I were to hazard a guess, he sold his shadow to a rouge darkling before he died, and then took on a monster of the Ruins as his shadow after he died. In death, he recreated himself and erased his story. He was a Legend, but no one remembered his name or the bloodshed that tainted his story."

"How do we kill him?" Evadne asked.

"Well, the incredibly vengeful, petty side of me is suggesting you chop him into pieces. Make sure you split his shins and femurs apart while he's alive. I know from experience that hurts like a bastard bite from a MooreFly. But that would take time and effort we do not have. I would suggest cutting off his head, then cutting out the heart and burning both it and the head. There's no telling what Darke magic he's bound to his lifeforce. If he's smart, he'll have done quite a few. But be careful, his shadow has teeth and claws. It will rise and fight to defend its human. It feeds off him and everyone in his path—especially the ones he tortures."

She turned to Evadne. "You carry darkness, daughter of Grimm. I can hear it inside your racing heart. It's there in your bones. Do not let it prevail over you. Do you understand me?"

Evadne nodded and took a hurried sip of her water.

"I know you sense it. You're clearly affected by such things. Be on your guard against the seeds he's planted in your mind. It leaves the door open for greater evil to invade. I was made from darkness. I recognize the echoes like I recognize my hideous face in the looking glass every morning. You carry a *great* taint of Darke magic."

Well, that's disturbing. Poor Evadne.

"Is there a way to be rid of it?" Evadne asked.

"Your only hope of that lay with the witch. Since we're all on less than cordial terms now, what with your trying to kill her in self-defense, I'd say you should just accept it and keep the monster locked up, tight. Throw away the key while you're at it. The Mooresmith might be able to give you some relief, but it will never truly be gone."

Evadne nodded, turning back to her food. She, too, seemed to have lost her appetite.

"Well, now that this disgusting conversation is over," Raz interjected. "Why don't you tell me how many dinosaur clouds you saw today."

Nyra made a face, as if protesting, but then began a detailed description of the three separate dinosaur clouds she had seen while working her shift.

If only the world was as simple as dinosaur clouds and arm wrestling. I miss home and the simplicity it carried.

I sat weeping on the thick stones of a well. Gray mist obscured the world around me, save for three oak trees around the well and the bright moonlight overhead.

Where am I?

Why am I crying?

Forget the crying. What am I wearing? This is not what I went to bed in.

The offending outfit in question happened to be a gorgeous, sky-blue evening gown with long sleeves that trailed down toward the ground and a neckline that touched the hollow of my throat.

I must be in a Dreamscape.

A branch cracked somewhere nearby, and I jumped to my feet, startled. A large cloud passed over the moon as I reached for a thin white cloth that lay drying on the grass.

The world around me grew heavy, as if everything stood frozen in time. My own body froze a second away from snatching the material off the grass as arms wrapped around me, pulling me backward.

NO!

I was terrified.

What if it's Darcy? What if he's found me?

"It's me," Artemis' voice whispered soothingly. "It's just me, Em."

"Don't," I choked out, finally able to find my voice as the dream fully froze.

"Don't what?" he asked gently.

"Don't say my name like that," I whispered. "Don't say my name like you care for me."

"You know I do."

"Why are you here?"

"Where are you?" he countered.

"Lost," I murmured. "Let me go."

"You know I can't. I can't let you go. I can't return to the Realm without you. The monarchs will kill Jack."

"He chose for us to come."

"I cannot let him die. I cannot let the Moores bear their wrath...and most of all, I cannot let you go."

"You have to," I hissed, my voice ragged. "You have to let me go."

"I will never let you go, Ember. I promise you, I will never let you go."

"Don't make promises you can't keep."

The dream was trembling, fragmenting around us. Artemis couldn't hold the Dreamscape much longer.

"I'll keep it," Artemis murmured. "I'll keep it, even if I die trying."

"Don't die for me," I whispered, tears sliding down my cheeks. "I'm not worth it, Artemis. Just let me go."

The dream at last shattered and I woke with a cry, tears on my cheeks and Artemis' name on my lips. I knew at last the truth within myself as I faced this impossible decision. The possibility of a better path, a different life was within grasp, but I didn't think I wanted it if it meant a future without him.

36

The Scars We Carry, The Revenge We Crave, The Ones We Love

EVADNE

"You don't have that fire in your eyes anymore and you know it."
-incoloure

The morning dawned blood red on the horizon, promising violence and tears in the crimson blaze.

I hadn't slept at all.

I spent the night lying out on the deck, watching the stars through my undamaged eye. Bright, swirling galaxies surrounded us as we sailed through the sky. They looked so close, it seemed I could almost reach out and touch them. The crew on the graveyard shift didn't notice or even care about my presence. If anything, they seemed to be purposefully avoiding me—giving me the space I so desperately craved.

I felt guilty for abandoning Ember to her nightmares, but I couldn't bear to be near her. The darkness inside of me craved her—it wanted to hurt her, punish her. It wanted to steal her away. The voices inside my head, that monster I sought to keep locked up, that hunger of Darcy's, tainted my being and for the first time I was afraid of myself.

I was afraid of what Darcy had done to me.

I could hear her tossing and turning, then a cry that cut at my aching heart—Artemis' name.

I missed Marcus so much I was forever aware of the hole in my life where he should be standing. But I didn't know where or when I'd ever see him again.

Why did we leave them? I understand, but I don't. Why did you send us here, Jack? Things don't make sense.

Why does nothing make sense?

The world's gone all topsy-turvy and I don't know which way is up.

I feel like Alice, falling through the rabbit hole...and everything is confusing and wrong.

A lullaby Mum used to sing for us was drifting around the back of my mind as I watched the sky expand endlessly above me.

'Hush my darlings, don't shed a tear, tomorrow will come, there's no need for fear...tomorrow we'll find our way back home, hush my darlings, you're never alone...'

But I'm alone now, Mum. I'm alone, I'm so alone in this.

'The morning will dawn, and we will find our way, no matter the monsters, we will be okay. So don't you fear, and don't you fret, Momma's right here, and I'll always protect. Even in pain and sorrows so great, I'll always love you to my dying day.'

I was lost in the memory as tears silently slipped from the corner of my uninjured eye and slid down the side of my face. My injured eye was shedding a black poison, the closest thing it could produce to tears, but it burned like acid against my skin as it slipped down my cheek.

I can't even cry without remembering what happened.

Mum was there. She was there. He was holding her.

When I'd told Ember about Mum being trapped in that place, the grief on her face had been enough to break my heart.

How do we get her back? How do we save her?

It always came back to my never-ending questions, and like always, I had no answers as I watched this lost Realm around me awaken and come back to life. Some small part of me felt connected with this place. It was a lost world, made up of outlaws and outcasts. Yet, despite their disadvantage, they still found their way. They still made a life for themselves in the Moores. It wasn't just a life, a barren survival—they were *thriving*. The resilience of these Fey gave me a small fragment of hope. If they could find a way to move on and live, despite everything, then maybe I could, too.

"Land ho!" a voice shouted from above. I vaguely recognized it as Nyra's.

Groaning, I pulled myself to my feet.

"Evadne?" Ember called, her voice frantic.

I'm fine Em, I just needed some space. Cool your heels, I'm not a helpless child.

Using my staff for balance, I began to slowly make my way back toward the crew's quarters. Ember met me in the doorway, her eyes wide and afraid. "Are you okay?" she whispered, pulling me into a tight hug. "I woke up, and you were gone, and, and..." She was babbling, tangling up her words in her haste to try to speak. "I..." Tears were in her eyes as she pulled back. "I'm sorry," she whispered. "I just, you were gone and my nightmare...it..."

"Sorry," I sighed. "I didn't mean to worry you. I just needed some air."

Ember forced a smile. "I mean, I know I smell bad, but you should just tell me to shower instead of leaving."

"You showered last night," I said as I laughed. "Remember? The water was so cold, your lips turned blue. You couldn't even get them to work right so you could swear."

Last night was the first time I'd fully seen the mark the Moores left on her shoulder blade near Ryver's marks. It was a glorious phoenix and, to be completely honest, I was a little jealous. I wanted cool marks that meant something great and amazing. Instead, I had a damaged eye and a deep vine and flower scar burned into my skin.

Ember gets to have all the fun. Why does she get to be the hero?

I pushed the thought away. I didn't want the divisiveness it carried, and I was fairly sure it came from the monster locked in the back of my mind.

Ember laughed, then grimaced. "I despise cold showers," she grumbled.

"They are quite literally the worst," I agreed, wrapping an arm around her for balance as we made our way back into the crew's quarters.

The crew's quarters were below deck. The space was divided with women on one side and men on the other. Smaller, separate rooms were reserved for couples, and thick oak doors kept things private between the multiple quarters. But most nights, everyone slept with the doors open to allow for better air flow. Usually, they were only closed when people were changing or bathing. Wide windows lined the outside wall, and unless it was raining, they were kept open to allow a breeze into the space. Hammocks stretched out against one of the other walls, anchored into thick beams that helped support the weight of the deck above.

Slipping inside, the sound of swearing met my ears. It was quite an elaborate concoction that made my ears tingle. I suspected there was some sort of magic woven through it.

I wonder where Raz learned to swear like that. Is there some sort of faerie swearing class you can take? Or perhaps you learn it while working in certain places.

Honestly, I'd expect nothing less from a pirate.

I wonder if she can teach me to magic swear. That would be awesome.

Raz was currently taking a freezing cold shower, ensuring that everyone in the room knew how much she hated them.

"You should comb your hair, Em," I said to Ember, making my way toward my hammock to put up my WyrldCloak. "You look like you got into a fight with a raccoon."

"I do not!" Ember protested.

I turned back to lecture her on why I was right, and my words fell silent. My attention had caught the two vertical scars running down Raz's shoulder blades as she dried off. They were jagged and black, and something inside of me broke as I stared at them.

Rage, the likes of which I hardly recognized, filled me.

How dare they do this to her.

I was staring, but I couldn't look away.

Stop staring! Stop staring at them!

I couldn't look away. I couldn't tear my eyes away from the sight of the atrocity that had been done to her.

Ember elbowed me in the ribs, her gaze urgent. "Stop staring!" she whispered.

"It's okay," Raz said quietly, her back to us. "I'm not ashamed of my scars. What was done to me was unforgiveable, but I am not ashamed of my story."

"What happened?" I asked, unable to stop myself.

Raz pulled on a loose undershirt and turned to us with sad eyes. "Quillon cut them off, to make an example of me. I defied Lillith, a little bit of treason if you will. So she ordered the king to carry out an unnecessary, bloody deed." Raz scoffed. "He would have done it without her urging. Such is the way of things when you crave bloodshed. I did not deserve such an extreme punishment."

"Oh no," I whispered. Lillith's bloodthirsty revenge was not something I ever wanted to witness.

"What did she do that prompted your...dash of treason?" Ember asked hesitantly.

"Lillith killed my forest in a skirmish. My sisters were casualties that never should have happened. I stabbed her through the chest, but it wasn't enough. There's a wrong sort of magic to her. Something dark and sinister. No doubt the meddling of her sister, the *great* Lady Nightshade. Instead of killing me then and there, she decided to prolong my torment. She had him steal away my one true joy in life—my wings. After he took them, she used my own blood to curse me while they burned my wings to ash." Raz shuddered. "Some days I can still smell the stench. My beautiful wings, destroyed. My freedom, stolen from me... I can't die until she does, and I can't kill her. The curse prohibits me from doing so."

Raz's gaze was fixed on a spot on the floor. Her long, waist-length, curly hair dripped water into a puddle at her feet.

"I'm so sorry," I whispered.

"Rosamond watched," Raz replied, lost in thought. "She watched. She *let* them. She did *nothing*. I can never forgive her for that, when, at one time, we, too, were sisters. She said she would change things from the inside. It was a delusion I could never agree to. You can never change a corrupt system from the inside. All you'll ever do is compromise, again, and again, and again... You will watch the people you love be destroyed by them." She paused. "You have to burn the whole thing down from the ground up to truly make any change."

Raz smiled softly. "Someday, maybe I'll help set its destruction. Perhaps I'll light the match myself. Or maybe I'll just watch from a distance, listening to their screams as the Realm is destroyed."

"Do you want the destruction of the Realm?" Ember asked. She was swinging gently in her hammock, fingers twisting and untwisting, then fussing with the bracelets on her wrist—a nervous habit she indulged when she was anxious.

"I carry within myself a number of contradictions and possibilities. I want it, and yet, I do not. For a great many innocents would be slaughtered on such dark days. The carnage would stain the Realm an uncleansable red..." she paused, "though, all the blood on the monarchs' hands...it's already uncleansable. You can't save the Realm Ember; you can only try to fight for what's right. But most days I don't know what's right anymore."

"We offered to set the Summer Realm ablaze," Rune said. "Huxley had it all planned out...the bombs she stockpiled for the occasion are absolutely glorious, but the good Raz wouldn't let us."

"They'd kill you," Raz replied as she began to scrunch her wet, curly hair with a towel. "It is not worth the death of those I now call my family. Revenge never brings solutions; it only brings sorrow."

"Oi!" A woman's voice called out. I couldn't quite place the name it belonged to. "Breakfast is on, and if you don't hurry up, the guys won't leave anything for you."

"We're coming, Huxley!" Raz and Rune shouted in unison.

"JINX!" they yelled, pointing at each other. "Double jinx!!" Again, their words were in complete unison. "Triple Jinx, on top of every other cursed jinx!" It did no good. Neither could catch the other out of rhythm. "Fine! Truce!"

They began to giggle as they hurriedly put on the rest of their gear.

Ember's hair was still in a rat's nest, sticking up in multiple different directions, but I wasn't about to bring it back up. Ember combing through long hair was a nightmare. She'd likely cut it all off before she was through, and I rather liked her with longer hair. It looked so stunning on her; I wasn't about to play a part in its demise—even if that meant she went to breakfast looking like she got into a fight with a crazy raccoon.

37

The MooreSmith

EVADNE

"You robbed me of my life. I could have been human—I could have
been alive, but you took my heart and you murdered it. You made me
into this."
-Emilie Autumn, The Asylum for Wayward Victorian Girls

The floating island was comprised of trees—trees so massive they looked as if they had
been undisturbed for eons.

"Caaaarl, I'm home," Raz muttered under her breath, flexing her mechanical fingers
anxiously.

"Does the Mooresmith make you nervous?" I asked hesitantly.

"No, we're very close he and I. But such magic is not a pleasant experience. It's very,
very painful. I'm anxious because of the bad memories I've lived through in this place."

"That's...comforting," I whispered. My chest felt tight, heartbeat pounding against
my ribs as I struggled to get a breath in.

Panic or asthma?

Both. Either way, I need my inhaler.

Sensing my distress as I began to dig through my cloak pocket for my inhaler,
Fireheart appeared with it gently clamped between his teeth. I gave him a grateful

scratch beneath the chin as I took the medicine from him.

"You'll never be the same after this," Raz said softly. Her eyes were sad as she looked at me.

"I'm already not the same," I choked out. "There's no going back from what...*he*...did to us. The only choice I have is to keep moving forward." I inhaled the medicine, pausing as I waited for it to take effect.

Darcy, Darcy, Darcy...I will break this curse, I will say his cursed name. I will not be controlled by his curse.

"That's the spirit," Raz encouraged as she took hold of the rope. "Now, you're going to grab the rope like so, and go down, hand over hand. If you slip, or fall, or don't make it, or something else happens and you go plummeting, I'll be right there to save you. Okay?"

I nodded, unable to find the words as I took the rope from her.

"Just focus on what you're doing and don't look down. You can do this; I believe in you."

It was my first time accomplishing such a feat, and for a few moments I was dead certain she was wrong, and I was going to fail and fall to my death.

I can do this, I can do this.

Who are you kidding? I can't do this. Maybe I could have when I was fine. But things are different now. I'm half blind, and my balance is off. There's no way I can do this.

Why can't Theron just carry me? I'd rather live through the embarrassment of being a sack of potatoes than the humiliation of failing. Why is she making me do this? I can't!

Yes. I can. I can do this. I can.

I took as deep a breath as I could manage and carefully clambered over the edge of the ship, using the side like I was rappelling, and began to descend.

I was grateful for my gloves, but by the time I reached the bottom, my skin felt raw and bruised.

That is my least favorite way to get off a ship. Why can't we just use a rope ladder? That would be so much simpler.

Raz landed on the deck beside me, her wings tucking in neatly against her shoulder blades, the tips gently brushing the ground. "Very well done," she praised as she gently pried the rope from my clenched fists. "Proud of you," she said, grinning.

I sighed, staring at the forest ahead of us, dread filling my body.

Ember landed on the deck beside me with a thud, wobbling slightly and swearing under her breath. "I am *not* a pirate! Stop trying to make me act like one!"

Theron landed next, laughing as his wings tucked back into the pack on his back. "Nonsense, Sparks. You just need a little more practice is all. You'll still make a fine, swashbuckling pirate one of these days.

"I will not," Ember hissed angrily. "Why don't *I* get a pair of wings to fly with?" she demanded. "Why do I have to come down with the rope?"

Theron simply laughed at her indignant questions, which only increased her ire.

It took all my self-control not to join Theron and laugh off her crabbiness.

She clearly needed more coffee to be anywhere near civilized, and while we could all tell, pointing it out was the wrong way to go—a fact Theron learned the hard way when Ember swung her staff at his head.

Theron and Ember bickered the whole time we journeyed through the woods. The further we went, the stronger Raz's anxiety became evident, and the worse mine also grew. If the fearless Raz was nervous about something, I knew I had better be terrified.

What's going to happen? What have we gotten ourselves into?

At last, after half a day's journey in, we reached a series of trees that were larger than all the rest, but completely different.

"They're mechanical," I whispered, awestruck.

The trees were metal, full of gears and mechanisms that hummed and whirred. Various rope ladders led up into the mechanical canopy of the trees then branched off into an intricate network of pathways, high off the ground.

"CAAAAAAAARL!" Raz yelled, startling all of us. "CAAAAAAARL COME DOOOOWN HERE!"

"Raz!" Theron hissed. "Do you really think that yelling is the wisest choice? You just gave away our position!"

"What, what is Carl dearest going to do? Eat our hands?"

"He *might*!" Theron snapped angrily.

"Carl would never do something like that. That is his least favorite thing to do."

Theron took a deep breath, looking as if he was about to give us all a very long lecture about Carl.

"Here we go again," Raz muttered. But much to her delight, he was unable to begin his lecture. A large metal net snapped up from the ground, capturing us in a neat little boobie trap.

Well. I wasn't expecting that.

"CARL!" Raz screeched. "You put us down *THIS INSTANT!*"

"This!" Theron yelled angrily. "This is exactly what I was worried would happen. We haven't seen him in ages."

"Bologna!" Raz retorted hotly. "We saw him last month!"

Theron ignored her. "For all you know he isn't here anymore, and someone's taken up his workshop."

"Nonsense!" Raz snapped, whacking him on the top of the head from her cramped position.

Why, when we're clearly in a trap, are they spending their energy fighting, instead of getting us out of this?

I began to struggle, trying to get myself in a better position to get out. "If we all work together and stop *fighting*," I snapped, "we might be able to get free."

"Rubbish," Raz said airily. "Nobody can get out of Carl's traps."

As if proving her point, the net's fibers began to twist and squeeze. The more I moved, the tighter they became.

"See?" Raz said triumphantly. "I *told you* so!" She cleared her throat. "CARL! If you do not let us out of this trap this *instant,* I will destroy your plaything with my handy dandy laser fingers. Laser fingers that, I will remind you, you kindly bestowed up on me."

"Raz," a new voice called irritably. "If you destroy my net, I will take away your laser fingers."

It was a man's voice, with just a hint of an accent clinging to the edges of it. He sounded young.

Raz screeched in absolute indignance. "You wouldn't *dare!*" she yelled back, seething.

She seems to know the voice. This must be the illusive Carl.

The net was rising, up toward the massive treehouse nested in the canopy.

"I've rigged the ladder," the voice continued. "Too many raiders after my work. The only way to get help is to get caught."

Ember looked like she was about to be sick from the tumultuous, spinning journey, and the more the net swayed in the air, the more I began to wonder if I agreed.

"CARL!" Raz shrieked. "You put us down *this INSTANT!*"

"As my lady wishes," the voice replied cordially.

Ember and I screamed as the net dropped us onto the porch of the treehouse.

A cacophony of laughter echoed around us. Voices were everywhere, with no one in sight.

"You turn off those blasted automatons," Raz demanded as she struggled against the net. "And let us out of here!"

"Patience, patience," Carl scolded, laughing. "All right you hooligans, you've seen the show. Now go back to work."

A flickering scurry of movement in the shadows of the metal foliage was there and then gone in an instant. The laughter began to fade, and soon it was nothing more than an echo, lost on the wind.

The net released and lifted off us, and there stood a young man somewhere in his early thirties. Knowing the Realm, he was likely ages older than that. He was tall and thin, wiry in build, with muscular forearms and calloused hands. His cheekbones jutted out from his face, and dark brown hair hung in wild waves to his shoulders. A dark brown mustache, soul patch, and goatee finished out the pointy angles of his face. Vibrant royal blue eyes glowed in the dim light; they were mechanical. Metal copper plates lay in a haphazard pattern across the left side of his face and down his neck. They disappeared beneath the collar of his button-up shirt. Lights and wires glowed dimly under his skin in places. He looked part Fey, part robot.

"Well Raz, what have you broken today?" Carl asked, leaning heavily on an ornate staff. "Is it the wings, or your *oh so dangerous* digits?"

"Neither," Raz replied loftily. "I haven't broken anything in *months.*"

"Thirty-four solstice suns," Carl interrupted.

"Over a month," Raz corrected with a snort of indignation.

Carl rolled his eyes. "Fine then, why have you come to disturb my sanctuary? I know you didn't make that trek just because you missed me. Your oh so scary husband would protest."

Raz laughed, then sobered. "No, my friend needs help. She was cursed with Darke magic. She lost her eye. You're the only one who can help her now."

Carl's gaze flicked rapidly over our group before quickly settling on me. He stared at me for a moment, then his attention began to hop from me to Ember then back to me.

"Grimms," he stated.

"Nevermind who they are, they need your help."

"You know I do not deal with those who belong to the Courts," he replied icily. "I can't help you. Find someone loyal to the cause."

"They're unmarked," Raz pressed.

"No."

"Please," I rasped, stepping into the argument. "I need your help."

"Are you a fool then? Begging for help, asking a favor from a Fey?"

I wanted to shrivel, wilt under that fiery gaze that seemed to hate me—despite the fact he didn't even know me.

The Courts must have hurt him so badly.

"I give no allegiance to the Courts," I replied, my voice growing stronger with every word. "I am unmarked, unnamed. Yes, we are pursued, but we have not found our path yet. I do not know what side of the abyss we stand on. But I cannot stand as weak as I am. Without your help, the tide is overwhelmed. Please, help me so I have a chance. Give me a chance to make my choice."

"You do not want the fate they have planned for you."

"Nevertheless, it is mine to face or forfeit."

Carl sighed. Centuries of rage was buried in the sound. He still wasn't convinced.

"Bluebeard hurt her, to get to me," Ember choked out.

I reached back, grasping her hand. This was the first time she had been able to speak of it.

"You're under a curse," the Mooresmith replied. It was a statement rather than a question.

Ember nodded. "Yes," she whispered. Blood was trickling down her chin from the corner of her mouth.

The curse is unraveling. This is the first time she's been able to speak of it at all.

"Twins of fate," the Mooresmith spat. "Why do I bother with this Realm that has destroyed everything? They will one day use you to destroy the Moores."

"I will decide my own way," Ember replied defiantly. "I don't want to destroy the Moores, I want to help it."

"That's what you don't understand, child," Carl replied sadly. "None of us decide our own way. We are simply pawns in fate's hands. Though, perhaps she has been death in disguise all along."

"I was marked by the Moores," Ember countered.

At this, Carl stilled. "You what?" he asked quietly, his voice deadly calm.

"I was marked by the Moores," Ember repeated.

"Show me."

Ember quickly shed her cloak, then her armor, vest, and shirt, until she stood in an undershirt. "Help me, Eva," she said.

I stepped forward as she turned, helping to pull the material of the undershirt down until the phoenix across her shoulder blade and back was revealed.

Carl sucked in a sharp breath. "You have indeed been marked."

Ember turned back around. "I need you to help my sister," she stated.

"Cursed though the outcome may be?" Carl asked evenly.

"We won't know unless we try. You're the only one who can help her."

"That I am," Carl sighed. His attention turned back to me. "Come, child, there is much to do. I will take the damaged eye as payment. You cannot keep it. The toxin bleeds into your body even now. Yaga could not stop it." His gaze was keen, pained even as he continued to stare at me. "Once you start this, there is no going back. It is the worst pain you will ever endure. Are you sure you want to do this?"

I squared my shoulders and took a deep breath. "Yes," I whispered, my voice trembling despite my effort to be brave. "You are my only hope."

"What a curse lies heavy upon my shoulders," he replied wryly. "If I am your only help, you are doomed indeed."

"You were my only hope and now look at me," Raz piped up, trying to be helpful.

"My point exactly," Carl replied with a wry smile.

Raz's spluttering protests followed before he turned and began to limp back into his house, one footstep heavier than the other as he led the way into the darkness.

38

The Divide Between Realms

EMBER

""Forests have secrets" he said gently. "It's practically what they're for.
To hide things. To separate one world from another.""
-Catherynne M. Valente, Deathless

I couldn't stop pacing as Evadne's screams echoed through the intricate workshop. Carl had demanded that we not disturb him—in fact, he'd made us promise not to. At the time, it seemed extreme, but now that I was forced to listen to her agony, I knew why. My promise physically prevented me from wrenching that door open and rescuing my sister from his hands.

Her agony was mine, and I could hardly contain myself as I felt every ounce of his work on her.

Raz also paced, her face ashen as she clenched and unclenched her hands. "It's almost over, it's almost over," she whispered again and again as tears streamed down her cheeks.

At last, we both slid to the floor, exhausted.

Meanwhile, Theron was busy arm wrestling with a tiny little robot. Much to my petty pleasure, he was absolutely losing. He was swearing under his breath as he struggled and strained, cursing the Mooresmith for his genius.

"You okay?" Raz asked quietly, wiping her cheeks with the back of her hand.

"No," I whispered as tears poured from my eyes. "You?"

"Nope. Not one bit," Raz replied, her eyes glued on the door. "It brings back a lot of bad memories. That was me at one point. But I can't imagine what it's like having it be your eye. My hands were closed off from me, so while I could feel everything, there was a certain level of disconnect. But it's not the same when it's your face. Something you constantly sense and see out of."

I nodded, trembling inside. I felt tightly wound, as if any second I was going to explode.

"It was the best decision I'd ever made, but also the worst. Your sister had no choice. Without his help, she'd be dead before the next solstice. Dead or possessed. Bluebeard knew what he was doing. He wasn't just hurting her to get to you. He was making sure she was tainted with enough Darke magic that she would eventually be sucked into the Shadewyrld. After such a success, he would then take her to the Ruins."

"The Shadewyrld is by the Ruins?" I asked.

"Not exactly," Raz replied. She reached over and snatched a loose piece of paper and a thick pencil off one of the Mooresmith's many work benches.

She drew a circle in the middle of the paper. "This is the Central Kingdom," she said softly as she then drew two more circles—one on the far left, and one on the far right of the middle circle. "These are the Summer and Winter Realms. This is where the Courts go, when they are not in power." She then drew lines from the Summer Court to the center and the Winter Court to the Center. "These are the protected, magic bound paths they take from the Central Kingdom to their Realms." She then drew another circle at the top of the page. "This is the Ruins," she said quietly. "From the Central Kingdom there is a path that goes from the Eastern Gate to the Ruins. That is the path you all were taking. It is not defined like the paths to the Summer and Winter Courts. It has a mind of its own and can be somewhat unreliable as the Knight's power grows." She drew a semi-circle off the back of the Ruins' circle. "This is the Shadewyrld. Its magic is wild and Darke—they have a law and a land of their own, though they send diplomats to the Winter Court often. They try to stay in good standing with the Winter Realm, because Shadowthieves are a valuable asset in times of war." She began to connect the bubbles. "Around all of this is what contains the Realm itself. It is what we call the borders. The magic of the borders is old and unchallengeable. It is the magic that keeps the Knight contained and it was woven by the sisters three. Now, this side of the Central kingdom," she said, drawing another semi-circle, connecting the back side of the circle, and putting two slashes at the center, "is called the Wiyldes. It isn't Moores, but it isn't kingdoms either. It's a... more reliable form of Moores if you will. The Moores are dangerous and volatile, the Wiyldes are where you go if you don't want to be in the Realms, but you're Fey and want a, well, a more pleasant place to live. It is governed and protected by the Central Courts for the most part, but generally, it is left under the jurisdiction of the Legends—those who remain in good standing, that is. As well as the societies that created themselves within the Wiyldes." She scoffed under her breath. "There aren't many of either left, from what I hear. They're finally coming to their senses."

She pointed at the two slashes across from the central kingdom at the bottom of the page. "Now, this is the Main Gate. This is where you get into the Realm, from the Borderlands." She drew another semicircle at the bottom of the page around the outside of the Wiyldes. "This is the Borderlands. The Borderlands are where the portal takes you from the human realm. That way, if humans accidentally wander into the Realm, they aren't taken directly into one court or the other, they're just sorta dumped in the middle of the woods without realizing they fell in the first place, then they're snatched. Though, I haven't heard of any humans within the last few decades..."

"The portal is on our property," I replied. "We keep it fenced off. That way no one will get hurt. Though monsters and Fey folk get through it and roam our woods freely—they've caused us a fair bit of trouble over the years."

"That's not supposed to happen," Raz replied, confused. "The borders and the portal are supposed to keep the Fey in the Realm. That's one of the reasons the brother created the borders in the first place—to keep the Realm contained so humans would stop getting hurt."

"What do you mean?"

Raz pursed her lips. "I shouldn't speak of it, certainly not here. We are in between Realms in this place."

"What?"

"The Mooresmith's magic flows within multiple Realms. His particular type of magic can't be sustained on just Fey magic. When the borders were put into place, he suffered greatly. He had to relearn how to weave it and find a way around their magic. He takes some pins and needles from human genius, as well as shadows from

Shadewyrld, and beauty from the central courts. His magic can't survive on just one form; it must have all. So, he created a portal with the mirrors, and he pulls your sister's blood and her magic through multiple Realms as he spins her a mechanical eye. The Shadewyrld magic will also help pull the Darke magic from her bones."

"When will it be over?" I whispered, desperate to hear my sister stop screaming.

"I don't know," Raz said, arms wrapped tightly around herself. "It could be days; it could be ages... There's no way for anyone to know how long it will take."

The Mooresmith worked for seven days straight—not once taking a break—until at last, my sister's screams fell silent and he emerged from the room, withdrawn and haggard.

"It is done," he rasped, gasping for air.

Raz caught him as he stumbled, his legs gave out beneath him, and he fell.

"Why don't you heal yourself," she muttered under her breath as she helped him settle into a chair.

"I was my first test subject," he replied, gasping. "I will carry my failures with me, so as to never falter again."

"Sounds like some self-sacrificing pixie dust to me," Raz replied irritably. "Come on, I've got some food cooking."

He shook his head. "I need only a moment to rest, then I must check the mirrors. Her magic is unique. I wouldn't be surprised if it pinged on someone's radar as I rewove her eye. The Grimms have a particular crimson thread of fate tied to their elements. Hers is indeed magnificent. It glowed such a crimson and sapphire blue...you should have seen it; it was radiant with galaxies and stars." His voice was full of wonder as he stared up at Raz. "Such beauty despite the tragedy woven into the destiny."

Raz sighed and nodded. "There's no escaping fate," she replied quietly.

He turned to me. "She's asking for you," he sighed. "Be gentle with her, she is weak."

I nodded and then hesitantly made my way toward the door as Raz and Carl continued their quiet conversation. I couldn't explain why I was scared, but something inside trembled as I pushed open the door.

Evadne lay motionless on a small bed in the center of the room. Tables and mirrors were scattered all around in a haphazard disarray. Her eyes were closed, but as I came closer, they flew open.

Her damaged eye was a network of copper disks, wires, and gears within a pale, milky white orb. Dispersed around the copper were flares of bright blue, pitch black, and florescent opal green. It was beautiful and heartbreaking all at once. Her eyelid and socket had been completely replaced with a gold plate. The rest of the scar from Darcy's dagger still ran up and down her face, but now, instead of a jagged black weeping wound, it was filled with gold.

He made her into a living kintsugi.

"Hey," I murmured as I went to the bedside and gingerly sat down.

Hey. She mouthed back.

Her voice was gone, exhausted from all the screaming.

I pulled her hand into mine. "Two squeezes for no, one for yes," I said softly.

She blinked, once, twice, and the golden eyelid moved fluidly with the movement, smooth as real skin.

What kind of marvelous magic is this?

"Are you still in any pain?" I asked.

She squeezed my hand twice. *No.*

"That's good," I sniffed, trying not to cry. "Does it work?"

Again, she gave my hand a tight, hopeful squeeze. *Yes.*

"Do you want anything to eat?"

Two squeezes. *No.*

She looked at the door, then back to me. "You want to get out of this room?"

A quick squeeze, conveying her urgency. *Yes.*

"Okay. Hang on, let me go get Raz."

In a matter of minutes, Raz and I had Evadne out of the room and into another room graciously offered by Carl. Evadne's eyes drifted closed in a matter of moments, and soon she was out cold, clutching my hand tightly to her chest—as if she was afraid she was going to lose me if she let go.

39

Lost Legends And Stories Rewritten

EVADNE

"Bury your past, let flowers grow where you lay."
-Unknown

My dreams were a chaotic landscape of pain and comfort. A wolf chased me through the darkness, but I always stopped running, turning to face the beast as I held out my hand. My mind screamed at my body to run, but every time I thought I was going to die, the wolf changed, morphing into a man who wrapped me in his arms and held me tightly to his chest—as if he was afraid of losing me.

When I awoke, I held Ember's hand with the same desperation. The ache in my chest only intensified as, for a moment, I thought I was perhaps holding Marcus' hand.

He's not here. He may never be here again.

What if we never find each other again? What if I never see him again?

And what if he does? Will he still want to stay by my side when he sees what Darcy's done to me? Will he still think I'm beautiful?

Will any of that matter when our future holds no hope? When I can't choose the one I love?

Ember was asleep on the floor beside my bed. Her legs were curled underneath her, and she was draped across the bed to continue to allow me to hold her hand.

Oh Em, you're going to wake up so sore and grumpy. You should have just let go and gone to bed yourself.

I gently pulled my hand from Ember's, and she stirred, mumbling about coffee and gremlins while making dark threats at any creature who dared touch her precious coffee.

Oh Em, what am I going to do with you?

I climbed out of the bed gingerly so as not to disturb her, and quickly dressed, trying to avoid the sight of myself in the mirror. But once my eyes caught on my reflection, I couldn't look away. It was like nothing I'd ever seen before. The mechanical eye was stunning and terrifying all at once. It was not my eye, and yet it was. The clarity with which I could suddenly see the world seemed impossible. I had even better eyesight than before my injury. I narrowed my eyes, and the mechanical eye suddenly zoomed in, giving me a detailed inspection of my eye in the mirror.

How did I do that?

I widened my eye, and my focus returned to normal.

That's amazing.

My balance still seemed off, but it was an off-kilter that seemed far more manageable than before.

Ember was awake now, groaning as she clambered to her feet. "How are you feeling?" she asked carefully, coming to stand behind me in the mirror.

Well, that is not the grumpy Em I expected to be greeted by. Did Carl give her a brain transplant while he was working on me?!

"I..." my voice was raspy and faint. "I don't know," I whispered. "I don't know what to make of it."

"Give it time," Ember replied gently. "You'll get used to it. Let's go see if he can make coffee as well as he can make body parts."

I laughed quietly, amused by such a strange statement as we made our way out of the small bedroom. Raz and Carl were talking in low voices by the fire, holding steaming mugs of something.

Whatever it is, it smells amazing.

"Well," Carl called, exhausted. "What do you think?"

"Thank you," I said. "I don't know what to say."

Carl inclined his head. "You're welcome. At least my curse can help someone."

"It's not a curse," Raz scolded gently.

"It is to me," Carl replied, staring pensively into his mug. "If you understood how my magic flows, you'd know it for the curse it is. The brothers condemned me to live this way with their borders and boundaries. The Realm was never meant to be reduced to this." He turned his attention back to us. "There's stew in the pot over the fire, coffee in the first kettle, cocoa in the second. Tea in the third. I wasn't sure what you liked, so I made some of everything. Raz tends to rotate between all three, so I try to keep it on hand for whenever she drops from my net."

Raz scoffed, annoyed. "That cursed net," she muttered under her breath.

"Come have a seat when you're ready. Evadne, you'll want to keep your staff close—your body is still adjusting to the new sense of balance. It will take a while, so just be patient."

I nodded, opting for a mug of cocoa over tea. Something about it reminded me of home, and right now I needed something familiar and comforting—even if it filled me with longing and heartbreak.

We will likely never go home again.

After putting my mug on a table by one of the various recliners scattered about the room, I went back to the fireplace for a bowl of stew. My stomach growled hungrily as I filled my bowl. Thick chunks of stew meat and potatoes, with carrots, rice, and sausage, created a heavenly aroma, and beneath the savory aroma, I could make out the multiple layers of spices woven throughout. It was exactly the way Oma used to make her stew.

The bowl was hot in my hands, but I welcomed the warmth. My fingers were stiff and aching, having been clenched for so many grueling hours while Carl worked. He was right. It was the most excruciating thing I'd ever been through, but having come through it with an eye that now worked, the horror inflicted upon me by Darcy had been given a sense of purpose. Though I couldn't undo what'd been done, making something out of the wreckage made it seem as if maybe, just maybe, it wasn't all for nothing. At least in some way, Darcy no longer had power over my future. I felt as if I had taken a piece of myself back and thwarted his efforts to destroy me.

"When do you leave again?" Carl asked Raz.

"We'll likely head back in the morning. We've been gone almost two weeks now."

"What?" I spluttered, choking on my cocoa.

"You were both asleep for five days," Raz replied patiently. "Which seems a little short to me. I slept for a week after mine, and my procedure only took a day and a half."

I blew on a potato chunk, trying to resist the urge to scarf it. My stomach was giving bad advice to my brain, while my tastebuds screeched in terror. They remembered all too well what happened the last time I didn't wait long enough for a potato to cool down.

Carl sighed. "I suspected as much. I do value my privacy, but it gets lonesome out here."

Raz nodded empathetically. "I won't bother trying to convince you to come have some adventures with us."

Carl shook his head, sighing again. "My machines would suffer without my care. They are smart, but they tend to make lots of stupid decisions. I have to rescue them on a daily basis."

Raz laughed. "Creatures after my own heart."

"I think you were a bad influence on them last time you were here," Carl replied ruefully. "They were giving me all sorts of backtalk and rude gestures after you left."

"I have a question," Ember interrupted softly. She was staring down at her stew, eyebrows scrunched together in concentration.

"What is it, child?" the Mooresmith replied.

"Well, Raz said your magic couldn't be sustained through the Fey's magic alone. Why is that?"

Carl sighed, suddenly seeming ancient in the firelight. "That is a very long story."

"I've got all the time in the world," Ember replied impishly. "These potatoes are scalding. If I don't have something to distract me, I'll end up throwing caution to the wind and searing off all my tastebuds because I'm so *incredibly* hungry."

Carl laughed. "You are right about that. I hope the stew is to your liking."

"It's impeccable," she replied. "I already burned off a few, but it was totally worth it."

"Well then, I guess I shall indulge your curiosity for the sake of your remaining taste buds," he replied ruefully. "My story begins long before the Realm was formed. Before the Darke Knight rose. Long ago, there was a young Fey, whose gift was transformation. Anything he sought to change, he could. Whether it was rope to chain, grass to grain, or, perhaps, straw to gold. All he needed then was a spinning wheel."

Rumpelstiltskin.

"This Fey loved a woman, but his love was hopeless. In those days Fey and mortal did not mix. We were evil or benevolent to them—never anything but something to use or fear. Her father was a greedy man, and he cared not who he destroyed in his quest to gain more. One day, upon seeing the royal carriage ride by, he boasted a great and terrible lie. He told the king his daughter could spin straw into gold. The king, also a greedy man, wanted a demonstration and put the daughter's life on the line. If she could not spin straw into gold, he would kill her and exile the man. Now, to the man, exile was no great cost. He could con others just as easily in another place as there, and perhaps the prospects would be better. The fool cared not for his daughter. So, he readily agreed to the terms and let the king carry his daughter away."

Carl's face darkened. "I couldn't let her die," he said softly, changing tense as he owned up to the story being his. "I loved her too much to let that filthy mortal destroy her. So, when night came, I went to her. I thought of myself as a knight in shining armor; she saw me as a way out. We bargained for my assistance, and she agreed to give me her ring in exchange for my help. I knew how much that ring meant to her—it was one her mother gave her before she died and I, in my *great* chivalry, planned to give it back to her when the ordeal was all over with to prove I hadn't done it for my own gain. So, with the terms of the night set in place, I went about my work.

"She watched me, awestruck, as I wove my magic. My magic cannot be defined. By its very nature, it defies the Realms. Fey magic morphed with the Mortal Realm, it was something of legends..."

My skin prickled at the words as Carl carried on with his heartbreaking story.

"I thought I was winning her over," he admitted quietly. "When in reality, I was only feeding the seed of greed I knew not was inside. It was an impossibility to me that she could ever be like her father. When morning came and the king found her with nothing but gold, he was pleased, but his wretched heart wanted more. So, he took her to an even larger room and locked her inside, again threatening her life if she did not weave this magic for him once more.

"Once again, I came, and so we bargained. Having nothing to give me, I impishly suggested a kiss. Desperate for her affection, I would have spun *ten* rooms of straw just for a kiss. She readily agreed and after my work was done, she kissed me. She kissed me like she loved me," he added in a whisper. "I left, high as the moon in the cursed sky and certain the prejudiced barriers between Fey and human could be demolished. I was sure, with the sincerity of the kiss she bestowed upon me, that she really, truly loved me."

Carl stopped and rose from his chair. "I need more coffee," he said gruffly as he limped over to where the kettles sat. His shoulders were hunched as he stood in front of the kettles, arms wrapped tightly around himself. He seemed to be holding himself together. After a long few moments had passed, he refilled his mug and came back to his chair.

"Now, where was I?" he asked, his voice forcefully uncaring. "Ah yes, the third day." He cleared his throat and then began again. "When the king came the next morning and found this massive room filled with gold, he was ecstatic. But his greedy heart still demanded more. So, he put the girl to the final test. Unbeknownst to me, he promised her his hand in marriage. She would be queen if she succeeded, and he locked her in his throne room—which had been filled from floor to ceiling with straw. Left to herself, she began to weep in earnest. This feat seemed too great, even for her bewitched Fey helper. But it was not. When night fell, I again came. She showed me such great affection, I had no suspicion about where her desires *truly* lay. So, we again set to bargaining. Encouraged by her affection and thinking myself incredibly clever, I bargained with her for her firstborn child. I thought it was a great irony. For, I had plans to propose to her when the night was through, and she was at last free of the greedy king. I planned to use the very ring she had given to me in the first place, after which, we would be wed. The child I bargained for would be mine regardless, making the bargain doubly sweet and costing her nothing, for we would be together. We would be...happy," he whispered.

"Her hesitation to agree should have tipped me off, but I was too drunk on hope for the future to realize. When the sun rose and all that remained were the mountains of gold, I proposed." Carl's voice shook with sorrow and rage. "She laughed in my face. She said she would *never* wed a Fey, let alone one like me..." he paused. "I had already been a victim of a tragedy, and my body was disfigured. I had rewoven my skin with this metal and mechanics, but it was my first project, and still crude work." He pointed to his face. "It is not work I am proud of, but it got me to where I am today, so for that I recognize its worth." He sighed. "But back to my sad sob tale."

"Sob story," Raz muttered.

Carl rolled his eyes. "*Fine*, sad sob *story*. It wasn't enough for her to reject me. No, she had to kick me while I was down. She bragged of her cleverness, how she used me...how gullible I was and how she was going to be a queen. I left, enraged and determined to never see her again. But our bargain. That *cursed bargain*," he hissed. "It pulled me back to that place not ten years later. It dragged me back to that sweet child that now belonged to me. I didn't want her. I didn't want that reminder of what I'd lost, and at that point, the Erlking was rising. To bring a mortal child to the Realm, where she would be in constant danger, would be foolish. So, I offered her an easy bargain. Say my name, and I would let her keep my child. I had told her my name the first night we officially met, and it seemed a simple bargain to me. I did not realize she would forget it so easily. She guessed a million names, but never once the name I had told her.

"As the days ticked by, I began to despair ever being free of her, or the small child's heartbeat I was now bound to, burning, burning, burning for me to take it away from the woman I once loved. So, I concocted a plan. I made sure when I left her castle, upon hearing the latest list of ridiculous names she had for me, that her servant tailed me. I persuaded him with my magic, planting the idea in his puny mortal brain that he should follow me, and follow me he did. I led him out into the woods, and then, with as much obviousness as I could muster, I began to dance around my little campfire and sing a song that revealed to the world my true, cursed name."

"Rumpelstiltskin," I whispered.

He winced, and then nodded. "Yes, child, but I prefer that you do not use it here. Names have power and I do not want the curse tied to my Fey name to find me here. I adapted the name Carl on a whim, and it suits me in some strange way."

"Sorry," I replied, horrified at putting him in danger.

"It is quite all right; you couldn't have known. It is not a story I tell many. The true lore of the Legends is steeped in magic. Even in speaking it, I can feel my powers growing."

"Why wouldn't you speak it more then?" Ember asked around a mouthful of stew. I had been so entranced by his tale I had forgotten to eat. Ember, on the other hand, was on her third bowl of stew, eating it the way one would eat popcorn for a scary movie.

"Because it is a curse I do not wish to revisit."

I wanted to ask him to elaborate, but I was afraid to. There was probably a reason he was speaking in riddles.

Ember, however, held no such inclination. "What curse?" she asked.

Carl sighed. "My, aren't you curious," he scolded gently.

"Sorry," Ember muttered, shoving more stew in her mouth to silence herself.

Carl smiled, as if to reassure her it was fine, but returned to his story instead of answering her question.

"The next morning, she sent for me, and on the third guess she triumphantly uttered my real name, releasing us from the tainted bargain. I didn't want to tip her off about my ruse, so, to give myself an out, I began to scream and rage, stomping my feet until the floorboards morphed and gave way, sending me down into the depths of the castle. After that, it was an easy matter of changing stones to a door, and back to stones where I then made my escape. I intended to never see her again."

"What about the child?" I asked hesitantly, sensing there was more to the story.

"She grew up the spitting image of her mother. Her mother finished growing up, too, and chose to raise her daughter better than she herself had been at such an age. When the greedy old king died, Thara ruled—which was unprecedented. Years passed and peace reigned. The country *thrived* under her reign, but still the people rioted. They were incited by priests who claimed it was by witchcraft that the queen ruled so wisely. My Thara called on me through the mirrors. How she had learned such magic I never could find out, but she found me, even after all those years. Seeing her tears, hearing her call my name, my *true* name, I could not abandon her cry for help. She begged me on her hands and knees, weeping bitterly, as the mob got closer and closer to the castle walls and the men loyal to her tried to fight them off. I could not abandon her...I could not abandon the child either. So, I came... Even free of the bargain, my heart was still tied to the child in a way nobody would ever know. She was not my blood, but my heart did not recognize that truth...to my very heart and soul, there was no escaping what had happened when she was born. The magic had written her into my bones...the child was indeed *mine*.

"What I also didn't know, was since the magic marked the child as mine, it gave her a spark of her own Fey magic. That spark lay buried and dormant, waiting for the call to rise.

"My magic was strong, but I couldn't weave the spell and hold off the mob. I also couldn't transport people through a mirror—I didn't know how yet. So, Thara decided to reason with them. I told her it was a foolish idea. I told her to hide with us, that her men would hold them off. I *begged* her to stay. But she was so sure she could bring the people back to her side...these were people she had helped and cared for, for decades." He paused. "She foolishly still believed in the goodness of humanity, and while I wove the spell around the child, my Thara died to protect her." He paused and took a deep breath, steadying himself. "I gave the child, who by then was a young woman, what I believed to be a fighting chance. In the far tower of the castle, I pricked her finger on the spindle of an enchanted spinning wheel, and when she fell into a deep sleep, I rewove her lore. I could not erase her memory, but I could protect her from those monsters and their senseless thirst for innocent blood. After they murdered Thara, the humans left. My spell had already made them forget the queen ever had a daughter.

While she slept, the child wept. But I couldn't afford to wake her, even though the danger was past. The spell to reweave her lore required her to sleep for a hundred years. So, as a precaution, I wove a protective spell around the castle that hid her in the tower. The spell turned every inch of dirt into vines and thorns that would come alive and impale anyone who tried to reach her before those hundred years were up. Having done everything I could think of, I left her there, convinced no one could find or harm her. I thought that, when the hundred years had passed, she would wake up and find the world a better, kinder place. I thought...I would be by her side when she awoke."

Raz reached out and gently held Carl's hand. His head was bowed and tears now flowed freely down his cheeks. He choked on his words, regret filling every syllable. "I was *wrong*," he whispered. "I was so, *incredibly* wrong. The Mortal Realm still harmed her. A hundred years passed, but what I didn't know about my desperate spell was that it was tied to *my* magic. She needed *me* to return to wake properly after the hundred years."

He stared down at his calloused, scarred hands. "It is here I must deviate from my horrific story. There is more that must be explained for the rest to make sense. You know of the sisters three, who bound the Knight, do you not?"

Ember and I nodded.

"The sisters three bound the Knight, but by then there was too much violence, too much bloodshed. They needed help, damage control if you will. So, the mighty three sought out a poor weaver to rewrite history itself."

My gasp was audible as I stared at him.

"Yes, child, *I* am the reason the *unbreakable* prison crumbles. I told them it would happen; I told them it would crumble, but they refused to listen. In their pride, they carried on and left the Grimms to carry the weight. You cannot build a prison on magic that is rewritten and steeped in lies. For, as history forgets and adapts to the new truth, the entire system breaks, for it cannot sustain lies. So, it crumbles and falls. Because it inherently *knows* it is built on falsehoods. I *told* them," he hissed angrily. "But they. wouldn't. *listen*." His voice was low with rage now as he remembered. "They forced me to help them, but by helping them, the spell in turn smothered my magic. But it wasn't just my magic, it was all magic. The borders they created to contain the Realm, and in turn the Knight, *crippled* all of the Fey folk, Seelie and Unseelie. The Fey were never meant to be confined to such basic categories. Summer, Winter... Seelie and Unseelie, they are too broad for any parameters. The Fey are wild and unpredictable, just like their magic. It is what makes them Fey. If you reduce and confine them, it will destroy the core of who they are. But they wouldn't *listen*. The borders they wove together almost destroyed my magic. I was not meant to be contained to one Realm or another, for I am a part of every Realm. My magic moves and flows throughout the world as a whole."

"What do you mean when you say you rewrote history?" I asked. I was almost scared to voice such a question. "What did you rewrite?"

"Everything," Carl replied softly. "Everything, child. The brothers were not from the eighteenth century. They were from *my* century. The thirteenth century."

His words hung in the air around us, until at last he found his words and, with a great sigh, resumed the harrowing tale. "The brothers Grimm stumbled upon the magic of the Fey and the two took different paths. One became greedy with what he found. He saw not only an opportunity to profit from the tales and stories, but to obtain power for himself. The Knight, sensing a betrayal among his court, and fearing the Seer's words, began to corrupt this brother. In turn, Wilhelm, craving the lure of power, fell prey to the Knight's poisonous promises.

"Meanwhile, Jacob, sensing a shift in his brother and already seeking a way to put an end to the Knight, chose a different path. He wanted to end the violence being wrought upon the world by the Knight. Millions of innocents were being slaughtered. So, he came deeper into the Realm, seeking the help of three of the most powerful witches in history. The sisters three. Fool that he was, he begged for their help and help him they did. But he did not ask the cost. He killed his brother, and when Yaga ate his heart and bound his bloodline for all time, it was too late to turn back. The Darke magic the sisters wove to bind the knight have several linchpins." Carl waved his hand toward where we sat. "The Grimm bloodline, bound to fight at the Last Gate and keep him contained. The sisters three—the magic is tied to their lifeforce. If they die, it will begin to crumble. Lastly, *the* twins of power."

His eyes were sad as he looked at us. "The first two linchpins are crumbling. The Grimms cannot last much longer at the Last Gate. The sisters three are reduced to two. Artemis' arrow carried a desperate sort of magic. A prayer of love and hate aided by the poisonous darkness in his mind. He did the impossible and killed a Wendigo." Carl was staring at us now, his eyes intent. "So, it all hinges on you—what you do, or don't do. Whether you fall prey to the lure of darkness and the Knight's Darke magic, or you resist and stand with what remains of the untainted Realm...you are the linchpins, my dears."

I don't want this kind of responsibility.

"Why though?" Ember asked, confused. "Why does it rest on us? Surely we're not that important. We're just two people. Anyone could do anything we do."

"Maybe not, but maybe so. Most of all, your blood is what's important. Your heart is what matters. The magic knows you are capable of great things. Fate has marked you as her own and make no mistake, she will ensure you meet your destiny—whether you run from it or not, you will meet it."

Ember began muttering under her breath about the stupidity of bossy fate and I patted her on the hand. It was just like her to show such grumpiness toward an unstoppable, unseeable force of power.

"There is more to their tale, but I do not have the energy to pick it apart for you. I should finish the tale of the lost princess. With my magic crippled by the border, I did not realize that I needed to return for her to wake. The spell of protection crumbled after a hundred years, but still she slept. Her screams of agony as she at last woke were the last things I heard before the borders finally closed themselves around me." Carl hung his head. "I sought only to protect her, and in the end, I was the reason she was harmed. I could not sense the flaw in my spell. When she realized what had happened, when she saw the bodies of her stillborn children, her screams woke her spark of magic. The vines came to life once more, and after killing the perverted thief, they bound themselves to her—mutating themselves in the tangled magic. Determined to protect her and never again let anything harm my precious child, they made her into a Legend, into something entirely new. A protector of the woods and those within. So that no one would ever be harmed under her watch.

"So, though the story has been recreated twice over, it was enough to transform her into a Legend. Her magic was unraveled and recreated twice, and my regret is that I didn't protect her better. I wish I had seen the holes in my logic when I put her in that tower..." He sighed, wringing his hands. "But time was so short. The mob was there at the castle, with torches and ropes, ready to kill the queen and her daughter. I had such little time to come up with a plan to save them...save her," he corrected, his voice choked. "I could not save my Thara."

"You still loved her," Ember whispered.

"I still loved her," Carl confirmed. "I still love her now. She is forever the scar on my heart, the thing even I cannot heal or mend."

"The princess," I said hesitantly. Is that—" My unfinished question hung in the air around us. It seemed an impossibility their stories would be so closely affected.

"You know her by Rosamond," Carl replied. "She changed her name when the magic recreated her, trying to leave the tainted memories behind. But once, in the time I knew her, her name was Aurora.

40

Shenanigans And Malarkey In The Face Of Great Danger

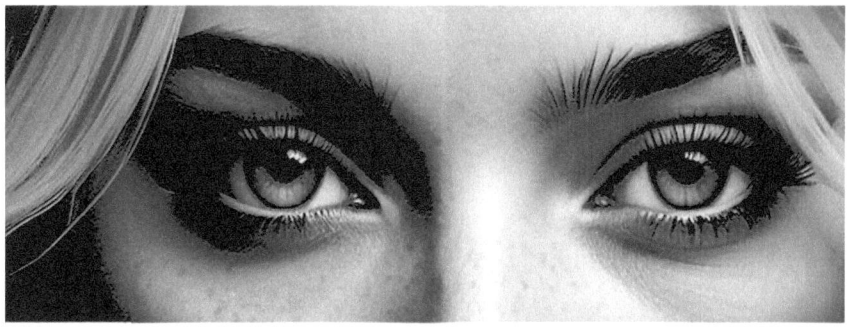

FAYE

""We look brave," said Frog. "Yes, but are we?" asked toad."
-Arnold Lobel

So far, a month had passed in bright and brilliant chaos, and with every day that sped by, Meghan got better and better at self-defense and fighting. With this newfound level of capability, I stopped taking it easy on her and began to let myself actually train. A few, sparse nights, Ronan joined us, and together he and I put on a demonstration for how a real fight went. Demonstrations that, much to my growing pride, *I* usually won.

I was growing addicted to Meghan's gleeful cheers when Ronan had to tap out during our spars.

Meghan was an easy student. Despite being exhausted from working all day in the kitchen, she still applied herself diligently, though she always fought me when it came to pushups and jump squats.

I took a tainted satisfaction in making her do just those. If Artemis made me suffer through them, she could suffer too, and thus my life had come full circle in petty satisfaction.

Meghan reminded me so much of Ember and Evadne it hurt. Every time she burst out laughing, unable to stop, an unbearable wave of homesickness hit me. But, despite the homesickness, her company consoled the ache in my heart that wept to see my sisters.

Meghan swore worse than Ronan (much to his annoyance). He always frowned whenever she began to rant, and I found the deep divot of disapproval that formed between his eyebrows incredibly adorable and hilarious. I began to hope she'd swear more in his presence, just so she'd cause the frown and little divot to make an appearance.

Much like Evadne, she hopped between languages in her colorful outpourings, but unlike Evadne, she had no fluency of language, only awareness of the worst words. It often took all of my self-control not to bust out laughing when, after being knocked on her butt, she let out a conglomeration of words that made absolutely no sense, yet were completely terrible in their meaning.

Her personality matched her style. She had dark black hair that matched Ronan's, but she had dyed the tips teal. Her nails were painted a pristine black with metallic galaxies that popped out when she turned them this way and that. I was very envious of her fabulous nails, but there was no way for me to get mine painted. I was supposed to be in solitary confinement with no access to amazing nail polish. Which my brain cells decided was absolutely unfair. They wanted cool nails.

Meghan matched the dark and bright with flares of sarcasm and absolutely deadpan, depressing comments. But she was a quick study, and I had no doubt that she was going to be just fine when we got her out of here.

Soon, desperate to win, Meghan began to rely on the not-so-subtle tactic of distraction, otherwise known as sabotage—which was absolutely *cheating*. (A scheme I knew Artemis would approve of quite heartily.)

"Ronan says you're cute when you're pissed," Meghan said out of the blue, as I aimed a punch at her exposed ribcage.

My concentration faltered and Meghan blocked the distracted blow with an incredibly evident smirk.

"He said that?" I gasped in shock. "Why would he say a thing like that??"

Meghan slammed her fist into my gut, and her foot was a blur as she swept my feet out from under me. "Beats me," she replied smugly as my back slammed into the floor.

OW!

That no good, dirty rotten, stupid little PUNK!

I did a quick kip up and landed in a fighting stance, ready to beat the ever-living crap out of her.

"Oo, scary," Meghan taunted.

"Child, you are about to regret that," I threatened darkly.

"Oo, double scary, the old woman makes threats," Meghan replied, pressing her hands to her face in mock fear.

She should be on a 'Scream' poster.

"He also said you were a pain in the butt," she continued as I forced her to go on the defensive.

"Sounds about right," I laughed, grinning as I delivered a quick series of punches. With every strike, I forced her to go back a step.

"*AND,*" she crowed, continuing her faltering quest of sabotage. "He said that you were, and I quote, 'terrifyingly beautiful' when you were being all scary powerful with your great and impossible magic."

My fists fell, failing to protect my ribcage.

He said I was terrifyingly beautiful? He thinks I'm beautiful??

Who cares about beautiful?! He thinks I'm TERRIFYING!

My life has been made complete. I am terrifying.

"He then proceeded to say that the lightning also crackles in your eyes, and you look like a *goddess.*"

My mouth fell open, and I didn't have time to block her front kick. Her foot slammed into my gut and before I knew it, I was propelled backward into a large pile of books stacked against the wall.

I, being the adult in the room, resorted to the petty tactics of a four-year-old, and threw a book at her head.

Three points to Faye for ingenuity and cleverness.

She just Sparta kicked you into a stack of books because you got distracted by her useless prattle about what YOUR KIDNAPPER thinks about you.

He thinks I look like a goddess.

He kidnapped you. You've sworn to loathe him for all eternity.

This eternity perhaps, but maybe in the next I'll think about kissing him... After all, he thinks I look like a goddess.

Much to my disappointment, she ducked, and the book went sailing over her head. But the damage was done. Hit her or not, she was utterly furious. "Do NOT throw—"

I interrupted her self-righteous rant and clocked her square in the face with her heavy paperback volume of *Harry Potter and the Deathly Hallows*, which was quickly followed by the less hefty classic, *The Hollow Kingdom*.

She lunged and *In the Coils of the Snake* missed her by a foot.

I cackled and dodged, brandishing my hastily stolen handful of books as I danced out of her reach.

You wanna play dirty, I'll play dirty.

"Did he tell you I'm dangerous? That I nearly killed him? He's foolish to let his one-track man brain tell him I look like a goddess. You shouldn't listen to your brother. I am not his friend."

Liar.

Also, the three brain cells would like it to be noted that you didn't 'almost' kill him, you DID kill him. That's what got us into this mess in the first place. If you had watched your power and simply struck him without killing him, he would have been unconscious and incapable of following us into the Borderlands.

The three brain cells can take a number. My schedule is booked and they'll have to wait their turn to have their observation properly put into the books of 'notes.' Besides, I think it's an absurd note. I might not even consider it.

That's against the rules. You have to consider it.

Fine. I'll consider it, then I'll throw it out immediately as slander and libel.

"He might have mentioned that," Meghan replied nonchalantly. "But he also told me you look fragile when you're sleeping, so that balances out the venom."

"HE SAID *WHAT*?!" I shrieked.

She once again took advantage of my distracted state of mind and tackled me, sending the books flying. I had to give it to her, the girl was trying very hard to win.

I've taught her well. She's truly learned everything, even what I didn't teach, which was always fight dirty.

She had a knee on one of my wrists but was struggling to catch and pin the other arm.

I decided the best course of action was to taunt her, the way a cat would taunt a mouse. Reaching up this way and that, I lightly poked and slapped her body—all for the sheer joy of aggravating her more.

"He also said you were lethal when you're mad, but also kind of adorable—in a very menacing sort of way."

Now she's just making it up. There's no way he's talked about me this much to his sister. He said they hardly ever see each other.

She did say he talks when he's making my obnoxiously healthy meals.

At last, tired of playing around, I rolled and pinned her in a matter of seconds.

"He said he'd take it all back," she heaved, her stormy gray eyes searching my face. "He wishes he'd never taken you." She trembled slightly, her eyebrows scrunching together. "I wish he hadn't either. Because no matter how Jeremiah threatens me, that doesn't excuse the bad things that follow. I don't want to be the reason he gets himself killed. I don't want to be the reason he taints and poisons his soul."

"I know," I said gently as I picked myself up and began to slowly gather the fallen books. "I believe you. There are a lot of things he and I would take back, if we could."

The clock on the nightstand read 3:48 a.m. and the silence stretched between us, and the heartbreak we shared.

Meghan shook her head, her eyes lingering on the Lichtenburg figures on my hands. "How often do we fight to stop a thing from happening," she whispered, "only to have our efforts become the thing that brings it about all along? Will we forever run to escape death, only to meet it at our afore destined meeting place? Will we ever escape this empty cycle of bloodshed and violence?"

I don't know Megs, I don't know.

There was a sound at her door. The locks were turning back, one by one.

Meghan's eyes went wide, and she looked frantically at the poster. We didn't have time for me to dive through, and for her to cover it back up. It would be a dead giveaway. She pointed to under the bed. "Hide," she breathed.

41

What A Father's Love Should Have Been

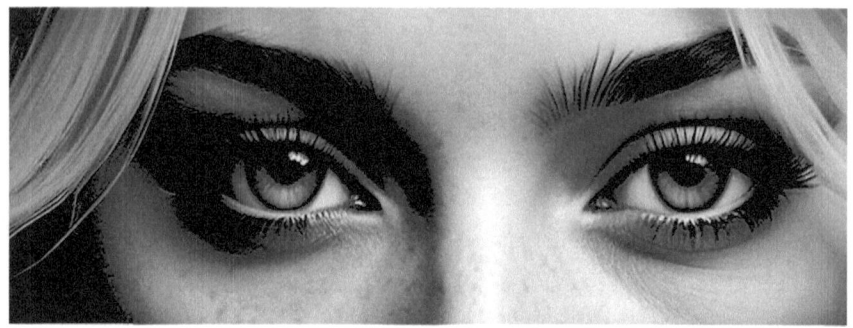

FAYE

"All my grief says the same thing: this isn't how it's supposed to be. *This isn't how it's supposed to be.* And the world laughs. Holds my hope by the throat. Says: but this is how *it is.*"
-Fortesa Latifi

There had been no knock to signal that it was Ronan entering the room. He always knocked in code before entering so we knew it was safe.

Click-click-click-

Meghan lunged for the shelf as I dove under the bed. She quickly raced back and shoved a phone into my hand. "Call Ronan," she whispered urgently. "And no matter what you do, don't you dare come out. No matter what you hear, no matter what he does. Don't blow the plan. If Jeremiah finds you here, I'm done for. Call Ronan. He'll get here."

I turned on the phone, desperately looking for the contacts logo. There was only one contact listed, Ronan.

I urgently clicked on the contact and pressed call, turning the phone volume down so low as to not be heard.

Ronan picked up on the second ring as the knob turned. "Hello?" he grunted, out of breath.

I couldn't make my voice work as Jeremiah walked into the room. If he heard me, that was it. The entire farce was up, and he would kill us all.

"Meghan?" Ronan's voice was urgent now, as if sensing something was wrong.

"Help," I breathed so low I wasn't even sure I had spoken, let alone clearly enough he would be able to hear me.

"Faye?" His voice went ragged, fear tearing at the edges. "Where's Megs? Are you okay?"

"He's here," I whispered.

He was running now. I could hear the sound of his feet, the desperate gasp of his breath as he sprinted. "Hold on," he heaved. "I'm coming, just hold on. Stay on the line, okay? Just stay on the line."

I can't. If he hears anything, we'll be dead.

I hung up, hands shaking as I ensured the phone volume was set to silent.

It was.

I flattened myself to the floor, sliding back as far as I could to see what was going on without giving away my hiding spot.

The phone screen lit up, Ronan's laughing face filling the screen. He was calling back.

I can't risk it, Ronan. I can't risk our plan failing. I can't use my inheritance and if something were to happen to her because I mess up, or he kills her before I can get him in a chokehold...I can't risk it.

"Do you know what today is?"

Jeremiah's voice was a rasping whisper, choked and full of rage.

Meghan's eyes were wide with fear. She didn't move as she stared at her father.

"I asked you a question!" he roared.

Meghan flinched. "It's my birthday," she replied, a sob clinging to her voice.

Even from where I lay, I could smell the alcohol on him as he drew closer to where Meghan stood, shaking. "It's the anniversary of the day you *murdered* your own mother. The very one who gave life to your miserable body."

I scooted to the back of the bed and crept out from under it, determined to catch Jeremiah by surprise and kill him. Plans or not, I was not about to let him kill her for his delusions. I was not about to let this man destroy the one thing that Ronan really, truly loved. The one thing he was fighting to protect. Maybe I couldn't save my sisters, but I could save his.

Meghan's eyes caught mine for a brief instant, begging me to stay back. The look was so quick Jeremiah didn't even notice it in his intoxicated state.

I'm sorry Meghan, I can't.

I can't just crouch here and let him kill you. Ronan would never forgive me. I would never forgive myself.

It was then I noticed the gun in his hand.

Well crap. That's going to make this much harder. I have to make sure he doesn't shoot her in his attempt to fight me, or startle him so that he shoots her. So many possibilities to avoid.

"I've tolerated your existence long enough," Jeremiah seethed. It's time you repented of your wrongdoings."

Someone's delulu.

"I'm sorry," Meghan whispered. "You have no idea how sorry I am that I'm here and she's not."

Oh honey, it's okay. I'm sure your mother doesn't think that. She was probably glad that you were okay, even if she didn't make it. She's your mother. She cares for you no matter what, and wants the best for you, no matter what...

"Sorry doesn't bring her back, you sniveling murderess. Sorry doesn't change what you've done. What you've stolen from me!"

I have to help her! I have to help her!

Her eyes flicked to mine again, telling me, begging me to stay.

I can't, Meghan. This is so wrong. I can't. Don't ask me to do this. Ronan where are you?!

"I'm going to bury you alive," Jeremiah sneered. "You'll suffocate. You'll die alone in a box, eight feet underground where no one can hear you scream. No one will save you, not even your deluded brother. Your tainted magic that sways him won't be able to reach him from underground."

I will. I will. I would die to save her. I will save her, you monster.

I eased around the bed. He still hadn't noticed me.

If I tackle him from behind, and she dives out of the way of potential gunfire, I could yank him backwards and strangle him.

He escalated the situation by pointing the gun at her head, jamming the barrel into her temple. "Maybe I'll just end it all now. Do what I should have done eighteen years ago.

I crouched, desperate to help, but unsure how. He had his finger on the trigger. One wrong move and he could kill her.

Is he going to simply threaten and monologue?

Doesn't matter. We'll just break his neck. That will take care of the problem. We can figure out what to do from there.

How many of Jeremiah's men are loyal to him? How many would fight us? Besides, how do we get the zappers disconnected? What if we can't?

We'll burn that bridge when we get to it.

In order to break his neck, I have to be close.

"You do not deserve the mercy I've given all these years. You do not deserve the time I've let you live." He lowered the gun, shoving it into her gut. "Maybe I'll put a bullet in here, and leave you out in the woods to rot as the wolves smell your blood and tear you apart, or perhaps the maggots that eat you alive from the inside out."

I crept up closer, silently, intent on his decimation. I was directly behind him, and he was so intent on Meghan, he didn't sense my presence.

Tears were streaming down her face as I slowly, silently reached up. My fingers were half an inch from his exposed neck. He was monologuing, I was certain he would continue to do so and give me thirty seconds more to make sure I took him down as cleanly as possible and protect her. *Is his finger on the trigger? If I break his neck, will the gun go off?*

I was wrong.

The gun exploded just as the door burst open and Ronan barged into the room. Meghan screamed, masking the sound of my own shriek as Ronan yanked me back from Jeremiah.

The message was clear—hide.

I dove behind and underneath the bed, ducking out of sight just in time.

Ronan wrenched Jeremiah away from Meghan. "GET AWAY FROM HER!" he roared.

Meghan fell to her knees, clutching her side, blood seeping out through her fingers.

"Ah, the ever valiant protector," Jeremiah sneered. "I am beginning to tire of this rift that *thing* puts between us."

Ronan looked murderous. "How about I end this now," he hissed, chest heaving.

You're going to blow it, Ronan. Just get him out of here. We have no way out; we have no idea who is loyal and there are only so many bullets in your father's gun. I haven't disabled the zappers yet.

"Marcov is in my office," Jeremiah countered. "He's got his fingers on a particularly nasty electrode that can deliver a deadly amount of voltage. If I don't return to him, and he finds out I'm gone, he'll kill her."

We have got to get these zappers disabled. NOW.

"Get out of here," Ronan growled.

"Don't," Meghan coughed. "Ronan, don't. It's not worth it."

Jeremiah gave Ronan a cold, knowing smile. "It saddens me to hear you talk that way, son. I shall think of how best to handle this. When I have thought of the appropriate consequences, I shall let you know. I don't want to...but you leave me no choice. You must be taught. After all, you are my son, my only child."

He's insane. He's utterly insane.

A vein pulsed in Ronan's temple as he stood between Jeremiah and Meghan, seething in rage.

Jeremiah left, laughing menacingly as he went.

Ronan kicked the door shut behind him, putting the locks back in place, one after the other, before taking one of Meghan's chairs and jamming it under the doorknob.

I was already out from under the bed and at Meghan's side, trying to help staunch the flow of blood. Ronan knelt beside me, his breath warm and minty on my cheek as he gently moved me aside and began to inspect the wound.

"Just breathe, Megs," he said soothingly, his voice calm and low.

His hands shook as he gently turned her, looking at her back. "It looks like it just tore through your side, in and out... it was almost a graze... I should get you to the hospital to get it checked out."

Meghan shook her head. "I can't leave, and he won't let you take me...you'd never come back."

"I would," Ronan countered hotly. "Just not with you. I still have to get Faye and her father out of this mess."

"Is she badly hurt?" a new voice whispered. It was familiar, as if I had heard it before.

I jerked at the sound, searching for its unfamiliar owner. A flicker of movement in the darkness under the bed and a face of swirling shadows slowly emerged.

Ronan jerked and my mouth fell open in shock. It was the monster from under my bed back home—the one I had attacked with my book. "Hello Kleiner," he said softly.

"Show me the child."

"What the, who is, what, I?!" Ronan was spluttering so much his words no longer made any sense.

"It's a monster, Ronan," I replied evenly, trying to stay calm. "They're typically bad, but this one seems to have a soft bone. I think it came out of the monster factory defective."

"I am there for the ones who need me most," the monster replied. "It is what I have always done. I am not capable of eating the dear children, as my brethren strive to do."

"I am never going under my bed again," Ronan whispered in horror.

"You shouldn't," I replied saucily as I gently began to pull Meghan closer to the monster. "Monsters are downright evil. When you give them a finger, they'll take your whole arm." I snickered. "Usually they want to take my arm because my finger was a particularly insulting finger."

Ronan shuddered, ignoring my clever joke. "What does he want?"

"To help my child, you ignorant meat sack," the monster growled irritably.

Ronan looked visibly offended by such a title, and I stifled a cackle. This was no time to be laughing, but the monster had definitely gained points in my book. Anyone who called Ronan a meat sack and pushed him to such indignation was a winner as far as I was concerned.

"Hey there, Drysdyne," Meghan whispered. "It's not the worst you've ever seen me. But he's definitely getting bad again."

Drysdyne growled under his breath. "Bring him to me, and I will make an exception to my oath not to harm the mortals. He alone deserves to be eaten, slowly, from the toes up."

Yaaassss! You go monster!

I like this one. Does he have a waiting list? I'd like him to be my monster from now on.

Shadows swirled around Drysdyne's hands; his face scrunched in calm concentration. "No organs were hurt. It is in and out. I cannot heal it, despite my desire to do so. But it will heal on its own if you give it time."

"Thank you," I whispered.

"You're welcome, daughter of Grimm. I warned you the scales were shifting, and what do I get in return?"

"Sorry about that," I muttered, embarrassed. "In my defense, I didn't know nice monsters existed... I did what came naturally. I could have grabbed a thinner book."

"It is a marvelous book," Drysdyne replied happily. "I did not mind being attacked with it. I consider it my honor. Do you know if the next chapter has released after the small in between book..." his words fell as he contemplated. "The one with worm and fork, or some such strange title."

"Yeah, the latest one is out now. I'm surprised you don't know that."

"It is hard to check the mail when watching the house. The brounie does a noble job, but checking the mail is outside its job qualifications. I believe the post office has been holding it back for your parents."

"Is everything okay there?" I asked hesitantly.

"We have placed all living beings into a suspended sleep. Someone from the family must come home and request the brounie release the spell to wake them. The brounie has made a truce with the cat, and together, they guard the sleepers."

Relief crashed in my chest. At least something was okay in the midst of all the chaos.

"But," Drysdyne continued. "There have been visitors. Men who smell tainted of shadows. They are looking for your sisters."

A knot formed in my stomach.

"They have not checked under the beds. If they had, I would have disposed of them," Drysdyne continued. "Even so, they shall not succeed. Your sisters are in the Moores. They belong to the Realm now."

I nodded, too exhausted to find words.

"I shall check on her periodically. If she does not heal and it grows worse, then perhaps I will go rogue to summon a Shadowthief to assist us."

Ryver.

Could he help us if I called him?

Would he hear if I called?

"You may have to sacrifice a few fingers," Drysdyne continued.

I stared at him in horror and he began to laugh. Apparently, he thought his joke funny.

"I'll go get my medical kit," Ronan said quickly, clearly unnerved by the conversation.

"Cursed medical kit," Meghan and I chorused in unison as Ronan turned to go.

He turned back, frowning. "I'll have you know that medical kit has saved both of your lives on multiple occasions."

Meghan and I rolled our eyes as Ronan went into his room to find said cursed medical bag.

"It's gonna be okay," I said soothingly, brushing back strands of hair from Meghan's sweaty face as I helped her sit up. "You were so brave, sweet girl."

Meghan sniffed, tears rising in her eyes. "I don't know why he hates me so much. I'm his own daughter, the spitting image of my mother. You'd think that would be a comfort...but still, he hates me. Logically, I know he's crazy, but my mind wants to know why. What did I possibly do to deserve this kind of treatment from my own *father*."

"Your father is insane," I replied quietly, holding her close. "There is no logic in any of this. Nothing you do or don't do could sway him."

"I just want him to love me," Meghan whispered. "He hates me, and I can't stand him... I hate him too...but it doesn't change what I want deep inside. I just want him to love me." She was sobbing now as she whispered the confession.

"I know, sweetheart," I murmured. "I know. It makes sense. He's your father, and all a girl ever wants from her father is his love and approval—no matter how much of a monster he is. It's all you ever want."

Tears streamed down her cheeks as she stared up at me, her eyes questioning and afraid.

But I had no answers left to give as I continued to hold her close.

Together we wept for what life was and what it should have been.

42

The Language Of Dragons

EVADNE

"I wonder if I will ever find a language to speak of the things that haunt
me the most."
-Bao Phi, Thousand Star Hotel

The wind carried a song that resonated deep in my bones, stirring something in my
mind as I stared out across the deep blue skies. Colors were more vibrant through my
new eye and the imbalance between the two turned the world into a slightly distorted
picture. Slowly, however, my brain was filling in the gaps and creating an altogether
new image.

Despite Carl's work to drain the Darke magic from my body, bits and pieces remained. The shadows were still there in the back of my mind. But now they were firmly
under lock and key. They were contained. I was the master over them now, and though
I couldn't yet find a way to destroy them, the pressure had decreased.

The manipulation of my memories, however, was still something I couldn't quite
decipher. I felt like a jigsaw puzzle that had been haphazardly shoved together—a
picture that no longer made sense. My memories were unreliable now.

The endless expanse of skies stretched out in front of me, but I lacked the energy
to appreciate it. I had yet to rekindle the fire of my emotions. Everything was damped

down, vague and colorless.

Run child, run. The darkness comes.

Would any part of me be untainted by the time death claimed me? Already the horrors I had lived through seemed like too much for one person to handle.

"You're miles away again," Raz said from beside me. Her dark gold eyes searched my face, looking for answers. I hastily turned away, returning my attention to the material in my hands.

I was supposed to be holding the ends of the ripped sail together so Raz could mend them, but it was all I could do to keep breathing. I was wrapped within so many violent emotions, buried beneath a great cloud of nothingness.

How do we come back from this? Will we ever be okay?

Raz's long fingers were a blur as she murmured a spell into the fabric beneath her hands. The torn fibers grew and stretched, while a green moss sprouted beneath her fingertips and spread across the rip, pulling it together until all that remained was an intricate pattern where the rip had once been.

"Good as new," she stated with a grin.

I managed a small smile, doing my best to imitate her good humor and kindness as I followed her muscular frame to the next sail.

"We've got company!" Theron bellowed from beneath us. Together, he and Ember grabbed their ropes and slid down, careful to keep it within the palms of their leather gloves.

Theron must have given her a burst of extra courage. That was amazing.

Raz began climbing higher, heading for the crow's nest, and I followed. The company in question was a small ship, miniscule in comparison to Verity's rig, but there was a certain hum of energy that surrounded it as it approached. Something familiar that called to me.

Verity strode across the deck, closely followed by Theron and Nikos, both of whom had their weapons drawn. Ember stood with Rune, whose hand was buried in the leather bag on her belt. I had a sneaking suspicion there were a fair few explosives hidden inside.

The small boat pulled up beside the deck and my heartbeat stuttered as I took in the sight of Ríonach standing tall on the ship's deck. She looked healthy and healed—nothing like the way she had looked when last we'd seen each other. She stared at Ember and shock flashed across her face; there for a moment and gone in the next.

Then her gaze quickly found me in the crow's nest. Her lips curved into a small feral smile, revealing the tips of her sharp canines.

"Ríonach!" I yelled happily as I began to descend the rope ladder to greet her.

"Hang on," Raz ordered. "Verity hasn't given her permission to board."

"Oh, right. Why wouldn't she? Ríonach is our friend."

"Because Ríonach belongs to the Courts, and Verity is currently hiding two stowaway Grimms. Ríonach could be under orders to slaughter everyone to bring you two back. Friend or not, Ríonach is a danger to everyone here."

"But she wouldn't," I protested, confused.

"If she's ordered and bound, she would," Raz replied sadly. "Many a subject of the Courts is forced to do great horrors at the rulers' command. Their own heir is not beyond such tactics of control."

The ship fell silent as Verity and Ríonach assessed each other. At last, Verity spoke. "My regards to the Winter Court," she stated.

It was neither an invitation, nor a question.

Ríonach inclined her head in a small bow. "My respect to the brave Moore voyagers of the skies. I mean no harm to any aboard your ship, stowaway or not. I simply request your permission to board. I wish to speak to you."

"Are you bound in any way?" Verity asked sharply.

Ríonach shook her head.

"I'll take that in the form of a verbal promise," Verity pressed. "I cannot be too careful when the lives of my crew depend on my discretion."

"I swear by the stolen blood that binds me, that I am under no curse no compulsion to harm you, nor any on your ship. I do not seek the Grimms. I was not even aware of their presence on this vessel. I only wish for a conversation with you, and perhaps to have some of Logan's fine cooking."

Verity nodded once. "Thank you, I can't be too careful."

Ríonach shrugged as she began to skillfully tie her little vessel to ours. "I understand completely. I would have done the same."

"Okay, now you can go down," Raz said, letting go of my arm. "Try not to get tangled in the ropes."

"I won't," I replied, eager to get to Ríonach.

She stepped aboard the ship just as I reached the deck. She gave Ember a searching look. "It seems you have encountered much trouble since we last saw each other,

Grimmling. I'm proud of you. But tell me, where did you abandon your prince?"

"Somewhere in the Moores," Ember replied quietly, shame overtaking her voice. "Jacques sent us on the ship to seek answers."

Ríonach pursed her lips. "A desperate choice," she said under her breath. "He would not begin such anarchy lightly... Is the prince hot on your trail?"

"I don't know for sure," Ember said softly. "I believe he is."

"Well, I wish him luck on his wild goose chase. Jack knew what he was doing. We shall see what fate makes of this twist. Though, I do not believe he will ever give up the chase, child. Your magic is entwined. He will not surrender you—he will hunt you to the ends of whichever Realm you hide within."

She turned to me, just as I rushed into her, giving her the biggest hug I could manage.

She stiffened, and then hesitantly wrapped her arms around me. "You continue to amaze me, child. Tell me, who do I kill for hurting you?"

"He's not dead," I choked out.

Ríonach pulled back. "You don't mean?"

"It's a long story," I replied, tasting blood.

When will I break the curse? When will we be free of this tainted silence that holds so much pain and sorrow?

"One I doubt you can yet tell in its fullness," she replied cryptically after a few moments had passed.

I shook my head, understanding what she meant. "But the curse is splintering. We're almost through."

Her fingers gently traced the golden corner of my scar. "So much for one so young. I recognize this handiwork. You found Rumpelstiltskin; I have not seen the maker in centuries. He is the finest craftsman in all of the Realm's history. You could not have been in better hands." She stared down at me, her face pensive and eyes sad. "I am sorry for the pain this Realm has caused you," she said softly. "I would protect your fragile heart from it, if only I could."

At a loss for words, I hugged her again and was quickly joined by Ember. "We missed you!" she said happily as she wrapped Ríonach in a hug of her own.

Ríonach laughed quietly. "You will ruin my reputation if you continue this ridiculous display of affection."

"Let it be ruined," I replied emphatically. "We've missed you."

Ríonach laughed again and at last returned our hugs. "All right girls, I'm sure Verity has duties for you aboard her vessel, and I have business to attend to."

"Are you going to stay long?" I asked hopefully.

"No," Ríonach replied, casting a wary glance out at the endless skies around us. "No one knows I am here. My absence from the central realms must not be noticed, so I will leave as soon as my business is completed. I cannot put Verity at such risk. Had I known she possessed you, I would not have come."

She turned to Verity. "Verity, if you don't mind, I'd like a word with you in private. I have a growing concern with your Moores."

"As do we all," Verity muttered under her breath. "Come, this way. I believe Logan is cooking up a mess of sweets. I'm sure he has something that can tempt your ever present sweet tooth."

"Excellent!" Ríonach crowed. "Last time I was here he created the most amazing crème brûlée."

"Carry on about your business," Verity called to the crew as she, Theron, and Nikos escorted Ríonach to Verity's quarters.

Theron paused for a moment, speaking quietly to Rune and Ember. Ember pursed her lips in annoyance as he turned to her. "You'll be fine," he soothed.

Apparently, he was no longer going to be helping her fight her fear while he was in the meeting.

Ember shook her head vehemently. "I will not!"

Theron poked Ember's shoulder. "You will, too. You have to learn to do this without me, Sparks."

"I don't *want* to," Ember protested. "I can't do this without you, Theron."

"Your life may well depend on it. If we're under attack, I won't be able to do what's required of me and keep your fear at bay. Things will explode with your prince. He's going to find us, and when he does, he will try to use your fear against you."

"He's not *my* prince!" Ember snapped.

Theron arched an eyebrow. "Why are you calling out his name in the middle of the night, then?"

Ember began to splutter indignantly as her cheeks flushed a deep red.

Heh, he's got her there. Oo, look, her ears are absolutely crimson. He should tease her about Artemis more often.

Theron gave Ember a little push toward the rope ladder. "Just be glad I've entrusted you to Rune and not Raz. Raz would make sure you fell just so she could prove she'd save you."

"YUP!" Raz replied impishly.

Ember made a face but began to make her way to the ladder going up the mast. "My prince," she muttered angrily. "He's not *my* prince."

"I mean," I taunted, following her, "he did say quite a few *interesting* things while he was having his little identity crisis. I seem to recall him stating he would tear the entire Realm apart to find you...that he couldn't bear to lose you. Plus, there was the whole, holding you to his *very* muscular chest that happened to be deprived of a *shirt*...any of this ring a bell?"

Ember glared down at me, her face the color of an incredibly ripe tomato. "You can just shut up," she snapped. "Nobody asked you."

Theron's laughter echoed from below as he followed Ríonach and Verity toward the captain's quarters. "Play nice little skye kraken," he called before disappearing from view.

Ember and I split at the first set of masts, where Rune began to give Ember a basic lesson on ship navigation and I continued to climb, letting muscle memory carry me forward. My body had begun to sense the odd rhythm of the ship and I was starting to adjust and move freely. At times it felt like a dance that only I could feel.

The wind seemed to sing as I began to help Raz repair another sail. Words slipped in and out of my mind, so fast I couldn't piece the syllables together. It was a haunting lullaby that begged to be understood, but no matter how hard I tried, I couldn't.

Hours passed, and by the time Verity, Ríonach, Theron, and Nikos emerged from the captain's quarters, the light around us was failing.

Over the course of the day, Rune had taught Ember how to swing on a rope, from mast to mast—all without throwing up, and Raz and I had finished inspecting the sails. The ship carried twenty different sails in all, and while we worked, Raz had taught me their proper names and what they did. The names escaped my memory as soon as she said them—it was too much information—but their purpose and location stuck with me. I knew what she was talking about when she pointed to one or the other.

We were all on the main deck now, learning how to tie a series of important knots. Despite my interest in this lesson, I was distracted. The song was back at the edge of my mind, but now it was a constant, steady hum. It grew clearer and clearer by the moment, until at last it swelled into a song that seemed to soar with the growing wind.

'Skies around us, Moores below, Chasms within our hearts,
as we ride the wings of storms, and slowly fall apart.
We seek a place of refuge, we seek the one of hope,
Our fire cannot fight the darkness, We long to find our home.'

"Something's coming," Ríonach said sharply.

Verity turned, scanning the skies. "Eyes up!" she shouted.

A steady hum was overwhelming the wind's soft rise and fall, and beneath that, a rhythmic beating. Like great wings cutting through the sky. Shapes, so vague they could have been a mirage, loomed on the horizon, fading in and out of focus, the longer we watched.

"All hands on deck!" Verity yelled.

"What is it?" I called, following Raz hurriedly.

"Dragons," Verity snapped. "They're out of their migration pattern. They shouldn't be in these portions of the skies."

Ríonach bared her teeth in a feral smile. "I have longed to see the Moores dragons. It seems I get many a wish today."

Verity rolled her eyes. "You won't be saying that when they destroy our ship and kill my crew."

"I fear no monsters in this place," Ríonach replied.

"That's because you are one, Princess," Verity snorted. "Those of us who are mortal carry a healthy dose of fear regarding the ancient creatures of this place."

The song was getting louder, growing stronger as the shapes solidified. The dying sunlight reflected against their scales like a spotlight. Shades of black and gray with undertones of navy and teal.

"They won't hurt us," I said softly.

"You know nothing, Grimm," Verity snapped. "Dragons are volatile. They do not speak our language, and they cannot be bargained with. They bring nothing but death and destruction. They have no intelligence with which to communicate. All they crave is blood, and we do not have a magic wielder on board who is strong enough to control a pack that large."

"We linger on the edge of sorrow,
as darkness calls our name,
we search and search,
but nothing's left to claim,
burning hearts, fade to ash,
no, nothing is the same."

"Raz!" Verity barked, "I need you and the Grimm up top." She turned to me. "If they set anything on fire, I need you to put it out, am I understood?"

Raz nodded then took to the skies. Her wings beat powerfully through the air until she landed on the rail of the crow's nest.

They won't hurt us.

How do I know? I don't know anything about dragons. How do I know?

I don't know, I just do.

"Weapons!" Verity yelled, still shouting out orders. "All warriors on post! Theron, get higher. See if you can quell the bloodthirst."

Theron nodded and pulled Ember close to his side. "Hold on tight, Sparks," he grunted as his wings exploded from his pack and flared out from his back. She muffled a startled shriek as he launched them up into the air, toward the crow's nest where Raz waited.

Fireheart flew down from one of the lower masts, abandoning his quest to eat the magical birds that foolishly flew too close to him.

He landed on my shoulder, grinning excitedly. He was moving his head side to side, staring at the sky as his throat vibrated.

"What if she's wrong," I whispered, running a finger down his spine. "I can hear them...I think. They're not violent, they're just...they're searching, Fireheart. They're looking for a place to call home."

"We seek the one whose heart is captive, The one who changes tides, The one who holds the fate of worlds, The one whose heart will die..."

I began to climb up a rope ladder, Fireheart clinging to my neck and shoulder as I tried to get higher. If there was a fire, height would likely help me put it out.

The dragons were larger now, bigger than Verity's ship, with long necks and tails. Long, sharp horns ran down the length of their necks. Huge black and silver eyes took in the sight of our ship as the sound of their song grew into a chorus, drowning out all thoughts as I struggled to keep my footing on the rope ladder.

"They're singing!" I yelled, but my words were carried away on the roaring wind. The dragons' huge wings sucked the air from around us, and the breeze we sailed on turned into a tumultuous gale. The ship rocked violently back and forth in the tumult.

"Archers, ready!" Verity yelled.

Go around us, please go around us. I don't want to see you get hurt.

Half the crew drew back massive bows, their arrows trained on the monstrous beasts. The ship fell silent, waiting to see what the dragons would do.

They continued to advance.

"STEADY!" Verity called, raising an arm in the air as she watched the dragons. "Do not shoot unless they attack first!"

"They're *singing*," I yelled again. "Verity! They're not going to harm us!" But again, my voice was gone, carried away in the tumult.

The dragons hovered in front of the ship, their massive wings tossing the boat like the stormy waves of a sea. Everyone struggled to keep their footing as they awaited Verity's command.

The monstrous faces did nothing but stare at us as the song drowned out everything. The agony and longing within the words filled me with such sorrow that I wanted to fall to my knees and weep.

"We seek a place free of the darkness that rises."

I gasped as the growling voice cut through my mind, overwhelming the song.

"EVADNE!" Verity screamed as the largest dragon drew closer, until it was face to face with me.

Terror cut through me. One quick move of its neck, and the dragon could swallow me whole. But despite my fear, my hand raised, reaching out to brush the tip of its nose. My fingertips were inches away from its smooth scales.

"We rose from myth and legend," the voice cut through again. *"Yet we cannot stand against the darkness that rises."*

'What do you want?'

"Nothing but peace. Nothing but freedom. Nothing but a home that is free. We wander the skies endlessly, searching, searching, ever searching."

Tears were streaming down my cheeks as my fingers brushed the face of the dragon. Fireheart growled excitedly on my shoulder, his claws digging into my skin. The energy between us vibrated in the air around us as the ship rocked and pitched.

An arrow flew out of nowhere, piercing the dragon's neck. It roared and jerked back, a stream of fire rushing from its mouth and onto the sails.

"HOLD YOUR FIRE!" Verity roared.

My balance wavered as the dragon drew back and the fire raged above me on the sail and rope ladder.

I have to put out the fire.

I turned, water leaking from my fingertips.

Too late. The rope snapped, reduced to nothing but ash, and I went flying.

The ship disappeared from sight as I plummeted down.

Ember's desperate scream followed me.

'HELP ME!'

I could see Raz and Theron racing toward me, unheeding of the danger from the dragons around us.

'HELP ME!' I screamed again, desperate to communicate with the dragons. Surely, if they spoke to me, they would be willing to help. Why else would they have been there?

Their song swelled around me as the world began to grow blurry at the edges.

> *"We seek the one whose heart is captive.*
> *The one who changes the tides,*
> *The one who holds the fate of worlds,*
> *Whose love and fate shall die."*

43

I Do Not Have The Energy For Your Cryptic Warnings

EMBER

"Forget them Wendy. Forget them all, come with me where you'll
never, never have to worry about grown up things again."
-Peter Pan

Time slowed to a standstill. I was screaming, of that much I was sure, but I couldn't
hear the sound over the roar of my heartbeat and the desperation of my thoughts as I
watched my sister fall.

Theron and Raz had already jumped, trying to reach her before the ground did.
They had been so intent on the dragons, no one had noticed my sister out there all
alone, seemingly conversing with a monstrous dragon hoard.

The dragons hovered in the air, watching her body plummet. Then time snapped
back into place and the one that had been in front of her tucked its wings against its
body and dove—joining the race for my sister.

"EVADNE!" I screamed again as I grasped a rope and swung out across open air.
Fear was a distant memory, though Theron's magic muffler was nowhere to be found.

The fire was rapidly spreading and the crew was now working in unison to get it put out.

If I can get to the deck, maybe I could control it and make it leave the ship.

My rope hit the flames, and it snapped. Before I could realize what was happening, I was plummeting down toward the deck.

This is NOT how I thought this was going to go down.

Ah yes, what did you imagine? A stunning, heroic display—like something out of Pirates of the Caribbean?

I did picture myself somewhat like Jack Sparrow, thank you very much.

My shoulder hit first, and I curved into as tight a ball as I could manage, trying to disperse the injuries throughout to lessen their severity.

I forced myself to my feet as I plunged my hands toward the hungry flames, calling them to me. My only thought was Evadne, but my help was needed.

The flames trembled, as if contemplating such a feat, and then continued to devour the ship.

I should be helping Evadne.

They've got her. Right now, Verity needs me here. I'm no use hanging over the rail sobbing. I can sob over her when they get her back. If these flames don't get put out soon, the ship will be too far gone.

I intensified my call to the flames, my fingers curling into claws as I fought against their will.

Come to me. Come to me.

Half of the flames leaned toward me, then, in an instant, raced back to the rest.

NO!

Mine. You are mine. I claim you. I own you. I control you...

Suddenly, all of the flames raced toward me, and braced myself for their attack.

Mine. You are mine.

The flames hovered in front of me, flickering and snapping as they wavered in the dim twilight. It was all I could do to keep them in one organized ball, let alone figure out what to do with them now.

What do I do? What do I do?

My hands trembled and the flames leaned toward the ship, hungry to consume.

NO.

I pulled control back to myself, and my stomach rocked and plummeted.

Mine. You are ***MINE.***

The flames shivered for a moment, and then began to morph and transform, until a flaming phoenix flapped in the air above me.

I held out my hand, and the phoenix landed. The fire was cool and comforting against my skin. I pushed my memory back, back to that time all those ages ago in the clearing, when Artemis had taught me how to control and disperse my fire.

Return.

The phoenix was dissolving into ash and smoke, drifting away on the tumultuous wind.

My limbs sagged and I sunk to my knees, staring out at the skies. I had put out the fire, but my sister still had not returned.

Verity and Ríonach were at the edge, staring down into the clouds.

"Come on, come on," Verity muttered under her breath.

The dragon that had dived burst through the clouds and soared through the air above us. I jerked to my feet, rushing to stand beside Verity and Ríonach.

Where is Evadne? Is she there?

I couldn't see her.

Evadne, Evadne, where are you? Please be okay, please be okay.

Tears were streaming down my face as the dragon drew closer. Looming over us, it stretched out a clawed leg toward the ship.

Please, oh please.

Evadne's limp body tumbled out onto the deck from the dragon's claws.

"Eva!" I yelled, rushing to her side. Verity and Ríonach were hot on my heels as I pulled her head into my lap. Her face was ashen, but she was breathing.

Still alive. She's still alive.

Ríonach knelt beside me, fingers probing her neck and forehead. "Fainted," she stated as she grabbed her arm. I watched, confused, as Ríonach bit the inside of Evadne's wrist.

Everything logical inside of me said I should be pushing Ríonach away from my sister, but I trusted Ríonach enough to know that she knew what she was doing.

Ríonach sucked for a moment, then pulled away. "She's not harmed beyond oxygen deprivation. There's no inflammation in the cells; the blood is clean."

My mouth fell open in shock.

That is seriously cool.

"Not everyone can sense wounds like your summer prince can," Ríonach said wryly.

"We all must find our ways to problem solve." She grinned at me, her teeth stained crimson with Evadne's blood. "This way just happens to be one society frowns upon. She should wake soon. The fall was simply too much for her system to handle."

We waited in silence as I cradled Evadne in my arms, pushing the straggling curls away from her face. The wind had torn most of it loose from the French braid she had contained it in.

Fireheart was curled around her bicep, his eyes fixed on her face as great, big dragon tears rolled down his face and dripped onto her shirt.

"It's okay, Fireheart," I said gently, stroking his scales. "She's okay. She just passed out. She's going to be okay. You couldn't have done anything, it's okay."

He continued to cry, and I began to hum quietly, trying to pull my mind from my anxiety and soothe both of our fears. It was the lullaby Faye used to sing for me, before she was taken, and soon the tune morphed into words. "The ring-dove sang from the willow spray, well-a-day! Well-a-day! He mourn'd for the fate of his darling mate, well-day!" I began humming again. Here was where the song shifted into another language, and I could never remember how the foreign words sounded. "Till the prisoner is fast and her doom is cast, there stay! Oh stay! When the charm is around her, and the spell has bound her, hie away! Away!"

"You and that depressing song," Evadne mumbled as she stirred.

"You stupid idiot," I sobbed, pulling her into a smothering hug. "Theron told you skye dragons were a no-no for your petting zoo! Why did you have to be so stupid and try to pet one?!"

"Good grief, woman, your bedside manners need some help," Evadne muttered as she hugged me back. "You're supposed to ask if I'm okay, and weep about my amazing recovery. *Then* you can call me stupid. Get your priorities straight."

I was laughing and crying and scolding her all at once. "I thought I lost you," I cried. "I thought I lost you again."

She clung to me. "I'm sorry," she whispered. "I'm so sorry Em, I didn't mean for it to happen. Something happened, then the rope snapped, and I was falling. I didn't mean for any of it to happen."

"What happened?"

"The dragons were speaking to me. They were singing when they came. But the one that caught me was speaking to me. I was so enthralled by all of it I didn't realize how much danger I was in…"

Fireheart bumped her face with his and glared indignantly at her.

"You have wings," she replied reprovingly. "I did not put your life in danger."

Fireheart continued to glare, sticking out his tongue in annoyance at her.

"Don't be petty and stupid," she scolded. "Dying with me won't get us anywhere. Someone needs to live and keep Ember in line. Just because I'm falling, doesn't mean you have to fall too."

Fireheart crossed his little arms stubbornly, his wings flaring. Evadne rolled her eyes.

Her attention quickly shifted to the dragons. "I can hear them," she said quietly. "But why can't I hear you?"

Fireheart's head drooped and he buried his head against her neck.

"You don't speak?" Evadne asked.

Fireheart shook his head, burying it further.

"You...*can't* speak," Evadne whispered, understanding dawning on her face. "You should be able to...but you can't. You're mute..."

Tears were falling from his eyes again and she hugged him closely.

"It's okay," she murmured. "It's okay. Just because they can speak, and you can't, doesn't change how amazing you are. You are still my favorite dragon.

"The dragons don't mean us any harm," she said to Verity.

"Child, I understand that dragon saved you for some unknown reason, but I have never known a skye dragon that doesn't mean any harm."

"I can hear them," Evadne pressed. "They're not looking for a fight. They came because of me."

"That's ridiculous. You can't, wait, what?"

Ríonach looked at Evadne sharply. "What did you just say, child?"

"I can hear them," Evadne replied. "They speak. They were singing when they came to us."

"You continue to amaze me," Ríonach murmured. "What in all the Realms is fate doing with the likes of you? I shudder to think what the future will hold."

She turned to me. "What about you? Have you experienced any new powers emerging? Anything out of the usual?"

"Noooo?" I replied questioningly. I had no idea what she was getting at.

"I think your sister may be developing a new Inheritance. Dragons are...a class all their own. To speak with one, or to train them, or ride them...that's unheard of. Fireheart is a rare creature. He is the last of his kind, but skye dragons belong to another world. Nobody knows where they came from. They just appeared." She sighed, staring out at the wind. "In all my years, I have never seen skye dragons hover like that."

Huxley was making her way toward us. "Ríonach!" she called in greeting. "Nobody told me you were coming."

"Didn't you hear the hullabaloo when I pulled up?" Ríonach laughed.

"No, I work nights most of the time. I was sound asleep in my hammock, dreaming of flying. I only woke up when I heard Ember's scream."

Ríonach pulled Huxley into a tight hug, and a thousand words seemed to pass in the span of a moment. "I miss you," Ríonach said at last. "When are you coming home?"

"When the queen is dead, I will be by your side in an instant," Huxley replied. "I cannot until she is gone. She'd kill me as soon as I set foot in the *proper* Realms."

Ríonach scoffed and rolled her eyes. "I tire of Realms and politics. Why can't we just be at peace?"

"Now you see why she thinks I am a bad influence," Huxley snorted. "Heaven forbid the heir's best friend thinks that fighting is stupid."

Ríonach pulled her into another hug. "I miss you," she repeated.

Huxley hugged her back. "I miss you, too. More than words can say."

The crew was a flurry of movement around us. Theron and Raz had landed on the ship and were helping with the work. Weapons were put away, and they had begun to clean up the wreckage.

Faolan was making repairs, singing new wood around the damage, while Verity chewed out the archer who had failed to keep his arrow under control. The poor crew member looked green with guilt.

"I have to go help," Huxley said after a moment. "I'll talk to you later, okay?"

"All right, try not to have too much fun without me out here on the skies."

"Fun? Me? Never," Huxley replied sarcastically as she walked away.

Ríonach turned back to me. "I have never known *anyone* who could talk to skye dragons. Even Hemming cannot speak with them."

"What does it mean?" I asked, watching as Evadne began to scale a rope ladder to get closer to the dragons.

"It confirms what you are," Ríonach replied softly. "The manifestation of two gifts only cements you are the ones of the prophecy. The powers your siblings display, also confirm how important you *all* are." She still didn't look at me. "Jack should not have sent you here," she said, shaking her head. "They'll kill him for it, and traitor that I am,

I hope the prince catches up with you, if only so Jack will not suffer...after all we've been through, I cannot bear to watch him be tortured so. The Realm will crumble, but in what way...for what cause, I cannot yet discern." She looked at me then, electric green eyes piercing down to my trembling heart. "Pledge allegiance to Winter," she said suddenly. "Pledge allegiance to my claim to the throne. I will help you get your father back. We will rescue your sister, and together we can all stop the evil that rises...we can change the fate of the Realm."

My heart pulled painfully in my chest. If I pledged allegiance to Winter, it would put Artemis and I on opposite sides of the world. We could never be together then. Not when he was destined to rule Summer. If I pledged allegiance to her, it would destroy all chances of finding another way to survive that didn't end at the Last Gate. To pledge allegiance before I knew of my options, would destroy my chance of saving Evadne from that fate as well.

"I don't know," I whispered. "Ríonach, I trust you with my life. I trust you, but I can't make any decisions right now. I just can't. I'm sorry. Jacques wanted us to come here, and I have to see this through. And..."

"Artemis," Ríonach finished, her eyes probing mine.

I nodded, tears welling in my eyes. "I think my path leads back to him..."

"If he is your choice, then so be it. But you must decide for yourself what you want," Ríonach replied soothingly.

"Am I traitor if I go back to him?"

"No, not if it is your choice." There was a deep sadness buried in her eyes. "Though I fear for you, for what the future holds. I cannot hold my silence on my fears. Child, I doubt the truth of the summer prince's affection."

"What do you mean?"

"After what happened...after what Uledia did to him, I'm not sure he could ever truly love again... Perhaps I am wrong, but if I am not, I would spare you that heartache. If you come with me, you can save your heart before he shatters it. We will be sisters and friends when this war is over."

"We will be sisters and friends when this war is over regardless of where this takes me," I replied quietly. "You will always be my friend, Ríonach."

"I know, but I fear for you. I fear for what Babushka saw in the bones."

"What did she see?"

"The prince's name will be on your lips as you fall," she replied, staring down at the rope in her hands. "I do not wish such an end upon you. I wish to find a way to stop the rising flood. I wish to save all of us from the darkness the monarchs have drawn to our doors." She began to untie her rig. "Think on my offer at least. You do not have to pledge now, but perhaps there will come a time when I may have such an honor. You are yet unmarked; there is still hope."

"Why don't you just mark me, if you want my allegiance so badly?"

"It doesn't work like that," Ríonach replied. "A monarch's mark means you are compelled to follow orders given by the monarchs, but especially by the one who gave it. It was agreed that, since Jack was marked by Winter and Faye by Summer, you two would be unmarked till the magic claimed you. So as to not influence the claim, it is a...subpar attempt to not twist the prophecy. I could mark you if I so pleased, but I would spare you that trial. I want your oath willingly, not by compulsion. An oath given willingly before the claiming, tells the magic how to claim. A marking given before the claiming influences the claim, but it is not an absolute surefire way of getting you to that Court."

Evadne was clambering back down the ladder. "Are you leaving?" she called, interrupting our conversation.

"Yes, I must away," Ríonach replied sadly. "I have already tarried too long." Much to my surprise, she wrapped me in a hug. "Fly well, daughter of Grimm," she whispered. "May you follow the threads of fate and evade her twisted plots. Even if you do not join me, you are still a sister and my friend."

Tears rushed to my eyes at those words. It was an honor to become so trusted by this fearless warrior.

Ríonach wrapped Evadne in a tight hug. "No more petting zoo," she said sternly. "I mean it. Find a different hobby. Maybe you should take up origami, or perhaps knitting."

"Knitting is fun," Evadne replied, laughing. "You get to stab things."

"See, knitting it is," Ríonach replied as she got into her boat.

A large black raven landed on the rope ladder beside us as we watched Ríonach's ship sail out across the sky, getting smaller and smaller with every moment.

Is that the bird from the Moores? Erebus?

The raven took a deep breath and then screeched. "Shadows loom, on edge of ruins, prince of vengeance, comes for you."

YUP. Stupid Moores raven has decided to once again ruin my day.

Go away Erebus, I do not have the energy for you today, or for your stupid, cryptic warnings.

44

Constellations Of Sorrow

EMBER

"My heart is a cathedral. Windows, ghosts, and lovers sit and sing in the dark, arched marrow of me."
-Segovia Amil

I was exhausted, but I couldn't sleep. Evadne was sleeping, but it hardly seemed restful. She tossed and turned, whispering Marcus' name as she begged him to stay with her.

If it wasn't for me, she would still be with him.

The rest of the dayshift crew slept soundly, unheeding of her nightmares or my insomnia.

I need some fresh air.

Careful not to wake anyone, I slipped on my boots and my cloak and made my way out to the deck in search of the stars and the cool night air.

My heart was a tangle of emotions. Ríonach's words ran a frantic loop around my memory as I tried not to think about Artemis. His confession on that beach had made it seem as if he was over Uledia, but what if he wasn't? What if Ríonach was right?

"You should be sleeping."

I jumped at the sound of Huxley's voice. She was lounging on the railing on the deck above me, watching the skye dragons as they hovered around the ship, sleeping.

She laughed quietly, turning her attention away from the dragons. "My, you startle easily."

"I was under the impression I was alone," I muttered, annoyed at having been surprised.

"You're never alone here, Evadne. A ship never sleeps, not truly. Someone must watch over her even as she herself rests. Care to join me? I'll show you some of the Moores' constellations."

"Sure," I replied as I made my way toward the ladder. My fear was a background noise, and I pushed it aside. By now, being out in the open was nothing new. It was only when I was up in the rigging or near the edge that it tried to take control.

"See up there?" Huxley said, pointing to a grouping of stars. "That's the lovers. Legend has it a Fey fell in love with a mortal. He loved her every moment of her brief life and no magic he poured into her could keep her alive. When death claimed her, he took his own life and the Moores' magic bound them to the stars—where they are finally together for eternity."

She pointed to another grouping. "The sisters. Twins, light and dark, bound by love but separated by fate. They fought to protect each other, and in the end, they died to protect each other. Over there, are the brothers. Myth has it they fought the rising tide of evil, but darkness still took them, and in death the magic snatched their life threads and bound them to the skies to protect the Realm. On the far side, way over there, is where the darkness *should* be."

"Should be?"

"Yes, it disappeared nine solstices ago." Huxley shrugged, nonchalant. "The Moores are ever changing—it does what it pleases. Who am I to question why it destroys a constellation? Perhaps the evil has finally been done away with."

"What was the lore behind the constellation?" I asked, almost afraid to hear the answer.

"The Darkness was created by the Knight as he attempted to escape. The monarchs bound it, intent on using it to kill the Grimms when they strayed too far from the Realm...gave away too many of the secrets to mortals..." her voice trailed off, full of sorrow. "It was a great evil that could not be stopped, so it was bound with Darke magic and exiled to the skies, where it continues to seek its revenge on the Realm for containing it."

A shiver ran down my spine at her words and I was certain that such an evil was one I never wanted to encounter.

"The rulers are over on the other horizon. They were the ones who sought to make a difference, whose hearts were broken in the tainted process and whose fates were tied to the ever-burning constellations. Over by the sisters is the weaver. The weaver is the one who wove destinies and stole fates. He was exiled to the stars, where he can only reweave the galaxies and stars. It's why our skies are never really the same, no matter how we try to say they are. The last one of notable importance is the flower-singer—the maiden of tragedy, whose story holds naught but heartbreak. She fled to the stars for relief from her bleeding soul, but the tragedy followed her there."

"I'm sensing a theme," I commented dryly.

"What was in our stars that destined us for sorrow?" Huxley quoted, staring up at the skies. "Our stories are all bound by tragedy in some way or another."

"What is your story with Ríonach?" I asked, unable to contain myself.

Huxley sighed, "I'll need a cup of coffee for that story, perhaps a cookie too."

"I could go for coffee," I piped up happily.

Huxley laughed. "Do you ever sleep, child? If you drink that enchanted brew, you'll be up for another fourteen hours."

"It's the best coffee I've ever had. I might as well enjoy it while I can."

"You're not wrong about that. Come on, let's get some coffee and then I'll share my story."

After coffee and cookies had been acquired, Huxley and I made our way back to the upper deck where we both sat on the wide beam of the railing.

"Ríonach and I were born around the same time. My mother was her nursemaid, so we grew up together. She was like a sister to me and my best friend in the whole Realm. Nightshade, however, considered me a liability to her precious daughter's reign." Huxley pointed to the scars on her face. "She gave me these when she exiled me. That was before Ríonach was attacked and turned. She and I have kept contact through the mirrors. The moment her mother dies, Doyle and I will return to the Realm."

"Who's Doyle?" I asked. The name didn't sound familiar at all.

"My husband," Huxley replied with a quiet laugh. "He's off on a scouting mission for Verity. We're picking him up tomorrow."

"What do you mean when you say you keep contact through the mirrors?" I asked.

"It's a very old form of magic. There are two forms, one-way and two-way. Two-way mirror communication is where you and the other person talk. It generally only works in the Fey Realm as a whole. One way is the means by which you can spy on someone without their knowing."

A chill ran down my spine. "Could Artemis be spying on me while I'm on the ship?"

"No, there are certain spells interwoven on the ship that block such forms of magic. Nobody can spy on anyone on this ship." She wiggled her eyebrows. "But you can still spy on others. Do you want to see your prince?"

I hesitated, pondering the question. "Yes," I said at last.

Huxley grinned and took a small, handheld mirror out of her pocket and handed it to me. "Think about your prince and repeat after me. Use the same sort of concentration and power you do when you're summoning your Inheritance."

I nodded, fingers trembling.

"*Ostende mihi, corporis delictum,*" Huxley said in a clear voice.

"*Ostende Mihi, corporis delictum,*" I repeated softly, picturing those bright green eyes in my mind. Something pulled deep in my gut, and the surface of the mirror began to swirl until at last, Artemis' troubled face came into focus. He was talking with someone, but the words were too far away. He looked upset, desperate even as he spoke.

"Your prince is a handsome one," Huxley teased.

"He's not mine," I protested weakly, staring at those emerald-green depths. I was enamored; I couldn't look away. There was something surprisingly vulnerable about him in this light. I could scrutinize him all I wished without his knowledge, without him returning my stare. I missed him, I couldn't deny it. I missed him terribly.

I don't think I made the right choice to leave him. I want him by my side...but I want my sister safe, too.

"There's no need to deny it. I can see it in your eyes. You care greatly for him, but you're conflicted in that care."

I nodded, disheartened.

"It's all right, child. If you're meant to be, it'll happen."

Suddenly, Artemis' attention focused intently on me. He was staring at me through the mirror.

I jerked, shoving the looking glass back into Huxley's hands.

"He can sense you, but he can't see you," Huxley said soothingly. She moved a hand over the glass. "*Corporis deletum*," she said quietly.

She handed me the small mirror. "Here, I have others. Hang on to this. Maybe it'll help you figure out what it is you truly want."

I want Artemis, but I don't want to die at the Gate. I want the best of both worlds...I want what is impossible.

The confession came unbidden, and I shoved it away. It was a wish I couldn't bear to think about, not when everything in the Realm sought to destroy any shred of happiness I might take for myself.

45

Run Little Bird, The Darkness Comes

EMBER

"There is hope, but not for us."
-Franz Kafka

By the time the sun rose, Huxley and I had consumed six cups of coffee, and she had taught me how to do a front flip off the railing. It would probably be safe to say we were both starting off the day punch drunk and high on just a little too much sugar from the copious number of sweets we had consumed.

Huxley was pulling an all-nighter, since we would soon reach the island to pick up her husband. She was practically vibrating with excitement when, after breakfast, the boat began to descend toward an island covered in trees and fog.

"I don't remember there being fog on the island," Verity commented, scrutinizing the landscape. "You can barely see the dock. Doyle's ship is there, but he's not on it."

"Do you think it's a trap?" Theron asked warily.

"I don't know, but we'd best proceed with caution." She turned to Huxley, who was excitedly bouncing over toward us. "Huxley, I want you with us. Nyra, Nikos, mind the ship and keep the archers at the ready. I don't like this. There's something wrong."

Huxley's exuberant energy immediately died, and a calm warrior took its place. "Yes, ma'am," she replied, drawing her sword.

"Try to get ahold of him through the mirror; see what's happening."

Huxley nodded and pulled a small, silver mirror out of her pocket.

My coffee was quickly wearing off, and a sense of foreboding began to grow. There was indeed something off about the whole situation, but I couldn't put my finger on what it was that bothered me.

"Huxley, have you managed to get ahold of him?" Verity asked after a few moments of Huxley staring at her mirror.

Huxley shook her head, eyebrows scrunched in worry. "I can feel his heartbeat—he's here. But it's far away, almost a nonexistent echo."

"Right then, we treat this as hostile territory until we have proven otherwise. Ember, Evadne, stick to your people and do not deviate. We will stay together until we reach Doyle. Am I understood?"

"Yes ma'am!" the crew chorused.

Verity pursed her lips, staring out across the dense fog. "I don't like this," she said, frustrated. "I don't like it one bit."

Hours passed as we carefully attempted to navigate the foggy island and find Doyle. Verity's compass wouldn't work the moment we set foot on the island. It just spun and spun. The fog was so thick, the only course of action left was to hold onto each other, while the last person held onto a long rope that was tied to the ship. Holding onto each other instead of a rope ensured we knew where the next person was. That way, if something happened and somebody got hurt, we'd know immediately.

Given the circumstances, it was unsafe to call for him, so we followed Huxley's senses through the treacherous, shrouded landscape. She could sense him, but the connection between their bonded heartbeats was faint enough it had us all worried.

"Over here," Huxley's voice called at last.

Everyone raced forward.

A man's bloodied and battered body was collapsed in the dirt.

"Curse it to the Gate," Verity swore angrily. "He's half dead."

Huxley was sobbing, gathering him into her arms as Theron tried to find the worst wound.

An unnatural silence fell around us as they tried to draw him back to consciousness.

"Come on baby, come on," Huxley whispered desperately. "Just talk to me. Just open your eyes. Please, please, please, just talk to me."

"We need to get him back to the ship," Verity said urgently. "It could be a trap."

Doyle's eyes fluttered, and he groaned. "Hux, is that you?" he muttered. "Please, don't be here. Don't let it be her...by the Gate, don't let it be her..."

"It's me," Huxley murmured as she bent over him, cradling his head in her hands. "It's okay, I'm right here, Doyle. I'm right here. It's okay, I'm right here."

"Run," Doyle gasped raggedly. "Run Hux. It's coming."

"Theron, put him on your back. The rest of you, form a circle. We go out in a defensive stance."

"Yes ma'am," the crew chorused in a whisper.

It was then that the trees around us started to weep blood.

"What the—" Theron growled.

"No," I whispered. "No, it can't be."

"What is it?" Verity asked sharply.

"The monster," I gasped. "It's here."

"What do you mean?"

A terrible screech, like nails on a chalkboard, echoed around us. The crew jerked, covering their ears with their hands, desperately trying to block out the sinister noise.

"We have to run!" I cried frantically.

"What's coming?"

"The creature from my nightmares," I hissed. "Verity, it haunted my dreams. I know what this is. We have to get out of here, or it's going to kill all of us!"

"Let's move!" Verity yelled. "Theron, you take the lead and set the pace for what you can manage. I want everyone on guard; we follow the rope and get back to the ship."

"Sparks, can you give us some light?" Theron grunted as he hauled Doyle across his shoulders. "Maybe you can burn some of the fog away."

I nodded and summoned my Inheritance, trying to provide the best light possible as we began to go back.

The rope went slack, and then, the severed end reached my fingertips.

"Oh no," I whispered.

"Verity, the rope's been cut," Theron yelled.

Verity swore. "Find the other end," she ordered.

Evadne and I began to frantically search. My locket was burning against my chest.

Please don't let it be here. Please don't let that monster be here.

Please just let it be a coincidence.

The other end of the rope was nowhere to be found.

"All right then, change of plans," Verity barked. "Keep forward, and watch your steps. We'll have to reach an edge eventually. When we do, we'll follow it until we reach the dock."

"Got it," Theron grunted. "I'm going to set a faster pace for as long as I can. Tell the crew to keep up."

He began to jog, and the crew kept a steady pace behind, holding onto each other so no one got lost.

We continued for another five minutes before the hand holding mine jerked and wrenched away from me.

"Theron!" I yelled, as a scream echoed out through the stillness behind us.

Theron stopped. "Roll call!" he yelled.

There was no answer, only the unnatural silence.

"ROLL CALL!" he roared.

Still nothing but silence.

Theron gently lay Doyle's body on the ground. "Sparks, you need to protect him," he said urgently. "Evadne, guard her back. I have to find my crew. Keep your fire lit, and if anything comes at you, you torch it, no questions asked. Am I understood?"

I nodded, terrified. "I don't want you to go," I whispered raggedly. "Theron, I'm scared. I need you."

"I know, and that's okay. It's okay to be scared. But you have to do it scared. You can do this; I believe in you."

"I don't know how to do it scared," I gasped. "This monster has killed me in my dreams, over and over."

"I won't let it hurt you, okay? Dreams are just dreams. You have the power here, you don't in your dreams."

I was trembling. "I don't know if I can," I choked.

"You keep that fire lit, and you keep making noise, do you understand me? Burn the fog away and protect Doyle. He's bleeding, so whatever this is, it will be able to track you."

I don't think it's after Doyle...I think it's after me.

The locket Marcovester Red had given me was burning against my chest, so cold I was sure it was giving me frostbite.

I can't do this Theron, I can't do this.

"You can do this," Theron said gently. "I have to find the crew."

I nodded, fighting back tears as I urged my Inheritance to burn brighter around my hands. It flared a bright, vibrant orange.

"That's the spirit," Theron said encouragingly, and then he was gone.

Doyle was delirious, crying and yelling about shadows and darkness.

"I'm scared," Evadne whispered as she pressed her back against mine.

"Me too," I replied, hands shaking and teeth chattering.

There was no sound in the dense fog, and the longer Theron was gone, the thicker it became.

Something hissed in front of us and my adrenaline spiked as I pulled Doyle tighter against my chest, determined to protect him.

I will protect you. I won't let the monster harm you. I won't let it harm you.

Something was solidifying in the fog, a dark shadow that smelled of decaying flowers and water rot.

My flames roared higher in my hands.

I will not be afraid. I will not be afraid. I will fight this monster, and I will not be afraid. I have the advantage here.

My terror intensified as the details began to form.

Wake up, wake up. Maybe I've just been dreaming this whole time. Wake up!

Evadne gasped in horror.

"Guard our back," I said steadily, trying to control the sound of my voice and stay calm. "I've got the front. Don't look. Just keep your eyes behind us, so nothing can sneak up on us. Okay?"

"Okay," Evadne whispered.

"Don't look, okay?" I repeated.

"Okay," Evadne gasped, her voice trembling.

Theron where are you? We need you!

The monster continued to rise, and I decided it was better to act instead of waiting any longer. I urged my fire into a roaring inferno, creating a shield between us and the creature.

It drew back with a shriek of rage, and I poured more energy into the fire until it was a circular wall around us.

The monster's vague silhouette bounced against the flames, testing for weak spots.

Not today. You will not hurt us. I won't let you!

This is not my nightmare. I can fight you! I will not let you hurt us!

Claws pushed through my flames and the monster screamed in agony as I urged my fire to burn hotter and hotter.

Protect us. Incinerate the beast.

Theron where are you! Help us!! It's here!

My thoughts were quickly becoming a jumbled storm of panic and fear. Soon the wall was quivering.

It's going to give if I don't focus and control my fear.

I took a deep breath and blew it out through my nose as slowly as I could manage. In, out, in, out. I forced my breaths to return back to normal. Evadne's hand was on my shoulder, helping ground my emotions.

In my mind's eye, Artemis stood beside me, sword drawn as he glared at the beast. 'That's it, my Flamín,' he said encouragingly. 'Deep breaths, just stay steady. You can do this, okay?'

"Okay," I whispered to my phantom prince. "Okay. It's going to be okay."

The monster's arm was flaming now, its cloak set ablaze as blood seeped across the ground in a rising river.

You will not pass. I won't let you harm him.

Suddenly, in a desperate move, the monster stopped moving slowly and plunged its whole arm in. Razor sharp claws sliced deep into my chest. The wall wavered as I fought against the pain, but it held.

My phantom Artemis was yelling. His words were indecipherable, but his meaning was clear. Hold on. Just. *Hold. On.*

Evadne sliced at the arm as it reached for Doyle's unconscious figure.

I urged more and more into the flames and the monster drew back.

Relief crashed through me. We were going to make it.

Just hold it a little longer. We're going to make it through. It's going to be okay.

"Just hold on, my Flamín. You're doing great, just hold on a little longer. Help will *come."*

Where are you? Where are you? Help me!

My flames roared in pride at his words. Claws raced through the wall all at once and grabbed me around the throat, hauling me to my feet. Doyle's body fell from my arms as I kicked and struggled.

"Run little bird, run," the monster screamed in my mind.

"Ember!" Evadne screamed.

My flames spluttered and died.

"EMBER!" Artemis' phantom voice roared in my mind.

The claws were so tight around my throat I couldn't breathe, let alone scream.

I swung my arm, and the knives hidden in the forearm of my armor whizzed out and sliced into the monster's throat.

It drew back with a shriek, dropping me, as black, rancid puss poured out of the wound. I drew my sword, and the edge burst into flames as I swung it at the monster, desperate to protect us.

Get back!

I will not let you harm me. I will not let you harm the ones I love!

Help us! Help us! Somebody help us!

Evadne lunged at the monster with her sword, throwing a wave of water at it with the strike, trying to push it back.

The monster lunger at her, backhanding her across the face and sending her flying.

"Evadne!" I screamed.

The monster lunged for Doyle's body, and I slashed, trying to shove it back. It didn't do any good. The monster batted away my sword, unheeding of the razor-sharp edge. Claws closed around my throat again, but its other hand closed around Doyle's and lifted us both off the ground.

Doyle spluttered and wheezed, his body limp in the monster's grasp.

I desperately called my Inheritance back. Raising my hands, I poured a wave of fire over the creature.

C'mon, c'mon. Why isn't this working? Why isn't the monster affected by the flames??

Air was quickly becoming a desperate necessity as the monster's claws cut into my skin. Blood was pouring from Doyle's throat.

Evadne was on her feet again, running at us with weapons drawn.

The monster lowered its head to Doyle's throat, its mouth wide and full of razor-sharp fangs.

NO!

I slashed again, intensifying the blast of fire.

Evadne was throwing her daggers, one after the other, but the mortal blows didn't faze the creature.

Blood spurted from Doyle's neck and the monster dropped his body, laughing.

Evadne and I both drove our swords into its body, but it only laughed harder as blood poured from its maw.

No, no, no!

The locket burned and burned against my skin, a raging inferno that I feared would melt the skin to the bone.

The monster drew back, hissing.

"Run little bird, run, the darkness comes..." it screamed as it again reached out. This time, it touched a single, curved talon to my undamaged collarbone.

NO!

The monster screeched and drew back, as if burned.

I threw the wall of fire at it. I knew it was pointless. The monster had been uncaring of my flames when I had tried so hard to protect Doyle.

"Ember!" Evadne yelled. She was desperately trying to staunch the flow of blood pouring from the gaping wound in Doyle's throat.

The fog was receding as the monster drew back, laughing.

My collarbone burned where its claw had touched me, but I paid it no mind as I urged the fire to burn higher and higher until it roared around us in what seemed an impenetrable dome. It was useless, but I had to try. The monster could still get through, but I had to try. My fire wasn't enough, but I had to *try*.

Tears streamed down my face as I stood sobbing, because I knew it was already too late. We had done everything we could. We had done our best and still it hadn't been enough.

Doyle lay dying in Evadne's arms, coughing and spluttering as crimson bubbled from his lips, his throat, his eyes.

"Hang on, Doyle, just hang on," I whispered.

But my desperate pleas fell on deaf ears. Doyle's ragged gasps had fallen silent.

He was gone.

46

A Mourning Of Dragons

EMBER

"There is something bleak and barren about a world that is missing the person who knows you best."
-Jodi Picoult

Sunset burned crimson against the horizon as we floated in the open air. Ten crew members had been slaughtered by the monster on the island. They had all been buried in its soil, as per their written wishes within the last will and testaments Verity kept stowed in the safe in her cabin. But now it was time for the final funeral of the day, and it was all I could do to breathe, let alone stand among the crew while my failure ate me alive.

Huxley knelt on the deck, draped over Doyle's lifeless body. Tears streamed down her face as she sobbed her goodbyes in a language I did not understand.

My fault. My fault. If I had just...done something. Done something different, something more...he would have made it. He would have made it.

This is all my fault, and I cannot bear the guilt.

The dragons hovered at a safe distance around our ship, so as to not disturb the vessel.

Verity laid a gentle hand on Huxley's shoulder and Huxley rose, still sobbing. She turned and motioned at me. "Ember," she called, a sob breaking the syllables apart. "Please."

No. I can't. Please, don't. I can't bear my failure. I can't bear what happened and my part in it.

"Please," she repeated gently.

I stumbled forward, my steps hesitant and afraid.

My fault. My fault. He would still be alive if I was a better warrior.

Verity held out a bow and arrow to Huxley, the end of which was wrapped in cloth. "Light it," Huxley whispered raggedly holding the arrow out to me. "Help me send him on."

"I can't," I whispered raggedly. Even if I wanted to, I couldn't. My Inheritance was nothing more than a shred that wept and writhed deep in my chest.

"It wasn't your fault, Ember," Huxley said gently. She handed the bow and arrow back to Verity and wrapped me in a tight hug. "It wasn't your fault," she repeated.

Tears streamed down my face. The dam of grief in my chest burst open and I wept against her shoulder. "I'm sorry," I sobbed. "I'm so sorry, Huxley. I did everything I could. I did *everything* and it wasn't enough. I fought that monster, I did *everything* I could, and it still wasn't enough. *Why wasn't it enough?*"

"I know," Huxley whispered, holding me close. "I know. Sometimes, even when we do everything, and we do our best, the odds are still stacked against us. It doesn't mean we failed, it just...it means that was the fate and destiny of the one we loved."

"But it was such a terrible way to go," I whispered raggedly. "I...I tried."

"I know," Huxley replied. "I know. I do not blame you, child. We dance across a tightrope with death every day on this vessel," she continued. "Death gave us many daring adventures that will be sung into legend. He knew the risk, as did I...and we regret nothing. My only sorrow is that we were not given more time together." She pulled back, forcing me to look her in the eye. "This guilt is not yours to carry. Do not bear it."

I nodded, still sobbing.

Huxley took the bow and arrow back from Verity. "Light it for me," she said softly. "Help me send him on."

Theron and Verity pushed the small lifeboat with Doyle's body out into the skies.

My hands trembled as I pulled at the fragile string of my Inheritance.

Come to me. Please. Come to me.

Orange flames burst across my fingertips, and I held out my hands to the arrow's tip. It caught fire and Huxley raised the bow, tears streaming down her face as she took aim.

The ship was in her sights, but she hesitated, trembling. "I love you," she whispered raggedly as she finally let the arrow fly.

The arrow's aim held true, and Huxley fell to her knees with a scream of grief as the small vessel erupted into flames.

The air was vibrating around us.

It's coming from the dragons.

They were singing.

Then, Evadne's voice cut through the silence. She sang quietly at first, eyes closed and voice trembling as she swayed in the rising breeze. "Farewell, farewell, farewell to thee. We mourn the loss, of a soul so free." Evadne's voice rose, gaining strength as she translated the dragon's song. "Heart of fire, you burned so bright. Always of courage, through darkest night. Bravery, honor, with a love so fierce. The widow stands weeping, with heartbeat pierced. Make death fear to take you, make her scared to come. Live your life with courage, burning bright as the fiery sun."

Now, Huxley and the crew had picked up the flowing tune and began to hum along. "Farewell, farewell, brave warrior of skies and wind, may death fear to take you, for in another life, we shall meet again."

Huxley's trembling alto joined Evadne's and together they repeated the last stanza as they held each other and wept.

"Farewell, farewell, brave warrior of skies and wind. May death fear to take you, for in another life, we shall meet again."

47

I Wish I Were A Monster, A Monster's Never Glum, Cuz How Could You Be Sad, When You Eat People Just For Fun?

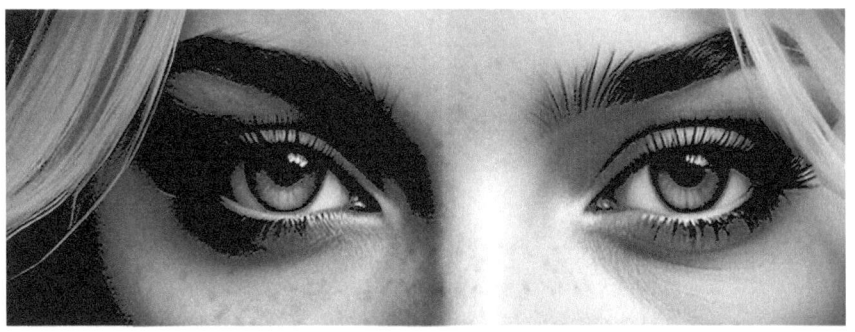

FAYE

"You have never had to steal my breath or take it away, somehow you
have always managed to convince me to hand it over freely."
-Tyler Knott Gregson

Training was put on hold while Meghan healed, and Ronan was nowhere to be found. After a week came and went and there was still no sign of him, I began to worry.

Did something happen? Did Jeremiah kill him? What if Jeremiah did something terrible to him?

He wouldn't. Would he?

We passed the time amicably. I read to her while she rested, but it was really for the intention of keeping myself awake. Every time I closed my eyes, we were back in that room, but this time Ronan didn't save her. This time, it all fell on me, and I was always too late. My fingers half an inch away from Jeremiah's neck, half a second too late as the bullet shattered her skull, or her heart. In the nightmares, I was always too late. I wept as I cradled her broken body while Ronan raged over me.

Finally, growing restless and bored, I decided to investigate what was behind the last door. Perhaps it would give me some sort of clue as to what was going on.

Meghan told me what was behind this door...but I can't for the life of me remember what it was.

You could just ask her again.

Yes, but then I'd look stupid. So we're not going to do that. We're going to be sneaky and find out for ourselves.

My three brain cells donned their black outfits, which had been dubbed 'the most sneakiest-sneaking garb.'

The lock was easy enough to pick and soon I was through—much to the ever-growing glee of my brain cells. It was immensely pleasing to me that human locks were child's play. They were nothing compared to the magical locks that were used within the Realm.

This would be the worst time to discover this is where they keep their dead bodies.

That is a disgusting thought.

Then this would probably be a really bad time to think about how large the possibility is that a spider will run across my hand.

YES! This is absolutely the wrong time!

I had opted to leave the light off in Meghan's room, so as to not give myself away. I was beginning to wonder if that was a mistake as I slowly crawled through the room on my hands and knees, fingers desperately groping and searching.

Where am I??

My eyes were slowly beginning to adjust, and soon vague, dark shapes began to form around me.

Something creaked and I froze, listening.

This was a very, very bad idea. What if there's something terrible in here?

If there was something terrible in here, why would it be connected to Meghan's room?

Fair point.

It's probably just the building moving...or a monster deep in the underground...

OR it could just be the earth shifting and moving. Stop thinking about monsters, sheesh!

It was a point of comfort to me that the earth shifted and moved, even as its inhabitants slept. It breathed in and out, deep within, both in the Fey and Mortal Realm.

I inched forward, trying not to think about spiders, or bodies, and my fingers touching disgusting, terrible things.

A light flicked on, and I froze, momentarily blinded while my eyes tried to adjust. The room fell into sharp focus as I finally managed to clear the dark spots out of my vision.

A dresser, a bookshelf, a nightstand with the cursedly bright lamp. A bed, and sitting upon the bed, a shirtless Ronan, who stared at me in sleepy confusion and annoyance.

"Faye...what on earth are you doing?" His face darkened for a moment. "You're not trying to escape, are you?" he hissed.

"Don't be ridiculous," I snapped quietly as I turned back and closed the door leading into Meghan's room. I didn't want to wake her, and I had half a mind to chew Ronan out.

"I haven't seen you in a week, a *week*!" I whispered angrily as I turned back to him. "You were in here sleeping and you didn't even bother to stop in to let me know you were okay? That is not cool, Ronan! I was worried sick! I didn't know if—"

My words stopped abruptly as I finally noticed Ronan's disheveled state. "What happened?" I gasped in horror. I was moving before I realized what I was doing. "What did he do to you?" I whispered, my fingers trailing down his swollen cheek.

Ronan pulled back sharply, shocked for a moment, and then closed his eyes and leaned into the touch for the briefest moment.

"I thought something terrible happened to you," I scolded. "Why didn't you at least let us know you were okay?"

"I didn't want to worry Megs," Ronan said, his voice bleak. "I didn't want her to see what happened and get upset."

"What did happen?" I asked, sitting down on the bed beside him.

Ronan hung his head and massaged the back of his neck wearily. "He punished me, like he said he would. But the only thing I learned is the continued lesson that my father is an abusive psychopath."

"We're running out of time," I said softly as I leaned back and absentmindedly examined the intricate tattoo on his shoulder blade. "What's the symbolism behind the ink?" I asked, unable to help myself.

It was layers upon layers of images, all woven within each other. A lighthouse, a phoenix, a wolf, a lion, a compass, an anchor, a woman's eye, a rose, swirls of shadow, rays of light, ravens and wings, hands reaching for each other, the phases of the moon, a tree with roots that trailed down his ribcage. The closer I looked, the more I saw.

"I got it while I was in nursing school," Ronan replied. "I had to be away from Meghan at that time, and I was worried sick about what my father would do to her while I was gone. I'd go through my day, terrified that when I called to check on her that night, it wouldn't be her voice that answered the phone. Finally, she told me to use the credit card Jeremiah sent with me for expenses for something incredibly stupid, but meaningful all at once. She suggested I get my eyebrow pierced, and when I balked at that, she insisted on a tattoo. So, I told her if I was going to get one, it had to have meaning. So, she wrote down everything she could think of, and I did too, and what each piece meant. It's the light and dark of me, fighting against each other as I try to become who I'm meant to be. It's the bits of pieces of myself, and my story, and what I want to be...what I aim to be..." His voice trailed off, and he swallowed. "Megs would tell me that every time I felt afraid, to look in the mirror at that tattoo. Look, and remember that everything was going to be okay. That I was going to get through nursing school and the additional training Jeremiah had laid out for me...and then I was going to come home to her. That the ink was a reminder she would always be waiting for me, and things were going to be okay."

"I had a saying," I whispered. The words slipped out before I could consider what I was about to share with him. "When I was trapped...there..." I was afraid to speak of the Realm, lest it mark me, but I could tell by the look in his eyes that Ronan knew exactly what I was talking about. "I had a saying...a phrase that an unlikely friend gave me to help me be brave. I would whisper to myself in that darkness, to keep me alive and grounded when I thought I wasn't going to make it. I would say, 'I am Faye Narah Grimm. I am a wolf with a lion's heart, and I will not be afraid.' I don't know why, but it helped me keep going."

Ronan nodded. "It makes sense."

"We're running out of time," I repeated, changing the subject. We had to talk about this before Meghan woke up. "If I continue to train your sister, we're likely going to lose our window. She's as ready as she can be, but if we tarry much longer...Jeremiah will kill her."

Ronan shuddered. "I should have run faster."

"I should have snapped his neck," I countered. "I should have killed him then and there."

"I'm glad you didn't. If he was telling the truth about Marcov, then we'd really be in trouble. Marcov wouldn't have hesitated to kill Meghan. He's just as psychotic as Jeremiah."

"Meghan tried to protect me," I said softly. "Even though she was the one in danger. She's so incredibly brave."

"I know," Ronan agreed ruefully as he gave me a crooked smile. "Sometimes you'd remind me of her, and it was shocking to remember you two had never actually met."

I laughed, cheered by the thought.

Has his smile always made me feel so light and fluffy?

Fluffy? Good grief, girl! Get ahold of yourself! We admire nothing and accept no fluffy feelings. None. Nothing. Zilch. Nada. He is your kidnapper, who, I will remind you, you have decided to loathe for all eternity.

At this thought, the three brain cells rioted. Unbeknownst to me, they had apparently decided to fall head over heels for the man.

It was then that fate decided to throw a wrench in our lovely little stolen moment of time and insert a monster.

I had been so absorbed in our conversation, and so stupidly enamored by his smile, that I failed to notice how the shadows were growing at the edges of the room.

Crap.

I yanked Ronan down off the bed just as the shadowy creature lunged at him.

Double crap. This is not supposed to be happening.

Ronan scrambled back, eyes wide as the shadows lengthened, growing claws and fangs and lashing out at us, shoving us this way and that.

"What the freaking heck," he yelled. "I have to get to Meghan!"

"No!" I shouted, summoning my Inheritance with a snap of my fingers. "If you go in there, it will likely expand the territory. We have to keep it in here. Besides, Drysdyne guards under her bed. He will protect her."

"How do we keep it here?" Ronan asked desperately.

"Entertain it," I hissed as I shot a bolt of lightning at what appeared to be the face.

The monster ducked, laughing, and I swore under my breath. It was a smart monster.

"What do you want?" I called, trying to goad it out.

A hissing cackle filled the room. "I wish to devour the human; I want the flesh stripped from his bones. I want to eat every bloody morsel."

"Do you enjoy your life as a monster?" I pressed, monologuing as I spun in quick circles, searching for the heart.

"I enjoy my existence quite often. It is tender and sweet; the screams warm my icy soul. He has promised to give me my fill of such delicacies if only I heed his call and lend him my strength. If I aid in the rise, he will give me the children without the interference of the cursed thieves."

Yeah, those thieves are there for a reason, you dumb shadow. They keep idiots like you in line.

"That sounds *so* delightful," I muttered as lightning crackled across my fingertips.

Oh, how I wish I had a dagger. Who is the illusive he?

I think we both know the answer to that question—we just don't quite want to actually acknowledge it.

Nope. Not one teeny-tiny, solitary bit.

I aimed another reckless bolt, guessing, and once again missed.

I think this counts as a monster going rogue. Where is my assigned Shadowthief?!

"Faye!" Ronan warned as he shoved me out of the way. A tendril sliced past my ear and slammed into Ronan's shoulder, dragging him back.

A mouth was opening along the wall, razor sharp fangs materializing on a monstrously deformed face.

Ope. There's what I'm looking for.

"Faye!" Ronan yelled.

I waited. I had one shot. I had to wait for the monster to materialize more.

Almost there.

"Faaaaye!" he screeched in terror.

Be patient, you impatient human.

Make him wait longer. He sounds like a little girl when he screeches like that.

Your opinion, while right, is not appreciated. We tarry only for the purpose of killing the monster.

"FAYE!" Ronan screamed as the monster's mouth opened over his head.

There's the little girl screech!

I released the bolt, striking the monster through the heart.

The monster screamed, its body dissolving into a pool of hungry, poisonous shadows.

I lunged in front of Ronan, taking the flood of shadows into my palm, shielding him from the residual echoes of evil.

I have it in me already. That's what's in the serum.

I swayed, and Ronan's arms encircled me just as my knees buckled.

He looked down at me in horrified amazement. "Thanks."

"You know, based on what the monster said, it might be fun to be a monster…" I replied deliriously. "Hey, there's this song the girls used to sing…it was about a glow worm…but I think it works better for a monster." I cleared my throat and began to sing in a warbling, off kilter key. "I wish I were a monster, a monster's never glum, 'cuz how could you be sad, when you eat people just for fun?"

A slow, patronizing clapping filled the room, and I rolled my head sideways, half fearing to see Jeremiah there, exposing our whole charade. But it was only Ryver. "Ten points for creativity, my dear, but you need to work on your vocals a little more."

"Gee," I coughed. "It's not like I just got done doing *your* job."

My accusation hung in the air between us and Ryver raised his hands in surrender. "Fair enough, Faye, fair enough. But I'll have you know I was trying to get in here the moment my senses started tingling. Something was blocking me."

"I didn't know you could be blocked," I mumbled.

"I didn't either," Ryver seethed.

"I'm sorry, who are you?" Ronan asked, confused. "And…how did you get in here?"

"I'm a magical Fey, come to steal your shadow," Ryver replied, giving Ronan a toothy grin.

Ronan looked as if he was fighting the urge to step back.

"Uhm, no thank you?" he said after a moment. "I…I don't know what I'm using my shadow for, but…I think I'll keep it."

"Hence the term *steal*," Ryver replied sarcastically.

"Ryver, you're not allowed to steal his shadow," I panted, trying to find air. The room was incredibly hot and stuffy and oxygen was suddenly a precious commodity.

"Fine, I'll just think about stealing it," Ryver replied, his eyes crinkling with laughter.

"Now, for introductions," I rambled. "Ryver, this is Ronan. Ronan, Ryver. Ryver is my Shadowthief, Ronan is my human. I expect you two to behave and become best friends."

Ryver arched an eyebrow. "My, how the tables have turned my lionhearted girl. Last I checked, you hated him."

"Not anymore," I sighed, staring up at the constellations painted on Ronan's ceiling as I leaned back against his chest. "It's more of a quiet sort of loathing now, tinged with our mutual hatred of his father and a wee bit of anarchy and treason. Maaaybe a bit of a schoolgirl crush because of his alluring smile…it makes me feel fluffy."

"Is she okay?" Ronan asked, clearly shaken. "She's…not acting like herself."

"No, she's not. She just took a very potent dose of shadows. It's going to kill her in a moment."

"WHAT?!" Ronan yelled.

Not so loud, Ronan, my dear, sweet, brave, strong Ronan…Ronan who screeches like a girl…my head hurts so much right now. Please don't yell in my ear.

"Never fear, the Shadowthief at last is here," Ryver said ruefully.

"Anaaarchy and treeeeason…" I whisper-sang, trying to find my air. Everything felt heavy around me, and I was quite certain I was going to regret this particular moment in time when I was myself again.

"You always had a soft spot for anarchy and treason." Ryver chuckled as he sat down on the floor beside us. "Here, let me take the shadows out."

"Noooooo," I moaned angrily. "That hurts worse than all of Ronan's infernal medical poking."

"It'll kill you," Ryver lectured.

"It'll kill you," I mocked back in my best imitation of Ryver's voice.

Ryver rolled his eyes, a smile twitching at the corner of his lips, as he took my hand in his. "Hold her," he instructed Ronan.

"Don't boss *my* human around," I snapped.

"Don't worry, you can go back to bossing him after I've got the poison out."

"So, the shadows she…somehow absorbed…its poison?" Ronan asked, trying to put the pieces together.

"Yes," Ryver replied tightly, his eyebrows scrunched together in concentration. "You're pretty quick for a human."

I was beginning to squirm in Ronan's grasp. My hand was all sorts of pain and spasming discomfort. Ryver's shadow exorcism was making my whole body cramp up and ache.

"Let me go," I hissed.

"Nope, don't listen to her for the next thirty seconds," Ryver instructed. "She's about to say some very rude and nasty things—usually about your face—none of which she really means. She's just going to be so desperate she'll say anything to shove you away."

Much to my annoyance, Ronan's grip tightened.

I began to swear at him, annoyed he would listen to Ryver instead of me.

Ryver was right. The final thirty seconds were not thirty seconds I was proud of. But relief flooded my body as, at last, the shadows faded. I was drifting, floating, as everything in my body seemed deliriously happy.

"Funny that," Ryver mused, staring down at the spiky shadows contained in the palm of his hand. They were lashing out at him, but he held them contained in some sort of sphere. "This isn't just a solitary shadow...it's been enhanced...and there's more than one type in here..."

"It's the drugs," I replied, slightly deranged. "His father is a psycho who has a door...a special, *magical* door. I think it leads to the Ruins. He's been using me as his lab rat...and let me tell you, I do not make a good rat. I'm much too cute to be a rat...I would rather be a...a guinea pig." I stared up at Ronan. "You called me cute like a guinea pig...do you still think I'd make a cute guinea pig?"

Ronan's mouth fell open in speechless shock, but I was too far gone to realize he never answered my question.

I was clinging to his muscled forearm and examining it closely. "Has anyone ever told you, you have very nice forearms?" I whispered, staring at the flow of muscles. "They are so incredibly beautiful, and the veins...you have lovely strong hands. I bet you would tear the world apart to help me if you needed to..."

"Uhm..."

Ronan's surprise was enough to make me giggle. "Silly Ronan, he doesn't know what to say..."

Ryver rolled his eyes. "Give it another thirty seconds. I've just taken every drug out of her system. She's essentially high. I could record her for you if you'd like to use this as blackmail later. She's going to be saying some of the most random, true things she's ever thought. Enjoy it while it lasts. She's bound to be extra spicy to make up for it when she realizes what's happened."

I was oblivious to everything as I continued to stare up at Ronan. "Your eyes are the most beautiful shade of gray, but they're so sad. Your eyes are sad like mine, but sometimes I just want to hold your face and kiss it until the sadness goes away..."

"Ten seconds now," Ryver said, rolling his eyes again.

My fingers trailed the Lichtenburg marks on his chest. My handprints burned into his skin. "We both have these ugly marks from my mistake," I whispered. "My hands are ruined, and your lovely chest is too...but I guess that's okay. It keeps you humble. If you didn't have my ugly marks, your chest would be so beautiful even the elves would be jealous. I wonder what would happen if I just—"

"And right about now..." Ryver's voice monologued from some distant part of my mind.

The disconnected words died in my throat and I stopped, blinking. The world came crashing back and I jerked myself back into reality. I felt as if I had been trapped in a very, very bad dream. My hands were on his chest, but why, and what I had been about to do, I had no clue.

"What, I..." I yanked my hands back away from Ronan's chest, as if they burned. "I uhm. Ryver, what did you do to me?"

"What do you remember?" Ryver asked, his voice teasing.

"I...I remember defending Ronan and taking the shadow so it wouldn't corrupt him...then you came in, too late, and took the shadow. Then you subjected me to your torturous magic to get it out of me..."

"Anything else?"

"Not really, it's all rather hazy. But somehow, I ended up here...and..."

"You don't remember anything? Not even your ravishing thoughts about Ronan's body?" Ryver prodded.

My mouth fell open in shock as my cheeks flamed. "Not anything...oh gosh, what did I say?"

"You were giving your human here all sorts of lovely compliments," Ryver replied smugly. "Especially about his arms and his *lovely* chest...you even told him how you wanted to kiss him."

"Oh, dear heavens no, please tell me I did not."

"Come now, Faye, you're going to hurt his feelings after you just made his ego sing. You should have heard yourself. You went into *such* great detail about his chest muscles, too."

"Oh my gosh, kill me now," I whispered as I quickly pushed out of Ronan's arms and hid my face in my hands.

"I'll kill you later," Ryver commented saucily. "I can get years of blackmail out of the last two minutes. It'd be a shame to waste it."

He dissolved into a laughing wisp of smoke just as I lunged, intent on wringing his neck.

48

Curse Breakers

EVADNE

"You are a church of broken glass and hallelujahs. You are haunted
like every other holy thing. What tried to destroy you didn't have the
strength. Still you stand. Sturdy and smelling of smoke"
-Little Bird, Clementine von Radics

Ember was screaming, writhing in pain, and nothing I did would wake her up.

"We could always throw her off the edge of the ship," Raz suggested unhelpfully,
rubbing her eyes sleepily as she wandered into the room. "Maybe the jolt would wake
her up and then I'll save her."

"How about no," Rune muttered angrily as she curled around a pillow and pulled
her blanket over her head. "It's just a Dreamscape. You remember how Theron used to
scream when he first came to us?"

"That was a guilty conscience," Raz replied hotly.

"*Sure* it was," Clarice muttered. "Child, you know he doesn't possess a single re-
morseful bone in that stubborn body of his, don't you?"

"He does, too. They pop out when I break his fingers."

Clarice muttered a muffled curse and was soon snoring once more.

"Sorry," I said softly.

"Hey, no problem," Raz replied cheerfully. "She'll wake up eventually. Isn't that right, Ember?"

As if hearing her name, Ember bolted upright with a scream, eyes wild, but awake.

Apparently, all Ember needed was for Raz to call her name.

"Hey, hey, it's okay," I said reassuringly. "It's okay. You're safe."

"Alive," Ember managed to choke out.

Darcy.

"I know," I whispered, rubbing circles on her shoulder blades. "Still...alive."

The words were a stilted jolt on my tongue. Still his curse prohibited us from speaking freely.

I've had enough of this. The curse is already unraveling. I'm going to make it unravel all the way.

I sat down beside Ember, pulling her into a hug. She began to cry. Slowly at first and then harder and harder as she rubbed at her wrist. The scars we shared because of that monster were more than I ever wanted to think about. The horrors we had endured in this Realm at his hands were things no one should ever live through.

"Let's go sit out on the deck and look at the stars," I suggested. "I'm guessing you don't want to go back to sleep anytime soon."

Ember shook her head vehemently. After grabbing our cloaks, and making sure Fireheart and my dangerous little petting zoo were safely tucked into a fuzzy blanket in my hammock, we made our way out.

Ember was still crying as we sat down, and I pulled her close. "Tomorrow will be kinder," I sang softly as I gently rubbed her back. "It's true, I've seen it, before. A brighter day, is coming my way, yes tomorrow will be kinder..."

It was a song Mum used to sing to us when we got particularly upset. She would hold us close and sing to us until the nightmares were nothing more than a distant memory. It hurt to be the one singing when I knew Darcy still had Mum for ransom.

"Today, I've cried a many tear, and pain is in my heart," Ember sang, her quiet soprano a gentle lullaby around us. "Around me lies a somber scene, I don't know where to start. But I feel, warmth on my skin, the stars have all aligned."

I joined her then, allowing the wind to carry our voices out as I harmonized with her melody. "The wind has blown but now I know, that tomorrow will be kinder. Tomorrow will be kinder. I know, I've seen it before. A brighter day is coming my way. Yes, tomorrow will be kinder..."

Our voices faded to the faintest whisper as we repeated the last stanza. "A brighter day is coming my way, yes tomorrow will be kinder."

"I feel so hollow," Ember whispered. "The mark on my chest was burning during the nightmare." Her eyes were wide and afraid. "Eva, that monster on the island was the same one from the nightmares. It marked me..."

She pointed to the strange constellation burned into her skin. It had been left there after the monster had touched her on the island, before it killed Doyle.

Rune had been incredibly alarmed to see it and had dragged Ember over to Huxley, who had then shared a whispered conversation with Verity, who proceeded to tell us it was nothing to worry about. Ember challenged her lie, stating they were all full of crap, until, clearly exhausted, Huxley at last told her the truth.

Somehow, the constellation was the same one that, up until recently, had been in the skies of the Moores. It had disappeared a while back, and the fact that the monster had marked Em with the same constellation did not bode well. No one knew for sure *what* it meant, because nothing like that had ever happened before. But they did know it meant something incredibly bad.

What does it mean? The monster was in her dreams, then on that island...the constellation was in the skies representing a monster, and now it's on her skin? What does it mean?

"That *thing* is haunting my nightmares again and now...*he*—" Ember choked on the word, and her tears resumed harder than before. "And I can't even *talk* about it," she cried. "I can't even talk about what happened."

"We need to break the curse," I replied resolutely.

"How?" Ember demanded angrily. "How?" she sobbed. "Eva, we can't."

"Yes, we can," I replied, doubling down on my certainty. "The curse is already crumbling. We're already breaking it. We just have to...to try a little harder. I think after everything, his continued assault has only weakened it further because he didn't bind up the events that followed with the silencing curse. We just need to keep pushing at the wall."

Ember hung her head, defeated. But I was unwilling to give up.

"Mum was there," I whispered. "The Knight had Mum trapped in that darkness...he was torturing her, trying to get me to break. D—"

My words were cut off, falling silent as I tried and failed to say his name.

"See, I told you," Ember whispered raggedly.

"D—" I swore under my breath as a metallic taste began to grow in my mouth.

No. I will not let you control me. I have not lived this long and survived this many horrors to allow you to haunt me any further. I will not let this curse stand.

The shadow monster in the cage hissed and roared as I stood outside the cage, contemplating the events that led us to this place. This monster was here now because of Darcy.

His monster is here, but I've locked it up. I will not let it harm or control me.

Darcy. Darcy. Darcy. I will say what I want, and you will not stop me.

I began to stab at the monster through the cage as it howled and roared.

Die. Die, die, die. Get out of my mind!

The cage crumbled and the monster began to dissolve as I continued to stab it. I would not be a victim to his curse any longer.

"D—" I gritted my teeth, forcing my voice to stay with me. "Are...see!"

Ember stared at me in wide-eyed shock.

"Darcy tried to kill me," I whispered raggedly. Blood was gathering in my mouth, but I didn't care. I was done letting this silence me any longer.

"Sisters break, curse of pain" Erebus screeched above us, making us jump. "Fight the silence, death will stay. Face the rise, fate lies slain."

You need to work on your cheerleading skills, Erebus.

Ember's lips were moving, but no words would come. She glared down at her wrist, at the mark that shimmered beneath her skin.

Come on, Em. Come on. You can do it!

"Let me go, let me go," Ember whispered. "I won't be bound any longer, I won't be bound. Let me go... Let go of me..." Her voice was rising as she stared down at her wrist.

"***Break,***" she yelled.

The words trembled in the air around us as Ember fought against Darcy's curse.

"***BREAK!***" she screamed. A flaming phoenix burst from Ember's fingertips and hovered in the air in front of us.

"Help me," Ember whispered, holding out her hand for the phoenix.

"You do not need my help," a voice whispered. Her phoenix was talking.

My mouth fell open in shock.

"You have already broken the curse. Once again, you have broken the curse upon you and the ones you love. You, child, will break the curse that binds our Realm. You will be the savior of the bloodstained Moores."

Ember was sobbing as she at last whispered the long-silenced secret. "Darcy hurt me," she gasped as blood trickled from the corner of her mouth. "Darcy..." she repeated with a disbelieving gasp. "Darcy tried to kill me, he tried to kill me and silence me..." she sobbed, in joy and pain. "He tried to kill me...he did such terrible, awful things to me, Eva."

I pulled her close, tears streaming down my face. "I know, Em. I know."

"He will not have any power over me any longer," she whispered. "I will not let this control me. I will not let it destroy me."

"I'll destroy him myself," I hissed, making a dark promise to myself to end the monster's life.

The phoenix lowered, touching its head to Ember's forehead, and then drifted behind and down, settling onto her shoulder. It was gone in a whiff of smoke, leaving an ashen imprint on Ember's cloak.

The night stretched on, and as it did, we shared the horrors that had been buried within us. The many ways Darcy had tried to reduce us to a tomb. We dug up those shallow graves and buried the bodies properly, until all that remained was the memory of the horror, and the graveyard we had created to at last lay the curse to rest.

49

Carrying On

EMBER

"You must not permit sorrow to destroy you."
-Mary Shelley

Now there's hope beyond the wreckage,
and these things I thought I'd be,
I've pulled myself up from the rubble,
and crawled back to my feet.
I'll find my way back from this,
though I'll never be the same,
but I will find myself again,
I will find a way.
'Why me, why me', my heartbeat cries,
but it's not for me to know,
I simply must continue on,
even though I'm painfully slow.
I'm headed back for the child,
the girl I used to be,

I cannot leave her there alone,
I cannot bear her screams.
I'll take her and protect her,
I'll teach her how to fight,
until nothing else can harm her,
and fear has taken flight.
Step by step, we'll make it,
For her I'll fight and try,
one breath, then another,
I'll overcome that 'why'.
Hope is a constant effort,
Each moment, an intentional choice,
but I must continue forward,
and believe I'll find my voice.
The path ahead's not easy,
It's unending fire within,
but there's still hope within the wreckage,
as the healing journey begins.

50

Bounty Hunters

Ember

"I wish people had half the honor of dragons."
-Terry Goodkind

Timing is everything, and it was soon decided that Evadne and I had picked a terrible night to pull an all-nighter, when out of nowhere, another ship joined us in the skies.

"COMPANY!" Logan roared from the crow's nest.

Raz swore beside me on the rigging, and we quickly made our way down. Verity had switched us for the day, though Theron was still giving me some aid with my fear levels. I was beginning to feel as if maybe I had a handle on my terror.

The crew was quickly gathering on the deck as Verity strode from her captain's quarters, eyebrows scrunched together in anger. "Who dares come at my ship?" she growled.

"Well, the skies aren't endless, isn't it inevitable someone would go by us?"

"Yes," Archer replied as he dug through several bags at his feet. "But they would be flying colors of peace and journey." He pointed up to the bright blue, purple, and yellow flag flying high above us. "They would be flying a flag like that, or something similar. They're flying with no colors, which means trouble. They're likely raiders."

"Or bounty hunters," Verity growled as she stared at the rapidly approaching ship. "They're coming at us too fast to be merchants. They're light traveling...so not raiders. Raiders play the long game. They want your load...all of it. We've got bounty hunters on our hands. Rune, fire a warning shot, keep it twenty degrees off. Enough to send a message. Perhaps they'll think twice."

She turned to us, her frown deepening. "Jack will kill me if you're hurt, or worse killed. But we need every hand we can get. If it's bounty hunters they're likely after you. Theron, Raz, take the girls up. I want you to attack the sails, cripple them as much as possible."

She turned to Evadne. "See if you can call your dragons back. If you can, find out if they'll fight for us. If not, that's fine. We are not their master, but we would greatly appreciate their help. They can eat their fill of the scavengers. It takes quite a monster to hunt their own kind for gain."

Evadne nodded and we took to the rigging.

"Do not let the girls out of your sight," Verity instructed Theron and Raz. "We cannot afford to lose them."

"We could lock them in the brig," Raz suggested cheerfully.

That is a terrible idea!

Verity shook her head. "Too much risk of getting hit by cannon fire. They'd be at more risk as a casualty."

Oh, thank goodness.

"Best they stay with us and help fight. Ember, as soon as they're close enough, send a fireball and set their sails on fire. Okay?"

I nodded.

"Evadne, send a wave, as big as you can muster, and shove them back."

Evadne nodded and we resumed our climb, with Raz and Theron hot on our heels. The two were joking as they climbed, comparing current events to the last raid they had fought. "This vessel is half the size of the last," Raz said lightly. "We'll have them crippled in no time."

"BUGS!" Archer yelled from beneath us, just as an unfamiliar figure landed on the mast above us. Another quickly joined the first as Evadne and I drew our swords.

I have no idea what I'm doing, but it's probably smart to have a blade in my hand. At least then I can somewhat defend myself.

"DUCK!" Theron yelled.

Evadne and I ducked and there was an explosion above our heads. Gore splattered and I gagged.

Theron had thrown an explosive and caught one of the Fey. The other took off, then quickly dove at us, hands reaching for Evadne.

She spat out a curse and slashed.

The raider dodged and she sent a stream of water next, as quick and sharp as her blade. The jet hit the raider square in the chest, and he was propelled backward. "WE'VE GOT 'EM UP HERE!" he roared toward the ship as he tumbled through the sky.

Well crap.

Maybe using our Inheritance was a bad idea?

I am too tired for this. Why couldn't they have raided tomorrow? I need more coffee before I can deal with something like this.

Evadne and I quickly climbed up to the mast, standing back-to-back as we stared in openmouthed shock at the hoard of flying Fey pelting toward our ship.

"Well, isn't this fun," Theron commented dryly.

Beneath us, the crew was a flurry of activity on the deck.

"Bloodthirsty fiends, raid the ship," Erebus screamed above us. "Stab, destroy, and let death be thy welcome gift!"

That's more like it, Erebus! That's a war cry I can get behind!

"Eva, dragons?" I called as I gave Erebus a thumbs up.

"They're on their way," Evadne yelled. "They'll be here in a couple minutes. They were busy destroying another ship."

"Oh?"

"Yeah, apparently the idiots tried to steal one of the babies..."

I hissed in rage at such a thought. The babies were essentially defenseless. From what Evadne had been able to gather, they couldn't breathe fire until they were past a year old. Most rode on top of the larger dragons since their wings couldn't maintain the miles of flight the dragons covered in a day.

"I hope they ate them all," I muttered darkly.

"Yes, there was much blood and gore in the response," she replied distractedly. "There was also a great amount of pride. I think they accomplished their goal."

Raz and Theron were shooting arrows at the flying Fey, picking them off one by one. Down below, Rune, Faolan, and Sora launched a barrage of grenades. Soon, the crew were jumping off the ship and meeting the bounty hunters in the sky with screams of fury.

The ship was close enough now, and Evadne and I set to work. "We have to make sure your water doesn't put out my flames." I called.

"Yeah, not sure how we're going to do both," she replied grimly.

"Send the water in the form of a waterspout," Theron suggested before jumping off the mast and tackling a raider who got too close.

"Okay," Evadne whispered, staring down at her hands. A little waterspout began to grow in between her hands, gaining speed and power the longer she held onto it.

I conjured up a ball of fire in mine. "I'll go for the mast, you go for the hull, okay? We can take it down two ways."

"What about the crew that's fighting with the other crew?" Evadne asked hesitantly.

"Uhm..."

"Send it," Raz yelled as she sliced the throat of an unfortunate raider. "I'll call out a warning when you do, our crew will know what it means."

"Okay," Evadne and I chorused together.

"COCAROACH!!" Raz roared as our twin balls of power sped toward the ship.

Verity's crew members dove at once, abandoning their fights. The raiders looked around in confusion, but they were too late to dodge.

Evadne's waterspout continued to grow as it raced toward the vessel, and together our twin powers wreaked havoc on the bounty hunter's ship. The swirling column of wind and waves blew a gaping hole in the side as my ball of raging fire slammed into the masts.

Rune hurled a bag at Raz, and I watched in openmouthed horror as Raz sped toward the ship. She hurled the bag at the flaming masts. As soon as the fabric touched the flames, it exploded. The ship was utterly crippled in the sky, black smoke marking their location as the Aurora began to speed away from the wreck.

A roar shook the air around us, making the hairs on the back of my neck stand on end.

The dragons had arrived.

They slammed into the raider's ship, unheeding of the flames. Crew members began to pour out the sides, trying to escape. But it was no use. They were picked off one by one as the beasts systematically destroyed them.

Down on the deck, one bounty hunter had been taken alive. Steadily bleeding from a wound in his side, he wasn't long for death, but Verity had a knife to the side of his face, demanding answers.

"Who sent you?" she seethed. "Why did you attack my ship?"

"The bounty," the man choked, blood coating his lips. "There is a king's ransom for the sisters Grimm, the twins of power, alive. The bounty wants them alive. Someone knows you have them. The Aurora has been named. Your days are numbered *Captain*." He spat the word as he glared up at her, furious.

"I know of the bounty," Verity seethed, ignoring his threat. "Where is the drop off for the ransom? Who put up the bounty?"

"The Darke one," the man whispered raggedly. "His right-hand man, with the crooked shadow. He listed the reward. He and the tainted wraith seek the girls. They seek to set the Knight free. One way or another, they will succeed."

"Not if I can help it," Verity muttered angrily.

"You cannot stop the tide. We rise and rise again. No matter how you snuff out our flames, the resistance rises against the cursed reign."

"You spread like the plague, seeking to destroy the home we've made for ourselves here."

"It is no home, if you live in fear, awaiting destruction. The monarchs have us under their thumb. But we will not abide their rule any longer."

"The monarchs turn a blind eye to our home here. It is only when you make trouble they notice their negligence. You will only bring their wrath."

"We will bring their destruction," the man spat.

"But you will not live to see it," Verity snarled. Her blade was quick as she dispatched the man and dumped his body off the side of the boat. "It's no use arguing with fools. They refuse to listen to truth."

"Sound off," Logan yelled. "Are we missing anyone?" He began to call out names, to which each was answered with a resolute battle cry.

"None, ma'am," Logan said, turning to Verity. "We survived the scrape with no casualties."

"For once," Verity grumbled. "I don't like how quickly they snuck up on us. Why didn't our radar ping them? Faolan?"

"Yes, Captain?" Faolan called.

"Inspect the ship and reinforce the spells. I want to know of anyone within a twenty-mile radius of my boat."

"Yes ma'am."

"The rest of you, about your duties. Clean up this blood. I do not want to attract scavengers."

"Yes ma'am!" the crew chorused.

"I am proud of all of you," Verity continued. "You fought valiantly and bravely. Logan!"

"Yes, Captain!" Logan yelled from across the ship.

"Make something special to go with dinner tonight!" she called.

The crew roared in approval and she gave them a grin that promised violence.

She turned to me and Evadne. "Well done, girls. You've survived your first raid and also gave the crippling blow." She turned to Raz. "Good flying out there. I would be surprised if your wing tips weren't a little singed."

Raz smirked. "It wouldn't be a true fight if I didn't put my life in some sort of danger."

Nikos was making his way toward us, eyes blazing as he stared at Raz. I expected anger, indignation at how she'd put her life at risk. But his grim face broke into a hungry smile as he pulled Raz into his arms. "Look at you out there, kicking their tail!" he crowed before kissing her fiercely.

"It's one of the reasons why you fell in love with me," she giggled as she broke away. "If I remember correctly, it was a similar feat of danger that had you stating to Verity that you were going to marry me."

"Darn right!" Nikos agreed before kissing her again.

Verity rolled her eyes at the PDA and turned to the rest of the crew who watched in amusement. "All right, carry on, all of you!"

"Yes ma'am!" they chorused as they broke into a flurry of activity.

Theron gave Evadne a fist bump. "Way to go, my vengeful kraken. You should learn to make your Inheritance look like octopus tentacles."

"Oo!" Evadne whispered, her face alight with ideas and possibilities. "That is an *awesome* idea. Don't you think so, Em?"

I nodded, giving her a smile. I was too drained to give her more enthusiasm as I followed Theron toward the rigging. "We need to check the sails," he called back. "Make sure no damage was done to them while we were occupied."

I nodded, utterly exhausted, and Theron smirked at me, amused. "I bet you wish you'd slept through the night, instead of being up at all random hours, chugging coffee and spying on a certain *prince*, huh?"

"Who told you about that?" I asked grumpily.

"Archer told me."

"Of course he did," I muttered. "Everyone on this ship is a bloody tattletale."

"If you don't want us to think he's your prince, you really should do your spying in private," Theron teased.

"If you don't want me to bite you, I suggest you stop being stupid," I countered.

Theron's deep laughter drifted down to me as I followed him up the rope ladder.

"You'd have to catch me, Sparks, and we both know you're too exhausted from stalking your dear prince."

I didn't deign to give him a reply. Instead, I allowed my hands to give him my thorough opinion of his ridiculousness as I angrily made my way up.

51

Honor Among Thieves

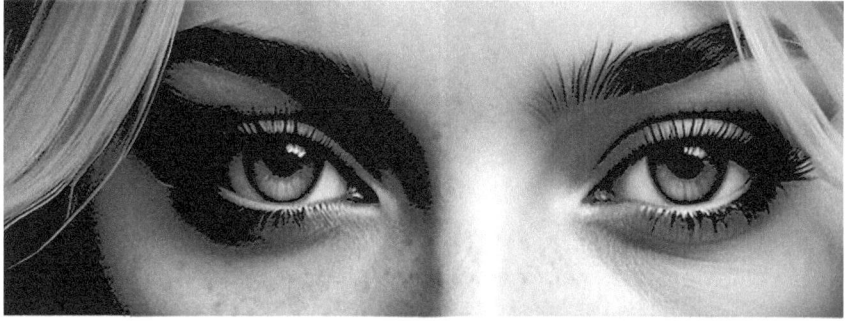

FAYE

"You love him despite the burden of Atlas resting on his shoulders, and
he loves you despite the death still clinging to your lips, and the blood
drying at its corners. What a pair you make. -The greatest lovers in all
of hell."
-L.H.Z.

Ronan and I sat together on the floor with our backs against his bed, watching the hours
trickle by. The sun would be up soon, and I would have to go back to my cell. Ronan
knew for a fact his father was coming for me later in the morning. He was done letting
me stew. It was time to implement the next phase of our plan.

I didn't want to admit how much I dreaded going back into that darkness. It was
comforting sitting here, sharing these quiet moments with Ronan. Our fingers were
mere centimeters apart as we traded stories and memories, beating around the bush and
avoiding the dangerous truths that lay buried just below the surface.

"Ronan," I said quietly. "I'm going to blow everything up when I get back to my
cell. You'll know when it happens. The whole system will be down. Don't come, be
somewhere else, but stay close. Jeremiah will come. I'm going to pretend to be weak.
He's going to take me to his office, at which point I will stage a coup and escape. You

are going to try and fail to stop my escape, but at least it will cement you in your father's good graces, okay?"

Ronan nodded. That little line was forming between his eyebrows as they scrunched together, but now I was too anxious to find it adorable.

"I'm going to seal you all in that office and get a head start. I'll let you catch me. But make sure you're the one who catches me, okay?"

"Got it," he said, his voice shaking.

He's afraid. My Ronan is afraid.

The silence stretched around us.

"Faye," he began, his voice taking on a different tone. "Faye, I would take it all back if I could. I know I've tried to apologize, but I don't think you believed me. I am so, *so* sorry for my part in all this. For not finding a way to get Meghan out before it came to this. I...I never should have taken you. No matter what I thought, no matter how I believed it would come to nothing... No matter how scared I was. I never should have taken you. I'm sorry Faye, I am so, *so* sorry."

I was staring at the partially open door, listening to the muffled sound of his sister's soft snores. I wrapped my hand around his and gently squeezed. "I forgive you, Ronan." I whispered. "I forgive you, and I mean it. I would have done the same thing if I was in your shoes, and all my hot air saying otherwise was just that. I would have gotten as far as you did. I really, truly forgive you, Ronan. You need to let the guilt go. We've found our way through the labyrinth..." I turned then. "We found our way through the labyrinth and it's going to be okay. We have a plan. It's going to work. We just need to work together and hold on a little longer. It's going to be okay."

Tears were gathering in Ronan's eyes. "I'd take it all back," he whispered.

"I know you would," I replied softly. "But who knows, maybe in the end, you taking me will be how I find a way to save my sisters... My original plan..." I looked away. "It would have saved them, but it would have destroyed...everything."

"It would have destroyed the Realm, and you with it, wouldn't it?" Ronan asked quietly.

I nodded, unable to find the words.

"Then maybe my taking you did some good. It saved your life. Maybe your plan would have done more harm than good..."

"Maybe," I whispered, remembering the dark nights where I searched for answers. The bloody, desperate path I made for myself. Had it all been for nothing?

"Sometimes the way out isn't what we plan, it's what we fight against the whole time. If...if you had told me last year that I would be getting help from the spitfire girl *I* kidnapped...I'd have told you to go check your facts...because there was absolutely no way that beautiful girl would ever work with me, let alone help me."

"You think I'm beautiful?" I asked, unable to help myself.

"Yes," Ronan replied softly, brushing a strand of hair away from my face. "Kinda cute, too, in a guinea pig sort of way."

I snorted in laughter, effectively ruining the moment. But Ronan didn't seem to care. He continued to stare at me.

"What?" I demanded, still laughing. "What are you looking at?"

"If you had told me a year ago, that I'd find my lifeline, my lighthouse on the ocean, I would have never believed you..." Ronan whispered. "You are my lighthouse in this churning ocean, Faye," he murmured as he lightly brushed his lips against mine.

"Oh my *gosh*," Meghan's voice squealed from the cracked doorway. "You totally just *kissed* her!!"

Ronan and I jumped a solid ten feet combined as we quickly jerked away from one another.

"You totally just kissed her," Meghan cried, wrenching open the door and rushing into the room. "I was *right,* you *DO* like each other. Faye, someday when you guys get married, can I be one of your bridesmaids?"

I was laughing and crying all at once, too mortified and giddy to find words as Meghan raced across the room and wrapped me in a tight hug.

"You were already like a big sister to me," Meghan continued, unheeding of Ronan's spluttering protests. "Now you're *actually* going to be my sister! I can't wait, what kind of dress are you going to wear?"

"Slow down, hon," I said gently, hugging her back. "There are a lot of milestones that have to be crossed before we get to marriage. First and foremost, we have to get out of here. Secondarily, we need to convince my sisters not to kill him for taking me in the first place."

"Oh, that's easy. I have a feeling your sisters and I will become best friends. I'll have them swayed in no time."

Much to my chagrin, Ronan's face was as red as a tomato. "What were you doing? Spying on us?" he demanded in mock irritation.

"I was doing exactly that," Meghan confirmed. "I was not about to let you make secret plans without me."

"We weren't making secret plans," Ronan protested.

"Well, maybe not. But you were certainly up to *something*." She wiggled her eyebrows suggestively and Ronan once again became an incoherent ball of spluttering goo.

"Megs, we're out of time," I said gently, changing the subject.

"It's time for the jail break?" she squealed excitedly.

"Not exactly. I'm going to disable the zappers so we don't get fried like bugs. After that's done, we'll be on to the next stage of the plan."

"What is that stage called?" Meghan pressed exuberantly.

Good gravy, this child has more energy than me when I've had six cups of coffee. I must be getting old.

I just need to move straight to espresso.

"Uhm... We'll call that stage jailbreak."

"Okay, so what's this stage called?"

"Uhmmm..." I was stalling, drawing out the sound as long as possible while I tried to think. "How about honor among thieves?"

"What?" she scoffed. "That doesn't make any sense."

"Uhm...sure it does." I was rambling now. "There's nothing but honor among us...your brother stole me from my home, thus making him a thief. I stole...uhm...his heart? And you stole...all the energy from both of us."

Meghan squealed appreciatively at my random, on the spot explanation. "I *love* it," she gushed.

"I'm...not surprised," Ronan teased. "You love everything."

"You two are something straight out of a rom-com!" Meghan screeched.

"Shhh!" we whispered in unison. "We can't risk getting found out," I said gently.

"*ROM-COM*!" Meghan whisper screamed.

Ronan rolled his eyes, and I clapped a hand over my mouth, trying to muffle my laughter. My mind was combing back through the tangled history between us.

There is way too much violence for it to be a rom-com.

Ronan took advantage of my absentminded pondering to lecture his sister on the great evils of eavesdropping and spying, to which Meghan and I both rolled our eyes.

"I need to get back to my cell," I said, interrupting Ronan's moral spiel. "Jeremiah will be showing up at any moment."

Meghan's smile died. "You'll protect her, won't you Ronan?" she asked urgently.

Ronan's glanced at me, his eyes worried. We weren't going to tell his sister how much danger I was actually going to be in, with this next phase of our plan. "I'm gonna try, Megs."

It's not a promise he can make, Megs. We can't compromise our plan. If he protects me, it'll compromise everything.

"Promise me," she insisted.

"Megs..."

"*Promise me,*" she repeated angrily, tears gathering in her eyes as she grabbed my arm and clung to it. "Promise me you'll protect her. I need her, Ronan. I. *Need.* Her." She snarled, pouring every ounce of vehemence into her voice.

She is so much like Ember. So much like her it hurts.

How did I ever get so lucky to have someone like her on my side?

Just promise her, Ronan. It's okay if she doesn't know it's a lie...your promises aren't binding like mine are.

Yes, but he likely takes his promises very seriously.

"I promise," Ronan said quietly, fingers brushing mine for a heartbeat.

A promise he cannot keep...but that's okay, because there is no honor among thieves.

What Meghan doesn't know won't hurt her...what we can't tell her is the truth. We can't tell her what's going to happen to test if I've successfully disabled the zappers... If I succeed, his father will be incredibly angry and Ronan will have to bring me back to face his wrath...

Ronan won't be able to stop his father, because we need to get her out...she can't know that there is no honor among thieves and Ronan won't be protecting me...not this time.

52

To Choose Your Path And Decide Your Fate

EVADNE

"Do not ask the price I paid, I must live with my quiet rage, tame the
ghosts in my head, that run wild and wish me dead."
-Mumford and Sons, Lovers eyes.

The ship was flooded in moonlight as we sailed gently through the night sky. I was
exhausted, but too restless from the day's excitement to sleep. I knew I needed to
rest, pulling two all-nighters at once was a bad idea. But I had reached the point of
exhaustion where sleep would no longer come.

*I'll probably pass out sometime tomorrow while I'm in the rigging and Raz will have
to rescue me.*

How humiliating.

Oh well. That's tomorrow's problem. Future me can deal with past me's terrible choices.

The dragons hovered around us, and though sleeping, they followed our ship, wings
gently beating in the air. I told them they could go, but they wouldn't. They were afraid
we would get attacked again.

They sang as they slept, and it broke my heart to listen to the haunting strain over and over again. Snatches of vibrant dreams floated through my subconscious as well as their music. Bits and pieces of their memories passed between all of them. Together they dreamed, together they remembered.

It all passed through my mind the way an audiobook would when I was focused on something else. I knew it was playing, and if I applied myself, it was all I heard. But I kept it at the back of my mind as much as I could. Their songs made me want to weep. Their ache and love for the skies, their adoration for the moonlight—it filled me with such a violent need to have the wind on my face and my body floating through the stars.

Fireheart dreamed with them. He was curled around my neck, sharing their story, while in turn sending out his own. I saw his story through their minds—what he shared with them in the language in between that was their dreams. It was a tale of love and loss, of lives he had bound himself to, mortals he had cared for. I saw my face repeatedly, and it was strange seeing myself through his eyes. I hardly recognized the fierce person he projected.

The wind became a song, with lyrics that pulled through my blood. Their dreams...oh their dreams made me want to run and never look back. To forget who I was and what I loved. They made me want to forget everything I fought for and simply have a life that existed to answer their potent call to adventure, that hungry ache for more. They made me long for things I could never have, desperate for some happiness of my own.

I missed Marcus, and their song reminded me of the joy I'd felt in his arms. The music reminded me of his, and the way he made such beautiful melodies.

It's better we're apart. He's safer without me.

My fingers anxiously twisted the promise ring around my finger. It hardly seemed real. How could he be so certain about where his heart lay? We had only spent a solstice together and yet my soul felt as if it had known him my entire life. There was a connection that I could not deny, and it scared me. The need and dependance on another person that I couldn't explain. It was all so uncertain and terrifying.

'Consider it a promise...A promise that no matter what darkness we face, I will always stand by you.'

If only, if only.

We left him, and if I had been in Ember's shoes...I still would have left him to protect her.

Everything is such a mess...how will we ever come back from this? Will he forgive me?

What if he thinks I'm ugly with this mechanical eye? What if he doesn't want me anymore?

"What are they saying?" Theron asked, drawing me out of my thoughts.

His fingers moved deftly, tying a complex knot as he stared at the dragons. "All my pirate years, they've only ever been a terror to us, beasts we tried to avoid...and now?" His question hung in the air around us.

"It's not so much saying, as feeling," I replied as I stared out at the magnificent creatures. "They speak in words yes, but mostly pictures. Their heartbeat is a song, their minds whisper the words...it happens all at once."

Theron nodded. "That seems complex," he mused.

"They long for a home," I replied. "But there's nowhere for them in the Moores. It's not safe, and they're not safe in the Realms. There's nowhere that's untouched by the darkness..." My voice trailed off as I allowed their thoughts to become my focus. Their emotions washed over me as they dreamed of the world they used to know.

"They want the moon, the wind, and stars...they long to explore...they're voyagers, on a journey, but now there's no end in sight. They can't find their way back home..."

"Now they're wanderers," Theron said sadly.

"They're not meant to be wanderers..." I whispered. "They need a home."

How did he escape the only home and fate he ever knew? How did he escape his fate? How do we escape? How do we get away?

"No one is meant to be a wanderer," Theron murmured, his eyes fixed on the dragons.

"Theron—"

"I know what you're going to ask," Theron interrupted gently. "I can't help you."

How could you possibly know that?

"Your emotions changed. They went from desperation to hopeful questions...now they're absolute indignation." He turned to me, arching an eyebrow. "Am I mistaken?"

I huffed and he laughed, a deep rich sound that the wind carried away as it played with the loose strands of hair around his face.

"Well, if you know, you might as well answer me."

"I don't have an answer that can help you," Theron sighed.

"Jack sent us here to get answers," I pressed.

"Jack didn't know the cost," Theron replied firmly. "If he did, he wouldn't have sent you here. It's already too late..."

"How do you know?"

"My path is not one you should take. It has a great cost." His hands fell still as he stared up at the stars. "I chose my end, but it is not one I would encourage you to make."

"But Jack wouldn't have sent us here if there was no hope," I pressed desperately. "Why would he send us here if there was no hope?"

"Because he's your brother, and he doesn't want to watch you die."

"All men die," I countered hotly, tears gathering in my eyes.

Oh Oma, I sound just like you. What would you say to him?

Loss slammed into me as Oma and F floated through my mind. Guilt attacked me next. I had been so desperate to survive, that it felt as if I had betrayed them by not mourning them every second.

F and Oma are gone, Mum held captive...when will this end?

Theron looked at me sadly, eyes full of understanding. "Don't feel guilty for living. We cannot mourn every second of our lives and expect to survive. They would not want you to live in such sorrow for their sake."

I quickly wiped the tears from my cheeks, desperately trying to be okay.

"All men die," Theron said softly. "Jacques sent you to me, because he wanted you to have a chance to live before death takes you as her own." He paused, considering his words carefully. "He didn't realize that, while you are not claimed, to truly escape the claim of the Courts, is to answer the call of the Moores. If you answer that call, you surrender not only yourself, but your heart. It is to live a life without love, and in the end, you are cursed to be a wanderer. That is the cost of being a traitor to your blood. You're doomed to be a wraith that can find no rest, even when the earth fades." He regarded me sadly. "Your heart and love are already claimed," he said gently.

"How do you know?" I stammered.

Consider it a promise. A promise that no matter what darkness we face, I will always stand by you.

"I see it in your eyes. Your heart is miles away. Ember wasn't the only one who left the one she loved on that cliff. You abandoned your heart as well."

If I am to be harmed, let me choose my destruction. It is you. It will always be you...

I nodded mutely, trying to quell the tears that continued to rush down my cheeks.

"Are you saying that you would take it back?" I choked out. "Are you saying that, in the end, it was all for naught?"

"No," Theron sighed. "I denied them my fate and took back a semblance of my life. But in the end, it was never mine at all. I simply chose my end. I would rather have a lifetime of adventure, and wander beyond when death takes me, than live a life with an end that I did not decide." His silver eyes held mine. "I found peace to accept my decision, and I will live well before I face the darkness. I will live many, many centuries before I allow death to take me."

"What if you're killed?" I whispered.

Theron shrugged. "I've been lucky for the last four lifetimes. Fate and I have enjoyed a complicated dance. I think she's quite taken with me. Neither of us want our shenanigans to cease, or to let death cut in." He laughed. "Besides, I'm very hard to kill. If I'm going to die, it will be my decision to die, not because I wasn't a good enough warrior."

The silence stretched around us, and his hands fell back to their work as he continued his complicated set of knots. He was making something, but what it was I could not tell.

"Was it worth it?" I asked at last.

"I wake up every morning and feel the wind on my face. I seize opportunities, ripe for the taking. The world is at my fingertips and impossible realities dwell around me. There are dragons in the skies and they're not trying to eat me." He chuckled. "That alone makes it worth it." His tone became serious. "I have a captain that respects me, a crew that is my family, and I am free to live and die as *I* choose." He met my gaze again. "I would not trade it for the world... The only form of so-called love I knew was that of monsters. It was a poison I was willing to give up. I never tasted true love to know what I surrendered."

Marcus' face flashed through my mind—those kind eyes, that wry smile, the feel of his hand in mine. His arms around me as we danced, the agony in my chest as they tortured him in front of me.

I want nothing more in the world than to protect him...but if I gave him up, it wouldn't protect him. It would only break his heart. I do not have a heart to offer the Moores. Marcus already has my heart. I can't run any longer, I have to accept my fate. I have to face it...I think Ember and I both do.

Tears flooded my eyes and rushed down my cheeks as I at last realized the truth. There was no way out. We had no way to escape our fate.

"The choice is yours, Eve, but you must know the cost of weakening the Gate. There is a price to denying your blood. I am marked a traitor. The cost of such a mark is that I will be a wanderer, a haunt, after death. My heart belongs to the Moores."

I stared down at my hands.

"You can't keep running from who you are, my grouchy kraken. This darkness will find you. We can't escape who we are...because one way or another, it will find us." He shrugged. "I was meant to be a defender. I defend this ship and my family on board it with my life. But your destiny lies elsewhere. It calls to you. Do not deny your blood if you want to see this world changed. You have the power to change this Realm. Just because they say *they* get to decide who you are, doesn't mean it's true. They want you to believe it is, so they can retain their power over you." He stared down at his hands, his work falling quiet for a moment. "Only you can choose your path and decide your fate. The rest of their nonsense is just smoke and mirrors."

"How do I know which path to take?" I whispered raggedly.

"You do what is right, and you fight to make a change in this dark world. They want you trapped in the darkness. But as Dylan Thomas says, 'rage, rage against the dying of the light.' It is the only way forward. It is the only way to be the change."

53

I Can't Run Any Longer (Because Cardio Is Not My Thing)

EMBER

"No one wearing a crown comes in the name of peace-queens show no mercy."

-J.M.

I knew I was dreaming. I never would have worn such a ridiculous dress if I wasn't dreaming. But still, something about the setting was wrong. There was something within the dream that didn't belong, I just couldn't figure out what it was.

The room was exorbitantly decorated. Splendor surrounded me and my dress resembled a trail of glimmering stars. It was intricate and gorgeous, as if it had been woven with magic and starlight. Long blonde hair, the color of gold, spilled over my shoulder. The pale skin of my arms almost seemed to glow it was so translucent. The man I was dancing with was tall and handsome, with dark black hair and bright green eyes. He looked vaguely familiar, but I couldn't place where I'd seen his face before.

Perhaps in a different Dreamscape? I've had a fair few dancing Dreamscapes...

A golden crown sat on top of his head, so I figured it was safe to assume he was the king. Why I was dancing with a king, however, was beyond me.

The girl I had become kept trying to pull away from the King, but he held me tightly, his eyes staring intently down at me, as if trying to memorize my face.

I have to get back...I have to get away or I'll be missed.

Phantom girl's thoughts swirled through my mind. There, then gone in an instant.

Where does she have to go?

I wrenched myself from the king's arms and shoved my way into the crowd. He lunged after me with a shout, but I was faster. I burst from the ballroom and pelted down the empty hallway, losing him in the many twists and turns. I was running toward a large door now. The sounds of cooking and clattering could be heard inside. Beside the large door, a massive staircase led to an upper floor. There, in the curve of the staircase, a small door was hidden, leading into a tiny little cubby.

Am I Harry Potter now? Living under a staircase?

I rushed inside the little space, chest heaving as I pressed my ear against the door and listened. Several moments later, footsteps rushed past the door. I had just barely managed to stay ahead of the king.

The cubby was miniscule. A small mat was spread out on the floor, with a thin, ragged blanket folded neatly on top. My hands were a flurry of movements as I grabbed a thick, mottled coat. It was made like a patchwork quilt, with bits and pieces of many different types of animal pelts haphazardly sewn together. I hastily pulled it on over my dress.

A bucket of ash sat on the floor by the doorway. I quickly grabbed a small handful, then hastily smeared it all over my arms and hands, then across my face and neck. Soon, I was absolutely filthy. My skin and body were unrecognizable from the polished splendor that, moments before, had held an entire ballroom in awe.

I fastened my fur cloak, obscuring the dress entirely, then turned to leave. I stopped with a muttered cry of alarm and ran back to my little mat. Underneath the far corner sat a jumbled collection of items. I grabbed a small reel, which looked much like a bobbin, made entirely of gold, and then I was out the small door and through the large kitchen door.

"Where were you?" A man yelled angrily from the side of the room. He was elbows deep in pastry dough. "You have to make the soup!"

"I'm sorry," my voice called in a foreign lilting accent. "It was all too magnificent to leave."

"The king needs his soup!" the man scolded. "Next time I will not let you out to view the party if this is how you choose to repay me."

I made no reply as my hands began to quickly prepare the soup. Vegetables were swiftly chopped and thrown into a large pot as a bowl of bread dough rose on the far end of the table.

Hey look, dream me can cook!

There's absolutely no chance of me burning down the house in a dream...is there? Surely my poor cooking skills won't ruin the Dreamscape cook's abilities, will it?

The room blurred around me as I worked. Soon, the dough was formed into balls and placed in the oven to bake. Then, after about twenty minutes or so, the soup was done, and I was ladling it into a large bowl and setting the bowl on a tray.

"Take it out to the King," the angry pastry chef called. "I'm busy and he wants it delivered personally."

"The rolls are in the oven," I replied. "Watch them for me?"

The pastry chef nodded, his eyes on his work.

I glanced around quickly and after ensuring no one was watching, I dropped the golden bobbin into the bowl of soup.

Girl, what on earth are you thinking?

The tray shook slightly in my hands as I carried it out. Soldiers bustled around me as I made my way back toward the ballroom, but none of them gave me a second glance.

He's going to know this chick put the bobbin in. It's a dead giveaway. He's going to know. What on earth is she thinking?

Is she trying to get caught?!

Was she dropped on her head as an infant?

The ballroom shone alluringly, but my feet carried me off to a room on the side, where a large court was gathered around a long table. There, at the head on the far end, sat the king.

His green eyes were fixed on me as I walked forward. I could feel the weight of his gaze, though I kept my eyes down—focusing on putting one foot in front of the other.

Just deliver the soup and get out. Otherwise, he's going to know.

Thank goodness dream me isn't clumsy.

I set the tray in front of him and then backed away. His eyes lingered on my face and then fell to my hands. I kept my features neutral as I backed away, eyes lowered and expression blank.

He's going to know. She put the bobbin in there and delivered it herself. He's going to know, why would she do that?

Before I could make it back to the other end of the hall and out the door, he had finished the bowl of soup and was holding the golden reel in his hand. "Stop her!" he called.

I knew it. This chick is so incredibly dumb. What on earth was she thinking?

Guards stepped in front of the doorway, blocking my escape.

Stupid, stupid girl. Why would you let yourself get caught?

"Come here," the king commanded.

My steps were slow as I made my way back to where he sat at the head of the table.

"What's the meaning of this?" he demanded, holding up the golden reel.

"I know nothing, my king," I replied quietly.

He leaned forward and grabbed my hand, staring down at my pinky finger. I had missed it in my haste to get back to the kitchen. It sat pale as milk, a stark contrast to the rest of my dirty skin.

I struggled to free myself, but the buttons on the cloak were quickly coming undone.

He's going to see! Stop struggling, girl! Stop struggling!

It was no use. My body kept fighting, and soon the buttons slipped, revealing the undeniable shine of the starlight dress.

The king touched a thin ring on my ring finger and my efforts fell still.

Where did that come from? How long has that been there?

I couldn't stop him as he undid the last of the buttons and wrenched the cloak from my shoulders. The dress shone in all its glory and the entire room gasped.

This has to be the worst look possible. Beautiful dress, incredibly dirty lady...

The king was triumphant as he dipped his napkin in his waterglass and began to wipe the ash and soot from my face. "It is you," he breathed.

Yes, yes, you win Sherlock award of the year, Mr. King.

"You are indeed my dear bride, and we shall never part," the king whispered.

Okay Romeo, calm down. You don't even know me. You can't possibly want to marry me. Just because we had a lovely time dancing doesn't mean we're soulmates. We haven't spent enough time together to know if my chewing is going to drive you crazy, or if I can stand you when you get angry. Do you throw things? Do you yell?

I can't be with someone who gets angry like that.

The gray mist was gathering at the edge of my vision, and I braced myself for the dream to pull back and begin again. But it didn't. Instead, it paused as the mist gathered until we were the only ones left in the room.

The king still stared down at me, eyes shining triumphantly as he held me close.

Something isn't right.

His eyes. The green is changing.

It's Artemis.

CRAP.

I struggled against the dream, desperately trying to wake myself up.

"Hello, my Flamín," Artemis' voice said from a stranger's face. The only thing that was truly his were his eyes.

I continued to fight, trying to wrench myself from his grasp. I had control of my body again, but it was useless. I couldn't get away.

"Let's have a little talk, you and me. I would rather like to go back to the ballroom. It was magnificent and the dance was utterly delightful. You look quite stunning as a blonde, but I prefer your fiery locks.

Now is not the time for compliments, you stupid, moronic prince.

The dream was shattering around us, until at last we stood in our own bodies.

"Now, let's talk."

"I'd rather not," I snapped. "I have soup to make."

"While the soup was delicious, *you* didn't make the soup. Your blonde alter ego did. Last I heard, you couldn't cook to save your life."

"Who told you that?" I demanded angrily, my cheeks blushing in embarrassment.

How dare he insult my cooking. Even if he's right, he doesn't have the liberty to insult it.

"You just confirmed it by your reaction," he laughed.

Ember: zero. Artemis: one.

Shut up. Nobody asked you to keep score.

"It was a wild guess from a disconnected memory. Something your sister said about peanut butter and jelly..."

I rolled my eyes. "What do you want, Artemis? Surely you didn't come to talk to me about my cooking skills."

"No, I didn't," Artemis replied, staring down at our entwined fingers. "I came to give you a warning."

"Oh? And what is that?"

"Tell your captain I arrive tomorrow, and I intend to reclaim both of you peacefully."

"That's not going to happen," I growled angrily. "We don't want to come." My voice faltered, revealing my lie.

I don't want to come...but I don't want to stay away. I am a being of contradictions, and it is tearing me apart.

"Maybe so, perhaps not. Either way, you're out of time. You need to come back."

"No."

"They'll kill your brother if I come back without you. Surely by now you've discovered the other path of the Grimms, the denial of your blood. Surely by now you've discovered it's not a path you can take."

I was in denial as I desperately tried to pull away from him. "No," I whispered. "There's another way. There's another way."

"The path that Theron took sacrifices your love to the Moores. It dooms you to live without love and surrender your heart to the Moores. After death, you will be a haunt. That is not a path you can take."

"Why is that?" I whispered angrily. He was right, but I wasn't willing to admit it.

"Because your broken heart already belongs to me, just as mine does to you," Artemis stated gently. "But putting that aside, you must come back. We need to be done with this foolishness. I can't return to the Realms without you. Say your goodbyes and be ready to go."

"No," I hissed. "We won't. We will fight you."

"Are you willing to let your new friends die for you?" Artemis asked, his eyes probing mine. "Is that a price you're willing to pay for the illusion of freedom? What about the death of the Realms? Is that a price you're willing to pay?"

"I—"

"If that is the path you choose, it will bring you nothing but sorrow," Artemis pressed, pulling away. His hand was gentle as he cupped my cheek. "We can't change our fates, my Flamín. We can only rise to meet them as we fight for a better tomorrow."

His eyes were full of sorrow as he looked at me. "Say your goodbyes," he repeated. "Your time is up."

54

I'd Risk It All For You

EVADNE

"The question is, what color will everything be at that moment when
I come for you? What will the sky be saying?"
-Marcus Zusak, The Book Thief

It was an understatement to say that Verity was greatly displeased with Ember's report.
It took her a solid five minutes to put words together in a comprehensive manner that
didn't rabbit trail off into insults and swear words.

"Nobody tells me what to do," Verity snarled, outraged. "It's *my* ship, in *my* skies.
I'll stop when *I* want to, not a minute sooner. Certainly not because some stuck up, no
good, dirty rotten—"

"Verity," Theron cut in with an exasperated sigh.

"*Prince* of the cursed Summer Court," Verity continued, picking up her original trail
of thought, "orders me to."

She glared out at the horizon as Ember and I stood in anxious silence.

"Verity, I don't want anyone getting hurt," Ember began.

"None of your self-sacrificing heroism, please," Verity scolded, rolling her eyes.
"Answer me this. Do you *want* to go back to the Courts?"

We contemplated the question. I knew I didn't want to go back, not yet. But to be quite honest, after the conversation with Theron, I wasn't sure what I wanted anymore.

I want a future with Marcus...but I don't know if it's something I can have. Our chance of escape was never a chance at all...is there any point in continuing to run away?

"Not yet...?" Ember began quietly. "I think...I think eventually, yes? I...I do want a future with Artemis by my side..." she admitted softly.

It was the first time I had heard her admit the truth out loud.

"But I need to find a way to make it be on my terms, not that of the Last Gate...but I...I don't know enough to make that happen yet...I don't even know if it's possible." She sighed, trying to sort out her thoughts. "In all honesty, I don't think we have a choice. The path we thought we could take isn't an option...not anymore." Tears rushed to her eyes.

We had both been crushed by the truth that Theron's path was not one we could take. Neither of us had a heart to offer the Moores.

"You always have a choice," Theron snapped. He was staring down at the map spread across Verity's table. "Verity, there was a path on the edge of this cliff here." He pointed to a spot on the map. "Last we traversed this part of the skies...if we can get there, I can take the girls and run."

"Theron, I don't think splitting up is a smart idea," Verity cut in.

Theron pursed his lips. "Well, let's see what state we're in once we reach that path, deal?"

"Fine," Verity sighed irritably.

Theron turned back to us. "This crew will fight for you; we consider you our family and friends. If we're hurt, we're hurt. It's our choice, not yours, certainly not his."

"Theron—" Ember began.

"Embeeeer," Theron interrupted sarcastically. "Look, I know what you're saying, but I disagree. It's our choice to fight. We are not blindly walking into a situation without knowing the possibilities."

"And more than that," Verity continued. "I am not okay with the monarchs tromping through *our* Moores and telling us what to do. I harbor who I wish. He doesn't get to tell me what to do. Unless you're begging me to take you back to him, I will fight him on those grounds alone. He does *not* get to boss me around." She turned to Theron. "Take the girls up to the rigging. You guard Ember, tell Raz to guard Evadne. If we have any luck, we can cripple their ship and leave them floating in the skies for the dragons to find."

"Yes ma'am," Theron replied happily. "Come on girls, we have some pirating to attend to."

We followed Theron through the chaos on the deck as he happily whistled 'a pirate's life for me.'

The ship was within sight now, but Verity gave no indication of stopping. We were cutting through the skies at full speed.

I searched the outline of the ship for any sign of Marcus, even though it was still too far away to make out any details.

Please don't be on that ship. Please don't make me fight you.

The promise ring seemed to grow heavier on my finger as I wrestled against my thoughts and feelings. I didn't want anyone to get hurt, but I also didn't know what my actual decision was. There were too many questions left unanswered, and everything suddenly felt hopeless. I had to face my fate, yet now that it stood before me, I was hesitant to act.

Time dragged on and I watched with bated breath from my post as the sleek ship drew closer. No amount of speed we put on was making a difference.

Fireheart hummed anxiously on my shoulder, staring at the ship in contempt as he bared his little fangs. I could only imagine what his battle screeches were—they probably all referenced death by cheese and fire.

A ball of energy rushed at the ship, a glowing green orb that pulsed violence.

Verity barked a word, sending out a counter ball, but it was too late. The green orb slammed into the far mast and it exploded. Burning pieces of wood and rubble fell and the crew scattered, trying to avoid the dangerous rubble.

"Stop blowing holes in my bloody ship!" Faolan roared as he rushed to the damaged mast. He put his palms on the wood and began to quickly repair the damage.

Verity raised her hands, and a gust of wind erupted from her fingertips. Artemis' ship balked and bucked, fighting to get through the sudden tempest. We gained headway for a few minutes, but our defense was short-lived. Another burst of green light enveloped Verity's wind, and it cracked, dissolving into a flurry of snowflakes.

Verity swore and rushed to the ship's wheel, taking it from Nikos' control. Nikos drew his blades with a savage grin and rushed toward the main deck. Verity began chanting, and another wind rose behind us, pushing our ship forward.

Raz stiffened beside me. "This is bad," she muttered. "If Verity is already resorting to using her magic, then we are in very real danger of being overtaken."

"Why is this so much different from when the Raiders came?" I asked, confused.

"This ship has a very powerful sorcerer aiding it. Verity isn't taking a chance. We've been in countless battles; it's part of being a pirate and a voyager. But Verity only uses her magic as a last resort."

A plant was growing in Raz's hand, and after watching it grow for a few moments, she gave me a wicked smile. "Let's see how your sister's prince plays with this, shall we?"

She hurled the plant at his ship. As it flew, it began to expand. Tendrils rapidly grew until at last it collided with the ship's hull. Thorns sprouted, embedding themselves into the wood. A gigantic vine exploded, rushing across the surface of the ship.

Another set of vines exploded from the hull of the ship, attacking Raz's.

Raz watched the plants fight, glaring. "Well, this is an unfortunate turn of events," she muttered angrily.

"What?"

"Rosamond is on the ship," Raz replied icily. "I'd know her cursed magic anywhere."

My eyes at last landed on the figure I had been searching for. I knew the sharp jaw, the set of his shoulders, the way his body took up the space. I'd know my Marcus anywhere.

Despair cut through me as we locked eyes across the vast expanse of sky.

Why are you there? Why did you come?

I couldn't breathe.

Why would you come with Artemis? Why would you side with him?

The questions ran around my mind as I seized my Inheritance, readying myself for a fight.

"When they hit the ship, flood it!" Raz yelled.

A roar shook the air as a dozen dragons burst out of the clouds, colliding with Artemis' ship.

Raz whooped in delight as I searched for the strand of connection that bound my mind to the dragons. There, at last I found it. Their song had morphed into that of a battle roar—a rage filled scream of blood and fire that swore to protect the one who called. Flashes of past battles rushed through my mind. Teeth and claws, agonizing screams, and endless fire overwhelmed everything.

"Don't hurt them. Disable the ship and stop the pursuit. But don't kill them. The one I love is on that ship."

The dragons roared, accepting my instructions.

"You command our oath, Kaida," the leader growled.

What does Kaida mean?

There was no chance to ask what he meant. The link trembled and faded as the dragons turned their attention to a plan of action.

They broke apart, pulling back and up until they formed a circle high above us. They were preparing to dive again at Artemis' ship, but a clear dome rippled out from the middle of it, shielding them from the dragons' assault. I watched in horror as the circle grew, encircling ours as well.

It's like a force field...

I watched in rising panic as the dragons dove, pummeling the bubble with roars of anger, then pain. Every assault sent out a lightning effect of power, striking the dragons as it rushed from one body to the next—injuring them all.

He's hurting my dragons. It's going to kill them if they keep trying.

Pain was overwhelming my senses as the dragons fought against Artemis' magic. Over and over, they attacked the barrier, trying to weaken it or find some weak spot in its composition.

It did no good. The magic held, attacking them back with every strike.

I didn't mean for them to get hurt like this.

How can Artemis muster this much power?

"*RETREAT!*" I yelled through my bond, putting every ounce of authority and command into the words as I could muster.

The dragons drew back, hovering in the air around us at the edge of the forcefield as their questions rushed over me.

"*Find a safe place to go,*" I pressed gently. "*This is a fight I must win on my own.*"

"*We would serve you to our death,*" the commander argued.

"*I know, but that is not a price I'm willing to pay. I will have need of you in the future when we fight the darkness.*"

The leader bowed his head. "*If you need us, call. We will always come. No matter the distance, no matter the Realm. The bond is unbreakable. We will answer your call, Kaida.*"

I touched my heart and bowed.

In unison they dipped their heads, then turned and disappeared.

"Where are they going?!" Raz yelled in disbelief.

"His magic will kill them. It's too powerful. I couldn't watch them die, so I sent them away."

Raz nodded. "The magic he's using is raw and unfiltered. He must be desperate to use that much in one go."

I nodded. "I can't let them die, not like this. This fight is inevitable, but it's not the one that matters."

The ships collided and my balance wavered. Crew members were flying at our ship and swinging across on ropes.

"NOW!" Verity screamed. "Flood them!"

Water surged from my hands, rushing toward his ship at blinding speed.

Fire exploded from the mast across from us as Ember's phoenix raced toward Artemis' ship, screeching in rage.

Sheesh. Artemis must have really pissed her off in their dream conversation.

You go Em!

The masts and the upper decks caught on fire as my water encased the ship in an isolated bubble with Ember's phoenix. But what caught my attention was how my water did not douse Ember's fire. The two combined and worked together in an unstoppable force against Artemis and his crew.

Two figures broke through the water, swinging directly toward us.

"Heads up!" Raz yelled as she launched off the deck and attacked the first man.

They tumbled down, down, down, fighting tooth and nail until they disappeared beneath the ship.

"RAZ!" I screamed.

My concentration broke and the water shield fell around the ship, flooding the deck with a tidal wave of water. Men fell screaming into the sky, washed from the deck, desperately activating parachutes and wings to save themselves.

The second figure landed on the other side of my mast, sword drawn.

I turned, feral with rage, ready to tear the invader apart.

Marcus stood dripping in front of me, his chest heaving as his gaze locked onto me. "Eve," he rasped.

Why are you here? Why are you trying to take me back??

Does he still think I'm beautiful with this monstrosity of an eye?

How could you? How could you?!

The chaotic questions circled, a never-ending ball of anxiety.

I lunged across the narrow beam with a yell, trying to ignore the ache in my heart as our swords met.

How did it come to this? How did we become such monsters?

I slashed, blind with anger and he dodged, knocking the sword from my grasp with a sharp hit of his sword hilt.

Pain spread over my hand, and he caught the tip of my blade as it fell, flipping it up, end for end, before catching it out of the air.

I will protect my sister. I will protect my family.

Why are you fighting me?!

"Eve!" Marcus yelled.

I drew my daggers and attacked again, painfully aware of how much ground I was losing. He was pushing me back, seemingly without trying. It was infuriating to me that after all my training, he was still better. My feet were off the mast now, as he backed me onto the small platform that rested at the cross of the two beams.

My shoulders collided with the upward mast, and I desperately threw my dagger at him.

My aim held true, and the blade buried itself in his shoulder. He snarled in pain, but continued to advance, unheeding of the wound. His arms were a blur and before I could think how to block him, he had me disarmed. My remaining knife clattered on the platform and both the swords were crossed against my throat.

I can't get to my other daggers without him seeing...

"EVE!" he yelled.

I blinked, thoughts racing as I stared at him, anger and grief tearing my mind apart.

If I am to be harmed, then let me choose my destruction. It is you. It will always be you.

The swords swept down as he sheathed both behind his back, and before I knew it, his hands were on either side of my face and his lips crashed into mine.

The world faded for a moment, and before I could stop myself, I was kissing him back.

What am I doing?!

I'm kissing the enemy!

When did he become the enemy? When did my heart become the enemy?

I love you; I love you.

Why are you doing this to me?

I wrenched away, pushing him back a step as I drew two more daggers from the sheath on my back. I ducked under his blades in one quick move and stepped behind him. He turned to face me, only to find my daggers at his throat and his back against the mast.

"You know I'm not going to hurt you," he whispered.

"Your sword was at my throat!" I yelled. "You're attacking our ship! So, forgive me if I'm hesitant to believe you."

"I had no choice!"

"You always have a choice!" I screamed, raw with desperation and grief. "You could choose to say no and walk away."

He swallowed. "I couldn't leave you."

"So you decided to try to drag me back, regardless of what I want?" I demanded, my voice trembling.

"No," he snapped. "That's not what I'm doing. I came to help you."

"This is your idea of helping?" I scoffed. "Join forces with a prince who will clearly go to any length to ensure that we are in his court? Who will take us against our will, back to the Realm? Who plays with my sister's heart as if it's nothing, because their magic is bound? This is your idea of helping?"

I was trembling, caught in indecision and anger, torn apart by questions I couldn't answer.

"Artemis has no choice," Marcus replied urgently. "They'll kill Jack if he comes back without you. They will *destroy* the Moores to get you back. They will slaughter *everyone*. He has to get you back or the monarchs will wreak such indescribable hell on everyone here, there will be nothing left."

"We don't have a way forward," I sobbed. "We need more time to figure it out."

"There's no time left," Marcus said, his tone gentle.

"So that's it, you're just going to take me back?" I demanded.

"I'm not going to do anything," Marcus whispered. He leaned forward, uncaring of my blades at his throat. "I would not force your hand to anything," he said softly as his lips brushed mine. "It would break your heart."

"What are you saying?" I sobbed, pulling away from his kiss.

"Take your sister and go. But please, Eve, don't bind yourself to the Moores. Whatever you do, don't choose Theron's fate. It will mean the end of the Realm if you bind yourself to that cursed magic."

"Either way I'm cursed," I whispered helplessly. "What does it matter what curse I choose?"

I wasn't going to choose Theron's path, but in that moment of raw emotions, I couldn't find a logical course of thought.

"It will mean the end of us," Marcus murmured. Desperation clung to every syllable. "Please, don't destroy my heart."

I can't destroy you, I can't lose you.

"One choice might save millions of lives," Marcus continued gently. "One will destroy us all. Those are the choices that rest in front of you at the end of all this. Running will buy you a little more time before you decide what path you'll take. The Moores are lost. They hold nothing except the rising darkness. But if you run a little longer...you might find what you're looking for."

"I don't know what I'm looking for," I sobbed.

"You're looking for peace," Marcus said with a shrug. "Peace of mind to accept what you cannot change. Peace of heart to have the courage to embrace what you want most."

"I'm looking for you," I choked out. "But I can't have you. It's too much of a risk."

"It's a risk I'm willing to take if I had just a day, an hour, a moment," Marcus murmured, pulling me close. "I'd risk it all for you...don't run on account of me. We still have hope, even with the future that looms, there is still hope for us."

"Is there?" I whispered raggedly.

"There's always hope," he pressed. "There is always hope. Until the Moores crumble around us and the Realm is reborn or lost, we have hope. You still have a way out...it might buy you some more time."

Marcus was pointing, but I couldn't quite make out what he was pointing to. Then, it began to materialize. The ship was coming up on an island, and there at the edge of the island, stood a blood red door with an ornate knocker.

"What about Artemis?" I breathed, lowering my knives. "He'll know you helped us escape."

"What Artemis doesn't know won't hurt him," Marcus replied with a crooked grin. "We see the world a little differently at the moment. He doesn't want this cat-and-mouse game to continue." His crooked smile widened into a flirtatious grin. "I rather like the chase."

Marcus pulled my sword from his sheath and put it back into the sheath at my hip. My cloak billowed around me as I stared at him, conflicted and shocked.

He pulled the knife from his shoulder with a wince and cut off the bottom edge of his shirt, wrapping it tightly around the wound. "Tie it off for me, would you?" he asked, giving me a crooked smile.

My hands trembled as I grasped the ends of the fabric and tied it off as tightly as I could. "I'm sorry," I murmured. "I was so angry...I just wasn't thinking. I've been so conflicted I don't know what to do anymore."

"It was a good shot. I'm sure on some level I deserved it. Besides, I should take pride in it, since I'm the one who taught you to throw your knives so well."

I smirked. "I was aiming for your head."

He clutched his chest and laughed. "Well then, I should be glad that I didn't train you quite well enough." He pressed a kiss to my forehead. "Go," he murmured. "There may yet be another path no one knows of that will take you from this place and save you from the bloody fate they want for you. I'll find you again."

"Will you?"

"I can't possibly stay away," he quipped, giving me a wide grin.

"He's going to kill you when he finds out," I whispered raggedly.

"I meant it when I said I was willing to risk everything," he replied. "But now it means I have to let you go."

The world seemed to shatter around us as my heartbeat stuttered and ached. To leave him willingly felt as if I was leaving a part of myself.

"I don't know if I can leave you again. It feels like my heart is breaking."

"I'll find you," he repeated gently. "I promise, Eve, I'll find you again."

I pulled him close, stealing a final desperate kiss. "I love you," I murmured.

"I love you, too. Now go."

"I love you," I repeated. "I'll find *you* again," I whispered, repeating his words. "I promise."

"Go," he whispered.

My heart trembled in my chest, aching, as I at last turned and fled, trying to get to Ember before Artemis found her in the chaos.

55

When You Kick The Hornet's Nest, You'd Best Prepare To Die

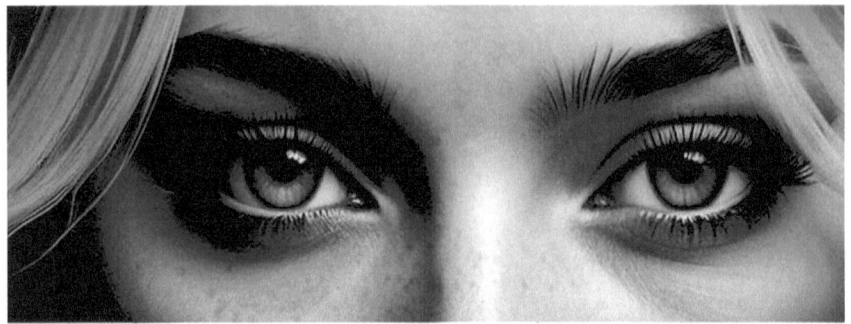

FAYE

"I think women are foolish to consider themselves equal to men, for
they're far superior and always have been."
-William Golding

Much to my disappointment, Jeremiah didn't follow the proposed plan and allow
Ronan to take me out of solitary. He also didn't pick a fight when he finally decided to
show up. If anything, he seemed distracted and disoriented. There was a heavy presence
around him now. One that hadn't been there last time, and it worried me how unlike
himself he seemed. Whatever he was messing with was consuming him at a much faster
pace. It wouldn't be long until the man himself was gone, and only darkness remained.
We were running out of time. I had no doubt that when the shadows consumed him,
he would try to kill Meghan.

Alone at last in my room, I paced anxiously, waiting for the noise to die down. I had
to be sure it wasn't some sort of a sick trick to make me feel comfortable.

Time to get to work.

My laptop was back in my bookbag, shoved underneath my bed. I knew Ronan had done what I asked and logged me into the internet, because it had been put back in the wrong place.

I pulled it out, hands shaking as I grabbed the cord and walked into the bathroom. The only outlet in my cell was by the sink. Plus, I could possibly hide the laptop underneath the sink if someone came in unexpectedly.

After putting my handy dandy Ronan alarm in place, my three brain cells began to bicker about whether or not it should remain named after Ronan, since Ronan had very quickly won them over with his little speech and, of course, the kiss.

I blushed crimson, remembering that kiss, as I grabbed the pillow and blanket from my bed and settled down on the floor to work.

I can't think about that now. I can't. I can't let myself fall for him. It's too dangerous. I'll be the death of him...he will only break my heart...I can hear the bloodshed that awaits us in the future...I can't love him, I can't. I can't bear the heartbreak of losing him.

It was no use lecturing myself. The three brain cells had pulled out a projector screen and were now rewatching the moment, over and over again, while they happily munched on popcorn and squealed in absolute delight. The hoard quickly joined them and soon, they were utterly out of control. The three had begun to plan our wedding and were designing what type of dress I'd wear. They mooned over how handsome Ronan would look in a suit and wondered what color tie would best bring out his stormy gray eyes. Eyes that, coincidentally, they had polaroid pictures of taped up all over the walls.

It took four hours and seventeen minutes, a bag of gummy worms Ronan had apparently smuggled into my bag, and an especially complex grouping of multi-Realm malware to destroy the Andersons' database.

It was a particularly nasty piece of work, considering I interwove some stolen pixie code in as well—there was a reason I was taking my laptop to the Realm. The pixies absolutely loved hacking the human Realm and causing general amounts of havoc and chaos. I had picked up some knowledge during long stints of boredom at the Summer

Court. But I planned to do more when I went back, just for the sheer joy of giving some very bad people in the Human Realm a migraine. After I was done with it, I had the grand idea to trade it to the pixies for some explosives.

It was my own personal vindictive and dastardly evil touch that, with the final click of my mouse that brought the database down, every device connected began to blare an endless loop of *Baby Shark* at top volume.

Jeremiah had made the mistake of interconnecting every device on the compound to his database, creating a monitoring system that allowed him to view what everyone else was doing. Once I was in his system, I was in every system. His own hubris allowed me to destroy everything in one go.

Soon enough footsteps began pounding down my hallway. The unmistakable sound of *Baby Shark* getting closer and closer.

Having returned my bed to its proper location, I sat down, placing my beautiful laptop beside me. It was covered in a bright array of amazing stickers I had collected over the years. My particular favorite was one I had gotten off of Etsy when I was sixteen. It featured an incredibly round raccoon with the title 'chonky.' The raccoon was closely followed by a switchblade with the caption 'feeling stabby,' and a screeching fox with a chainsaw, intent on mass destruction.

Who am I kidding? I love all of my stickers.

It was pointless to hide the laptop, even though I had wiped and destroyed it. Jeremiah was bound to search for it, and that would only lead him to discover everything else I had hidden around the room. I wasn't about to let him take *all* the contents of my backpack. Just to be safe, I had taken the extra precaution of hiding my iPod and headphones inside one of the towels under the sink. Of all my possessions, that was the most valuable one I possessed.

I squared my shoulders as a key turned in the lock.

I am Faye Narah Grimm, and I will not be afraid. I am Faye Narah Grimm, and I will protect Meghan from this monster.

Jeremiah strolled leisurely into the room, his eyes fixed solely on me. I watched in silence as he began to clap, slowly. "Come on men," he jeered. "Let's give our distinguished guest a hand, shall we?"

The men behind him shifted uncomfortably and then broke into a scattered smattering of awkward applause.

I bowed at the waist, opting to stay sitting. "I'd stand, but I find myself rather weak at the moment."

Jeremiah didn't acknowledge my sarcasm. "It seems I have underestimated you, my little Grimm," he snarled. "You are so much like your pathetic *dead* mother. I should have known better. She was wicked and crafty like you, always sticking her nasty, selfish fingers where they didn't belong."

Rage flared hot in my chest, I wanted to hurt him, like he'd hurt her.

Stick to the plan!

Baby shark, doo, doo, doo, doo, doodoo. Baby shark, doo, doo, doo, doo, doodoo...

Stick to the plan...doo, doo, doo, doo, doodoo...to the plan doo, doo, doo, doo, doodoo...

"Ronan was right, I shouldn't have given you your computer back all those months ago. But I admit, I never dreamed you to be capable of such destruction...I never thought you were smart enough. To be honest, I thought perhaps you'd play solitaire, make vlogs of yourself whining about your terrible luck...perhaps write some terrible poetry.

My poetry is amazing, thank you very much.

Here, let me show you. I think you're a jerk and Ronan thinks so too, we both give you a finger and say you're made of pooooo.

Jeremiah snatched the laptop off the bed. I made no move to stop him. I was much too busy composing insulting poetry.

You think that I'm trapped here, you think that I'm stuck, but let me tell you buddy, I don't give a—

"Perhaps I'll use this since it's not compromised. Nor is it singing that idiotic song."

"I destroyed it," I snapped, annoyed he'd interrupted my brilliant poetry. "After the final piece of code went into place, I trashed the system. I wouldn't be so stupid as to leave it usable for you. There's no undoing what I've done. You're stuck listening to the brain melting children's song."

I narrowed my eyes, taunting him.

Come on, take the bait. Take me to your fancy office with the door. I know how to get out of here from there. Ronan gave me all the directions.

Meanwhile, my brain cells were busy dancing to the song, complete with all the sharky hand motions.

Grandma shark, doo, doo, doo, doo, doodoo...Grandma shark, doo, doo—

I was too busy singing to notice the computer as it sped toward me. I toppled, stars exploding across my vision as it slammed into the side of my head.

It's the end, doo, doo, doo, doo, doodoo. It's the end, doo, doo, doo, doo, doodoo...It's the end...

Please, let it be the end, please...

Pain was everywhere as Jeremiah knocked me off the bed and continued to beat me with the laptop.

Worth it. She's worth it. I will protect her from you.

At last, the ruthless assault stopped, and Jeremiah hurled the computer at the wall, his face deadly calm as it smashed against the unforgiving steel and broke apart. Shards of plastic and glass exploded from the force and scattered over the floor.

"You two, pick her up and come with me. The rest of you, get back to work."

Finally. Take me to the office, oh human chariots.

Two men whose names I didn't know hauled me to my feet.

They must be new at this, they left my arms free.

Jeremiah took a step closer until he was inches from me. "You will regret what you have done," he hissed.

"I regret I didn't do worse," I spat, as I rammed my head forward and smashed my forehead into his nose. I quickly followed the first assault with a second, ramming my fist beneath his chin in a harsh uppercut.

Jeremiah stumbled back, blood pouring out of his nose. His hand was a blur as he slapped me across the face.

My lip was bleeding, as was my nose and other parts of my body, but none of it mattered. Nothing could quell my satisfaction of seeing Jeremiah bleeding before me. I smiled savagely up at him, letting the monster I kept carefully hidden out for the briefest moment.

That was for Meghan, you sick piece of trash.

The Realm made me into a monster. See me for what I am. I will eat you whole.

Jeremiah's men drew back, unnerved by the feral rage that was quickly overwhelming me.

Where's Marcov? I think maybe I'll pick a fight.

I glanced around the room. He was nowhere to be found.

Funny. I would have thought he'd be here to see the show.

Aw man, I wanted to pick a fight!

"I tire of this rebellious act," Jeremiah hissed. "You'll soon break beneath the shadows. My king has a *nasty* surprise for you, witch."

Well, that sounds ominous. Too bad for him we're not going to explore that particular surprise today.

Why does he keep calling me a witch? Clearly, I haven't eaten anyone or dabbled in the darkness. That's so incredibly rude. At least give me a chance to do something that rightfully earns the title of witch.

He turned away and I went limp, trying to catch my breath.

The men gingerly stepped forward and pulled me to my feet. I continued to feign exhaustion and weakness, ensuring the men were forced to drag my dead weight through the halls.

Hehe, carry on my gullible human chariots. You're going to wear yourselves out, whereas I'll be fresh as a spring chicken.

I wonder where that phrase comes from. Why are spring chickens referred to as fresh. Is it because they're born in the spring, or is it because they're sassy? What definition of fresh are they referring to?

Daddy shark doo, doo, doo, doo, doodoo...Daddy shark, doo, doo, doo, doo, doodoo...

Jeremiah's office was cast in shadows. It was so dark the lights around the room did nothing to penetrate the presence.

This is not good.

We'll think about it later. We have business to attend to. The men are going to take me in there, and then I am going to cause a scene. After which Ronan is going to try to stop me. At which point I shall then cause an even greater scene.

Yesss! I love causing scenes!

The two men dragged me in, and to pretend bravery, I pulled my feet under me and stood.

"Ah, the ever valiant warrior rallies," Jeremiah droned. "Michael, go fetch Ronan, would you? He should have been here by now. Once you've found him, go about your duties. The girl won't give us any trouble, of that I am sure. She can hardly stand."

To emphasize his point, I swayed slightly, allowing my eyes to go glassy.

"Yes sir," the man on my right replied as he entrusted me to the man on the left's care.

The door closed firmly behind him, and I began to count backward from a hundred. Ronan should already be on his way, so it wouldn't take the right-hand man long to find him.

Ninety-six bottles of pixie farts on the wall...ninety-six bottles of farts...take one down, spin it around...boom there's fifty bottles of farts on a wall...

The little ditty ran a deranged circle around my mind, and I began to wonder if I was going crazy.

Well, revenge is best served piping hot with a side of insanity. I'm only doing my due diligence to ensure Jeremiah gets my revenge in the best possible fashion.

My three brain cells were getting out of control with the bottles of pixie farts. I had lost count, and now they were just lobbing the highly fragile explosives around, blowing up everything they could in their crazed pyromaniac state of mind, all while cackling maniacally.

I think I've waited long enough. Time to act.

YES! Time to launch the bottle of pixie farts.

If only.

"You've gone awfully quiet," Jeremiah commented gloatingly. "Remembering what happened last time? I do have to admit, your screams were particularly sweet. Friedrich, bring her over here please."

He's starting to sound like a monster.

Come on, I'm tired of his monologuing.

In an instant the room was under my control.

Friedrich's loosely guarded gun was in my hands, pointed directly at Jeremiah's head as I jumped away from Friedrich's grasp.

"Friedrich, go stand by the desk please," I said calmly.

"Put the gun down, Faye," Jeremiah said nonchalantly.

"Go stand by the desk," I repeated.

"Put the gun *down*," Jeremiah repeated. This time there was force and fear in his tone. Jeremiah was afraid now. There was no Ronan, no hoard of men under his control to defend him. He was good and truly toast.

"*NOW,*" I snapped.

Friedrich complied as Jeremiah began to back slowly away from me.

"No, you stay put," I hissed. "I know you have a weapon on the other side. You'll both stay on this side of the desk. Now, give me the key for the door."

"There is no key," Jeremiah said coldly. "Besides, how do I give you the key if it's on the other side of the desk?"

"Fair point," I scoffed. "I'll just freeze the lock. It'll work just as well as locking it."

"You don't have control of your powers," Jeremiah said calmly. "The shadows have been infecting you in that dark cell."

"Not enough," I hissed. "I am far more powerful than your shadows realize. I thrive on what should kill me. They made me into a monster, Jeremiah. Do you think your poor attempts can stop me? I am the monster your master fears."

Where is Ronan?

He has to be in here, so his father knows where his loyalty lies.

What if we just…shoot Jeremiah? This whole nightmare could be over if we just disposed of him.

It's too risky. It puts Meghan in too much danger…We don't know where Marcov is. Jeremiah wanted Ronan here. For all we know, he could have nefarious plans for Megs. It's best just to stick to the plan…

But is it the best plan?

If I do away with him, it's for the better—it cuts out three steps of this plan.

That is a fair point.

Jeremiah, as if sensing my inner dilemma and argument, was beginning to edge around the desk.

"Stay there, or else I'll shoot," I threatened.

Jeremiah lunged and I didn't hesitate. I pulled the trigger.

The gun clicked.

My stomach dropped as I desperately yanked back the rack and pulled the trigger again.

Maybe there just wasn't a bullet in the chamber…

Again, it clicked.

There had never been any bullets in the gun.

Jeremaih began to laugh, a harsh, cruel sound. "Oh, you are so gullible. You should have seen your hopeful little face…you were so convinced you were actually going to get out of here. Do you really think that I would be so foolish as to allow my men to be so careless with their weapons?"

I am still going to get out of here.

"Forget this," I hissed as I hurled the gun at Jeremiah's head.

When the gun is empty, it becomes a club.

My pride soared as the gun slammed square into his forehead. I made a mad dash for the door. Ronan was late. It was time to improvise.

Someone was in the doorway. Familiar arms wrapped around me and drug me back into the room.

Ronan.

I allowed him to gain control. He pulled my back against his chest and his hand wrapped around my throat. I was moments away from death and yet I never felt safer. Ronan wouldn't hurt me, I knew it.

"Kill her!" Jeremiah roared, blood pouring down from the gash I'd made in his forehead with the gun.

That was not a part of the plan.

I was banking on Jeremiah wanting me alive. Crap. What now?

Ronan's hand trembled as his fingers pressed against my throat. "Sir?" he questioned. His body was so tense I could feel the outline of every corded muscle.

"I said kill her!" Jeremiah screamed in fury.

Apparently, someone doesn't like getting clocked in the face with an improvised handy dandy gun club.

"We need her! You won't get the information from anyone else," Ronan yelled. Fear covered every syllable.

My Ronan is afraid. I have to do something.

The talisman burned against my chest as I summoned my Inheritance and plunged the room into an icy blizzard. We couldn't see the desk or Jeremiah anymore. I squeezed Ronan's hand, and he carefully released me.

I delivered a quick set of blows, and Ronan exaggerated his response to them, I wasn't sure if Jeremiah could hear it through the storm, but we had to try for the sake of acting.

One quick move of my hand and a sheet of ice spread across the floor. Then, with a final meaningful look, and an impish wink, I pushed Ronan away from me with a strong gust of wind. He slammed into the far wall and mouthed a single word as he crumpled. 'Go.'

I blew him a kiss and turned to run.

There was a crack, and I jerked. Something shoved me backward as pain exploded across my leg.

It seems Jeremiah found the gun hidden in his desk. What an unfortunate turn of events.

What was he thinking?! He could have hit Ronan! He didn't know where we were! He just fired blindly into a room.

What an absolute idiot!

In desperation to give myself a solid head start, I summoned a storm, a hurricane that poured water all around me.

My strength was slipping; blood loss was against me now. I whispered a desperate plea as I dipped my fingers in the blood and drew a Rune on my arm. My skin burned beneath the magic mark as I summoned the water from the storm and sent it across the room in a tidal wave. As it rushed forward, I dropped the temperature to a dangerous negative twenty so the liquid froze on contact.

Jeremiah was facing away from me, covered in a thick layer of ice. His hands were thrown up over his face, as were Friedrich's. Ronan was the only one left mostly unscathed. He stood sideways to me, arms shielding his face in a defensive stance. He shook from the cold, icicles hanging from his arms and chin, but that was it.

Get up.

I can't. It appears I have been shot. I need a moment to gather my wits.

There are no wits left to be found, only slightly deranged brain cells. Now get up or we all die. You have to get up right now! The whole Swiss cheese plan relies on you getting out of here. We have to test if the zappers have been disabled.

I can't get up. I'm in shock. Don't I get a blanket for being in shock?

I want a blanket, darn it.

There's no time. Get up or all this effort is for nothing. Meghan and Ronan are relying on you. Get up, NOW!

I forced my legs to move, crawling to my feet as I placed a palm over my bleeding thigh and sent a blast of ice down into the wound, packing it as best I could. It would hold, for now.

The room was tilting, everything a disoriented kaleidoscope as I struggled to stand.

Ronan turned, his eyes wide in horror as he stared at me, then at the frozen pool of blood on the floor and my crimson stained fingertips.

'*Go!*' he mouthed again.

I didn't waste another moment. I ran out of the room, slamming the door shut behind me as I sent a final blast of ice through the door handle and latch—locking it in place. Then I shot another three-inch sheet of ice across the entire surface of the door.

That should hold. At least for a few minutes.

Time to find my way out.

How did Ronan's instructions go? Over the river and through the woods, to Grand-

mother's house we go?

Nope. Wrong instructions.

Baby Shark, doo, doo, doo, doo, doodoo...

NO!

Fine. Go straight, then left, then right, then straight again...dur, dur, dur...Ronan should have tried to make his directions more exciting and interesting. I'm bored already.

I began to follow the tangled instructions, running as fast as I could without further injuring my leg.

Getting shot was not a part of my genius plan.

I told you it was a Swiss cheese plan.

No, it's not. You know why?

Why?

Because I got out. That's why.

We are not going to tell Meghan about the bullet bit.

Nope. Absolutely not. She'll try to kill Ronan, and I quite like the idea of having her as a bridesmaid at our wedding.

Shut up!

I was utterly mortified that I had thought such a thing. My three brain cells, however, had once again taken up the idea with great vehemence and were now scrapbooking various wedding ideas, and making plans, all while humming the bridal march and waltzing around with little bouquets of wildflowers.

56

A Debt Repaid

EMBER

"You underestimate my ability to turn you into ruins. I will shatter your
soul into pieces like you did mine, I will burn your sanctuary destroy
everything you own. Don't ask the gods to help you because they're
afraid of me, their fear will rain down upon the earth your kingdom is
over and I will wear your crown too. -Don't test me"

-a.a.m.l

The battle raged around me as I used every ounce of strength to control my Inheritance. The flaming phoenix had nearly destroyed Artemis' vessel, but still its crew attacked.

Theron flew in and out of my peripheral vision, protecting me from their assault. His mechanical wings hummed loudly as he engaged the pirates that tried to board our ship.

I had yet to see Artemis, though his magic was evidently there. Rosamond's magic was there as well, but I hadn't seen either one of them.

Maybe I was mistaken. Maybe he isn't on this ship after all...what if it's a decoy?

My phoenix screamed as it plunged toward the ship again, setting another path of fire and destruction. Their ship couldn't hold out much longer, of that I was sure.

Suddenly, pain exploded across my body as a long, blood red arrow pierced my forearm and pinned me to the mast. Words were beyond me; comprehensive thoughts failed me as I stared at the unexpected wound in my arm. It looked like a giant locust thorn, identical to a sword I knew all too well.

Rosamond.

My phoenix screeched and faded as the world around me went hazy. Pain was tearing me apart and the damage hardly seemed real.

I...no. This isn't real. I'm dreaming. Surely, I'm dreaming. A shot like that isn't even possible...

"Sparks!" Theron roared as he rushed toward me, his wings sparking and smoking as he urged them to go faster.

Another bloodred arrow hissed toward me from the boat.

"Look out!" I yelled, but it was too late. The arrow caught on his wing, tearing through the complicated mechanism and sending him into a tailspin.

"NO!" I screamed, jerking forward.

I regretted the action immediately as pain overwhelmed me.

He caught the deck at the last minute and hauled himself up, swearing the whole time as he lunged toward me. "I haven't ruined a pair of wings in a solstice cycle," he snarled. "And now that stupid idiot has the gall to ruin them for me?! What a jerk!"

More profanities followed his griping as he saw the extent of the damage. "This is going to hurt," he warned.

I nodded, gritting my teeth. "Do it," I ground out. "I'm a sitting duck here."

His sword was quick as he sliced through the end of the arrow, leaving a clean cut and smooth end. Before I could process what he was going to do, he pulled my arm out of the arrow.

I screamed, watching the blood pour out of my arm. The hole went straight through, in between the bones. It had been a very lucky, almost impossible shot.

Theron ripped off the fabric from his ruined wings, and then quickly bound it around my arm.

"This will heal," he said decidedly. "But you're likely off rigging duty for a few days." He winked, his silver eyes laughing. "You didn't let this happen on purpose, just to get out of having to face your fear of heights, did you, Sparks?"

I shook my head, dizzy and exhausted.

"It's quite the battle scar, Sparks. Let's get you out of the open. We've almost got them now. The pretentious Summer Prince will run back to the Realm with his tail in between his legs soon enough. We've shown them what the Moores are made of."

Over his shoulder, I could see a dark shape speeding toward us.

I couldn't get the words out to warn him—I couldn't tell him to duck as pain tore my stomach apart.

Danger. Danger.

LOOK OUT!

I shrieked, fumbling with his arm and trying to drag him out of the way, but it was too late. An arrow slammed into his shoulder, knocking him sideways a step.

"NO!" I screamed as he teetered on the edge of the small platform, his arms windmilling.

He caught his balance after a moment, his eyes a blaze of fury as he searched Artemis' ship for the culprit.

Another arrow flew from the ship, grazing my cheek and burying itself into the wood by my head.

A warning shot.

"We have to get out of here!" I yelled. "Rosamond is on that ship!"

"I know," Theron yelled back. "But she'll have to try harder if she's going to finally kill me! Now let's go!"

Blood dripped down my fingertips from the hole in my arm. Everything was numb as I struggled to find my balance.

I am so incredibly tired.

I'm going to pass out.

I think I might be in shock...

There was another bolt headed toward us, and I screamed, desperately trying to warn Theron. It was going to pin me to the mast again. I couldn't move away fast enough.

Theron's eyes went wide, and he dove, trying to shield me from the arrow as his arms wrapped around me.

NO!

He jerked as the arrow slammed into his back and out through his chest. We toppled and fell off the edge of the mast. He curled around me, pulling me to his chest.

No, no, no. This can't be happening. This can't be happening.

"Live well, Sparks," he whispered as he closed his eyes and held me tighter to his chest.

No, don't talk like that. We just need to get you to Clarice. She can help you! Hold on Theron! Just hold on!

We slammed into the deck, and I screamed as the arrow in his chest impaled my side, sliding between my ribs and ripping me open as the force of the fall threw me away from him.

"THERON!" I screamed as I tumbled and rolled.

Blood was pouring out of my nose, from the corner of my lips, rapidly spreading through the fabric of my shirt. But none of it mattered. The only thing that mattered was the broken body that lay motionless on the deck of Verity's ship.

No, no, no. Please, no.

I was screaming his name, and I couldn't stop as I crawled toward him. A pool of blood was spreading out from his body. His eyes were distant and glassy as his chest barely rose and fell.

No! If he dies, he'll be a wanderer, a haunt.

He can't die. He can't die. Not like this. Not like this!

I wasn't worth it. Take it back, Theron. Take it back!

"Theron," I sobbed as I cradled his head in my hands.

His lips were moving, but no sound came out as his eyes struggled to focus on my face.

Don't die. Please, don't die. Please, I can't lose you too. I can't lose you too!

I searched Artemis' ship, desperately trying to find Rosamond in the wreckage.

Maybe it wasn't her. Maybe it wasn't her.

My hopes were useless, I knew it was her. The arrow was a unique kind I'd only seen her carry.

All my desperate hopes died in an instant, as I at last laid eyes on Rosamond. Her face was unreadable as she slowly lowered her bow.

I watched as Artemis raced up to her, his face furious as he stared at Rosamond. Then, as if sensing the weight of my gaze, he turned.

Our eyes locked across the divide and my heart threatened to shatter inside my chest.

No. No. NO!

"Theron," I whispered desperately, turning my attention back to him. "You have to wake up. I need your help. I need you, Theron."

Blood smeared his lips as his chest rapidly rose and fell. "I...I don't think I can walk away from this one, Sparks," he rasped as his eyes at last focused on my face. "Was it

Rosamond?" he whispered breathlessly.

"Yes," I sobbed. "It was."

Theron chuckled, then choked as blood bubbled out of his mouth and poured down his chin. "Tell her," he coughed. "Tell her, I'll still kill her in the next life...maybe then we'll have our forever...maybe then we won't be on opposite sides of the ocean...maybe then she'll want this twisted heart, cursed though it be..."

"I'll kill her," I threatened. "I'll kill her for this!"

"No," Theron choked, clutching my hand tightly. "Don't Sparks, *please* don't. Don't carry the hatred forward. Let it die with me...let it die with my heartbeat. I chose this...I chose my end. It's for you...you're worth it, Sparks...You can be the change. Go, be the change this Realm needs...don't be afraid of the future...choose your path and be willing to face your fate."

"I don't know how," I wept. "I don't know how. How do I do that?"

"Sparks, you have to go now," he rasped, ignoring my question.

"There's nowhere to go," I sobbed. "I'm trapped."

"Fate," Theron whispered, his voice growing weaker. "Your fate...is your own...don't be afraid of it. Save the Moores...save my Moores."

"I need your help!" I sobbed. "Please Theron, just hang on. Clarice will heal you. Please!"

"I can't," Theron whispered, smiling as his eyes stared up at the skies. "The wind...it's calling me...the wind...it's singing, it's—"

His voice fell away from his smiling face as the life at last drained out of his body with a bone-chilling sigh. Blood bubbled and overflowed from his mouth.

"THERON!" Raz's scream cut through my sobs as she slammed onto the deck and raced to my side. She draped herself across his chest and held his face in her hands. "NO!" she wailed. "NO! Don't you dare die on me. Don't you dare! You can't! You can't!" she sobbed.

But it was already too late.

No, no, no. Please Theron, please, no.

My fear and emotions came crashing back into my mind all at once. I hadn't realized how much Theron was still withholding from me.

I clutched my head, paralyzed.

"GRIMM!" Verity's voice roared through the overwhelming chaos.

I looked up, tears streaming down my face, trying to make sense of the blurred mess the world had become around me.

Fury was building up inside of me. Grief I couldn't contain. It was tearing me apart, ripping my mind to pieces.

I screamed again, clutching my head as the grief and rage tore me apart.

Artemis' ship exploded in a ball of flames. Men fell screaming into the sky as burning rubble fell down. But it didn't matter. The only thing that mattered was the figure that was swinging across the divide, tumbling through the air as the end of his rope caught fire, sending him plunging down, down, down.

A vine snapped down from the top mast of our ship. Rosamond had already boarded, and now she dropped Artemis onto the deck.

This can't be happening. All of this bloodshed, all of this violence, and for what? He still caught us in the end...

"GRIMM!" Verity screamed again.

I gently laid Theron's head down, then quickly placed a gentle kiss to his forehead. "Goodbye," I whispered before lurching to my feet. I was covered in blood and the world seemed blurred around the edges as everything slowed down around me.

My heartbeat roared in my ears as I surveyed the carnage, searching for Verity.

Blood. There's so much blood.

"RUN TO THE DOOR!" Verity's lips noiselessly mouthed.

She was screaming, I knew she was, but all I could hear was the roar of my heartbeat in my ears.

Figures moved and blurred around me—only Artemis remained whole as he rushed forward, his gaze locked on me.

"*EMBER!*" Evadne's voice screamed through my mind.

The world snapped back into focus, and I turned on my heels and fled.

"NOW!" Verity roared. The crew simultaneously dropped onto the deck of the ship, ambushing Artemis and Rosamond.

Evadne stood on the edge of a cliff, her eyes frantic as she screamed my name, over and over.

"DON'T DO THIS!" Artemis roared behind me.

Verity was pulling the ship away from the cliff, trying to cut off Artemis' access to me. Raz was racing toward him, her sword drawn and eyes murderous.

I'm not going to make it.

The deck was slick with blood beneath my boots. Fire raged around us. But all I could focus on was the beat of my heart and the desperate fight for breath.

I am Ember Natasha Grimm.

I leapt off the edge of the ship, fingers desperately reaching for Evadne's outstretched hand. The world faded, until all that was left was the frantic beat of my heart as it pounded out the mantra.

I am Ember Natasha Grimm, and I will decide my fate.

My fate is my own. I will decide my fate.

PART THREE
BROKEN DESTINIES

57

There Is Nowhere Safe

EMBER

"But the wolf, the wolf only needs enough luck to find you once."
-Emily Carroll

My feet hit the edge and slipped. I wasn't going to make it.

My fingers slid through Evadne's, but she dove forward, putting herself at risk to grab my arm with both hands. Pain coursed through my body as I slammed into the cliff face with the full momentum of my jump.

I was screaming, terrified, as my life flashed before my eyes.

"Don't you give up on me!" Evadne yelled, trying to pull me up. "Don't you dare give up and stop fighting! I did not come this far just to lose you, you stupid sister! Now crawl!"

I was sobbing, panicking, as my boots scrabbled against the rocks, trying to get some leverage to help Evadne pull me up.

Seconds dragged by and at last I was moving upward, pushing myself up with my legs as she slowly inched back, never once letting go of my arm.

We collapsed backward onto the grass, gasping for air as the reality of what had just happened slammed into me.

"Theron's gone," I sobbed. "Rosamond killed him."

Tears were pouring out of Evadne's eyes. "I saw," she whispered. "But Verity kept me moving. She told me to get to the cliff and wait for you. She must have known you'd be a crap jumper."

"Whatever," I laughed hysterically while simultaneously sobbing my eyes out.

Why do I laugh when all I want to do is curl up in a ball and cry?

"We have to go. We don't have much time."

I nodded and pulled myself up. It was the last thing I wanted to do, to keep running. But this was our last chance to see what the Moores had to offer us.

I glanced back. Artemis was engaged in a sword fight with Raz and Verity. Both women looked murderous—they tag teamed against him as he tried to get to a jumping point. The rest of the crew kept Rosamond occupied. We had time, but it wouldn't be long before Artemis and Rosamond overpowered them and were hot on our heels.

There was nothing on the small island but the door and tall, dead grass around it. It swayed and shook in the rising wind.

"Where does it go?" Evadne whispered?

"I don't know," I gasped, reaching forward. "But we're gonna find out."

Evadne's hand wrapped around mine and together, with bloodstained hands, we turned the knob. Everything on the other side of the door was obscured by thick fog, and with a final, hesitant glance back, we stepped through the door and closed it firmly behind us.

All of a sudden, my body felt as if it was dying. The full measure of my injuries slammed into me. "Eva," I gasped.

She was on her knees beside me. "I can't breathe," she rasped. Fireheart hissed and dove into her cloak pocket.

He returned almost immediately, inhaler clutched gently in his teeth. She took it from him, giving him a grateful scratch beneath the chin before inhaling the lifesaving medicine.

So, we're probably somewhere in the Mortal Realm, since we are suddenly dying...the only question is where?

I scrutinized the dense fog. Through the shadows, I could just barely make out the shape of a familiar-looking wrought-iron fence.

"Evadne," I whispered. "The door took us home."

"That's impossible," she gasped. "There are a million places it could have taken us.

There's no way home was one of them. That's too convenient!"

What if it's a trap? What if the Moores wanted us to come here?

Don't be silly...the Moores can't do something like that...can they?

But it wasn't impossible. We stood in front of the large, wrought-iron gate that surrounded our home. The same gate I had opened, closed, and locked for years. I knew it like the back of my hand.

Everything was silent, the house dark and formidable, and we stood in shock, vulnerable outside the gates.

"We need to get inside the gate," I whispered.

Evadne nodded, her eyes fixed on the house as we slowly made our way forward.

The gate was unlocked; the iron chain had simply been wrapped around it several times.

That's not how Mum and Dad would have left it...is it?

The gate screeched as we pushed it open, giving testament to the neglect of time past.

How long have we been gone for?

Will it still be home without Mum and Dad?

Evadne wept silently beside me. "I thought we'd never get to come back," she whispered raggedly. "But now that we're here...I'm not sure I can go inside...not when they're gone."

"Hey, they're not gone, not really..." I whispered. "Mum's still alive...sort of...Dad's just being held prisoner. Besides, we should go inside—it's safer. We need to regroup and figure out what we're going to do. We can't stay here, but we need to figure out what we're doing."

Evadne nodded and we slowly shuffled forward.

The house loomed over us, silent. The flower garden was overrun, and the yard resembled a ragged field.

We left at the start of fall... now it looks like it's high summer again. Everything green and thriving has taken over.

What month is it?

How long have we been gone? Will it still be home?

The front door was unlocked, which didn't seem right.

Maybe Mum and Dad left it open for us, in the hope that we'd escape Rosamond and come back?

There is no escape...surely they'd know there was no escape. Not when Faye spent eight years trying and failing to escape. Faye is much cleverer than we are.

Evadne was having trouble breathing again, but her inhaler didn't seem to be working. She scrutinized the side, looking at the numbers. Her eyes went wide with fear. "It's empty," she said softly.

"Do you have your spare?" I asked.

"I..." she pondered for a moment, her chest rising and falling in rapid little gasps. "No. But there's one here at the house...I just...I remember now...I forgot to pack it. Mum handed it to me as we were getting ready to leave...but I set it down... It feels like that was years ago...it's on the desk."

I nodded. "Go sit down, I'll get it. Just rest, okay? I'll be right back."

"You're injured," she protested.

"I'm fine," I lied as I limped down the hall toward the stairs.

The house was still around us, silent like a tomb with a layer of dust that coated everything.

How long have we been gone?

The climb up the stairs was torturously slow. Every inch of movement pulled at my injured ribs, and it was all I could do to stay on my feet. But I forced myself to keep putting one foot in front of the other. Evadne needed her inhaler.

Evadne needs me. She needs that inhaler.

I can die after I get her the inhaler.

Our room was silent, curtains drawn, reducing the furniture to vague shapes. I flipped the switch as the lights blazed, painfully bright.

I made my way to the desk, trying not to let the emotional wave of being back in the safe haven that my room had once been drag me under.

There's nowhere left that's safe.

My fingers closed around the inhaler the exact moment I noticed the smell that clung to the room. It was that of cigarettes and strong black coffee.

That doesn't belong here.

I turned slowly. There, by the window, sat a chair, a large rifle and scope, and last but not least, a large pile of cigarette butts.

Someone's in the house.

I left Evadne downstairs, alone.

Someone's in the house!

My feet were a tangle beneath me as I turned and fled, desperately trying to get to

Evadne.

A scream echoed through the house.

EVADNE!!

Evadne was screaming my name.

Then came a single word. "RUN!"

58

Monsters In Our Midst

EVADNE

"Murder is like potato chips; you can't stop with just one."
-Stephen King

Being home was like having all the air sucked out of me. Like someone was hitting me in the chest, over and over and over again, all the while asking why I didn't get up, why I couldn't process the grief that rushed over me as I took in the details that reminded me of Mum.

What if we never find a way to get her out of that place?

What if she never comes home...

Every painting on the wall was a piece she had created. Every photo was an image she had lovingly selected. Every object of furniture had a memory of her tied to it and it all threatened to tear me apart as I remembered how she had been held captive at the Ruins. The way she had screamed. My inability to save her.

Nothing will be the same again...will we ever free her? Will she ever come home?

I can't escape the heartache. I can't escape this hole in my heart.

The letters and numbers on the digital clock shone brightly, reading June 19th, 6:15pm.

It's June...how is it June?

Smells and shadows that didn't belong to the house crept over me as I sat numbly, staring out the window into the foggy morning. Never mind the fact that I already couldn't breathe, the new element of grief had apparently reduced me hallucinating.

Why does the house smell like burnt coffee?

Why does it smell like cigarette smoke?

I can't breathe and so my mind inserts smells that don't belong. Lovely. What's next? Will I hallucinate people in the house too?

A floorboard creaked behind me and Fireheart bristled on my shoulder. "It's just Ember," I said soothingly.

"Em, there's no need to be so quiet, you're scaring the crap—"

Fireheart wouldn't be scared of Ember... He knows her.

My voice fell silent as I took in the shadow that stood in the hallway. It wasn't my sister. It was a man. A man I didn't recognize.

What do I do?

We had no one to help us, I could barely stand, and Ember was grievously injured. She couldn't possibly fight him.

I have to draw him away from her. She has to run.

I rose slowly, assessing my options as he stalked toward me.

My sword was on my hip, but he could easily overpower me if I didn't get him on the first shot. I could throw my knife at him, but there was no guarantee it would take him down.

Throw the knife, two or three if necessary, then run.

I slowly reached for my knife, and he lunged.

I screamed as loud as I possibly could, letting my voice carry through the silent house.

"EMBER!" I screamed as I swung my forearm, activating the knives hidden in the armor. "RUN!"

The man roared as the razor-sharp blades cut across his chest. He stumbled back a step, swearing, and I hurled my knife at him. It flipped end over end, as if in slow motion, before finally burying itself deep into his thigh. He yelled in pain, and I dodged around him, avoiding his sloppy grab.

Get out, get out, get out!

Ember was above me. I could hear her frantic steps on the hallway floor as she raced toward the stairway.

I glanced back, checking to see where my attacker was. He was standing up, chest bleeding heavily. Swearing profusely, he wrenched the knife out of his thigh.

Stupid move. You'll bleed out. You should never pull out objects you've been stabbed with.

I ran headfirst into another figure. "Hello, Princess," he sneered. "So, you've finally decided to come back home, did you?"

I stabbed a dagger into his other thigh as his fingers closed around my forearm.

Not good.

He hurled me sideways with a roar of rage, and my head collided with the corner of the doorway.

Run, Em! Ru—

My thoughts fell apart as everything went black.

59

When The World Goes To Hell, You Can Only Expect It To Get Worse

Ember

"The truth is this, every monster you have ever met or will ever meet, was once a human being with a soul that was as soft and light as silk. Someone stole that silk from their soul and turned them into this. So when you see a monster next, always remember this. Do not fear the thing before you. Fear the thing that created it instead."
-Nikita Gill

The stairs betrayed me, and before I could catch my balance, I was tumbling head over heels down the steps.

NO! Why?! I haven't fallen down the stairs in years!

I should have just slid down the banister!

That would have looked cool as heck! Swooping off the banister, sword drawn, to save my sister from whoever is here!

The only thing you would have managed to do is impale yourself with the drawn sword and fall off.

You can hush up. You're ruining my delusions of grandeur!

Every turn sent explosions of pain through my body, but the disconnected rambling thoughts kept the pain in the back of my mind, until at last I collided with someone at the bottom.

They fell, spluttering and cussing. The voice was strangely familiar.

I know that voice. Where have I heard that voice before?

Forget the walk down memory lane! Where is Evadne?!

I struggled to untangle myself from him and get away. But the man had turned his full attention to me and was now trying to overpower me.

No, no, no. This can't be happening. What is happening?! Where is Evadne??

"Hello friendly hobo," the man sneered.

The connection at last clicked into place. This was the man who had hurt Faye. The one they had called Marcov.

"*You,*" I seethed.

Fire erupted across my fingertips, and he drew back with a startled yell.

That's it. Fear your friendly elvish hobo!

My fire disappeared as quickly as it had come, smothered by pain and the lack of magic in the Mortal Realm as my heartbeat faltered and spluttered in my chest.

I quite literally feel like I'm dying. How did Faye survive for a month here?!

Faye didn't have grievous injuries when she came.

Marcov shoved me back and my head collided with the banister. Stars jumped and danced in front of my eyes as the world turned on its axis. Fingers were closed around my throat and suddenly, I couldn't breathe.

He's choking me. Why is he choking me? Did they come here just to kill us?

Where is Evadne?!

I clawed at his hands, trying to get free of his grip and force him off me.

Help me! Please, someone help me!

My chest was burning, burning, burning. My throat was collapsing. My lungs ached. Air. I needed *air.*

I slashed with my forearm, driving the curved blades hidden in my armor into the side of his face.

He screeched and drew back,

Precious air flooded my lungs and I rolled over, coughing and gasping.

I'm going to throw up.

I think that's a bad idea. You'll stain the rug and then Mum will be most cross with you.

I think she'll forgive me...besides, there's already blood on the carpet...quite a lot of it.

Whose blood is it?

Is it mine?

I think it's Evadne's...

CRAP! EVA! Where are you?!

"Ember!" Artemis' voice roared.

Great. Now I'm hallucinating.

Thanks Marcov, you deprived me of so much air I'm hallucinating about my pissed off boyfriend.

He's not my boyfriend!

Well, what is he?

I don't know. We're going to have to revisit this conversation when my life is in a little less danger.

Fine. But you are not getting out of that conversation.

Blood was pouring down Marcov's face, but he was on top of me again, his face contorted in agony and fury. Then, the weight was gone. Marcov went flying, colliding with the door at the far end of the hallway.

"Ember! Can you hear me?!" Artemis yelled as he pulled me up.

Ah, now I'm hallucinating that he's here. Perfect.

Maybe hallucination Artemis will save me.

I was gasping, desperately trying to get air into my lungs.

"Ember!" Artemis yelled again.

"Evadne," I wheezed, ignoring the fiery pain. "They've got Evadne."

Eva, go help Eva, Artemis!

Marcov was on his feet and scrambling out the side door as a dull roar overtook the house, loud and deafening.

"Eva," I whispered, voice barely present.

"Stay here!" Artemis called as he raced after Marcov.

Not a chance.

I crawled to my hands and knees, then stumbled to my feet, trying to go after him.

Please don't let it be too late.

Everything was spinning as I stumbled outside. There was a crack, and I jerked back, screaming.

Artemis knelt on the grass; four dead bodies lay on the ground around him. But the helicopter was still pulling away. Artemis' hands were raised as he tried to stop the machine, but nothing he did seemed to help. Evadne's bloody face was pressed up against the glass of the helicopter's small window. Her eyes were closed, shallow breaths fogging and unfogging the glass by her nose. Fireheart was wrapped around her neck, his eyes begging me to help her as he lay completely still, trying to avoid detection.

No. No. This can't be happening.

Artemis' hands were shaking with exertion as the helicopter pulled away and sped off into the sky.

Artemis' hands fell, and he clutched his shoulder, his face shocked.

"The bullet landed," he whispered in shock. "It's impossible...the bullet landed."

"Forget the freaking bullet!" I yelled. "You didn't save her!"

Artemis gestured to the bodies on the grass. "I tried...but then the one I threw shot me...he actually shot me..."

"I'm going to kill you," I seethed.

"You can't," Artemis replied quietly.

"What do you mean I can't?" I raged as I drew my dagger and advanced.

"Go ahead then," Artemis whispered. "Show me how much you hate me...but know that I'm the only hope you have of getting your sisters back."

My arm swung.

He sat unmoving in the grass, staring out at the foggy forest beyond the fence. "You have a beautiful home," he said softly, uncaring of my promised violence.

My hand stopped, shaking, my blade hovering an inch from his chest. If I had stabbed him, it would have been a mirror mark from where Baba Yaga's blade had landed on me.

"I'll make you wish you were dead," I threatened, voice trembling. It was a useless threat and we both knew it.

"I'm already there," Artemis replied raggedly. "Come on, my Flamín, you can hate me later. You can kill me later... But right now, I need medical attention. I need to get some strength back before we go back into the Moores. If I go back now, it might kill me."

"Why?" I scoffed. "It's never been an issue before."

"A bullet has never hit a Fey," Artemis replied with a shrug. "And the closer we get to the Ruins, the more volatile the magic becomes. If I go back wounded from something in the Human Realm, I'm not sure what it'll do, but I can't risk it."

"What do you mean getting my sisters back?" I asked, finally processing what he had said.

"It's the same man from the beginning," Artemis sighed. "He was there with the others when they took Faye. I saw his face in the bird's report. It's the same man. The same person who holds Faye, has orchestrated to have Evadne taken. For what I cannot say, but there is clearly a darker, more sinister hand beneath it all. No human would be so determined to get the Grimms, and no mere bullet could hit..."

"What does it mean?" I asked.

"I don't know, but I don't like it. Things are worse than I ever thought... I think the Knight is orchestrating all of this. I can't prove it, but I have a bad feeling."

I fell on the grass beside him, overwhelmed and distraught.

"I'm sorry," Artemis murmured. "You have no idea how sorry I am."

I was crying now, fear for my sister, frustration, and grief shutting down my body with every sob as Artemis gently pulled me into his arms.

"I hate you," I whispered. "I hate you."

"I hate me too," Artemis replied quietly as he stared out into the fog. "I hate the monster they've created. I hate that you're caught in the crosshairs...I hate what this Realm has done to you...I hate the monster they made me to be. But most of all, I hate that I cannot let you escape."

60

Run

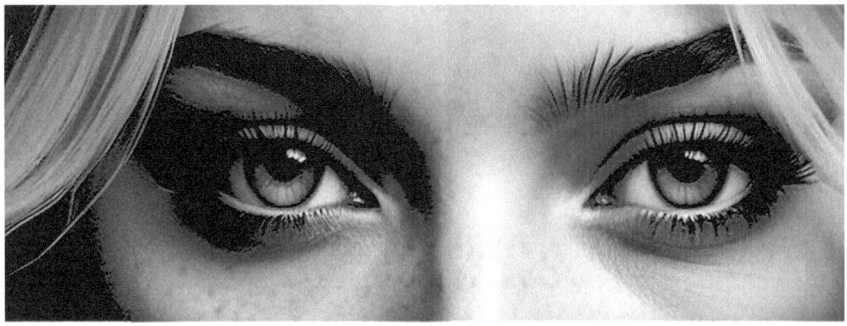

FAYE

"Manon met Sorrel's eyes, then Asterin's. And Manon gave the thirteen
her final order. "Run.""
-Sara J. Maas, Empire of Storms

The sunlight was too bright on my eyes as I burst through the door and made my way toward the outdoor training area. There were trees behind it; they would hide me for a little while.

So far, I hadn't been turned into a living bug zapper, but I needed to test it further. It could just be dumb luck.

I have a small head start, but not much.

I was in the trees and away, lungs burning as I forced myself to keep running.

We did it. We actually did it! The zapper is disabled. We're going to make it.

"Faye!" Ronan yelled. He was already hot on my heels.

Come on Ronan, hurry and catch up. I'm tired of running.

Gotta keep up appearances.

Boo, I hate this idea. I HATE running!

I kept running, intent on keeping up the charade in case there were others with him.

I could hear him now, breaking through branches as I at last broke free of the woods and raced out into an open field full of tall grass and wildflowers.

It's so beautiful out here.

The ice was rapidly melting, and my thigh had begun to burn.

Stupid Jeremiah and his stupid trigger-happy fingers. How dare he shoot me!

I mean, technically it's probably revenge because I shot him and tried to shoot him again... But STILL! He didn't have to get his stupid revenge.

Ronan was closing the gap now; I could hear him close behind me.

Run, run as fast as you can...you can't catch me, I'm the gingerbread man...

That rhyme is problematic. I most certainly am going to get caught, and I am no man...

I AM NO MAN!

I giggled, feeling slightly deranged as Ronan turned into an ugly Nazgûl in my mind and I became the ever-brave Éowyn, defiantly yelling 'I am no man' as she faced certain death and still triumphed.

Arms wrapped around me. I was caught at last.

I didn't bother to fight as I went limp in Ronan's embrace. I would recognize those arms anywhere.

"Took you long enough," I whispered.

He was shaking as he held me close. "Are you okay?" he whispered raggedly.

"I haven't been turned into a living bug zapper yet," I snorted.

"Your leg?"

"Quite thoroughly shot," I griped. "You owe me, big time. I expect a whole box of treasures. All the bribery and rewards from the worldy-widey-web for such great feats of bravery."

Ronan let out a stressed laugh as he scooped me up into his arms. I wrapped an arm around his neck to make it easier for him to carry me back.

"This is strictly because your leg is injured," Ronan joked solemnly. "Otherwise, I'd make you walk."

"I shall forgive you for the transmission of cooties," I replied primly. "But I would remind you that, last time my leg was injured, you carried me like a stupid, freaking, sack of potatoes."

"Would you like me to carry you like a sack of potatoes?" Ronan scoffed.

"No," I replied quickly. "Definitely not. I'd rather not relive such a horrendously humiliating experience."

"I think damsel-in-distress-carrying suits you better, don't you think?" Ronan joked.

"I don't think I'm quite the damsel in distress."

"Oh? Then what are you?"

I thought about it for a moment. "I believe I am the dragon that will eat you whole. Probably with ketchup."

Ronan laughed, shaking his head. "Just do me a favor and eat Jeremiah and his men while you're at it."

"It's a deal," I snorted. "I'll eat you last," I promised, giving him a toothy smile. "That way I get my full use out of you."

"Oh, and what use is that?"

"Carrying me around for one. Also, building my dragon hoard," I scoffed. "Perhaps some hugs and cuddles. Haven't you been paying attention?"

"Not really," Ronan confessed cheekily. "I was too busy planning what color of tie I'd wear to our wedding."

"Not you too!" I groaned as a blush spread up my cheeks. "Meghan is such a bad influence."

"The worst," Ronan agreed, laughing. "Come on, let's get back. We have a sister to save."

I sighed, resting my head against his chest. "I don't want to go back," I whispered.

"I know, but it'll be over soon," Ronan replied softly. "Just hold on a little longer. It'll be okay."

I listened to the steady rhythm of his heart, the way it calmed my own frantic heartbeat as I let his words wash over me.

Just hold on a little longer... It's gonna be okay.

It's gonna be okay.

For once, things will be okay. We did it. We're going to get out of here. We actually did it!

61

My Snooping Prince Adores Pop Tarts

EMBER

"I have illuminated this ruin by my own light."
-Forough Farrokhzad

I couldn't decide whether or not I was furious with Artemis. I wanted to blame him for Evadne getting taken, and while the accusation simmered in my mind, it just wouldn't stick. Artemis had done what he could to save her, but it just wasn't enough. He was right. There was something wrong with the whole situation. His power outside of the Fey Realm was inexplicably depleted and there was no explanation as to how Marcov had successfully shot him. There were too many unanswered questions surrounding everything, and I was too busy trying to decide what emotions I was feeling to find the answers.

Forever ago I had left him on that cliff, with nothing but heartbreak and a desperation to find another way. Jacques had wanted me to make the choice whether to be of the Realm or of the Moores on my own.

I had left him seeking answers, seeking a different path, but now as I looked at him, I began to wonder if my deviation had only cemented the fact that my heart led back to him...that he had always been my path, my fate.

I came out of the bathroom, having taken an incredibly hot shower to get all the blood off me, to find a clean Artemis exploring the house. He had apparently made use of the secondary bathroom I had shown him.

"I need you to rebind my arm," I called as he poked his head into the library. "I can't even bear to look at it." Seeing the hole go clean through my skin, and then watching the slow process of my arm knitting itself back together from the inside out with the help of Artemis' magic, made me want to retch.

"Sure, if you'll kindly take me in the direction of food," Artemis counter offered.

I led him to the kitchen, and he stared in wonder at the pantry. "I think I've found my favorite part of your house," he said as he reached for a box of pop tarts.

"You can have food after you fix my arm," I protested.

"No, I can have it *during*," Artemis countered as he quickly unwrapped a frosted strawberry pop tart and shoved it into his mouth. "I see why Jacques likes all his junk food," he said around the incredibly large bite.

"It's the chemicals," I sighed, distracted. "It makes the food addictive."

Artemis shrugged as he wrapped his hands around my injured forearm. I tried and failed not to shudder as he worked his finger inside the hole.

"Grooooss," I whined, thoroughly irritated.

"Almost done," Artemis chided. "There, now it's a little more healed. I should be able to finish it out next time I look at it."

I pointedly kept my eyes averted. "I'll need you to wrap it for me, too."

Artemis laughed, but quickly began to bind the wound with a clean bandage. "I managed to get the bullet out," he said by way of conversation. "I think I'm going to keep it as a trophy."

"I think I'm going to take a nap," I sighed as I slowly stood and made my way toward the living room and the most comfortable couch. I didn't have the energy to go up the stairs, and my room just wasn't the same with the echoes of those men still in it. They had tainted my safe place.

Artemis followed me, watching in silence as I dragged three blankets out of the ottoman, and after making myself a thorough layer of blankets, crawled underneath and curled into a tiny little ball. Artemis settled onto the cushion by my head and began to absentmindedly stroke my damp hair.

"Rest, my Flamín," he said softly. "I will keep watch."

I was already drifting. Lost, far away in an unfamiliar castle.

I awoke in disoriented confusion. Nothing made sense around me as I stared at the familiar surroundings.

Maybe it was all just a dream...maybe the last fifteen years have just been a long, continual nightmare.

Something moved next to me.

Artemis.

I stared up at his face, unable to stop the tears that rose.

"You were hoping it was a dream?" he asked quietly.

I nodded.

"I'm sorry, my Flamín," Artemis replied gently. "Come on, I'm half starved."

I watched in disconnected silence as he made his way back toward the kitchen.

How long have I been sleeping?

I followed, my steps unsteady and stilted as I wrapped a blanket around my shoulders.

By the time I made it into the kitchen, Artemis was already busy raiding the cabinets for food.

I watched in silence as he grabbed two boxes of pop tarts and began to once again explore the house.

I decided I needed something more substantial than pop tarts and settled on protein granola bars—the special kind Mum bought only for me, since they were dairy free.

"What are you doing?" I called, irritated as I went to find my obnoxious prince.

"Exploring," Artemis replied as he began to climb the stairs. "I...I have an unexplainable curiosity to see where you grew up...we may never have this opportunity again, so I plan to take advantage of it."

"Artemis, my sister is in grave danger, you're injured, and your solution is to snoop through my house?"

It didn't make sense.

Artemis shrugged and began to eat his eighth pop tart. "These are de-wightful," he crowed, his mouth full. "Are there any more?"

He just took two boxes of pop tarts from the pantry and then has the audacity to ask if we have more?

Good grief, I'm so glad he doesn't live with us permanently. He'd eat us out of house and home.

We'd never be able to afford it...

Can you imagine what the cranky people in town would say if they saw us in the grocery store now? Grocery cart full of junk food, Artemis wandering the aisles in hungry delight?

They'd probably call the police.

I bet he'd give them a run for their money.

"Those were our only boxes," I replied halfheartedly.

Does he ever get full?

"And before you ask, no, I will not share my box of protein bars. They're special, just for me."

Artemis made a face as if to protest, then turned back to his pop tarts.

It hurt how much the mannerism reminded me of F when he would come visit. He, too, would raid the pantry for sweets and the two-liter bottles of soda Mum would keep on hand, just for him.

"This place is under a strange spell," Artemis mused. "My magic won't work right... I got shot. None of it makes sense. I'm inspecting the world around me. There's nothing wrong with that. You can call it snooping if you like, but I'm simply trying to figure things out. Besides, I need to get my strength back before I try to heal, and like I said, I can't go back into the Moores like this. Something might happen."

"There's everything wrong with it," I snapped. "We have to get back to the Moores and get to the Ruins to get my sisters back."

Artemis waved a hand dismissively as he walked into the bedroom Evadne and I shared.

"Time moves differently here. We're not going to miss anything while we delay in the Mortal Realm. We've already tarried a day or two while you got some much needed rest." He stopped, staring in wonder at the murals Evadne had painted all over. Then the pictures I'd developed that hung on strings from the ceiling. "What is this place?" he asked in wonder.

I clung to the doorframe, exhausted. "It's my sister's and my bedroom. We've lived here since Eva and I were nine."

Artemis was moving carefully through the room, his fingers brushing the photos. "These are phenomenal," he said softly. "Did you take these? I assume the paintings are Evadne's."

I nodded weakly, staring at the camera case on my desk. It seemed a lifetime ago that I had left it there, abandoning it at the last minute. It was almost more than I could bear to come back into this room and meander. I wasn't the same person anymore, and it hurt to remember the illusion of peace we had once held here. It hurt to return to what had been my sanctuary and find nothing but fragments of the life I once loved.

What is left of the place I called home? The people who made it a home...we're all separated. Oma and F are gone...the rest captive. What does it mean? What does it all mean?

My gaze lingered on the family photo I'd taken the week before Faye left. Bright happy smiles were on all our faces, and we were gathered around Oma for her hundred and third birthday. Faye had insisted on shoving the cake full of exactly one hundred and three candles. The blaze had been glorious, and Oma and Faye had both cackled in absolute delight when the last candle had been shoved onto the cake and lit, despite the fact the cake was completely out of room. Oma was grinning ear to ear, her arms wrapped around Faye. She didn't understand anymore what had happened to Faye, or that she would be forced to return to the Realm. As far as Oma understood, Faye had gone to college in another country, and this was a short summer break.

She was so happy to see Faye...that goodbye was so hard for Faye... she cried all night. Oh Oma, it wasn't fair what happened.

Artemis had stopped his perusal and was now staring at one of the only pictures Evadne had taken. It was of me. I stood, grinning, sunlight streaming through my hair, making it all colors of bronze, gold, and crimson. It was a moment of pure, unfiltered joy. Evadne had stolen my camera and then done the most absurd little dance that had me rolling with laughter. She had snapped the picture while I wasn't expecting it, and to date, it was one of the best photos that had ever been taken of me.

I look so happy...untouched by the Realm's tragedy, unstained by the violence and bloodshed...you can't see the sadness in my eyes...

When was the last time I felt that happen? When was the last time our family was whole?

Artemis was pulling the picture down from the paper clip. "Can I keep this?" he asked hesitantly, still staring at it.

I pondered the question. He could just take it; I was in no shape to stop him. Why would he bother to ask?

"It's not doing me any good hanging in here...this is probably the last time I'll ever be...be home," I whispered, trying to suppress a sob.

I pulled the picture of us and Oma down, quickly followed by one I'd taken of Evadne and me, one of my parents, one of Dad and F. Soon I was pulling down photos left and right, every piece of the life I once knew and loved.

Artemis stared at the photo in his hand and then began to help. "Is there anything else you want?" he asked.

"I want to stay," I whispered raggedly. "I want my family to be whole again. I want...I want..." I was sobbing now as I stared down at moments of my life that were gone forever.

I'll never hug Oma again. Mum is trapped in the Realm...Dad's captured...we will never be whole again. Even if we get through this, Oma and F are still gone...we are still destined for the Realm. We will always be fractured.

Artemis approached me hesitantly, hands full of photos, face full of remorse. "Your heart can't stay," he said gently.

"My heart is here," I snarled, furious. "My heart *belongs* here. This is my home, my family, my *life*." I was crumbling, the shattered pieces of everything I thought I was lying broken between us. Everything I had left behind lay in shallow graves at my feet.

"You have to accept who you are," Artemis replied. "The longer you run from it, the harder it becomes to move on."

"I am Ember Grimm!" I yelled, spiraling. "I am the daughter of Amaris and Ruslan Grimm. I was born in the Mortal Realm. I *am* a mortal! Your cursed magic of your cursed Fey Realm changed me without my permission. Your cursed magic made me into a...a monster! This is *not* who I am. I am something more. Something your stupid, pompous Realm will *never* understand. I am the love of my parents, I am the daughter they raised, I am Ember Grimm and *nothing* more. No matter what you say, I am *not* of your Realm. My heart is in this home. My heart is with the ones I love. My heart...my heart..."

My words were spiraling, my breaths a jagged burn in my chest. I couldn't breathe. My chest was so tight, I couldn't get any air in or out, my lungs wouldn't move.

I'm having a panic attack.

No. I don't have time for this. We have to get back to the Realm, we have to save

Evadne.

I need to get my pictures together so I can have the pieces of my heart in one place.

"Ember," Artemis said gently as he pulled me close. "Hey, Em, it's okay. It's okay."

It's not okay. It most definitely is not okay.

Stop saying it's okay when everything is wrong. Nothing is okay, least of all me.

The photos fell from my trembling hands as I struggled to get air into my lungs.

Artemis carefully set his stack on the end of my bed and wrapped his arms around me. My ear was pressed against his chest, and gradually the beat of his heart began to pulse through the frantic, spiraling thoughts. Slowly, the echo of his deep, even breaths began to calm my ragged gasps.

Slowly, ever so slowly, I came back to myself and returned Artemis' hug. Sorrow overwhelmed the panic, and soon all that was left were tears. We held onto each other as I mourned the people I'd loved and lost, the life the Realm had stolen from me, and everything in between. I wept in the ashes of everything I thought I would be, holding the broken pieces of the possibility of a life that could never be mended.

There was no going back from this moment in time.

"Leaving what we thought would be is the hardest part of moving forward," Artemis murmured.

"I don't want to move forward," I whispered desperately. "I want to stay here. Trapped forever in a moment of time that isn't trying to wrench me away from the only home I've ever known."

"I wish I could let you," Artemis replied softly. "But you have a destiny in the Realm, whether you want it or not. The darkness is rising, and the Realm needs you to fight for it. If you don't, millions of innocents will die. Moreso than they already die under my father's reign." His arms tightened around me. "Em, if you stay here, it will kill you."

I don't care. I don't care. Let it kill me, let it destroy me.

Music pulled at the edges of my mind, a symphony that sought to soothe and hold. "You may not care," Artemis whispered. "But I do. I cannot let you destroy yourself. If you stay, it will kill you. You have no choice but to move forward. You and your family are inherently important to the Courts. You were never supposed to be separated from the Fey. You cannot escape your destiny; it awaits you in the Realm."

"Then why are we here?" I demanded. "It would have been easier just to drag me back, kicking and screaming, and force me to face that fate, whether I want to or not."

"My father would force you," Artemis said softly. "But I am not my father. I want to be better than he. Yes, I came to get you and yes, I found you. But I had no choice. I can't let Jack face the repercussions of such a rebellion. I can't let the millions of outcasts in the Moores be destroyed in the monarch's rage to find you. Furthermore, dragging you back kicking and screaming will not get us where we need to be. You need to come to terms with what is. Accept your place in the Realm, and realize I am behind you every step of the way..." He paused, contemplating his words. "We also linger because I know you need a chance to say goodbye."

"Goodbye to what," I scoffed.

"Goodbye to your home, your life...and something else... There is something else I need to show you," Artemis replied. "Rosamond told me some things while we were tracking you."

"Like what," I snapped. My panic and pain were quickly morphing into frustration and anger, trying to bury the vulnerability I'd shown. I wasn't sure I wanted to see anything Rosamond had told Artemis about. She had killed Theron, and I still had a score to settle with her for it.

"Let me show you," Artemis repeated carefully.

Theron's words washed over me as I wrestled with my anger. *'Don't carry the hatred forward. Let it die with me...you can be the change.'*

I don't want to be the change, Theron. I want to avenge you. I want to hurt her the way she hurt me...

But I wouldn't be justified in doing it...not if it's something he didn't want.

How do I move forward from this past that ripped my heart out? How?

I felt as if I couldn't bear the contradictory weight of everything as I followed Artemis out of the room and down the stairs.

I wish I could forget everything. I wish I could undo the past and go back to the way it was.

62

Goodbye My heart, Goodbye

"The only thing I know is this: I am full of wounds and still standing
on my feet."
-Nikos Kazantzakis

A rowan tree stood swaying in the wind, and at the foot of the tree, a small mound of
rocks lay.

"Rosamond buried your Oma," Artemis said quietly. "She happened upon the body
on her way to collect you two, so she buried her on the way. That's why she arrived when
she did. She was delayed. She intended to arrive *before* F got there, to prevent things
from becoming complicated."

"She wanted to avoid F?" I whispered, confused.

By my own unwilling hand...

"Quillon put her under compulsion that, if she came across F trying to warn your
parents, or get you girls out, to kill him... He's had F under scrutiny since we came and
took Faye. Quillon knew of the visits, but decided to let him continue to go...why, I
never found out... I often wonder if he thought nothing would come of them. Perhaps
he thought F's power would activate your powers faster?" Artemis shook his head. "I

don't know. I have nothing but theories. My father rarely consults with me."

"Rosamond didn't want to kill him," I stated.

"No," Artemis replied. "But she had no choice. She buried her self-loathing with an uncaring disguise. She had a job to do, so she did it. There is much the monarchs have forced her to do over the years, and she has buried her ire deeply to protect herself."

"Why would she tell you any of that?" I whispered. "Surely telling you, the future ruler of the Summer Court puts her life at risk…"

"Rosamond is a complicated being. She has faced much hardship in her life. She and I both seek a better future for the Realm we are bound to."

"Bound to?"

"We, too, cannot survive outside the Fey Realm," Artemis replied sadly. "Our destiny lies on the bloody foundations the monarchs have created. We both seek to create a better future, one that survives the rising darkness and makes a way forward. As the future ruler of the Summer Court, I try to build relationships on trust, not force obedience with compulsion." He looked down at his hands. "I almost marked you," he said softly. "When I finally caught up to you, I almost marked you as Quillon did to Faye when he came all those years ago."

"Why didn't you?"

"Because you would have never trusted me if I did. Yes, our paths are entwined. I believe you are my future. But I cannot build the foundations of our relationship on compulsion and fear. If I marked you, you would have been forced to obey my every command…and you would have hated me. That is not what I want for us. I had to get you and your sister back, but that is as far as I was willing to take it."

"And if I fought you, kicking and screaming?"

My question hung between us as I stared down at Oma's grave.

"Then I'd be forced to bear your ire. I cannot change the fact that you must come back. I took a shot in the dark and guessed you wouldn't hate me…that maybe by the point I caught up to you, you'd realize that you hadn't found another way, you'd only cemented the truth that you were already on your destined path. I think we both know you found no answers on that ship. I also think we are both aware that, even in the endless running, you found no peace. Our paths are bound, Em, and no amount of hiding and fleeing will change that."

"And if I don't want you?" I breathed, my voice barely a whisper.

Silence stretched as my question hung in the air between us.

"I am beside you regardless, for that is a fate we cannot avoid," Artemis said at last. "Quillon bound our magic...I am bound to you."

"Did you know?" I asked softly.

"Not until after the deed was done. He did it in secret. I was furious when I found out. It was not the way I wanted to win your heart."

I had too many thoughts, too many questions I couldn't decipher. I was trapped between anger and hopelessness, still desperate for another option. Yet, beneath it all was the longing that maybe there was hope for us. Maybe there was a way through this...maybe I didn't need to run anymore.

Am I stupid to have feelings for him? Am I stupid for wanting a future with him?

The path stood before me, but now I saw it in a different light. No longer was it simply death at the Last Gate, but now it held a future. A future with a green-eyed prince who offered hope and strength...who offered his heart with outstretched hands. But was I a fool to believe him? Was I a traitor to take his heart and give him back my own?

Was I betraying everything we had ever fought for? All those years we tried to avoid the Fey and escape the Realm? Was I betraying my family if I let myself fall for him?

What would Mum say if she was here? What would Dad think?

"Do you want me to give you some space?" Artemis asked hesitantly.

I shrugged, tears gathering in my eyes. "It doesn't bother me that you're here," I replied as I knelt beside the grave. "You can stay," I added before putting my hand on the smooth stones. Runes were burned onto their surface, but what they meant I didn't know.

"Hey Oma," I whispered, my voice cracking.

I had so much to say, but didn't know where to start. I knew she couldn't hear me. All that was left of the woman I loved was a shell, buried deep in the ground beneath me. But there was a certain kind of relief spreading across my chest as I began to speak to the stones, as if I was speaking to her. It was a balm to my broken, bleeding heart, giving me closure to unpack everything I'd never had the chance to say before it all went wrong.

Artemis settled on the grass beside me, listening as I told Oma about everything that had happened since we'd left. I voiced the guilt that ate me alive, the agony that I hadn't gotten there in time, and if I had, things might have been different. I spoke of my regret that I hadn't been able to save her. Then I told her about the fire that sang and danced across my fingertips, Evadne's water and the way it flowed around her. I spoke in a ragged whisper about the monster that hunted us, and Artemis' fingers gently closed around mine as I at last spoke of what had happened in the darkness—the horrors Evadne and I had been forced to face both together and apart. I told her of the pirate ship and the Moores, the crew I considered family and the complexity that bound them all together. I told her of the Phoenix on my shoulder blade, the constellation on my collarbone, and what they meant. Then finally, as the story stretched to a close around us in the quiet clearing, I spoke of the emerald-eyed prince that had the power to destroy me. I spoke of how he fought to protect me, and how much it hurt to fall in love and still be afraid. I told her about the way our paths had found each other again, and how I dared dream of hope in a place that harbored fear. I shared with my oma how I was struggling to find a way through my questions, how it felt as if I was betraying her, and my family, by falling in love.

I spoke until my voice faded and the sun had sunk below the trees, and there in the dim twilight I imagined my oma beside me. I could almost feel her there, with one hand on my shoulder, and the other wrapped around a steaming mug of tea. I could almost hear her as the daylight fled, reassuring me that it was okay. That if Artemis was a good man, it didn't matter whether he was Fey or human. In the growing dusk, I could feel my oma there. As darkness fell and the presence faded, I found all I had left were tears as I at last mourned the loss of my Oma, my F, Theron, and everything else the Fey Realm had stolen from us.

I say goodbye in twilight,
I do not want to leave,
but I find that I must go,
and flee this place I grieve.
It used to be my safe place,
a calming place of peace,
but fate has torn it from my grasp,
and destroyed my sanctuary.
My mind and soul plead to stay,
but my heartbeat begs to go,
this world I love is killing me,
it cannot be my home.
Home is where the heart is,

and where my loved ones go,
there I find my peace at last,
their love is my true home...
No matter where fate takes me,
no matter where I go,
if my loved ones are beside me,
my heart will have its home.
I still fear what the future holds,
I fear the grief the tides will bring,
but if they are still by my side,
I can stand against anything.

63

Meet The Paths Of Fate

EMBER

"I feel my ancestors in my blood. I am a body of people that are asking
not to be forgotten."
-BEINGUPILE

It was pitch dark outside and still we sat deep in the forest beside the grave. Instinctively, I knew we should leave and get behind the fence, but something had changed. Yes, there were monsters in the woods, but I wasn't afraid of them anymore. I had seen and lived through so much, what might come prowling was a distant concern—especially when I had Artemis by my side. Though his wounds were healing slowly, I still had a hunch that he was the most dangerous thing in these woods.

"I need to show you one more thing," Artemis said gently as he took my hand and pulled me to my feet.

I nodded, too drained to ask any questions, and followed as he led me through the woods. At last we were through the gate, but instead of going inside, he guided me toward the back of the house, where Evadne's wild, magical garden had taken over most of the back yard. After the raven incident, she had slowly surrendered her garden to the strange magical flowers. The ones that smelled of rot and death eventually disappeared and strange, but wonderful, flowers took their place. Though wild and unmanageable, they were gorgeous, so she didn't mind the surrender too much.

There, amid the blazing colors and strange glowing shapes, a space had been cleared. Large stones were piled up in a thick, long line. A large square piece of wood had been shoved into the ground. I instinctively recognized it as a grave. Burned into the polished surface was my mother's flowing penmanship. The inscription read: *F—Beloved father, grandfather, friend. Taken too soon, but loved beyond measure. May the wings of death give you rest.*

Tears rose to my eyes as grief overwhelmed everything. Death had taken so much from my family. I couldn't bear the graves that held the ones I loved.

"Rosamond went back to the Mortal Realm after she found the source of the magic in the cursed forest," Artemis said. "She figured your parents had buried him; she went to pay her respects and apologize."

"She sure kills a lot of people for someone who says she regrets it," I muttered, wiping away the new tears that had begun to flow.

"She is her own being," Artemis said with a shrug. "Her revenge on Theron was a toxic, mutual agreement between the two of them. Torn by festering hostility, they hunted and hated each other because they couldn't acknowledge that they still loved each other. She just got to him first. Their story was one bound by heartbreak and fury... Theron knew she would keep her word, just as she knew he would keep his. I don't think he would have wanted it any other way. Rosamond is an enigma; there's no way to fully understand her actions."

I stared down at the wood. "I want to hurt her," I confessed. "I want to make her pay for what she did to him. Pinning me to the mast was bad enough, but killing him...why?"

Artemis frowned at his boots. "I told her not to harm you or Evadne. I told the crew, and her, not to kill *anyone*. We were trying to incapacitate the ship. I didn't want anyone to die. From what I gathered, Rosamond pinned you to that mast to draw Theron out. She knew it was likely you'd be paired with him, given his gift and your fear of heights."

Anger burned in my chest. "Why did you bother?" I muttered, staring down at my injured arm in rage. "Besides, your aim to limit the bloodshed was in vain. From the looks of it, you got most of your crew killed. Verity showed no mercy."

Artemis shrugged. "They were all criminals on death row, anyway. I told them what likely awaited us when we met your ship, and I told them they weren't allowed to give any killing blows themselves. They seized the bloody day regardless, with fangs bared."

"That's insane."

Artemis shrugged. "That's the Moores, and in a way, that's the Realm. The Fey live and die and seize every moment in between... F knew that when he came to warn your parents. He knew every time he visited, he was putting his life in danger. He knew the scrutiny he was under, but he came anyway."

"Then why did he do it?!" I demanded angrily.

"Because he wanted to help. He wanted to find a way around the curse."

"You don't want me to find a way around the curse?" I whispered.

"No."

I threw up my hands, furious. "Why?" I shouted. "Do you even care about me?!"

"I do," Artemis replied gently. "I care about you more than you could ever know. But what you can't see is that your destiny isn't to be under that curse. Your destiny is to meet the curse and break it. Your ancestors have been waiting for you—all of you. You and your siblings have a destiny to free the Grimms and set the Realm free from the Knight's power."

"What if I don't want that destiny?" I whispered, desperation flaring.

"It is yours, whether you want it or not. You can't run from fate. You'll always meet it in the end."

"I can, too," I hissed, suddenly furious.

Artemis arched an eyebrow, which only enraged me further. "You ran, my dear *Flamín*, and where did it get you?"

La-la-la. I'm not listening!

"You ran from your destiny, trying to find another path, and your desperation only brought you back to the Realm...back to me," he added softly. "The only question that remains is, are you going to meet your fate the easy way or the hard way? The hard way will only increase the bloodshed. Running from your fate will only hurt you and the people you love." Artemis took a step closer. "The Realm is your destiny," he whispered. "I am your destiny. Ember, you *can* save your sisters from the Last Gate. You can save each other from that end, but not in the way you think. You will never save them if you keep running. The cards are nearly on the table...the knight rises, and we no longer face him at the Last Gate. We will face him in the Central Realm."

"Why me?" I sobbed. "Why me? I don't want this! I don't want anything to do with the Realm, or the Fey. I don't want it!"

"I know," Artemis sighed. "I know how you feel, but it's the truth. The Realm has been waiting for you. That's why the Knight wants you all so desperately. He wants to escape and ruin you, because you have the power to destroy him, once and for all." He took another step closer, until we were a breath away. "Your destiny is in the Realm, my Flamín, and I will be behind you every step of the way."

I pulled away, conflicted, choosing instead to turn to the grave. "He'd tell me to cut out your heart and leave you bleeding to death on his grave."

"He'd tell you a great many things. But one thing he knew, that he never told you, was your destiny. He knew what you mean to the Realm."

"Then why was he always looking for a way out? If he knew that I had the power to set my sisters free, to set the Grimm lineage free from the curse, why would he continue to search for a way out?"

"Because he knew the cost of such deliverance was steep, and he wanted to save you from the heartache... There is a conundrum that, you would let the whole world—a world that destroyed your life—burn, if only to save the few precious lights you desperately love. He wanted a different way, one that would not break your heart in the end..."

"And you want the end that breaks me?" I whispered.

"I want a way that truly sets you free," Artemis countered. "The Grimms have been wrongly enslaved by the sisters' magic and the monarchs since the brothers helped bind the Knight. Though there is pain, this is the only path left for you to take. If you pledge yourself to the Moores, you will sacrifice a heart that you do not possess and doom the Realm as well as your family. If you stay in the Mortal Realm, your heart will give out, the Realm will be doomed, and I will lose you. Would you ask me to stand by and do nothing but watch as you kill yourself?"

His words hung in the air between us as I wiped away my tears, trying to find an answer. At last, I shook my head.

"Now do you understand why I had to come find you?" Artemis asked, voice sad. "I know why you're running, but it will kill you. I can't stand by and watch you die. There is hope for change if we stand together. That is the only way forward that has *any* hope for the future."

"Do I really have any say in my future?" My words were stilted, filled with anger and heartbreak.

"You have a destiny to meet, and how you meet it, though it will happen regardless, is what matters. That is what makes the difference for the ones you love."

I sniffed, staring down at the stones. "I don't know if I'm strong enough to meet my destiny."

"I'm here," Artemis said quietly. "As are Evadne, Faye, and Jack. Together we can save the Realm and defeat the Knight. But only if we work together. Divided, the Realm crumbles. It crumbles now because of the division the monarchs have sown. But you're not alone, Em. Your destiny awaits you, but you don't have to meet it alone. You don't have to be strong enough to meet it alone. We are right here with you."

"I guess I should get ready to go back then," I whispered, defeated.

"We have time yet," Artemis replied. "I'm still not healed enough to go back into the Moores."

"How do you know we'll be able to get back to the Moores?"

"Rosamond is in the doorway; she guards the bridge between Realms. Jacques is with her guarding her back. I should be strong enough for us to join them in a few hours. Until then, we can twiddle our thumbs or perhaps exchange riddles."

"I detest riddles," I griped.

"Twiddling it is, then," Artemis laughed.

We spent the remaining hours in the Mortal Realm sharing bits and pieces of our lives as we wandered around my house. While we meandered, I gathered a small collection of things I wanted to take with me. I was certain this would be the last time I went home again.

The house was under a spell. The animals slept, undisturbed and unaware. They would eat and drink as they slept, the food magically appearing in their troughs and the water never running out. After some careful examination, and some crawling along the floors, Artemis let out a cry of triumph.

"It's the brounie!" he crowed. "The brounie is taking care of your home!"

"Frankie the evil one?" I gasped, shocked. "Why would he take care of our home? I have been locked in a battle of wills with him since he came to us."

"Brounies care for the homes they choose. If the owners are away, the brounies take control. That's why their possessive nature within the house, even while the home-owners are there, is so strong. They have decided upon joint ownership of the dwelling, with or without the actual owner's consent. I'm surprised the spell hasn't broken since we're here, but I'd wager they woke and he put them back under. He knows you're not here to stay. Look," he pointed to the dusty row of shoes by the door—a pile Mum was forever getting after all of us for. "There's no shoelaces."

"Oh, that no good, dirty rotten little scoundrel! He was just waiting for me to leave so he could eat the shoelaces!"

Artemis smirked. "I'd guess so. Brounies are very partial to shoelaces as well as mortal junk food. I'm honestly surprised the tarts of pop survived this long."

I rubbed my temples. "They're called Pop Tarts, you moron."

"It's the same thing!" Artemis cried, laughing. "I'd be surprised if you had any socks left in your drawers."

I let out a cry of indignance and raced for the stairs, intent on finding the little monster.

Artemis followed, still laughing.

I was furious, until I actually found the furry little creature sleeping soundly in a nest made in my sock drawer. Various articles of clothing had been woven together, until nothing but a bundled nest remained. Small, shiny knick-knacks surrounded the drawer, rather like a packrat's nest.

I'd never actually seen the brounie before, and what I saw I was delighted with. It looked like a cross between a chipmunk and a man, with large ears like a jerboa and sharp little claws on its hands and feet. About the size of a large packrat, with a fluffy bunny tail, it matched the image I had in my mind of the little creature.

I had no doubt that if Evadne were here, she'd be trying to add him to her portable petting zoo.

Oh Eva, where are you?

Curled around the brounie, Maladroit slept peacefully in the nest, purring softly.

"They're so adorable," I breathed.

"Brounies typically are," Artemis mused, peering over my shoulder at the ball of fur. "For such tiny beings, they exude a great amount of power in the Mortal Realm. It's phenomenal, really."

The brounie stirred and then opened two vibrant purple eyes, staring up at us in a sleepy haze.

"I have to go away again," I said, tears gathering in my eyes. "I'm not sure when I'll be back, or when my parents will be back... Take care of the house while we're gone, okay?"

The brounie nodded and yawned, before curling into a tighter little ball against Maladroit.

"Thank you," I whispered as I quickly took off one of my bracelets and dropped it into the drawer as a thank you gift. "Thank you for taking care of my home, Mr. Frankie."

I scratched Maladroit gently, careful not to wake him. "I love you, Maladroit. You're definitely *my* cat. Always have been."

Maladroit's purrs intensified, as if he could hear me while he slept, and I wiped away the tears that rose. I was going to miss my cat.

Goodbye was harder than I realized it would be—harder than it had been the first time. Because now, I wasn't being dragged away. I left of my own volition and, though I knew it was the right choice, it still felt like a betrayal.

I took an absurd number of pictures using my polaroid camera, trying to preserve a moment in time I knew I could never return to again.

Artemis gave me space as I took picture after picture and buried them in my cloak pocket. Finally, after laying a two-liter bottle of soda on F's grave, and a jar of strawberry preserves on Oma's, I was ready to go.

"Wait," Artemis said suddenly. "Let me take one of you in front of the house."

I handed him the camera, but as he raised the viewfinder to his eye, I found I couldn't bring myself to smile as he snapped a picture.

He handed it back to me, and on impulse, I raised the camera and took two pictures of us. I still couldn't smile in the first, but for the second I managed to pull the corners of my mouth up, even though the tears were still trickling down my cheeks.

Good heavens. I've done enough crying today to last a year.

What happened to the girl who hated when people saw her cry? What happened to the girl who wouldn't cry in front of others?

Gone, she's gone far, far away...

Home, home, will I ever come home again?

Home is with my family, not in a house or material things. My heart is with my family. My home is in their love.

I looked back a final time as we walked away, trying to memorize the image of the house, buried in a landscape of fog.

Goodbye, goodbye. I love you, goodbye.

Though I was crying as I turned my face forward again, there was hope buried beneath my sorrow. It was time to face who I was, and everything I could be. It was time to see what the future could look like, with a green-eyed prince at my side who had crossed the Moores to find me.

64

Well If It Isn't The Consequences Of My Own Actions

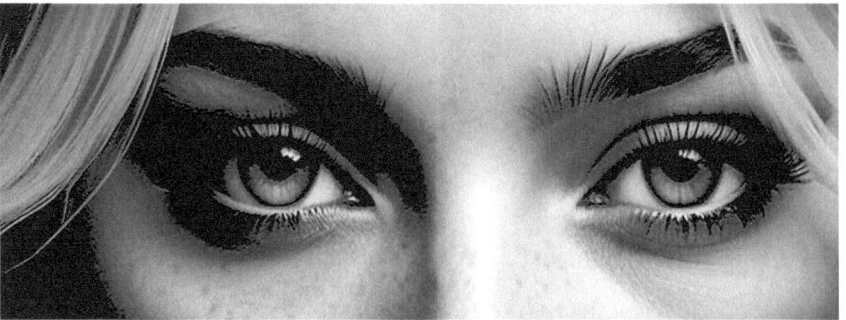

FAYE

"Look here comes the consequence, consequence, consequence, consequences of my actions chasing me right now...I don't want no consequence, consequence, consequence, I don't want no consequences chasing me right now...Someone take this consequence, consequence, consequence, someone take this consequence chasing me right now!"

-Look Here Comes The Consequence,

-Unknown

My three brain cells had decided that they were ridiculously, head over heels in love with Ronan. Despite the fact that, in the not distant past, they had been planning a gruesome, horrifying death for him followed by a less than honorable funeral.

I, thoroughly mortified that my brain cells were arguing over what design of wedding dress I'd wear when I walked down the aisle, had decided the best course of action was to ignore them entirely.

It wasn't long before the dress was completely forgotten because the argument had turned into an all-out brawl—complete with spiked baseball bats and folding chairs.

Thankfully, none of them had decided to once again take up admiration for the man and the way he was chivalrously carrying me.

Ronan shifted my weight as he waded through the wildflowers. Pain flared in my leg. Agony, my leg was in utter agony.

An unchecked sliver of electricity fled from my fingertips and into Ronan's back.

Oh no!

"CRAP!" I yelled. "Let go of me!"

It was too late; it had already hit him.

He swore and, surprised at being electrocuted, dropped me.

Well, he obeyed.

There was no point in dropping me after the shock. It was only to save him from the shock. Now it's just pointless!

I screamed as I hit the ground. The pain was unbearable now.

Clumsy, stupid human!

He's only clumsy because you accidentally electrocuted him. He was quite doting before your powers decided to ruin the moment.

Fair point.

Ronan dropped to his knees, profusely apologizing as I both laughed and cried, trying to get a handle on the pain.

"Oh my gosh, Faye, I'm so sorry. Are you okay?" He was rambling as he tried to pick me back up.

"Just, just give me a second," I gasped. "It's my fault. I'm in enough pain that my power's leaking out." I looked down at my clothes. The timing had been terrible. Ronan had dropped me right in the middle of a giant mud puddle and now I was absolutely filthy.

That's not fair. Why do I have to be the one all dirty?

Maybe I should make him all grody too.

No. That is not the right course of action. This is your fault, anyway. If you hadn't shocked him, he wouldn't have dropped you.

I was losing strength and, in a moment of unchecked intrusive thoughts, I flopped back onto the ground and stared up at the bright blue sky. "Just leave me here to die," I sighed. "I would rather die here than in that compound."

"Don't be ridiculous," Ronan spluttered. "We have not gone to all this trouble for you to give up now."

"Your father bloody *shot* me, Ronan! That was not part of the plan."

"No, it wasn't, and I plan to increase your dragon hoard when we get clear of this mess, remember? Bribery at its finest is the solution to make up for unexpected problems."

I rolled my eyes. "Yes, yes, I remember."

"Come on," Ronan sighed. "We need to get back so I can convince Jeremiah to let me take you to the hospital."

"Good luck," I griped as I sat up.

"Now you're absolutely covered in mud," Ronan sighed disapprovingly. "Why did you lie down??"

"I dunno. Moment of weakness, intrusive thought won out, my brain cells needed a good mud bath to cleanse them of their violence...and delusional thoughts...or perhaps all of the above?"

Ronan sat back on his heels and sighed. "This is not how I imagined today would go."

"What did you expect? Roses and sunshine? Rainbows and butterflies with unicorn farts?" I demanded. "I can assure you unicorn farts are *not* magical. They smell absolutely *horrendous!*"

Ronan chuckled. "You're something else, Faye."

It was then another intrusive thought won and, without further contemplation, I lay down again. Then, I arranged myself neatly on one side, putting one leg over the other to accentuate what little curves I had. Propping my head up, I gave him the best pickup line I could think of. "Paint me like one of your French Girls," I saucily stated.

Ronan laughed outright and my heart summersaulted in my chest. I would say and do a whole multitude of ridiculous things just to hear him laugh like that for the rest of my life.

Engines roared somewhere in the distance and Ronan's smile died as quick as it had come.

Stupid Jeremiah. Ruining my attempts to make Ronan's life better.

"Come on," Ronan sighed. "Jeremiah's coming. It might look bad if he were to happen upon us like this."

"Stupid Jeremiah," I muttered. I made a face as I wrapped my arm around Ronan's neck. Ronan made a face in return as he carefully picked me up.

"You're absolutely filthy," Ronan chortled as he stared down at me with laughing eyes. "You need to stop listening to your impulsive thoughts."

"*Sometimes* my intrusive thoughts have very good ideas," I stated loftily.

He chuckled and once again began to walk as the sound of vehicles grew louder.

Well. If it isn't the consequences of my own actions...I run, Jeremiah shoots me, and then, unable to wait for Ronan to return, chases me down himself.

Three off-road vehicles roared toward us, coming to a violent stop ten feet away. Marcov leapt out of the first vehicle. He was limping, his left pant leg soaked in blood from an obvious stab wound, and his face held a set of nasty, deep gashes. He looked absolutely livid.

Well, well, well. What did Marcov stick his nasty little fingers into? Whatever it is, it looks as if it put up a fight...

Jeremiah followed, his face a tangle of fury and calculation.

Jeremiah ordered Ronan to kill me. He hesitated. We have to play this carefully. Think. Think fast.

The rest of the vehicles emptied out in a matter of seconds, with every man pointing a gun at our exposed bodies.

Well. This is an unfortunate hiccup.

"Why didn't you kill her?" Jeremiah seethed. "I told you to kill her."

"I tried," Ronan sighed. "When she produced the blizzard, it startled me and she knocked me away with a blast of raw power. I wasn't aware she had the strength to pull that kind of magic off with the shadows feeding on her."

"She shouldn't have been," Jeremiah replied, glaring at me. "Put her down," he ordered.

I gave Ronan a subtle squeeze on the shoulder, warning him not to argue.

Ronan carefully put me down, and I struggled to keep my balance and weight off my injured leg.

"Perhaps I spoke rashly," Jeremiah mused. "After all, she will be the leverage I need for the other."

What other? Does he mean Dad?

"Sir?" Ronan asked, questioningly.

"I had another iron in the fire, one I chose not to tell you about in case it came to nothing. I have captured one of the other sisters, *fresh* from the Realm. She will give me the information I desire, especially when I have her sister's life in my hands. The young ones are weak-willed and easily manipulated."

No, no, no. This was not part of the plan. What does he mean?

He's got to be bluffing. He has to be bluffing.

Who does he have? Ember or Evadne?

If I ask, it'll make me appear vulnerable and desperate. I'll have to wait and have Ronan find out.

"You will be punished for your rebellion," Jeremiah seethed, still glaring at me.

"Bring it, psycho," I drawled, holding onto my thin façade of rebellion.

Jermiah lunged, fists colliding with my body over and over.

Don't do anything, Ronan. Don't you dare.

I screamed, unable to help myself, and Ronan stepped in. "Leave her alone!" he yelled.

Fine. Plan B it is then. We will use this display of protection to cement my affection for Ronan and make it believable that I'll tell Ronan the truth.

Ronan's arms wrapped around me, pulling me to my feet, and I intentionally leaned into his embrace, chest heaving as I struggled to get a handle on the pain.

"That's enough," Ronan snarled. "She's been through *enough*."

Jeremiah's gaze jumped between me and Ronan, as a slow smile spread across his face.

That's it. Realize Ronan's finally won me over. Realize that you two can manipulate me to get what you want.

Time to plant the idea.

"You should thank Ronan for not killing me," I hissed.

"Why is that?" Jeremiah scoffed. "Do you really think so much of your puny life?"

"Yes."

Jeremiah arched a disbelieving eyebrow.

This is going to hurt.

"I am the only chance you have of getting your dead wife back," I gasped, laying the groundwork in place for the next phase of our plan. "Why do you think I came back to the Human Realm from that cursed Fey Realm?" A trickle of blood crept down my chin from my split lip as I struggled to get air into my battered lungs. "I was coming back to give my parents the power to resist," I lied. "A way to save us...but you could use it to revive her."

Fire was overtaking my body. I had spoken just enough truth to get myself marked.

Good. He'll know what that means. He'll think I've shared a secret.

Jeremiah took a hungry step forward as I was branded, once, twice, three times for the singular secret. His eyes were feral as I fell to my knees, screaming, clutching my arm as the letters carved themselves into my skin.

Traitor.

But this time, I wasn't a traitor. I was a wolf ready to swallow him whole.

Jeremiah took another step forward and I spat blood on his boots. "I'll never tell you," I hissed. "Torture me, kill me, anything you like. But you will never break me. Surely the last few months have revealed that to you. You cannot break me, no matter what you do."

"Maybe not, but I don't need to break you anymore." Jeremiah's gaze flicked between Ronan and me. I could feel the shift as Ronan gave his father the subtlest of nods, confirming Jeremiah's idea.

That's it. Trust your traitorous son. Believe your deformed delusions. It will be your downfall, your ruin.

I will be the death of you, Jeremiah Anderson. One way or another, I will destroy you.

65

The Horrifying Reality Of My Inability To Drink Water Without Drowning

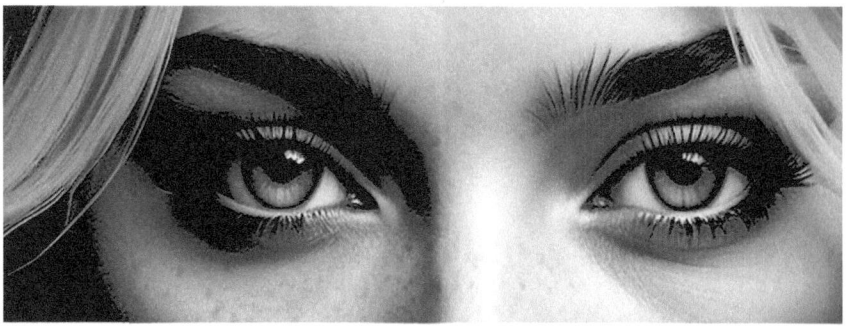

FAYE

"I'll keep all my emotions right here, and then one day I'll die."
-John Mulaney

Turns out human doctors are pretty dupable. All it took was Ronan's desperate cries for help as he rushed me into the emergency room, and a frantic, garbled explanation about a home invasion, and the nurses and doctors jumped into action. Turns out Ronan was a born liar and actor. He even managed to start sobbing. It was a good enough performance that my three brain cells began suggesting perhaps I should give *him* my Oscar award. That idea was rapidly shot down with great threats of violence and mutiny. I had earned that Oscar fair and square. I would not be sharing it with anyone.

Much to my annoyance, fishing the bullet out required surgery under general anesthesia, which trapped me in a particularly horrifying Dreamscape.

WAKE UP!

I wrenched myself from the magic induced dream with a screech, nearly startling Ronan out of his skin. He jumped several feet in the air before wrapping me in a tight hug.

My mouth was as dry as a desert and tasted absolutely awful. I swatted at his back weakly. "Water!" I protested.

He ignored my demand and continued to hug me.

I balled my fists and hit him harder. "Water!" I demanded angrily.

Did Jeremaih give him a concussion after I passed out? What the heck is wrong with him?

My leg was screaming in pain from the odd angle he was putting me in, and my words wouldn't come. My throat was too dry to get words out.

Maybe I'm still dreaming?

Alarms and machines blared and a nurse at last rushed to my rescue. "Mr. Anderson, did she—"

Mister Anderson...which pill are you going to take...what, are we in the Matrix now?
Ronan's shoulders were shaking.

What the heck, is he crying?

Enough with the theatrics, you've already put on an Oscar-worthy performance.

"Mr. Anderson, I know you're in shock and relieved your wife woke up, but her injuries are not life threatening. She really is going to be okay."

HIS WIFE?!?!?! He told them I was his wife?!

I most certainly did not consent to marrying him...did I?

My brain cells, however, took the thought in a completely different direction. They were gloriously giddy to find that we'd finally married their beloved Ronan, and though they were upset about missing the ceremony itself, they had great and glorious plans for the future. The honeymoon was to be at a lovely island beach, and during our time in paradise, they planned to force Ronan to learn how to dance, teach him the joys of glorious junk food, and lastly, much to my mortification, force Ronan to give me big hugs and kisses every night.

I need my brain cells to shush. I can't take their lovey-dovey thoughts anymore.

"You need to let her lay back. I need to check her vitals and you're going to hurt her if you put her leg at that uncomfortable angle."

"Sorry," Ronan whispered.

"What..."

"You don't remember, do you love?" she asked casually. "Can't say I'm surprised. Brains block out such things. The trauma is just too much to allow remembrance. You went through a horrible ordeal. You're lucky to be alive."

It took me a minute to put the pieces together. The anesthesia was stronger than I had given it credit for, and finding my mind was a challenge. Currently, other than the three love drunk brain cells planning a make-believe honeymoon, the collective hoard was stumbling around, slurring their words and singing little ditties about their adoration for cookies and Ronan that didn't make sense. They were all in a total state of disorientation.

Right. Jeremiah shot me...we came to the hospital to get the bullet out...Ronan told them I was his wife...Jeremiah has my sister...crap. Jeremiah has my sister. Who? Ember? or Evadne?

Ronan pulled away, easing me back down onto the pillows. His eyes were red rimmed, cheeks tear streaked.

Wow. He really is putting on quite the performance.

Never mind, give this man my Oscar. He's earned it.

At this, the drunk collective immediately began organizing the event. A mock 'Ronan' came up in a tux, and began giving a long, meaningful speech. At least it would be if I could understand it. The speech itself was nothing but a garbled set of mumbo-jumbo words and noises, with plenty of fart sounds sprinkled in. Clearly, the anesthesia was still making a fantastic mess of things.

Good grief.

"I'll be honest love, we didn't expect you to have such a severe reaction to the anesthesia," the nurse continued as she began to take note of my vitals.

Say what now? What reaction?

"We've put a nice big note on your chart to never give you that form of medication again. We almost lost you on the table."

Excuse me, what?!

All this time nearly dying in the Realm and putting my life on the line, and it's human anesthesia that almost kills me?

That was not in my bingo cards for this year.

"Are you in any pain, love?" the nurse asked kindly.

Well, yes, I am. But I can't afford to be doped up and foggy headed. Jeremiah has my sister.

I hope whichever sister it is, she bit him. HARD.

No, I think I'll keep my pain right here in my chest, with all my suppressed emotions, until I die.

The nurse was still staring at me expectantly. I stared back, my mind blank.

What was the question again?

Pain levels, you dummy.

Oh, right. I have a valid excuse for my foggy headedness. I've been shot.

Your excuse is denied. The brain cells are writing you up for your stupidity.

That's a load of bull—

"Any pain?" the nurse repeated kindly.

Right. Answer the question.

"One to two," I lied. In all reality, I was closer to a six or seven. "Not bad, really," I continued nonchalantly.

The nurse raised an eyebrow and glanced at my elevated levels on the computer screen. "Are you sure?"

"Oh, yeah. I've always, uh, run high…" I stammered, trying to keep the lie together.

Every word was hard to get out. My mouth was so dry, my throat so tight, I was bound to burst out coughing from lack of moisture.

Ronan was pouring a glass of water, and I watched him anxiously, mouth growing drier by the second. I had never felt so parched in my life.

Hurry up, you stupid human. I'm dying of thirst!

At last, he turned toward me with the paper cup.

I lunged forward, ignoring the outcry of pain from my leg as I snatched it out of his hand and gulped it down. I couldn't risk the odds of him adding terms and conditions to the precious liquid such as, 'be careful,' 'go slow,' or 'one swallow at a time.' I didn't have the patience for such nonsense. My mouth was so dry it might as well have been the Sahara Desert. I was fairly sure some unsuspecting animal had crawled in my mouth and died from thirst in that desert.

"Easy!" the nurse and Ronan scolded, as I simultaneously choked and dumped the water on my face.

Now you look stupid and ridiculous.

Ronan laughed, then quickly clapped a hand over his mouth, trying to hide his outburst of amusement as I spluttered and coughed.

How dare he laugh at me!

I mean, you do look pretty ridiculous right now.

You can take your critiques and shove them where the sun doesn't shine.

Sheesh, you're grumpy.

Hmm, I wonder why. It's not like I was just SHOT or anything!

"Easy love, just nice, slow sips now..." the nurse said gently as she pried the cup from my fingers and held it to my lips.

Cursed terms and conditions! I'm not a child. I can drink water without assistance!

Says the person who literally just spilled water down her front like a toddler.

Shut up, nobody asked you.

I glared daggers at Ronan, blaming him for the catastrophe. It was infuriating he found my predicament amusing.

The nurse was carefully administering the precious hydration, controlling how much I could gulp at a time.

I am not an invalid. I know how to drink water.

My three, unhelpful braincells decided it was the perfect time to pull down their large projector screen and replay the moment of humiliation on repeat. They watched in horrified embarrassment as I repeatedly snatched, choked, and dumped the water all over myself.

The nurse pulled away as I once again began to cough and choke, desperately trying to get the water out of my lungs.

"I believe I said drink it, not breathe it in," the nurse teased gently, trying to ease my discomfort as she firmly patted me on the back.

There was a snort of laughter somewhere in the room, and I looked around. There was no one else there, and neither Ronan nor the nurse, whose nametag I could now see read Meredith, indicated they had heard anything.

Great. Now there's monsters here, too. Is nowhere safe from their nosy little claws?

My fingers twitched, longing for my confiscated dagger.

Stupid Ronan. He never should have taken my daggers away!

I think, since Ronan and I are back on good terms, he should give me my daggers back!

"I'll have the kitchen bring you some broth," Meredith said happily as she handed the water cup to Ronan. "The doctor will be pleased to know you're awake. I'm sure he'll be in to see you after a while." She arched an eyebrow at Ronan. "Small. Slow. Sips," she instructed firmly. "Now, I've turned off your bed alarm. If you need to use the bathroom, use these crutches. If you need any help, turn on the call light and we'll be right in."

"I can help her if she needs it," Ronan replied cheerfully.

No. Absolutely not. There's no way in any cursed Realm I'm letting you help me use the bathroom. I would rather fall on my face because of those stupid crutches than let you help me.

"I figured," Meredith replied with a smile. "Well, I'll leave you two alone. Just use your call light if you need anything."

"We will," Ronan reassured her with a grateful smile.

The nurse left, and I glared at Ronan. "Give me back my water at once!" I demanded.

"I don't know if that's such a smart idea," he snorted. "You've already tried to drown yourself multiple times in the space of five minutes."

"I know how to drink water," I growled as I snatched the water cup from his hands.

Timing is everything, and my body had apparently decided to choose violence sprinkled with constant, terrible timing.

Just as Ronan smirked at me, I choked on my water again. Another coughing fit rose, only proving the snarky point he was about to make.

"Obviously not," Ronan countered as he patted me firmly on the back and took away my precious water.

In retaliation, I maturely imagined myself throwing him headfirst into a giant glass of water.

Yes. Full of crocodiles.

And snakes.

Oo, and spiders.

Now that's just cruel.

He shouldn't torment me. Then I wouldn't have to resort to such drastic measures.

Wait...what was I thinking before the water incident? I had a question for Ronan...what was it?

"Welcome back to the land of the living, my dear."

What was that about crocodiles?

Forget the question, I have violence to attend to.

The water had quite revived me, and I decided a reminder of what happened when he called me 'my dear' was necessary. I lunged forward, ramming his chest with my finger horns.

My petty victory was short-lived as I realized I was falling off the bed.

Crap!

Ronan caught me just before my poor choices turned into an all-out catastrophe.

"Easy!" Ronan chuckled as he carefully helped me settle back onto the bed. "How about we save the attacking for later."

I'll attack you now, if I want to. You're not the boss of me.

Ronan arched an eyebrow. "You know, I would have thought, given the whole kiss situation, you'd stop attacking me."

My cheeks flamed crimson, and I decided a solid punch to the gut was necessary to reclaim my dignity.

Someone chortled and I scrutinized the space. "Show yourself!" I called out.

Ronan gave me a confused look. "Faye... maybe you should rest. I think you've overdone it. Nobody else is here."

I rolled my eyes, choosing to ignore his stupidity. "Show yourself!" I repeated angrily.

"Faye, it's just the machines. Look around. It's impossible that someone else is here. There's nowhere to hide. I think the drugs are making you hallucinate; you should just lay back and rest."

I shot him a blank look, giving him a moment to consider how absolutely stupid he sounded. "Impossible is reality, Anderson," I snapped. "That's what happens when you, as the curious cat, get yourself killed."

"I'm not curious here, you are. Besides, satisfaction brought it back."

"Do you feel satisfied?" I demanded. "Do you feel like you have all the answers to your many, and may I add, stupidly impertinent questions?"

"I'm not asking questions," Ronan sighed. "Clearly, you've overexerted yourself. You're not making sense."

Forget the stupid human for a moment. He's going to give me a migraine. We have bigger issues at hand. Something is here in the room with us.

Could be a ghoul. We are in a hospital. Ghouls love cold, dark places that smell of blood and death.

Oh no, please don't be a ghoul. They're incredibly hard to kill and I don't have any weapons.

"Come out!" I growled. "Before I make you come out!"

Ronan had the audacity to roll his eyes. "Faye, come on, just rest—"

Ryver stepped out of the shadows and Ronan's mouth fell open in shock. "Oh," he said softly.

"You should listen to Faye," Ryver scolded. "When she says there's something else here, she means there's something else here."

"Hello again," Ronan replied quietly.

Ryver grinned and nodded. "Hello, foolish human." He turned his smirking attention fully to me. "Hello, my Faye dearest, I see you've managed to stay alive without me."

I gave him a rueful smile. "Not for lack of trying, though."

"I can see that. Tell me, what foolhardy idea have you got in your magnificent brain now?"

"Oh, just one of chaos, madness, and a possible murder."

"Intriguing." He sat down on the edge of my bed. "Well, tell me my lionhearted girl, how long do you think you can evade death before he turns the odds against you completely?"

"I think I can evade *her* for quite a bit longer."

"Come now, Faye. Don't be stupid. We all know death is male."

"I don't think so," I replied primly. "Men do plenty of killing, but who comes to gather and mourn the bodies? Who wipes blood from the well-loved faces, who closes the lifeless eyes, who weeps late into the night? War may be a manmade horror, but death is a woman. Woman brings life into this world; I believe death is she who takes the souls out again."

Ryver laughed. "Well, aren't you poetic today. When we meet him or her, we can settle our argument."

"We both know *I'm* going to die first. After all, you're the one who gets my shadow."

Ryver rolled his eyes. "You wound me when you act as if the only reason I care for you is the shadow I am owed."

"I mean..."

Ryver huffed a sigh and shook his head. "Impertinent girl," he muttered.

"Yes, well, surely you didn't come to insult me. Why have you come this time?"

"I have news," Ryver stated as shadows began to leak out of his fingers and surround us. Ronan watched in wide-eyed fascination as Ryver's shadows created an impenetrable bubble around me and Ryver. We were now unheard and unknown—even from Ronan.

My gut plummeted. If he took the time to secure our conversation, chances were the news wasn't good.

"The Moores are shifting," Ryver sighed. "But you know that already. My neutrality is no longer an option. I have been marked. I spied on the Knight for the Winter Court as long as I could, but Nightshade turned a blind eye to my reports. The Knight knows who I am now and the traces of my shadows."

"The monarchs won't act?" I asked in shock.

"To put it bluntly, no."

I sighed, irritated, and my collective hoard of brain cells booed.

Stupid, stupid monarchs.

"What's more, the Moores are uniting, morphing together. Someone is controlling the Moores and I think you and I both know who."

"The Knight," I whispered.

Ryver nodded, looking disturbed.

"From what I've been able to gather, he's draining power from the Mortal Realm through doors he's been scattering around the Moores. They're portals and they suck the energy around them—draining the life of those nearby. The door that is at the compound leads directly into the Ruins. He's draining you as well, my lionhearted girl."

"I know," I sighed. "We're working on getting out of there. Ronan has a sister. We have to get her out as well."

"I'd help, but the shadows at the compound are on high alert. The Knight put a bounty on my head. The only place I'm somewhat safe is within the Summer Court. Even the Winter Court has been compromised. Though she turns a concerning blind eye to the growing darkness, Lady Nightshade has granted my request to leave until things even out."

"But they won't."

"No, they won't," Ryver agreed. "Not until war is pounding on their door, and when it does, they will be unprepared. They refuse to see the truth."

"Why though?" I murmured, pulling the pieces apart. "You don't think they're complicit in his rise? Aiding it?"

"No, I don't think it's that...but Nightshade is hiding something...something she doesn't want anyone to know... He's got his claws in her somehow."

"Ember and Evadne were sent into the Moores," I whispered, realization crashing into me like a blow to the gut.

No, no, no. This can't be happening.

"That they are. I believe the whole hairbrained quest was manipulated by the Knight."

"You think the Council has been compromised?" I gasped, shocked.

Ryver nodded.

"Oh no. They're in so much danger," I whispered.

Ryver nodded again. "But the prince is with them. He is more powerful than he lets on. Far more than anyone senses. He will not allow them to be killed or taken, though all the Moores strive as one to steal them away. His magic is bound to Ember's."

The words settled over me and rage slowly grew in my stomach.

"Did she know?" I asked, my voice deadly calm.

"Neither of them did. The King did it in secret, and then informed his son of what he did. If my sources are correct, Artemis was so angry he destroyed the throne room in his fury. They had to cancel court and rebuild everything."

"Why? Was he displeased with the prospect?"

"No, quite the opposite. He cares deeply for the girl. He viewed it as a violation since she had no say in the matter."

"Strange," I mused. "The monarchs bind the magic of Grimms all the time."

Ryver shrugged. "Artemis is different from his parents... How he came away unstained by their taint, I'll never figure out."

"She can still go against the bond. I went against mine when they bound me to Eryx."

Ryver nodded. "That you did. Nightshade's fury was unending for a whole solstice when you did that."

I grinned. "I wasn't about to have their stupid magic tell me what to do."

Ryver smirked. "I quite enjoyed the tantrum. It was about time someone defied her."

"I do love a good mutiny," I giggled.

"Ever my rebellious girl," Ryver agreed ruefully. "Ember can break the bond if she's decidedly against it and has enough mental clarity...but she's falling for him."

"Odd," I murmured. "That doesn't sound like her."

Ryver shrugged. "When it comes to love, we often aren't ourselves. She's definitely conflicted about the matter, but I think Artemis' anger will be the saving point for the hope of any relationship. The fact that he didn't want to force it on her, the way he wants to win her heart, may play out in his favor."

"What did he want?" I snorted. "Sunshine and roses?"

"He still foolishly dreams of true love," Ryver sighed. "He wanted her to choose him willingly. Poor, heartbroken prince...he was head over heels the moment she challenged him in the throne room with that fiery gaze."

I sighed, annoyed by all of it. Stupid meddling rulers. Stupid lovesick princes. It was enough to make me want to scream.

"I think Ember is embracing the bond, however," Ryver continued nonchalantly. "She's accepted her place in the Realm at last, and is going back with him to set out for the Ruins in search of you and Evadne."

That was the question I forgot! How could I possibly forget to ask about her?

Blame it on the anesthesia.

"So, Jeremiah took Evadne?" I asked, my mind spinning.

"Yes, he took her in the Mortal Realm. She's at the compound now."

My list of people to save from Jeremiah was rapidly growing—quickly becoming absolutely overwhelming.

"It's an old curse, may you live in interesting times," Ryver mused as the shadows began to dissolve around us. "We certainly live in interesting times, don't we?"

"Unfortunately so," I muttered.

"Good luck with your human," Ryver chuckled. "Though, I do have questions about a certain aforementioned kiss..."

I spluttered and swore as he disappeared into a cloud of shadows, his laughter still echoing around the room.

"What was that about?" Ronan asked in confusion.

My cheeks burned as my three brain cells and the collective hoard began to review the kiss in question on the projection screen. I was utterly mortified when they started to scream for an encore.

"Nothing," I muttered, trying to silence their begging that I kiss him right then and there. "Now give me my water."

I had some brain cells to drown. I was *not* about to admit my feelings for Ronan.

66

The Strange Realm Of Anderson

Evadne

"The only thing we have to fear is a tarantula hiding in our glove."
-Welcome to Night Vale Podcast

I stood on the edge of a cliff, gasping for air as the world shifted and swayed around me.

I'm going to fall.

"Evadne!" Ember's scream was there and gone again. So far away, it could have been something I imagined.

Where are you?

Come back! Where are you?

The mirage around me was flickering at the edges, breaking apart. Darkness was clawing its way toward me, threatening to break through the fog and overtake me.

No, no. Not again. I won't! Not again!

I drew my daggers, preparing to fight, terrified and alone.

I will not go with you. I will not go with you!

The monster lunged and I slashed, desperate to keep it at bay.

Wake up! Wake up!

"EVADNE!"

Ember's voice was screaming my name again, over and over as I fought the monster.

No matter how many times I stabbed it, it kept coming back. Again and again, and again, it resurfaced, unfazed by my blows.

Wake up! Wake up! I can't keep fighting this much longer!

Why can't I wake up?

My feet slipped on the edge. I had lost track of my surroundings. It was too late. The momentum from the fight pulled me backward and then I was falling, screaming as my fingers clawed open air.

The monster laughed above me, the sound a rasping scrape as it jumped off the cliff and plummeted down toward me.

I woke with a scream, clawing at empty air.

It was pitch black, so black I couldn't see my hand in front of my face.

Where am I?

What happened?

Why does my head hurt?

Memories came back to me in bits and pieces. The house, the men, the banister.

Right. Stupid meddling humans.

Where am I?

I have absolutely no idea.

"Are you all right?" a voice whispered hesitantly.

I shrieked, then clapped a hand over my mouth, afraid to have made a noise.

"It's okay," she laughed. "I'm not going to eat you."

Given what I've seen in the Realm, that is not a comforting statement. Since you said it, I'm more concerned that you do indeed want to eat me.

"Why should I trust you?" I demanded.

"Because eating people is a disgusting pastime, you distrusting goober."

Wait, why am I a distrusting goober in this situation? I think that's an unfair assessment.

She sounded young, and reminded me of Ember with her dark sense of humor and petty insults.

"That's true..." I replied, unsure of what to say.

"So, what's your story? Why would they bring you here? Do you have magical abilities like Faye?"

"I...well..." My words trailed off. I wasn't sure what I could or couldn't say. The fact that she knew Faye meant I was likely in the same place she was. "I don't even know where *here* is. Is this in the Human Realm?"

"Is there any other Realm?" she asked sarcastically.

Yes.

"Next thing I know, you'll be telling me you're actually like a Faerie or something," she snorted, laughing. "Did Jeremiah finally get his wish and catch himself a Faerie?"

No, yes...maybe?

"Where am I?" I asked, ignoring her question as I tried to put my thoughts together and force my ducks to stand in a row.

That is a hopeless endeavor. My ducks are quite scattered and I'm pretty sure one of them is a pigeon.

"You have been abducted to the awful *realm* of *Anderson*," she replied happily. "Are you hungry?"

"I mean, yes?"

"Good," she crowed. "I have some cookies in my room. I'll share, but only if you ask nicely."

"Can you turn on a light?"

"Negative, my fellow prisoner. This is the ultimate no-no cage. Jeremiah put Faye here when she was greatly misbehaving. Seems you one upped her and earned yourself a stint in the no-no cage as well. Which, on a sidenote, I'd like to know what you did. Jeremiah didn't put her in here for months. You've been here, what? All of a day, and you landed yourself right in the cage of despair? You must be quite the accomplished troublemaker."

Hope leapt wildly in my chest. Faye was here. This must be where she was being held prisoner.

"There's no lights on purpose," the girl continued. "It's his twisted idea of psychological torture. Solitude and darkness."

"I mean, it would be really nice for napping."

"Yeah, but you can only sleep for so long before you're bored out of your mind."

The way my body felt, I wasn't sure if I agreed. My body felt heavy, my heartbeat aching slightly in my chest. I wasn't sure I could ever get enough sleep to truly become rested.

"I mean, I guess you're right. Besides, it is kind of scary not being able to see anything. What if there's a tarantula in here and I don't know it?"

"Well, oblivion is bliss," she quipped. "Unless you have a good imagination, in which case oblivion is your worst nightmare because you *can't* know if there's a tarantula or not."

I shuddered at the thought of such a large spider in the darkness.

"Come on, let's go to my room."

"How...well, how do you have access to this room?"

"It's kind of a long story," she replied with a sigh. "But I'll give you a crash course in our tale of woe. Essentially, Faye has decided to help my stupid brother get me out of here, despite the fact he kidnapped her. They've also decided to fall in love, and I'm going to be a bridesmaid at their wedding."

"WHAT?!" I shrieked. This was a turn of events I never would have predicted. I'd think my sister would have more sense than to fall in love with her kidnapper.

"Yeah, I know, right? It's something straight out of a romance novel! She hated him, but then she finally saw him for who he was and realized that he's just as trapped as she is. He only ever did anything because he was trying to protect me from my demented father... which, is actually *our* demented father. So, they started working together, and then the other day, he. *Kissed. Her!*"

Her story cut off in an excited squeal and I rolled my eyes. This wasn't a romance novel, this was clearly Stockholm syndrome. My sister was too smart to be so incredibly stupid.

"I was spying, but it was necessary spying," she continued. "Anyway, she's been teaching me how to defend myself so when I get out of here, I can protect myself until she and Ronan get back to me. She came up with an absolutely *brilliant* escape plan. Jeremiah locked her up in this cell, not knowing that Ronan had put a way between our rooms so she could come train me. Ronan made a secret hidey hole, but it only proves we're terrible cliché criminals. Man, I am so happy she decided to listen to him. They've been fighting for *months*. He was in an absolutely horrendous mood for most of those months, and it was just *torture* to be around him. He was *so. GRUMPY.* And his obsession with making her eat healthy food? Come on, it's so stupid. I mean, I know you want to take care of the girl but give her a *twinkie* every once in a while. *SHEESH.*"

The story kept going back on itself and seemed quite a bit out of order. I was having an incredibly hard time keeping track of everything.

"But anyway, you can come over to my room if you like."

"Oookay...how?"

"Let me show you."

A sliver of light appeared in the room. It was a hole.

Interesting.

I followed the small figure through the light and into another room.

"So essentially, Ronan made a secret tunnel, and he put a poster over it on my end. Her end is a little more disguised. But mine is the most cliché thing I've ever seen."

I had to giggle with her at the absurdity of the large Taylor Swift 'Era's Tour' poster.

"Ronan even had the *audacity* to fib and say that Faye was the one who came up with the idea."

That does honestly sound like something she'd come up with.

I took in my surroundings, immediately feeling at home by the vast collection of books and the cozy-looking bed piled high with blankets and pillows.

The voice belonged to a short girl with dark, shoulder-length black hair, the ends of which were dyed a bright teal. Wide, stormy gray eyes stared at me, scrutinizing me as closely as I was scrutinizing her.

"Well," she said at last. "It appears you *are* a Faerie...but you're Faye's sister, aren't you?" she asked.

"Uhm..."

"You have the same sort of face shape, and your ears...they're pointed like hers. But your eye..." her voice trailed off in wonder. "Your eye is wicked cool," she stated at last.

"If you knew how I got it, you wouldn't think it was wicked cool," I muttered.

"So, you're Faye's sister?" Meghan asked again, changing the subject back.

I figured it didn't do any good to hide the truth. "She's my older sister, yes. Is she here?"

"Yes and no. She and Ronan are off initiating the next part of the *super-secret* plan to save us. This phase is called honor among thieves. Your sister came up with the name."

"So...why do you need her to get out? If Ronan is the one who kidnapped her, why doesn't he just take you out?"

"Because my father is trying to kill me," the girl said with a shrug.

"Uhm..."

"It's a long story. I'm Meghan, by the way. I don't think I actually introduced myself."

"Evadne, nice to meet you."

What on earth is going on? I'm so confused...she's definitely not giving off prisoner vibes...and if she is a prisoner, why does she have such a nice room?

As if reading my mind, Meghan gestured to the bookshelves. "Ronan knows how much I love to read, so he feeds my addiction. Jeremiah is annoyed by it, but he doesn't put a stop to it. Ronan uses our father's credit card to get me books...it's about the only thing he can use the credit card for. I wish Jeremiah didn't monitor the orders. We could get out of here with some weapons if he didn't. But for now, he lets it slide. Every once in a while, he comes in and destroys my books...I think that's why he lets Ronan get me things...so he can take them away." Her voice went soft as she recalled the incidents. I could see the fear in her eyes as she remembered.

"So, Jeremiah is your father?" I asked, still slightly confused.

"Unfortunately so. Jeremiah Anderson, the psycho, is my father; Ronan Anderson, the saint, is my brother. We are in an underground compound that is very closely guarded."

"It all sounds very complicated," I sighed, massaging my aching temples.

"You can clean the blood off your face if you like," Meghan offered. "My bathroom is just over there."

"Would it be suspicious if I cleaned myself up, though? Wouldn't someone put the dots together?"

"No, there's a tiny bathroom in your cell, too. Theoretically you could have given yourself a sponge bath in there, even though it's dark."

"Can I take an actual shower?" I asked hesitantly.

"Absolutely. Just be quick. I'm not sure when Jeremiah will come back for you."

I nodded.

My cloak had been taken, as well as all my weapons, but I still had my armor.

My petting zoo is in the cloak. Oh dear. If Jeremiah hurts any of them, I'll kill him.

There was a strange scratching on the door and Meghan turned, wide eyed toward it.

I dove for the hole leading back into my cell.

"What the heck!" Meghan screeched as a dark shape wiggled through the tiny crack underneath the door and hurtled toward me.

Fireheart.

I caught the tiny dragon in my arms and held him to my chest. "It's okay," I whispered reassuringly. "I'm okay."

"Is that a *DRAGON*?!" Meghan squealed excitedly. "Oh my gosh, oh my gosh, ohmygooooosh!" She was hopping up and down with every word.

"Yeah, this is Fireheart. He's...well, he's my dragon."

"My whole life is a lie," Meghan whispered, coming closer. "It's all a lie, and I couldn't be happier."

Fireheart hissed menacingly and I shushed him soothingly. "It's okay, she's a friend."

Meghan held out a hand, letting Fireheart come to her. "Hi, Fireheart," she whispered in amazement. "My name is Meghan. It's an honor to meet you."

Fireheart puffed out his chest in pride at her words and gently bumped her fingertips with his nose.

"You are *so* cool!" Meghan whispered ecstatically. "I can't believe what I'm seeing."

"If only you knew," I replied with a sigh. "The world is so much more than you could even begin to imagine."

"Can you tell me about it?"

"No...if I did it would hurt me."

"Hurt like the marks Faye has?" Meghan asked quietly.

"I...I don't know. I haven't seen my sister in a long time. The scars she has are from monsters masquerading as people."

"She had lines burned onto her skin on her forearms. The word 'traitor' was carved into her biceps...she tried to hide it from me, but when she got too hot training with me, she'd shed her layers... I saw what my father's interrogation did to her."

She didn't have those scars when she was home...that must have happened to her while she was here... F and Faye always said if they gave away too much information they'd get hurt...but they never elaborated on how. I bet that's what happens. Poor Faye.

"I think I'd like to get somewhat cleaned up before Jeremiah comes looking for me. Fireheart, could you hear if someone comes this way?"

Fireheart nodded, then began to gag.

I stared in worry as Fireheart heaved up a particularly large pile of cloth. Vomiting done, he stared down at the drool-covered clump in pride.

"Uhm..."

I picked it up carefully and stared in wonder as my cloak began to unfold. "It can be condensed?" I asked skeptically.

Fireheart nodded proudly and did a little bow.

Oh dear, I hope Elvie is okay in there...

I wonder if that was satisfying for Fireheart—in a way, he finally got to eat Elvie...

"Okay, I'm also going to rinse off my cloak. I love you, Fireheart, but I don't want to smell like dragon drool."

Fireheart looked at me with indignation and I shrugged. "Feel how you like, it's true."

After a moment, Fireheart shrugged and turned toward the door.

"If it sounds like someone's coming, come get me and I'll make a run for my cell. I'll be super quick."

Fireheart nodded and took up a post by the door, laying an ear on the floor as he stared intently at the metal surface.

"I'll just be a couple minutes," I sighed. "I need to get this blood off of me."

"You do look pretty rough," Meghan replied. "I can only hope the other guy looks worse."

That depends on how you look at it.

67

Embarrassing Ronan To Death Is My New Favorite Hobby

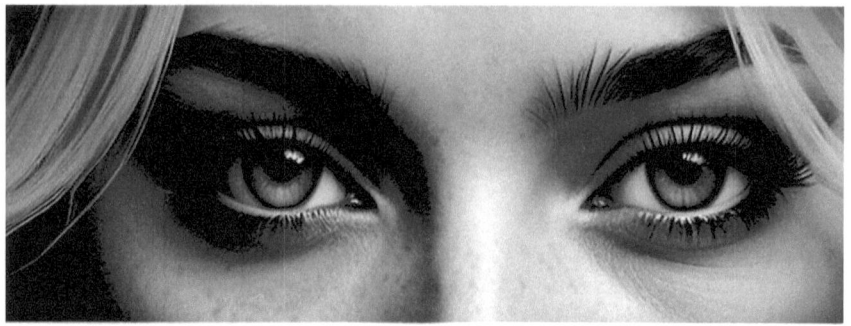

FAYE

"She has the laugh of an angel and the smile of the devil. She's a wicked,
wild, and reckless thing."
-Jordan Sarah Weatherhead

Ryver had disappeared about five minutes ago, but Ronan was still lost in thought, staring aimlessly at the place where Ryver had disappeared. I, having finished my Jell-O, was growing tired of looking over and seeing his fishlike expression.

"Helloooo?" I called. "Earth to Ronan." I waved my stolen spoon in his face for added effect.

Ronan blinked. "Where did the spoon come from?"

I gave him a savage smile, making sure my extra pointy canines showed for dramatic flair. "I just had a secret meeting with my Shadowthief, and the only question you can come up with is to the background story of my beloved spoon?" I licked a stray bit of delightful cherry gelatin from the handle. "Humans, absolutely ridiculous."

Ronan's gaze flicked to the nightstand, where, up until just recently, four Jell-O cups had been left unsupervised. "Where's the Jello-O I left there?" he demanded.

I, the ever-honest maiden that I was, feigned innocence. I was not about to own up to stealing them when it was absolutely my right to take them.

"Faye," he said in a patronizingly questioning voice.

"Huuuuuman?" I retaliated mockingly, threatening him darkly with my spoon.

"You haven't been cleared to eat food yet."

"And you haven't been cleared to be all up in my business," I retorted hotly. "So, mind your own beeswax. I had a bullet removed from my leg, not my gut. There's nothing wrong with my amazing, no, *impeccable* digestive system."

Ronan began to protest further, but I cut him off with a sharp flick of my spoon to his nose. "Relax, Anderson. It was Jell-O, which is comprised of gelatin, sugar, food coloring, and water. I'm not going to die. It's not my time to die yet, and until then I shall enjoy whatever I wish. Which currently happens to be your poorly hidden Jell-O."

"It's me again, loves," Meradith announced as she bustled in and interrupted our argument. She carried a large, covered tray.

Perfect timing. I'm starved and that looks like food.

"She ate my Jell-O while I was in the bathroom," Ronan tattled. "Is that going to be a problem?"

How dare he. Doesn't he know what happens to snitches?

Yeah. They get stitches and end up in ditches.

With the FROGS.

Yes, because clearly the frogs are the worst part of this scenario.

"Well, it shouldn't be too much of a problem," the nurse replied as she set down the tray.

HIS Jell-O...so THAT'S why he's so upset. It was HIS Jell-O.

How dare he tattle on me!

Well, he lied and left a window WIDE open for me to crawl through. He said he was in the bathroom? Let's elaborate for our dear nurse, shall we?

"You shouldn't have taken so long *pooping* sweetie," I retorted in a tauntingly sweet voice. "You *know* I can't resist unsupervised Jell-O. I'm so hungry right now I could eat a horse."

Ronan's face turned a delightful shade of crimson, and I decided my new favorite pastime was to give him such a complexion.

Oo, he's sensitive about poop. Good to know. I shall use and abuse this bodily function to my advantage.

How strange for a nurse to be sensitive about such a normal part of life.

The nurse patted a very embarrassed Ronan on the shoulder, giving him a sympathetic look. "It's all right, love. Everyone poops." She laughed. "You won't find a nurse here who's embarrassed about such things."

Ronan's face turned an even deeper shade of red and I smothered a delighted cackle. This was so much better than even *I* could have done.

She didn't know he was a nurse, who was *clearly* sensitive about fecal matters.

But is it all fecal matters, or just HIS fecal matters?

"No doubt it's the relief of her waking up that eased the constipation. I know you haven't left her side since she got out of surgery."

Ronan squirmed and I began to lose the battle against the cackle.

Must. Resist. The urge. To. Cackle.

Meradith turned an appraising eye on me. "You're not going to make his job of keeping an eye on you easy, are you?"

Nope. Not one bit.

I clasped my hands to my chest and looked up and to the left. "I'm an angel," I said piously.

"Satan was an angel, too," Ronan muttered.

I ignored him. I had a nurse to win over. "I was just really, *really* hungry. I reckon all that surgery and almost dying gave me *quite* an appetite."

"How many Jell-O cups?" Meradith asked, smiling.

"One," I lied, not willing to risk my chances of getting at that dinner. I would stab Ronan if he stood in between me and that food.

"*FOUR*" Ronan cut in.

The nurse laughed. "Well love, I hate to tell you this, but maybe we should wait and make sure you can keep the Jell-O down."

"No," I snapped. "Absolutely *not*."

"You should listen to the nurse," Ronan cautioned.

"I will stab you," I threatened darkly.

"With what?"

"A spoon," I snarled.

"Oh, like that's going to work," he scoffed. "Why a spoon?"

"Because it'll hurt more, you *ninny!*"

"Someone's got the hangry," Meredith laughed.

"You have no idea," Ronan replied good-naturedly. "One time she threatened to eat me with ketchup."

The nurse laughed. "Well, okay then. How about this—you can eat, but only if you promise to take it slow. If you throw up, then I'll come say I told you so."

"Deal!" I cried as I turned to Ronan. "Gimme!" I demanded.

Ronan chuckled as he brought the tray over to me.

"It's good that you have an appetite," the nurse commented. "I wouldn't be surprised if the doctor sends you home today if everything continues to look good."

I tried to ignore the dread that rose, making my appetite plummet. I did not want to go back to the compound.

"All right there, love?" the nurse asked. "You've gone white all of a sudden."

"I think you were right," I whispered.

Ronan shot me a quick, sympathetic look. He knew exactly what was going on. It wasn't the food that brought me to my knees, it was the thought of going back to the compound and the shadows that now called it home.

"Well then, just lay back. The food will still be here when you feel like eating."

I nodded weakly and lay back, comforting my frantic thoughts with the mental image of Ronan turning bright red at the thought of his imaginary pooping.

68

This Endless Cycle Of Bloodshed And Revenge

EMBER

"I have made the obscene decision to do something unforgiveable for the sake of our survival. Listen to me: I was a child who only wanted to heal things- now, I want to be an abomination."

-s.b.l.

I stood over Rosamond's sleeping figure, dagger in hand. Hatred pulled me apart with every pulse of my pounding heart. I wanted to hurt her. I wanted to destroy her for stealing Theron from me.

I want to hurt her. I want to make her pay for what she did to him.

Why did you kill him? What gave you the right to take my Theron away? He's a wanderer, a haunt now because of you!

Florescent purple eyes suddenly stared up at me through the darkness, glowing softly in the dim light of the Moores.

"Are you going to kill me, daughter of Grimm?" Rosamond asked quietly.

The dagger trembled in my hand.

This is not who I am. This is not who Theron wanted me to be. This is not who I want to be.

Theron's dying words swirled around my mind. *Don't carry the hatred forward…let it die with me.*

"No," I whispered, fighting back my hatred as I at last lowered the blade.

A soft laugh emerged from the darkness. "It takes great strength and courage to lower the blade that begs for revenge. When retribution is so close, you can almost taste the spray of blood, the copper within." She paused. "It is a strength I do not possess. I am not capable of mercy and forgiveness. It is not in my nature. I was reborn into violence and bloodshed. I came into my magic as the vines gave revenge and retribution to a human pig. I am the woods; I consume. It is all I am capable of."

I sighed and sat down beside her. "Artemis called you a healer," I countered. "Surely there is some strand of good within you."

"You won't find a bit of good in this pitch-black heart," she retorted coldly. "I heal only to amuse my tainted humor."

It seemed like a feeble excuse, but I was too tired to pursue it.

"I want to hurt you," I whispered angrily.

"It will not bring back the dead."

"Do you regret it?" I asked, restlessly flipping the blade in my hand.

"No," Rosamond sighed. "I do not for a moment regret it. I swore to him I would kill him for what he did in a burst of anger. That promise has burned in my heart for too long. He knew his day was coming and so both of us greeted that bloody dawn with blades drawn."

The silence stretched between us as I chewed over the memories. Theron's bloody lips, his ragged breaths and courageous words.

"He told me to tell you something," I whispered.

"Oh?"

There was an edge of longing in her tone, one I could tell she was trying to block out.

"He said to tell you he'd kill you in the next life and maybe then you'd have forever. Maybe then you wouldn't be on opposite sides of the ocean…maybe then you'd want his twisted heart, cursed though it may be."

Rosamond sighed. "Hopeless. It was only ever hopeless and yet, he always longed for me to come back. Despite what I'm sure he told you, his letters give testament to that."

"He said he hated you," I said softly. "He said he regretted nothing… But his final words would say otherwise."

Rosamond sat up and leaned against the tree next to her. "He did hate me...but beneath the hate was a love he harbored. He always hoped that, though we swore to kill each other, we'd manage to find a way back to what we were..."

Rosamond gave a lifeless laugh. "He was lying to himself. Such damage cannot be mended...there are just some things that cannot be healed, and we were one of them. I loved him...I *loved* him," she repeated raggedly. "But I hated him more for what he did. It was something I could not forgive—not ever. I was never the same after that night, crawling back to the Realm with nothing but stumps left of my precious wings... All I could do was weep and scream...my wings, my heart, my *love*...everything I had ever cherished was destroyed on that night. He had no idea I was under compulsion. He had no inkling of understanding or mercy to deduce it was not my willing hand that dragged him back. It was not my willing silence that didn't explain what was going on. He jumped right to the worst-case scenario. He assumed..."

She paused, staring up at the stars. "I waste my breath trying to explain. I don't expect you to understand, child."

"I want to understand," I pressed.

"There was no coming back to what we were when I dragged him back...but he dragged us into a cursed abyss when he took my wings... It is a deception you never recover from, a betrayal that is only solved when you silence the heartbeat that sings your name...the one that your traitorous heart still pines for—despite everything."

She glanced over, giving me a pained smile. "We constantly run back to the things that break us, don't we?" she asked softly. "We lie to ourselves, believing the delusion that, if we just try harder, if we just bury ourselves a little more, this time it'll be different. We constantly lie to our broken hearts, when the answer before us is to walk away."

Silence stretched between us as we stared up at the stars. "I loved him," Rosamond whispered. "But any hope of reconciliation died when he took my wings from me."

"Am I a fool to fall in love with Artemis?" I asked at last. It was a question I had been ignoring since returning to the Moores.

She was quiet for a moment, pondering my question. "Do you question the act because he's Fey, or because even though you love him, it can't save you from the Last Gate?"

"Both?"

"If we run from choices because we fear they will take us to a future we dread, it will not save us from the future. It will only place us there alone, with no one to guard our back. The prince changes. I see in him the makings of a great ruler, for he seeks to be more than he is...more than the monster he was made to be. Do not fear him simply because he is Fey, or because of what the future might hold. If you feel nothing for him, that is one thing. But if you hesitate simply because of what others might say, or because of your fear, you will never find your footing. Decisions made in fear always lead you astray."

Rosamond stared down at her hands. "I should know...my revenge was rooted in fury, but it was also rooted in fear."

"Do you regret it, then?" I asked hesitantly.

"No...I have no regret...only an echo of what could have been and the heartache of what never was. So tell me Grimm, have you decided to walk away and save your heart, or meet your fate, painful though it might be?"

"I can't run any longer," I replied.

She hummed in quiet approval. "Brave girl. You've finally come to terms with who you are. You've come to meet fate in the crimson dawn that looms." She was still staring at me, scrutinizing my face. "You give me hope, child. Hope that maybe there is more to this Realm than bloodshed and sorrow. You give me hope that maybe we'll make it out of this alive...maybe there's more than death waiting for us at the end of all this."

I couldn't find the words as I stared up at the swirling stars and galaxies that churned in the sky above us.

As the night stretched around us once more, I drifted. I was miles away, sailing through the open air on Verity's ship, reckless and free. I didn't want to admit how scared I was. Running had been an easy solution to my problems.

I was afraid of what the future held. What waited for us at the end of all this? Would I regret this choice to come back?

69

I Have Been Promoted To Quality Blackmail Material. I Should Start Charging My Kidnappers a Fee to Use Me

EVADNE

"I was no one's sacrifice. Not then. Not now. Not ever."
-Shelby Mahurin, Serpent and Dove

After getting myself cleaned up and eating my fill of Meghan's cookies, I went back to my cell. I was worried, despite Fireheart's keen watch, that I wouldn't get back to my cell in time and Meghan would get hurt.

Thankfully, my gut inclination to go back was right. Within five minutes of my returning to my cell, the lock clicked back, and the door swung open.

A tall, menacing figure stood in the doorway. "Oh good, you're awake," a man's voice drawled as I shielded my eyes from the bright florescent light. With the light behind him, his face was masked in shadows. But his voice sounded harsh and cruel.

"My name is Jeremiah," the man drawled. "You and I are going to be spending a lot of time together, especially if your sister proves difficult."

He's going to use me as leverage against her. What a jerk.

There was an unnatural presence around him. Darkness clung to him, a darkness I was all too familiar with. He reeked of the Ruins.

What did he get himself into...he's human...what on earth is going on?

"We're going to pay a little visit to your precious sister," Jeremiah drawled. "If you tell anyone what's really going on here, I'll kill her and your father."

This is not good.

"Let's go," he instructed harshly.

"Go where?" I whispered as I picked myself up.

"Good, you were smart enough to clean yourself up," Jeremiah snapped. "One thing you will quickly learn, is that you are in no position to ask questions."

Yes, but that's not going to stop me from asking them.

I don't think that's the smartest idea.

I pulled myself up to my feet, resisting the urge to groan. I wanted to appear as indifferent as possible. I had a terrible feeling it was going to be a long day. I could only hope that Fireheart was content to stay hidden in my corset pocket—which also happened to be enchanted. My only worry was its lack of cheese.

Much to my surprise and immediate worry, Jeremiah's ridiculously large Hummer took us to a hospital.

Oh no. Is Faye hurt?

Jeremiah turned back to me

"Now, like I said. Not a word."

I nodded, too worried to say anything.

I followed him inside, trying to ignore the strange looks from the staff and patients. I stuck out like a sore thumb.

"Oh now, I declare!" a nurse cried, stopping us. "It's good to see you so soon, Mr. Anderson." She turned to me. "You look like a sibling of Mrs. Faye. You have the same sort of face shape and nose. You must both be into fairytales. I find your commitment to cosplaying quite remarkable. Her ears were glued on so seamlessly, I couldn't even find where she put the tips on...and your eye?!" She leaned in, examining Carl's handiwork. "My, you must have worked hard on that makeup...what an incredible contact lens..." she tsked. "That lens must have cost you an arm and a leg."

She was beaming at me. "I heard there was an event on the edge of town. Did you enjoy yourself?"

I coughed, nervously. "Yeah," I replied quietly. "I just came back from that convention. I heard the news and came as soon as I could to see her..."

"Oh, that's lovely! She should be released today or tomorrow; the doctor is undecided as of right now. You remember the way over?" she asked Jeremiah.

Jeremiah nodded, giving her a smile that didn't meet his cold blue eyes. "I remember, Meridith. Thank you very much."

"Of course, just let me know if you need anything."

"I will, I will," Jeremiah mused amicably as he led me down the hallway.

We stopped in the doorway, and it was the sheer force of Jeremiah's grip on my arm that stopped me from running to Faye's side.

Her eyes went wide as she saw me, the utensils in her hands clattering down onto her plate.

"Not so fast," Jeremiah snarled softly.

"Eve," Faye whispered.

There was a man standing beside Faye, with dark, stormy gray eyes like Meghan's. This must be the elusive Ronan.

Faye's frantic gaze jumped back and forth from me to Jeremiah and back to me.

"It seems fate has looked favorably on me this week," Jeremiah said casually as he pushed me into the room ahead of him and firmly closed the door behind him. "Because now, I have the means to get what I want." He pulled me closer, lording his advantage over Faye. "Hello Faye, how are you feeling? I see you're awake, and look, I've brought your sister to see you. Aren't I nice? I'm sure you've missed each other terribly."

Faye swallowed, anxiety radiating from her body. She looked ready to tackle Jeremiah and throw up all over him simultaneously.

Tackling him and then throwing up would be amazing.

Jeremiah's grip tightened on my arm, bruising the skin. "Don't be scared, child, she isn't upset to see you...just the company you happen to find yourself in." He laughed at his own confusing joke, and irritation swirled within me.

It's rude to laugh at your own jokes. You'll get the hiccups. Besides, it wasn't even funny. I have no idea which one of us you were talking to.

"Let go of me," I snapped.

The spell broke and the supposed Ronan lurched to his feet. He pulled me from Jeremiah's grasp. "What are you thinking?" he hissed. "We barely scraped by without the police being called to investigate the story and you decide to drag her sister in here? She could scream and flip the entire situation."

I took advantage of the argument between the two and launched myself at Faye, wrapping her in a tight hug and burying my face in her shoulder as the world unraveled and rebound itself in a matter of moments. All the words I wished I had said the first time around came bubbling to the surface. The apology for running away the morning she left. The confession of how afraid I was. The horrors we'd endured in the Realm. But my words were soon forgotten as her arms wrapped around me and blocked everything out.

Faye was subtly slipping something into my hand. It was a butter knife. Even now, she was trying to protect me. I didn't want to risk Jeremiah hearing me tell her I had a whole arsenal stuffed in my cloak. I shifted and pushed the blade into my pocket that held the cloak. No doubt Fireheart would find the silver amusing.

"Don't give in," I breathed. My voice was masked by the sound of Ronan and Jeremiah's continued argument. "No matter what he does to me, don't let him use me against you, okay?"

"I'm so glad you're safe," she whispered. "I was so worried. I—"

Hands closed around my arm, fingers sharp like claws, wrenching me from Faye. "No secret conversations," Jeremiah snarled.

Excuse me. That is my arm. Take your hand off of me before I chop it off.

Or sick my dragon on you.

Yeah, he'll bite your sharp fingers clean off.

Jeremiah was flickering at the edges, shadows drifting off of him like smoke on the breeze.

What is wrong with him?

"Now then, let's get down to business, shall we?" Jeremiah sneered. "Faye, you're going to tell me exactly what I want to know, or else I'm going to hurt your sister in the most inhumane ways possible."

Oo, blackmail. Classy.

I'm going to put this on my resume. Quality source to use as blackmail against people. Maybe then I'd actually get paid to tolerate this nonsense.

Ah yes. Because I'm sure charging kidnappers to use you as blackmail is really going to take you places.

Faye looked as if she was about to leap out of bed and kill Jeremiah right then and there with her fork and spoon. "No," she snarled at last.

Jeremiah laughed. "No?"

"Let her go, and then I'll tell you everything you want to know."

"Not a chance," Jeremiah snarled. "She's the only leverage I have on you at the moment, and I'm not about to let that disappear." He looked down at me. "You and I will have some fun when we get back to the compound," he promised menacingly. "I'm sure it will help loosen our dear Faye's tongue. She'll come back to us ready to talk if she's had all night to ponder what on earth I've been doing to you. Oh, I know. Maybe we'll let father dearest join the fun."

A low vibration trembled against my chest as Fireheart let out the softest growl.

It's okay, Fireheart, it's okay.

Hush little dragon, don't say a word, he's just a no good, dirty, rotten jerk…and if that jerk tries to hurt me today, I'll let you come and bite off his face…

The delightful, little ditty ran circles around my head, getting more unhinged and out of rhythm the longer it went on.

"Don't you dare!" Faye yelled.

"Faye," the likely Ronan hissed. "You can't yell in here, it'll alert the nurses."

"Let them hear," she growled. "They'll lock him up faster than you can say the word Mum."

"And Marcov will kill your father. He's under *very* specific instructions. If anything is amiss, he'll kill him and the girl to boot."

Ronan stiffened and Faye's fury dimmed slightly.

Is he talking about Meghan?

I have to find a way out of that compound before Jeremiah uses me against Faye.

"Consider this your final, and *only* warning, Faye. When you return, we will begin. Don't for a second think I won't let your little sister bear the consequences of your outburst here, either."

He's demented.

We do not negotiate with terrorists.

Nope. We sick our dragons on them and let the dragons eat their fingers and faces.

Fireheart is going to love me when I let him loose to commit great feats of mayhem and bloodshed.

As if sensing my threatening thoughts, Fireheart hummed in approval against my chest, promising violence with every subtle vibration.

I took a deep breath, fighting off the fear. There was so little time left in which to figure out an escape.

We began to walk toward the door and Jeremiah took my hand. I resisted the strong and sudden urge to bite his arm. It would likely only get me in deeper trouble. Besides, I didn't want his germ-covered skin in my mouth. He likely carried the plague. I settled on a gagging sound, ensuring he knew of my annoyance at such impertinence.

"Hold your breath," Jeremiah commented dryly.

Why? Are you going to fart? Did you fart?

Either way, we can't risk it. I do not want a fart in my mouth. Especially not his.

I subtly held my breath, not wanting him to know I was obeying his instruction. My sarcasm was lost in an instant as Jeremiah wrenched my fingers apart and, in one deft motion, wrenched the pinky sideways. There was a sickening pop as it dislocated.

Oh my gosh. No!

I crumpled, biting my hand as I swallowed a scream. My hand was still in his, but my mind was in the past. This time however, Ríonach was not there to save me.

Faye's cry was cut short. Through my tears I could see Ronan's hand covering her mouth, muffling the sound as she struggled against him, trying to get out of bed. There was a fork clenched in her fist, and it promised violence.

Faye, now is not the time for stabbing kidnappers with a fork. Though I absolutely approve of such methods.

Ronan's eyes were wide and afraid as he stared at me.

"Think about what I've said," Jeremiah said coldly. "I mean what I say, and I don't go back on my word. If you don't tell me how to gain the magic, I'll let Marcov handle her torture. You will watch *every* second," he snarled. "You will watch until you *break* and I can assure you, she will be in pieces by that point."

"Get up," Jeremiah spat as he stared down at me in disdain. "If you think this is bad, just wait until you meet Marcov. He's not quite right in the head. He craves the violence."

I have faced worse and survived. This man is nothing compared to the horrors of the Realm. I will destroy him. I will not be afraid.

I will not be afraid. I will not break.

I am Evadne Averyn Grimm; I am a dragon that cannot be caged, and I will not let you break me.

70

I Love You Rosebud

EVADNE

"I would have come for you. And if I couldn't walk, I'd crawl to you,
and no matter how broken we were, we'd fight our way out together—knives drawn and pistols blazing."
-Leigh Bardugo, Crooked Kingdom

Much to my annoyance, Jeremiah did not return me to my original cell with the hidey hole that led to my new friend's room. Instead, he shoved me into a completely new, dark cell and left without so much as a word. Not that I was complaining. After the whole dislocating my poor finger stint, I wasn't looking forward to the other punishment he had promised Faye.

The closer we had gotten to the compound, the more distracted he had become and the darker the shadows around him had grown. They began leaching out of him in earnest as we stepped through the door, with sharp claws that pulled and sliced at me as we made our way deeper into the compound.

I wasn't sure what he had gotten himself mixed up in, but I knew it wasn't pretty. He clearly had some connection with the Ruins, and that alone was enough to make me wonder about the integrity of our being sent to the Moores to begin with.

What if the Council was compromised?

The small cell had a tiny window with bars that let in small strands of moonlight. The moon was full, and it sent a thrill of joy down my spine as I stood on tiptoes and looked up at it. I had missed the moon so much. It wasn't quite the same in the Realm. The Realm's moon was beautiful, the Moores' moon was terrifying, and neither of them compared to the moon I had loved all my life—the moon of the Mortal Realm.

The cell measured ten shoe lengths by eight shoe lengths and, after listening for a moment, it became apparent that I wasn't alone. Someone else's quiet breaths were a background noise that, up until now, I hadn't noticed.

My heartbeat picked up.

"Hello?" I whispered as loud as I dared. "Is someone else there?"

What if it's a monster? What if it's someone that will hurt me?

"Rosebud?" an all too familiar voice whispered hoarsely.

"DA!" I cried, launching myself in the direction of his voice.

"Hey there, Rosebud," Da whispered weakly as I threw myself into his arms.

"Are you okay? Did he hurt you?" The frantic questions were pouring out of me as I felt his face and neck, then down his arms and chest, trying to assess for any injuries.

"I'm okay," Da groaned. "My last interrogation session with Jeremiah ended in some broken ribs and bruising, but I'm okay."

I pulled away, feeling guilty for aggravating his injuries with the force of my hug.

"It's okay, honey. It's okay," Da said gently as he carefully pulled me back into a hug. "I'm worried you're just a hallucination…"

"I'm real," I sobbed. "I'm right here, Da. I promise I'm real."

"Have you seen your mother?" Da asked, yearning filling his voice. "Jeremiah's holding her. He's kept her from me this whole time…" He gasped for a moment, trying to get more air.

Guilt hit me. I knew what had happened to Mum. I knew where she was held captive now, but all of this I couldn't relay to Da. Right now he needed to hold onto what little hope he had.

"I haven't seen her," I lied. The guilt sat acidic in my gut.

"Well, that makes two of us," Da joked weakly. "I miss her. I don't know how long I've been locked up in this cell…I try to keep track of the sunrises and sunsets, but I've lost count…" his voice trailed off as he tried to catch his breath again. "But enough about me, tell me everything that happened. Well, tell me everything you can."

"I'm not sure what I can say," I sniffed, fighting back tears.

"Are you doing okay in the Realm?" Da asked after an eternity.

"Yeah," I whispered. "We're doing okay."

"How did you get here?"

"We...ended back up in the Human Realm," I said hesitantly. "It's a long story, but essentially when we did come back, Jeremiah had men waiting to ambush us at the house. They kidnapped me, but I think Ember got away. I screamed at her to run."

Da nodded. "We need to get you out of here," he said decidedly. "They'll use you against me or against Faye. I'm so doped up, I can't bend the bars, or else I would get you out of here."

He was right.

"Jeremiah dislocated my finger," I said. "Do you think you can reset it?"

"I can, but it's going to hurt," Da warned.

"It hurts either way," I replied ruefully.

Da chuckled and pulled me into the moonlight to better see what he was doing. "Look away, I'll count for you."

I held my breath as he counted forward. "One, two..." On three he skillfully maneuvered the bone back into place with a disgusting pop.

I crumpled for a moment and he caught me, pulling me into his arms. "There, honey. It's all over. You did it. It's done now."

If only it were done. Life goes on and everything hurts in between. There is no end to the pain.

"We need to find a way to get you out of here," Da said urgently. "I need to get you out of here before he hurts you worse." He bent close, examining my face in the darkness. "There's something off about your face," he murmured. "Did they do something to you?"

"Something happened...and I lost my eye," I replied carefully, trying to figure out what I could say without getting in trouble. "A very powerful person, a friend of a friend, gave me this to replace the damaged eye."

"Incredible," Da whispered. "Perhaps that place isn't all bad."

"There is good mixed in the bad," I sniffed, thinking about the crew. "I have met some phenomenal people...there are phenomenal creatures there too...Oh, Da. If only you could see what lies beyond the darkness. There's a whole separate world out there and it takes your breath away."

Something stirred against my chest. It was Fireheart.

I wonder if he could do anything about the bars...

Fireheart crawled out of my vest and eyed my father with bright eyes.

"What's this?" Da asked in amazement.

Sensing his wonder, Fireheart began to preen.

"This is Fireheart. He's my dragon," I said softly. "He's one of the breathtaking wonders that belongs to that place."

Da's eyes were full of wonder as he stared at Fireheart. "First puppies and now a dragon. My, you have a knack for this." He held out his hand to Fireheart. "It's a pleasure to meet you," he said quietly.

Fireheart touched his nose to Da's fingers and bowed.

"Hmm," Da mused. "Dragons can breathe fire, can they not?"

To answer his question, Fireheart proudly shot out a tendril of flame, lighting up the dark cell for a moment.

Da laughed, then winced. "That is amazing, my friend. Tell me, do you think you could melt the bars on that window up there? Can you aid in my daughter's escape?"

Fireheart gave Da a toothy grin, flicking out his tongue in pleasure, then jumped off my shoulder. He swooped around the room, clearly showing off for my awestruck father, before landing on the tiny ledge. He ran a claw down the metal bar, causing it to emit an earsplitting screech.

I winced, clutching my ears. "Fireheart, can we decimate the bars without the pre-decimation gloat?" I called. "I hate that sound."

Fireheart stuck out his tongue and made a face. His chest glowed orange in the moonlight as he took a deep breath. Blue and green flames spewed from his mouth and the bars began to melt.

"I'm going to lift you up and you're going to go," Da said firmly.

"Not without you," I said savagely.

"Yes, without me, young lady. I am much too big for that hole."

"Then I'll blow a hole in it," I retorted hotly. "I am *not* leaving you."

Da wrapped me in a hug. "Yes, you are. You need to get out of here and find help."

"I *can't* leave you," I sobbed. "I can't lose you."

I can't lose you, too. I can't lose you, too, like I lost Mum. He's going to kill you if I leave you here.

"Sweetheart, it is a father's duty to protect his children, and it is a duty I take seriously. I have failed to protect you in so many ways. Let me finally have a chance to protect you. I couldn't save you from the monsters in the Fey Realm, but I can save you from the monsters in the Human Realm."

"I can't leave you," I repeated.

"I love you, Rosebud," Da said softly. "I am so incredibly proud of you, of *all* of you. If...if you have a chance for happiness in that place, take it. Okay? I know we fought the Realm all those years, but now that it's done...it's okay." He choked on his words, and I hugged him tightly. I knew what he was trying to say.

"I love you," he whispered. "Get out of here and get help, okay?"

I nodded, sniffing.

Fireheart was already through the bars. The metal had run down the wall and pooled on the floor at our feet, and my little dragon was looking at me in smug satisfaction.

"Marvelous," Da breathed. "You are a prince among dragons, my brave friend. Protect my daughter, please?" His voice wavered on the last syllable, hitting my chest with a sharp pain. I didn't want to leave him. I had the terrible feeling Da knew something might happen.

"Here," Da offered, knitting his fingers together. "You're light as a feather. Let me give you a hand up."

I would have declined, but I seriously doubted my ability to hoist myself up and crawl out the window without help.

After giving him a final goodbye hug, I scrambled through the window, ignoring the way Fireheart rolled in the dirt, pointing and laughing silently as I struggled.

Having made it through, I pressed myself up against the building, reaching back through the bars to grab Da's hand.

"I love you, Rosebud," he whispered. "I love you so much and I am so *incredibly* proud of you. Be strong, my sweet girl. Be brave and never forget that your mother and I love you, okay?"

Tears were streaming down my cheeks again. "I love you, too," I whispered.

"Now go," he said firmly. "Go before they find you. Stick to the shadows and don't look back."

I nodded, sobbing. "Okay," I whispered weakly. "Okay."

I counted to three, and with a final squeeze goodbye, let go of my father's hands and raced to the next shadow. But I couldn't obey my father's instructions. I did look back, desperate for a final glance at the man who had been my rock growing up. My father meant the world to me, and it felt like a betrayal to leave him behind.

I'm coming back for you, Da. I'm coming back to get you out of here. I'll come back. I'll come back. Hold on, I'm coming back.

71

I Am An Excellent Liar

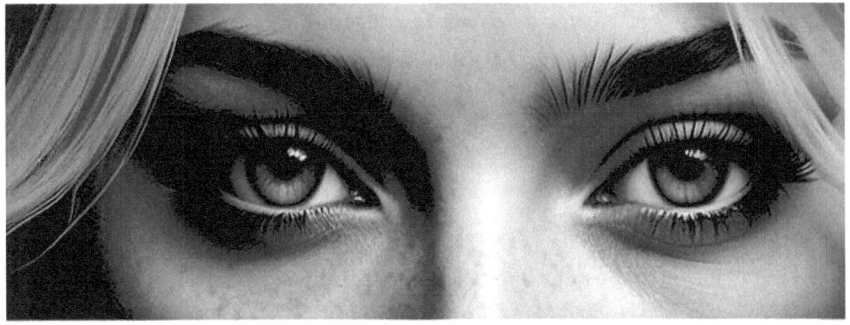

FAYE

"I enjoy talking to you. Your mind appeals to me. It resembles my own
mind except that you happen to be insane."
-George Orwell, 1984

A final, tiny piece of the situation that neither Ronan nor I had thought to consider was
how incredibly caring the hospital staff was. They had wisely grown suspicious of my
many injuries and scars.

Not long after Jeremiah had left with Evadne, a kindly old man entered my room. He
introduced himself as Dr. Morrey, the hospital's psychiatrist. Apparently, the hospital
staff thought that I was in some sort of distress. They were right, but I wasn't about to
tell them that.

"Jane, are you listening?"

I turned my attention back to the sympathetic Dr. Morrey who sat beside me, pen
and notebook at the ready.

*Whoopsie, I got lost in thought. Is that normal? What is he writing on his notepad?
What is he saying about me? Does he think I'm insane? I want to know what he's writing.*

*Furthermore, what kind of stupidity was Ronan smoking when he told the hospital my
name was Jane?*

How obvious is Jane?

The concern was practically oozing from the kind doctor. He clearly knew some-thing was up, but he couldn't prove it. Not unless I confirmed his suspicions. Which I clearly couldn't do.

Watching Ronan sweat outside the door, however, was certainly entertaining. He looked as nervous as a lamb in a den of wolves, and I fully planned to drag out his torture by taking my sweet time with the good doctor. We might be on the same side now, but my favorite activity to date was still tormenting my Ronan.

"Jane, you seem to be lost in thought. Are you all right? Do we need to take a break?"

I certainly am lost in thought. I'm preoccupied with thoughts of torture for my kidnap-per turned hero.

At the thought of Ronan being a hero, my brain cells adamantly began taking their various pictures of Ronan and tying a cape around the frame, while they hummed the 'Hero Guy' theme song from *Sesame Street*. Soon, they were racing around the space with their pictures, making him 'fly' through the air as if he was a superhero.

"No," I sighed, distracted. "I'm sorry. I'm just tired. I'm fine, we can go on."

"I'd like to talk about what happened."

"How many times do you want me to relive that nightmare?" I whispered. While tormenting Ronan was delightful, I was growing tired of the roundabout interroga-tion.

Just get to the point. Say you suspect something. Just spit it out.

He's too chicken to say it bluntly.

Five bucks says you're wrong.

Deal. When I win the bet, we get to buy something fancy from the gift shop.

And where are we going to get this imaginary money from to pay for such a thing?

From Ronan, of course. Do you think I'm going to get out of this hospital without strong arming him into getting me some quality giftshop loot? We are going to spruce up my cell.

Dr. Morrey sighed. "Jane, I'm going to get straight to the point."

Ha! I win.

He hasn't said anything just yet. Hold your horses.

"The staff noticed some disturbing scars when they were taking care of you, as well as some fairly recent looking cuts and bruises. We are rightly very, very concerned."

I win. Give me five bucks.

Well, my losing is also my winning. I love loot.

Now, what do you think he's going to suggest? Abusive husband or is he smart enough to suspect I've been kidnapped and I'm here against my will?

No way he guesses the latter.

I squirmed in my bed as Dr. Morrey reached out a hand and patted it. "What you say here is confidential, my dear."

Finger horns activate!!

NO! Absolutely not! We are not poking an elderly gentleman in the gut for calling me 'my dear.' it is a term of comfort to the older generations, and we are not going to mortify him.

Boo, you're no fun.

"If he's hurting you, we need to know. You need to think about your safety. We can get the law involved and get you out of danger."

I licked my lips; my mouth was once again as dry as a desert.

"I can see your husband is visibly distressed out there and you look uncomfortable. If he's threatening you, we can help."

"Dr. Morrey," I began hesitantly as I cleared my throat. Dr. Morrey handed me one of the steaming mugs of tea one of the nurses had brought in for us.

I am a very good liar. I can do this.

"He's distressed because, well, he's worried," I sighed. "My past is very, *very* hard for me to talk about. You see, my father...he was very abusive."

The doctor took a long sip of his tea.

I imagined myself in Meghan's shoes. A girl whose father that despised his child, whose every breath threatened violence. Soon, tears were pouring down my face. "My father was horribly abusive," I choked out. "And I was trapped with him until I was eighteen. My husband...he's the one who got me out." My voice broke as I choked on my tears. "The only reason he's worried is because he knows about the PTSD, and how hard it is to talk about what happened when I was young. I've been in therapy for quite a while, but this break in..." I shuddered. "It brought all these horrible memories back, front and center."

The doctor nodded, making a sympathetic noise. "That answers the scars, but the newer wounds that are too old to be from the robbery?"

"I'm very clumsy, and anemic." I choked on a forced laugh. "I take iron, but I still bruise if I bump into something."

Dr. Morrey nodded. "Do you happen to have a phone number for the therapist you've been seeing? I'd like to pass on my notes to them, so they can continue to help you."

But what ARE your notes? What do you think about me? What have you been writing in that little notebook? I want to knooooow!

My three brain cells offered to snatch the notebook from his hands and run away as fast as they could, but I firmly shut down their ridiculous idea. I was not about to rob a kind, elderly man.

"I don't have my phone with me." I sighed as I picked at the edges of my blanket. "I don't even have my purse or a pair of clean clothes. All I remember is trying to defend myself and the next moment I'm here. My husband hasn't left my side. Can I call the hospital tomorrow after I get home and give it to you then?"

"Of course, my dear, that will be just fine."

"I don't want you to think badly of him," I whispered. "He's done everything he could to protect me. He blames himself for not getting me out sooner. We were neighbors you see...but it's not his fault. Nobody knew what was going on, my father was a psychopath. Fine with others, murderous toward me."

Dr. Morrey nodded. "What if, is the worst enemy of peace," he said gently. "We offer ourselves no forgiveness when we look back. There is no recognition of what could or couldn't have been done. There is only the accusations of our failure." His eyes were lost, somewhere in the past, as if remembering something he wished he could change. He pulled himself to the present with a quick shake of his head. "Get some rest, my dear. You're healing at a phenomenal rate, and since you've stabilized it will be best you heal in your own home where you're most comfortable." He hesitated, as if debating whether or not to say something. "Being back home may bring up some traumatic memories from the break in. If you find it too much, you should consider taking some time away from home. Go on a trip or stay with friends until you feel as if you can confront those memories. It will be painful, but you are not alone. Reach out and continue to get help."

I nodded, chewing my lip. "It won't be the first time confronting my demons. When my father died, we had to go back to the house and settle his affairs. I was his only heir."

"Even so, be careful. The human mind is fragile, it is not a thing to take lightly."

I tasted blood as he stood up. I had torn my lip apart without realizing it.

"These are dark times we live in, but there is always hope. There are always things worth fighting for, worth living for. See that you don't lose sight of that, okay? If you need help, please reach out."

"I am," I said quietly. "I'm reaching out, Ronan's holding my head above water."

It was the first true statement I had uttered during the entire interview.

72

Trauma Goblin Brain Manipulates Ronan

FAYE

"It's the thought that counts. So think real hard about why you got me
this terrible gift."
-Night Vale Podcast

"You want something from the gift shop?" Ronan asked incredulously.

"Well, the proper thing to do would be to get me a t-shirt that reads 'I got shot and all my kidnapper got me was this lousy t-shirt', but I'm guessing the hospital is running low on very specific designs like that. So, I'd suggest you raid the gift shop for trinkets to appease me and my goblin brain."

"We're getting ready to go back to the compound, where we are in worlds of trouble, and your solution is to crack jokes and demand treasures?" Ronan asked in disbelief.

"Trauma baby," I said snidely as I took a sip of my tea and made a face. I hated herbal teas, I much preferred cocoa. "It turns one into a goblin, thus giving me a skewed sense of humor and an eye for shiny things. Now, go find me something that says you're really *really* sorry for kidnapping me in the first place."

"I already said I was sorry!" Ronan protested.

"Yes, but my love language is gifts. If you don't get me something to prove you're sorry, then you're not *actually* sorry."

Ronan laughed, shaking his head.

"And bring me back hot cocoa. I can't believe they expect me to drink this liquid salad of disgustingness."

"Faye, that's a very powerful blend of herbal tea. I specifically requested it for you. It will help your body heal."

"That explains why it's so awful. Health-food boy got his green fingers on it. I refuse to drink this pond scum."

Ronan rolled his eyes as I forcefully handed him back the mug. "Take your liquid death and go. Cocoa and trinkets. Now." I demanded. "Trauma goblin brain is thoroughly traumatized by both the shooting and your disgusting tea. She now wants shiny things." I was making names up. First it had been goblin brain, then trauma brain, and now the best descriptor of all—trauma goblin brain.

Ronan's shoulders were shaking as he tried and failed to contain his laughter. "I don't know whether to laugh or cry," he chortled.

"Bit of both never harmed anyone," I quipped. "This wouldn't be the first time I've reduced someone to mirth and despair in one go. I'll consider it a personal best if I can make my *ever stoic* kidnapper bawl his eyes out like a baby."

"Fine. I'll get you the cocoa first. Then I'll go raid the gift shop. Although, I might have to buy the whole shop to express how incredibly sorry I am."

I clapped my hands in glee. "Goblin brain is pleased by this suggestion. Go use and abuse your father's credit card."

I managed to find three more Jell-O cups hidden in the drawer of the nightstand, and much to my outstanding chagrin, I promptly stole them. These were extra special—they were chocolate Jell-O cups.

Wouldn't they technically be pudding cups?

I mean...yes? But it says right there, Jell-O...

This is so confusing. How am I supposed to be clear on what I'm stealing if the packaging is sending conflicting messages?

Ronan would get over it. After all, I was the one who got shot. I had infinite amounts of manipulation at my disposal. I could almost hear Ronan's complaints as I gobbled them down.

Why are you eating my Jell-O? Dur-dur-dur.

Why are you so mean to me? Dur-dur-dur.

You're going to make yourself sick. Dur-dur-dur.

"Faye," Ronan's voice called in exasperation from the doorway. "You're going to make yourself sick."

Dur-dur-dur.

Ronan carried a steaming mug and a lecturing expression, which I fully planned to ignore.

"Here is your cocoa, oh mighty trauma goblin brain," Ronan sighed as he placed the steaming mug of cocoa on the rolling table beside the bed.

"It has marshmallows!" I squealed in delight.

"It has marshmallows," Ronan confirmed with a small grin as he headed for the door. "Don't make yourself sick."

"Bring me back shiny things!" I countered hotly. I was in no mood to be lectured. I would make myself sick if I pleased.

It wasn't long before Ronan returned, carrying an oversized gift bag.

Yeaaaaaasssssss!

I should guilt trip him more often. This is fun.

"I wasn't exactly sure what the goblin would require for apology trinkets," Ronan said sheepishly. "So, I got a little bit of everything."

"Gimme!" I snapped, reaching for the bag.

"Did they give you brain damage while you were in surgery?" Ronan chortled. "You've never used that expression before, and now you've used it at least four or five times in the space of a day."

I arched an eyebrow and primly snatched the bag from his hands. "Gimme," I repeated loftily.

Ronan burst out laughing, and it wasn't long before I joined him. It felt good to laugh, and in this hospital room, away from the chaos and madness of his father, it finally felt safe to laugh.

I began to excitedly peruse the bag full of gifts.

"Secondary note to self, bribery is *absolutely* possible," Ronan chortled as he sat on the edge of the bed.

I stopped my exploration and glared at him. "This is not bribery; it is an emphasized apology for kidnapping me. If anything, it's proof that you're incredibly susceptible to blackmail. Now, stop ruining the moment."

"Faye, when is your birthday?" Ronan asked suddenly. "I knew what it was when I kidnapped you, but I can't remember now."

"June 21st," I replied distractedly. I was too engaged with the gift bag to really wonder why he'd ask such a random question.

The first item at the top of the bag was a squishmallow stuffed animal. It was a cat, with large green eyes, and a body that looked like a cross between a loaf and a bowling ball.

Delightful. Utterly delightful.

It was the perfect size to hold against my chest. Underneath the first plushie was a secondary, slightly smaller cat plushie that was identical in everything but size.

What absurd, inflated, gift shop price do you think Ronan paid for these?

I don't know, but I don't care either.

Do you think Jeremiah will notice? Or is he too busy being crazy to care about charges on his card from the gift shop?

"The sign said they were stress plushies," Ronan snorted. "I'm not sure how they would help you manage your stress, but I thought they were cute."

I promptly whacked him upside the head with my new plushie. I swung again and he tried to duck, which only managed to make him fall off the bed.

"Oof!"

I almost fell off the bed myself I was cackling so hard. "I feel so much better already," I crowed at last, finally able to get air back in my lungs as I stared down at him. "My stress is ten times lighter. Hold still—if I hit you a few more times I think it would disappear entirely."

Ronan rolled his eyes but couldn't keep his smile contained as I gave him a few more whacks while he got to his feet.

Next was a large bag of peanut butter M&Ms, followed by an equally large bag of Swedish fish.

How did he know what my favorite type of candy was?

Creepy level thirty-two obtained.

Eh, I'll allow it. It means I get candy.

Next came a gorgeous leather-bound notebook and a box of colorful felt-tipped pens.

"I had to get you felt tip, because I didn't quite trust you not to stab me with a ballpoint pen."

"I promise you, I can still do damage with a felt tip," I threatened darkly.

"Yes, but the damage would be less severe."

Challenge accepted.

Ronan shook his head ruefully as I came to a change of clothes. Yoga pants and a long-sleeved, teal colored shirt with the word 'fighter' scrawled across it in bold cursive. It was a caption that seemed very fitting for a hospital's gift shop. There were also fuzzy pink socks, a light gray undershirt, and the softest black hooded sweatshirt that said: *Don't tell me I can't eat pizza and cake for breakfast. I'm an adult.*

I laughed, absolutely delighted. "It's so perfect!" I whispered excitedly as I pulled the sweatshirt on over my hospital gown.

"Well, I remember that you said you liked to eat pizza for breakfast," Ronan said sheepishly. A blush was steadily creeping up his cheeks with every word. "I saw that, and it practically screamed your name."

"I love it," I stated decisively as I turned back to the bag and what remained. A crystal ball attached to a wooden stand, with holographic image of the moon in it. A small knob on the side indicated it was a music box, and I excitedly cranked it. I instantly recognized the beginning strains of *Swan Lake*. As the little music box inside the stand played, a light came on beneath the moon, casting synthetic rays of moonlight around the room.

"It's so beautiful," I breathed.

"Glad you like it," Ronan replied, his voice thick with emotion.

"Goblin brain finds this very pleasing," I quipped, trying to lighten the mood as I took out a jewelry box. Inside was a pair of round studs, with a very realistic-looking opal, surrounded by what looked like tiny blue sapphires.

"This is some gift shop," I muttered. "Sheesh, it would be hazardous to your budget to go in there..." I examined the box more closely. "Ronan, this says they're real opals with sapphires set in gold."

"I noticed you were missing a pair," Ronan replied quickly, "so I deviated from the gift shop in search of those."

I grimaced. "Yes, they came out during one of your father's...rants," I sighed.

I pulled my earrings out of my first lobe piercing and moved them to my second, and then put the new studs in the first. I was grateful that none of my other piercings had been compromised. I was rather fond of the assortment I had collected over the years. Most of them were from the Realm, and they possessed enchantments and charms woven into the stones. The pair from my seconds that I had lost was one of the few I had obtained in the Mortal Realm. It was no surprise to me they hadn't held up under the strain of Jeremiah's abuse.

I'll get these enchanted when I get back. Then I won't lose them. I can keep them forever to remember him by.

What will we do when we're free of this? He can't come to the Realm with me...we're doomed...there's no hope for us.

I shoved the thought off. The inevitability was just too sad to think about. I didn't *want* to think about it. Not now, not ever. I didn't want to think about what my future would look like without those stormy gray eyes and his contagious smile.

Lastly, there was a woven bracelet of brightly colored thread. "I'd have gotten something nicer, but I was worried that too many purchases at a jewelry store would alert Jeremiah," Ronan said sheepishly. "I have an excuse for these trinkets because I'm winning you over. But too much, and it would be overkill."

"I love it," I replied softly as I pulled the bracelet on and tightened it. "Now, let's talk about the next phase of the plan. When we get back, we move on to the next part. No delays, understood?"

Ronan nodded, his eyes distant. "I'm worried," he whispered. "What if it doesn't work? What if—"

I cut off his words by impulsively wrapping him in a hug. "It's gonna be okay," I said, trying to hold the fragile remains of my hope together with determined optimism. "It's going to be okay."

But what if it's not okay. What if nothing works out and I lose you in the end?

I shoved the thought away. I didn't want to think of my world without him.

Ronan stiffened for a moment and then relaxed into the hug, wrapping his arms around me.

"I'm scared," he admitted, his voice muffled as he buried it in my hair.

"I know," I replied soothingly. "I am too, but we have to do it afraid. We're the only hope our family has left."

Ronan's grip tightened. "Is goblin brain satiated?"

"For now," I laughed. "You still owe me a box of internet trinkets for my getting shot, you know."

"My budget is going to hate me this month," Ronan chuckled. "But it's a price I'm willing to pay. Though, I still call it bribery, my dear."

Apparently, he had become too comfortable in our friendship to remember what happened when he called me 'my dear.' Once again, he was not fast enough to avoid my finger horns as they slammed into his gut and knocked him off the edge of the bed.

73

The Wolf And The Man

EMBER

"...No one wants a remembered tragedy. You must know the width of
the knife and how it ruined you, name the organs it kissed"
-Life of the Party, "addendum II to no Baptism" Olivia Gatwood

The day dragged on, and as the butt of the group, I had the ample ability to stare at Rosamond without it being weird. I couldn't stop staring at her new wings. They were gorgeous. Huge, with a vivid forest-green and black onyx pattern on a dark brown surface. They resembled the wings of a lunar moth, with added bits of bark, leaves, and branches interwoven into the surface, as all the while, a jagged skull leered at me.

Why did she wait until now to regrow them? If she could have had them all this time?

Was she waiting until she killed him?

Is this her way of letting go of the past?

"Artemis," I asked suddenly. "Where is Marcus?"

"Oh, uhm. He had some business to attend to for me," Artemis replied offhandedly.

He's lying.

"Why won't you just tell me the truth?" I asked in exasperation.

"Just tell her," Rosamond sighed. "You can't keep it quiet any longer."

"It's not for me to tell," Artemis protested.

"Fine then," Rosamond snapped. "Let me give her a riddle. She's a smart little cookie, she'll figure it out."

That sounds like a terrible idea. I hate riddles.

Artemis sighed and I was fairly sure he was rolling his eyes.

"At the full moon's rise, cursed magic takes place," Rosamond began. "A monster rises and a man is erased. He reappears suddenly, at break of crimson dawn, the heartbeat he loves, pulling him on."

Rosamond is wrong. I most certainly am NOT a smart cookie.

Boo, I want to be a smart cookie.

Artemis held up a fist, and I was grateful for the distraction as we stopped. A bright green door stood just off the path.

"That's the third one in the space of an hour," Jacques muttered.

"They're getting more frequent," Artemis replied, scrutinizing the door.

"Are you going to see where it goes?" Rosamond asked.

"No," Artemis replied. "Every door so far has led to the Mortal Realm. I have no doubt that this one does as well."

"What does it mean?" Jacques asked.

"I think the Knight is trying to get out," Rosamond replied quietly. "The enchanter's realm with the cursed princes was under the control of the Daughter, though she's imprisoned in that cursed moon. Her return is inevitable, as is his rise."

"Do you think there's a reason they all lead to the Human Realm?" Jacques asked tightly.

"I can't say for sure," Artemis replied. "But I don't have a good feeling about it."

Rosamond gave a humorless laugh. "There's nothing about this situation that gives good feelings. The good vibes have rotted; we're left with a corpse of what could have been."

"Yes, hello Mr. Knight," Jacques chortled. "I'd like to file a complaint. None of your evil plans give good vibes—you really need to work on your people skills."

We continued to follow the path, trading back ideas about how to best file complaints with the Knight and what exactly we'd say.

It wasn't long before I began to get the uncertain feeling that I was being watched. The hairs on the back of my neck prickled, but every time I looked back, there was nothing there. Nothing but dark green foliage that shifted and swayed in the gentle breeze.

"Em, what is it?" Artemis called out sharply. "Your magic just went on high alert."

"I..." my voice trailed off as I continued to scrutinize the landscape. "I don't know. I just, I feel like I'm being watched."

"Trust your gut," Artemis replied, coming to stand beside me.

"What are you going to do?" Rosamond asked tightly, drawing her dark red blade.

"We should keep moving," Jacques stated. "No sense starting trouble."

"If we keep moving, we have to walk in formation. I don't want anyone's back getting compromised."

"UGH!" Jacques griped. "I hate walking in formation. It's so slooooow," he whined.

"So we call it out then," Rosamond replied.

Artemis frowned in concentration. "I can sense something there, but it's masking itself quite well. It's just a slight disturbance in the air. Breaths in and out, moving against the flow of the breeze shows someone's there."

"All right," Rosamond yelled. "The game is up. Come out, nice and slow. If you don't, I'll come find you, and I promise, you do *not* want me to do that. I will be most cross with you then."

A chuckle came from somewhere far away in the bushes. "Look at you, traitor," a male voice called out. "Helping the prince. You've regrown your wings even. Have you forgotten what they've done to you? Have you forgotten the monster you're meant to be? Your fangs should be at their throats, but instead you walk at their heels, docile as a *pet*."

Rosamond snarled in rage. "Show yourself!" she yelled. "Or I come after you."

"I have the high ground," the voice called back. "I know these Mooreland woods like the back of my hand. Would you be so foolish as to go where the woods do not heed your call?"

"I am the woods," Rosamond hissed.

Artemis nocked an arrow and sent it flying into the underbrush. "That was a warning shot," he yelled.

A large figure began to rise out of the dense, knee-length foliage. It seemed impossible, given his size, that he had remained hidden as he did.

"Hello, Princeling," he called as he slowly clapped. "You've won the game of hide and seek, this time."

"Hemming," Rosamond snarled, brandishing her sword. "I should have known it would be you."

"I should have known you would pick the losing side," Hemming retorted hotly.

He was tall, standing at what I guessed to be over six and a half feet, with black hair and bright yellow and black eyes.

"There are no sides, not yet," Artemis replied coldly. "We are not here to pick a fight."

"Oh, but you are," Hemming replied as he strolled toward us. He pointed to me. His fingers were curled like claws. "There's a hefty bounty on that one's head and she's been marked by the darkness to boot. I can smell the poison on her skin. The constellation is there beneath her shirt, I'm sure of it."

Artemis stiffened and his music became a worried buzz in the back of my mind as his thoughts clouded over. He knew about the mark, but the mention of it was enough to make him afraid.

"The Knight rises, and here you are, trouncing through his claimed territory. I'd say you were trying to pick a fight."

"We're following the path," Jacques cut in.

"Ah, Jacky boy. Don't think I've forgotten you. It's been a long time."

Jacques walked forward. "Still being incredibly stupid, I see," he sighed as he clasped Hemming's hand and pulled him into a quick hug.

Jacques turned to Artemis. "Ignore his prattle. He's just trying to get a rise out of you. He plays both sides. Whichever side caves first is the group he devours."

Rosamond bared her teeth. "I'll be the judge of that," she threatened darkly as she pointed her sword at Hemming's chest.

"Oh please, healer," Hemming said. His words were soft, but his tone was menacing, begging for violence as he stared her down. "Bring out the monster. Let's play. I promise you, you won't win. I'm especially hungry today."

"Where's Autymn?" Rosamond asked coldly, ignoring his threat.

"Out murdering something, no doubt. I haven't seen her in an age."

"Liar," Rosamond snapped. "The beast cannot leave her. You are bound in the most explicit way possible."

"She hates me right now," Hemming sighed. "I ate her grandmother."

My mouth fell open in shock and Hemming laughed, slapping his thigh in amusement. "This one doesn't get around much." He stared at me, tilting his head to the side.

"She's new. I've never seen her before. Pretty, too."

Artemis took a protective step in front of me.

"Easy, Princeling, I was simply complimenting her."

"You were thinking about how her blood would taste," Artemis countered hotly. "You were wondering how her hair felt. I can sense your thoughts."

"That was the beast. He craves the flesh, especially the blood of redheads." He shrugged, "I've got a type, who am I to argue it?"

"What are you doing following us?" Rosamond asked with a sigh. "Let's get to the point before the prince loses his temper and we're forced to kill you."

"I came to warn you," Hemming replied. "There's an ambush up ahead, and they have a siren."

Artemis' eyes went wide. "Is there any way around it?"

"Nope. Not unless you want to lose your way to the Ruins. You're close. I'll give you bonus cookies for your efforts. You've made the Knight quite desperate. He sent some men out to kill you and take both of the Grimms."

"Both?" Artemis questioned. "Not just Ember?"

"Both," Hemming confirmed. "The bounty is on her and the other twin, but he wants them *all* alive." He glanced at Jacques, his eyebrows wiggling. "Feel important, Lieutenant?"

"Very," Jacques snapped.

Hemming laughed. The sound was harsh and snarling as he pointed at Jacques. "Though, why they'd want this useless sack of bones is beyond me."

Jacques scoffed. "I am the most useful sack of bones you'll ever meet, you dirty, rotten jerk. The Knight must want me for my good looks."

"Yes, perhaps, but you don't *taste* good," Hemming shot back. "You taste so bad the monster never wants to bite you again. It's all that junk food, no doubt."

"I'll have you know, I am what I eat, and since I eat sugar, I am incredibly sweet."

"No, you're incredibly disgusting."

Jacques rolled his eyes.

Hemming was eyeing me again and I brandished a dagger at him. "Stop looking at me like you want to eat me," I growled. I was in no mood to be ogled.

He snarled, the sound low and menacing. "That's exactly what I want to do, little girl." He leaned forward, smelling the air. "I want to eat you whole."

He was flickering around the edges, and for a moment his face morphed into a wolf, then back to a man. He shook his head and smirked. "Sorry about that. The beast gets carried away sometimes. He likes watching you squirm."

"Do that again and I'll kill you," Artemis threatened softly.

"You'll *try*," Hemming corrected. "And when you do, you'll put all your lives in danger, just to fail to prove a point. We both know the monster can't be killed."

"I can certainly try," Artemis replied hotly.

"And ruin the little party we're having?" Hemming shot back with a laugh. "Before I've even had a chance to make tea and find the crumpets Jack's squirreled away in that magical cloak of his? Well, in that case, I can see my hospitality won't get us anywhere good. I'd better move on. I just thought I'd warn you...perhaps I shouldn't have. Maybe I should have let them destroy you."

"We appreciate the warning," Jacques sighed. "But *why* do you have to be such an arrogant bastard when you drop in? If you would just, play nice, then you could stay and have some decent company."

"I am all the company I need, pretty boy," Hemming countered hotly. "The monster keeps me entertained." His gaze flicked toward me, but he pulled it away with a final, hungry smile at Artemis that made my skin crawl.

Artemis took another threatening step forward and Hemming began to back away, palms raised. He stopped after a moment, his golden eyes narrowed at Rosamond. "You've killed him, then." It was a statement, not a question.

Rosamond nodded and Hemming laughed. "So it begins," he said, tone menacing. "Keep your wits about you. Even with your knowledge, you're in for a nasty surprise."

With the cryptic warning still hanging in the air around us, he stepped back and sunk into the undergrowth—there, then gone in the blink of an eye.

Artemis swore and stared at the path ahead of us. "Do you think he's bluffing?" he asked Jacques.

Jacques frowned. "I don't know. But I'd treat this like he wasn't, just to be sure."

Artemis shook his head. "Cursed Legends," he spat angrily as we began to cautiously move forward.

Rosamond rolled her eyes and brandished her sword at him. "Careful Princeling, you happen to have a *cursed* Legend in your company."

Artemis shook his head angrily. "As if I could forget."

I couldn't resist sharing a conspiratorial glance with Rosamond, who was mocking Artemis behind his back. 'As if I could forget,' she mouthed with exaggerated facial expressions.

I chortled and Artemis shot me a venomous look, to which I maturely made a face and stuck out my tongue at him.

74

The Woods Are Lovely, Dark And Deep, But I Am A Chicken, And I'd Like To Leave

EVADNE

"When the fox hears the rabbit screaming, he comes running. But not to help."
-Thomas Harris, The Silence of the Lambs

I hadn't quite comprehended during my daring escape that fleeing in the middle of the night, while smart for not getting spotted, was a blow to my courage. Trying to make my way through the woods, with a full moon shining above me, was the last thing I wanted to be doing. Robert Frost's poetry was running a terrified loop through my mind as I dodged branches and trunks. The moon gave enough light, despite the thick branches, that I could safely set my pace to a steady jog.

The woods are lovely, dark and deep, but I have promises to keep and miles to go before I sleep...and miles to go before I sleep.

No. That rhyme is incorrect. Here's how it should go. The woods are lovely, dark and deep, but I am a chicken, and I'd like to leave. I am a chicken, and I want to leave... There. Much better.

The moonlight was bright enough to help me avoid smashing my face into a tree. It was not, however, enough to stop me from falling headfirst into what happened to be a very deep bog.

What the actual crap?!

The water was heavy and unnatural with an oily sort of feel.

This is absolutely disgusting.

Stop complaining and get out of here.

I'm working on it. Just be patient.

I was kicking and struggling, trying to pull myself back to the surface, but my efforts were in vain. Something was dragging me down.

My lungs were screaming, already desperate for air.

Fireheart squirmed against my chest, aggravated about getting wet.

Just hold your horses Fireheart, it's not like I planned for this to happen.

What the heck is even happening??

The water was dark, but my eyes were slowly adjusting. There, down beneath me, a pair of yellow eyes glowed dimly in the murky water.

Well. That's not good.

I pulled my foot up, and the eyes came closer. A webbed hand was wrapped around my ankle, intent on dragging me down. I kicked and struggled, trying to wrench the long, sharp fingers free from my ankle.

Why me? Why today? I do not have time for this right now! I'm supposed to be getting help, not putting myself in a position where I'm the one who needs help!

My lungs were burning. I was going to drown soon. But no matter how hard I fought, I couldn't get away.

I'm such an idiot, I'm literally in water! I can get out of this!

Oh. Right.

The water churned and swirled around me as I gathered a ball of water and threw it at the creature. It drew back with an ear-splitting scream that vibrated through the water and made my mind ache. My ankle burned as its claws sliced through my skin.

One more blast and it'll be knocked off.

I shot another wave and at last my ankle was free. Blood swirled in the water around me and my mouth fell open as more eyes began to rise through the water.

I was surrounded.

That's it. I'm toast.

I raised my hands, ready to fight, only to realize that my hands had shifted and changed. No longer were they slim, delicate fingers. They were now webbed. My nails were stained a dark blue, and ended in sharp claws.

What the heck?

Am I dreaming?

"Why have you come?" one of the creatures hissed. "We will give no homage to you."

I don't want homage. What the heck is it talking about?

"We will not recognize you as our queen. We have no ruler but the one we choose."

Look lady, or, erm, mermaid? I think you have the wrong person. I was minding my own business and then I fell into your bog.

It took me a moment to realize that I was still underwater, and my desperate need for air was, in fact, gone.

My fingers probed my face and neck. There, along my cheekbones and the sides of my neck, gills had opened up.

So...I get in water and I turn into a mermaid? What the heck is going on??

I mean, yes, what's going on? But also, this is stinking cool!

So...can I talk underwater?

"I don't want any trouble!" I yelled. My voice sounded garbled, full of phlegm and water, but it was there, nonetheless.

"Lies," the mercreature hissed. "Such lies from the false queen. I told you." It hissed to the others. "I told you about the dark one. The power she possessed. I told you she would come and bring ruin to us all."

I am so incredibly confused right now.

"I'm just trying to get home," I called. "I...I come in peace; my being here was an accident."

"Drown her!" the other merfolk yelled.

"She has transformed. The landwalker has morphed."

"Then she is our queen!"

What? No, this is not how this is supposed to work. Don't choose the first person who adapts to your conditions! Judge them by character and acts, not physical change.

"We have no queen but the one who already resides on the throne. I will not allow this, this *mortal*," the mer who tried to drown me spat, "usurp the throne."

"I'm going home!" I shouted. "I'm not here to take over your kingdom."

"Then you forfeit your stake to the throne?" the mer asked sharply, eyes blazing in the darkness.

That...seems like a loaded question. I don't want it now, but what if something happens? I shouldn't give definite answers I may regret later...something about that question seems like a trap.

"I'm leaving," I said. "I will make no promises, nor will I answer such a question. It is not yet...uh...time."

The group drew back, hissing.

I'll take that as my cue to go... If I can control this water, then perhaps I can tell it to throw me out.

I pulled my Inheritance back to myself, and with a final confused glance around, urged it to push me back to the surface, back to dry land.

I burst out of the water and lay heaving on the soggy bank. Now it was my precious oxygen that betrayed me. I couldn't breathe as the gills on my body desperately fluttered and heaved.

C'mon. Work!

I belong on land, not in the water!

At last, after what seemed like an eternity, my body slowly adjusted to being back on land.

So, does this mean I'm part fish?

What on earth just happened?

"Looks like you're no end of trouble," a new voice commented drily.

I jerked, startled, and stared up at the familiar face.

"Hello, daughter of Grimm," Scarrington purred. "I was told I could find you here."

75

My Sister's Escape And Ronan's Lopsided Cake

FAYE

"There is so much stubborn hope in the human heart."
-Albert Camus, The Myth of Sisyphus and Other Essays

It was with great displeasure that I viewed the empty houses marking where the compound lay buried. I sighed, annoyed, and Ronan shot me a quick glance, one eyebrow slightly raised.

I do not want to go back to my prison.

Hold on, just hold on. We'll be out of there in no time.

Being in the hospital had given me a brief disconnect from my fear, since it was a situation I couldn't control. But now, returning to the compound, everything came rushing back. All the things I didn't say or notice suddenly raced to the front of my mind.

I didn't ask Evadne about her eye...I was so worried about her safety it didn't even cross my mind...

I am SUCH a terrible sister.

At this thought, my brain cells began to wail. They absolutely hated the terrible sister accusation. They prided themselves on being the best at everything.

What am I going to do? I have to get Evadne out too.

My list of people to save was growing longer, and I was beginning to wonder if I could pull it off.

It's so long it's just making me tired.

The closer we got, the more I noticed the oddities. Men were everywhere, racing back and forth across the grounds.

"What on Earth?" Ronan muttered, staring at the chaos.

"I haven't even caused any mayhem yet," I whined. "I expect to see that, but only if I'm at the root of it."

Ronan's mouth pulled into a tight line as he parked the car. James ran up, his face flushed and eyes wide as Ronan opened his door.

"What's going on?" Ronan asked in a low voice.

"The girl escaped," James replied. "Your father was in a strange space last night. He seemed...distant, disconnected. He put her in the cell with her father, and now she's gone."

"That cell had a window," Ronan replied. "Do you think she went out it?"

"There's no doubt she went out; the bars were completely melted. There was nothing left."

That's an interesting development...

Ryver said Fireheart had bonded to her...I bet she had him with her and he helped her escape.

Ronan chortled, then quickly covered it up with a cough. "Well, I guess that's what he gets," he mused.

"He's in an uproar," James replied. "Absolutely livid."

Ronan shrugged. "I can't help him. He made a terrible choice; these are the consequences of his terrible choices."

James nodded. "I know, but I just thought I'd warn you."

"Thanks, keep me posted."

Ronan shut his door and made his way around. I, opting to continue my charade of hating his guts, shoved my door open at the last second, ramming it into Ronan.

James let out a surprised laugh, then clapped a hand over his mouth. Ronan was having a hard time containing his amusement. He opted for glaring, but his eyes were laughing beneath his lowered brows.

I smiled up at him sweetly. "What's the matter?" I cooed. "Cat got your tongue? Surely you know to treat your valued prisoner with less glares and more smiles."

"Let's go," Ronan snapped, his voice wavering slightly with barely contained laughter.

"I've got to get back to searching the property," James said abruptly, his voice strained as he quickly walked off. Much to my delight, once he was a little distance away, Ronan burst out laughing.

"A cat hasn't got my tongue," Ronan said under his breath as he led me toward the metal door that went into the compound. "But a saucy Grimm does."

"We have to keep up appearances, you know."

"Yes, yes, I know."

As the doors opened, the lingering song *Baby Shark* drifted down the hallway, indicating the system was still down.

"Apparently," Ronan said with a sigh, "Jeremiah got so infuriated by the song, he had all the technology piled in the tech room and locked the door."

"Isn't he trying to get his programmers to undo the hack?" I asked smugly.

"He did..." Ronan's voice trailed off and he frowned at the floor. "But when they failed repeatedly, he killed them all in a fit of rage. Now he doesn't have anyone to try to fix it."

My mouth fell open. I meant to harm Jeremiah, but I never meant to get anyone killed with my virus.

"Don't feel too bad," Ronan said gently. "They weren't good men. There's a reason Jeremiah employs ghosts. He holds their past over them; he grabs men away from life sentences or those on death row. They were monsters of their own making and agreed to Jeremiah's madness eagerly."

"I guess it truly was a virus," I mused, distracted.

"How *did* you do it?" Ronan asked, shaking his head.

"I mixed uh, *places*," I replied cryptically.

Ronan nodded, understanding dawning on his face.

"None of *his* hackers will be able to undo it," I bragged. "Now, if he were to hire an especially spicy pixie with the promise of an irresistible bonus, he'd have it undone in an hour. I can't hold a candle to the pixies, though I copied some of their greatest code. They love infuriating humans and infecting their tech. They use the money they steal on an absurd amount of candy and other ridiculous things. Once they figured out online shipping and bulk buying, it was really over for the Mortal Realm. They're way too jacked up on the sugar." I giggled, amused by the look of utter bewilderment on Ronan's face. "Long story short, don't piss of the Fey." I stopped suddenly, my amusement gone. "Oh no," I whispered. "Did I just..."

I waited in anxious anticipation, but surprisingly, nothing happened. I had spilled Realm secrets, but I hadn't been marked.

Maybe this compound is being turned into part of the Knight's Realm? If his magic is strong enough here...but is that even possible?

Not sure, but it doesn't bode well, whatever it means.

"If I've learned anything in this stupid escapade," Ronan muttered, pulling me back to our original conversation, "it's that you are an expert at teaching me not to piss off the Fey." He paused, a smirk growing. "Though, I think perhaps it's better phrased not to piss off *my* Faye." He laughed. "Do your parents know how ironic that name choice is?"

I ignored his question and returned to the prior subject. "You're an incredibly poor student, by the way. You'd think your 'learning' would manifest itself better."

We continued to trade insults back and forth until we reached the door to my cell. Ronan unlocked it and followed me inside. We stopped and stared in horror at the wreck the room had been reduced to. Everything was in shambles. Someone had completely trashed the room while I was gone.

"Seems Jeremiah threw a temper tantrum," I whispered, trying to stay calm and maintain my good humor.

My spirits dove and crashed headfirst into the wreckage as they saw the ripped up ruins of what had been a purple bedspread.

"Oh, the purple bedspread," I whispered, oddly devastated.

It was just a bedspread. Why do I care? Why does it matter?

Ronan swallowed, clearly jarred. "I...I wanted to surprise you," he replied softly. His face was ashen as he stared at the mess. "When do you implement the next step?" he asked at last.

"I should be healed up enough in a couple of days to cause enough mayhem," I replied, my eyes fixed on the debris.

"Do you want help cleaning it up?"

I shook my head. "No, he'll suspect. It's fine, it doesn't bother me..." My voice trailed off as I stared at the torn remnants of my backpack and there, among the ruined towels, my smashed iPod on the floor. My headphones had been ripped apart, my journal torn to pieces and scattered.

I saved for months to buy that iPod...years and years worth of music was on that... I wonder if the memory card is still intact.

I crouched, inspecting the broken pieces. There beside them was the deliberately snapped memory card.

That's it. I'm gonna sue for destruction of property.

Forget suing. I'm going to break every single bone in his wretched body.

Fun fact, there's 206 bones in a human body, as opposed to Elves, who have 210 bones. Pixies only have 199 bones.

Okay. Focus. We are plotting great revenge and mayhem.

"Here," Ronan said suddenly.

I looked up in shock at the small black box and the little headphone case in his hand. It was *his* iPod. The same iPod I had tried to steal the last time I'd been outside the compound.

"But don't you need it?" I asked hesitantly.

"Nah, I don't. I barely touch the thing."

If you barely touch it, why do you have it in your pocket?

Oh, to have men's pockets. It's not fair! Clothing companies make sure men's pockets can actually hold things, but what about women's clothing?

Why are you whining? You have WyrldCloak pockets on most of your things. It's an endless exciting experience of 'what did I forget I put in my pocket today?'

I miss my WyrldCloak. I wish Ryver hadn't taken back that cloak.

"Here," Ronan repeated, pushing the iPod and headphones into my hand. "I want you to have it."

"Thank you," I whispered. "I'll keep it safe."

"I need to go, but I'll be back, okay? Guard yourself. If anyone comes in here who isn't me, kill them."

The bluntness in his words and tone stopped me short, but I nodded. I was capable of great and terrible things, and I could not afford to be taken out. Not when everything rested on me.

I nodded. "I will. Go make sure my father is okay."

Ronan pursed his lips, his face grim. "I'm worried about exactly that. Meghan too. But, if I were to guess, I'd say he would take any manner of torture if it meant getting his daughters out."

"Have you talked to him at all?" I whispered.

Ronan nodded. "I explained everything. He told me to get you out if it was the last thing I did."

"I'm not leaving until Meghan is out, and my father."

"I know, but he said to tell you if need be, to forget him."

"That's not happening," I snapped.

"I'm not saying it is," Ronan cut in gently. "I'm just telling you what he said."

"Right, sorry."

"It's okay." Ronan pulled me into a brief hug. "I've got to go," he said gently, his voice muffled.

"Keep my treasures safe," I replied. "I left them in your car."

"I'll guard them with my life," Ronan promised valiantly.

"Don't be stupid," I chortled. "You can just guard them with *some* of your life. Not all of it, though. I still get to kill you last."

Ronan rolled his eyes and shook his head, and with a final, lingering, worried glance back at me, he left, closing the door carefully behind him.

Ronan's iPod proved to be the balm I needed to give me the energy to tidy the wreckage Jeremiah had made of my cell. I returned to the playlist entitled 'Stupid Pain in My Butt,' happily listening to Ronan's mix as I cleaned. Then, after carefully gathering the pages together, I decisively shredded what used to be my journal. Even torn up, it was legible, and I was not about to give Marcov a chance to read *this* journal. My heart was poured onto those pages, from my time in the Realm, to my month at home...it was all there.

Jeremiah's an idiot. He might have gotten some useful information from those pages. Who knows, maybe he read it before he destroyed it.

I shuddered at the thought, and my three brain cells began to promptly plan his brutal murder. Anyone who read a girl's journal deserved the worst kind of punishment.

Journal destroyed, I made myself a nest in the shower with the torn remains of my pillows, blankets, and the precious purple bedspread. Even though I had put the decimated parts of my cell in front of the door to warn me if anyone came in, I still didn't feel safe enough to sleep out in the open.

I was curled up in a ball in my little nest. The lyrics to the song "This isn't final" by Lily Kershaw played softly through Ronan's earbuds. *'Don't give up, on all that you love, just because it's getting hard... Don't give up, on the person you've become, just because it's getting dark...'* It was a beautiful song. Completely new to me, I found a strong comfort in it as I drifted off to sleep.

What was that noise?

Nothing. The noise was nothing.

No, I definitely heard something.

Grumbling, I pulled out one of the earbuds and heard a soft, yet distinct knock on my cell door.

Thoroughly annoyed, I clambered to my feet with a groan. My leg was all forms of angry and did not appreciate its well-deserved rest being interrupted.

It must be Ronan, but what does he want?

What if it's not him? What if it's a trick?

I grabbed a piece of my bed from the pile of rubble I had put in one corner of my room, brandishing the thick wooden leg like a club as the lock slowly slid back.

"Who is it?" I whispered. "If you come in here, I'll gut you," I threatened darkly.

"It's me," Ronan's voice laughingly replied. "Don't gut me, I have a surprise."

What is he so happy about?

Ronan always turns on the light...what if it's not him? What if he's trying to distract me with the thought of a surprise?

At the word surprise, my brain cells had gathered in an excited mass, screeching and jumping up and down at the prospect of a surprise.

Still suspicious, I pulled against the wall, my heart racing.

Who else could it be? What other reason would anyone else have to come here?

Lots of other reasons.

I should teach him the code song, so I know for sure it's him and not a trap.

The door began to open, pushing the broken parts of my bed across the floor with a loud screech. Then, someone slipped into the room.

That shadow doesn't look or move like Ronan.

Fear won the argument, and on instinct I swung, terrified it was a trick. My aim held true on the dark figure and Ronan's startled cry and profuse swearing in German informed me I had made a drastic mistake.

Well. Now we know for sure.

"What the heck, Faye?!" Ronan hissed. "I almost dropped it!"

"Dropped what?" I demanded. "How was I supposed to know? I thought it was a trick. You always turn on the light when you come."

"Yeah, but I don't want anyone to know I'm here. I'm supposed to be on shift."

"So why aren't you?"

"I said I had a headache and was going to go lie down. James is covering for me. I wanted to give you an update."

"Is Dad okay?" I interrupted, worried sick.

"Yes, he's safe, and we haven't found your sister. She made it out free and clear."

"Go Evadne!" I whispered excitedly.

"I also wanted to give you well...this."

In the dim light from the bathroom, I could make out a rather misshapen blob in his hands.

"Whaaaaat..." my question fell flat as Ronan stepped closer to the bathroom. There on the plate in his hands was a lopsided birthday cake. The frosting was a weeping mess, and scribbling, loopy letters spelled 'Happy Birthday Faye!'

"I guess this is where I start singing," Ronan joked.

I clasped my hands behind my back, suddenly giddy and excited.

The silence stretched.

"Well?" I giggled. "Go ahead, I'm waiting. Start singing."

"Are you serious?" Ronan asked in disbelief. "I was only joking."

"Yes! Sing!" I demanded. "It's not a proper birthday celebration if you don't sing!"

My brain cells all began screeching happily and dancing in a circle. The prospect of hearing Ronan sing was utterly delightful to them.

"Happy birthday to you!" Ronan sang softly in a rich baritone. "Happy late birthday to you! Happy Birthday dear Faye...Happy birthday to yooooou!"

The brain cells screamed their praise, giving him a standing ovation and demanding an encore. I hushed them, watching in wonder as he pulled a lighter out of his pocket and lit the singular candle on the cake. "There was only one," he said sheepishly.

I blew it out, grinning ear to ear. "It's perfect," I said reassuringly.

"I didn't quite realize I missed your birthday," Ronan replied. "I'm sorry. For some reason, I was thinking your birthday was in August."

I laughed, suddenly nervous. "So, are we going to eat the cake or what?"

"Absolutely...but I think I forgot a fork."

"That's what fingers are for," I replied, taking a swipe of the pink frosting with my finger. It was strawberry flavored and delicious. I closed my eyes, savoring the taste.

"Tell me, oh wonderful human, are you going to partake in this delightfully unhealthy cake, or are you going to rudely abstain?"

"I'll be unhealthy," Ronan chortled. "Just this once and only for you."

I giggled, uncontainably happy as Ronan sat down on the floor. He set the cake in front of him and I slid down the wall and settled beside him. Our shoulders were just barely brushing as we stared at the cake.

"It looks so delicious," I whispered, trying to take it all in. It didn't seem smart that Ronan had gone to all this trouble, but here we were regardless, and some part of me was immensely grateful he had. Sifting through the wreck of my room had left me feeling incredibly sad and sorry for myself. Ronan's iPod also possessed a sad music playlist, and it was just as good as mine had been.

"What would you have done if Jeremiah had caught you?" I asked absentmindedly.

"I would have said that I bluffed about my shift to make you a cake and was doing some extra trust building with you. He would have bought it without a question. He knows now that the key to his problem, if the interrogations fail, is our relationship."

"What news of the world outside?" I asked as I pulled a chunk of cake loose. It was still warm.

That must be why the frosting melted. He didn't wait for the cake to cool.

Ronan was watching my face anxiously as I shoved the chunk into my mouth. He was clearly waiting to see what I'd say about the cake.

Aww, he's worried. How cute.

"This is the most dewishious cake," I announced around my incredibly large bite, "I have evewr had."

Ronan's face lit up and a smile spread across his face.

"Mind if I have some?" he asked.

I pretended to think about it as I chewed. "Hmmmm..." I swallowed the monstrous bite.

I should really think about my bites before I just gung-ho shove them in my mouth and then swallow them much too soon.

I could have choked.

At this thought, my three brain cells began to scheme. Unfortunately for them, they had their facts and terms mixed up. Their brilliant plot was to *purposefully* choke, so that Ronan would be forced to give me CPR and, of course, the life saving kiss. When the collective hoard reminded the three about how choking meant the Heimlich maneuver, the three promptly and impulsively exiled the hoard once more. They didn't care what the real world said, they wanted an excuse for Ronan to have no choice but to kiss me again.

"Well," I mused, forcibly pulling myself away from the brain cells' idiotic plotting and the hoard's wailing. "I guess I can behave like a mature adult instead of a petulant child and share. But let me tell you, this is delicious enough it's a struggle."

Ronan laughed and broke off some of the cake. "I'm worried about the next step of the plan," he said as he stared at the bite.

"It's going to be okay," I stated firmly. "It has to be."

"I'm worried it won't be. I'm worried about all the moving pieces. Between you and Meghan, your father... how can I possibly protect you all from Jeremiah?"

"You can't protect me, Ronan," I pressed gently. "You protect your sister, I'll protect myself. My Dad can worry about himself, too. If you try to protect me, it'll compromise her safety. She's more important than I am."

"You're both important," Ronan replied stubbornly. There was a desperate edge to his voice. He was truly afraid.

"You can't protect me," I repeated. "And that's okay."

"I want to protect you," Ronan insisted.

"I know. But right now, you need to protect her. Between the two of us, she's more vulnerable and helpless. I can take care of myself. All my time in the Realm gave me enough experience to keep me alive here. You have no idea what I've lived through. I'll be fine. Meghan needs all your strength right now."

"And you don't?"

"I need you by my side," I replied quietly. "But it looks different than you think. We have different roles in this situation as we work together. If you're protecting her, it leaves me free to defeat your father."

"Some father he is," Ronan scoffed around a mouthful of cake. For some reason, I found it incredibly adorable, and I was willing to let him devour the whole cake if he kept doing it.

That's it, you've lost your mind. You hate it when people talk with their mouth full.

Yeah, but he makes it cute.

That's probably just because he himself is cute.

My cheeks warmed at the thought and after a moment, I realized Ronan was still staring at me.

"I'm scared," he whispered. "I am really, really scared, Faye. What if I lose you?"

I shrugged, at a loss for words as the cake turned to stone in my stomach. "Then we'll find each other in the next life. I will never truly be lost to you, if we are meant to be."

"What if we do everything right, and I still lose you in the end?" Ronan murmured fearfully, still circling the question.

"Life is full of loss, it's unavoidable." I laid a gentle hand on his cheek. "The future is uncertain, but we have each other now, and now is all that matters. We can only do our best and hold onto hope...while there is life, there is hope. We're still alive Ronan, and there is hope. There is always hope."   .

It was something Ryver used to say to me when I was spiraling.

"I don't know if I can bear it," Ronan pressed.

"You can," I said gently. "You will find the strength to make it through this, with or without me."

Ronan was staring at me, eyes full of fear. "I don't want to make it, if you aren't with me."

"Ronan, you can't pin your survival on another person. Because sooner or later, that person will fail, or fall, or disappear...sooner or later you'll lose them. You must find the strength within yourself to survive. Meghan needs you, Ronan. You can't give up just because you've lost me. Do you understand? I need you to promise me that you'll keep living and protecting her, even if you lose me."

Tears were gathering in Ronan's eyes. "I promise," he whispered, his voice tight with tears.

"It's going to be okay. We have the most daring plan. It's genius and brilliant and it can't possibly fail." I was bluffing, using my most courageous voice possible to try to lay his fear to rest. I wanted him to carry some measure of bravery forward.

Ronan nodded. "You have frosting on your nose," he said, abruptly changing the subject.

"What?" I spluttered.

"You have frosting on your nose," he repeated, laughing.

"Yes, well, you have it all over your face," I snorted, allowing the serious subject to fall away.

"You put some of it there," he retorted.

I took careful pains to give him a rather large blob on the end of his nose. "Now it's on your nose."

"Turns out I'm a wonderful cook," he boasted.

"Well, you're good at cake at the very least. Your eggs leave something to be desired," I teased.

"My eggs are a healthy combination of nutrients and protein!" Ronan protested, unable to keep a straight face.

"A healthy combination of nutrients and protein," I mocked under my breath as I took another mouthful of cake. "I'll stick with eating my eggs inside cake, thank you very much," I said loftily.

"How are we going to make it through this?" Ronan asked. His tone was serious again as he stared down at his frosting-covered hands.

"For starters, we're going to finish every bite of this delicious cake. Then, we're going to take over this compound."

"How?"

"One bite at a time, silly."

Ronan laughed, but the sound was strained. The weight of the burdens we bore only seemed to grow as we silently finished the cake. Ronan's fears, and the desperation in his words, pulled at my mind.

You can't protect me, Ronan, don't try. Please don't try. I can't bear to see you get killed trying to protect me.

If anyone has to go, let it be me. Please, let it be me.

76

The Stranger In The Moores

EMBER

"We can simultaneously be human and monster—that both of those
possibilities are in all of us."
-Matthew Quick

We arrived at the scene of the ambush to a pile of bodies. Artemis stared at the carnage with narrowed eyes, picking the scene apart.

"Is this the ambush?" Rosamond asked under her breath. "The bodies are fresh. I can feel the warmth coming off them."

"Is it a trap?" Jacques countered tightly. "They make us think the danger is over, we go on, then they ambush us?"

Thick arrows stuck out of every corpse. Some carried five or six.

"There's no one else here that I can sense..." Artemis said quietly, his voice trailing off as he turned his head, listening intently.

My stomach was churning, unease spreading through my body. "I don't like this," I whispered.

"We're safe," Artemis replied suddenly. But something about his tone was off. He seemed distant, dazed almost.

His music in the back of my mind was gone.

Hemming said they had a siren.

I shoved my fingers in my ears. "They have a siren!" I yelled. "He's under the thrall!"

Rosamond snarled softly, as vines and flowers wrapped around her ears in the blink of an eye.

Artemis turned on me, his green eyes a dull and glassy. "Come on, Em," he said quietly, his voice strained. "We need to go, it's safe."

"It's not," I called, backing away as I desperately shoved the ends of my cloak in my ears. "Wake up, Artemis. This isn't real."

"We need to go," Artemis repeated. His voice was lifeless.

Wrong, wrong, I need to wake him up.

Jacques was singing as he desperately dug through his pockets. "I have cloth in here somewhere," he cried.

"There's no time, commander!" Rosamond yelled angrily. "Shove your cloak in if you must."

"I can't!" Jacques yelled. "If I have to fight, the movement could pull the cloak out and then I'd be compromised." He was frantically digging now as his voice rose. Soon he was singing *Living on a Prayer* at the top of his lungs, trying to drown out any of the siren's call.

Jacques came out with a Ziplock baggie with miniature donuts.

"This is no time for snacks!" Rosamond screeched, enraged.

Jacques swore, ignoring her, and broke one in half. With a regretful glance at the broken pieces, and a muttered curse, shoved the doughnut halves into his ears. "It's not perfect, but it'll do. But it's a waste of a perfectly good doughnut!" he yelled angrily.

Gross!

"Subdue the prince!" Rosamond yelled as Artemis lunged at me. "You can whine about your stupid snacks later!"

I stumbled backward, but Artemis was faster. His fingers wrapped around my arm, yanking me to his chest. "We're safe, Em," he said firmly, a breath away. "Come on, let's go. He's waiting for us."

"Artemis, you need to wake up," I whispered urgently. My dagger was drawn, the blade at his gut, but it was a useless threat. I couldn't hurt him. "Wake up," I whispered. "It's not real."

His eyebrows scrunched, face flickering to confused, then back to calm. "Em..." he whispered, his voice hesitant.

"That's it," I said calmly. "Wake up. I need you. I'm in terrible danger."

Rosamond's vines were around his torso, trying to yank him back.

"Guard us!" I yelled. "I'm almost through. This is likely a distraction!"

Arrows whizzed out of the underbrush, only proving my point.

"Em, it's okay. We need to go; they're waiting for us. It's okay. I know them."

"I know you think you do," I said evenly, forcing myself to remain calm as my heart raced in my chest. "This isn't real," I whispered as I held his face in my hands. "It isn't real."

His features flickered, indecision tearing him apart. "How do I know you're not the illusion?" he asked suddenly. "How do I know you're real?"

I pulled his face closer to mine, resting my forehead against his. "I'm real," I said softly. "I'm right here, Artemis. I'm real."

His lips brushed mine hesitantly and the thrall shattered. His eyes cleared and he stared at me in shock as fear danced across the bright green depths. "What's going on?" he whispered.

I shoved my fingers in his ears. "Find something," I yelled, trying to emphasize the words so maybe he could read my lips.

He ripped the bottom of his shirt and tore it in half, shoving the fabric into his ears. "You saved me," he mouthed.

"I'll always save you," I replied gently. Embarrassed by the sweetness of my words, I decided an insult was in store. "Because apparently you're too stupid to save yourself," I continued as I drew my sword.

Artemis laughed, his eyes bright with joy. "I'll live and die by your hand, and your hand only, my Flamín. Death shall not take me today."

"You're utterly ridiculous."

The element of surprise gone, our attackers had apparently decided on a more direct approach. They swarmed at us from every direction and soon we were surrounded.

"Prepare to die!" Jacques yelled savagely. "No one makes me waste a perfectly good doughnut and lives to see the sunset."

An arrow whizzed out of the underbrush, striking a burly-looking Fey with bright blue skin.

"Whose arrow was that?" Artemis yelled.

"Who cares," Rosamond replied. "They're helping us!"

"How can you be so sure?" Artemis cried.

Another arrow whizzed out of the dense forest, striking another attacking Fey.

"That's how!" Rosamond yelled angrily. "Stop wasting our time!" She lunged forward with a savage battle scream, vines exploding out of one hand, blood-red sword swinging from the other.

The fight lasted a matter of minutes. The bodies dropped one after the other, as arrow after arrow soared out of the dense forest and struck them down around us, until nothing remained but corpses.

"Well, that was easy," Artemis panted, wiping blood off his sword.

I was cleaning my own blade, chest heaving. Even after so much training, I never felt prepared for fights. The adrenaline rush left me shaking, and I didn't care for how close I came to death with every day that passed.

The threat destroyed, we pulled the various items out of our ears. Jacques was disgusted by the mushed pieces of crumbs and goop. When he couldn't get his water to clean his ear, he turned to Rosamond in despair.

"Told you it was a bad idea," she smirked.

"Heeeeelp meeeee!" he whined, pleadingly.

Rosamond rolled her eyes but pointed to the ground. "Kneel," she ordered.

Jacques quickly knelt and in a matter of seconds her vines had cleaned the crumbled mess out of his ears.

"Perhaps you're right," she mused. "Perhaps my plants do need powdery goodness."

Now it was Jacques' turn to smirk. "Told 'ya,"

"I would like to remind you guys that the threat isn't quite cleared yet," Artemis called out. "Someone is still in those woods. They helped us, but that doesn't necessarily mean they're here to help us. They might have just taken out the competition."

Rosamond nodded then brandished her blade. "Come out!" she yelled.

"That's no way to thank someone who helped you," a male voice jovially called back from the Moores.

"I'll thank you when I can see your face," Rosamond snarled. "I don't trust good Samaritans."

A cloaked figure walked out of the woods, face hidden in deep shadows by the cowl of his cloak. "My name is Kieran," he said, drawing back his hood with one hand. The other held a thick longbow with ornate carvings etched across the surface.

"Kieran of the Crow?" Rosamond asked tightly.

"My, word gets around fast, doesn't it?" the stranger, Kieran, asked lightly.

"You tell me," Rosamond growled.

"Ah, healer, you can't choose your family—you can only do damage control with their magic. My mother is her own being; you can't hold me accountable for who she is."

Rosamond rolled her eyes. "We still can't trust him."

"He just saved our lives," Artemis replied. "Plus, he's right. If you hold someone accountable for the deeds of their parents, you'd never be able to trust me, either."

"What makes you think I trust you?" Rosamond asked tightly.

Artemis arched an eyebrow but didn't bother to respond.

"The prince of the high-and-lofty Summer Court has a point," Kieran said with a taunting grin at Rosamond.

"Kieran is nothing but bad luck," Rosamond snapped. "Everywhere he goes, he leaves a trail of bodies in his wake."

"All self-defense, darling. Just look around you. I was defending you all from that attack. You acted quickly on the siren, I'll give you credit on that...but it could have been much worse."

"His help worked in our favor," Jacques mused, though he didn't lower his blade.

"*This* time," Rosamond replied angrily. "It won't continue to be so."

"Such prejudice," Kieran said, rolling his eyes.

"Rosamond has a point," Artemis sighed. "I've heard of Kieran, and more importantly, his mother."

"You too?" Kieran pouted. "After I just saved your life to boot? How incredibly *rude*."

Artemis rolled his eyes. "How are we going to trust you?" he sighed. "I don't have the energy for this."

"Does anyone have energy when they spend it being overly suspicious of other people, who, might I add, just saved their lives?"

I stifled a giggle. Kieran's humor reminded me of Jack's absurdity. Jack also looked as if he was smothering a laugh.

"Tell you what, I tag along and steal some of the heir of Grimm's doughnuts, and if you think I'm going to harm you, then you can kill me. Sound fair?"

Artemis looked dubious, and Rosamond looked furious, but after a moment's thought, Artemis sheathed his sword and held out a hand.

Kieran shook his hand and after a few more moments, Artemis shrugged. "Seems fair," he mused. "I'll let Rosamond kill you if you give us any trouble."

"She'll just be looking for an excuse to say I was going to harm you."

"Then that should keep you on your best behavior."

"My mother wants to see you," Kieran announced. "She's right along the path. She wants to know what you're about this far into the Moores. She also wished to give you a warning."

"We have no business with her," Artemis replied tightly.

"Nevertheless, she has business with you. Do not hinder her message. It would be most unwise."

"Is that a threat if we don't?" Artemis snapped.

Kieran arched an eyebrow. "No, but you would be a fool to ignore the Morrigan."

"If she has business with us, we'd best stop in," Rosamond said, her voice low. She locked eyes with Artemis and a quiet conversation passed between them. "We would be fools to land in her bad graces," she added.

"She resides by the Last Gate at the moment," Kieran replied. "She is not away from your path. It is your destiny to meet her, she has seen it."

"Is she the Seer?" I asked hesitantly.

"No," Artemis replied as his fingers intertwined with mine. His eyes were distant as he surveyed the woods around us, as if searching for something. "She is something far worse. She is a harbinger. A banshee and one of the most powerful sorceresses of her time. She, like the sisters three, is an Olde one."

77

I Am Incredibly Clever, So clever, I Should Get a Treat.

FAYE

"The 6,800 rabbits – more rabbits now than students – are running amok throughout campus. They have disrupted lectures and shown *flagrant* disrespect for faculty, they have joined academic and social organizations, and are engaged in *irresponsible drinking*. There are even reports that these vulgar, cuddly rodents broke into the college president's office and licked viciously on President Sultan for several minutes before her administrative assistant could free her."
-Welcome To Night Vale Podcast, Episode 50,

Three days later, a day later than I had hoped, I was healed enough to live up to my namesake and become the ultimate chaos bunny and cause, you guessed it, a catastrophic amount of chaos.

My plan was simple: get out, cause mayhem, get caught, let my little secret slip, at which point Ronan would come rescue me, having safely deposited his sister in the car where the spare tire goes. She was small enough she'd fit, and the spare tire would go on top of the compartment. Its random placement in the trunk would be excused as laziness. The last thing we needed was a flat tire with no spare available.

Zip-a-dee-dah-dee-dah-doe-doe...Dee-ba-dee-dee-doe...Shoopadoop-pa-do-ba-dee-da-doe-doe...Shoe-ba-dee-da-dee-da-dee-dee-doe...

Much to my absolute delight and amazement, I was currently sneaking through the compound. I had, at long last, successfully blasted the cursed door of my cell off its hinges. Now, swinging my handy dandy bed leg club around and around in the most menacing fashion possible, all I needed was for someone to successfully wander into my path and then the chaos would begin. All bets were off as soon as some poor, unfortunate soul found me. I intended to hurt as many of these low-life jerks as possible. They would rue the day they decided to work for an evil overlord.

Poor, unfortunate soooouls...in pain...in need...

There was a shout up ahead. Someone had spotted me.

Bingo!

The unfortunate man took off running, screaming his head off, and I took off after him, adding my own savage war cry to his terror. The noise echoed so loudly through the corridors it wouldn't be long until I was surrounded. Hearing the commotion, Ronan should have Meghan out the door soon. I just had to hold out until he came back.

Two men lunged at me from open doorways. They were quickly dealt with, their skulls smashing against the unforgiving wood of my club.

Too bad I can't use my Inheritance.

Yes, well, you can't be trusted with your Inheritance.

The original man was getting ahead now, still screaming.

Ha, he screams like a girl.

Time to pay Jeremiah a visit. It's time he learned not to mess with a Grimm.

It's time he learned not to hurt my sister.

I took off running again, making sure my presence and escape was known. The closer I got to his office, the more the men tried to ambush me. Still, I prevailed, knocking them out cold and breaking their bones liberally. I was done playing nice. The Realm had made me into a monster; it was time I reminded Jeremiah what I was capable of.

The office door loomed in front of me. It had been easy—too easy —and some part of my brain began to worry it was all an elaborate trap, that Ronan hadn't gotten Meghan out and they would be waiting for me in the office. What if Jeremiah was smarter than I? What if my plan didn't work?

Don't be ridiculous. You're much smarter than Jeremiah.

Yes, but he's got the Knight on his side.

I threw a bolt of lightning at the cursed wooden door, blasting it open and knocking it off kilter on the hinges.

Here's Faye!

Men were running toward me from behind, and I turned, screeching as I threw a torrent of wind at them, knocking them back against the wall.

See, I can still use PART of my Inheritance.

Yes, well, I still don't trust you.

Several fell and didn't rise again, having hit their heads. The other rose and came again, but this time with more caution.

I grinned savagely, letting my muscles go loose as I swung my club. "Come on then," I yelled. "Who's brave enough to fight me before I go after your little master?!"

The men rushed forward all at once, and I let muscle memory take over, giving no mercy as I took them out one by one until none remained conscious.

I turned to the darkened office.

"Show yourself, coward!" I yelled.

There was no reply.

That is not what I had planned. Where is he?

I raised my bat, ready to attack Jeremiah, as I crept into the room.

Where is he?!

This is not part of the plan! Where is he?! He's supposed to be here!

What if he's where Meghan is? What if he found out? What if he's there?

My eyes were slowly adjusting to the room around me. Shapes and shadows took form within the space as I searched for Jeremaih.

"Hello, Princess," a voice snarled in the darkness.

Marcov.

I screamed in rage and lunged toward the sound of his voice. My bat collided with something solid and I grinned as Marcov grunted in pain. I had an advantage over Marcov. Even though the Winter Court was not in power, I could still see in the dark better than he could.

He was trying to creep around and get behind to knock me down.

I spun, club swinging, and landed a solid blow on his wretched face. He crumpled. I waited, expecting him to crawl to his feet again. But moments passed and still he did not stir.

Well, that takes care of that disgusting, measly problem.

I turned to the door against the wall, where the strange, but familiar symbol glowed faintly.

How much you want to bet Jeremiah is there, having tea with the Knight.

Ah yes, and crumpets. We mustn't forget the crumpets.

I took a deep breath and grabbed the door handle. It was time I finally found out what actually lay on the other side. I had a terrible feeling I already knew what was there. But I had to be sure.

No time like the present.

Today is a gift...that's why it's called a present...

My three brain cells rallied their courage around the little saying and, donning their battle armor, screamed at the door with weapons raised.

The door opened slowly, and I stared into the swirling shadows. Someone was screaming close by, as ghosts and spirits drifted around the edges of the room.

I know that scream. That's mum's scream.

No, no. He can't have her. No! NO!

I took a step inside, and somewhere within the room, someone began to laugh.

The hair on the back of my neck rose.

"So, at last we meet, daughter of Grimm," a cold, harsh voice whispered. "At last, you come to my Realm in all your self-righteous glory to destroy me."

"Where is Jeremiah?!" I hissed.

"He's having his fun with your beloved mother," the Knight replied. "He liked killing her so much he's trying to do it again."

"Where is he?" I yelled, brandishing my makeshift bat.

Change of plans. He dies. NOW. I'm in the Realm; I can kill him fair and square.

"Right here, darling," Jeremiah whispered from beside me.

I swung, but my club only met empty air.

Laughter churned around me. Both Jeremiah and the Knight were laughing at me.

"Come out now," I yelled. "Or else you'll never get what you want."

"She's lying," the Knight said calmly. "Don't listen to her."

Jeremiah ignored the Knight and took the bait.

A shadow lunged at me, and I slammed my bat into Jeremiah's knees with as much force as possible. Given my enhanced strength, the damage was considerable. I stepped back just in time to ensure he fell through the doorway and back into the Mortal Realm.

"I'll be back for you later," I hissed to the shadows. "And I *will* kill you."

"No, you'll die trying," the Knight laughed. "You and all your cursed siblings will rise and fall trying to stop the flood. Run, child, run while you still can. The darkness comes and nothing can stop my return."

I gave the Knight a defiant gesture with my fist and finger before slamming the door shut. Seething, I turned to where Jeremiah lay swearing on the floor. I was fairly certain I had been successful in shattering his kneecaps. As much as I enjoyed hurting him, the wound had been measured and intentional. I had to make sure he was injured enough that he wouldn't be the one to take me to the house to obtain the false information I was about to give him.

"I've come to bargain," I snapped as I savagely kicked him in the ribs. There was a crunch, and I smothered my wince as his ribs cracked against my boot.

I hate breaking bones. It just sounds SO disgusting.

He screamed and rolled over, coughing.

"I have information you want," I continued angrily. "I know how to bring back your beloved wife."

"How do I know you're not lying?" Jeremiah hissed.

"I can't lie anymore. I've been bound to the Realm," I snapped. "Much to my annoyance, I can't lie to your sniveling carcass."

Jeremiah scrutinized my face, and I glared at him, letting my unending anger seep through. "I'm done playing games. I'll give you what you want. In exchange, you will let me, my father, *and* Ronan go."

"Ronan?" Jeremiah hissed. "What do you want with him?"

"Much to my vexation, I have come to enjoy the stupid mortal."

"You genuinely care for him," Jeremiah gasped. "I've seen the affection you display."

"It was an act then," I snapped. "I thought I could use him, but I can't. He's too loyal to turn on you. But now, I find I do genuinely care for him. He kissed me, and now I can't leave him here with the likes of you. You'll get him killed with your meddling within the Realms. You don't know what you're messing with. It will be the death of you, Anderson."

Jeremiah rolled his eyes at my warning, so I continued on my trail of lies and delusions. "I want Ronan to come with me. If he decides to leave me to come back to you, I won't stop him. But he comes with me at the first."

"What about his sister?" Jeremiah muttered angrily.

"What about her?" I challenged. "If Ronan wants to take her with us, she comes, and you'll let her. You'll have your wife; it won't matter where the girl is."

Jeremiah stared at me, his eyes narrowed.

"Do we have a deal, mortal?" I growled.

"Why bargain?" he gasped. "You have the high ground. Why not just kill me and forget the whole matter?"

"I don't know which men are loyal to you," I replied with a shrug. "I can only hold the high ground for so long. Besides, if I kill you, there's no telling how Ronan will react. He would probably never forgive me. Why he cares about you is beyond me. But he cares regardless. I figure this way, I'll have Ronan's heart for sure. If I spare your life and give him a way to have his mother back. If I help him give his father what he's been searching for, he'll never leave my side." I gave Jeremiah a savage grin. "I win."

"You truly are a deceptive little Fey, aren't you?" Jeremiah spat in disgust.

I shrugged again, letting my actions speak louder than my words. "My name is literally Faye. It doesn't get more obvious than that."

Jeremiah shook his head. "Magnificent creature," he whispered.

"I am what they made me to be," I hissed. "A monster, inside and out. I want him, and this is the only way I can get him away from the likes of *you*."

"We'll see," Jeremiah scoffed. "He'll come running back to me. I'll have the mother he loves and misses."

"I doubt it," I snorted. "He'll come visiting. That's all." I paused and glanced at the door, as if paranoid. "He knows nothing of our bargain," I said urgently. "Am I understood?"

Jeremiah stared at me, scrutinizing my face. "Why not tell him?" he whispered, his voice ragged.

"I don't want him to know. I want him to think I gave the information you want up to him willingly, because I love him."

"Faye!" Ronan's voice yelled. He was running; I could hear his steps getting louder and louder, that singular, distinct squeaky shoe giving his location away.

"Do we have a deal?" I hissed, brandishing the club.

"Fine," Jeremiah coughed, spitting a wad of blood out on the floor at my feet. "We have a deal, death-touched witch."

I trembled at the words; they did not bode well for a mortal to speak. I had heard those words before, and they were not ones I ever wanted to hear again.

I raised my club. "Good," I snapped before taking a hard swing at Jeremiah's exposed face.

Time we rearranged that smug grin.

Ronan slammed into me, stopping my chaotic quest for bloodshed.

"Well done, Chaos Bunny," he whispered in my ear before we toppled and slid across the floor.

"That's enough!" Ronan yelled, picking up the charade. "Stop this!"

"Make her talk," Jeremiah groaned, clutching his broken ribs. "She knows how to get your mother back."

That's it, that's it. Almost there.

Ronan stiffened in shock as he stared down at me. I winked, giving him the smallest of smirks.

That's right, I duped your father. I did it. I'm guessing by your reaction you didn't think I could actually do it.

How rude of him to doubt me.

"No one can bring back the dead," Ronan breathed. He was effortlessly picking up the narrative.

"She can," Jeremaih insisted as he pulled himself up to his elbows. "Make her talk and she'll tell you."

"I don't need to *make* her talk," Ronan whispered angrily. He turned back to me, his expression gentle. "She'll tell me."

Yes, that's it. Coerce me as if you don't know about the bargain I already made.

Ronan cusped my face with his hand. "Please Faye," he said softly. "Tell me. Please, tell me. I want my mother back," he sobbed, allowing real emotion to bleed into his voice. "Please," he murmured before dipping his head lower and kissing me gently. "Please," he whispered against my lips.

The tactic was that of manipulation against Jeremiah. It was a front and we both knew it. But my brain cells didn't care. They began to screech and riot in absolute joy. Popcorn was liberally thrown about as they pulled out the projection screen and replayed the moment over and over again.

"Okay," I relented. "I'll tell you..." I hesitated for a moment. "There's a spell," I whispered. "But it's at my home. Hidden in the house, protected by a brounie... He'll give it to me, and me only. You have to take me home, Ronan."

Ronan sobbed on my shoulder, letting the supposed relief and hope show. "We did it, Dad," he sobbed. "We're going to get her back."

I locked eyes with Jeremaih as Ronan continued his charade.

'Remember our deal,' I mouthed.

Jeremiah glared back, but at last, he nodded.

The pieces had at last fallen into place. We were going to make it out of this.

I can't wait to see Jeremiah's face when he realizes I've double crossed him, and Ronan has too.

That will be a glorious day of revenge.

I am so clever. So, incredibly clever.

So clever I should get a treat!

Oo! Yes, more treats! Ronan owes me ever so many treats and bribes for all my hard work.

78

Elven Blood, Elven Magic

"And men said that the blood of the stars flowed in her veins."
-C.S. Lewis, The Silver Chair

I had decided about fifteen minutes ago that murder was not beneath me, when it was the murder of an incredibly saucy, snarky cat. I had a justifiable defense; I was soaking wet, and despite the warm summer air around me, I was absolutely freezing.

I could blame it on a bout of insanity. Or, I could say I was threatened...

Threatened by what? His ego? That will be an incredibly hard case to prove.

Nobody asked you.

Fine. Commit a heinous crime and rot in prison. I'm simply giving you logical feedback for your stupidity.

I trudged through the woods, growing more irritated with every step. "Where are we going?" I demanded angrily.

It's not as if I've asked him at least ten times and he's refused to answer me...what's one more time asking if he's not even going to answer me?

"Well, if you must know, mistress of impatience, we're going back to the Realm."

Oh, he is going to answer me this time.

"But there happens to be a band of Winter Elves that have migrated to this area of the Mortal Realm. The edges of the Borderlands are bleeding into the Mortal Realm. The elves came in through a back door, so to speak. We're going to them, and they will send you to the Central Gate through the mirror."

"Why to the Central Gate?" I asked. "Why not just send me back to the Central Realm?"

"You need to go to the Gate," Scarrington answered cryptically.

"Fine," I muttered, angered by his roundabout answers.

Stupid cryptic cat, with his stupid cryptic answers.

"They're around here somewhere..." Scarrington was a distant blur in front of me.

Are you sure we can't just get rid of the cat? I feel like that would make my life better. It would certainly make the walk quieter.

My traveling petting zoo was currently pouting as they sat on either side of my shoulders. Neither Elvie, nor Fireheart had been pleased about the impromptu bath. But, sensing my mutinous thoughts, Fireheart perked up and shot me a conspiratorial glance. One that clearly offered to roast and eat Scarrington and all his sarcastic commentary.

If only, but that wouldn't solve our problems.

He IS helping us, and even if he's being incredibly irritating while he's doing it, that doesn't justify letting him get eaten.

I shook my head and Fireheart resumed his pouting.

There, there, tiny dragon. You can eat someone later. Right now, we need this annoying cat.

Maybe he could eat the annoying cat after said annoying cat stops being useful...

No, that wouldn't be a kind thing to do.

What if we just...let Fireheart pull a Maladroit, and he relieves Scarrington of some of his fur.

I have the feeling Scarrington has an ace up his sleeve. Fireheart would probably get hurt.

"Ah, here we are," Scarrington mused, interrupting my inner argument as he stopped at the edge of a cliff.

I stared down in amazement at the massive encampment beneath us. Large tents stood in a small circle around what appeared to be a main hub, and people milled around, laughing and talking. Some danced on the far edge beneath the light of the waning moon.

A heavy presence seemed to dwell around the area, thick with raw power and possibility. It pulled at my Inheritance, begging to be harnessed.

"You should feel right at home here," Scarrington noted with a smirk. "Your mother spent the second half of her time in the Realm here. The head elf, Oryn, claimed and rescued her. He loved her dearly, and when she escaped with the wretch, Oryn was heartbroken for ages. I don't know if he's recovered, even now."

"She never spoke of her time here," I said softly, staring down at the elves.

"Her heart belonged to the Mortal Realm. Even though she found comfort here, she always belonged to the humans. She left this place, desperate to forget. Oryn has been waiting for years, hoping in vain she would return to the Fey Realm...to him. They were always passing ships in the night, destined to circle each other forever. He continues to search for her. You of all the girls look most like her. He recognized who you were at once."

"The elf at the door," I said quietly.

"Yes," Scarrington mused. "Won't he be surprised to find you walking up to his camp. Be careful, daughter of Grimm. You may be just the balm to a broken heart, the daughter he was never given. Do not let him keep you."

"Are you leaving me here?" I asked, confused.

"My job is completed. I was instructed to bring you here."

"Who instructed you?" I asked, suddenly concerned.

"Wouldn't you like to know," Scarrington taunted as he turned and sauntered off into the dark woods.

Fireheart hissed on my shoulder, throwing an expressive hand gesture at the cat that seemed to say 'now can I eat him?'

I shook my head. "No, you can't eat him." I sighed.

"A wise decision," Scarrington called back.

"*YET*," I added, just for spite.

Scarrington's haughty laughter followed me as I turned and began to make my way down toward the elves' camp.

My cheeks heated in embarrassment as one by one, the elves stopped what they were doing and stared at where I made my clumsy way toward them. At last, I stood at the edge of the camp. "I..." my voice trailed off. I wasn't sure what to say. "I need..."

At last, a familiar face began to walk toward me. It was the one Scarrington had called Oryn.

"Child," he said gently, his dark eyes searching my face. "What in all the three Realms are you doing here?"

"I was brought here...by a cat," I finished weakly. "Uhm...I need some help. I must return to the Central Realm."

"You're supposed to be with the prince," Oryn stated. "What happened?"

"We were separated...I was taken, but I got away..."

Oryn's eyebrows scrunched together as he pondered my words. After a moment he raised a hand and waved it. "Carry on about your business," he called. He turned back to me. "Come child, you look worn to death. We will figure out a plan after you've slept."

He was right, I was so exhausted I felt ready to drop. The fight with the Merfolk, the escape from the Andersons, it was beginning to hit me all at once.

I nodded weakly. "Thank you," I said quietly as I began to follow him. Relief lodged deep in my chest. At last, I felt safe. Exhaustion chased me, threatening to knock me to my knees.

Oryn glanced back just as my knees buckled and in one quick move, caught me before I hit the ground.

He stared down at me in quiet compassion as he carried me.

"Sorry," I whispered. "You wouldn't believe the day I've had."

"I think I would believe it," Oryn replied softly. "There is no need for apologies, child. It is not right what they've done to you. You are a bright, beautiful thing in this world, as your mother is. I would not let them snuff you out as they sought to extinguish her all those years ago."

What do you know about my mother? What role did you play in her life?

He speaks of her in the present tense. Does he know?

I sighed and began to drift off despite my best intentions.

Oryn began to sing gently in a language I barely recognized. It faded in and out of my consciousness. It was a song about stars and moonlight, seeking your path, and seizing your fate in the stars.

I woke disoriented and unsure of where I was. A thick fur lay over me. It was comforting despite the warm summer air.

I rose slowly, feeling surprisingly refreshed and renewed. It was dark outside, but the camp seemed awake and alive.

I wonder if the elves stay awake at night all the time, or just during the winter?

But it's not winter right now...it's summertime.

Is it all elves, or just the winter elves?

"Did you rest well?"

I jumped at the sound of Oryn's voice. He sat outside the tent, weaving a garment on a slender loom.

"I did, thank you," I replied, yawning.

"You should, you slept for three suns," Oryn stated with a quiet laugh.

I what?!

Holy cow I must have been exhausted.

"Come, eat. There is food at the fire. Eat without shame until you are satisfied. You need the nutrients. Your body is starving. Your Inheritance is bleeding you dry."

I sat and began to eat the bread, meat, and cheese laid out. It was warm and savory, with flavors that exploded across my tongue. I didn't realize how hungry I was until, with a little embarrassment, I saw that I had eaten everything available and was looking for more.

Oryn laughed from where he sat. "The appetite of a Grimm always amazes me. The raw power that flows through you is more than food can sustain. But still the body tries. It's been far too long since you had a decent meal."

I nodded. "Yeah...it's been a little bit."

When was the last time I ate? Was it when I was with Verity?

Surely it hasn't been that long...cookies. I had cookies with Meghan.

"Now, suppose we talk truths. What happened that separated you from the prince and the mission given to you by the Lady?"

I stared down at my hands and sighed. "It's a long story."

"We have nothing but time," Oryn replied lightly. "The moon is still young."

So, with as few details as possible about our little mutiny, I explained about the doors and the one that took us home, how there had been a trap waiting there, and how the same humans who kidnapped Faye, had spirited me away too. I told how the compound reeked of shadows and my fear for Faye, locked up in that place. My fear began to grow as I shared how I had escaped, and the guilt of leaving Da behind. I spoke of how Scarrington had found me in the woods, the way the Merfolk had tried to kill me, and my confusion over the matter. My story circled around to the beginning. I had forgotten to tell him of that horrible place of shadows and the monster that lurked there, the one that held Mum. Oryn's face fell.

"Can you help her?" I asked desperately.

"No," he replied, his eyes distant and sad. "She is beyond my reach, and to go to that place would be a foolish mission for you. She dangles in front of you and if you take the bait, he will have you at last."

My hope plummeted and I quickly wiped the tears that spilled out.

"How do I save my father?" I asked. Perhaps I could still save one of my parents.

"Your best hope is to return to the Central Realm and garner the aid of the monarchs," Oryn replied after a moment's consideration. "I must protect my people against the storm that grows."

"Scarrington said you could take me to the Central Realm through a mirror?" I asked, getting to the point. If the only way to help Da was to go, then I'd best be going.

Oryn laughed softly. "I often forget how smart that feline is. You would probably be shocked to know he's an Olde one. Not many remember who he is..." Oryn shook his head. "Oh, he knew what he was doing when he brought you here. He remembers how I loved your mother. He likely guessed how tempted I would be to keep you. You look just like her."

His stare was piercing, and I met it unflinchingly. "I know," I stated.

"I could tip the scales of fate," Oryn said, yearning buried in his voice. "If I kept you, perhaps you could be spared from the prophecy. I could teach you to weave magic; I could raise you as my own. My *daughter*..."

"I do not belong here," I pressed. "My heart yearns for home, for my sister and family. I have a destiny to fulfil, Oryn. I cannot run from fate. Even here, she would find me, and I fear what she would do to you and your people when she comes to drag me back."

"I know," Oryn sighed. "But you cannot fault me for trying."

I shrugged. "No, I can't."

"I wish to save you...as I wished to save your mother...it seems I cannot save either of you."

"I need to travel to the Central Gate. I was told you can help me do that."

"It's shadow magic, of which I am most skilled." Oryn stared at me, pondering. "You have a touch of darkness, child. I will teach you to weave the spell. It might save your life one day... Perhaps that is my destiny, to give you the tools to save yourself."

"We can only hope," I sighed, overwhelmed at the thought.

Oryn reached out, touching the bracelet on my wrist—it was the moonstone Mum had given me before we left for the Realm. "I gave her this," he said quietly. "I sought to protect her from the monsters that haunted her nightmares...I did not claim her soon enough. She was taken in the rule of Summer..."

"You helped," I replied. "I know you helped."

"Did she speak of me?" Oryn asked softly.

I shook my head. "No, she tried to forget, but I know that your kindness made the forgetting easier."

A long moment of silence passed. "Did she find happiness in the Mortal Realm?" he asked at last.

"Yes," I sniffed, tears gathering in my eyes as I remembered the years we had together before the world imploded. "She was very, very happy before the Realm tore us apart...even after it did, we still had moments of happiness."

Please let us have those happy times again. Please, let her make it home again.

I don't want to lose her again.

"That is all I wish for her," Oryn replied, staring up at the stars. "All I ever wanted was for her to find happiness, even if I was not the one who could give her such joy..." his voice trailed off. "I find rest in the knowledge she found it with another," he said at last. Tears were sliding down his cheek as he gently took my hand. "All I ever wanted was for her to find peace."

Tears gathered in my eyes as I looked up at the stars he gazed upon.

"I am so relieved she found it," Oryn repeated. "And I am so glad I was given the chance to meet and visit with you, her shining light."

79

The Odds Are Against Us, But I Have An Ace Up My Sleeve, And I Think We've Managed To Sufficiently Stack The Deck

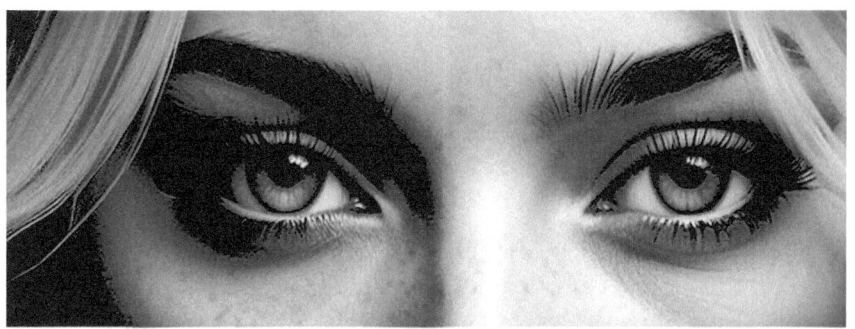

FAYE

"The gods envy us. They envy us because we're mortal, because any moment may be our last. Everything is more beautiful because we're doomed. You will never be lovelier than you are now. We will never be here again"

-Troy

It seemed impossible that we were out. I kept pinching my arm, over and over again, desperately trying to make myself wake up. It couldn't be real. We couldn't have actually pulled it off. But the more time passed and the further away we got, I began to realize that I wasn't dreaming. It was reality.

Clearly, I managed to stack the deck in this card game against death...and for once I WON!

"Faye," Ronan began hesitantly. "I want you to leave with Meghan. I'll go back to the compound and get your father—or die trying. Go with her and protect her. I can't have you getting hurt."

"No."

"Faye—"

"Stupid heeeead," I replied saucily. "I'm not leaving you. I will not leave you to fight that monster alone. Meghan will be fine. I'm sending her to a close friend. She will protect your sister. I'm going with you. You need someone to guard your back."

Ronan shot a glance at the rearview mirror. "I keep expecting a car to race up behind us, to discover the ruse and stop us."

"I know, but it's okay. We don't have to be afraid anymore. We did it, Ronan. We got her out. Now we just need to get my father out, and everything will be okay."

"Will it?" Ronan asked. Fear and grief filled his voice with every syllable. "You have my heart, but you're bound to the Realm. Faye, we're on opposite sides of the world."

"You could come to the Realm with me," I said quietly.

The words slipped out before I realized what I was saying, what I was suggesting. It was impossible, utterly impossible. There was no way he'd willingly leave the Mortal Realm, or his sister.

"And leave my sister alone?"

Stupid, stupid, stupid. Why would I suggest that?

"You're right," I whispered, trying to stifle the sudden disappointment and tears that rose.

"Faye, I—"

"It's okay," I interrupted. "It's, it's really okay. I shouldn't have suggested it."

"I have to make sure she's safe, that she'll be okay without me...but after I do..."

Ronan's voice trailed off. He was staring at me now and I couldn't bear it.

"Eyes on the road," I choked. "Just, keep your eyes on the road. Stop looking at me, you stupid idiot," I whispered.

"Faye, I'll come to the Realm," Ronan stated, at last turning his eyes back to the road. "I *want* to come. I would follow you anywhere, whether you want me to or not. But I have to get Meghan situated first. That's all. The question came out before I could think about what I was saying or how it sounded. If you didn't mind waiting for me..."

What will the rulers do to him? Will they allow me to choose who I love?

Could he come to the Realm without them killing him?

"I didn't think about what I was saying," I stammered. "You can't come. You *can't.* They'll kill you."

"They can try," Ronan scoffed.

"I can't lose you," I whispered raggedly.

Ronan ignored me. "I have not lived this long just to let a stupid Fey kill me." He shot me a meaningful glance. "That includes you, my dear Chaos Bunny."

I laughed despite myself as Ronan pulled off on the side of the deserted highway into a dense wooded area.

"We've been on the road two hours now. I think it's far enough away that we can risk getting Megs out of the trunk."

"She's bound to be cranky," I murmured. "Being cooped up all this time. I have no doubt the ride has been anything but comfortable."

"I came prepared," Ronan laughed. "I have cookies."

"Bribery?" I scoffed.

Ronan arched an incredulous eyebrow. "Says the pot to the kettle."

I rolled my eyes, refusing to answer the statement.

A muffled screech interrupted our discussion. "Let me out of here, you stupid jerk-faces!" Meghan yelled angrily.

"Like I said, cookies," Ronan laughed.

"Seems like a smart choice," I giggled as Ronan popped the trunk.

Meghan was irate. "You two can have your heartfelt conversations *after* I've been liberated from the trunk, thank you very much!"

Ronan held the bag of cookies up and Meghan eyed the offering critically. "Do you really think you can bribe your way out of trouble?"

Ronan glanced at the cookies, then back at her. He raised his eyebrows, as if to say yes.

"Okay, fine. Give them here. But I would like it to be noted that I do *not* like to be kept out of conversations."

"Noted," Ronan laughed. "Now come on, we have a long trip ahead of us."

"That's because somebody lives in stupid *Alaska!*" I snorted.

"I've told you, it's not in Alaska," Ronan snorted. "We live in *Oregon!*"

Oregon?!

The drive was long and exhausting, but hope kept us awake and in good humor as Ronan and I took turns driving. At last, I recognized the landscape around us. We were close to home.

"I know where we are," I whispered excitedly as we drove through the outskirts of town.

"So, this is the town where you grew up?"

"No, not exactly. We moved here when I was a kid...this place gave my family a lot of trouble. They were never kind to them."

"We have an extra five minutes," Ronan mused. "How about I let you out, and you walk around. You're the scariest thing here, and small towns remember. You're nothing but a ghost to them. How about you make them regret their poor life choices?"

I shot him a conspiratorial look. "I do think we could use some more snacks, plus you have some cash saved up. We'll pop into the grocery store. I wish I had my armor and blades, though. That would really add to the effect."

"Oo! Snacks!" Meghan cheered from the back seat. "This is the best road trip ever!"

"Plus, we need to get Meghan some things for the trip."

"But I don't want to go," Meghan protested. "I want to stay with you guys. You're way more fun."

"We'll have plenty of fun. But there are a few things that need to be done first," I replied soothingly. "Right now, you can't stay with us, okay? I know you don't like it, but that's how it is. If you aren't out of the picture, Jeremiah can continue to use you against us. We need to be able to defeat him."

Meghan sighed. "Yeah...okay."

"That's my girl," I said encouragingly. "We won't need to get you clothes since you're about the same size as Ember and Evadne. You can pack from their closet."

It's not like Em or Eva are going to need their clothes anymore now that they're in the Realm...

"How am I going to get there?" Meghan asked.

"There's a Greyhound bus station at the edge of town. It'll take you to my friend."

Meghan looked as if she was going to ask something else, but changed her mind at the last minute and lapsed into silence as we pulled into town.

It was an understatement to say I enjoyed the looks of shock and surprise on people's faces when they saw me strolling through the grocery store's doors. Covered in scars, sporting my pointed ears and an especially feral grin that promised violence. I took great, *wicked* delight in making sure these people remembered me, and perhaps regretted the isolation of my family. Playing on the guilty consciences they already possessed was my ally. Now, it would be a long while before they went anywhere without looking over their shoulders, wondering if I was waiting in the darkness, intent on making them pay.

"That was the most amazing thing I've ever seen," Meghan laughed as we carried shopping bags into my home. I stopped, staring in dismay at the disarray. Something had happened. The house was covered in a layer of dust, but parts and pieces had been disturbed. Some spots were downright wiped clean while others remained untouched.

I sighed. "Mum's gonna have a cow when she gets home. She worked so hard to keep the house clean..." my voice trailed off as I stared at the floor. It looked as if someone had cleaned up a puddle of something here and there.

There was something strange about the house, beyond the mess and chaos. Something else had happened. I licked my finger and traced a rune on the door, seeking the last important moments this house had held. A gentle wind blew through it stirring up the fine layer of dust that lay on everything. The dust took form. Ember's face stood in the doorway, and beside her, Artemis. She was saying something, but her words were lost, unreachable by the spell. Artemis took her hand, his expression gentle, and together, they turned and left the house.

"They were here," I whispered.

There were so many missing pieces. I had no idea how any of this was possible, but clearly when they left this place, she left *with* him on good terms.

"He's falling for her," I whispered in amazement. "He's actually, truly falling for her."

I had never seen such tenderness from Artemis before. But I had seen glimpses of the care he tried so hard to hide. It honestly didn't surprise me he had taken a liking to Ember. If she was bound to the Realm, being with him was her best shot at staying protected. Perhaps he could find a way to keep her from the Last Gate.

"Whoa, that is seriously cool," Meghan whispered beside me. "Can you do it again?"

"There's no need to," I replied quietly. "My question was answered…mostly."

"So, what's the plan now?" Meghan asked.

"Well, we're going to unload the stuff, and pack you up. You leave on the eight o'clock bus. I'm also going to equip you with some self-defense items I know are stashed here in the house. Ronan is going to take you to the bus stop and make sure you get on and away safely. I am going to stay here and create the spell for Jeremiah."

Meghan sighed. "It's such a mess," she muttered. "I wish it wasn't…then we could be a normal family."

I pulled her into a hug. "We are a family. We made our own," I added softly. "You've got Ronan, now me. Someday I'll introduce you to my sisters, if we can find a way to do that…you won't be alone. Sometimes the family we're born into isn't the one we carry with us. But the family we choose, is the family that stays by our side no matter what."

Meghan nodded and her eyes filled with tears as we began to pull stuff out of the shopping bags. While we worked, I gave her a detailed plan as to where she was going. We had lucked out. The bus ticket was a one-way trip without any changes or transfers. Other than rest stops, it would take her straight there.

Soon, we lost track of the hours, and it was time for Meghan to leave.

I pulled her into a tight hug. "Keep your wits about you, and your head on a swivel. Don't trust anyone, and I mean *anyone*. Listen to your gut. If it tells you something's off, it's off. Okay?"

Meghan nodded.

"My friend's name is Branwenn. She has silver eyes and bright, silvery white hair. She knows you're coming, so there's nothing to worry about, okay?"

Meghan pulled her backpack onto her shoulder; Ronan had her duffle in his hand.

"Be careful. I'll see you soon, okay?"

"*You* be careful," Meghan countered. "You have the most dangerous job of all."

"Pfft, such dramatics," I said lightly, trying to ease her anxiety.

"I'll see you again, right?" Meghan asked tearfully.

"If I have anything to say about it, yes. Don't worry. I have a plan. Everything's going to be okay."

"Okay," she whispered, tears sliding down her cheeks. "If you're sure."

"I'm sure, stop doubting me," I giggled as I wrapped her in one last hug. "Now shoo, an adventure awaits you. Give Branwenn my hello."

As they left, Ronan gave me a quiet, lingering glance that seemed to speak volumes.

"It's going to be okay," I whispered.

"I know," he said softly as he gave me a quick hug. "I know."

They were gone for what felt like hours, and as I waited, I began to put the pieces together for the spell.

It was a complicated piece of old Rune magic that would give him an apparition of his wife. He would have five minutes with her ghost, nothing more. But I had some small, demented hope it would give him closure and bring peace to his fragmented mind. Maybe I could draw him back from the abyss and save some part of him.

I was chewing over the whole thing as I carefully carved the runes onto a curved stick. Then I strategically ruined a piece of paper so it looked old and scrawled some instructions on it.

The door creaked, and Ronan came in.

"Did she get off okay?" I asked as I put the finishing touches in place.

He nodded and sighed. "Yeah, she's safely on her way. I just feel like a terrible brother sending her off."

"It's the best thing you can do for her right now."

"How goes your end of things?" he asked, peering over my shoulder.

"Just about done. I only need to apply the finishing touches."

"Do you think he'll buy it?" Ronan asked quietly.

"I can only hope," I replied ruefully. "If he doesn't, we'll have to shoot our way out."

Ronan nodded. "I don't relish the fact, but I'm prepared to, if need be."

"If I knew the combination to Dad's safe, we could *literally* shoot our way out," I replied.

"Well, at least you're honest," a terrifyingly familiar voice drawled from the doorway.

I turned, shocked. I hadn't heard anyone else come in.

Jeremiah stood in the doorway, his face livid, eyes wild.

The game was up. Death had found I'd rigged the deck, snatched the ace from my sleeve, and taken matters into her own hands. She'd blown the whole thing up and tipped off Jeremiah.

At least Meghan is out of the picture. At least she's out of harm's way.

80

All The King's Horses And All The King's Men, Couldn't Put Us Together Again

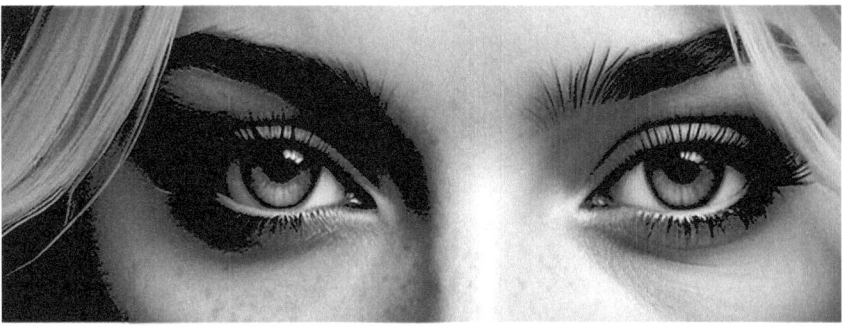

FAYE

"Don't smile. Stare intensely. Speak like you don't car about your own death."
-Miracolina

"Hello son," Jeremiah said softly. "You and I have some talking to do. This witch has put you under her spell. I'm sure you don't understand what I'm talking about, but I'm going to break the curse she's put over you."

Ronan's not going to play along now that Meghan is out of the way. I guess we'll just have it out here...we can storm the compound and get dad rescued...

Not really according to plan, but maybe it's better this way.

My heart was racing in my chest, eyes wide as I glanced frantically between Ronan and his father.

Ronan's face had drained of all color.

It's okay Ronan, she's safe. Meghan is safe.

"Where's the girl?" Jeremiah asked, his voice cold as ice.

Ronan didn't answer.

"I said, where is the *girl*?!" Jeremiah roared.

"Safe," Ronan hissed, finding his voice. "Safe at last, away from you."

Jeremiah had a gun in his hand now. He was pointing it at Ronan. "How dare you!" he seethed. "How dare you defy me."

Is it defying if you believe he's under a spell?

His logic isn't making any sense.

"How dare you refuse to care for your own daughter!" Ronan yelled back. "How dare you threaten her life when you should protect her. You're her *father*! You should protect her with your *life*!"

The gun went off and the shot went wide, shattering something in the cabinet by Ronan's head.

Man, Mum's gonna be pissed when she comes back and finds out Jeremiah shot up her house.

"How dare you!" Jeremiah repeated. "If you weren't my son, I'd kill you now."

"What's stopping you?" Ronan roared, furious. He was advancing on Jeremiah with every step. "What is the difference between me and my sister? Why would you hate her and love me? What did she ever do to you?!"

"She killed your mother!" Jeremiah screamed.

"She was a baby!" Ronan yelled. "She was a helpless, innocent baby! She didn't kill *anyone*! She was a helpless child, who should have been protected! The circumstances surrounding her birth do not negate the value of her life and your duty to protect her! You're her *father*!"

"Her birth killed your mother!" Jeremiah screeched, taking a menacing step forward.

"No!" Ronan yelled, coming nose to nose with Jeremiah. "You did," he hissed. "You killed my mother by refusing to get her to a hospital. You refused to call the ambulance. You refused to get her help. I was *there*! *YOU* killed my mother!"

Jeremiah took a step back, shocked. "So, this is what you really think?" he whispered.

"Yes," Ronan hissed, his chest heaving. "This is what I have always thought. I only ever kept silent to protect my sister. But she's out of your clutches now. Now at last, I can speak the truth."

"This isn't the truth, Son. You're under a terrible spell. She turned you against me. It's the nature of the evil Fey. She turned you against me. There was nothing between us before I brought her to our home. She's a curse, a blight, a disease!"

"She is my heart!" Ronan yelled. "*You* are the curse!"

Someone else was on the porch, steps heavy and stumbling.

Likely one of the men.

I screamed in heartbroken horror as Marcov shoved a bloodied Meghan through the door. His gun was pointed at her head.

"I warned you, son, what would happen if you tried again," Jeremiah hissed. "And now you leave me no choice."

I jumped into action, grabbing a knife out of the butcher block and with a yell, threw it to Ronan.

He caught it by the blade, and without even so much as a wince, flipped it so the handle was in his palm.

Marcov shoved Meghan away with a curse and I lunged forward, covering her body with my own as Jeremiah fired a wild shot at her.

The bullet went wide, just barely grazing my side before embedding itself in the wall. I pulled her close, ignoring the agony that burned across my skin. "Don't look," I whispered as Ronan knocked the gun from Marcov's grasp and buried the knife in his chest. "Don't look," I repeated. I watched in growing horror as Ronan yanked out the blade and, in one decisive movement, slit Marcov's throat.

Jeremiah kept his gun trained on me and Meghan, watching in bored disinterest as Marcov's lifeless body toppled to the floor.

"Well done, son. He was becoming a liability anyway," Jeremiah commented drily.

Ronan advanced on his father, blade dripping crimson.

"Don't watch," I whispered, keeping Meghan's face buried against my side.

No daughter should have to watch her father die—even if the father was a monster.

Meghan was sobbing. "He killed everyone on the bus," she whispered.

"What?" I gasped in horror.

"Marcov murdered *everyone* on that bus. Even after I got off to try to save them...he, he murdered them all...the children, women...everyone."

"Leave my family alone!" Ronan yelled as he raised the blade and lunged at Jeremiah.

"I am your only family!" Jeremiah roared back as he turned the gun on Ronan and fired.

81

The Morrigan

EMBER

"There is immeasurably more left inside than what comes out in
worlds."
-Fyodor Dostoevsky

The path led us to a little stone cottage that sat unbothered in the middle of the woods. Every window was a beautiful collection of stained glass. Flowers and swirling colors spread out across every surface. It seemed homey and safe. Completely out of context for the dangerous Moores.

A middle-aged woman came out to greet us with a wide smile. "Kieran," she called. "I've been waiting for you!"

For someone Artemis and Rosamond seemed to fear, she was almost too normal. Soft, chin length, gray hair with streaks of silver and pure gold framed her smooth face. Laughter lines lingered at the edges of her eyes and mouth. Her fingers were odd. They were long, and ended in sharp, curved nails. Streaks of black wandered up her hands from the tips of her fingers toward her palms.

Kieran grinned and wrapped the woman in a hug. "Mother," he said affectionately. "You knew exactly when I'd be home."

She laughed. "That I did, that I did. I see you brought our guests."

"Saved their hides, more like. You should have seen the size of that ambush."

"I told you it would be so," she chastised.

"Yes, and you are never wrong," he replied with a lazy grin.

Artemis gave her a careful bow, fist over his chest. His eyes never left her face. "My lady," he said cautiously.

Jacques, Rosamond and I followed suit, putting our fists over our hearts to show our respect.

I have no idea who this lady is, but she's even got Artemis bowing...she must be a very, very powerful person.

"Hello, Prince of the Summer Court, heir to the cursed Realm," the woman replied. Her golden eyes were calculating as she stared at us. "To what do I owe the pleasure?"

"We are just passing through, but your son said the Morrigan requested to see us."

"That I did."

"You're the Morrigan?" I asked, unable to help myself.

"What, is it a surprise? What did you expect? A bloodthirsty monster that would attack you for passing by? No, those are not my ways. Do you care to tarry and share a cup of tea?"

"We cannot spare a moment. Time is of the essence right now," Artemis replied smoothly.

"All time is a sacrifice. You must decide what you are willing to lose," the Morrigan replied cryptically. "I have a gift for the girl." She held out what appeared to be a shirt of deep green. "It's freshly washed," she stated.

"Uhm, thank you?" I whispered, taking the garment from her.

She wanted us to come so she could give me a shirt?

"We would be most grateful for your guidance or input for the path that lies ahead," Artemis said after a moment.

"You would seek the counsel of one your king exiled?"

"I would. I am not my father."

"That you are not...you are a great many things he is not...you will fight the tide, but it will be in vain, my sweet summer prince. You will lose. I have seen it. Death circles you, and she closes in for the kill. You must choose what you are willing to lose."

A chill ran down my spine at her words.

"Nevertheless, we must do what is right," Artemis replied tightly.

"What defines right and wrong, in a world drowning in grey?" the Morrigan countered. "Your hands are already covered in blood. Why do you seek to stop the rising flood? What righteousness do you dare cling to that was not stolen in the beginning?"

"I..." Artemis' voice trailed off.

"I have seen it," the Morrigan said. Her eyes were distant as she stared out at the trees. "I have seen what comes. You cannot stop death. She comes."

Someone forgot to take her optimism pill this morning.

"Do you want my guidance, Prince?" the Morrigan asked, turning to him with eyes narrowed.

"Yes," Artemis replied.

"Stand out of the way. You cannot stop it. Let it come."

"The Knight will destroy everything," Artemis protested.

"He will destroy everything you love if you stand in his way. Run while you can. Take the girl and flee; it is the only path left that will leave you with a small measure of happiness."

"What of me?" Rosamond cut in smoothly, pulling the Morrigan's attention away from Artemis. "What do you see of my future? Do you see death waiting for me?"

"I see a sacrifice, but only you can decide if you will give of your heart or not. I see a shadowy figure that screams your name. I see death...but I do not know if she comes for you or those next to you. Your path is undecided, and the bones are silent."

"Thank you," Artemis replied reverently, bowing. "We appreciate your guidance."

"Don't thank me yet," the Morrigan replied wryly, giving Artemis a sharp grin. "You do not as of yet know what it means. You have no idea what's coming, little boy."

Artemis bristled, but he held his temper. "Nevertheless, we thank you," he replied. He turned to Kieran. "Thank you for your aid in the ambush."

"Of course," Kieran said with a grin. "I have been dying to meet the prince and the much talked about Grimm." He grinned at Jacques. "Your reputation precedes you, Lieutenant."

Jacques smirked. "That it does, whether for good or ill, it does."

"I'll be seeing you," Kieran said, giving us all a friendly smile.

We all gave a varied arrangement of farewells and turned to leave. "Guard your heart," the Morrigan called. "Fate has marked your bloody, broken path. Destiny hunts you all."

"Just what we need," Jacques muttered. "More cryptic warnings to feed my nightmares." He angrily shoved a cookie in his mouth as he continued to gripe.

I had no mirth left within me to laugh at his ridiculousness. Something inside of me felt very heavy and I couldn't escape the ominous feeling that there was much left unsaid as my fingers rubbed the soft material of the shirt she'd given me.

What does it mean? What does it mean?

82

The Man In Disguise

EVADNE

"Lovely-eyed. Death-touched. Witch."
-Odysseus Elytis, The Dream

The surface of the tall mirror swirled in front of me. Oryn stood near, his eyes fixed on the shadowy depths. Three moons had passed as he taught me how to weave the magic required for mirror travel. The spell that would take me to the Central Gate was a spell of my own weaving, and some part of me was terrified to try it out. What if I had done something wrong?

"Do you want me to go with you?" Oryn asked, as if sensing my hesitation.

I shook my head, staring at the mirror. "No," I said at last. "You need to stay with your people. Protect them. A storm is coming."

"When it comes, I will return to you," Oryn said quietly. "I would fight by your side until death claims me."

"I don't want you getting hurt," I whispered.

"Death comes to us all, my child. If I refuse to fight for what is right as the darkness rises, am I not just as bad as that evil? Silence and fear give approval. I will not die a coward's death. I will fight with blades drawn and teeth bared. I will ensure death is scared to take me."

I nodded. "Then I'll see you on that dreadful day when the darkness comes," I whispered, my voice catching. "Goodbye."

He pulled me into a tight hug. "Even if you are not my daughter...I feel the responsibility as if you are. Be safe, child. Do not let the darkness extinguish your light."

"I won't," I replied, my voice muffled.

"The spell is sure and stable. It will take you to the Central Gate."

I nodded. "Goodbye then."

"Goodbye, daughter of Grimm," Oryn said softly as I stepped into the mirror.

It was the most disconcerting feeling. My body felt heavy as lead, yet dizzy and weightless all at once. Everything spun, but I kept my concentration together, continuing to envision the Central Gate as I took a step forward, and then another. Walking through the thick fog that swirled around me, I waded against the current.

A flash of light and then I was through, collapsing onto the grass on my hands and knees, heaving.

"I did it," I whispered in amazement. "I actually did it."

It was dark outside, and bright moonlight streamed around me from the full moon overhead.

There was a low growl behind me. I was not alone.

I turned, staring in horror at the monstrous, scarred wolf that loomed on the edge of the trees.

Fireheart hissed on my shoulder as I pushed to my feet. I had nothing to give the Gate. I had forgotten to get something to give.

I had one dagger in my hand, one that Oryn had pressed into it before I left. But if I gave that, I would have nothing with which to defend myself until I found the few weapons that might be hidden in my cloak.

What if I gave my shoe, or a shirt? I can't get them off fast enough and I don't have time to dig through my cloak.

Crap. I'm screwed, I'm really screwed.

A wild thought raced through my mind. There was one thing I could offer quickly.

I pushed to my feet and raced toward the Gate as the wolf let out a horrifying snarl and took off after me. The dagger was in my sweaty hand and, without any further thought, I sliced my braid off at the base of my skull and threw it onto the roots of the Gate.

The magic shuddered and heaved, and after a moment of resistance, I was through.

Loose strands of hair fell around my face as what remained of my French braid slowly came unraveled.

I wish I had my armor back. Stupid Anderson. How dare he take my things!

The wolf stopped and snarled at the edge of the Gate, staring me down. One of its eyes was badly damaged, milky white with a jagged scar that ran down its face.

I bared my teeth and let out the loudest and bravest roaring scream I could manage, trying to scare it off. Perhaps wolves were like bears and could be intimidated.

The wolf lunged.

Apparently not.

I dropped into a crouch, raising my blade. My mark held true, and I sliced through its underbelly. The dagger was wrenched out of my hand as the blade caught on a bone and momentum carried the beast forward. It snarled and howled, injured. But still, it turned and advanced.

I scrambled backward, afraid as I frantically dug through my cloak pockets.

There has to be another weapon in here. Why did Jeremiah have to disarm me? Darn it!

A huge form leapt over me, meeting the wolf in the air and tackling it to the ground. It was a second, pitch black wolf.

They both went rolling and snarling, biting and snapping at each other as they faced off and began to circle one another. The new wolf looked familiar. Deep brown eyes glanced at me for a moment.

That's the wolf from the Moores. But what's it doing here?

An arrow whizzed out of the trees behind me, striking the first wolf in the shoulder. It yelped and drew back a step as another quickly followed.

A Fey with bright crimson hair and a gruesome scar on the right side of her face stalked out of the trees. She came and stood beside me, her dark silver eyes fixed on the wolf.

"Get out of here, before I kill you!" she yelled.

The wolf snarled a challenge, and she spat a curse. "So be it. Today you die."

I watched amazed as she raised her longbow and, without another moment's hesitation, let the large arrow fly.

It struck the wolf in between the eyes, burying itself deep in its skull. The beast howled and toppled sideways.

The night was quickly drifting away. Nothing more than a dim dawn remained, with an ever-fading full moon.

The second wolf was limping away, back toward the trees, and we watched it leave. It stopped, body trembling, and fell to the ground.

"No!" I yelled, jumping to my feet.

It must have gotten hurt defending me...I don't see any blood, though.

The woman's hand wrapped around my bicep, pulling me back sharply. "Not yet, child. The beast hasn't departed yet. If you go over there now, you will regret it."

Departed? What does she mean?

The wolf shuddered again and as the moonlight faded around us, the wolf disappeared, leaving in its place a familiar, shirtless man.

What? That can't be possible...that can't be real.

Pieces I had missed were rapidly falling into place. Details that I had shoved away in my fear suddenly came rushing back.

Oh no. No, no, no, no.

I wrenched my arm out of her grasp and raced to Marcus' side, pulling his head into my lap as I searched his face.

"Marcus!" I whispered desperately. "Marcus, are you okay? What just happened? Oh my gosh, oh my gosh...you, you, you..."

"I must be dreaming," Marcus groaned. "At least if I'm dreaming, there's a chance you'll kiss me..."

He was dazed, delusional.

"It's no dream," I whispered as I pressed my lips to his. "But I'll kiss you anyway."

The red-haired lady made a sound of disgust. "Lovers," she muttered in annoyance.

"Oh, hello Autymn," Marcus groaned. "Fancy you to invade my dreams. I'd better watch out, you'll turn it into a nightmare. You're not going to kill me, are you?"

"It's no dream or nightmare, wolf boy. You went in search of the girl again. As for killing you, I haven't decided yet."

Again.

"The wolf won't hurt her," Marcus sighed as he stared up at me. "It just can't bear to be parted from her."

Autymn crouched by us, toying with an arrow. "You'll pardon me for not believing you," she said, pointing at the gruesome scar on her face. She glanced at me. "Seems you got lucky. You found the Mooresmith before it was too late."

"Doesn't she look stunning?" Marcus groaned as his fingertips traced the lines where metal met skin on my face. "I didn't think it was possible for her to get even more beautiful, but she did."

I could almost hear Autymn rolling her eyes, her disgust was so palpable.

My cheeks burned at the compliment. I had been so worried about what Marcus would say about my mechanical eye, and if he would still think me pretty, I hadn't even considered that he would find it attractive.

"She looks like she's capable of cutting a man's heart out."

"Let's hope her actions match the vibe," Autymn commented drily. "Come on, wolf boy, we have a lot of ground to cover."

"I have a name," Marcus muttered as he pushed himself up.

"But do you have a shirt?" she replied sarcastically. "You look like you stumbled out of a Harlequin romance."

Marcus' cheeks went crimson, and he muttered something about not having his enchanted shirt on at the time of the shift.

"Well," Autymn replied icily. "Be glad you had your pants."

The crimson shade of Marcus' cheeks deepened and he shot her a glare.

Completely unfazed, she returned his glare with a wink before turning to the second wolf.

Marcus' fingers wrapped around mine and he pulled me into a tight hug. "Are you hurt?" he asked, his voice muffled.

I shook my head, and he sighed in relief. "Good, I was so scared the Direwolfe would hurt you."

Autymn was pulling my dagger out of the Direwolf's gut and, after cleaning it on the long grass, handed it back to me.

"Thanks," I panted.

"You'd think a Grimm would have more weapons on her than just a measly dagger," Autymn teased.

"Well, it's a long story. I got disarmed."

"The prince should have trained you better," Autymn countered, rolling her eyes.

"He tried...it's a really long story."

"As all stories are," Autymn replied mirthlessly.

I turned back to Marcus. "It scared me, but it didn't hurt me," I said, answering his question. I stared at him. "You were a wolf...you're a Werewolf?"

Marcus nodded and sighed. "Yes, that is the curse I bear and have borne for the last six years."

"That's how you found us in the Moores," I said quietly, putting the pieces together.

"Yes, every full moon I morph, no matter which Realm I'm in. Human Realm has more full moons, so I morph more often than Fey born Werewolves. I morph with both Realm's full moons."

"Is it painful? Does it hurt you to change" I asked.

"You find out I'm a Werewolf, and your only question is about my wellbeing?" Marcus asked in disbelief.

I shrugged. "What were you expecting? Hysterics? Perhaps a declaration of my sudden prejudice and hatred toward you?"

Marcus shrugged. "Kind of...most people don't take to werewolves kindly."

I punched his arm, offended he would expect something so ridiculous from me. "Take it back!" I snapped.

"Okay, okay," Marcus raised his hands in surrender. "I take it back." His fingers brushed the ragged ends of my hair. "I'm sorry I didn't get here in time to save your hair."

I shrugged. "That's okay. It was overdue for a trim...I just, took it a little too far."

"It looks stunning on you," Marcus replied.

"Any day now, lovebirds," Autymn groaned from the edge of the trees.

"I don't care that you're cursed," I said, desperate to reassure him as we walked toward Autymn. "I love you regardless. In a way, we're both cursed with magic we don't want. But we bear what can't be changed. This plot twist doesn't affect how I feel about you."

"Autymn, you should go," a new voice called out.

We turned; a cloaked Fey was coming toward us. She dropped what looked like a loose handful of change onto the roots of the Central Gate and walked through.

"I need to see them safely to the Summer Court," Autymn replied. "It's too dangerous now. Someone *sent* that wolf after the girl. If Marcus hadn't gotten here, I would have been too late."

"I'll protect them," the mysterious woman replied. She pulled back the deep hood of her cloak to reveal her face. She had bright silvery eyes, a shade lighter than F and Theron's eyes had been, that almost disappeared into the whites. Her pupils, however, were a deep shade of purple, causing a sharp contrast. She had pale, porcelain skin covered in light gray scars, and her hands were blackened at the tips of her fingers. The black swirled up and down her fingers, as if she had dipped her fingers in ink and, after raising them, let the ink slide down her hands.

"It's not safe, Branwenn," Autymn replied gently. "You can't take that risk. It's okay. I'll escort them."

"No, it's not time," the woman, Branwenn, replied. "Trust me. Now is the time for my return. The rulers need this wake-up call. The Realm is in great danger. Go, see what the Moores hold. Find Hemming, before he makes a stupid decision. He lingers on the edge."

Autumn swore under her breath. "Foolish, foolish beast," she muttered angrily. She touched her forehead and bowed. "Thank you," she said softly.

"Go now," Branwenn replied. "We don't have much time before the darkness comes. The prince is soon to find how far the corruption goes. We have almost reached the pin."

Autymn's face drained of color; she must have understood what the cryptic phrase meant. "I think I'll find Hemming," she stated. She turned and, without another word or glance, left.

Branwenn turned her attention to where Marcus and I stood. "Come, we must away. More monsters seek us and we cannot let them catch up. You must live, daughter of Grimm. It is not yet time."

Marcus' hand tightened around mine, nervous.

With those ominous words, Branwenn pulled up the hood of her cloak and walked past us, entering the deep woods.

Marcus and I followed in uncertain silence.

I pondered the last time I had journeyed through the woods. Then I had been terrified, alone, and lost. Now, with Marcus' hand in mine, I wasn't afraid. With him by my side, I felt as if I could overtake the world and leave it burning behind me.

83

The Grimms At The Gate

EMBER

"A burning sense of injustice, sobs, sorrow: desire to fight back, and no
time or energy to do so."
-Sylvia Plath, The Unabridged Journals

The Ruins loomed ahead of us, its broken, jagged edges jutting up into the sky like the jaws of a monster. The Last Gate stood well in front of the foggy landscape, blocking the Moores off from the cursed place. In front of them a large bonfire burned, around which figures sat.

"Time for a family reunion," Jacques muttered. "How I loathe such events."

"Family reunion?" I asked quietly. "What do you mean?"

"These are Grimms...some of many. They're camped at different locations all around the Ruins to strengthen the barriers."

"There's other Grimms?" I asked, confused. "But whose kids are they? How are they related to us?"

"F and Theron had other siblings, and there were lots of other Grimms before F and Theron...they in turn had children who were born and raised to be warriors. The monarchs have used the Grimms as breeding stock to protect the Last Gate since the brothers' bloodline was bound to the curse. Often, the duty is spun by the monarchs as a noble sacrifice. The Grimms who disagree were locked away and silenced."

I turned to Artemis, suddenly uncertain and unreasonably furious. "Did you know about this?" I demanded.

He stared down at the pommel of his sword. "I knew," he replied hesitantly.

Anger burned in my chest, but I couldn't find the words to decipher the churning thoughts.

"Who goes there?" a voice called through the darkness.

Jacques muttered a curse, then began to sing in a steady baritone. "I tell a tale of a lovely lass, one who wondered, till the last. Abandoned by the one she loves, cursed to live and dwell above..."

"Ah, it's a Grimm," the voice laughed. "The loathsome Lady's Lieutenant to boot! Come, tell us what news you bring from those on high. Or are you here to spy and tattle on us to your great Lady?"

Jacques rolled his eyes. "Fortunately, these Grimms don't care for the noble calling. They thrive on spite and strong, enchanted coffee."

Yes! Coffee!

Artemis took my hand, and I stared down at our entwined fingers in confused frustration. I wanted to yell at him, but I wasn't sure what about.

Just give him a chance to explain...I don't know everything about this situation. He doesn't seem okay with it.

"Snitches get stitches, you ignorant lot," Jacques called out as we stepped into the firelight. "You should all know by now, I'm not a snitch."

"But you brought the prince," one snapped angrily.

"Hush," another replied, swatting the first. "You know how the prince has tried to help. He protected us the best he could from the rulers."

"Didn't save Mum, now did it?"

"No one could save her," a woman replied. She held out a hand to me. "I'm Annie," she said with a small smile. "The grumpy one is Felix." She went around the circle, giving basic introductions. "Philip, Archer, Alexander, Brooke, Felicity, Mary, Willa, and Griffin."

Jacques stepped forward. "You all know me," he said with a quiet laugh. "If you don't then you need to go read your history books. There's some pretty murals of my gorgeous face in there somewhere. This, of course, is Prince Artemis, Rosamond, and my baby sister, Ember."

"She was raised on the outside as well?" Felix asked with a gasp.

"Yes," Jacques replied. "I have two other sisters besides Faye."

"Why didn't you tell us?" Griffin whispered.

"I was hoping they'd be forgotten...I was hoping they wouldn't get dragged to this place."

The group grumbled in agreement. "Cursed lot we are," Brooke mumbled as she stared down at her boots.

"Well, enough moping," Annie said cheerfully. "Let's have some coffee. I doubt they're here to see us."

Artemis shook his head. "No, unfortunately we're not."

"Aw, c'mon prince boy, we were hoping you were here to set us free."

"Not yet." Artemis sighed. "I'm still looking for a way."

"Ah, such traitorous words from the ruler to be," Felix called as he poured a cup of coffee and handed it to me. "We're something of cousins, I'd reckon. Pleasure to meet you, Ember."

"You too," I replied distractedly. I was trying and failing to process the sudden onslaught of new information. The Realm as I had known it had suddenly shifted and changed.

Why did I never think there would be other Grimms elsewhere?

"You didn't know about any of this, did you?" he snorted. "You're pale as a wisp, and the way you keep glancing at your prince, I'm betting you're feeling every stage of anger right about now. If you're gonna fight him, give us a chance to place bets first. I'll put my money on the prince, no offense to you. If you were raised on the outside, he has a definite advantage on you."

"I..." my voice trailed off. "I don't know," I admitted as I savored the warmth of the cup in my stiff fingers. The rich smell of coffee reminded me of Verity's ship and a shot of pain cut through my heart.

Oh, how I miss that ship. It felt like home for the first time in forever. If only there was a way to have that and Artemis...

"Do you want me to tell you the truth?" Felix asked, staring at me over the rim of his cup.

I nodded.

"Your prince is not the monster in our story. He's responsible for saving at least a dozen of us from bad marriages to abusive Fey. He saved my sister Annie from the dungeons, and set our mother free from those dungeons. It didn't save her life, but at least she died in the Moores where she wanted to be. Our fate is decided, but he gave us a better future than what the monarchs would have forced on us."

"How many Grimms are there?" I asked, amazed.

"Right now, there's a hundred and twenty-five of us guarding the Gate. We have no littles in training... Against all reasonable logic, the Grimm bloodline seems to have dried up. Despite what the monarchs try to brew and torture...we are all that remains."

"And the ones...in the dungeons?" I whispered.

"Artemis faked the deaths of every one of them. My mother was the last. No more Grimms remain in the dungeons for Nightshade and Lillith to torture. They're either here or passed. He made sure of that."

Tears were gathering in my eyes and suddenly I was extremely glad that I hadn't blown up at Artemis and assumed the worst.

He really is trying to make a change, to be better than the monarchs.

Artemis came to stand beside me, his eyes searching my face. Clearly, he was still worried I was angry with him.

"I'm sorry I jumped to conclusions," I whispered.

"You didn't," Artemis replied.

"I did, in my thoughts..."

"But you controlled it. You paused and gave me the benefit of the doubt. I understand why you'd think I was the worst... I have much ground to gain back to prove I am not my father."

Annie held a steaming mug of coffee out to Artemis. "Majesty," she said quietly.

"Artemis will do just fine, Annie. After everything we've been through, you owe me no title."

Annie smiled softly. "I still can't thank you enough," she whispered.

"You have no need to thank me—it was unquestionable. How are you and Rand getting along?"

"Very well, it was a good match. He's incredibly kind and after what I've been through...it is what I love about him the most."

Artemis laughed, relieved. "I thought you two would get along."

Artemis turned to me. "I paired her with a Fey named Rand a few Solstices ago. It saved her from the dungeons and the dark magic that goes unchecked there."

"Whose magic?"

"Lady Nightshade's. After learning how to save Ríonach if something were to happen, she dove further into the Darke magic. She found a way to force Grimms to have more and more children, using them like breeding stock. The magic was violent and bloody. It was the beginning of the end for the Winter Court. I believe that's how the Knight has gained such a foothold over the courts. I think she's brought on his rise. It's through the darkness and corruption of those meant to fight to protect the kingdoms and their subjects."

"Princey boy has put the pieces together at last," Philip muttered as he sipped on his coffee. "If only there was a way to stop the rising storm."

"I'm working on it, I'm working on it," Artemis replied absentmindedly.

"So, two sisters, where's the other?"

"She was taken."

"What's Faye up to these days? Did she get posted to the Summer Court?"

"She was also taken."

Philip threw up his hands. "Don't they teach you anything in the human world about not getting yourself kidnapped?"

"There's a direct connection to the Knight," Artemis replied. "It wasn't any ordinary kidnapping in either situation."

"In these days, what *is* ordinary?" Annie scoffed. "Stop speculating and drink your coffee before it gets cold. Then we'll attend to business."

Business comprised of bad-mouthing the monarchs and their horrible, hair brained plans, and then deciding how on earth we were going to get through the Last Gate and get to my sisters. As soon as the gates were opened, it was bound to be a disaster.

"The monarchs sent you on fools' mission," Annie snapped angrily.

Artemis was finishing up his sixth mug of coffee. "I know," he replied wearily, rubbing his eyes. "I have been trying to figure out how we're going to do this since they sent us on said fool's mission.

The Last Gate resembled the Eastern Gate, covered with strange and powerful symbols. It, too, radiated power and darkness that promised death. In the darkness, the wrought iron surface glowed a dim crimson.

"Tell me you aren't thinking of doing something stupid," Rosamond said, bored. She was currently occupied with glaring at the fire. She and Annie had gotten into a heated argument about it, but much to my joy, Annie hadn't caved an inch, not even when Rosamond hung her upside down by her toes and lectured her for fifteen minutes. It was only when Annie told her of what happened when the fire went out at night, that Rosamond relented. The monster Annie described was one I was not keen on meeting, whether in broad daylight or at night.

"Well, something stupid may be our only hope. We have to open the Gates. Rosamond, if you stay here with the Grimms and guard the Gate while I am gone with Jacques and Ember, it may be enough to keep them safe when they open the doors."

"Do you know how powerful that magic is?" Rosamond demanded. "You can't just harness it on the first go."

"Well, I'm going to try," Artemis replied sharply. "I don't have any other choice."

Rosamond pursed her lips. "I don't like it," she snapped.

"I don't think any of us like it," Jacques replied with a shrug. "But, at the end of the day, it's his duty, because he's the future king, and it's ours, because it's our family."

Rosamond sighed. "Fine. But I still don't like it."

"I think you said that already," Annie quipped impishly.

Rosamond glared at her, but Annie, unperturbed, smirked back.

"We'll leave first thing in the morning," Artemis stated. "The daylight may give us aid."

"We can only hope." Rosamond sighed, glaring at the burning logs. "What has become of the Realm I once loved?" she said softly.

"It was sacrificed for power," Annie replied sadly. "Only the monarchs aren't the ones to pay the cost. It's the ones beneath them. We suffer, but they don't care."

"I care," Artemis whispered, his face unreadable. "I care."

84

A Tale Of Crimson Sorrow

EVADNE

"You deserve someone who is terrified to lose you."
-r.h.Sin

Despite the warmth of the day and its bright sunshine, my fingers were blocks of ice. I welcomed the heat of Marcus' hand in mine as we followed Branwenn through the dark woods. I was unwilling to let go. Whether for selfish or practical reasons, I planned to mooch every ounce of enjoyment from our time together. Holding his hand definitely fell into the enjoyment category.

It seemed like ages since we'd last seen each other, even though it had only been a few days since I'd given him that desperate goodbye kiss on the beam of Verity's ship.

We passed the time in quiet conversation, sharing everything that had happened since we'd been separated. I told him about Verity's ship, the broken curse, and Carl. He told me about Artemis' desperation to find us and his fear of losing Ember when he inevitably found us. Every once in a while, Branwenn would speak up and offer some sort of cryptic enigma, before lapsing back into silence.

"Branwenn," I asked hesitantly as the sun sat high in the sky.

"About time you asked," Branwenn replied.

"What?" I stammered. "I, uh...I haven't asked anything yet."

"No, but you're going to," Branwenn stated.

"I was just wondering why Autymn would have been arrested," I replied quietly. "I haven't heard her story."

"There are many stories you haven't heard," Branwenn replied. "You would do well to learn them all, especially those of the Legends. It may well save your life one day."

"What is your story?" I asked.

"One best left unspoken in these times."

What's the point of telling me to learn the stories, if she won't tell them to me?

"Even here, the woods are not safe," Branwenn continued. "Autymn's story, however, is one I can share freely. You may know her by another name. She is, in the lore, known as Red Riding Hood. But contrary to common belief, her being rescued from the wolf's stomach was not the end of the story. Haunted by the memory of what she endured, Autymn set out to ensure it never happened again. She became a warrior and defended the helpless. Her grandmother was a witch, one you might know as Marcovester Red. As the third Yaga, her story is shrouded in mystery and misconceptions. But what is not a secret is how she aided her granddaughter. She wove magic around the girl and turned her into a Legend."

"So, did she get the scar on her face when the wolf ate her?"

"No child, she got that scar when the wolf returned."

"But it was killed, wasn't it?"

"Hemming is no ordinary monster. He cannot be killed. In a fit of rage and desire, the wolf bound itself to Autymn. Forced to satiate the monster, Hemming followed at the edges of her life for years. She could sense him there, but couldn't find him. Finally, tired of the games, she set a trap for the man, and the wolf answered the call. She, by all human means, killed him again, but as I said, the wolf cannot be killed. Time passed and every time she set her snares, he came, knowing it was a trap. Soon they were caught in a tangled dance of bloodshed and romance. She laid the bait for the wolf, but her longing was for the man behind the fangs... I'm sure you can figure out the rest."

"So, she went from trying to kill him, to liking him?"

Branwenn shrugged. "They share a unique, though toxic, bond. They love and hate each other simultaneously. He wants to be freed of his curse, but the wolf will not let him go. She wants the man and not the monster...around and round they go."

"So—"

"Why can't she come into the Central Realm?" Branwenn asked, beating me to my question.

"Yeah."

"Because she's wanted for murder, as well as aiding and abetting a criminal."

"Who did she kill?"

"The last queen of the Summer Court."

My mouth fell open in shock.

"Quillon had another wife before Lillith. She was a vicious creature named Visha, but she was barren. Attempting to make her womb fertile, Visha began to practice dark, evil magic. The further she went, the more she lost her sanity. Her attempts were futile, no magic, no matter how bloody, can produce life in dead places. Growing desperate, Visha set a trap for Autymn. She made the foolish choice to kidnap Autymn's sister, Victoria. Hemming, head over heels in love with Autymn, set out to rescue poor Victoria. He impulsively followed the trail of Victoria's blood left by Visha's brutal guards. But by the time he got to her, it was too late. Victoria was already dead. Visha's guards had left her corpse out as bait to catch Hemming's monster. It was all a trap. Hemming and Victoria were both pawns in a greater hunt for Autymn. The mad queen was convinced it was the blood of a powerful, female Legend—one gifted magic by one of the sisters three—that would reverse her infertility. On the night of the equinox, under the light of the full moon, Visha planned to sacrifice Autymn in a *terrible* spell."

I shuddered. "That's awful."

Branwenn nodded. "Indeed it was. Autymn showed up ready to destroy the Summer Court and destroy it she did. Winter was in power, but Quillon was in the Central Realm on business. In a matter of hours Autymn laid waste to the Summer Court. With several unnamed accomplices, she burned the Summer Palace to the ground and set Hemming free. Hemming's wolf took control and together they killed the queen." Branwenn sighed. "The revenge was justified, but it was not recognized as such. The casualties slaughtered in their quest for vengeance were far too great." She turned sad, silver eyes on us. "You see, daughter of Grimm, we are all monsters of our own making...no one here is really truly good, and the ones we seek to save, are always lost in the end."

"What are you saying?" I whispered.

"You cannot stop fate," she replied sadly. "Death comes to all. You cannot slow her steps."

"I don't seek to stop death," I said, my mind spinning.

"But you will, daughter of Grimm," she whispered as she turned back to the path. "Oh, how you will try."

85

Brenna

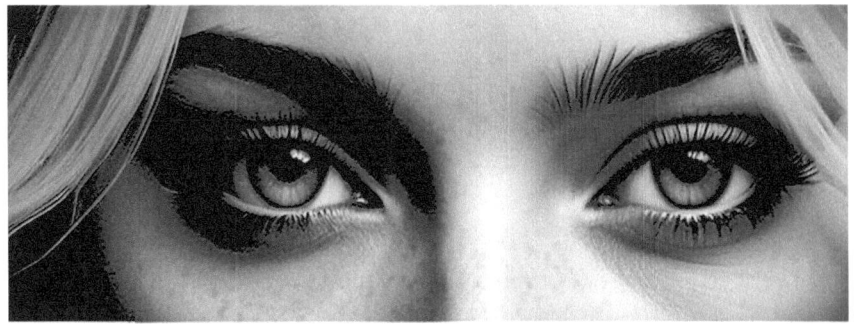

FAYE

"Seek for me never, keep your course true—when I am needed I'll come
to you, then I will show you road without end—why do you fear me, I
am your friend."
-Death, Clarence E. Flynn

I watched in horror as Ronan's body fell. Meghan screamed, shoving her way out of my arms and rushing to his side. I was screaming, I knew I was. I could feel the strain on my vocal chords, but I couldn't hear anything. All I could process was Meghan's terrified voice.

Ronan's eyes were wide as he looked at me. For the first time, I saw true despair and hopelessness etched in his features.

No. No, no, no.

I'm still standing. I can still fight.

I'll kill Jeremiah. We'll get Ronan to the hospital. We'll call an ambulance. We'll find a way out of this. I'll find a way through this. We're not going back. We're not going back to that place!

This ends now.

I turned on Jeremiah, my heart breaking as I realized the consequences that awaited me. My only advantage against Jeremiah would mean my death—The Darkness would come for me.

She's worth it. Meghan's worth it.

I won't let him hurt her. I won't let him take us back there.

"Help her," Ronan's choked whisper cut through the panicked thoughts, blocking out everything.

Help her. Help her.

I raised my hands, lightning dancing across my fingertips as I sent one bolt, and then another at Jeremiah.

Shadows jumped from his back, counteracting my attack.

That's impossible.

Jeremiah raised his hands and pure, unfiltered power rushed from his palms. Poisonous shadows from the Ruins ripped through my chest, silencing my power.

That's not possible. He can't...he can't...

My Inheritance went silent. Gone from my grasp.

NO!

Abandoning my first plan, I decided on brute force. Stumbling forward, I snatched the knife from where Ronan had dropped it on the floor.

Meghan cradled Ronan's limp body, her hands pressed against his torso, desperately trying to staunch the welling flow of blood that spread across his shirt.

My steps were unsteady, heartbeat uneven in my chest as my talisman burned against my skin, fighting to keep me alive against the darkness that sought to destroy me.

We're not going back there. We are not going back to the place! I won't let you take me.

Another blast of shadows and I fell to my knees, weakened beyond belief.

No, no, no.

I hurled the knife, end over end, intent on burying it in his heart.

The shadows rose, knocking the blade aside.

Jeremiah advanced, his eyes crazed.

Shadows poured out of him and materialized into burning chains of iron that bound me in a second.

"You will *never* escape," Jeremiah hissed. "You're going to meet the King, my dear. He has quite the present for you. His plans for the future are glorious. All will fall beneath his feet and you will be his weapon."

I screamed in defiance, fighting against his hold, searching, searching, searching for my Inheritance. Something, anything to help me.

It was nowhere to be found.

I was still screaming as the shadows pierced my mind and the world went black.

The sound of sobbing woke me up.

Where am I? What happened?

Reality came back in bits and pieces, and I jerked, searching for Ronan.

He was on the floor beside me, Meghan huddled at his side, pressing worn kitchen towels to his wound, trying to keep pressure on it as best she could with her wrists handcuffed in front of her.

The middle seats of the vehicle had been removed, and all of our hands had been handcuffed and then chained to the seat anchors.

Jeremiah's shadows still held me immobile; they now gagged me as well. Sharp edges dug into my face, and I could feel them under my skin, feeding on my blood, draining my strength.

He drove in furious silence, breaking every speed limit to excess. As the hours dragged on, I began to wonder if something was also shielding our vehicle from detection. There was no way he could drive at over double the speed limit in such an incredibly reckless manner without being pulled over.

The madness had taken over completely; the Knight was clearly in control. Jeremiah was too far gone.

Meghan's face was white, and she couldn't stop crying as she tried to keep Ronan stable. Unable to help, I prayed to what powers may be that he would survive.

Let him live. Please, please, let him live.

In my mind's eye, I was standing over Ronan's body, arguing with death herself that she couldn't have him. I wouldn't let her take him from me.

If you must have a soul, take mine. We both know I'm well overdue for our teatime. I'll stay with you forever. I'll be good. Just don't take him!

"I'm sorry," Meghan whispered, over and over as Ronan drifted in and out of consciousness. "I'm so sorry, Ronan."

"You're worth it," Ronan whispered back breathlessly. "You're...worth...it...every ounce of blood and pain, Megs...be brave...try to be brave..."

I longed to whisper my own apologies to him. *I'm sorry it didn't work, Ronan. I'm so sorry.*

As if sensing my regret, Ronan murmured his own reassurances. "Not your fault, it's not your fault, chaos...bunny."

It was an excruciatingly gruesome drive back. Sitting in the same position for hours on end, my legs were nothing but a distant memory. There was no water in the vehicle, and we quickly became dehydrated. As the night dragged on, Jeremiah began to mutter in another language. Old, powerful words, full of darkness and hatred spewed from his mouth as the edges of his body began to flicker. His shadows danced, hungry for violence and bloodshed as they fed on me.

I wouldn't admit it to anyone, but I was terrified.

At last, the sun rose, and the dreaded compound came into view. Jeremiah had completed the two-day drive in the span of a single night, and we hadn't been pulled over once.

I watched in anxious silence as Jeremiah's men poured out of the building and stood at attention.

Swearing, Jeremiah swerved, nearly hitting several of his men as he recklessly parked the vehicle. The shadows receded, and I nearly cried in relief as the darkness within my mind and body lapsed for just a moment.

Meghan whimpered as Jeremiah jumped out.

"It's okay," I whispered, taking advantage of a moment without the monster. I scooted forward as much as I could with my body aching and numb. "Be brave, sweet girl, it's going to be okay. I'm going to try to find a way out of this, I—"

Jeremiah wrenched the passenger door open, cutting off my words.

"Take him away," Jeremiah spat at James and another man, throwing him the keys to the chains that secured the padlocks.

I held onto Ronan's arm tightly. "You can't just take him!" I protested. "He needs help. Your son needs medical attention, Jeremiah. Take him to the hospital! Don't just throw him into some cell to die!"

"If it's the will of death to take the boy, I will not stand in his way," Jeremiah spat. "Ronan is my son; this is a lesson he must learn. You've turned him against me, witch.

I must break the spell you put over him."

"I didn't do anything!" I seethed.

"Take her to my office and put the despicable filth of my bloodline in the box."

"No," Meghan breathed, her eyes filling with tears.

Jeremiah heard her desperate whisper, and his face broke into a cruel grin. "Don't worry. Death will soon come for you. You'll remain in the box until he comes for you, or until I come up with a more suitable end."

"Don't you dare!" I yelled, lashing out, trying to protect Meghan. Between protecting Ronan, and protecting Meghan, I knew Ronan would want me to protect Meghan.

My protests were useless as the men lunged into the vehicle and dragged me out. I could barely feel my limbs, but still I fought and struggled. "No! NO!"

I reached for my Inheritance, but it was still gone. My mind was nothing but an empty echo, a tomb that had been robbed.

It took four men to hold me back as they dragged Meghan away from me.

"Be brave!" I cried, trying to give her something to hold onto. "Be brave, we'll find a way out of this!"

"No, you won't," Jeremiah hissed, grabbing my chin and forcing me to look into his cold blue eyes. "Your time is up, Grimm. Tell me how to weave the spell." He was waving the coffee-stained paper in my face.

He doesn't know the truth...he doesn't know it's partially a ruse...there's still hope I can twist this...maybe?

My mind was spinning, desperately trying to pull the pieces back together. "You went back on our bargain!" I cried. "He chose me. Ronan chose me," I cried. "You went back on our bargain!"

"No, I didn't," Jeremiah replied calmly.

"He chose to take his sister out, that was part of the deal. If he chose to take her away from here, you weren't allowed to stop him."

"I agreed to let him take her out if he so wished, *after* my wife was returned to me." Jeremiah's cruel smile widened. "Of course, I was going to kill her before we even reached that point. She was going to go...in a body bag."

"You monster!" I yelled as the men began to drag me back through the cursed doors of the compound. "I'll kill you for this," I screamed. "I'll make you regret doubling back on our bargain!"

"No," Jeremiah replied calmly. "No, I don't think I will."

There was no way out. We were good and truly doomed. Tied to a chair and unable to move, I watched in horror as Jeremiah's men dragged my father into the room.

"Let him go!" I yelled. "He has nothing to do with this!"

"Tell me how to work the spell," Jeremiah stated. "And maybe I'll let him live."

"You only have half the spell," I whispered, desperate to make him understand. "You have to have the stick."

"Here's a new stick," Jeremiah mused, offering me a jagged branch from a cedar tree. "Create it again."

"Free my hands," I whispered. "And reinstate our bargain."

"Don't help him!" Dad cried out.

Jeremiah nodded to his men, and in an instant, they roughly gagged him.

It's okay, Dad, we're gonna get through this. I'll give him closure, it'll be enough.

"I'll reinstate our bargain when I have my wife back," Jeremiah growled. He grabbed my face, forcing me to look into his eyes. "I won't have you deceiving me again."

"I didn't deceive you to begin with!" I yelled, furious. "You jumped the gun! We were coming back!"

"You turned my son against me!" Jeremiah screeched. "You turned my own son against me!"

"You're going back on our bargain!" I continued, furious.

What are we going to do? What are we going to do??

Jeremiah freed my hands, but my elbows and torso were still tied to the chair. With my feet bound to the legs, I couldn't get enough momentum to topple and break the wood. My hands shook as I carefully carved the runes into the stick with a dull knife.

If I tried to cut my bonds, it wouldn't work...they'd subdue me...maybe I can find a way to kill Jeremiah if I get him close enough?

Jeremiah cleared his throat, giving me a meaningful look as he turned to my father. A man stood behind him, hands at the ready to snap his neck.

No. I can't try anything. They'll kill him.

This spell isn't going to work. This will only give him a few minutes. He's going to know, he's going to know!

It wasn't supposed to be this way. This wasn't how it was supposed to happen.

My brain cells had fled, disappeared entirely. There were no ideas left to be found, no chaotic inspiration. There was nothing left but the empty echoes of my footsteps and the sound of my pleading screams as I searched for an idea.

"Here," I whispered as I finished the last rune. "Now let us go. Let Ronan, my father, Meghan, and me go. *That* was our agreement. Honor our agreement!"

"No," Jeremiah snapped. "Weave the spell. Maybe then I will let you go." He stared down at the stick and then the paper. "You do it."

"I won't finish the spell," I threatened. "I won't do it, unless you let them go!"

"I'll kill your father," Jeremiah hissed as he raced around his desk and pulled a long knife out of a drawer. "I'll kill him," he panted as he pushed his man away and pressed the blade against Dad's throat.

No, no, no.

"This wasn't the bargain!" I yelled as the shadows around us deepened.

"You manipulated that bargain," Jeremiah replied. His eyes were bloodshot, crazed as he stared at the knife. "You manipulated it, witch, by turning my son against me. Now finish the spell, or he dies."

Maybe if I finish it, he'll get closure. Maybe it'll give him closure and he'll let us go.

And if he doesn't? What then?

I don't know. I don't know.

My powers were gone. There was nothing left as the shadows in the room drained my strength.

"Don't hurt him," I whispered, my voice trembling. "Please," I sobbed as I stabbed the end of my finger and wiped the blood on the runes as I whispered the complicated words of the spell.

It was a desperate prayer, a plea to the spirits held captive at the Ruins. Brenna's name echoed in the sudden silence around us as I held my breath and waited.

Please, let her come. Let her come.

The Knight hadn't done his duty to death's realm since he'd been bound to the Ruins. As the guardian bound to the cemetery, he was supposed to ferry the souls to whatever end lay after death. Neglecting his duty meant the souls of the dead endlessly wandered the Ruins and the Shadewyrld—cursed to nothingness.

The air shimmered around us as an ethereal form took shape in the dark office.

Jeremiah stiffened, his mouth falling open as the spirit of his wife materialized in front of him. "Brenna," he whispered hoarsely, falling to his knees. "Brenna?"

The woman was crying as she knelt in front of Jeremiah. "What have you done?" she murmured. "What have you done, Jeremiah?"

"I brought you back, I brought you back, my love. My heart, my love, my life."

"No," Brenna whispered. "You can't bring me back. You can't...I'm gone. Stop trying to kill what remains of me. Please, stop. Our children bear the weight of your madness. Don't do this."

Jeremiah lunged forward, as if to grab her, but he passed through her as if through smoke. "No," he whispered. He turned on me. "What did you do?" he screamed. "What did you do?!"

"Don't!" Brenna yelled, racing in front of me as Jeremiah advanced.

"The child killed you! The witch tricked me! She promised to bring you back...she..." he stopped short. "*Promised*," he whispered. "No, she never promised...she *never*..." his gaze turned murderous. "You *tricked* me!"

Tears were leaking out of the corners of my eyes as I desperately sawed at my bonds with the rusty knife, trying to get free.

Jeremiah wrenched the knife from my fist. Something cracked and popped as he turned it backward in his rage.

"Stop!" Brenna yelled, sobbing. "Please, my love, stop! For me! Stop for me!!"

"I can't!" Jeremiah screamed. "I CAN'T! I've lost you! The only thing that ever mattered! I lost you and it's all her fault!"

"*You* killed me!" Brenna cried, her voice breaking as she stood in front of Jeremiah, weeping. "*You killed me*," she wailed as she began to disappear. "Let go of your hatred—it's driving you mad. Please, don't do this. Don't do this. Don't—"

Her sobs were the only sound left in the room as the spell crumpled and she disappeared.

Jeremiah stood, dumbfounded, staring at where his wife had been.

"What did you do?" he whispered numbly.

"I can't bring back the dead," I sobbed. Perhaps if I told him the truth, it would make him realize. "It only brings the souls back briefly, because they're not bound like they're supposed to be...the magic's been corrupted in the Knight's rise."

"Bring her back," Jeremiah hissed.

"I can't," I whispered. "I can't...the spell only works once. It's meant to give someone closure, a goodbye...it's a very complicated piece of magic and it can only be woven once per soul."

"Bring her back!" Jeremiah yelled.

"I can't!"

"LIAR!" Jeremiah roared

"You can't bring back the dead!" I cried.

"LIAR!" Jeremiah screeched.

"*Please!*" I screamed as he turned on Dad. "*PLEASE!*"

The knife was still in his fist as I screamed, fighting against my bonds as he plunged the blade in, again and again, beating his rage into my father.

My fingers were desperately tracing rune after rune on my clothes, trying to summon my magic. But every time it rose, the shadows smothered it. The Knight was ensuring I couldn't access my powers.

Dad locked eyes with me as I struggled and sobbed. "Look away," he whispered. "Don't watch, sweetheart. Don't watch."

I was sobbing, screaming—desperately trying to explain to Jeremiah and save my father's life.

It was hopeless.

It wasn't supposed to be this way! It wasn't supposed to end this way!

"It's okay," Dad gasped as his head lolled forward and he slumped against the ropes, passing out for a moment as the pool of blood on the floor grew wider and wider.

Lightning flickered around the room, but the harder I tried to harness it, the further it slipped from my grasp. The shadows were all around me, feeding off my agony and pain, stealing my strength.

"Dad!" I sobbed. "Stop Jeremiah! Please, stop! He doesn't know anything! He's an innocent!"

Blood splattered and Dad came to for a moment, whispering the same thing over and over as his words grew weaker and weaker. "It's okay, sweetheart," he whispered. "Just close your eyes, okay? Don't look, don't look."

At last, I obeyed and screwed my eyes shut. I couldn't watch any longer.

"Bring her back!" Jeremiah roared as his fist collided with the side of my head.

The room spun as everything threatened to collapse. "It was a lie," I whispered, blood pouring down my face. "It was all a lie to get us out. It was supposed to give you closure. I can't bring back your wife. She's gone, Jermiah. I'm so sorry, she's gone."

"Liar!" Jeremiah screamed as the world around me at last went dark.

86

The Ones We Cannot Save

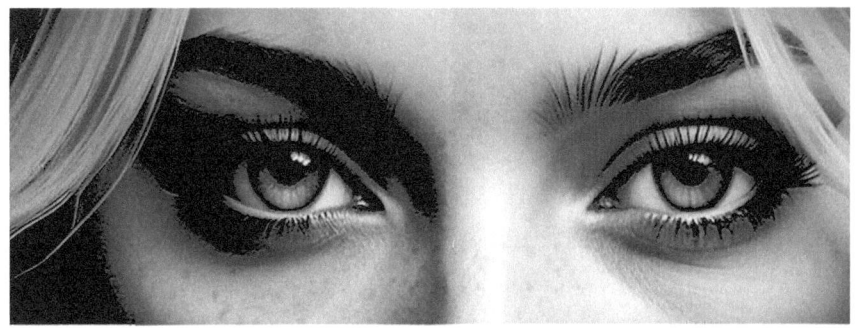

FAYE

"May the sins of our fathers be hung out to dry, cleansed by the waters
that swell from our eyes. So listen well daughter it's alright to cry, let go
of the monster, that you foster inside."

-Jimmy Osborne

I awoke in agony. Every inch of my body was on fire, but it didn't matter. The only thought I had was of my father.

Where is he? Where am I?

"Dad," I whispered, pulling myself up to my hands and knees as I began to grope around in the pitch-black cell. "Dad, are you there?"

There was no answer.

Jeremiah wouldn't have put us in the same cell.

"Dad!" I rasped.

My head hit the wall, and I rocked backward as the world seemed to explode around me.

"Dad," I sobbed as I began to follow the perimeter of the wall around the cell.

"Please, please, please," I whispered as at last, my hands hit something solid.

I was not alone in my new cell.

The face felt familiar against my fingertips, and I sobbed in relief as I summoned my Inheritance. With the last ounce of my strength, I sent a bolt of lightning across the ceiling.

Light flashed across my father's gaunt, bloody face. He appeared to be unconscious.

"Thank goodness," I whispered. "Dad, wake up. You have to wake up."

Seconds passed and I slowly became aware of the strained silence in the room. I couldn't hear him breathing.

My fingers hastily scrabbled at his throat, desperately trying to find a pulse. His skin was icy cold to the touch. I waited, holding my breath, frantically trying to find a pulse.

There was no pulse. No breath in or out. Nothing, there was *nothing*.

I pressed my head against his chest. Searching, searching, searching for the sound of his heartbeat, no matter how faint.

Please, please, please.

Minutes passed. Still nothing. No thud or tap vibrated against my ear.

He was gone.

No, no, no. This can't be happening. This can't be real.

Maybe this is a nightmare. Maybe I'm just dreaming.

I was pinching my arm, nails digging into my skin, trying to force myself to wake up.

Wake up, wake up. Please, someone, wake me up!

Time crawled as I continued to search, waiting for any sign that he was somehow, against all odds, still alive.

Please don't be gone, please don't be dead.

I was sobbing as I curled up against him, ear on his chest, still looking for any sign of life.

He was so still, and so cold against me as I choked and sobbed.

He's gone. He's actually gone.

I'm sorry. I'm so sorry. I should have protected you. I should have done something, anything.

Why couldn't I save you? Why was I given these gifts, when in the end, I still cannot save the ones I love?

Please come back to me, please, please, please. Come back to me.

Eternity passed as I clutched his stiff, icy hand and wept against his chest. Mourning the senseless murder of the man who meant the world to me.

87

Behold! The Worst Plan Of All Time—In Which I Get Eaten By A Cloak

EMBER

"Pull the lever Kronk!—WRONG LEVER!!—Why do we even *have*
that lever?!"
-Yzma, The Emperors New Groove

Artemis stood, sword drawn, in front of the Last Gate. "Ember, I won't tell you again. Get in my pocket."

"This is the worst idea you've ever had," I countered hotly.

"Excuse me little sis," Jacques called out from Artemis' cloak. "I will remind you that this is partially my plan, and you are being incredibly insulting to my cleverness and ingenuity right now."

"I cannot believe we're doing this," I hissed as I relented and stuck my foot into Artemis' WyrldCloak. My leg sunk down into the cloth and with a grimace, I stuck my other foot in. It was like being willingly eaten whole. "This is the worst idea ever."

"The Knight can't try to take you if he can't see you," Artemis replied with an anxious grin down at me.

"He could just steal your cloak and get two birds with one stone," I snapped.

"Look, as soon as I get in there, I'm going to harness the magic and channel to Faye."

"What about Evadne?"

"We'll start with Faye."

"Fine. Whatever." I didn't bother hiding my irritation. I had woken up on the wrong side of the campfire and Artemis' insistence that we act immediately meant I didn't get to drink a cup of coffee before facing the world. Grumpiness engaged, I fully planned to make sure Artemis never made that same mistake again.

How dare he deny me my fundamental right to have coffee when I wake up.

There should be a law against such ridiculousness. It is hereby illegal to do anything, or make anyone do anything, before they've had two cups of coffee.

Stupid Artemis, and his stupid cloak, and his stupid coffee denying stupidness. What a jerk.

I peeked up through the fabric, watching Artemis' face in annoyance as he stood in front of the Gate.

I sure hope this works.

"Open the Last Gate!" he commanded as the shadows swirled and grew on the other side, preparing for a fight. The insignia on the bicep of his armor glowed a deep crimson, and the runes on the gate began to glow.

This is the worst idea possible. This is never going to work.

The Gate slowly pulled open, screeching from misuse, and Artemis rushed through the narrow opening. "Close the Last Gate!" he yelled.

The air was different here, strange and haunted.

"Channel me to Faye Narah Grimm," Artemis commanded as the shadows lunged at him.

88

Prophecies And Desperation

EVADNE

"There's something disturbing about recalling a warm memory and
feeling utterly cold."
-Gillian Flynn, Gone Girl

The large doors of the throne room loomed in front of us, and I stared at them in trepidation. I couldn't pinpoint why I felt so *incredibly* anxious, but something told me this was not going to be a pleasant meeting. It certainly wouldn't have tea and biscuits, and given my current hungry state of existence, I would kill for a cup of tea and a biscuit or five.

I need to eat something before we talk to the monarchs, or else I'm going to go feral, hangry Eva on them.

As if sensing my violent thoughts, Marcus glanced over and gave me a sympathetic smile. "We'll eat our way through the kitchen after this is over," he whispered.

At the mention of food, Fireheart woke up and looked around. He was clearly disappointed when upon his perusal, he found no food.

"What are you, a mind reader?" I growled as I glared at him.

Fireheart joined my annoyance and shot a spurt of flame at Marcus.

"No, your stomach just spoke for itself. It was so loud, I'm sure the guards heard it down the hallway."

"Then take heed, or else I might just decide to eat *you*," I replied primly.

Fireheart nodded and bared his teeth, emphasizing my threat.

Marcus raised his hands in surrender. "Forgive me, oh mighty dragons. I shall not insult your hunger again."

I nodded primly. "That's more like it."

Branwenn glanced at us, arching an eyebrow. "I will remind you, Evadne, that eating a monarch is strictly out of the question."

Fireheart stuck out his tongue at her and I resisted the urge to giggle.

"I wasn't going to *actually* eat them," I protested. "I was just *thinking* about doing it."

Branwenn rolled her eyes and turned back to the door. "Well, let's get this over with. Maybe then we can find some food and avoid the question altogether."

Well, she sounds optimistic, but she also sounds worried. Why is she worried?

Marcus' hand wrapped around mine and he gave it three reassuring squeezes. All thoughts of eating him out of spite disappeared as I shot him a grateful glance. My anxiety was suddenly doing summersaults in my stomach and even though I wanted to hold his hand, I was unwilling to be the one to put him in danger.

It's not safe to love in a place like this...

Three squeezes. I, love, you...I wonder if that's what he means...

I sent back three squeezes and Marcus smiled. "If there's danger to face, we face it together," he said softly. "I love you, Eve. Let the monarchs see us united. I don't care what they think."

I love you too.

I gave him a grateful smile and squared my shoulders, preparing to face the crowds.

Branwenn pushed open the doors and, without another glance back, strode straight into the middle of court proceedings.

Is she allowed to do that?

Dunno, but we've got to follow her.

All eyes turned on our little group as Marcus and I followed her forward. The room became eerily quiet, and the crowd parted before us as Branwenn made her way toward the dais.

King Quillon and Queen Lillith stared in shock as Branwenn stopped before the monarchs and pulled back her hood.

The crowd gasped and screamed as her face was revealed to the room.

Both Quillon and Lillith's faces had turned white as they stared in openmouthed shock at the Seer.

She didn't bow.

"I have returned," Branwenn announced.

"Leave us," King Quillon boomed at last.

No one dared protest and the room emptied in a matter of minutes as a strained silence grew.

Quillon stared us down, rage visible on his features.

I felt vulnerable and exposed. Quillon was rattled, and I had no doubt he did not take kindly to Branwenn's *very* public appearance. Marcus gave my hand another set of reassuring squeezes, bolstering my courage as the message wove itself through my heart. *I love you.*

"What are you doing here?" King Quillon asked at last. "From what I heard, you were in hiding like a coward, and have been since before the Knight was imprisoned."

"Of course I hid," Branwenn replied icily. "I was acting in the best interests of future generations. Rulers do not take kindly to those who know the mistakes their future holds. I knew to stay away, lest *you* also try to kill me."

"You dare," Queen Lillith seethed.

"I *dare*," Branwenn cut in forcefully. "You know as well as I do, I cannot lie. You *would* have killed me centuries ago, if only to protect your Darke magic. You have dabbled too much with your sister, my queen. Do you have the gall to deny it?"

"Why have you come?" King Quillon interrupted, ignoring her question for Lillith.

"I have come to ensure the Grimm arrives at the Summer Realm safely, and to warn you of the cost of your blindness."

"You've returned the Grimm," King Quillon snapped. "Now leave us."

"I have not delivered my warning," Branwenn replied icily. "And delivering her is not what I came to do, I came to ensure her safe arrival. She is not yet *safe*."

King Quillon rose, scoffing, and stalked down the stairs toward us. "You're supposed to be in the Moores," he hissed, staring at me.

He turned to Marcus. "And you're supposed to be dead."

Marcus' face was blank and he shrugged, not giving King Quillon an answer.

I should have made him wait outside. I shouldn't have brought him in here. What if Quillon tries to kill him?

Quillon glared at both of us. "Give me your warning," he spat to Branwenn as he stared at our entwined fingers. "And then rid us of your presence."

"She is not yet safe," Branwenn repeated coldly. "I will not leave until she is safe."

King Quillon drew a sword faster than I could blink, laying the edge of the blade across Branwenn's throat.

No! Don't you dare hurt her.

I pulled my hand from Marcus' and, drawing my daggers, lunged.

Quillon threw out a hand, freezing me in place. Agony overtook my body as Queen Lillith worked her painful magic in retribution for my rebellion.

"I will not leave until she is safe," Branwenn replied calmly. "Put it away and release the girl. She acts in my defense."

"I could kill you now and rid this Realm of your toxic existence," Quillon snarled.

"You cannot intimidate me, for I have seen the end. I have *seen* your death, oh king."

"Ah, so you outlive me, is that it?" Quillon snapped. "You've come to gloat?"

"No. No boast leaves my lips. Only sorrow for what you have brought upon yourself. Only desperate hope that perhaps you will turn. I have come to *warn* you," Branwenn said softly. "Lower the blade, Quillon. There is still time. You still possess a chance to change the tides of war that rise."

Quillon sheathed his blade and released me. I crumpled to my hands and knees with a cry, gasping for air. My body felt electrified, and every inch of my being was in agony.

"Grimm, you owe me a debt," Quillon said suddenly.

"What, I..." dread plummeted in my stomach. I didn't like the sudden tone of spiteful glee that popped up in his voice.

"Marcus, step back," Quillon instructed. "This doesn't concern you."

"I'm not leaving her," Marcus replied fiercely.

The blade switched hands. Now it lay against Marcus' exposed throat.

"Leave him alone!" I yelled. I moved before I even knew what I was doing. This time I was faster. I knocked the sword away with my daggers and I lunged in front of Marcus. My Inheritance rose and water raced out of my blade, forming a wall around the three of us and blocking us off from Quillon. Dark shadows swirled in the pale, churning waves.

"Ah, the dragon grows fangs," Quillon mused, his eyes narrowed.

"Eve," Marcus said quietly, his voice urgent.

"It's okay Marcus," I said gently, tapping his hand with a finger. Three taps—*I, love, you*— "Just stay here. I'll deal with Quillon. He's right, I owe him a debt."

"What if he has you do something horrible?" Marcus hissed. "What if he has you kill Branwenn?"

"She will not harm me," Branwenn replied, her eyes distant. "He has chosen his path, cursed though it may be."

"I love you," I whispered. "It'll be okay."

I stepped out of my wall of water, leaving it behind me to protect Marcus and Branwenn.

Protect them. Protect my heart. I commanded my Inheritance.

"What debt do you require?" I asked, gathering my courage.

"Hold out your hand," Quillon replied, not answering my question. "I'm going to take my payment right now. Someday, you'll thank me. This will save the Realm."

Shaking, I placed my hand in Quillons. If I didn't honor the bargain, it would kill me. But I had a very bad feeling about his secretive plans.

As long as Marcus and Branwenn are safe, that's all that matters.

"Branwenn was right. I still have a chance to change the tide."

"You mistake my words," Branwenn angrily called out.

Quillon paid her no mind. His attention was on me now.

"Repeat after me," Quillon instructed. "A promise of debt, I on this day."

"A promise of debt, I on this day," I whispered, my voice ragged.

"Fulfill at last, I willingly waive."

"Fulfill at last, I willingly waive."

"What the King demands, I surrender today."

My voice faltered and Quillon stared down at me expectantly. "Your life, Grimm. If you do not fulfill the bargain, it costs you your life."

"What the King demands," I whispered. "I surrender today."

But what is he asking me to surrender? What is his request?

Ember still needed me; the Realm needed me. I had to fulfill this twisted bargain even though everything inside of me was screaming *no!*

I have to protect Marcus. I have to protect him.

I love you; I love you. Please know I love you.

"This memory I give," Quillon hissed in triumph.

"This memory I give," I sobbed as my head began to ache and throb.

What's happening to me? What's going on?!

"My debt is repaid."

"My debt...is...repaid." I collapsed, falling to my knees as I cradled my head in my hands. The world was churning, breaking and screaming around me. Something was wrong, very, very wrong. It felt as if someone was tearing my mind in half.

What's happening? What's going on?

"Fool!" Branwenn yelled behind me as the world unraveled and shattered around me.

In a matter of moments, everything fell back into place, and I looked down at my shaking hands.

I...What?

"What just happened?" I whispered, confused.

Quillon stared down at me, his face triumphant.

What did he do? What did he take?

The words of the bargain slipped through my mind like oil. I couldn't grasp them to remember what I'd given.

I stared at the strange ring on my finger.

Where did I get that? I don't remember that ring...was it given to me to protect me? Is it a ward of some kind?

It must have been.

Forget the ring, what happened? What did he do?

"I've stopped the prophecy," King Quillon crowed to Branwenn.

"Fool!" Branwenn snapped. "You stopped nothing. You brought it to bear."

"Impossible," Quillon snarled. "Without love, she cannot be used against the Realm."

"What do you mean?" I whispered.

"You'll figure it out," Quillon laughed coldly. "Well, no, you won't. But the ones around you will."

"I have to get to my sister," I whispered.

"You will stay here until she returns," Quillon replied dismissively.

"I will not," I hissed, pushing to my feet. "Get me a mirror."

"Why? You can't weave Wyrld magic," Quillon scoffed.

I looked around the room. Branwenn stood beside me. A stranger stood on her right, likely a guard of Quillon's meant to intimidate her, or perhaps her own personal bodyguard. Hulking guards stood at the door, watching the show with interest. There on the far wall, a floor to ceiling mirror stood.

I stalked over to it, fury pulling me apart. I was angry, so *incredibly* angry.

Why? Why am I so angry?

The surface of the mirror churned and writhed as I hissed out the spell Oryn had taught me. "I'm going to find my sister," I snapped. "If you try to stop me, I will follow in Autymn's footsteps."

King Quillon scoffed. "You wouldn't kill your king."

I pointed my dagger at him, shadows churning inside my mind and at the edge of my blade. "I might. Don't test me."

"Eve," the brown-eyed stranger next to Branwenn whispered.

He must be a guard.

"Don't call me that!" I snapped. "I don't even *know* you." I stomped over to Branwenn, pulling her away from the guard. "He might hurt you, Branwenn. Get away from him."

"Eve!" the guard whispered in confusion.

My arm was a blur as I lunged and pressed my dagger against his throat. My Inheritance rose, blocking the blade from his skin.

Move! Move darn it! What are you doing?!

"Leave. Me. *Alone*," I hissed.

The guard stumbled back, tears gathering in his eyes, and Quillon laughed in glee. "Isn't she magnificent?" he crowed. "I've stopped the fall. No one can use a prophecy against her now."

"Your desperate measures will be your downfall," Branwenn replied angrily. She turned to me. "I'm going home. I will see you soon, daughter of Grimm."

"Will you be okay?" I asked, worried about her getting back safely.

What if Quillon sends men, or an ambush after her?

"I will be fine. You need to worry about yourself. He's done something terrible to you."

"What do you mean?" I whispered. "I don't remember him doing anything...I...I..."

"That's just it, dear one," Branwenn replied gently, cutting me off. Her silver eyes shone with unshed tears. "You don't *remember*."

"That's enough!" Quillon yelled.

"Don't trust what you think you know," Branwenn said softly as she turned and left.

"Evadne, don't you *dare* go through that mirror," Quillon ordered as I turned back to the mirror.

"I'm going to save my sister," I snapped as I finished the final sentences of the spell. Buildings stood tall in front of me.

Strange. It looks like a housing complex.

Quillon's voice thundered behind me, but I ignored it as I stepped through the surface.

Just as the spell began to shudder and collapse behind me, Quillon's brown-eyed guard uttered a strangled cry and raced through the mirror after me.

"Eve!"

Together we ricocheted toward my sister.

89

Let The Darkness Take Me

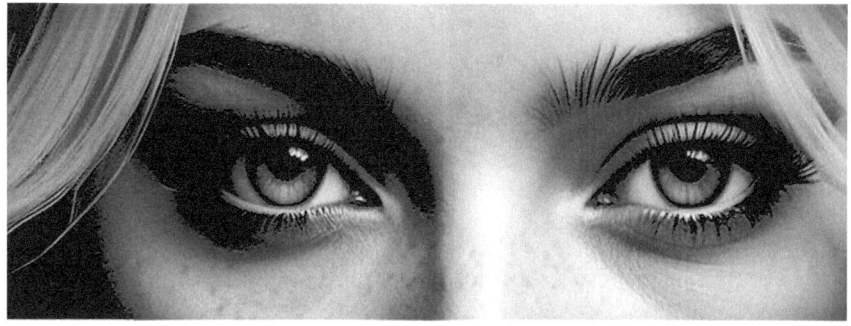

FAYE

"We fall from womb to tomb, from one blackness and toward another, remembering little of one, and knowing nothing of the other."
-Stephen King, Dance Macabre

The silence shattered around me as five men came crashing into my cell and dragged me away from my father's lifeless body. I had little strength left to fight as they took me out of the compound and out into the bright morning sunshine.

I looked around, frantic and terrified.

What's going on? What is Jeremiah doing?

My panicked gaze spotted Ronan first. He was a wreck, his face a discolored mass of bruises, nearly unrecognizable beneath the swelling. His shirt was in tatters, and what remained was soaked in blood. I knew the image well. He'd been whipped. His hands were behind his back, chained to a thick, wooden post behind him. He knelt in the dirt, blood soaking into the earth around him.

Much to my dismay, the men led me to a similar post a few feet away from his. I kicked and fought, using up what precious little energy I had, but it was useless. Soon, I too was kicked into the dirt and chained to the post with my hands behind my back.

"Faye?" Ronan rasped. "Are you okay?"

"No," I whispered numbly. "I'm not." My voice was ragged from hours of scream-ing. My head ached from all the crying. "He killed my father. He *murdered* him."

"I'm so sorry," Ronan whispered. "Do you know where Megs is?"

"No, he took her away...I don't know where she is. We're trapped, Ronan. There's no way out."

There was a scream, and I jerked, searching for Meghan. I watched, horrified, as Jeremiah drug her out from the compound by the hair. She was bloody and bruised as she stumbled and scrambled. She was clearly trying to keep her feet under her, but every time she managed to get her bearings, one of his men cruelly knocked her legs out from under her to allow Jeremiah to continue to drag her by the hair.

What is he doing? What is he going to do?

I looked around, frantically searching for the purpose of all this.

"Oh, cursed gate," I whispered, horrified.

"What," Ronan whispered.

"Ronan, there's a pyre. Look. He's lost it. He's insane. Utterly insane."

Ronan began to struggle against the chains as I tried to summon my Inheritance. The darkness could take me. I would not let Jeremiah kill Meghan.

Jeremiah threw Meghan on the ground in front of us. "Meghan Anderson, cursed child who bears my blood and name. You are found guilty of the crime of murder. You will burn for the abomination that you are, and the witch who stole my son from me will follow suit. Only then will my son be freed from the tainted thrall of her spells."

"NO!" Ronan roared.

"No!" I screamed. "Take me first!"

I'll end you before you have the chance to kill me.

"Wouldn't you like that?" Jeremiah hissed, crouching down to look me dead in the eye. "You will not be granted a chance to save her. You will *watch* her die. I will make you listen to her screams."

No. I won't. I won't! I won't let you kill another innocent person! I will not let you harm her.

My Inheritance was far away, leached from my very bones.

C'mon, c'mon. Please, please. Come back, come back to me.

Jeremiah was dragging Meghan toward the Pyre. I watched, horrified, as he and his men bound her to the post. I was fighting the chains, trying to break my hands to get out of the tight binding as Jeremiah's men threw what appeared to be gasoline on the wood and twigs piled high around Meghan.

No, no, no.

My nails scrabbled against a scab on the top of my hand, tearing it open. Blood dripped over my finger, and I desperately traced the rune on my leg.

COME.

Jeremiah lit the match, as I at last grasped the tiny, frantic thread of my Inheritance. The final spark untainted by the Knight.

He stared at the flame, letting Meghan's trepidation and terror grow as he gloated.

It was all the time I needed.

With the last of my strength, I sent a bolt of lightning at Jeremiah's chest. I would kill him before I let him harm Meghan.

Let the darkness take me. It will be worth it to protect her. I will not let someone else die because I am afraid of the darkness.

Let the darkness take me. Just don't be too late. Please don't be too late.

90

The Never Ending Nightmare

FAYE

"When day becomes the night and the sky becomes the sea, when the clock strikes heavy and there's no time for tea, and in our darkest hour before my final rhyme, she will come back to wonderland and turn back the hands of time."
-Alice, through the looking glass, Lewis Carroll

Jeremiah dropped the match with a scream as my bolt hit him square in the chest.

I watched in horror as a cloaked figure materialized out of thin air in front of him. The glint of silver in the bright morning light flashed, and the stranger plunged a dagger into Jeremiah's chest, directly over the lightning's strike.

Jeremiah's body crumpled and fell, but all I could see were the hungry flames that engulfed the pyre as it suddenly exploded. Jeremiah had added more than gasoline.

The stranger was propelled backward by the force of the blast.

Meghan screamed as the flames rose and obscured her from view. They were unnatural, hungry.

They're not mortal flames. Something is carrying out Jeremiah's dark wishes.

The hood fell off of the stranger and a head of wild blond hair met my desperate gaze.

It was Artemis.

"HELP HER!" I screamed desperately as Artemis shrugged off his cloak and raced toward Meghan. His body was a blur, but it wasn't fast enough. He couldn't outrace the twisted flames.

I dug deeper into the scab, drawing another rune over the first, and the chains on my wrist broke. I lurched to my feet and staggered as fast as I could toward the flames. Ronan's agonized roar urged me on as he fought to break his own chains and get to his sister.

The world didn't make sense, I was hallucinating as I ran. Ember was clambering out of Artemis' cloak pocket. A familiar blond guy pushed his way out of the other side.

It's Jack. That's Jack. It has to be, he has Dad's nose.

Artemis was wearing a WyrldCloak. He was carrying them in his pocket, likely because they came through the Ruins...

I sobbed in relief. Help had arrived, but it wasn't over yet.

Help her, please help her!

I couldn't even see Meghan through the flames.

Ember was ahead of me, racing after Artemis and holding out her hands. The fire swayed and shifted, fighting her command. Then, with a roar, the flames lifted off the pyre and raced toward her.

I watched, amazed, as Ember screamed and clapped her outstretched hands together. The flames disappeared with a hiss, dissolving into a whiff of smoke.

Meghan sagged against the post, skin blistered and red. Artemis broke the chains and caught her body as it crumpled.

She must have passed out from the pain.

Help her Artemis, please help her.

Jacques raced toward me, cutting down every man who lunged at me and Artemis. Jeremiah's men began to scatter, fleeing the savage warrior.

A quick blow from his enchanted sword and Jacques freed Ronan from the chains. Taking Ronan's arm over his shoulder, Jacques helped him limp toward us.

Artemis gently laid Meghan's lifeless body on the grass. I fell to my knees beside him as he pressed his head against her chest, as if searching for a heartbeat.

No, that's not the right gesture. She needs healing, not searching. Pull the smoke out of her lungs, Artemis. Heal her.

Artemis' face screwed up in concentration. He was still listening, searching. His lips moved soundlessly as he wove a desperate spell around her broken body.

No, no. Not her. Please, no.

Artemis looked up, his face anguished.

"She doesn't smell right. She...she smells like poison," he whispered. "She smells like the *Ruin's* poison. There was never any hope of saving her, Faye."

"Help her!" I cried desperately as I fell to my knees beside her limp body. "Help her, Artemis! Please! I'll give you anything you want. I'll pledge my unfailing allegiance to your reign in the Summer Court. I'll do *anything*! Just *save* her."

Ember let out a yell and raced toward another figure that suddenly appeared and began to stumble across the field. It was Evadne. She looked distraught and angry. There was someone with her.

Marcus.

Evadne shot Marcus an angry glare, but soon Ember tackled her in a hug. After a moment they turned and ran toward us as I wept and begged Artemis to help Meghan.

Artemis was silent, pondering something. His face was pensive. "I could possibly save her, if I could get back to the Ruins...the power is raw there...raw enough I could weave such a strong, Darke spell. Her soul is there since he hasn't performed his duties...but I have no way back, Faye. I can't get there in time. We traveled through the Ruins to get here, but we came in through the Moores."

"There's a door," I gasped. "Jeremiah has a door in his office. It leads to the Ruins."

Artemis jerked. "This is worse than I thought," he said quietly.

"You have no idea," I sobbed. "You have *no* idea."

Artemis scooped up Meghan's lifeless body. "We don't have time to waste. I'll take your promise as payment for the spell."

I didn't waste another moment. "I, Faye Narah Grimm, swear fealty to the rule of Artemis, heir of the Summer Court. I pledge my loyalty, strength, and Inheritance to the Summer Court during his reign. I will serve him to my dying breath or cursed be my blood to the darkness."

It was the promise I had held and denied everyone for so long. But it didn't matter anymore. The *only* thing that mattered was the girl I'd adopted as my sister, who lay lifeless in Artemis' arms.

I didn't care about my supposed ideas of grandeur and resistance. I couldn't lose her, not when we'd lost so much already.

"What about Da?" Evadne called as she and Ember came up to us.

My stomach dropped. They didn't know. They didn't know what had happened.

"He's gone," I whispered. "Jeremiah killed him."

Ember's face went white, and Evadne dropped to her knees with a wail. "*No*," she cried. "*NO!*"

Her scream echoed around the clearing and tears raced down my cheeks.

Artemis looked distraught and conflicted. "Em?" he whispered hesitantly. "I'm so, so sorry. But we have to keep moving. If we don't get to the Ruins, we'll lose the girl as well. There's no time, Evadne. I'm sorry. I'm *so* sorry."

Collecting herself quickly, Evadne pushed herself up. "Let's go," she gasped. "Maybe there's hope for her still."

Artemis turned to me. "Show me the way," he said urgently.

I pushed myself to my feet and, with a spurt of adrenaline, raced back toward the compound. The door stood open, but in a fit of vindictive rage I sent a bolt of lightning and knocked it off its hinges completely. The rune burned against my skin as the summoning spell fragmented and died. I had exhausted its use completely.

Marcus and Jacques were behind us, helping Ronan, and together we all made our way into the depths of the compound.

The office was in ruins. Everything had been destroyed in a rampage. The shadows fled before us, receding from the compound and back to the cursed place they'd come from.

Only the door remained unscathed in the wreckage. Runes glowed ominously across its surface, and Jacques' mark burned bright in the swirling darkness.

"What the heck?" Jacques whispered. "Am I blind? Has that mark been on every door?"

"Yes," Artemis replied tightly. "It just hasn't glowed."

What does it mean? What does it mean?

"Come on, time is running out," Artemis called. "Her soul is at the Ruins with the others. There's still time, but not much."

Ember, Jacques, Evadne, Marcus, and Ronan all gathered around me and Artemis.

With a final deep breath in and out, Artemis pulled the handle down and opened the door.

91

What Once Was Mine

EMBER

"Things we lose have a way of coming back to us in the end, though not
in the way we expect."
-Harry Potter and the order of the phoenix, J.K. Rowling

Cruel laughter surrounded us as Artemis knelt on the black stones and began to weave the spell. A shadowy girl stood beside our group, sobbing.

It was the girl Artemis was desperately trying to save.

"I need blood from both of you," Artemis instructed as he pulled back the tattered remains of the girl's shirt and cut a thin line from her collarbone to her solar plexus.

Faye grabbed a knife from the sheath on my thigh and sliced it across her palm. The dark-haired man followed suit. They grasped hands and together, their blood fell toward the girl's body.

Artemis began to chant in a low voice as the laughter around us grew.

The Knight was coming.

A whirlwind raged around Artemis as his eyes glowed a bright, florescent green. On and on the spell trembled around us, until at last the shadowy girl beside him disappeared and the girl's dead body jerked.

She coughed and gasped.

"Meghan!" Faye and the dark-haired guy chorused as they wrapped her in a tight hug. I could only assume he was her brother,

Artemis fell back, and I caught him before he crumpled to the ground. "Thanks," he whispered gratefully.

"I would have laughed if you fell," I replied jokingly. "And it would probably be terrible timing to laugh considering the situation we're in."

"There's no time for reunions," Jacques said tightly. "He's coming. We need to get out of here, *now*."

Evadne was staring at Marcus, her eyes narrowed. She looked confused.

Marcus was staring back, pleading, no, *begging* for her to just talk to him.

What's going on?

Did they get into a fight?

What happened?

The dark-haired guy scooped Meghan up into his arms and we ran through the Ruins, desperately trying to get to the edge of the courtyard where the Last Gate lay.

I could see the blurry outlines of people on the other side.

The Grimms were waiting for us.

There was a scream, the sound of which was all too familiar. It was my mother's.

"RUN!"

Faye stumbled, hesitating.

"Keep going!" Artemis yelled. "We can't help her!"

No! We have to get her out of here! We have to save her too!

The Knight emerged out of the shadows, and I buried a scream. It was the man from my nightmare. The nightmare where I ended up killing Evadne.

Evadne let out a strangled scream of her own and took off at a dead run. Her face was ashen, eyes wide with terror.

We were close, so close, and yet so far.

Jacques' foot caught on a stone, and he went sprawling. "Keep going!" he yelled.

I grabbed hold of his hand, unwilling to let him go as the Knight advanced.

"Go Emmie!" Jacques yelled. "I'm fine!"

A shadowy arrow went through his shoulder, knocking him back down to the ground again. He roared in pain, but started to push himself up. "GO!" he cried as the Grimms opened up the Gate from the other side.

Another scream from my mother and I watched horrified as Jacques scrambled to his feet, only to come face to face with the Knight.

"Hello, Grimm," the Knight screeched. His voice was the sound of razors on a chalkboard, slicing my mind to pieces. "I've been waiting for you."

Something slammed into the Knight, pushing him back. It was my mother's shadowy form. She had broken free of his bindings.

"GO!" she yelled.

Another figure rushed at the Knight—a dark-haired woman who bore an uncanny resemblance to Meghan and her brother.

Jacques pushed himself up, hesitating indecisively for a moment.

"Go!" Mum sobbed as she pushed Jacques toward the Last Gate. "Go, my sweet boy. GO!"

I grabbed his hand, and we raced toward to the Last Gate.

"Hurry up!" Artemis roared from the other side. His hands were raised as he and the Grimms fought to keep the Gate open.

I glanced back just as the Knight's blade went through her shadowy chest and protruded out the back.

"I love you!" she called, her voice strangled.

The other woman leapt on the Knight's back, pummeling him with her fists while Mum held onto the Knight's cloak, trying to hinder his advance.

In one quick move, he jerked his blade from her body and turned, slicing it through the other woman's neck.

Jacques and I slid through the gate just as it slammed closed.

The Knight roared in fury, as he crashed into the barrier not a second after. My mother's shadowy body crumpled to the ground. The other woman caught her, silvery white blood leaking from her mortal wound as she comforted Mum.

"MUM!" I screamed.

Mum looked up, her lips bloody, and smiled. 'It's okay,' she mouthed. 'I love you all, it's okay, it's okay.'

We all stood in silence, watching in agony as the shadowy forms of our mothers dissolved. They held onto each other, crying, as they stared at us and mouthed three words over and over again. *I love you. I love you. I love you.*

We all wept as at last they disappeared completely.

"We need to go," Artemis whispered as he gently squeezed my hand.

I was holding up Jacques as Rosamond tended to his wound.

"Hold *still*," she snapped.

"I'm trying," Jacques hissed. His eyes were distant as he stared at where Mum had been. "She did that for me."

"She loved you so much," I murmured softly as I wrapped him in a hug, careful not to disturb Rosamond's work. "They never stopped looking for you, Jack. They were always waiting for you to come back home."

Jack was crying as he hugged me back. "There was so much I wanted to tell them, so much I regret."

I didn't have the words as I held onto him.

Faye, Meghan, and the dark-haired man were hugging one another and crying.

"I'll be back," Artemis was saying to Felix.

Felix rolled his eyes. "That's what all rulers say. I'll be *back*, and then do we see them again? No."

Annie smacked him on the back of the head. "Have some respect," she chastised. "Did you not see what he just did? This king to be is different."

"How are we going to get back to the Central Realm?" I whispered, staring at the darkened Moores around us as I fought back tears.

"I'm going to use a very old, very complex form of travel called Wyrld jumping...it's similar to what is done with a mirror, but well, without the mirrors bit. It's a form of magic that belongs to the Shadowthieves."

"Can you do that kind of magic?" Felix gasped in wonder.

"Only on occasion. Being this close to the Ruins, I think I can steal some of the power to channel toward the spell."

"What are you going to do?" Annie asked anxiously. "You look ready to kill someone."

"I am," Artemis hissed as he took my hand. "I'm sorry, everyone. We can mourn later, but we're in danger here. The longer we stay, the more likely the Knight is to concentrate his efforts to get out. The borders are already fractured. I don't want the Grimms getting killed."

The Grimms around us chorused their distaste at such a sentiment.

"We can take care of ourselves," one piped up.

Artemis rolled his eyes. "I know you can, but I don't want to risk it. Now, everyone, hold hands," he ordered.

Everyone but Evadne obeyed. She was staring in disgust at Marcus' outstretched hand.

Man, he must have done something terrible to make her that pissed off at him. But even pissed off...that's not like her. What's going on?

"Evadne, I don't have time for your lover's quarrel right now," Artemis sighed.

"What the freaking heck are you talking about?" Evadne snapped. "This man followed me from the Summer Court. He's one of Quillon's guards."

Confusion slammed into me. What was she talking about?

"Evadne," Artemis sighed again in exasperation. "I don't have time for this nonsense. Stop pretending you don't know him. That's Marcus. You've been in love with him for ages. From the moment you met him, if I recall correctly."

"It's been absolutely nauseating the way you look at him all lovey-dovey moon eyed," Jacques added unhelpfully.

"I don't know any Marcus'," Evadne replied angrily. "I have *no* idea who this man is."

What on earth does she mean? She knows who he is. This is downright crazy.

Artemis' face darkened; he was losing patience. "Cut the games Evadne, we have to get out of here."

"Artemis," Marcus cut in. "Something isn't right. She's not herself... Quillon called in his debt...the debt she owed him for setting me free from the service of the courts...she hasn't recognized me since he called in the debt." Marcus' voice broke as he stared at Evadne's face.

Oh no...

Artemis' anger evaporated as he scrutinized Evadne. "Evadne, come here a second." He sighed.

She rolled her eyes, but complied, though she chose to stomp the whole way over to him.

What's gotten into her? This isn't like her...

Artemis stared at her, his face deadly serious. "You don't know who this man is?" he asked carefully, pointing at Marcus.

She shook her head. "I told you, he followed me here. I don't know him at all. I think he's one of Quillon's guards."

Oh no, what did Quillon do?

"What do you remember of when Quillon called in the bargain?" Artemis replied.

She shook her head. "I can't remember anything, it's all blurry…Branwenn was there. I remember that."

Artemis jerked. "Branwenn was with you when you were with the monarchs?" he asked quietly.

"Yeah, she met me at the Central Gate…there was a wolf, but Autymn killed it." She shrugged. "Branwenn took me to the monarchs because she said it wasn't safe."

"What comes to mind when you look at Marcus?" Artemis asked carefully. He pointed to Marcus. "For the record, this is Marcus. He's my best friend. I uhm…I told him to…to keep an eye on you."

What's going on?

"He could have given me a heads up, instead of acting like a total *creep*!" Evadne snapped angrily.

"What comes to mind?" Artemis repeated.

"Distrust," Evadne finally admitted. "I don't like him. Not one bit. He gives me the heebie-jeebies and I kind of want to *stab* him until I make him go away." She raised her dagger for emphasis, giving him a pointed look.

Artemis swore under his breath. "He stole your memories."

What?! What does he mean?

"What?" she snapped. "I think I'd remember if he stole my memories."

"No, you wouldn't." Artemis replied.

He's right, you wouldn't remember memories that have been stolen from you.

"I don't know him whatsoever," Evadne stated stubbornly. "I've never seen him before."

Artemis sighed, massaging his temples. "Okay, we'll…we'll fix this when we get back to the Courts. But right now, we need to go. We have to get out of here."

The Knight was attacking the Last Gate outright now, trying to get through to us. The Grimms had rallied around the Gate and were now pushing back against his assault with their mixed Inheritances.

"Join hands," Artemis instructed, placing himself between Evadne and Marcus.

We all joined hands, and he stared down at the ground, drawing a quick rune in the dirt with his foot. "*Home,*" he muttered as the rune began to glow.

Power slammed into us all at once, compressing and decompressing my bones as, in an instant, the world turned on its head.

We crashed down in the middle of the throne room, and the Court drew back with cries and screams as Artemis rose to his feet, glaring up at the dais as he wiped away the blood that trickled from his nose.

"I bring the lost Grimm," he called angrily. "And I bear news of the coming war. The Moores are rising, and the curse of three is broken."

The room gasped, drawing back from us as if we carried a plague or curse.

"The Knight is coming," Artemis yelled.

92

Farewell

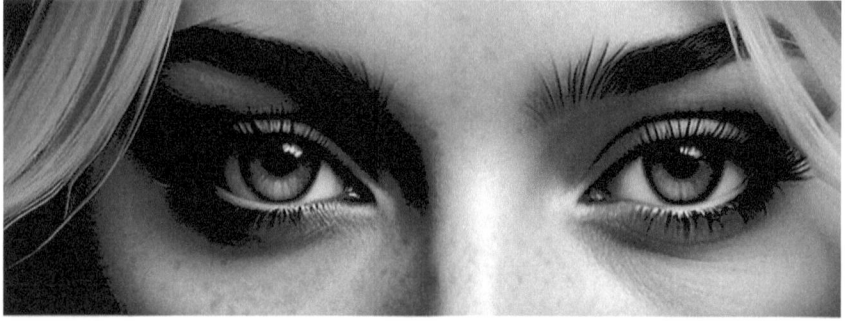

FAYE

"Death doesn't discriminate between sinners and saints. It takes and it
takes and it takes."
-Hamilton

We stood in the woods before three graves. One belonged to Oma, the other two my
parents. It seemed only fitting that we buried them beside her, though part of me wished
there was a way to put F with them as well. That way everyone could be together. But
I was fairly sure F wouldn't have cared about being on his own. After all, he'd been a
loner all these years.

The hospital had left a voicemail on Ronan's phone, notifying him of the unexpected passing of our mother. When she sacrificed herself for us at the Ruins, her heart had
stopped in the Mortal Realm. After a brief discussion with my siblings, we decided to
have her cremated since we were so far from home.

Artemis had gone back with us to retrieve her ashes and then went on to the
compound. The issue of the door still remained, and Artemis was intent on destroying
it. We also needed help with Dad's body. Too much time in the Mortal Realm had
passed during our seemingly brief time at the Ruins and the Central Realm. His body
was already too far gone, and we were forced to cremate him there and bring his ashes

home.

Jacques, Evadne, Ember, and I stood silent, staring down at the cairns. At last, all four of us were home, but our parents weren't here to be a part of the reunion.

"It's not fair," Evadne sniffed. "It's...it's not *fair*."

I pulled her into a hug. "I know, sweetheart, I know."

Even now, I couldn't escape the guilt of losing Dad.

His death was pointless, fruitless. He died for nothing, saving no one. Why? Why does it end like this?

We all stood weeping before the graves, mourning the loss of the ones we'd held dear.

I wish Ronan was here. Having him here would make this bearable.

Ronan and Meghan were busy having a funeral of their own. After rescuing Meghan's books from the compound and the few items from Ronan's room that he wanted, they were going to burn the husk of the compound down and their father's body with it. Their leader destroyed, Jeremiah's men had scattered. But unwilling to let them get away with what they'd done, Ronan gave the local enforcement hotline an anonymous tip, and most of the men had been apprehended.

James had turned himself in. In return for his cooperation and testimony he'd been given a reduced sentence. Jeremiah had an *extensive* crime ring—larger than anything I could have imagined.

I wanted to be there with them, but my family needed me here. In a spurt of kindness, Ember had loaned Meghan her WyrldCloak, so she could stow all her books in the pockets and make transporting them easy.

After they were done, Meghan and Ronan would come back here. Branwenn would notify Artemis, and he would return and take them to the Fey Realm.

Fate had once again stepped in and rearranged the deck, ensuring Ronan and I stayed together. The spell Artemis had woven to save Meghan's life, entwining my blood with his and Ronan's, had pulled out the poison and re-bound her soul to her body. In the strange magic of the Ruins, she and Ronan had somehow been given Grimm Inheritances of their own. They were now guardians, and their human hearts had been bound to the Realm.

It wasn't really something my selfish heart was currently complaining about. Being in the Realm was awful, but having Ronan there with me made our chances to be together in the future possible—especially under Artemis' impending rule.

Ember was crying on Jacques' shoulder, and as he held her, he wept. Staring down at the graves, he held nothing but remorse.

"There was so much I wanted to say," he whispered raggedly. "There was so much I wanted to apologize for...I ran away, and we never had the chance to make things right again."

"They never stopped looking for you," Ember sniffed. "Even after all those years...Dad was looking for a way to get you out of there. He didn't care about the fights anymore. He forgave you for running and was sorry about everything. All he ever wanted was for you to come home."

Evadne nodded, anxiously twisting the promise ring Marcus had given her. It seemed a cruel twist of fate that she'd finally found happiness, only to have it ripped away from her. Worst of all, she didn't even know what she'd lost.

Artemis had been unsuccessful in restoring her memory. There wasn't a block on her mind. The memories were completely *gone*. Artemis' fury at his father was met with cruel coldness. Quillon refused to restore the memories he'd stolen, claiming he was stopping fate and the rising flood. A flood that he immediately went and denied.

"I think Da would want you to have this," Evadne said gently, handing Jacques an incredibly thick, leatherbound notebook. It was Dad's journal from over the years. "He...he gave it to me before we left, and when they came back, I left it sitting in the house... Well, I found it again and I read it last night. He talks about you a lot...there's a lot he wanted to say to you, and I think you should have it."

Ember nodded as she and Evadne pushed it into Jacques' hands. "It'll help you get closure," Ember said softly.

Jacques stared down at the worn leather as tears slid down his cheeks. "We should go," he said at last. "It'll be dark soon."

Why should we care about being caught in the dark forest? We're all monsters now...monsters within something we once feared, facing an even greater evil... But can we withstand the flood?

We slowly made our way back toward the house, quietly exchanging thoughts and stories as we cut through the woods.

Artemis and Branwenn were waiting for us just inside the iron fence.

With Mum and Dad gone, no one was there to watch over the house. The brounie had done an amazing job, but it was time for someone else to step in. It was only a matter of time before people forgot their fear and came poking around the property. Branwenn had offered to live at the house, ensuring the borderlands that had bled over into our world would be protected from the foolishness of these humans.

"Ready to go?" Artemis asked Ember gently.

Ember sniffed and he pulled her into a tight hug. Her shoulders shook as she once again started crying.

I still couldn't quite comprehend how much Artemis had changed. The character that he often hid beneath his uncaring demeanor now shone for her without hesitation. He was no longer afraid to be the change. With his rising fury at the monarchs for their negligence, he embraced who he was becoming with open arms, though I had the sneaking suspicion Ember had something to do with his newfound courage.

Branwenn held the reins of the horses. Ember and Evadne would be taking theirs, and Jacques and I would take Mum's and Dad's. Branwenn would take care of Oma's horse and have a reliable form of transportation around the property, since vehicles were unreliable within the woods.

Evadne had stopped at the edge of the yard and was staring out at the woods, a puzzled expression on her face.

"You okay there, Eva?" I asked softly.

"Yeah…" she whispered, her eyebrows scrunching in confusion. "I just… I feel like I'm forgetting something. Something important."

Oh, honey. You are. You are forgetting. Except it's not something—it's someone.

Artemis was worried about what Quillon planned to do with her memories. Memories were a powerful blessing, or a terrible curse in the hands of a skilled sorcerer, and considering how they had no hesitation in corrupting the Realms with their Darke magic, he was right to be concerned.

It was a cruel irony that she gave the King that promise of debt to try to save Marcus, and in the end, it was that promise which had ripped him from her entirely, and now she didn't even know it.

Evadne wrapped Branwenn in a hug. "I'll see you later. Keep in touch, okay?"

Branwenn nodded. "I will. Here, this is for you. I know you're an artist and will appreciate my work. But you can't open it. Not yet."

"When can I?" Evadne asked, pondering the thick leatherbound sketchbook.

"When you're desperate and need hope," Branwenn replied. "You'll know when the time is right."

That's my Branwenn—infuriatingly cryptic.

Evadne pursed her lips, then shrugged and slipped the notebook into the pocket of her WyrldCloak.

Fireheart was perched on her shoulder and he cast a mournful glance at the house.

"I know," Evadne whispered sadly as she gently rubbed his nose. "I don't want to go either."

He seemed to be wheedling with her to go back inside—likely so he could raid the pantry again. Between him and Artemis, there wasn't much food left in the house.

Perhaps he wants to try to give Maladroit another haircut...

Evadne had been incredibly sheepish when she told me about that incident—Ember, on the other hand, had been absolutely indignant. She had ranted for five minutes about how Fireheart had tried to eat *her* cat.

He better not try that stunt again. I'll have Ember put him back in the time-out cage if he tries to hurt our cat.

"What are we going to do when we get back to the Realm?" Ember asked as she swung up into the saddle.

Artemis mounted up behind her, wrapping his arms around her to grip the pommel. It didn't escape my notice how she leaned into his embrace. "We convince the monarchs to listen. War is coming. They cannot ignore it any longer."

I settled into my saddle. "They are experts at ignoring," I replied, rolling my eyes.

"Then it will be their downfall," Artemis replied in a low angry voice as he stared out at the trees. "If they refuse to listen, we will still prepare for war. If they continue to disregard the warning signs, I cannot stop them, nor do I have the energy to argue with fools. We will walk forward with our eyes open. We are the only hope the Realm has left to survive what's coming."

93

Remember, Please Remember

EVADNE

"Tell me, father, which should I ask forgiveness for: What I am, or what
I'm not? Tell me, mother, which should I regret: what I became, or
what I didn't?"
-Dvoyd

The wind carried a secret. I could smell it there, dancing along the edges of my mind as
we made our way through the forest—back toward the portal.

Remember, remember. It seemed to say. But I couldn't. I couldn't remember. There
was something missing. A piece of myself that ought to be there. Something that
burned within my heart and wounded my soul.

Remember. Remember.

But no amount of racking my brain could bring it to bear. No amount of pleading
returned it to me.

There was a hole in my heart, an empty tomb in my mind, an open grave someone
had robbed and left barren.

Someone had stolen the life and joy from my bones and only shadows remained in
my mind.

Remember, remember. Please, remember.

I can't...I can't...

The only thing I remembered was the pain of my mind splitting apart, the throne room floor beneath me, and the hollow ache of something torn away.

Something I loved was gone forever.

Something I *needed* was lost.

But I just couldn't remember *what*.

Remember, remember...please remember.

"Out of the night that covers me, Black from the pit from pole to pole,
I thank whatever gods may be, for my unconquerable soul.

It matters not how straight the gate, how charged with punishments the scroll,
I am the master of my fate, I am the captain of my soul."
-Invictus, William Ernest Henley

TO BE
CONTINUED

Acknowledgements/A Letter From the Author

"The night may be dark and full of terrors, but I've got a big stick."
-Ben Aaronovitch, Foxglove Summer

My Dear Readers,

When I finished writing this book at the end of 2024, I was in a completely different place in my life. Things were hard, mind you, but they were not what they are now. Sitting in the present, finishing up the edits and wrapping up this book, it seems a lifetime ago that I poured my heart and soul onto these pages. I was a different person then. Then, it seemed a given to have my characters find hope in the midst of great darkness. It was easy to help them move forward when everything was breaking inside and the question of fighting to remain who you are when you're utterly destroyed, was one I answered without hesitation... In this story my main characters go through unspeakable horrors and yet they still find a way to retain their sense of self. They hold onto courage and keep putting one foot in front of the other.

I have come to realize that these reminders were a letter to my future self. I think I subconsciously knew when I was writing this book that my whole world was going to implode. So, I put my characters through hell and then intentionally pulled the silver strands of hope and courage through that pain, to give them a way out. In reality, I was giving *myself* a way out. I think I *knew* that my future self would need these reminders of courage and hope—even if she doesn't want to hear them right now.

I'll be perfectly honest with you, I definitely don't want to hear it right now. Because courage and hope are *hard* when everything inside of you is breaking. When the odds are against you and it's all you can do to keep breathing, holding onto hope feels like an impossible mountain that you just *can't climb*. It was incredibly difficult for me to read through this draft again, because hope is a *painful* thing to hold onto when life is agony.

You see, hope and I have a complicated relationship. It often leaves a bitter taste in my mouth, because it comes with the awareness that I may not get what I desperately pray for. I might *not* make it out of this whole, and that knowledge strangles me.

So, here we enter the valley of my life. Here is my *Ebenezer* stone. At the beginning of this year, 2025, my husband Drew, whose health had been in a steady decline, was diagnosed with heart failure. Since then, other areas of illness have begun that only add to the problem. We have been to numerous doctors, and sought many forms of help and possibilities, but so far it's been nothing but dead ends and apathy. The only solution offered has been medication—medication that only seems to make him sick. It's been five months at this point, and by the time you read this at the end of August it will be almost nine. Despite the medication, there is no change nor relief from the debilitating symptoms and the constant state of illness that plagues him.

So, we wait in prayer and attempted patience—for I am not good at patience. At this point, there's nothing anyone can do for us except pray, and there's nothing doctors can offer except periodically upping the medications to see if it helps. It is a constant cycle of hurry up and wait. I *loathe* such a cycle, because it forces me to acknowledge that I am *completely* out of control. While still doing everything I can, I must surrender the outcome to my Heavenly Father, and trust that in the end, He will do what is right.

I do not share all of this with you to obtain your pity or sorrow, but to simply try to convey where I'm at in life, in the hope that maybe if you're walking through something painful, you can find comfort in knowing you're not alone. It is also to explain what's going on because all of this directly affects my writing. Tomorrow is the beginning of June, and I barely have anything written on the fourth book. I feel as if I've lost myself and all the beautiful words I called mine. I have lost the flow and the joy, the snark and sarcasm...and while I have stubborn determination to make it, and publish the books within my predicted timeline, I stare at this page with real doubt in my heart. For the first time, I actually don't know if I'm going to be able to make it, and for that I am so *so* sorry.

My heart is shattered and as I struggle to put the pieces back together, all while taking it day by day, my words *fade*. My whole world imploded with the words 'heart failure,' and something inside of me *broke*. I didn't think I'd ever be able to stop crying...but after a few months, I did. I can only hope that the same is true with my words. Right now, I don't feel as if I'll ever get my words back, but, I will continue to take it day by day and *try*. I will *try* to have hope—even though it's painful, even though it hurts worse than the disease itself. As I fight to have hope, I will continue to trust that my words will come back to me and we will make it through this.

The night may be dark and full of terrors, but I've got a big stick. Right now, my life is dark, and full of terrors, but I have a big stick, and as I face these circumstances, I plan to use it. If my life is a terror, then perhaps I shall be a terror in return. Perhaps that will help me find my hope—or maybe it will help me find my words. Maybe all I need is a little less tears and a little more violence aimed at the things that scare me. (I'll keep you posted.)

And so, with all this in mind, I come to my acknowledgements.

First and foremost, I have my Heavenly Father to thank for this book coming to completion. It is by His grace and for His glory that this story carries on. But secondly, I have my husband to thank.

Drew, you are the most wonderful gift that God has given me. The way you constantly selflessly love and support me and my writing, the way you always show up for me, and listen to my woes and triumphs, rambles and plans. I'd be utterly lost and alone without you. This last year has been incredibly hard, but I am grateful to stand by your side and fight through it. No matter what we face and no matter what happens, you are and *always* will be the *best* thing that has ever been added into my life. Looking back, and knowing what I know now, I wouldn't change a thing. No matter the sorrow, tears or pain, sickness, trials or loss. You are *my heart* and I *love* you.

I am immensely grateful for my wonderful family. Your love and support through this project is no doubt a labor of love—for I am not an easy creature to deal with. I would not trade our love for all the accolades or riches in the world.

Teresa, thank you for being my friend and staying by my side. You gave Raz your vibrant *Heyo* personality. Laser fingers and anything goes Tuesdays are all because of you, and I'm fairly sure the *Aurora* would be lifeless without the chaotic Raz keeping things spiced up and throwing poor Grimms off the mast.

To all my dear, amazing friends, thank you for your constant love and support, for always being on my side, and cheering me on. I am so incredibly grateful for each and every one of you. Though I haven't named each of you individually, you know who you are, and you should know you mean the world to me. I am so *incredibly* grateful for you. More than words can say.

Thanks to my amazing editor, Allison. You really are the best editor an author could ask for. Your interest and care in this series, the endless encouragement, suggestions and feedback is all such a gift to me and I am incredibly grateful for you.

Thanks to Hannah, my awesome proofreader. We both know that I'm hopeless at proofreading. Thank you so much for helping me.

To all my awesome internet friends on TikTok, Instagram, and beyond. You are the most supportive, encouraging bunch of people I have ever met. If someone had told me ten years ago I'd have friends from all over the world, who were constantly cheering me on in my writing, I'd never have believed you. But now that I'm here and see it for myself, I have nothing but gratitude to hand back to you. Thank you for believing in me, and my story. Thank you for checking in and cheering me on, telling me you're proud of me and my work. It is an incredible blessing to live in the technological age, and I cannot wait to continue this journey with you guys.

Lastly, I have to thank you, dear reader. Thank you so much for your love and support of this series. Every note, every message, every, 'Hey I'm reading your book I love —', makes my day. I am so *incredibly* grateful for each and every one of you, and I hope you don't hate me too much for the cliffhanger...I'll get book four done as quickly as I can...but for now, perhaps you'll be satisfied with this promise: The story isn't over yet, there's still violence to be had.

With unending gratitude and many, *many* hugs to *all* of you,

-E

About The Author

"Do not let numbers tell you what to do. You are blood and earth, not theory and chalk."
-Welcome to Night Vale Podcast

I happily live in Kansas with my absolutely wonderful husband and two dogs. A snuggle-pup, (who is most definitely spoiled,) and a chaos gremlin, (who is also most definitely spoiled). I spend the long winter months trying to figure out how to fill my yard with wildflowers so I never have to mow again, and this year I think I might just succeed. (I have great and unrealistic expectations for a vast cacophony of colorful mayhem.)

When I'm not working with my beloved elderly clients, I'm turning blood into ink, talking to people who don't exist, creating entire worlds and spending way too much time plotting how to cause the most pain with my stories—all while making a general nuisance of myself and eating far too many cookies...(which isn't actually possible, because there's no such thing as too many cookies.)

My existence is dependent on Jesus, copious and questionable amounts of magic bean juice, and grace, while I rearrange all 26 letters of the alphabet (under a pen-name) and gleefully use semi-colons liberally and incorrectly. (Thank goodness I have an amazing editor.) Often I compare myself to a horrible goose or a crow—for I hold a great secret desire to chase people around while screeching as I collect shiny things.

You can find me at erbrookesauthor.com or on just about every social media platform under erbrookesauthor. I have a love hate relationship with social media and I do my best to post... but it's often hit and miss.

You can follow the QR code to my linktree and it will take you just about everything.

Thank you so much for continuing to take an interest in me and this series. It really means the world to me. I've held this dream close to my heart for as long as I can remember and I am both thrilled and terrified to continue putting my brain babies out into the world.

Seriously, Y'all are the literal best.

Pronounciation Guide :)

Faye — F-aa-y
    Ember — Em-ber
    Evadne — Ee-vad-knee
    Jacques — Jah-qu-ace
    Rionach — Ree-oh-nagh
    Ryver — Rye-ver
    Rosamond — Roz-ah-mund
    Ronan — Roe-nin
    Artemis — Are-ta-miss
    Quillon — Kill-on
    Isla — Iss-lah
    Kenna — Kin-nah
    Aberdeen — Ah-ber-dean